Justin Zaruba

Penelope Salvo
and
Untouchable Orange

Also by Justin Zaruba

Penelope Salvo and Impossible Red

Penelope Salvo and Unknowable Yellow

Penelope Salvo and Incorruptible Green

Io, Kung Fu Hipster

ISBN-978-1-7351749-0-7

Text set in Gentium Book Basic
Cover Art designed by Justin Zaruba; back cover layout by Claire Andersen

Printed in the United States of America
First edition 2018,

For Kyle

Punk rock died

when the first kid said,

punk's not dead

punk's not dead

-Silver Jews

You will not be punished

for your anger.

You will be punished

by your anger.

-Buddha

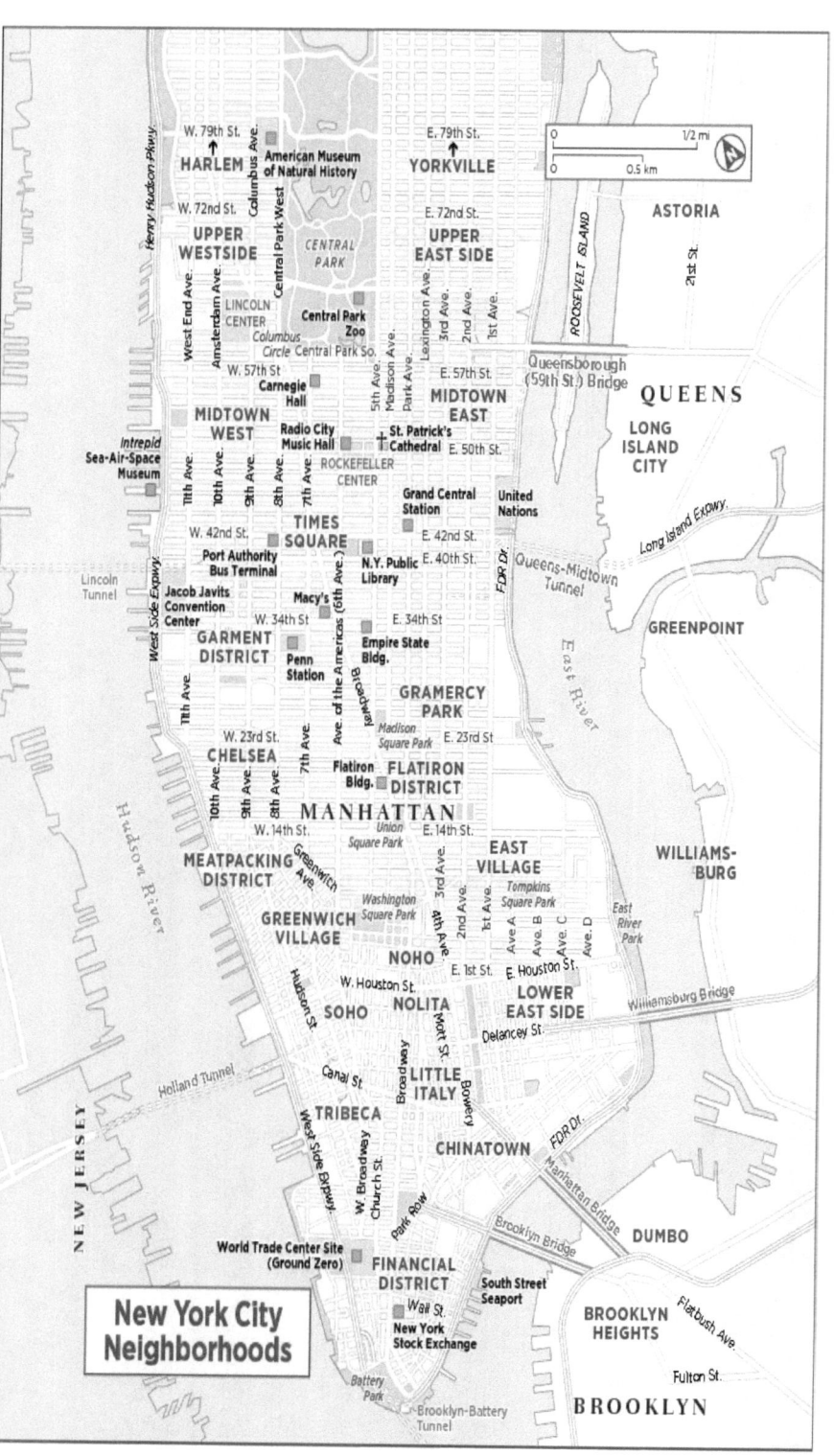

New York City Neighborhoods

Chapter 0

When you're born on a major holiday, it pretty much guarantees that your birthday will be a mess, everyday, for the rest of your life. If you're born on Christmas, you'll spend your whole life wondering if you're getting ripped off in the gifts department. How many of your gifts are Christmas gifts, and how many of them are birthday gifts? Would you have received more gifts if your birthday was on June 25th instead of December 25th?

You'll never know.

Or what if your birthday is on Leap Day? Sure, you can celebrate it on February 28th or March 1st instead, but that isn't *actually* your birthday. Those are fake birthdays. Your real birthday only exists once every four years.

Ilana Rittenberg, my best friend from high school, she was born on 9/11, which is a bummer of a birthday for any American, but it was worse for her because we lived in New York City. How does a New Yorker deal with having their birthday on 9/11? Your birthday party has to contend with a memorial for hundreds of dead people.

So that takes me to my birthday.

I was born on April Fools Day. Everyone sees this as an opportunity to fuck with me. I haven't had a single birthday where I wasn't the butt of some practical joke and ended with everyone laughing at me. And I'm supposed to just take it in stride with the dismissive excuse, "Oh, Penelope, don't take it personal. Your birthday's on April Fools!"

I know damn well when my birthday is. It coincides with a stupid-ass holiday based entirely on juvenile pranks; just another one of the horrible jokes fate decided to pull on me. My birthday has never been fun. It's never been awesome. I have never, ever liked my birthday.

One birthday, when I was in eighth grade, a bunch of girls covered a tampon with ketchup, put it in a shoe box and wrapped it up like a gift. I opened it at lunch. When I saw what was inside, those bitches had the audacity to laugh at me. I didn't deserve to be laughed at – I didn't do anything but open a stupid box – but somehow I was the butt of their joke. Now, I know a lot of girls who would have been humiliated in a situation like that and ran crying out of the cafeteria.

Not me.

I calmly walked over to their table, grabbed one of the girls by the hair – I'll never forget who it was, Juliet Novella, a notorious bitch – and punched her in the face over and over until blood gushed from her nose was all over my fist. It took the boy's gym team to drag me off of her and even then I was clawing for her, kicking and screaming. I got suspended, Juliet got detention, and they called my mother.

None of that was my fault.

Years before that, when I was in fourth grade and celebrating my ninth birthday, I was the victim of a prank orchestrated by my own father, Michael. Michael had planned a birthday party for me at our apartment in Little Italy. I didn't want a party. I was still only a kid, but I already wanted my birthday to just come and go so everyone could get on with their lives. Michael didn't listen. He said a good father would throw a birthday party for his only daughter. Funny, I don't remember anyone accusing him of being a good father. He made my mother call all the parents from school and invite my classmates to the party.

That April Fools Day, Michael sat me at the head of our dinner table and put a cone-shaped birthday hat on my head, the kind with the elastic string, and told me to wait.

"The party starts at noon," he told me. "Your friends should start showing up any minute."

My parents both acted odd that birthday. Ma, who showed me just slightly more attention than Michael, seemed distant and uninterested with the whole party idea. And Michael, who I don't think wanted a daughter, or didn't want me at all, suddenly cared a whole lot. Not so much that it would inconvenience him in any way, of course, but just enough so that he could look at himself in the mirror and say, "I am a good father," despite all evidence to the contrary.

I wanted a Spider-Man cake. The Toby Maguire version had come out the year before and I had a the biggest crush on him, but only when he was Spider-Man, not when he was Peter Parker. My parents didn't get me a Spider-Man cake. They weren't going to waste money on "nonsense." They said we were going to stick with tradition, which meant I got a plain white-frosting cake from Tony's Baked Goods yet again. It had HAPPY BIRTHDAY PENNY written across the top in pink frosting and had a candle in the shape of a nine. My party did end up with Spider-Man hats and napkins, but they were comic book Spider-Man, not movie Spider-Man.

Close enough, I fucking guess.

Noon came and the anxiety of having my classmates in my home slugged me right in the gut. I nervously fiddled with the elastic string on my hat, pulling it down and letting it snap against my skin. Noon came and went. No one showed up. Ten more minutes passed and no one buzzed for the door. I asked Ma where my friends were.

She kept her eyes down on the dishes. "Ask your father," she said. "This was all his idea."

So I asked Michael. He said, "I'm sure they're just running late. You're not worried, are you?"

"No," I said.

Twenty more minutes passed and I didn't know what to think. Twenty minutes is an eternity for a ten year old. I resisted the urge to run to the window and look for my friends on the sidewalk. Michael did it for me. He stood at the window, pulled the curtains back and peered to the street below.

"Gosh," he said. "Doesn't look like anyone's coming."

I looked him dead in the eyes, but I couldn't think of anything to say. If one kid didn't show up, that wouldn't be a huge deal. Or even if a couple didn't come, I could have lived with that. But *none* of them were coming?

"Are you sure you have friends at school?" he asked me.

"Yes," I said. My chest wrenched in a cocktail of emotions, none of them good.

"Real friends?" he asked.

"Yes, real friends!"

"I dunno." He peeked back out the window. "If you had real friends, they'd be here by now."

I pounded my fists on the table with tears in my eyes and I screamed, "I have friends!"

He shook his head like he didn't believe me. "I dunno."

"Michael," Ma scolded. "Don't tease her, please."

He grinned at Ma, quite pleased with himself.

I didn't cry. I had tears in my eyes, sure, but I wasn't going to cry. I grabbed fistfuls of Ma's lace tablecloth and squeezed. I knew I had friends. Real friends. Girls *and* boys. We played at recess together. We ate lunch together. None of them were coming to my party? No one liked me? Were they all just pretending this whole time? Oh, the next time I saw them at school, I was going to punch every single one of them in the face.

Then noon-thirty rolled around and there was a buzz at the door. My friend Lydia was at our apartment building with her mother. Shortly after, other kids showed up with their parents.

"April Fools!" Michael shouted at me. But I didn't understand. The confusion on my face made him laugh and laugh. "Your party was at twelve-thirty, not noon. Fooled you!"

My own father convinced me that I didn't have any friends. All the misplaced rage I felt towards my classmates was suddenly redirected at Michael. What he'd done wasn't funny. It was cruel.

I stood up and shouted, "Not funny!"

He could barely talk, he was laughing so hard. "April Fools!"

I stormed out of the dining room, marched to my bedroom and slammed the door. I threw myself on the bed and pressed my face into my pillow. I could hear my friends arriving one by one, entering my apartment. My mother awkwardly escorted them to the party table, but without me around.

Michael swung my door open and it slammed against the wall. This wasn't the first time he rage-entered my bedroom; it happened often enough that there was a hole in the wall from the doorknob hitting it. Michael wasn't laughing anymore. Now he was pissed. "Penelope Marie Salvo, you get out there and talk to your friends."

"I hate you!" I shouted.

"Are you crying?" he asked. "Here come the fucking water works. Your mother went to a lot of fucking trouble for this party, so get your ass out there."

I looked up and shouted, "No!"

Bad move.

4

He grabbed me by the arm and yanked me to my feet. He did that a lot. Sometimes worse. Depending on how troublesome I was being, that's how much he made it hurt. Sometimes he would leave bruises on my arms that would last for days. He dragged me into the dining room, right in front of all my friends and a few of their parents, and practically threw me into a seat at the table.

"You need to toughen up," he said, loud enough for everyone to hear. "You're acting like a baby."

So I toughened up. I didn't want to embarrass myself further by crying in front of my friends. I didn't want to give Michael the satisfaction. I would have fun at my birthday party, sure, but it was all just a performance. And I never forgive Michael for what he did that day.

Turns out I didn't need to forgive him. That was the last birthday I had with him around. The next year, there was a big archaeological discovery in Greece and he spent more and more time out of the country. Fine. Good riddance.

After that, I went into every birthday with deep suspicions that someone was going to trick me. Every present, a trap. Every birthday party, an evil prank.

For my tenth birthday, Ma asked me what I wanted.

"I just want to forget about my birthday forever," I told her.

And that broke her heart. She never forced me to have a party after that. She just overcompensated when it came to gift giving. That's how I ended up with a skateboard on my twelfth birthday, despite the fact that Ma dreaded the idea of me cruising around the sidewalks of New York City on a skateboard, but because of her silent involvement in what Michael had done years before, she felt like she owed it to me.

That's what it's like to have your birthday on April Fools Day. It's just one big hilarious joke that never ends. Even when I went on to high school and made new friends, they thought they were the first clever souls to draw the sick correlation between my birthday and April Fools. That's how Juliet Novella ended up in the hospital with a broken nose.

A lot of people hate their birthday because it's a reminder that they're another year older, another year closer to death. Some people hate their birthday because they don't like that much attention. I hate my birthday because my birthday sucks. If I never celebrated another birthday ever again in my life, that would just be fine by me.

Chapter 1

1

November, 2012.

Chuck Taylors aren't the best shoes to wear when you need to march through the muddy jungles of Guatemala. I learned that the hard way. And a black tank top with some denim shorts isn't all that great if you need protection from the elements. The mosquitoes in Guatemala get as big as hummingbirds and a lot of the jungle plants can be poisonous. I didn't have to worry about any of that, of course; mosquitoes can't pierce my carbon-nano-weave skin and I don't have allergic reactions anymore.

Not since swallowing Impossible Red.

The jungles I trailblazed were uncharted. Not meant for tourists. I worked my way through miles of towering mango and coconut trees. I leapt over mud puddles, I pushed through knee-deep bushes, and from time to time I had to kick a fallen log out of my way. Vines hung down from the tree branches and formed a kind of web that got me all tangled up, but I could slice through them with my bare hands. My skin got grass-stained and I smelled like a fresh-cut lawn, but them's the dues you pay if you want to explore a jungle, I guess. Tree roots grew above ground in big loops that threatened to trip me up.

The harder I pushed through the leaves and vines, the faster they seemed to grow back, as if they were trying to swallow me up. I'm not really the claustrophobic type, but between the humidity and the crowded plant-life, I felt like I couldn't get a decent breath. Which is fine, because I don't breathe.

I kept going.

Deep in those jungles, somewhere near the Mopan River, was the Forgotten Temple of Muzencab, the Mayan god of bees.

"Penelope," Corolla shouted from overhead. He'd been patrolling the skies for hours, where he hovered just over the treetops and searched for any signs of the temple. Apparently, he'd struck gold. "This way! I see something!"

Corolla floated off. I followed him by the blue glow of his hubcaps. I wedged my way through jungle trees. My tank top got caught on some kind of thorn bush and I had to stop to meticulously free the fabric from each individual thorn. I worried that I might lose Corolla from under the jungle canopy, but he was careful to stay where I could see him.

He led me around for an hour when I heard a strange noise, something like an army of chainsaws. I stopped and tilted my ear in that direction. I'd heard weird noises in the jungle before – distant waterfalls or cackling birds – but this was new. It definitely sounded like chainsaws, as if there was a lumber company out there cutting down acres of tress. But, no, it wasn't quite chainsaws. I closed my eyes and focused hard. The sound changed in frequency and intensity, as if it were throbbing, like it came from something alive.

If the noise came from a living thing, it would have to be huge. Maybe a monster.

Dope. I love fighting monsters.

But here's Penelope Salvo, wrong again. It wasn't a monster. It was bees. Trillions and trillions of bees. They covered every inch of an ancient Mayan pyramid.

The Forgotten Temple of Muzencab was only a legend, but I had found it. This wasn't like the smooth pyramids you'd find in Egypt. This pyramid was a Mayan pyramid; angular, blocky, and built from tiers of gray stone. I took a moment to drink in the sheer size of the thing. The Mayans had to cut down acres of jungle to make room for this thing; a plot of land the size of a football stadium. The temple towered thirty stories into the sky. The top just barely poked out over the treetops. At the very tippy-top stood a small cube-shaped shrine, covered in vines that grew in spirals and bloomed a bright yellow flower.

I needed those vines. More specifically, I needed those flowers.

I needed a Looping Bandis.

But in order to get to them, I had to climb thirty stories of stairs past an army of bees.

Legend has it that Muzencab, the Mayan god of bees, promised the bees that when they died, they could live in his temple and no one would ever bother them. This was his way of saying "thanks for all the honey," I guess. So even the living bees would visit here from all over the world, or come here to die, or just hang out. Whenever a scientist says that the bees are disappearing, they're disappearing to the Temple of Muzencab, which is like a never-ending Woodstock where bees can hang out, buzz around together, and have tons of bee sex.

"I am not going near that thing." Corolla descended from the sky and hovered over my head.

"What?" I said. He couldn't do that to me. "Bullshit, dude. Fly me to the top."

"Keep dreaming, sweetheart," Corolla said. "Do you see all those bees?"

"What do you care about bees?" I asked. "You're a car."

Corolla plainly replied, "A car that's allergic to bees."

I rolled my eyes and muttered, "Oh my god."

I turned and marched off towards the pyramid. Corolla was a huge coward, it was pointless to argue with him once he'd chickened out. I would just have to do it alone. At least the Mayans were thoughtful enough to build me a staircase. I took my first step up and craned my neck at the top of the temple.

"One down," I said. "Three-hundred sixty-six to go."

The bees covered everything. It sounded like I was walking through a wood chipper. They buzzed in my face and landed on my bare skin. They couldn't sting me, obviously, but that didn't stop them from trying. They crawled all over my arms and legs and got inside my clothes. They didn't actually bother me, but their tiny legs felt weird on my skin and I brushed them away.

I climbed fifty steps, then a hundred. Then two-hundred. And finally, after thirty minutes of climbing, I reached the top. The air was fresher up at the top, less humid, and it came with a refreshing breeze. Corolla watched me from a safe distance away, just above the tree line. I waved at him so he knew I reached the top without any problem.

The little shrine at the peak of the pyramid had four entrances facing north, south, east, and west. No doors, just open entrances that let me see the emptiness inside. The stone floor was stained brown with centuries-old blood. Human blood, if I had to guess. They had been sacrifices to Muzencab, maybe to keep the bees away, or maybe to honor the bees since they pollinate things. Whatever the reason, this room saw a lot of spilled blood. A small garden of Looping Bandis grew off the roof of this little structure. The spiral vines hung over the doorways in long coils, blooming with sweet-smelling, yellow flowers.

And then something startled me. A voice. The voice of a god.

"Who are you?" this voice asked.

I whipped around with a start and found myself face to face with Muzencab himself, in the flesh. Or, more accurately, "in the bees." Muzencab was shaped like a human, but he didn't have a body made out of skin and bone. His body came in a mass of swarming bees, all of them clinging together to create a head and a body and arms and legs. When he walked, his legs were made of bees. When he pointed at me, his arms were made of bees. And when he spoke, his voice came from the buzzing of the bees.

I backed away and bumped up against the wall of the shrine.

Answer him, I thought. *He asked you who you are. Answer him.*

I got my wits about me and cleared my throat. "My name's Penelope Marie Salvo," I said. "Nice cursed temple you got here. Love the blood stains."

"Have you come to release me from this prison?" he asked. "Have you come to summon me fully into this realm, that I might wash over humankind with blistering stings and painful venom?"

"Uh, no," I said, plainly. I tugged on one of the nearby vines. "I actually came here to steal some of your plants."

"Penelope!" Corolla shouted. "Hey, Penelope!"

"What?" I shouted back at him.

"There's a man made of bees talking to you!"

"Yeah, dude. I see it. He's right in front of me."

Muzencab didn't seem to notice or care that I was talking to a flying car. He kept on going with his apocalyptic monologue. "I will bless this world with poisonous stings that reduce even the strongest men to terrified children that spray foam from their mouths."

"Technically, bees are venomous," I told Muzencab with an insightful finger in the air. "Not poisonous. You're the god of bees, I feel like you should already know that."

"What's he saying!?" Corolla shouted at me.

I cupped my hands to my mouth to shout back. "This chooch doesn't even know the difference between venomous and poisonous! And he's the god of bees!"

9

"There's a difference?" Corolla asked.

"Poisonous is when you eat something!" I shouted back. "Venomous is when you get injected." I turned back to Muzencab and raised my eyebrows at him. "I hope you're writing this down."

Muzencab's doom-and-gloom monologue was just his way of getting attention. He reminded me of those guys in high school who talk about death and blood and worshiping Satan just to get a rise out of people. Muzencab was the same way, so the best thing I could do was ignore him. I walked away and scaled the walls of his sacrifice room. It wasn't a hard climb, really. The stones used to build the walls were rough-cut and provided a lot of hand-holds and foot-holds. I scaled the eight-foot walls without any trouble and sifted through the vines on the roof. I wanted the best samples of Looping Bandis, the healthiest and sturdiest ones.

"Spill blood in my name," Muzencab commanded me. "I will bring forth more bees than there are sands on all the beaches. I will bring forth more bees than there are stars in the sky."

I focused on my task and muttered, "That's a lot of bees."

"What's he saying now?" Corolla called out.

"I dunno, man," I replied. "He's talking about beaches and the stars or whatever."

"Beaches and stars are cool!" Corolla shouted.

I shrugged big enough for Corolla to see. "Yeah, but he's being kind of weird about it."

I only needed one Looping Bandis for Xin's shop, but there was no reason I couldn't bring back two. Better safe than sorry. The vines grew out of the cracks in the stone, which meant yanking them free would rip their roots out. I had a better method. I wedged my fingers into the cracks and split the ancient rock apart so I could pull two Looping Bandis free, roots perfectly intact.

"You have what you came for," Muzencab told me, victoriously throwing his bee-arms into the air. "Now return the favor and summon me fully into this world of soft flesh and flowing blood!"

I jumped off the top of the shrineroom and landed right in front of Muzencab. I looked his bee-body up and down.

"Nah." I brushed right past him and headed for the stairs. "I won't be doing that."

He didn't even try to stop me. He just watched me go.

I stopped to give him some parting advice. "Dude, honestly? You are wound way too tight. You need to, like, chill out."

I bounded down the stairs, two at a time. Even as I ran out of earshot, I could still hear Muzencab talking his nonsense. "Summon me forth" and "I'll sting the very soul of humanity." Shit like that. On and on he went. I can only assume he was still doing it as I ran away from the temple, rendezvoused with Corolla, and took to the skies.

"That guy seemed nice," Corolla said.

2

December, 2012.

There's this place in California called Area 5. It's where NASA dumps all the old space junk that they can't use anymore, but can't justify destroying it. If there's one thing NASA likes to do, it's catalog old junk. Are 5 has things there like old spaceship parts, entire sections of dismantled space stations, and astronaut suits from the '50s. They take all this useless crap and stash it in a warehouse just outside Burbank. No one really goes there. There's no reason to. It's all trash. The only time they open the doors is to add more junk to the collection.

That meant Corolla and I could poke around the warehouse without getting caught. Just inside the garage door entrance, I found a fuse box with these huge levers. Clack, clack, clack, I flipped the levers and these huge halogen lights flickered on overhead and started buzzing. This place was packed full with racks and racks of mechanical nonsense: little bolts, giant fuel pods, and cardboard boxes stuffed with empty water pouches that reminded me of Capri Suns. NASA kept everything. I mean, literally everything; even the "waste" from the astronauts' bathrooms.

Taxpayer money was well spent here in Area 5.

Their hoarding was so bad, it made the search for a space station panel pretty difficult.

See, there's this mold that only grows in space and the weird thing about it is that it only grows on the *outside* of space stations. It might grow on space ships, too, but they're not in space long enough. Space stations, on the other hand, are in space for years and years, and after that much time they end up with splotches of black mold all over them.

NASA scientists originally thought this was impossible, because of the lack of oxygen and cosmic radiation and whatever else, but they were wrong. Somewhere out there is an unidentified mold that can't be classified by science.

"Space Mold," Xin calls it. He uses it to make a potion that lets you breathe in space, or breathe underwater. It might have a scientific name, but I wouldn't know. I just call it Space Mold.

And it would be easier if NASA called it Space Mold, too, but they don't call anything what it is. Everything in the warehouse was labeled with numbers and letters; an organizational system I didn't understand.

The spaceship bolts were SSB-113.

The astronaut suits were OSA-33B.

The empty water pouches were individually marked, ranging from OSWP-11 through OSWP-1249.

"This sucks." I stuck my flashlight in a plastic tub to discover a treasure of rusty springs. "There's nothing here but garbage."

"No lie," Corolla said. He hovered over the racks and used his headlights to help the search. "Are you sure what we're looking for is actually here?"

"It has to be." I ripped open the plastic lid to tub BHE-17. "This is where NASA keeps all the crap they don't want anymore."

"I dunno," he said, floating off. "I don't see it anywhere."

"Ugh." I shoved plastic tub BHE-17 back into the rack.

We didn't have all night to search the warehouse, let alone the months it would take to go through every single box.

"You know what I do when a job gets hard?" Corolla asked.

"What's that?"

"Give up." He floated right over me and illuminated me in his blue hubcaps. "Yep. Nothing feels better than giving up. It's like this huge weight is just lifted right off your axles."

"Yeah." I exhaled and picked up the next box. "But we're not going to give up."

"Your call."

We kept looking. We had to. We didn't have the luxury of giving up. Xin asked for Space Mold and I was going to get him Space Mold.

"So someone's birthday's in a couple months," Corolla said.

"Who?" I asked.

"You!"

"My birthday's not for four months," I said. "That's forever from now."

"How old are you going to be?"

"Nineteen," I said in a flat tone. I hoped he would just drop it.

"Whoo-wee," he said. "The big one-nine."

I kept quiet and stayed focused on searching those boxes.

DSE-10012. Plastic hoses.

OFB-17. Shoelaces for some reason.

H-5-BE. Hinges.

"Cars have two birthdays," he said. "Did you know that?"

"Nope." BDU-91. Metal toggle switches for a control panel.

"Yep. Your first birthday is when you're assembled. Your second birthday is when someone buys you."

"Huh." OSM-83. Pillowcases. "So when are your birthdays?"

"I rolled off the line September 19th, 1997. Then that scientist lady from Japan bought me on November 11th of that same year."

I came across a rack of metal panels, arranged in slots like how they organize poster board at a hobby supply store. There were seven panels with bent corners and little specks of rust. I pulled one out and shined my flashlight up and down the sides.

Bingo. Little black dots of Space Mold.

"Over here!" I shouted. "Found it!"

Corolla flew over and pointed his headlights down at me. I pulled the panel all the way out and leaned it against the rack. It had a layer of fine dust and I brushed it off. This was Space Mold alright, one of the rarest substances on Earth.

"Here." Corolla spun around and pointed his rear bumper at me, then popped open the trunk. I wedged the panel inside. He asked me, "Do you think someone from NASA is going to realize they've been robbed?"

"Uh, I don't care?" I said. "And I don't think anyone is going to give a shit."

3

January, 2013.

Corolla and I floated over the deserts of Egypt. It's a big place, Egypt, and while the cities are well-mapped, the deserts not-so-much. I couldn't even guess where we were half the time. It felt like walking across a computer screen saver on loop: bright orange sand dunes, deep blue sky, bright orange sand dunes, deep blue sky. The desert stretches off for miles and miles and miles and it all looks the same; just sand as far as the eye can see. Sometimes I wondered if we were maybe flying in circles. But, no, I had a compass, and we were still headed east.

Corolla worried about overheating. I kept a few gallons of coolant in the trunk. He sucked down coolant like how a human would need water, but it kept him in good, working order.

I, on the other hand, didn't feel the heat. I noticed the heat, sure, but it didn't bother me.

We were listening to U2. I don't even like U2, but it was Corolla's turn to pick the music and he likes U2. Once his cassette was done, we were going to listen to Fight Like Apes.

We flew over the desert and worked on our one-liners.

Corolla asked me, "Okay, so you know what I would do if I was fighting an evil car?"

I was already grinning. "What's that?"

"I'd knock it into some power lines and say, 'Now you're a Volts Wagon.'"

I laughed and covered my face with my hands. How stupid. I regained my composure after a bit, then it was my turn.

"You know what I'd do if I was fighting the president?" I asked.

"What?" He was already laughing. I hadn't even got to the one-liner yet.

"I'd knock him into a big meat grinder..."

"Yeah?"

"Then say Hail to the Beef."

Corolla busted up laughing. I did, too. No better way to pass the time on a long road trip.

But eventually the game had to stop. We had reached our destination. Somewhere in the unexplored Egyptian desert was a Sphinx. Not *the* Sphinx, of course. A different Sphinx. The "real" Sphinx is right outside Cairo and is just something for the tourists. That Sphinx doesn't talk anymore. We were looking for Hobart, the Sphinx's idiot cousin. Hobart, like the Sphinx, was a riddle-telling oracle. No one ever visited Hobart though because, like I said earlier, he was an idiot.

Idiot or not, Hobart knew the secret location of the legendary Desert Strawflower. Strawflowers had oversized, beige petals and Xin used their nectar to make a special kind of burn cream that not only heals burns, it also prevents and removes burn scars.

We found him. Hobart. The idiot Sphinx.

Corolla landed in front of the giant sandstone creature. It towered over us, frozen in time, and cast a shadow that blotted out a part of the desert. I stepped out of the car and admired the craftsmanship. Hobart had the body of a lion and the face of a man. He resembled the real Sphinx, except Hobart still had a nose.

As I walked closer, I heard limestone scraping against limestone. Hobart opened his eyes and slowly moved his head in my direction. He opened his limestone mouth and at first I thought he wanted to eat me, but instead he spoke in a booming voice that echoed from deep within his ancient hallways.

"What brings you here this day, traveler?" Hobart asked.

I raised my head and looked him in the eyes. "I'm searching for for Desert Strawflowers. I heard you know where they're at, so start spilling those beans."

Hobart closed his eyes and frowned a little bit, like he was trying to remember. He took a deep breath, then opened his eyes and spoke.

"I will tell you," he said.

"Cool," I replied. "Thanks."

"If you can answer me this one riddle."

I sighed. Of course. "Okay, hit me with it."

He lowered his head down and glared at me like I was food. "If you fail to answer, I will swallow you whole."

"Oh yeah?" I said. "Well, you better pack a sack lunch and two cans of pop if you wanna go on that field trip."

Score! That was one of my one liners. I couldn't believe I actually got to use it. I looked back at Corolla with a huge smile and gave him a thumbs up.

Corolla whispered, "Nailed it."

Hobart wrinkled his forehead. "I do not understand."

I waved my hand at him. "Just ask your dumbass riddle."

He leaned even closer. His breath was a hot wind and it smelled like mummies. He said, "I am born in January, I live for twelves months, and then I die in December. What am I?"

I thought about it for a moment. Born in January. Lives for twelve months? Then dies in December?

"Uh. A year?" I asked.

Hobart leaned back, startled at how quickly I answered.

"Yes, well..." He paused. "You also have to tell me how you reached that conclusion."

"Uh." I ran my fingers through my hair. "Because a year starts with January, lives for twelve months, then the last month is December, so it dies."

He didn't speak for a little bit, then said, "You are correct."

I scrunched my face at him. "Was that supposed to be hard?"

He gasped. "No one has ever solved it before."

A laugh escaped me. "Well, that can't possibly be true."

"It's a good riddle," he said.

"Not really. A good riddle would be like..." I tried to think of some bullshit Sphinx-sounding riddle. "What's orange, then blue, then purple, then black?"

He raised an eyebrow at me and struggled to understand.

"What's orange...?" he repeated.

I said it back to him slower. "What's orange? Then blue? Then purple? Then black?"

"Uh..." He bit his lower lip and watched the clouds in the sky. He shut his eyes hard and made a low mumbling sound. He was really, really trying. After a while, he opened his eyes and answered, "A flower?"

"The sky," I told him. "Orange in the morning, then blue, then purple in the evening, then black at night."

His eyes went wide. "That's amazing."

I shrugged. "I literally just made it up."

"Are you an oracle like me?"

"No."

"May I..." He got quiet. "Use your riddle? It's quite good."

"Whatever, dude," I said. "But only if you tell me where the Desert Strawflowers are at."

"I agree."

And he told me. I thanked him. I got back in Corolla and we ventured out into the desert, off to find those little flowers.

Once we were out of earshot, Corolla said, "He's bad at his job."

I nodded. "No shit."

4

February, 2013

Demons are trapped in Hell. That's an unbreakable rule. But with help, whether it's cult-humans or some other supernatural force, that can change. Even then it's pretty rare, or so I'm told, because demons are unpredictable and letting them out of Hell never ends well for anyone.

There's two kinds of demons on Earth: demons *with* names and demons *without* names.

Demons Without Names are simple monsters and they come to Earth by possession. They jump inside a human (or sometimes a dog or a bear) and take control of their body. Then it takes a priest trained in exorcisms to send them back to Hell.

Demons With Names are far less common. These demons are summoned to Earth in their complete form, bringing their demonic body with them. They're far more powerful because they're not confined to a human host. Even the Pope can't send a Demon With Names back to Hell.

There are three Demons With Names living on Earth. Asag, the Skin Collector; Lylo, the Archdemon of the Army of Arms; and Voel, the Deranged Painter. They're the three that we know of, at least. If there are others, they're really good at laying low.

No one's heard from Asag or Lylo for years and years. People say they're overdue to cause a big heap of trouble. Who knows.

Voel on the other hand, she lives out of a fifth-story art studio in Astoria, Queens.

Her door was scratched all to Hell – haha – with red paint splattered in the symbols of some demonic language. I couldn't read Demon, so I had no idea what it said. I suppose there's a chance it wasn't red paint at all, but blood. It was tough to tell.

I pressed my ear to the door and listened. I heard the most horrible racket, something I suppose you could call music, but it was just high-pitched screeching and a deep, droning bass and electronic bleeps and bloops that didn't match the key or tempo.

I pounded on the door, hard enough to announce my presence, but not so hard that I bashed the door down. The psychotic noise immediately stopped and then there was silence. I heard the demon call out from inside the studio.

"Go away," Voel said. She sounded pissed off.

"I'm Penelope Salvo," I shouted at the door. "I need a favor."

She shouted back, "I don't do favors!"

And the music kicked back on, louder than before. It vibrated through the floorboards and rattled the doorknob.

I pounded again and said, "Xin sent me."

A brief second passed, then the music stopped again. The wood of the floorboards creaked as she approached the door. She opened it just a little, secured in place by the security chain. Her face appeared in the gap.

Voel looked radioactive, with lime-green skin, bright white hair speckled with black and red paint, and neon green eyes. She wore white coveralls also splattered with red and black paint, but more of it.

"Who?" she asked.

"Xin."

"Houng Xin?" When Voel spoke I could see her perfect teeth, as well as her vampire fangs.

"Yep."

Her eyes darted around. "Why didn't he come here himself? Why'd he send you. I don't know you."

"He's busy," I said. "I'm kind of like his assistant."

She sized me up, unimpressed. The door closed in my face. I heard the chain rattle, then she opened back up, swinging the door wide open.

"Get in," she said. "Quick. Before someone sees."

Voel's art studio was from another world. She had painted the entire inside black, floor to ceiling, even over the windows and the outlets and the light fixtures. The room was lit by a thousand candles of every shape and size: little teacup candles and candlesticks and birthday candles and even a candle in the shape of the Empire State Building. They were arranged all across the floor, some in clusters, some off by themselves.

Voel didn't own tables or chairs. The only furniture I saw was an easel for painting.

The easel sat in the middle of a ring of candles and supported a giant canvas. Buckets of red and yellow and black paint were arranged all around the easel, as well as paint brushes of every shape and size, and paint rollers, and toothbrushes, and paint-soaked rags.

I apparently caught her in the middle of painting something that looked like a bright orange woman.

She closed her apartment door and it boomed like a bank vault. The sound caught me off guard and I nearly jumped out of my shoes. I spun around to look back at her. She had her back against the door, bracing it shut.

"Nice painting," I said, pointing to her work-in-progress.

"No, it's not." She marched past me, went to her easel, and picked up a paint brush in each hand. She held them away from her body and waved them around like a wizard casting spells. Black and red paint swished through the air; some of it landing on the canvas, but most of it just splattering on the floor.

I took a cautious step backwards. A ribbon of red paint nearly ruined my shoes.

"It's terrible," she said. "It's bad. Everything I make is bad."

I shrugged. "I mean, I think it's okay."

She glared at me over her shoulder. "What did you say?"

"I'm just saying..." I paused. "I've seen worse."

She took a deep, cleansing breath, as if she was fighting a deep-down urge to rip my face off. She opened her mouth and released a horrible shriek – something painful and loud. She kept screaming, even as she tackled the easel to the ground and stabbed at the canvas with her paint brushes.

"This is pure mystery!" With every stab of the brushes, she added blots of red and black paint. "How can I kill mystery?" She stopped her attack, leaned her head back and shouted at the ceiling. "How can I kill that which will not die!?"

I stuck my hands in my pockets. I don't know if all demons are crazy, or if it's just Voel, but one thing was for sure: this chick was out of her goddamned mind.

She stood up and stomped her bare foot into the bucket of red paint. The bucket gurgled and paint splattered everywhere, all the way up to her knee. She pulled her foot out of the sucking paint and stomped on her canvas of the orange woman.

"This is hate painting!" She emphasized every word with another stomp of her foot. "I. Fucking. Hate. Questions."

"Huh." I took a step closer. "Why do you keep painting if you hate it so much?"

"Why?" She froze in mid-stomp. Black and red paint dripped from her bare foot. "Why do I do it?"

I shrugged. "Yeah. It seems to cause you a lot of stress."

She calmed down, but just slightly. "Because I have to. Because it's good for me. It's therapeutic, whatever that word means. Painting takes my mind off all the evil, horrible, fucked-up things I want to do."

"Oh."

"I want to kill dogs," she told me.

"O... kay."

"And I want to drown babies. And I want to push old people down the stairs at the subway. I want to find the sickest people in the world and slap the medicine right out of their hands. And when they ask for more medicine, I want to give them poison."

"Yeah. That's pretty intense. Probably good that you're painting, then."

For her, painting was some kind of self-therapy. Maybe resisting her demonic nature was what drove her crazy. Or maybe she was always like that. Who knows.

"Look," I said. "I hate to change topics on you, but I'm doing this job for Xin and I really need some demon blood. I know that sounds really weird, but-"

"Yes." She yanked the sleeve of her coveralls up to her shoulder and revealed her lime-green right arm. She came at me, leaving red footprints behind her. She waved her forearm in my face. "Anything for that Son of Adam. Do it. Slice me open."

"Oh." That was easy. I thought getting a pint of demon blood would require a little more convincing. I took a few steps closer to her. "Well... thanks for being cool about it."

"I like to bleed," she said. "I find it glorious."

I gave her a quick nod. "That's metal as fuck. I'm not a nurse or anything, so I don't have any medical equipment. I found this Big Gulp cup we can use. It holds thirty ounces."

"I will fill it," she said, staring into my soul with those green eyes. "The Big Gulp will overflow with the blood of my body."

"Hey, man, dealer's choice." I held the cup under her forearm. "I also didn't bring a knife or anything so-"

"No need." She grit her teeth and started breathing heavy. She used the power of her mind to open her skin and thick, green blood poured out. It drizzled into the cup like syrup, slowly filling it.

We stood there for a while, waiting to get thirty ounces out of her. It was kind of awkward, both of us just standing there in silence, face to face, while she bled out.

And it was taking a while.

"So you know Xin?" I asked.

"He hides my paintings," she said. "The ones I manage to finish. He hides them so they do not drive anyone insane."

"Oh yeah? That's cool."

I checked the cup. Half full. She didn't take her eyes off me.

"So..." I said. "You ever go out and do stuff?"

"I do nothing but paint," she said. "It is my passion. And it is also my prison."

I whispered to myself, "So metal."

I checked the cup again. Three-quarters full. This was taking a lot longer than I expected.

"You know what?" I said. "I think that's probably enough."

"No." She moved her arm closer to the cup. "We must see this ceremony to its conclusion." She kept bleeding into the cup.

"Of course," I said. "How silly of me."

So we waited as the cup slowly filled. I was done trying to make conversation. We just stood there in silence. Eventually the cup brimmed with green syrup, seconds away from overflowing.

"Alright," I said. "That's enough."

She grinned and showed me her fangs. "But, little mudblob, I have so much more blood yet to give."

"Yeah, you totally do." I moved the cup away from her arm. "You're totally full of blood. But I only have the one cup, so we're going to have to stop now."

A scream emerged from deep inside her guts and emerged from her throat like a dark creature. She threw herself at the splattered canvas and pounded her bleeding arm against it.

"I will drown the unknown!" she screamed. "Smother yourself in its warmth, foul secrecy! Gag and struggle for air and drown and die and we will bleed together!"

"So I'm gunna go ahead and take off." I backed towards the door. "Thanks for the cup of blood."

But she wasn't listening. She just continued to slam her bleeding arm on the canvas, adding her green fluids to the splattered red and black paint.

I reached the studio door and opened it.

"You want me to leave this door open or close it or...?"

"Die. Art." She punched her fists against the canvas. "Die, die, die and take your foul mysteries with you into the abyss!"

"You know what? I'm just gunna go ahead and close it." I opened the door and backed out. "Good luck with your art."

"Why?" she asked her painting. "Why won't you die?"

And I closed the door. It clicked shut.

Her nonsense screaming echoed down the hallway. Even as I went down the stairs, I could still hear her, just barely, but I could hear her.

Outside her building, street level, I climbed inside Corolla with my cup of demon blood.

"So how was it?" he asked.

"It was..." I had to think of the words. "It was really strange."

"Strange? Strange like how?"

"Strange like..." I had to think of the words. "Strange like Andy Warhol strange."

"Ew," Corolla said. "Gross."

"Right?"

5

March, 2013.

There's this secluded island out in the Pacific Ocean called Kula Kula. It's kind of close to Tahiti, around in that area. Kula

Kula is stupid beautiful. The weather is always perfect: clear skies, warm sunshine, and just the slightest breeze that rustles the leaves of the palm trees. The beaches are the cleanest white sand you've ever seen – no litter, no kids, no signs that read "PLASTIC BOTTLES ONLY" - just a perfect beach that stretches the whole way around the island. Then there's the ocean, so blue and so calm, like a private lagoon that covers the world.

Kula Kula is two square miles of paradise.

And no one wants it but me.

No one lives on Kula Kula. No tourists, no indigenous people. It's way smaller than Tahiti or Bora Bora. It's too small to build a resort. There's no dock, so you have to take a row boat to shore. It's the kind of island that someone would get stranded on and die. There's no phone, no lights, no motor cars, not a single luxury. It's just out there in the ocean, all alone, one of the few places left on Earth untouched by human hands.

And it's mine. I call dibs. I know it's technically a part of French Polynesia, but it's mine. I go there when I want to be alone. I can sit on the beach with Corolla and listen to music. I can smoke weed and watch the sun set.

I guess Kula Kula isn't technically mine. It's also Corolla's. We found it together in December when we were searching for the Typewriter Birds of Newspaper Island. Once we realized that Kula Kula was up for grabs, we started going there more often. Corolla likes to go there to "clear his head" and "just think about things," although I wonder if he just says that because I say that. Sometimes we'll sit on the beach together and talk about our adventures. Sometimes we just sit there and think. Sometimes we sit completely apart to be alone.

"Someone has a birthday coming up," Corolla said in a playful tone. He sat parked on the beach and faced the ocean. I sat cross-legged on the sand and took a spliff out of my book bag.

"Don't remind me." I put the spliff to my lips and sparked the lighter. I drew the smoke into my lungs and held it.

"You know, most people like their birthday," he said.

I didn't want to exhale, so I gave Corolla a whatever shrug.

"I was going to get you something," he continued. "But it's hard to buy things when you're a car."

I exhaled, releasing a cloud of positive energy into the world. I laid back and listened to the ocean waves hiss on the sand and the palm leaves rustle in the Pacific breeze. A tropical bird cackled somewhere behind us.

"Don't get me anything," I said. "Seriously."

We got a lot accomplished in the past four months, Corolla and I. We'd replaced Xin's entire collection of exotic plants and mosses and liquids, minus a few hiccups here and there. It was hard work, but the kind of hard work where you feel good when it's done. Now it was time for a well-deserved break and I couldn't think of a better way to spend it than getting high on the beaches of Kula Kula, just me and Corolla enjoying a sunset.

"I love it here," Corolla said. "No samurai ancestor ghosts. No Mayan blood gods. No two-dimensional paper people."

"I liked the two-dimensional paper people," I said.

"They were made of paper," Corolla said. "They smelled weird and they talked backwards."

I snapped my fingers. "Is *that* what they were doing? No wonder I couldn't understand them."

"Yep," he said. "They were talking backwards."

"Ohh," I said, nodding. "Wild and crazy stuff."

I took another drag off the spliff and gave up on talking. I kicked off my shoes and pulled off my socks so I could wedge my feet in the hot sand. Corolla turned on some Bob Marley and we watched the sun drop closer to the ocean. I heard that same tropical bird cackle again, one of nature's many musicians. Way out in the distance, I saw a whale erupt out of the water and crash back down. I wondered: are the whales trying to escape the ocean? Do whales look at the surface world the way human beings look at space? And, if so, does that mean that when a whale jumps out of the ocean, is that their space program?

"Did you see that?" I asked Corolla.

"Yeah," he said. "Looked like a humpback."

That word – "humpback" – made me laugh so hard, I started crying. I rolled in the sand and laughed like a crazy person.

"What?" Corolla asked. "What's so funny?"

I caught my breath long enough to point at him and shout, "Humpback!" Then right back to laughing, laughing so hard it made my stomach hurt.

"Oh my god." He sounded so judgmental.. "Grow up."

I laughed for an unreasonably long time, way longer than anyone should at the word "humpback." Eventually the moment passed and I regained my composure. I sat back up and watched the sun descend closer and closer to the ocean. I got real concerned when the thought occurred to me that the setting sun might crash into the sea. If that happened, it would boil the oceans and kill all life on Earth. Obviously that's not possible; that's simply not how the sun and the planets work. Still, as the sun got closer and closer to the water, my anxiety skyrocketed. I bit my bottom lip.

"Corolla," I said.

"Mm?"

"The sun's not going to crash into the ocean, is it?"

He sounded very confused. "Do what?"

"Just tell me the sun's not going to crash into the ocean."

"You're being paranoid," he said. "You need to stop smoking that stuff. I'm telling you, it's no good for you."

"Will you just say the words, 'The sun is not going to crash into the ocean.' Say that whole thing. Please?" Time was running out. The sun was about to crash into the ocean. We had to hurry.

He sighed. "The sun is not going to crash into the ocean."

The sun dipped behind the ocean and nothing happened. Once again, we'd saved the planet.

"Thanks, man." I gave him a pat on the driver side door. "We did it. Just in time, too."

"You are a strange, strange little girl."

I laughed. "Yeah."

The sun went lower, close to wrapping up it's adventure across the sky, off to light the rest of the planet. Day and night, on and on, so the cycle goes. It happened long before I was born. It would continue to happen long after I died. But through it all, I had Corolla.

I turned my attention to him – my talking, flying car and my best friend – and smiled. The sun took whatever little sunshine it had left and beamed it directly to the island of Kula Kula. Corolla looked orange, not white, in the final beams of daylight. He glowed like an angel. A car angel. I scooted across the sand and sat close enough to lean my head against his door.

"Penelope?" he said.

I kept my eyes on the sunset. "Yeah?"

"Why don't you like your birthday?"

"Why? Because..." I stopped myself. "I just don't."

Chapter 2

1

Rebuilding Xin's herbal shop was a huge pain in the ass. Xin obsessed over every single detail, trying to recreate the shop exactly how he remembered it. It was frustrating as shit, but I stuck with him through every step. He rebuilt his shelves by hand, nailing planks of wood together. I told him he didn't have to go to all that trouble; we had enough money to buy nice metal ones, but he refused. Xin didn't want new, fancy things. He wanted everything back the way it was.

While I spent months gallivanting across the globe, Xin kept busy with the rebuilding. I'd stop in every week or so to drop off shipments of exotic plants and I'd hang around for a day or two to help him out a little bit – do some heavy lifting or bend steel pipes with my bare hands – then be off on a new quest.

He hired a bunch of guys from the Bronx to repair the roof. I could hear them stomping around up there and could hear the hiss and thunk every time they fired off their their nail guns. I swiped a handful of roofing nails from them when they weren't looking so I had something to snack on between New York and Antarctica. After the roofers, Xin brought in a lady to replace the glass in all the broken windows. Then came the plumbers and electricians who redid the pipes and wiring. While those people were hard at work, Xin went shopping for a replacement toilet, same size and shape as before. After that he searched for the perfect bathroom sink. He rebuilt the shop slowly but surely, piece by piece, until things started to look like they did before the Westland Corporation blew everything to shit.

The only thing that didn't end up exactly the same was my bedroom. "It's your room," he had once said. "You can do whatever makes you happy."

For ten bucks I picked up the suede reading chair I'd seen down at the thrift store. It reminded me of a chair a Cambridge professor would sit in, surrounded by bookshelves and angled at a fireplace. I envisioned myself sitting in it, reading books far beyond my understanding. That rarely happened. I mostly used it to sit down and tie my shoes.

In December, right after Christmas, someone threw out an entire cardboard box of white Christmas lights. I found them next to a dumpster in the alley, so I scooped them up and tested them out. They worked just fine, so I strung them across the ceiling beams in my room.

In January, I took a few days off from my travels to help Xin get the jars ready. He knew exactly how many jars he needed, and what sizes. We collected exactly 537 jars of every shape and size, most of them donated from the local Chinese restaurants. We had 331 baby food jars, 181 pickle jars, 23 large mayonnaise jars, and five of those big three-gallon ones. Next came the 317 metal canisters. We rinsed everything out with bleach water and sorted them by size.

The only thing Xin couldn't replace to his borderline-insane OCD standards was the glass display counter. That bothered him a ton, not that he ever let on, but I could tell. We went to every pawn shop in New York City to scout out their display cases, but he frowned and shook his head at every single one. I'd told him that his old counter came from the '40s and the odds of finding an exact duplicate was one in a billion. Eventually we found something in Queens that he decided was "close enough."

I'll never forget Xin trying to buy that display case from the pawn shop guy. Xin stood there, analyzing every little chip in the wood and scratch on the glass. The pawn shop guy had no idea that Xin wanted to buy the case. He assumed Xin was shopping for the guns *inside* the case.

"Help you find anything?" the guy asked him.

"This case," Xin said. He put his old hands on the edges and pulled on it to test the weight. "How much for it?"

"You want..." The guy was pretty confused. "You want to buy everything in the case?"

"No," Xin said. "I don't want the guns inside the case. I want the case. The whole case. Just the case."

The guy looked at me for an explanation, but I felt like Xin was pretty clear. I shrugged and said, "He wants to buy the case."

"I can't sell the case," he said. "This is where I keep all my stuff. I use this every day."

"I will give you five-thousand dollars for this display case." Xin pulled out a tightly rubber-banded roll of money. He started stripping hundred dollar bills off the roll and laid them one-by-one on the glass counter.

The pawn shop guy watched the hundos stack up, probably wondering if this was some kind of prank. Eventually Xin reached five-thousand dollars and fell silent. The guy stared at the money, then at Xin. How does someone who owns a pawn shop turn down five-thousand dollars?

Just when I thought he was going to say no, the guy shrugged and said, "Alright. Let me empty it out."

After I searched the world for legendary plants, after I bleached hundreds of jars, after I carried our brand new display case into the shop, the big day had come. We were going to reopen. We planned on a very quiet, very on-the-down-low reopening. Xin scheduled it for April 1st.

"You scheduled it on my birthday," I told him.

"Is that so?" he asked. He wrote Chinese words across the masking tape stuck to the tops of the jars. He didn't even look up.

"Don't act like you don't know that," I said. "You know when my birthday is."

Still, he didn't look up. "I thought it was in September."

At first I thought he was joking, but moments passed and he didn't laugh. He didn't even grin at me. He was serious. How could he be my friend this long and not know my birthday? He wasn't even close. He didn't even get the month right.

"September?" I repeated.

He finally looked up, as if he were innocent of all charges. "I thought your birthday was in September."

I scoffed, now suddenly offended. "You seriously don't know when my birthday is?"

He placed his hands flat on the counter and locked eyes with me. "When is *my* birthday?"

"Uh." Fuck. Nice move, Salvo. Called out on your own bullshit. "Uhhh. January?"

He went back to writing on jars. "Now we are even."

I rubbed my nose. "Is it in October?"

"No."

2

It was the night before the grand reopening. Xin and I stayed up late to do some last minute cleaning. I propped open the front door to let in the cool night air and we worked in the yellow glow of our one-and-only light bulb. The radio was tuned to some '90s rock station, playing stuff like Foo Fighters and the Wallflowers. I swept the floors, getting in all the corners and behind the tables. Xin sprayed cleaner across the glass display case and wiped it down. We pruned the plants so they'd look fresh and healthy.

The big chores were done. All that was left were little things: replacing the toilet paper in the bathroom and straightening the jars into a perfect line, labels facing out. While I worked on the jars, Xin ducked under the counter and came back up with something wrapped in brown paper, something book-shaped, tied together with string.

He thumped the package down on the counter to get my attention. It worked. I looked up to see him waiting for me to come join him. I was immediately suspicious.

"What's this supposed to be?" I asked him.

"Birthday gift," he said.

"Xin." I gave him a disappointed look.

"Penelope," he replied, mimicking my tone. He pointed at my bar stool. "Sit. Sit. Open it."

Well, I couldn't say "no" now. He had already bought the gift and the damage was done. I gave him the most frustrated sigh in the world and stumbled over to the bar stool as if I were literally dying. I sat down.

He slid the package towards me and patted it.

"Open it," he said.

I rolled my eyes, pulled the string and undid the knot. Sticking my finger in the seam, I tore the brown paper wide open. There was a book inside.

"A book," I observed.

A leather-bound book, actually; hard backed, and the perfect size for a purse. The corners were worn thin and the spine was weak. It had four colorful strips of lace to use as book-markers – red, black, white, and gray – frayed and unraveling.

Also with the book was a small slip of yellow paper. Xin had written an inscription:

Penelope,
The Buddha teaches us that we are not given a good life or a bad life. We are given a life, and you make it good or bad. Please accept this gift. I hope the knowledge I pass on to you helps make your life better, as it has helped me make mine.
Your friend,
Xin Houng

Knowledge?
I flipped through the book. The pages were old and felt soft like paper towels. They were scribbled full with maps of islands and deserts and mountains, sketches of flowers and bushes and trees, as well as handwritten recipes. Lots and lots of recipes.

Ninjitsu Shadow
3 Soot Mushrooms from the Forest of Agony (Map on page 313)
One leg from a living mosquito
2 ounces of water from the Bindai River (Map on page 302)

On a night where there is no moon, combine the mushrooms, the mosquito leg, and the water into the mortar. Grind it into a paste and save in a jar.
When applied to the bottoms of your feet, your steps will be completely silent. You will not leave footprints in snow, sand, mud, or any other surface. The effects last until sunrise. Do not drink Ninjitsu Shadow, or you will be unable to speak until the next full moon.

"Is this for real?" I asked.
"This is my family journal," he said. He reached out and patted the book. "Given to me by my father, given to him by his mother, given to her by her father. It is over two-hundred years old. It contains every recipe I know and where to find the ingredients. And now I give it to you."

"Oh my god." I set the book on the counter and stepped back. This was sacred stuff, and I was getting my dirty fingerprints all over it. "Xin, I can't take this. This is like... way too important."
He pushed the book at me. "I want you to have it."

Honestly, I wanted to have it. But in the depths of my chugging mechanical heart, the responsibility terrified me. Still, Xin insisted. I picked it back up and turned to a random page. "You're serious?"

"I'm an old man. I don't have anyone else to pass this on to. And you already know the secrets of this place you call home."

I turned to a random page. It was a map of someplace called "the Caves of Boolg," hand-drawn by one of Xin's Chinese ancestors. The map took up two pages and detailed the maze-like caverns beneath a mountain called Boolg's Peak of Ancient Iron.

Wait.

"If this is an old Chinese book from two-hundred years ago..." I waved the book at him. "Then why is it in English?"

"It's not in English," Xin said. "It's in Chinese, written in Understanding Ink."

"Understanding Ink." I'd been at this game long enough to figure out the shtick. "Magic ink that anyone can understand, regardless what language it's written in, right?"

Xin nodded. "The recipe is on page 237."

As far as birthday gifts go, this one was a contender for number one, second only to the skateboard I got from Ma when I was a kid. I held in my hands more knowledge than the entire scientific humanity even knew existed, knowledge that would blow their little egghead minds. Knowledge that could possibly send global society into a fucked-to-death tailspin of chaos and confusion. Imagine what would happen if it ended up in the wrong hands.

I couldn't take my eyes off it. "Xin, I dunno what to say."

"Say thank you," he said.

"Thank you!" I snapped the book closed and bolted around the counter to give him a huge hug. He didn't hug me back – Xin wasn't much of a hugger, of course – but he gave me a respectable pat on the back. "I'm going to memorize the shit out of this book. I promise."

"I know you will."

3

The grand reopening to Xin's shop wasn't exactly what you'd call "grand." Sometimes when people hear "grand opening," they think balloons and spotlights and local celebrities. We didn't bother with anything like that. We weren't looking for attention and publicity. The herbal shop was a modestly-held secret, known only to a small community in Manhattan and we planned to keep it that way. We just needed enough human customers to seem legit, and to distract from the horde of dangerous weapons hidden in the basement.

So at 8 a.m. on April 1st, Xin unlocked the doors to a handful of locals from Chinatown. They were the same old customers we were used to: the restaurant owners wanted exotic spices, a few middle-aged people came in to buy herbs for medicinal remedies, and one lady bought four balls of Snow Cotton to completely eliminate the smell of her cat's litter box.

We helped eight people before lunch time, just like the old days, then things emptied out around noon. Xin settled in behind the counter and got to work crunching the numbers of the morning profits in his spiral notebook. I perched up on my barstool and studied my birthday book of magical mysterious mystery magic.

Xin and I sat there working quietly when someone knocked on the frame of the wooden screen door. The main door was propped wide open, so knocking was totally unnecessary. Xin glanced up from his notebook and pushed his glasses higher up on his nose. I looked over my shoulder to see Ilana Rittenberg, my old friend from high school, standing on the other side of the screen door.

"Holy shit!" I launched off my bar stool and bolted straight for her. "Ilana!"

"Hey," she said. She had a weird tone to her voice.

I threw open the door and side-hugged her tight – careful not to crush her bones – and escorted her inside. She walked a few steps into the shop and stopped with her arms crossed. Her fashion hadn't changed a bit; she had her Sluts t-shirt tucked into her black shorts and paraded around in torn up fishnets that barely held themselves together. When she walked, her combat boots thumped on the floorboards; the heels had ripped loose from the leather and flopped with every footstep.

All she did was glare at me. Her thick eyeliner made her look particularly unhappy.

"What?" I asked her, confused.

She gave Xin a sideways glance. Maybe she didn't like him, or maybe she just didn't want him to overhear.

She took one step closer and said, "Where have you *been*?"

Shit. Where have I *been*? Oh, you know. Around. The Sahara Desert. The Shadow Forests of Japan. The Seven Wind-Ripped Snowpeaks of the Himalayas. The forgotten jungles of Guatemala.

"Been?" I said, repeating the question and stalling for time.

"Yes, Penelope. Where have you been."

"Uh." I didn't have a good answer. "I've been out of town."

She squinted at me, as if our years of high school together gave her the power to see right through my lies. "For months?"

I shrugged and winced and offered the best explanation possible. "Shit be cray?"

"I haven't seen you since the day before Thanksgiving," she said. "You just fucking disappeared. And this isn't the first time."

"Yeah." I nervously rubbed my nose. "I'm sorry."

"So?" She arched her eyebrows at me, expecting something more than empty apologies. "Where did you go?"

"Uh." I glanced at Xin. He gave me a deer-in-headlights look. No help there. I turned back to Ilana. "I went to..." Had to think of something she would believe. "...China."

So stupid. She wasn't going to buy that.

"*China.*" She made the idea sound as stupid as I did.

But it was too late to backtrack. "Yup. China. For months."

"You. Were in China."

"Yeah."

"Where in China?"

"I was in..." Shit. I needed the name of a Chinese city. I couldn't think of one, not under that much scrutiny. I looked at Xin for a little help. "Xin, what was the name of that city?"

"Wang Chung," he said.

Wang Chung wasn't a city. Wang Chung was a band from the '80s. There I was getting interrogated and Xin was making jokes. I glared at him for a half-second, then turned back to Ilana.

"Wang Chung?" Ilana repeated. I could see the wheels turning. "Why does that sound familiar?"

"It's a..." I paused. "Popular city."

"It was popular in the '80s," Xin added.

I grit my teeth. "Yes. Thank you, Xin."

"Look," Ilana said, moving the conversation forward, thank Christ. "I'm not mad that you ghosted me for Thanksgiving and Christmas and New Years and the first financial quarter of 2013."

"Oh, good," I said. "Because you don't sound mad."

"I mean, I came down here mad, but I get it. I get it, Penelope. You've got this new... job... or whatever you call this thing you're doing. And with everything else you've been going through, I know you're busy. I just wanted to come find you and not wish you a happy birthday. And I didn't get you anything."

"You didn't?" I had a huge smile on my face.

"Nope," she said. "Not a damn thing."

"Dude. Thank you!" I gave her another quick side-hug. "You're the best."

"I know."

"Well, since you came all this way, do you want to go get some Chinese food?" I turned to Xin. "Hey, boss. Is cool if I leave for a little bit?"

He waved me along. "Go. Go. Enjoy."

Now I'm not one for birthdays, or presents, or celebrations, but if there was ever a reason to get lunch with my best friend – Corolla would be pissed if he heard me say that... my best *human* friend – then today was the day. I grabbed my black hoodie off the counter and me and Ilana were off.

4

We went to Liu's Peking Taste. Liu's doesn't have that dark ambient lighting like one of those fancy sit-down Chinese restaurants. Liu's was a deli-style operation that served food from behind a sneezeguard buffet table, with stained linoleum floors and daylight that spilled in through the large windows that looked out over the busy sidewalk. The business was mainly delivery and take-out, but they had a couple tables and chairs for the oddball customers who preferred to dine-in. We were treated to the racket of clattering kitchen utensils and hissing woks.

Ilana got a #4, which was some tofu-based stir fry and fried rice. I got a rice bowl with General Tso's shrimp, which I ordered to keep up appearances, but I couldn't actually eat at. The smell alone made me sick to my stomach. I eyeballed the silverware instead. God help me, that stainless steel looked delicious.

Xin says I eat like a pig, but I've got nothing on Ilana. She shovels food in her mouth like Yahweh is halfway to Earth and pissed off at everything we've done. She destroyed her #4. Halfway through, she asked me a question with her mouth so stuffed full of food, I couldn't understand a single word she said.

I couldn't even venture a guess.

"What?" I asked her.

She finished chewing, swallowed, then pointed at my food with her fork. "You're not going to eat?"

"Nah." I gave the styrofoam container a disgusted look. "I thought I was hungry, but I'm not."

She arched an eyebrow. I was Italian. It was in my DND to eat regardless of the circumstances. Ilana knew that. She wasn't buying my "not hungry" routine. Besides, who orders their favorite dish from their favorite Chinese food place just to sit there and not eat it? Half-robots like me, that's who. I had three seconds to give her a better explanation.

"Cramps," I confessed.

"Ah." She shoveled more food into her mouth, then asked, "What's with all the egg rolls?"

I had a to-go bag with ten shrimp egg rolls.

"Oh. These are for..." My car. My flying, talking 1998 Toyota Corolla who love egg rolls. "These are for my friend."

"What friend?" she asked. "The old man?"

Let's go with that. "Sure."

"What's his story?" she asked. "You've been working for him for almost a whole year."

"Xin?" My face lit up. Xin's my hero. Just talking about him put me in a great mood. "Xin's dope as shit."

"Dope as shit, huh?" She sucked down half of her Diet Coke until it gurgled deep into the crushed ice. "Isn't he, like, all elderly or whatever?"

"So? Elderly people can be dope. Look at Mister Rogers."

"How is your elderly old man dope?"

"I dunno. I have to give specifics? He knows a lot about rock music. And a lot about plants."

She nodded in agreement. "Plants *are* pretty dope." She chewed, then waved her fork at me. "Does he grow weed?"

"No, Ilana."

"Because if he grows weed, I'll buy some."

"He doesn't grow weed."

"He should." She used her fork to point at the people walking past the window. "Make a lot of money in this town."

"Xin's not really worried about making money."

"Oh, wow," she said with just a twinge of judgmental sarcasm. "The only guy in Manhattan not worried about making money."

"That's funny coming from you," I said. "Your parents are rich."

"They're not *rich*," she said. "They're frugal."

"You live in the Village."

34

She mocked my tone and said it back. "*You live in the Village.*"

"Well, you do."

"I make my own money, I'll have you know." She tore open a pack of soy sauce and dribbled it over her tofu and vegetables. "You're not the only one with a job. I uploaded my resume to work-manhattan dot com. It's like one of those career websites, but only for the Island. Manhattan businesses can contact you if they like your qualifications."

"When did you get qualifications?" I asked.

"Oh, hardy-har-har," she said. "I got a three-point-two at St. Mark's and I exaggerated all that babysitting stuff I did and made it sound like I ran a small business."

"Babysitting?" I said. "When did you do babysitting?"

"For my dad's boss."

"Ilana, that was a *dog*."

"Well, I didn't get into the *minutiae* of it, Penelope. It's a resume, not an application to NASA."

"And you're not worried they're going to find out you lied? They can nail you for fraud."

"Fraud?" She scoffed. "I lied about babysitting, Penelope. I didn't open a Ponzi scheme. What're they going to do? Slap me with a RICO? Drag me before Congress and make me testify?"

"Whatever, man." I poked at my food. "Good luck finding a job with babysitting experience."

"Uh, I'll have you know I already did. Today was my first day. Well, actually today was orientation. Tomorrow's my first day."

"*You* got a job?"

"Yes, I got a job."

"A *real* one?"

"Yes, Penelope. A real one. Why is that so hard to believe?"

"Doing what?"

"Receptionist," she said. "Basically answering phones for some company in Midtown. Stupid bullshit. Didn't they call you? I put you down as a reference."

"Call me on what? A tin can and some string?"

"You still don't have a phone?"

I shook my head. "Nope."

"Penelope Salvo, the only person in New York who doesn't need a phone." She scooped more food in her mouth. "Well, I already got the job, so I guess it doesn't matter."

"Working for some company in Midtown, answering phones." I gave her a sly grin. "Sounds punk as fuck."

She frowned and went for another packet of soy sauce. "Yeah, well, we can't all be janitors at a Chinese flower shop."

That was a little harsh. "Whatever. I was only joking."

"So am I." She stuck her fork in her stir fry. "Sorry, it's a sensitive topic. My dad's been a noodge since I'm not going to school. He says I have to either apply to NYU or find a job. And this job, it pays seventeen an hour. Can you fucking believe that? Seventeen an hour. So that makes me a sellout. Whatever. I'll play nice with Wall Street for seventeen bucks an hour. On nights and weekends, that's when I'll be punk as fuck."

Ilana Rittenberg got a real-life job with a real-life business? What was the world coming to? This was the same girl who snorted a line of crushed up Adderall and beat Grand Theft Auto 5 with a Guitar Hero controller.

She did it because she needed money. I used to need money. I used to need a lot of money. Money didn't really mean anything to me anymore, and I was alright with that.

Ilana's ADD must have kicked in, or maybe she had punk rock on the brain, because she quickly changed subjects.

"You wanna go to a show tonight?" she asked.

A show? I hadn't been to a show in forever. My new life consisted of traveling the world and interacting with magical forces that lay hidden from the rest of humanity. The things from my old life that used to get my adrenaline pumping, like shows, well, they just fell off my radar.

"It's at the Gold Mine," she continued. "The Sluts are playing tonight, and Space Station Forest Fire, and the Paris Sights."

Ilana had been fucking this dude from the Paris Sights off-and-on since junior year. And while the idea of going to a show sounded like a blast, I had to say no.

"I dunno." I averted eye contact.

"Bitch, come on. I haven't seen you in months. You can't go to this show with me? You got something better to do?"

"No." I tried to think of a good excuse why not. Nothing came to mind. "I mean, I want to go, but I can't. I just... feel weird."

"Crampy?" she suggested.

"Yeah." Not at all true, but when it came to plausible excuses, Ilana was doing all the heavy lifting for me. "Exactly."

Truth was, I didn't get cramps anymore. Without getting into too much detail, ever since I swallowed Impossible Red, there'd been no more Shark Week in Panty Town. Whatever those nanites did when they rearranged the molecules of my skin and bones and organs, it did something weird to my ovaries, too. I couldn't say what, exactly and it's not like I could just roll down to the discount OBGYN and explain that I'm a half-robot half-human and have them do a sonogram to find out if my ovaries had been converted into D-cell batteries.

And while it might freak out a lot of girls to suddenly be barren – if that was truly what was going on inside me – it didn't bother me in the slightest. I had no plans to have kids, ever, so all I was missing out on was that monthly feeling like someone blasted me in the guts with a shotgun.

I will say, however, even though I was cool with it... a part of me wondered, "What the fuck is going on inside my body?"

"You should come," Ilana said, still going on about the show at the Gold Mine. "Suck it up. I haven't seen you in forever."

"I dunno."

"A.J. and B-Gold are bartending tonight," she added. "They won't charge us anything. We can get fucking wasted."

I was running out of reasons to say no.

Approximately one year ago, this was everything I would have wanted from a Monday night: underage drinking, loud punk music, probably some moshing and making out. But, as they say, what a difference a year makes. Now my thoughts were wrapped up in getting egg rolls back to my talking car and ensuring that I was rested up for my shift in a supernatural plant shop.

I had an old life once, a normal life. But sitting there across from Ilana, I realized I could never go back to that. And if that was going to be the case, if I was doomed to be a supernatural robot for the rest of my life, it would have been nice to party like a regular girl one last time. I'd go to the Gold Mine with Ilana and do the things normal teenagers do.

"Penelope?" Ilana's voice snapped me out of my thoughts.

"Yeah?"

"You're..." She pointed at my mouth. "You're eating your fork."

"Oh." I didn't even realize it, but she was right. I pulled the silverware out of my mouth and looked at it. It was twisted and mangled with teeth marks deep in the metal. If I had chewed any longer, I would have bit the tines right off.

"Holy shit, Penelope." She snatched the fork out of my hand and held it up like some kind of forensics investigator. "You deadass chewed the metal. What're you, a fucking X-man?"

"I got strong teeth," I told her. It was time to change the subject before she started asking too many questions. "You know what? I changed my mind. I'll go tonight."

"You're serious?" She hit me with a million dollar smile; almost literally a million dollars. Her parents had spent a fortune on braces and retainers. Kind of a waste of money if you ask me, since it took an act of congress to get Ilana to smile for anything.

"Sure," I said with a shrug. "Why not."

5

Me and Ilana walked around Chinatown after lunch to catch up on the last few months. Ilana did most of the talking. She told me about how her parents caught her with weed and didn't flip out as much as she thought they might, and how her brother got grounded from Xbox because he kept calling everyone "fags."

I wanted to tell Ilana about my life, too, but I couldn't. My stories were so absurd and impossible. Stealing from NASA? Talking to Sphinxes? Scaling ancient Mayan pyramids? Don't get me wrong, the stories were awesome as shit and Ilana would have loved hearing the details, but I couldn't dump all that information on a regular human like her. She would have lost her mind, or assume I had lost mine. So when she asked me about the months I spent in Wang Chung, China, I just made up a bunch of nonsense bullshit and then found an excuse to go home.

I agreed to meet her at the Gold Mine later that night.

I got back to the shop around three and went back to work. The rest of the day went by normal, uneventful, and with nine more customers. Right as the sun began to set, Xin finished up with the days numbers and put his spiral notebook away. He then went through his daily closing routine: checking the basement padlock, putting on his 1982 knock-off Member's Only jacket, and saying goodbye.

"Goodnight, Penelope," he said as he went for the door.

I swept the floor around the Looping Bandis. "G'nite, Xin."

He reached the doorway and paused. I kept sweeping, but when he didn't leave I glanced up at him from the corner of my eye. He was just standing there staring at me.

"What?" I said as if I had done something wrong.

He said, "Someday, I'm going to turn this store over to you. You know that, right?"

"This isn't that retirement speech again, is it?"

38

"I'm simply pointing out how far you've come."

"Well, thanks." I shrugged. "If you say so."

"But the day will come when you'll have to run the shop."

I stopped sweeping to give him my full attention. "What the hell you keep saying that for?"

He closed his eyes and sighed, exasperated. I cursed again. Xin hated that, but old habits die hard. He didn't make a big deal out of it though; just a quick sigh and then he moved on.

"I am simply reminding you that one day this place, and everything in the basement, will be your responsibility."

"And I'll look after it. I'll do a great job." I turned my attention back to my sweeping. "When the day comes."

Xin gave me a smile and stepped out onto the front porch.

"Happy birthday, Penelope."

"Right back atcha, grandpeppers."

Chapter 3

1

The Gold Mine is a punk rock bar on Bowery, not too far from my old apartment building. I wasn't 21, but I'd been inside a couple times. Ilana had a pretty convincing fake and the door guys always seemed to have a crush on one of us. Ilana knew a lot of people there – and so did I – mostly other punks and hipsters from Manhattan, or guys who were a few years ahead of us in high school, or street punks from around town who sat on the corners and harassed tourists for money or smokes.

The Gold Mine let a lot of questionable stuff slide, and not just the underage drinking. It was an overcrowded shit-show of a bar, especially on the weekends, packed shoulder-to-shoulder with all kinds of troublemakers. It was impossible for the bartenders and door guys to keep things under control. Not that it mattered; they really didn't give a shit. When the bands started up and the lights went down, people would smoke weed right there on the floor, no fucks given. The bartenders were all fucking girls from the burlesque troupes and other bands, and those same girls would bring down all their strung out friends to drink for free. One time I caught this couple fucking against the wall in the girls bathroom. Fights broke out pretty regular and it was up to the crowd to break it up. Unwanted groping was a real problem in the mosh pit – and god knows what else – but thankfully that shit never happened to me.

I always wondered why the Gold Mine never got shut down, then Ilana told me this third-hand story about why. Apparently years ago, way before I ever started going there, some bad shit had gone down when this rockabilly-looking motherfucker grabbed one of the tip jars and bolted out the front door. He got away with, like, two or three-hundred bucks, but the owner happened to be right outside the door and chased him down. The owner dude, Bryan Reynolds, is this huge weight-lifting motherfucker who wears tank tops all the time, even in the winter. So this rockabilly thief bolts down Bowery with a full tip jar and Reynolds goes sprinting after him.

Reynolds catches up to the dude a block away. This rockabilly guy, scared shitless of the buffalo-sized human being chasing after him, throws the tip jar to the ground in hopes that it would get Reynolds to leave him alone. Wrong. Reynolds grabs the dude by his pompadour, spins his ass to the sidewalk, and jumps on top of him. From what I hear it was an absolute slaughter with Reynolds laying into this fuckwit with both fists, no fucking mercy.

Out of nowhere, this NYPD cruiser rolls up hot, because from their point of view all they see is one man bashing another dude's face in. They have no idea Bryan Reynolds owns a bar, or that this rockabilly dude stole a tip jar. These two cops show up and Reynolds jumps off the guy so they can arrest the thief.

Wrong again.

No, these two cops decide to go after Bryan Reynolds, and fucking hard. Reynolds is standing there doing nothing when suddenly, boom, out of nowhere this cop tackles him to the ground and throws him in a brutal choke hold. The other cop runs up and starts kicking Reynolds in the face and stomach and all kinds of shit. Meanwhile the rockabilly dude scrambles to his feet and bolts.

The cops kick the shit out of Reynolds so hard, they put him in the fucking hospital. They didn't do any permanent damage or anything – no coma or deaf-in-one-ear shit or anything like that – but he did have some broken ribs and his face was all fucked up. When the cops went to fill out a report, they finally heard the whole story about the tip jar and they realized, "Oh, fuck, we just beat the shit out of a bar owner who was just going overboard on some punk ass thief."

So the NYPD is totally expecting a lawsuit and some hellacious coverage on CNN. And who could blame them? If

Reynolds wanted to, he could have nailed those cops to a cross and raked the department over the coals for millions of dollars.

But he didn't. That's the kind of guy Bryan Reynolds was. He was actually super cool about the whole thing and said – so I heard – "It wasn't the cops fault. They didn't know who I was or why I was kicking the shit out of that loser. It was just one huge misunderstanding."

So no lawsuit. Those two officers kept their jobs.

Ever since then, the cops didn't fuck with the Gold Mine. Hell, the fire marshal wouldn't even come around to do inspections anymore. It's kind of an unspoken rule in the NYPD that no one bothers Bryan Reynolds. If you get a call about people smoking inside the Gold Mine, you ignore it. If there's fighting in the street, break up the fight, but the bar doesn't pay a fine. If you drive by and see young-ish looking kids drinking beer, you just keep on driving. Because after what they did to poor Bryan Reynolds, it's the absolute least they could do.

For those reasons and more, the Gold Mine had a reputation for being one of the roughest bars on Manhattan Island, but it also had its fair share of heroes; the middle-aged punk rockers and metalheads had zero-tolerance for dudes fucking with girls.

All in all, my kind of place.

2

The inside of the Gold Mine isn't much to look at; just a big square room with a bar and bar stools and a few '90s pinball machines that barely work. The windows are completely covered, inside and out, by layers of fliers that date all the way back to the '80s. The bathroom doors are painted black with "Penis" and "Vagina" written on them in white spray paint. There's a black stage against one wall, just barely big enough for a drum set and a few guitarists. The bar-top itself is completely carved up with initials and pentagrams and a dictionary of filthy language, and stacked behind the bar are a dozen styrofoam coolers filled with the shittiest beer New York has to offer.

They keep the lights low, so no one can really see how gross the place truly is. They pump punk rock through the speakers at concert levels, so no one can hear anything. It smells like piss and vomit and cigarette smoke and spilled beer.

There was a door guy that night collecting three dollars for cover and doing a half-assed job of checking IDs. The Gold Mine cares more about assholes on the banned list and shitty street kids who don't have any money than underage drinking.

I showed up and didn't see Ilana loitering on the sidewalk, so I figured I'd check inside. The door guy put his arm across the entrance and blocked me. He was a huge death-metal looking motherfucker with a goatee, long hair and tattoo on his forearm of Darth Vader force choking a stormtrooper.

"I.D.," he said.

"Oh." I patted my pockets, then rolled my eyes in a fairly convincing I-can't-believe-it sort of look. "I left it at home."

"How old are you?"

"Twenty-one." False. "Today's my birthday." True.

"What year were you born?"

Shit. Pop quiz. I was born in 1994, and that made me 19. So if I was supposed to be 21, what year would I be born in? I couldn't do that kind of math, not instantaneously, and not with the door guy staring right at me. I looked at the quadratic equation tattooed on my right bicep. No help there.

I shrugged and said, "I don't know?"

He looked me up and down to size up how much trouble I could possibly cause. I had on black shorts, two studded belts, and a black Star Fucking Hipsters shirt with the sleeves cut off. I had bracelets with spikes – the ones I got from East Village Thrift – and a necklace I made out of this lump of sandstone I found when I went to Egypt.

I didn't look like trouble. At least, not for the Gold Mine.

"Whatever." The door guy moved his arm out of the way and let me in. "You're fine."

The bar was half-full with punks and hipsters, busy enough that the bartenders cracked beers at a steady pace, but not so busy that I couldn't muscle my way through the crowd.

The bartender was this energetic guy who seemed to laugh at everything. We made eye contact and he pointed right at me. There was a speaker right over my head blasting gritty, lo-fi punk rock. I could barely hear him.

He either said "You're next" or "You're sexy." His smile was super friendly, so I guess it could have been either one.

"PBR," I shouted at him.

He nodded, stuck his hand in one of the coolers and sloshed around for a PRB. He found one, set it on the bar in a splash of water and ice, and slid it over to me.

"That'll be six," he said.

Jesus-fuck-me-running, six bucks for a PBR?

"B-Gold!" Ilana shouted at my bartender as she emerged from the crowd to put her hands on my shoulders. She shook me a little bit to say hello, but kept her eyes on the bartender. "B-Gold, she's with me!"

B-Gold gave us double thumbs up and moved on to take someone else's drink order. He didn't charge me anything and didn't bother to take Ilana's money.

"Dude, thanks!" I shouted right in her ear.

Ilana had some serious '90s ska fashion going on that night. She wore these god-awful plaid pants – black and white – complete with suspenders, except they dangled from her hips. Her combat boots were untied and loose and looked like they could just slip off with each step. She wore a white tank top over a black tank top and tied the look together with about a dozen necklaces of all length and size, decorated with pentagrams and skulls and all kinds of shit.

"Happy non-birthday!" she shouted. She swung her PBR into mine and smacked them together. Cold beer splattered on both of us. "Here, follow me! I want you to meet Ian!"

She grabbed me by the arm with intent to drag me around, but I can't be moved against my will, at least not by a puny human. She gave me a weird look, as if that half-second of supernatural immobility really fucked with her head. I quickly recovered by letting her "drag" me to where she wanted to go.

"Ian your boyfriend?" I asked.

She laughed. "He wishes!"

We cut through a sea of leather jackets and spikes and elbows. She led me over to this denim-jacket-wearing motherfucker leaned up against the front window. He had a beer tucked into his elbow so he could fiddle with his phone.

"Ian, this is Penelope!" she shouted at him, then turned to me. "This is Ian. He's in the Paris Sights."

"Ah." I sipped my beer. "Cool."

For what it's worth, while I couldn't eat normal food, I could at least drink alcohol. It didn't get me drunk, or affect me in any capacity, but it also never made me vomit.

"What kind of music do you play?" I asked the guy. "Punk or metal or something?"

This Ian dude scoffed, but didn't even look up from his phone. "I don't use labels."

"That's cool," I said, sarcastically. "You're a cool guy."

44

"What did you say to B-Gold?" Ian said to Ilana, suddenly looking up from his phone, suddenly a part of the conversation.

She gave me a weird look, then said, "Do what?"

Ian repeated himself in this snotty tone, as if she were stupid. "What. Were you saying. To B-Gold?"

"B-Gold?" She looked at the bar. B-Gold, our bartender, was busy cracking beers left and right for customers. She looked back at Ian. "Barely anything. I told him Penelope was with me. It's her birthday."

"Yeah?" Ian did not seem happy. He stuck his phone in his pocket and took a step closer to us. "That's all you said to him?"

"What the fuck are you getting at, Ian?" Ilana shouted. "What the fuck does it matter to you? Maybe I told him I'd suck his dick later in the bathroom. Is that what you want to hear?"

"Fuck this." Ian stormed off towards the door. He tried to shoulder-check me out of his way like a real tough guy, but he would have had better luck trying to shoulder-check an aircraft carrier. I didn't move. Good. I hoped it hurt. He was lucky I didn't snap him in half.

"I'm so sick of your shit, Ian!" Ilana yelled after him. The bar was so loud and chaotic, no one else noticed. "Grow the fuck up!"

Ian spun around and gave her both middle fingers.

Awkward.

"Well, he seems nice," I said to her.

"Fuck him," she said. "A week he doesn't text me, and now suddenly he gives a shit that I ordered a beer from Bryan Gold? Fuck that. He thinks he's a fucking rock star because he's in the Paris Sights, but go outside of Manhattan and you know who's heard of them? Fucking no one!"

3

The members of the Sluts - two grungy-looking dudes and some girl in a plaid mini-skirt - stumbled onto the stage, already half-drunk. The boys strapped on their instruments, the girl sat behind the drums with her legs spread, which meant her underwear was on view for everyone in the crowd. Everyone mobbed the stage. The drummer chick hit the sticks together over her head - "one, two, three, four" - and they all dove in to some of the fastest, loudest, heaviest punk rock I'd ever heard. I couldn't understand a single word they were singing; everything sounded like static through those shitty speakers.

For three minutes they bounced around the stage. They spit out the lyrics and leaned down to scream in the faces of the crowd. At the end of the first song, the lead singer – this thin, wiry dude with cocaine-levels of energy – yelled "fucking mosh!" and the band started in on the next song. After that, all hell broke loose. The crowd transformed into a shifting monster of shoving hands and bouncing heads. I wanted to get in there and fuck around – and I almost did – but I knew better. One careless bump from me and I'd put someone in the ER. If I hit someone in the face, better call the morgue.

"Let's mosh!" Ilana shouted at me.

"No way!" I held up my beer. "I don't want to spill this!"

So we just watched the mosh pit happen, which can be just as good sometimes. The crowd wasn't even listening to the Sluts anymore; they just moshed and brawled and thrashed around on their own free will. I loved it. It made me smile. For a moment – for just a brief moment – I felt human.

It wouldn't last long.

I don't know why, but something possessed me to peek out the window. There was a narrow gap between a couple of the fliers superglued to the glass, right about eye level. It gave me a slim view of the street outside.

Parked up the street, sitting under a street lamp, was a black SUV with tinted glass. Black SUVs aren't all that uncommon, but you don't usually see them parked in this neighborhood, especially not at night. The driver side window was down and I could just barely see the driver: a guy in a black suit, focused intently on the bar with some kind of electronic binoculars. It could have been nothing, I suppose, but why would a guy in a suit be running surveillance on a punk rock bar on a Monday night?

Ilana elbowed me in the ribs to get my attention.

"What's wrong?" She joined me in a glance out the window.

"Nothing!" I shouted back.

Probably nothing.

But also maybe something.

"I'm gunna go outside real quick!" I told her as I made my way to the door.

"Why?" she asked.

I couldn't give her a good answer. I didn't exactly know.

I turned back to her and said, "I'll be right back!"

I stepped out front. Immediately the music dropped to a muffled volume. A couple groups of cigarette-smoking punks and hipsters were clustered up in conversation circles on the sidewalk, checking their phones. They didn't notice me come out – why would they? – and they certainly didn't notice the SUV further up the road.

On the other hand, the guy in the SUV saw me. When I squinted in his direction, he lowered the binoculars. We locked eyes. He leaned back into the car and the window rolled up. Well, if that wasn't suspicious, I didn't know what was. In the back of my mind, I had a good idea who this might be – or, technically, who this guy might be working for – but I didn't want to jump to that conclusion. Not yet.

"Dude!" Ilana rushed outside and right up to me. "You okay?"

"I'm fine." I kept my eyes on the SUV. "It's nothing."

"Nothing?" she repeated. "You came out here for nothing? Don't bullshit me."

Alright. Fine. I couldn't keep lying to her. I turned away from the SUV and faced Ilana. With a whisper, I asked her, "Do you see that black SUV behind me? Parked half a block up?"

She peered over my shoulder. "Yeah. Why?"

"I think..." Here we go. If I tell her my suspicions, she's just going to ask more questions. "I think they're watching me."

"Watching you?" She gave me this sneer, like I was bonkers. "Why would anyone be watching you?"

"I dunno. Is it still there? What're they doing?"

"Who is 'they,' Penelope?" she asked. "You sound like one of those crazy subway hobos."

"Just tell me," I snapped. "What's the SUV doing?"

"They're leaving."

Yeah. Leaving, now that they've been spotted. Well, before they got away, I wanted to ask a few questions.

I spun around and speed-walked in their direction, cutting right across the street. Just like that, the SUV dropped into gear and went to speed away. I knew if I ran fast enough, I could get in their way and block their path.

"Hey!" I shouted at the vehicle. "Hey, I wanna talk to you!"

But the driver of the SUV wasn't taking requests. It built up speed, probably going 50 in a 35. That was fine. As long as I could get in front of it, I could shoulder-check it and wreck its entire front end, bring it to a stop, then crack it open like a walnut for the squishy guy inside. And just when I thought I could do it, just when I was smack-dab between the two headlights, the SUV swerved hard and off-roaded it onto the sidewalk. It crashed right through a newspaper dispenser and blazed right past me.

"Why the fuck are you following me?" I chased after them. "Fuck off and leave me alone!"

For a moment there, I had the idea to uproot a telephone pole right out of the sidewalk and chuck it like a javelin through the back window of the SUV, but how would I explain that to Ilana and everyone else standing in front of the Gold Mine? I had no choice but to stand in the middle of the street and watch them blaze through a red light, then disappear around the corner.

Just like that, the SUV was gone.

"What the fuck!" Ilana yelled as she marched after me in the middle of the road. "Penelope, what the fuck was that all about?"

"These people, man!" I shouted. That was as detailed as I could get. What more could I tell her? "These fucking people!"

"What fucking people?" she asked.

"They're just..." I was so pissed, I was shaking. I couldn't talk, or think, or anything. I wanted to punch a brick wall, but I couldn't even do that. "They're people from a long time ago and... and I just... they won't leave me the fuck alone."

Ilana was confused and scared and she shouted, "Penelope, you're not making any god damn sense!"

I took a deep breath. "I know. I know."

I ran my hands through my hair and tried to think. The real problem here was that I couldn't tell Ilana anything. Even if I did try to explain, she wouldn't believe me. And even if I showed her undeniable proof – if I ate a fork in front of her, or if I introduced her to Corolla – what would that accomplish? If anything, I would only be putting her life in danger. And I couldn't do that to her. Ilana was my only human friend.

I couldn't have humans friends anymore. I needed to be around people I could actually talk to, people who knew about the supernatural.

I turned to face her.

"Look, Ilana, I love you like a sister, but I'm just going through some weird life shit right now and..." When I started this sentence, I didn't know how I was going to finish it. "...I don't think we should hang out anymore."

She squinted at me as if I were telling a really offensive joke. But when she saw how serious I was, she frowned and her eyes watered. I might as well have slapped her in the mouth.

"What in the hell, man?" she whispered.

"I'm sorry."

Her voice was quiet. "What?"

"I'm just... I am so sorry. Ilana, I am so, so sorry."

"I don't..." Her voice cracked a little, almost as if she were on the verge of tears. That's something that's never happened. This was Ilana Fucking Rittenberg. Ilana Rittenberg laughed her way through the Saw movies. Ilana Rittenberg got the giggles at my own mother's funeral. But I'll be god damned if, in that moment, a black mascara tear rolled down the side of her face.

I thought I might cry next. But I heard Michael's voice. *Here come the water works.* I didn't cry. I shut it off. I took those sad emotions and swallowed them down into the pit of my stomach.

"Penelope," she said softly. "I don't understand."

"Look." I put my hands on her shoulders. "I'll explain someday. But not right now. Right now... I have to go."

And I hugged her. We were not the hugging type. Not at all. But this was different, after all.

This was goodbye.

4

I ran all the way back to Chinatown. I checked over my shoulder for black vehicles. Who was watching me? Was it the government? Was it Westland? Whoever it was, I *hoped* they were still out there, because I really wanted to crack a few skulls and send them a message that I'm unfuckwithable. But I got all the way home and didn't see anyone following me.

It was probably midnight or a little later when I got back to Forge Street. A lot of the places in Chinatown are open 24 hours – the restaurants mostly, for delivery, and the laundromats – but it was Monday and things were pretty quiet. I jogged down the sidewalk to Corolla, opened the passenger door and crawled in.

He said, "And just where have you been, young lady?"

I sat in the dim glow of his dome lights. "Corolla. Did you see anything weird tonight?"

"As a matter of fact, I did," he said. "A man in a spandex cat suit air-humped that mailbox for almost a whole hour."

"Did you see anything weirder than that."

"Jeez," he said. "How weird do you want it?"

"I mean cars, Corolla. Did you see any black cars?"

"Black cars?" he repeated, confused. I guess it did sound dumb. This was Manhattan. Of course he saw black cars.

"Did you see any Westland cars? Limos? Or SUVs?"

"Uh." He thought for a moment. "No."

"So you didn't see anyone around here scoping things out. No one's been spying?"

"No. At least, I don't think. I've been listening to the news."

"Huh."

"Why?" he asked.

I relaxed a little bit in my seat and laid my head back. "I was just down at the Gold Mine with Ilana and this dude in a black SUV was watching me with fucking binoculars."

"Oh." He paused. I let him have a moment so that could sink in. Then he said, "I bet it was cool to hang out at the Gold Mine. I wonder what it's like to get invited to do that. Sounds fun."

"Corolla."

"Maybe someday I'll have a friend who will take me to the Gold Mine. A really good friend."

"Corolla, stop." I turned in my seat and checked out the back windshield for strange or suspicious cars. Nothing. Everything seemed normal. "They're not here."

"Or maybe you're just being paranoid," Corolla said. "Maybe you were overcome with guilt because you were at the bar while your best friend was sitting here parked on the street."

"You have to park on the street!" I said. "You're a car!"

"I want to get parked in a parking garage."

"I can't afford to park you in a garage."

"Mister Chan from the stationary store and afford to park his car in a garage."

"Well, I'm not Mister Chan from the stationary store, am I?"

He muttered, "I wish I was Mister Chan's car."

"What was that?" I asked.

"Nothing."

"Do you want to live with Mister Chan?"

"No."

"Do you think Mister Chan is going to take you to Egypt? Or Ireland? Is Mister Chan going to hit up every thrift store in SoHo looking for Phil Collins cassettes? Is Mister Chan going to slam egg rolls in your car door?"

"No," he said, quietly. "Mister Chan only has one arm."

"Corolla, the only reason I went to the Gold Mine was so I could hang out with my old friend from high school. But after that SUV thing, I don't want to get her caught up in all our crazy bullshit. So I told her we can't be friends anymore."

Corolla's voice returned to normal. "Oh. That sucks."

"Yeah." I thumped the back of head against the seat. "Now I kind of regret doing that. I wasn't thinking."

"I didn't realize you were having a bad night."

"To say the least."

"Well, I've got something that might cheer you up," he said. "In the glove box."

I squinted at him. "What is it?"

"Just a little something."

I squinted harder. "Is this going to be a birthday gift?"

His replay was coy. "Maaaaybe."

"Corolla. We talked about this. No birthdays."

"I know. I know. But it's already paid for and I can't take it back, so you just have to accept it."

I gave him the longest, most frustrated sigh in the world. Then I felt bad. Corolla went to all the thought and effort to get me a gift - no easy feat for a car, obviously - and I wasn't being the least bit thankful. In fact, I was being a real bitch about it. Corolla was my best friend and I owed him better than that.

So I decided to play along. I popped open the glove box and rooted around inside. Mixed in there with the REO Speedwagon cassette tapes was a square blue envelope. I took it out. There was a card inside, so I slid it out and read it.

It was a gift certificate.

OHM BLISS YOGA
MASSAGE + YOGA
A gift to: Penelope Salvo
From: Mister Corolla
$100

"Yoga?" I had never, ever, *ever* in my life, ever expressed any interest in twisting myself into a pretzel or listening to seagull sound effects. Maybe this was some kind a practical joke. "You got me a gift certificate for yoga?"

"Yeah!" He sounded really excited about the idea. "And a massage, too, although that probably feels like massaging a bulldozer. But that's okay! You don't have to get the massage. You can use the hundred bucks on anything you want. Like yoga classes. Or... well... all they do is yoga and massage."

I hated to seem ungrateful. "I've never done yoga before."

"Yeah, I know!" Corolla wasn't the least bit discouraged. "Now you can try it! I hear it's very relaxing. And good for the body. And also good for the... attitude."

I arched an eyebrow at him. "Attitude?"

"Maybe attitude is the wrong word." He stumbled over his own words for a moment. "I'm just saying that sometimes you get real feisty. That's all. Yoga is supposed to be a very positive experience. Good energy, you know? It'll help you chill out."

"Feisty?"

"I said sometimes!"

"When am I ever *feisty*?"

"Well, right now, for example."

I was seconds away from showing Corolla "feisty" when I realized – holy shit – he was right. Maybe he had a point. Maybe yoga wasn't such a crazy idea. I gave the gift certificate a suspicious glance "Yoga, huh?"

"Plus, they put rocks on you. Hot rocks. They put hot rocks right on your face."

I had never heard of anything so ridiculous. "Why would they put hot rocks on your face?"

"I dunno," he said. "It's supposed to be good for you."

"How is putting hot rocks on your face good for you?"

"There's gotta be something to it," Corolla said. "Cuz they charge forty-five dollars to do it."

"Oh." I flipped the gift certificate around and looked at the back. Non-refundable, huh? I held it up where Corolla could see it. "I have a question."

"Okay. The floor recognizes Penelope Salvo."

"Where did you get this?"

He was quiet for a moment. "From the yoga store."

"That's not what I meant." I waved the certificate at his radio. "You're a talking car with no arms and you don't have any money. How did you get this?"

"I did it over the phone," he said. "They only heard my voice. They have no idea I'm a car."

"Okay. Follow up question."

"You have the floor."

"How did you use a telephone?"

"Huh?"

"How did you, a talking car with no hands, get access to... and then subsequently *use*... a telephone?"

Corolla cleared his throat. "I had my friend Gomez help me."

What in the... "Who the fuck is Gomez?"

"I'm not the one on trial here."

Chapter 4

Impossible Red runs routine maintenance on my body twenty-four hours a day, repairing the torn fibers of my industrial-rubber muscles, polishing my tungsten carbide bones, and flushing toxins out of my body. Since I'm in constant peak condition, I never fall asleep. I don't need to. In fact, I can't fall asleep, even if I try.

So I get a lot of time to myself in the midnight hours when it's just me and the city sounds of barking dogs and distant police sirens. That night after the Gold Mine, I hung out in my bedroom with the radio tuned to some lo-fi indie rock. I slouched in my suede Cambridge-professor chair and dangled my bare feet over the arm rest. In the dim glow of my bedroom light bulb, I flipped through the pages of Xin's old family book of recipes.

The ingredients were beyond fascinating, sure, but I was more fascinated by the maps of where to find them. They were hand-drawn and fairly well detailed, with elevations and important landmarks. Some of them weren't even on Earth. I recognized a map of the Guinee, the Voodoo afterlife, home of "Papa Pillory's haunted rum distillery" and "Baron Tobakko's condemned cigar factory."

There were also maps to places I had never has the pleasure of visiting before, like Hell, or the Hall of Ancestors, and some weird city called Chronopolis.

The book wasn't comprehensive. I knew that for certain after I checked for a map of the Muffincake Kingdom and couldn't find it. Well, if one realm was missing from the book, it was easy to assume there were others.

I got so drawn into the details of the book, time completely got away from me. Next thing I knew, the early morning sun was glowing through my bedroom window. I had barely scratched the surface of the pages, but the day was starting and it was time to get a jump on the morning chores. I tucked the book under the seat cushion and ran out to the shop.

I gave the Fire Lotus one cup of hot water. I rotated the Red Wattleseed so it could get sun on the opposite side. I plucked one leaf off the Hydra Bloom so two more could grow in its place.

Chores took about an hour, as they usually do, and then 7:30 rolled around. Xin should have been coming up the alleyway as he always did, but he didn't show up. It wasn't like him to be late. He'd never been late before.

I hovered on the front porch and watered the plants, occasionally glancing up the alley. 7:30 turned to 7:45 and still no Xin. Anxiety grew inside me like out of control bacteria. If the old man were five or ten minutes late, whatever, but the shop opened in fifteen minutes and he still hadn't shown up.

The thought occurred to me that maybe this was a test. Just yesterday he was giving me that "You'll have to run the store one day" routine. Maybe he wanted me to prove it. Well, if this was just a test, I wasn't cool with it; I was worried fucking sick. If he scared me just to make some kind of point, I was going to chew him up one side and right back down the other.

Worried or not, pissed off or not, it was 7:50 and the shop opened in ten minutes. It was up to me – and me alone – to get the orders ready for the day. I went around the store and gathered up everything I'd need for the daily customers.

For Liu's Beijing Taste, I needed one cup of fresh Szechuan Peppercorns and a small jar of Lord Emperor Xao's Ten Spice. I needed two pouches of Cloud Tea for Mrs. Zhang's swollen ankles; one cup for the morning and one cup at night. Her grandson, Kevin, would be by to pick that up on his way to school.

It was a Tuesday, which meant the ladies from Super Wash Dry Clean would be coming around for a pound of Chinese Borax and a small bottle of essential oils from the Looping Bandis and the Kofi Sweetgrass.

I had everyone's orders collected, bagged, and stored safely in a cardboard box behind the counter. I even wrote the customer names on them in Chinese, not because I knew Chinese, but because I'd seen the characters so many times, I could recreate them from memory.

8:00 came. I thought maybe Xin might show up late with some story about how he overslept or witnessed a car crash and had to give a statement to the cops or any of the other millions of things that makes a New Yorker late to work. He'd show up and the relief would wash over me and I'd make fun of him for being late. Maybe I'd give him detention.

But Xin didn't come.

Distracted and worried sick, I still managed to perform my duties flawlessly. None of the customers seemed bothered by the fact that I was helping them instead of Xin. A few of them asked a few curious questions.

"Where is Mister Houng?" Tommy, the guy from Peking Taste, asked me.

"He's taking the day off," I said. Then under my breath I added, "Apparently."

"He sick?"

I frowned. "I hope not."

Mrs. Zhang's ten-year-old grandson came in a while later and have gave me a funny look when he found me behind the counter instead of Xin. He stopped short in the doorway, but only for a second, then approached me and said, "Why are *you* behind the counter?"

I handed him a tin canister of his grandmother's tea. "I'm learning to run the store on my own."

"Oh." He looked at the floor for a moment, then peered up at me from over the edge of the counter. "Girls can do anything boys can do."

I smiled at him. "That's right."

The morning passed. Lunchtime came and went and things started slowing down. Xin was still MIA. It was officially time to start freaking out.

2

"I want to file a missing person report." The shop had an old rotary phone. I had the receiver tucked between my ear and shoulder, and I paced back and forth with the cradle in my free hand. I have a habit of pacing when I'm on the phone.

"Okay," said the officer on the other line. "What's the individual's name?"

"Houng Xin," I said. "H-O-U-N-G. X-I-N."

"And do you have Mister Xin's date of birth? Or maybe his social security number?"

"Uh." Shit. I did not. "He's old," I said. "He's not originally from here. He was born in China."

"You don't have his date of birth?"

God dammit. How could I possibly not know this shit? How much of a self-centered piece of shit could I possibly be that I don't know Xin's birthday, or even how old he was?

"I think he's, like, 87," I said. I seem to remember him saying that one time.

"Okay, what's *your* name?"

"Penelope..." I was about to give my last name. I hesitated.

"Penelope. What's your *last* name?"

I had to think. Was giving my name to the cops a good idea or a bad idea? "Do you really need that?"

"If you're filing the report," she said, "I need to know who to contact in case we find something."

Why was my last name important? What did that matter? I looked around the shop searching for something to use as a fake name. The vines of the Looping Bandis caught my eye.

"Bandis," I said. "Penelope Bandis."

"Alright, Miss Bandis. And what's your date of birth?"

"My date of birth? What the hell do you need that for? I'm not the one who's missing."

"Ma'am, if you want to help your friend, I need as much information as possible, okay?"

Out the window, I saw two police officers appear at the mouth of the alley and approach the shop, a lady cop and a dude cop. They were NYPD, and they looked pretty lost. Understandable. Most people assume the alley is a dead end. This was probably their first time in the courtyard.

No idea how the cops found the shop, but I didn't like it.

Silently, I hung up on dispatch and set the phone on the counter. I went to the front and stood behind the screen door. The cops saw me and kept coming.

"Is your name Penelope?" Lady Cop called out.

"Yes." I answered by reflex, perhaps too quickly. "Maybe."

"Do you know a Houng Xin?" She pronounced his name perfectly. I guess you don't work the Chinatown beat without picking up a little basic pronunciation.

"Yes." I pushed the screen door open and stepped out onto the porch. "He didn't come to work today."

"We're supposed to contact you in case of emergency," said Dude Cop. He stepped up onto the front steps and held out a yellow post-it note. "Your boss had a note in his pocket."

Did he say emergency? I took the note and read it.

In the event of an emergency
contact Penelope Salvo
at the flower shop on
83 Forge Street

That was all it said, and was in Xin's handwriting.

"Where did you get this?" I waved the note at them.

"Do you have somewhere we can talk?" Lady Cop asked.

"Right here is just fine," I said. "What the fuck is going on?"

"Miss Salvo," Dude Cop said. "Mister Houng collapsed this morning." He turned and pointed. "On the sidewalk. Just one block away from here."

"No." I backed away from them. Bunch of liars. "No no no."

Lady Cop chimed in. "He's down at New York Presbyterian on Gold Street. We would have come here sooner, but we had a hell of a time finding the place."

"What do you mean he collapsed?" I demanded to know. "Collapsed how? What from?"

"They're still trying to figure that out," Dude Cop said.

My hands clinched into fists. "How is it too early to tell? Did he have a stroke? Or a heart attack?"

"We don't know," Dude Cop said.

Lady Cop shook her head. "He just collapsed."

Fucking hell, man. No answers. I took a breath. "Is he okay?"

"He's alive," Lady Cop said. "When we found him, he was non-responsive." She paused, as if she couldn't think of what else to say. "Uhm. We haven't been in contact with the nurses at all since we left... so that's all we know."

"We didn't have anyone else to contact," Dude Cop said. He pointed at the note. "Just you. And the doctors at NYU have some questions if you think you could answer them. Insurance information and stuff like that."

Insurance. Money. Everyone wants your fucking money. This was just like Ma all over again.

I didn't say anything to the cops after that. What was left to say? These dipshits didn't know anything. My conversation with them was over. I pulled the shop door closed and locked it, then speed walked past them.

"Do you need a ride or anything?" One of them asked.

"I'll have Corolla take me," I said.

That was careless to mention Corolla by name like that, and it just slipped out, but I wasn't thinking straight. The cops didn't bother to ask me what I meant.

3

When Ma had her car accident in 2012, they rushed her to New York Presbyterian. Her accident was so bad, they started CPR in the ambulance and didn't stop performing CPR until she was in the ER and on an operating table. They didn't find my contact information in her purse until an hour later, long after my high school graduation ceremony was over and Ma was still missing. I knew something was wrong when she didn't show up, because my graduation was all she could talk about for weeks beforehand. When I finally got the voicemails from the NYPD and they told me she was in the hospital, I bused it across town just in time to find out they had already pronounced her dead.

I didn't even get to say goodbye. A surgeon came out and told me, plain as day, "We did everything we could, but..." Ma died of severe trauma to the brain, complicated by blood loss, further complicated by internal bleeding.

I did not take the passing of my mother well.

I ran out of insurance money, almost ended up homeless, and then Xin saved me.

For that reason alone, I have an aversion to hospitals, especially waiting rooms, especially the ER waiting room at New York Presbyterian. After Ma died and left me with no one else in the world, it never occurred to me that someday I would have to go back to that horrible waiting room with its disgusting pastel checkered walls, the counter tops filled with kids toys, and those stiff gray couches.

But I was wrong. I'd gone and found someone to new care about – someone elderly – and here I was, ten months later, back in the NYU waiting room.

Waiting.

God, couldn't they have at least taken him to a different hospital so I didn't have to relive these memories?

Xin's passing was, I suppose, inevitable. Death always is. Did I think the old man was going to live forever? It's morbid to walk through life constantly reminding yourself that the people you care about are going to die – people rarely think that way – but to ignore that fact is just a daily exercise in denial. Ma was going to die eventually; either in a car accident, or a plane crash, or of good old-fashioned cancer. And Xin was going to die, too, of food poisoning or getting run over by a subway or – in this case – collapsing for no good goddamn reason. That's the reality of things, but it wasn't not a reality I thought about until it was much too late.

I never worried about Ma dying, and then in a matter of hours she was gone.

And now it was happening again.

4

It took forever for someone to come out of the ER and give me an update. It was the surgeon, Doctor Jindal, who joined me in the waiting room. She was a slender Muslim lady with a white lab coat, matching white head scarf, and bright pink crocs.

"Penelope?" she asked.

I jumped off the couch, eager for news. "I'm Penelope."

"I'm Doctor Jindal." She spoke slowly and made strong eye contact. We shook hands. "I just want you to know that we have been working very hard to give your friend the best medical care possible."

"What's wrong with him?"

She swallowed and made a face that suggested I should brace myself for not-very-good-best news.

"We've run every test there is. MRI. EKG. His brain seems fine. There's nothing wrong with his heart." She shrugged. "At this point, I'm at a complete loss. I know this isn't what you want to hear, but I want to be completely honest with you. Currently, I have absolutely no idea what's happened to him."

"Is he going to wake up?" I didn't want to ask my follow up question, but I had to know. I lowered my voice to a whisper, "Is he going to die?"

"I can't say." She put her hand on my arm. "But for now, he's very much alive. His vitals are slow, but well within normal. His brain activity is very minimal, so it's impossible to say what might come next."

"I don't understand." I had to sit down. Doctor Jindal joined me on the couch. "How does this just happen?"

"Mister Houng is an old man," she said. "The human body does unpredictable things at his age. It does unpredictable things in young people, too. Maybe it's exhaustion? Maybe he's been working too hard?"

I shook my head. "I would not call what we do 'working.' We pot plants all day. The heaviest thing he lifts is a pencil."

"Penelope." She took both of my hands in hers and looked right into my eyes. "I can't begin to guess at what caused this, so our options for treatment are very limited. Right now we have him on an IV drip so he stays hydrated, and if his condition doesn't change by this evening, we're going to put him on a feeding tube as well."

"Then what?" I was starting to get hostile. "You gotta have some sort of plan."

"I'm not going to stop thinking." She wasn't making very good eye contact with me anymore. She looked at the floor a lot. "And I've emailed my colleagues to get their opinions, too. But like I said, your boss is a very old man. When people reach a certain age, sometimes the body just stops working."

I stared her down. "You think he's going to die."

She took a moment to consider her response. "I don't."

"Don't give me that bullshit." I stood up. "This is the shit you have to say because you're a doctor and you want me to stay positive, but deep-down you think he's gunna die."

"There are a lot of factors going on here," she said. "We're going to transfer him to a room and monitor his progress."

"Monitor his progress?" I paced in circles. I clenched and unclenched my fists. "You mean put him in a room where your jackoff NYU interns can study him like he's a test question. I bet if he was rich you'd figure out what's wrong with him. I bet if he wrote you a fucking check for a brand new MRI machine, you'd have him up and around in no time."

"Penelope," Jindal said. "Please."

Doctor Jindal did not appreciate my tone. She stood up and took slow, measured steps backwards, inching towards the safety of the ER. Two orderlies – big guys – loomed in the hallway. They weren't getting involved, not just yet, but they paid very close attention to my attitude.

They were about to kick me out.

"This is bullshit," I said to Jindal. "I wanna see him. I wanna see him now."

Jindal shook her head. "As soon as we move him to a-"

"I want to see him *now*," I repeated. "You let me see Xin or I swear to god, you don't know me, I *will* tear this whole floor apart and there is literally nothing you or your jamoke-ass guards can do to stop me."

She sized me up and weighed her options, then decided to give me five minutes with Xin, probably just to keep me from making a scene. Oh, and what a scene I would have caused, too. She waved her orderlies off and escorted me through the ER where I slipped through a thin curtain into his little area. Xin laid there in bed, comatose, hardly breathing, connected by wires to a bunch of machines.

5

I'd never seen Xin so helpless and frail, as if the simple act of putting him in a hospital bed made him twenty pounds skinnier and twenty years older. His blanket moved with each breath, which were evenly spaced apart by an alarming amount of time.

His ER room was small with a little sink, a counter top of medical supplies, and all kinds of machines. I dragged a chair to his bedside and carefully fixed his hair. Then I took his hand in mine and leaned in close.

"Dammit, Xin," I whispered. "Don't do this to me."

I laid my forehead down on his blanket and thought, just this once, I'd let myself cry.

"No no no." Cigar smoke puffed over the top of my head. Baron Semedi peered down at Xin from over my shoulder. "This doesn't look right at all."

It had been months and months since I'd last seen Baron Semedi, and suddenly there he was in his dusty tuxedo. He looked like he just crawled out of a grave. He probably did. He held a lit cigar between his teeth and puffed on it, and his white-gloved hand rattled a small glass of ice and rum. His top hat sat crooked on his head, casting a shadow over half of his Day-of-the-Dead-painted face.

"What're you doing here?" I asked him. I'm sure that came out bitchy. I didn't care much for having a death loa near my very sick friend.

"This *is* a hospital," Semedi said. He plucked the cigar from his mouth and blew a cloud of smoke up into the fluorescent lights. "I spend a lot of time here."

"Are you here for him?" I asked. "Is Xin going to die?"

"Well, of course Xin is going to die. All humans die. Knowing that is what separates the humans from the animals." He closely scrutinized the chewed up end of his cigar, apparently bored with our conversation. "Except for the dolphins. They know they're going to die. And so do the elephants. And most monkeys."

I stood and puffed up my chest. "If you're here for Xin, you have to go through me first."

Semedi rolled his eyes. "Please. I'm not here to take your precious Xin. I came here for someone else entirely. But I will say, these circumstances surrounding the old man's half-death are most intriguing."

Semedi strolled to the other side of the bed and picked up Xin's right arm by the wrist, holding it between his fingers as if he were checking for a pulse. He shook his head, disappointed, then laid the limp arm back down on the bed. He crossed his arms and took a step back.

I waited for him to say something. "Well?"

He said, "Well, there's absolutely nothing wrong with his mortal body. It seems to me that Xin here was the victim of some type of spiritual attack. Someone tried to destroy his soul completely, but they didn't quite get the job done. A sliver of life still burns inside him. Our would-be attacker underestimated the old man's strength of will, and an oversight like that reeks of human error. Yes, yes, this is definitely the handiwork of a human being. If a supernatural force was behind this, your dear Mr. Houng would be very dead. But make no mistake, human or not, whoever tried to pull this off is remarkably powerful." He puffed his cigar and arched his eyebrow at me. "For a human."

"Can you figure out who did it?" I asked.

"Hmm." He took a tiny sip of rum and looked down at Xin's body. "No. I don't believe so."

I gave him a long sigh. "Is he going to die?"

"Haven't you been listening? All humans die."

I grit my teeth. "Is he going to die *now*? Is he going to die because of this?"

"That is tough to tell. Maybe yes. Maybe no. Souls are quite unpredictable things."

"Well, do something!" I shoved him, not too hard, but enough to make him stumble backwards. "You're the Voodoo spirit of death. Work some damn magic."

"I can't." He turned away from me, defensively. "If he was all-the-way dead or all-the-way alive, then maybe I could help him. But he's half-dead and half-alive and that's not something I have power over."

"Then how do I fix it?"

"You? Fix it?"

"Yes," I said. "Me. Fix it."

He could see the determination in my eyes and sighed in defeat. "I can think of only one way," Semedi said. "Find whoever's responsible. If they have the power to destroy his soul, then they have the power to bring it back."

"Okay, how exactly am I supposed to do that?"

"That's the thing..." He squinted one eye shut and checked his white gloves for imperfections. "No offense, you're not a particularly good god of war, and you're certainly no detective. Tracking down someone this powerful will require resources and skill. Unfortunately, resources and skill are two things you have in very short supply."

Semedi was right. I wouldn't ever admit that to him, but this time it was true. I wasn't as smart as those detectives on TV who piece clues together and solve the case. I was completely out of my element and Xin, who saved my life when I needed it most, was going to spend the rest of his life hooked up to machines.

My face lit up when a solution popped into my brain.

"I got an idea," I said with new-found confidence. I poked Semedi right in his chest, backing him up inch by inch. "I might not have resources and skill, but I know someone who does."

I went for the ER curtains, then turned back around to say one last thing. Baron Semedi had opened a glass jar of cotton balls and was stuffing handfuls of them into his pockets.

"Will you..." God, I hated what I was about to ask. "Will you do me a favor?"

"Maybe," he replied. "Depends."

I pointed at Xin's body. "Will you keep an eye on him?"

Semedi shrugged and went back to stealing cotton balls. "Sure, why not."

Chapter 5

1

Corolla drove me up 6th Avenue, headed to Midtown. Traffic was ridiculous. Traffic is always ridiculous. It was that kind of traffic where the light half a block ahead of you turns green, but no one moves and you just sit there. Bumper to bumper, and we weren't going anywhere.

"I don't get it," Corolla said. "You hate the Westland Corporation. Now you're going to go ask them for a favor?"

"They have the skills and resources to figure out who tried to kill Xin's soul." I pressed my forehead against the window and watched the Westland HQ skyscraper in the distance: an unsuspecting rectangle of concrete and glass, tall enough to add to the skyline, but not tall enough to draw any unwanted attention.

"And you really think they're going to help you?" he asked. "Don't they hate you just as much as you hate them?"

"Kinda," I said. "But for whatever weird reason, Carl seems to like me."

"Carl just pretends to like you," Corolla said. "He's doing that keep-your-enemies-closer sort of thing."

"Maybe. But I don't think so. Besides, if it wasn't for Carl, you'd still be dead."

"I suppose." Corolla didn't like to be reminded of that.

Westland headquarters offers no real services, has no public bathroom, and doesn't boast a gift shop, which keeps tourists and randos from poking around and discovering the supernatural things no man was meant to know. The front of the building looks like everything else in New York: a set of revolving doors at the entrance, an unmarked awning of gray canvas, and a few Red Crape Myrtle shrubs growing in concrete planters out front. The first ten floors had full length tinted windows that functioned like mirrors against the afternoon sun.

Corolla parked right on the corner of 6th and 39th. The address numbers of Westland HQ – 1039 – were marked above the revolving doors, not because they wanted to make a big deal out of their address, but because that's how everyone else did it in Midtown and they wanted to blend in.

Men and women in black suits came in and out the revolving doors by the dozens, like some sort of CIA beehive. Field agents, probably, identifying supernatural threats around the world and wiping them out.

"Alright, dude." I grabbed Corolla's Boston's Greatest Hits cassette and clicked it into the stereo so he'd have something to listen to while I was gone. I pushed the driver side door open and climbed out. "I'll be back out after a while. Sit tight, okay?"

"Mmhmm," he said. "If you're not back in an hour, I'm calling the Feds."

"I'll be fine," I said.

I hoped.

At first I wondered if I'd even be able to get inside the building. I figured there would be keycard scanners by the revolving doors – something to keep the civilians at bay – but I was wrong. There wasn't much in actual security and I was able to waltz right through the main entrance.

The inside lobby looked like something ripped out of a luxury hotel. The floors were polished white marble, glass balconies hung overhead on the second and third floors, and Chinese oak trees grew right out of the floor. There was a three story waterfall that flowed into a sparkling swimming pool, home to red and blue fish. All around the pool were round tables and chairs – there to accommodate the nearby coffee station – so employees could sit and relax after a busy day of murdering innocent creatures.

To the left of the waterfall was a big atrium that led deeper into the building with mango trees and coconut trees and the sound of tropical birds. I wandered down that direction, admittedly a little lost.

Along the walls of the atrium were ten-foot-tall letters, solid steel, that spelled out *The Westland Corporation*; the "W" was flourished and more decorative than the other letters, like their corporate logo. Beneath their name was the company slogan, also in steel letters, "Protecting the World from Things."

The temperature in the atrium was perfect. Polite, corporate music came from well hidden speakers. Agents came and west through the atrium elevators and when they passed by me, they barely gave me a second look. I was an intruder, but they didn't seem to care. It's not as if they confused me for someone else. I wasn't in a million-dollar business suit; I was in a t-shirt and shorts and I smelled like Chinatown and patchouli.

But if they didn't care, then neither did I.

In the middle of the tropical atrium was a massive receptionist desk, circular, with a computerized tower above it that stretched all the way up to the ceiling. Flat screen TVs were mounted on all sides of it, displaying news from America, sports from Russia, stock prices from Japan, and even a channel of Baliwood celebrity gossip. *Information.* That's was the corporation's main commodity. Information. The receptionist desk – and I hesitate to call it a desk, because it was more like a small control station – looked like the information hub of an international airport.

I wandered that way. My sneakers squeaked on the polished floors and I sounded like a god damned basketball game. I worried that I might be drawing attention to myself, but no. No one gave a shit. I made it to the information booth with no problems. The receptionists there seemed busy; a dozen of them answered the phones that wouldn't stop ringing, and another dozen walked around to shuffle paperwork back and forth.

I approached the desk – a nice wooden desk, redwood maybe – and leaned against it to catch the eye of one of the receptionists.

"Excuse me," I said to the girl. "I'm looking for-"

The receptionist looked up and we locked eyes. My mind went blank. This girl looked exactly like Ilana. She even had the same glasses Ilana wore in high school. For a second I thought it was really her, but this girl wore a black pant suit, she had a Westland lanyard around her neck and a hands-free headset on her head. Her hair was washed and held up all prim and proper with bobby pins.

"Penelope?" the girl said, stunned.

Wait. Holy shit. This wasn't some girl who looked like Ilana. It *was* Ilana.

"Ilana?" I said. "What are you doing here?"

"What am *I* doing here?" she said defensively. "I work here. What are *you* doing here?"

"You work here?" I looked all around, then back at her. "At Westland?"

"Yeah? So?"

She didn't understand why this was weird. And why would she? She didn't know anything about anything. This couldn't be right. Someone was screwing with me.

"Why do you work here?" I asked her.

Admittedly, my question probably came off as super bitchy. To her this was just a job. She had no idea why this was a big deal to me and, on top of all that, I had just ended our friendship the night before. She shot me a dirty look.

"I work here because this is my job, Penelope. Now what are you doing here?"

"Uh." Okay, Ilana worked for Westland. I didn't have any choice but to just accept it. "Actually, I'm here to see Carl."

She frowned. "Uh, there's, like, a million people who work here. Carl who?"

"Carl," I said. "The CEO."

She stared at me and blinked. "Ha ha, Penelope."

"What do you mean 'ha ha'?" I snapped. "I'm not here to fuck around. I want to talk to Carl."

Some other receptionist must have overheard my F word and approached us, some dude in a tight suit and bald head. He looked middle-aged-ish with a narrow face and pencil-thin eyebrows. He might have been low-man on the totem pole as far as the corporation was concerned, but he walked around the reception area with his nose held high, as if he were Benjamin, Lord of Incoming Phonecalls.

"Ilana?" The guy tapped his pen on his knuckles. "Is there a problem here?"

"No, sir," Ilana said. "This street rat is just lost and she wandered in here on accident. I'm giving her directions."

"Street rat?" I growled at her.

The supervisor gave me a suspicious look and walked off. Ilana waited until we were alone again, then she gave me a stern, wide-eyed look that said, "See what you did? You almost got me in trouble."

"I don't know what you think you're doing here," Ilana whispered, "but I can't even see my shift manager without booking an appointment three weeks in advance. No one gets to see Mister Carl. Anyone who wants to see Mister Carl has to first schedule a meeting with his secretary, and she's got a waiting list six months long."

"Ilana, trust me," I said. "I know Carl. Just call him."

"I can't call him." She held out her hands and looked down at her phone. "I don't even have his number."

"But you have the number for his secretary, right?"

"Penelope..."

I matched her tone. "Ilana..."

"Dude!" She was getting loud again and realized it. She leaned forward and returned to a whisper. "Penelope, I don't know if this is some sort of joke or whatever, but if I call his secretary for your stupid ass, I'm going to lose my job."

"You won't lose your job." I held up my palm and extended three fingers. "Scouts honor."

"You got kicked out of scouts."

"Alright, I'm not on trial here. Look, I swear on my mother's grave, okay? Just call his secretary. Please?"

I wouldn't swear on my mother's grave if I was lying and Ilana knew it. She stared down at her switchboard and sighed. After a moment of thought, she adjusted the microphone on her headset and pushed one of the buttons that started blinking green. She muttered, "I can't believe you're making me do this."

Ilana bit down on her lower lip as she waited for the line to ring. Someone picked up on the other end and I followed the conversation through Ilana's responses.

"Miss Stegman, there's a girl down here in the lobby who insists on speaking to Mister Carl." Pause. "Ilana, ma'am." Pause. "No, this is my first day." Pause. "No, I went through orientation and I know the policy and I told this girl to leave, but she says she knows Mister Carl personally and she won't go away." Pause. "No, ma'am. Never again. I totally understand." Pause. "Her name is Penelope Salvo. Thank you, ma'am. I'm so sorry."

Ew. That didn't sound like it went so well. Ilana wrapped her fingers around her headset's wire-thin microphone and whispered, "Why are you doing this to me?"

"Trust me," I said. "You'll see."

Hopefully. See, once I had a chance to actually think about it, I realized getting an audience with Carl wasn't a 100 percent sure thing. The idea that the new CEO of the Westland Corporation would make time for me was kind of a wild assumption. It was equally likely that by simply trespassing onto Westland property Carl would call security, put the whole building on lock-down and Ilana would lose her job. I really hoped that wasn't how this played out.

Ilana returned to her phone conversation. "Yes, ma'am." After a quick pause, her concerned face changed to dumbfounded surprise. "You're serious? Okay. I'll... send her right up."

Still in a state of shock, she pressed her finger to the green button and the light blinked off. She stared at her desk, then moved her eyes up to mine.

"Mister Carl says you can go right on up. Take the red elevator to the 37th floor." She looked at me like I was a ghost. "He's waiting for you with bells on. He insisted we tell you the part about the bells."

"See?" I gave her a smile.

"But I don't understand." Poor Ilana looked totally bewildered. Here she was, a lowly receptionist at a major corporation while I – dumb old Penelope – was off to meet with the CEO. After mulling it over for a moment, she looked back at me. "How do you know Mister Carl?"

"That," I said as I left for the red elevator, "is a long story."

2

I'd been in Westland's elevators once before, but not this red one. This was the express elevator. The wall panel only had three buttons; one for the lobby, one for floor 37, and one for floor 41. The carpet was burgundy red and the walls were panels of polished redwood. This was the BMW luxury-ride of elevators, complete with orchestra music and the rich smell of pipe tobacco.

The doors closed behind me with a "ding" and the button for floor 37 lit up on its own. With a quick jolt, I was lifted up into the building. The numbers over the door increased one by one.

On floor 37, the doors opened up to the CEO's office, which looked more like a penthouse suite than an office. I'd been there once before and recognized it quite well: floors of black marble, couches of black leather, and gigantic paintings of "French dude leaning against a horse" and "half naked lady wrapped in white silk." I once sat at that very same wet bar while the CEO – the *old*, supernatural CEO – tried to intimidate into turning over

Impossible Red. I wound up impaling his hand with a ballpoint pen. That dude was dead now. Now the office belonged to Carl.

"Miss Salvo." Carl pushed his way into the elevator, blocking my exit and forcing me back inside. We suddenly shared the elevator. His arms were overloaded with a laptop computer and a stacks of manila folders. Carl hadn't changed since I saw him last; he still had the same billion-dollar suit, some gray hair above his temples, and a wry smile that reminded me of a politician up for reelection. He wrestled with the stuff in his arms and pressed the button for floor 41. Then he turned to me and said, "I'm glad you're here. Right now, you're the only person I can trust."

"Trust? What're you talking about?"

"I'll get into that later. For now, how are your power point presentation skills?"

"Terrible."

"Shoot." He fumbled through his folders and searched for something specific. The elevator doors closed and we started to move. He hadn't even bothered to make eye contact with me yet. "We'll just have to wing it then. Follow my lead."

"Wing *what*?" I asked. "Follow *what* lead?"

"Hey, that's perfect. Just play dumb." He found the folder he was looking for and stuck it in my hands. "Here. Give this the once over. Familiarize yourself with these materials. You're going to be my star expert."

"Expert in what?"

I turned the folder right-side-up and read the front.

The Westland Corporation: A Breech in Security

"What is this?" I asked him.

"The results of a three-month investigation. Long story. I don't have much time. Let me sum up. We've got a spy in the organization leaking information to someone on the outside. Just last month, someone gave our nuclear codes to a teenage girl and her pet astronaut."

"Pet astronaut?"

"A long story. I don't have time to explain that either. All you need to know is that the Board of Directors is furious and they expect me to fix it. I gave the order to dismantle our nuclear weapons before they fell into the wrong hands, but now the Directors want me to identify the spy so we can... you know... eliminate them."

I nodded. "I don't give a shit about any of this."

"Exactly why I need you. I can't discuss this with anyone else at Westland, not even my secretary Miss Stegman, because she might be a security risk. But I know I can trust you because you don't care."

"I super don't. I honestly give zero fucks right now."

Carl looked relieved. "Ah, thank you. That makes me feel a lot better. But mark my words, if we don't find this leak and soon, the whole world is going to be in a lot of trouble."

"Okay, look." I turned to face Carl directly. "I have some questions for you."

He anxiously looked at the numbers above the elevator door. "Do make it quick."

"First, what in the blue hell is Ilana Rittenberg doing working your reception desk?"

"Who?" Carl refused to look at me.

"The new receptionist," I said. "Ilana Rittenberg. She's my old friend from high school and now she's working here in your lobby, answering phones."

"Oh, her." Carl turned his attention down to his folders. "She put her resume on some employment website and listed you as a reference. Our computers are programmed to automatically flag anything with your name on it, so her application went straight to human resources. When the hiring manager sent me an email about it, I figured any friend of Penelope's is a friend of mine. So we gave her a job. Consider it a personal favor."

"You're doing me favors now?" I asked.

He finally made eye contact. "That's what friends do."

"I'm not your-"

I almost said it. *I'm not your friend, Carl, you shitbag,* but I couldn't say that to him. Not right now. Not when I was about to ask for his help in tracking down Xin's would-be assassin. I had to change subjects.

"And last night," I continued, "you had people following me down on Bowery. What's that all about?"

"This might come as a surprise," he said, "but not everything we do here at Westland is about you. They weren't following you, they were following Miss Rittenberg. It's all part of the screening process. I know she's young and I know she's new, but if she's going to work here at Westland, I needed assurances that she wasn't a spy."

"Oh."

"Mystery solved," he said.

Mystery solved, indeed. I took a breath and mentally prepared myself to ask Carl for a favor.

"Carl, you have all kinds of equipment you can use to track down supernatural people, right? Because I need to find-"

The elevator dinged. The doors to the 41st floor opened and revealed a board meeting already in progress.

"No time for that now," Carl ducked out of the elevator and into the boardroom. "Follow me."

"Follow you where?" I stayed in the elevator. "Dude, I don't want to be in your meeting. I'm just here to ask for a favor."

Carl spun on his heels, turned back to me and said, "Do me a favor and come to this meeting. Then, when we're done, I'll do a favor for you. Deal?"

He spun back around and power-walked into the boardroom. Ten other people were already seated at the round conference table, half of them men and the other half women, all of them from different nationalities. None of them were younger then forty and, in fact, most of them were elderly-looking. There was an eleventh seat open, apparently saved for Carl. He set up his laptop at the empty seat and plopped his folders down.

"You coming?" he asked, turning back to me.

I stepped out of the elevator. "Oh my god, fine."

The ten people at the table stared at me with haunting, creepy faces. They looked human, but they weren't human; there was something slightly off about them, something about their eyes. I walked halfway to the table and stopped, careful not to get too close.

"Penelope," Carl said. "Welcome to the 41st floor, home of the corporate entities. Right now we're between two worlds, halfway in New York City and halfway... somewhere else."

I looked out the windows. While I could see the surrounding skyscrapers of Manhattan, there was some kind of supernatural mist between us and the outside world. Maybe we were simply up in the cloud line, but it seemed weirder than that.

"Come, come." Carl came over and took my by the arm. "Meet the Board. And for Pete's sake, would it kill you to smile? These people might be the physical manifestation of corporate greed and profit, but they still have feelings. You're being rude."

I let him lead me closer to the conference table.

"Penelope, this is the Director of Accounting," Carl said. He gestured at some malnourished guy with super-pale skin. His black hair was slicked back and he wore a pocket protector.

"And this is our Director of Administration." She was a no-nonsense looking chick with total RBF. She barely looked at me and did not say hello.

"This is the Director of the Legal Branch." This guy was a textbook corporate lawyer with a glare in his eyes, like he would step on his own mother if that meant protecting company assets.

"This is the Director of Compliance." An elderly guy, but stocky, like someone who ate steak and lobster at every meal and wiped their mouth with hundred dollar bills. He leaned back in his chair, steepled his fingers, and glared at me.

"And this over here is our Director of Information." A middle-aged woman in a smart pant suit. She never stopped scratching notes down on her yellow pad of paper.

"This class clown over here is our Director of Marketing." He was a bright-eyed guy who looked a lot friendlier than the others, but I knew better.

"Then we have our Director of Security." This was a muscle-bound lady, like a gender-swapped Arnold Schwarzenegger. She wore jungle cammo, puffed on the stub of a cigar, and had two pistols laid out on the table in front of her.

"Our Director of Technology..." A guy in a white lab coat.

"...And our Director of Research and Development." A lady in a white lab coat. These last two could have been twins. Or clones. Either seemed possible.

"And finally our Director of the Supernatural." This woman looked like a cross between a wizard and a stockbroker, with mystical gold symbols burned into her black, silk pantsuit. Her hair was raven black with strands of silver.

"And that," Carl said, "brings us back to me, the Chief Executive Officer."

"Speaking of CEOs..." The Director of Legal stood and placed his hands on the edge of the table, as if these were his closing arguments to a courtroom. "Miss Penelope Salvo, it's our understanding that you murdered the corporate entity known as the CEO, which created a power vacuum and left us no choice but to promote this human to the open position."

The Director of Compliance stood up. "It was never our intention for a human being to join us here on the 41st floor. This is all your fault."

"Whoa whoa whoa." I waved my hand at them. "Let's clear the air on one thing right quick. I didn't kill nobody. Some

Voodoo spirit punched the CEO right through the heart, not me. I'm not taking a murder rap for something I didn't do."

"But that would not have happened," the Director of Compliance began, "if you didn't instigate the situation."

"I didn't instigate shit," I snapped. "That CEO jabroni tried to kill me with a space laser and he got his ass murdered. I'm not sorry about that at all. I didn't do it, but I'm glad he's dead."

Carl jumped in to de-escalate things. "Gentlemen. Ladies. Please. Let's not get tied up in the minutia of whether or not Penelope is guilty of second-degree murder. We need to focus on the matter at hand."

The Director of Legal sat back down. So did the Director of Compliance. They didn't look happy – none of the Directors did – but they didn't say much else.

"Now then." Carl opened his laptop and turned it on. "I spent a lot of time making this computerized presentation, so if you'll allow me..."

3

There were only eleven seats at the conference table; ten directors and one CEO. That meant no spot for me. But while Carl gave his presentation, I was allowed to steal his spot. He had a little remote control in his hand and with a push of one button, shades rolled down to cover the windows and block out the sunlight. He pressed another button and the fluorescent lights dimmed to fifty percent. The room went dark. Pressing yet another button, a white projector screen rolled down out of the ceiling and Carl moved beside it. Attached to the ceiling was a wireless projector; it flickered on and Carl's laptop display appeared on the screen.

Carl's laptop wallpaper was a bunch of adorable kittens in a basket. I nodded because... of course it was.

Carl's power point slide show looked like it was made by a 6th grader, complete with free, pre-loaded clip art. The first slide was simply the title of his presentation, in Jokerman font:

The Westland Corporation: We Got Ourselves A Spy
Someone's being a Naughty Nancy

Below the title was a clip-art drawing of a cartoon bank robber in a striped shirt stealing sacks full of money. You could tell it was money because the sacks had dollar signs on them.

"This..." Carl pointed at his title words with a laser pointer, "is my title. And this..." He moved the laser pointer to the cartoon criminal, "...is a funny little bank robber. Our spy does not actually look like this, so please don't be alarmed. This little guy is just here to lighten the mood."

He turned to us with a huge smile, but the Directors were not entertained. Neither was I. Carl realized his audience didn't like the cartoon bank robber and his smile faded. He pressed the button and moved to the next slide.

The next screen showed a bunch of folders that said CONFIDENTIAL. Then an animated "No Smoking" red circle came zooming in and landed on the folder with a loud "thud." The words "Do Not Steal Company Secrets" appeared, then it played an audio clip of a sassy woman saying "Oh, hell no, girlfriend."

This was Carl's corporate presentation about internal espionage? I looked around the room, like, this cannot be fucking happening. The Directors looked absolutely bewildered.

"Is this..." The Director of Accounting tried his best to formulate a question. "What are we seeing?"

"You told me to research the security leak within the company," Carl said. "And that's what I've been doing. Now, granted, I don't have any hard answers for you yet, but I'm getting there. Baby steps."

The Director of Security took out the biggest Bowie knife I had ever seen in my life and stabbed it into the table. "We don't need baby steps! We need big, huge, Buzz-Aldrin-bouncing-on-the-fucking-moon astronaut steps!"

"Frankly, I agree with you," Carl said. "But after tracking all incoming and outgoing communication for months, I still don't have a single suspect. Whoever is hacking into our system is some kind of gosh dang James Bond."

The Director of Research and Development shook her head. "Then we need to resort to more drastic measures. Mandatory brain scans of all the employees. Lie detector tests before and after work. We can put sodium pentathol in their cafeteria food and force the truth out of them."

"Jesus," I muttered.

"I suppose that's a thought," Carl said. "But brain scans, lie detectors, and swimming pools of sodium pentathol all cost human money. And we don't have human money because you guys converted it all to black money."

I was confused. "Black money?"

"Supernatural currency," Carl said.

He pushed the button and the next slide appeared on the screen: a big cartoon dollar sign with a sad face on it.

The Director of Accounting crossed his arms. "Carl, we've discussed this. We can get human money by developing our infinite energy system and selling power to the New Yorkers. Have you worked on a marketing plan for infinite energy?"

Carl frowned. "All I have is a slogan."

The Director of Marketing spoke up. "A slogan? That's all?"

"It's a good slogan though!" Carl said. He pressed the button again and the sad dollar bill zipped off the screen with a silly sound effect. His proposed slogan slowly faded onto the screen:

Westland Energy Solutions.
"You want power?
We'll show you power."

Everyone in the boardroom silently read the slogan.

Eventually the Director of Information spoke up. "That makes us sound like an evil corporation."

It was Carl's turn to look confused. "I don't see how."

I spoke up. "It sounds like you're threatening people, Carl. Like when you tell someone, 'You want dangerous? I'll show you dangerous.' That usually means you're about to kick their ass."

"The human is right," added the Director of Administration. "It sounds needlessly aggressive."

"I don't think you get it." Carl seemed a little flustered. "The people of New York need power. We have infinite power. The slogan is simply saying that we'll show the people of New York so much power! Power the likes of which mankind has never seen!"

The Director of Technology said, "That makes it sound worse."

"It's going to scare people," added the Director of Marketing.

The board room went silent.

Carl cleared his throat. "I think the slogan is fine. And with all due respect to the Board of Directors, if you're worried the slogan, then you've lost sight of what's really important here. We have a leak in the organization and we need to invest our time and resources into figuring out who our spy is. We don't have time for mandatory lie detector tests and truth serum in the cobb salad. We have a leak and we need to track it down as soon as humanly possible."

Director of Security asked, "And how do you plan on going about that?"

"Ah." Carl walked over to me. He put his hand on the back of my chair. "For that, I want to turn things over to my strategic planner, Miss Penelope Salvo."

All eyes were suddenly on me. Deer in headlights. I had no idea this was coming.

I squirmed in my seat. "I'm sorry, what?"

Carl rephrased his statement. "Penelope, you swallowed Impossible Red and now you're a god of war. Who better to sort through the meat and potatoes of strategy than a god of war?"

"You want me to think of a trap for your spy?" I asked.

Carl nodded eagerly.

"I have no idea, dude," I said. "Just start waterboarding everyone, I guess. Go waterboard crazy. Waterboard the hell out of people until someone confesses."

The security lady slammed her fists down on the table. "I like this girl!"

But Carl put a stop to that. "No no no, don't be absurd. You can't go waterboarding a bunch of innocent people. We don't have that kind of time. We need something quick... and concise... and tricky."

The Board of Directors all looked at me. These supernatural entities honestly wanted my opinion. The pressure was on. It felt like high school all over again.

"Okay," I said. "I dunno. What if you, like, put something out as bait. Then when the spy comes along to steal it, jump out of the shadows and grab them."

Carl just stared at me. The Directors grumbled unhappily to each other.

"That's it?" the Director of Security asked. She waved her knife around. "That's your brilliant strategy?"

"What do you want out of me?" I threw my hands up. "I'm not General fucking Eisenhower. I didn't go to military school. I got a D in government because I played too much Mario Kart."

"No." Carl silenced the room with a snap of his fingers. "You know what? I like where Penelope's going with this."

I looked up at him. "You do?"

"I do." His grin got wider and wider. "There are parts of this building with such high security clearance, only I have access to them." He pulled out a red keycard. On one side was the Westland "W" logo. The other side had his name and face and other vital information. He tapped the edge of the card on the table. "This is the CEO's passkey."

"What are you going to do with that?" the Director of Compliance asked.

"I'm going to 'accidentally' leave the door open to our infinite energy. The door that leads to Untouchable Orange."

Uh, what? I'm sure the surprise was visible on my face.

"Untouchable Orange?" I repeated.

That was a curve ball. The red god sphere – Impossible Red – turned me into the god of war. In all those months I spent traveling the world, no one knew where to find any of the others. In fact, I wasn't convinced the others were even on Earth. Come to find out the Westland Corporation had Untouchable Orange, the one that would turn its host into the artificial god of fire.

I asked, "You have Untouchable Orange?"

"That's what I just said." Carl patted me on the shoulder. "Do try to keep up."

"Don't touch me." I jerked my shoulder away.

Carl kept talking. "Penelope, we're using Untouchable Orange to solve the world's energy concerns. We've learned so much from it already: what it can do and what possibilities it holds. The beauty of your plan is that our spy won't be able to resist a chance to get their hands on that kind of information. And whenever Mister or Misses Sneaky-Peeky Blue Jeans comes sneaking along to take a sneaky peek at our infinite energy system – Boom! – we'll slam the door on them and trap them inside. Voila, one captured spy."

Sounds of approval came from the Board of Directors, along with a lot of nodding. Even the Director of Security, who seemed to enjoy more violent solutions, appeared pleased with the plan.

"You're a strategic genius," Carl said to me. "You really knocked it out of the park."

But I wasn't going to let Carl's praise distract me from the new information I just learned.

"How long have you had Untouchable Orange?" I asked.

"Still on about that, huh?" Carl asked. "Well, if you must know, we found it in California several months ago."

Several months? Imagine the kind of damage they could have done in several months. Carl said they were just using it for energy research, but I knew better than to take Carl at his word. I learned that lesson the hard way.

"I can't let you keep it," I told him. "You assholes can't be trusted with that kind of power."

"While I appreciate your opinion, that's not up to you." Carl had a self-satisfied grin on his face, like he just single-handedly saved the world. His white teeth twinkled in the reflection of his slide show presentation. "As the Buddha once said, finders keepers, losers weepers."

4

The meeting ended. Everyone pushed their chairs away from the table and gathered up their stuff. The Director of Legal stacked up his papers, tucked them inside his leather briefcase and clicked it shut. Both the Director of Technology and the Director of R&D scooped their tablet computers into their arms along with sheets of graph paper. And Carl, who was suddenly in a huge hurry to leave, tucked his laptop under his arm and dashed for the elevator.

A different elevator. This elevator was blue. Carl reached it and swiped his CEO keycard to open the doors. It was starting to feel like he was trying to escape, so I followed him.

"Hey," I called out. "What about my favor?"

"Oh, yes." Carl stepped inside the elevator. "Of course. I can't wait to hear all about it. Let's discuss it on the way down."

I followed him inside. This elevator had turquoise carpet and white wood paneling on the walls. He pressed a button and the doors closed. Slowly, the digital numbers counted down.

41.

40.

39.

38.

"Someone attacked Xin," I told Carl. "They did some kind of soul attack and now he's in a coma connected to machines and shit. Baron Semedi says the only person who can fix him is the person who cast the spell in the first place, so I need help finding out who that is."

"You think I did it?" He looked offended.

"What?" I asked. "No. I never said that."

"Well, why not? I'm quite capable."

"You're not the magical wizard type," I said. "And whoever did this to Xin tried to kill him. You wouldn't do that. You don't kill people."

He waved a finger at me. "Most astute."

The floors continued to tick away. 29. 28. 27. 26.

"Do you have any suspects?" he asked me.

"No."

"Do you have any clues?"

"No."

"Do you have any anything?"

"I have no nothing."

"Wow. You really do need my help." He glanced at me from the corner of his eye. "But I guess that *is* what friends are for."

I blinked at him. "What?"

He turned and faced me directly. "Wouldn't you agree that you and I are friends and, thusly, I would be required... as your friend... to help you. Wouldn't you agree with that?"

"I... uh..." The answer was no. No. Carl and I were not friends. Not now, not ever. But, fuck, he had me backed into a corner on this one. He turned away from me, stuck his hands in his pockets and casually rocked back and forth on his feet.

"You see," he continued. "I'm the CEO of an entire corporation. I have people asking me for favors all the time – promotions, raises, department funding – but I can't help *everyone*. It's simply not possible for me to help everyone. I only have time to help my friends. My best, closest friends."

I stared down at my Chucks and sighed. "God dammit."

"So what do you say, Miss Salvo?"

"Why do you even care?" I asked him. "Why's it such a big deal that you and I are friends?"

"Because I'm a friendly guy."

Technically, Carl didn't ask for actual friendship. He just wanted me to *say* we were friends. I could do that.

I crossed my arms and glared at him. "Fine. We're friends."

He arched his eyebrow at me. "Old friends?"

"Yeah, dude. The oldest."

"We go way back, you and I, huh?"

I rolled my eyes. "Back to the stone age."

"What a delight!" He clapped his hands together and gave me the biggest smile ever. "Tell you what, old friend. Let me send some people from Information Collection over to the hospital to take a look at Mister Houng. If we can figure out what kind of spell he's suffering from, that might give us a clue about who's behind it."

"Really?" A wave of relief washed over me. Maybe Carl, despite all his faults, wasn't actually a bad guy. "You're serious?"

"Quite serious. In fact, I'm going to fire off an email to the girls in that division right now."

Carl had one of those plastic cell phone holders on his belt. He snapped his phone out and immediately started typing up an email with his thumbs.

We reached the lobby and the doors opened to the tropical atrium. I didn't step out. We weren't done. Carl realized I wasn't going anywhere and he spoke up.

"Well, here we are at the lobby."

"Yep."

"So... goodbye?"

I pushed the CLOSE DOORS button and locked us back up.

"Show me this infinite energy," I said. "Show me Untouchable Orange. I want to see what you're doing with it. I want to know that you're not using it as a weapon."

He stared at me, as if he might call my bluff and tell me to leave. I gave him the evil eye, daring him to try me. It was Penelope Salvo versus Carl in a test of willpower. Eventually he caved and pressed the button for basement level five.

"Alright." He shrugged. "But just because we're friends."

Carl reached inside his suit jacket, pulled out a pen and a business card. He scribbled something on the back and handed it to me. It read: *Don't say too much. The walls have ears.*

5

The elevator dinged on basement level five and opened up to the howling winds of a deep underground canyon. Cold air blasted me in the face and smelled prehistoric. We stepped out of the elevator and onto this sprawling catwalk system that spiraled down the cavern walls like DNA.

This prehistoric chamber was certainly large enough to contain an energy system capable of powering the whole Eastern Seaboard. Standing at the top of it felt like being in the rafters of a basketball stadium.

I looked down to the bottom and got dizzy.

"Do be careful," Carl said. "It's a long way to the bottom. One of my technicians took a little stumble the other day and we had to clean him up with a mop and bucket."

"What is this place?" I asked.

"When the last ice age melted, the waters channeled through here. You're looking at 100,000 years of water erosion."

Stalactites the size of city buses hung from the ceiling. All along the walls were entire dinosaur skeletons fossilized into the stone. The walls had occasional dark tunnels – also from centuries of water erosion – that led off to god-knows what kind of horrible, sleeping monsters.

The Westland Corporation had apparently discovered this enormous cavern far beneath Manhattan and moved right in. They built loops and loops of catwalks to reach the bottom, twenty levels or more, and that's the journey that Carl set out on.

I followed behind him.

Below us, in the middle of the cave floor, was a cube of plexiglass the size of a two-story house. The plexiglass was super-thick and bolted together. The bolts were the size of concrete highway pillars. On one side of the cube was a plastic bank vault door. And instead of a combination lock in the middle, it had a key-card scanner.

CEO only, I'm sure.

Suspended in mid-air inside the plastic cube was a small orange marble. Untouchable Orange. The little god sphere puffed with fire and fueled a blazing inferno contained by the glass chamber. This heat was collected by circulating fans installed in the top of the cube where it was vented out of the cave through steel ventilation ducts.

They were using Untouchable Orange to harvest the power of nuclear fission.

Carl said, "We've been researching Untouchable Orange for months now. We've learned a lot – what it does, and what it can do – and we've only scratched the surface. Even our most brilliant scientists are struggling to comprehend the technology locked inside."

I kept pace with him down the catwalks. His stiff-heeled loafers thundered on the metal framework. My sneakers barely made a noise.

"It just makes fire?" I asked.

"For free," he said. "That's the amazing part. It doesn't require power. Once it's been activated, it generates hotter and hotter fire out of absolute nothingness. Just yesterday we got it up to 3,000 degrees. That's hot enough to melt steel. In another week, we should be able to get it up to 5,000 degrees. We're waiting to see if it has an upper limit."

"And?" I asked.

"If it has an upper limit, we haven't found it yet."

"This sounds dangerous," I said, quite plainly.

"Dangerous?" Carl repeated, offended. "What makes you think this is dangerous?"

"Dude, you're letting this advanced piece of alien tech create steel-melting fire out of nowhere. Has it ever occurred to you that it might explode? Or melt through the floor?"

"I don't worry about things like that," Carl said, dismissing my concerns with a wave of his hand.

"Well, you should! If something went wrong, you could end up destroying Manhattan."

"The whole Eastern Seaboard, probably," he corrected me. "This baby really packs a punch."

"You've gotta shut this down, man." I raced ahead of Carl down the catwalks and left him in the dust. "This is really stupid. You have no idea what you're messing with."

"Oh, Penelope, think!" He had to shout now, since I was outpacing him. His voice echoed off the cavern walls. "Did the first caveman have to understand fire before he could cook food? Or did the Egyptians have to understand the Universe before they could map the stars?"

"It's dangerous, Carl," I replied. "And you know it."

I broke into a sprint. Carl chased after me. It was a race to the bottom.

"Of course it's dangerous," he shouted. "That's the risk of research and development. But we learn new things about it every day. You of all people should understand why that's important! You swallowed the red one!"

I kept going. I wasn't going to listen to his bullshit.

"Don't you have questions, Penelope?" he shouted. "Questions about Impossible Red? Don't you want answers?"

That made me stop short. God dammit. I did.

Was my body done changing? Was I slowly becoming more machine than girl? Was I still aging or would I live forever? I had questions about the other god spheres, too. What planet did they come from? And how did they get to Earth?

If Westland had answers, I'd be lying if I said I wasn't interested. I'd never felt so conflicted in my entire life. I knew full well not to trust Carl. He was the blackest of snakes in a den of vipers, the kind of guy who would help you up with his right hand, then stab you in the back with his left. I'd seen it happen.

I'd even used it against him.

Then again, things down in Dinosaur Canyon didn't seem all that evil. If Westland wanted to turn this thing into a weapon, wouldn't they have done it by now? Like Carl said, they were just using it to generate power. Would it be so bad if the Westland Corporation discovered a cleaner, cheaper way to supply power to the world?

Power the likes of which man had never seen before?

A part of me knew the right thing to do was to smash my way through that plexiglass cube, rip Untouchable Orange out of the air and get the hell out of Dodge. Another part of me knew I had to stay on Carl's good side... for Xin's sake.

"If you have answers," I said to Carl, "I'm listening."

Carl and I reached the bottom together. The floor of the cave was polished smooth. There were fossilized seashells and pre-historic sea creatures visible in the stone. I looked up to where we started from; those elevator doors looked so tiny up there.

Carl led me up to the plastic bank vault door. He leaned in close to the transparent surface and stared inside. The crackling inferno on the inside of that plastic cube cast an orange glow across our faces, but I didn't feel any heat. I couldn't hear any sounds. Whatever box they built to contain the molten fire was apparently pretty sturdy.

As he stared inside, Carl started talking.

"We found a way to activate the nanites inside the marble without using a host body. Good thing, too, because the odds of surviving Untouchable Orange are remarkably low. Impossible Red gave you a metal skeleton and bullet-proof skin and mechanical organs. Turning into the artificial god of fire wouldn't be as forgiving. The host body would end up with liquid-hot plasma for blood, something around 10,000 degrees. Steel would melt in their bare hands. Their body heat alone would cook a human being like a Christmas goose. Whoever swallowed Untouchable Orange would have to live in the hottest deserts of the world, all alone, and even then their footprints would melt the sand into glass."

That must made it sound dangerous again.

"And you're just letting it run wild," I said. "You're pushing it to get hotter and hotter and you're going to end up blowing everything to hell."

"Penelope, try to understand. Untouchable Orange does not pose a threat to the world. The walls of this containment chamber are built from slabs of glorious glass, five feet thick."

"What the hell is glorious glass?"

"It's a celestial building material imported from Heaven," he said. "Quite expensive."

"Imported from..." I could barely say it. "Heaven?"

Carl nodded. "Hard to believe, right? But it's true. It's the same stuff they used to build Heaven. And getting our hands on this much glorious glass involved a lot of wheeling and dealing. As you might imagine, Heaven really doesn't like doing business with outsiders."

Well, that changed things. Now I was more interested in the glorious glass than I was in Untouchable Orange. "I've never seen anything from Heaven before."

"Between you and me, angels think an awful lot of themselves," he said "They're arrogant and not exactly fun to work with. The fact that I talked them out of four tons of glorious glass is nothing short of... well... a miracle."

"Holy shit. You're talking about real angels?" It wasn't a huge stretch of the imagination considering everything else I'd seen in my life. Just a few months ago I met my first demon.

"Have you never met one?" Carl asked. I was still so entranced by the heavenly building materials that all I could do was shake my head no. "Consider yourself lucky," he said. "I try not to work with angels if I don't absolutely have to. Unfortunately building this chamber was an 'absolutely have to' kind of thing."

I ran my fingers over the surface of the glorious glass. It felt cold and sent goosebumps up my arm. The oil from my fingertips left a streak across the glass which quickly evaporated.

I was awestruck. "It's glass from Heaven..."

"Completely impenetrable by anything supernatural," Carl boasted. "Ghosts can't pass through it, gods can't smash it open, and whoever stands behind it is protected from psychics. Even the all-knowing Oracles of the world can't see what's inside this containment chamber. Missiles can't crack it, bullets can't penetrate it, and it could probably shrug off a direct hit from a nuclear bomb if it had to. If you'll forgive the analogy, this is the Fort Knox of the supernatural world."

I flicked the glass with my finger. It resonated with a single crystal note. "This stuff is so cool."

"It's very difficult to build with," he told me. "Assembling this glass cage was a real... pane."

I shot him a weird look. "Was that a joke?"

He smiled. "I used it with the Angels. They didn't get it."

I pushed against the glass to see how strong it was. It felt solid. I thumped my fist against it a couple times, a little harder each time, but all I got was a deep, echoing boom.

"Satisfied?" Carl asked me. "As long as Untouchable Orange is inside this containment chamber, we are perfectly safe from it and *it* is perfectly safe from *us*."

Carl's cell phone began to ring. It's worth mentioning that his ring tone was an all-digital version of that old '90s song "Flip Fantasia." He snapped his cell phone off his belt like the fastest gunslinger in the Old West and answered it.

"This is Carl," he said. It's not every day you see a corporate CEO answer his personal cell phone. I wondered what the call could have been about. Maybe it was about Xin. Carl, who valued his privacy, turned away from me and lowered his voice. "When did this happen?" Pause. "And you're sure?" Pause. "Thank you, Miss Stegman."

Carl ended the call and stuck his phone back in his belt. For a moment he was lost in his own thoughts. He looked worried. When I cleared my throat and reminded him that I was still right there, he snapped out of it and gave me a smile.

"Terribly sorry, but we're going to have to cut the tour short. I have business to attend to." He angled towards the catwalks. I followed after him.

"Bad news?" I asked.

"Hmm?" he asked.

I gestured at him cell phone. "Bad news?"

"Oh." He glanced at his phone and then laughed. "Nothing serious. Just typical CEO stuff. You know me, busy busy busy."

And he kept laughing, but it wasn't a convincing laugh. It was a nervous laugh. Something was wrong.

6

Carl escorted me up the looping steel catwalks and to the elevator where he used his red CEO passkey to open the sliding doors. We stepped inside and Carl pressed the "Lobby" button.

The elevator lifted us up to the main floor and the doors opened. In the tropical atrium, field agents scrambled all over the place in a panic. Most of them were checking their phones. I spotted Ilana at the reception desk. She looked stressed out, answering phone calls as fast as she could. In fact, all the receptionists fielded phone calls, directing traffic in some kind of Westland disaster.

On the giant computer tower above the reception desk, the plasma screen TVs that earlier showed worldwide news and stock reports were now blue screens that read "No Signal."

I overheard a group of agents as they got off the elevators beside me and Carl's.

"...Definitely a hack job using out-dated access codes..."

"...A complete shutdown of primary and back up systems..."

"...Can't even contact the girls in Europe to tell them..."

"Alright, Penelope." Carl hurried me out of the elevator, "Thank you so much for coming. It was a real pleasure catching up with you. Don't be a stranger now. I would love to have you stay, but you are a very busy girl and you should probably leave immediately."

"Uh huh." My suspicion meter was through the roof. "I'm going to let you keep Untouchable Orange, Carl. For now. If I find out that you're using it for evil, I'm going to come back here and you're not going to like that."

He nodded. "Understood."

"And you're going to figure out what's wrong with Xin?"

"Oh, of course." He gave the cell phone on his hip a small pat. "You'll know something as soon as I know something."

A field agent sprinted up to the nearby vacant elevator, with his briefcase clutched to his chest. Papers fluttered out of his arms. His acted like we were minutes away from getting wiped out by an asteroid. "Oh dear Christ," he said.

What the hell. I looked back at Carl and asked, "You sure everything is okay?"

"Just dandy." He winked at me. "Bye bye, now."

"Hmm." I squinted at him. "Goodbye, Carl."

I elbowed my way out of the lobby through a complete clusterfuck of Westland agents. Everyone looked confused, or worried, or horrified. As I reached the revolving doors that led back out to New York City, I glanced over my shoulder one last time to see what Carl was doing. He was still there in the elevator, watching me with a nervous smile. He waved at me, confidently ignoring the chaos that surrounded him.

I gave him a small wave goodbye and left.

Chapter 6

1

By the time Corolla drove me back to Chinatown, the sun had started to disappear behind the Manhattan skyline. The glass skyscrapers glowed orange in that last hour of sunlight. The evening shadows of the Village highrises fell over Chinatown and I knew them well enough to use them like a sundial. I figured it was between 7:30 and 7:45; well past closing time for the shop. I had left the building locked up all day and got none of my work done. A few of our customers missed out on their afternoon orders, but nothing huge; nothing life-or-death.

With Xin in the hospital, this wouldn't be the last time I'd have to miss work. Still, I had a responsibility to my customers. I made a promise to myself that in the future, if I needed to close up shop again for whatever reason, I would make sure everyone got their orders first, even if I had to deliver them on foot.

Walking through the secret alley and crossing the court-yard, I couldn't shake the vision of Xin lying in that hospital bed, weak and unconscious. It was weird to see him that way. Sure, he was a million years old and moved slow, but his mind was still sharp. He seemed healthy. I worried about him a lot that evening. Would he ever wake up? Could Carl figure out who did this? And if Carl did find out, if I knew who was responsible, would I be able to get them to reverse this "soul killing" spell?

Worry, worry, worry. All I did was worry.

I distracted myself with the evening chores. There were flowers that needed watering, herbs that needed rotating, and a few plants that needed to be plucked and pruned. I kicked off my shoes, tuned the radio to some punk rock, and watered the porch plants in the golden glow of the Manhattan sunset.

That's when I realized I had visitors.

Right in the middle of the courtyard stood two strangers, a young teenage girl... and a bright red astronaut.

The girl looked younger than me, but not by much. She could have been Eastern European, with super pale skin and a menacing black eye patch over her left eye that made her look like a James Bond villain. Her hair was a chopped-to-shit mess, as if she cut it herself by the handful and without a mirror. She slouched in place, obviously unhappy to be here.

Sure, she *looked* like a human. She reminded me of the drama chicks I went to high school with: blue-and-black flannel over a plain black t-shirt, a denim skirt, and bulky combat boots. Perfectly normal except for that eye patch. Her one good eye was ice blue and super bitchy looking.

No, no, no. This chick was trouble.

An astronaut in a red astronaut suit stood next to her in a majestic pose, as if he were about to be immortalized in statue-form by an army of sculptors. His helmet was round and tinted so dark, I couldn't see inside. All I could see was my own reflection.

No way this was a normal girl. Normal girls don't wear eye patches. Normal girls don't pal around with red astronauts. Normal girls don't stare down Penelope Salvo as if they're looking to brawl. So I returned her bitchy stare and sized her up. What was she? A god? She didn't dress like a god, at least no god I'd ever seen. Was she a ghost? Or a psychic?

Please don't let her be a psychic. Psychics are the worst.

Carl mentioned something about a young girl and her pet astronaut at our earlier meeting. Damn, that sounded weird at the time and I should have asked some follow up questions, but I had other things on my mind at the time.

I said to the girl, "Can I help you?"

When she spoke, she had a slight, but definitely noticeable Russian accent.

"What is this place?" she asked me.

How to answer that? "You mean Chinatown?"

She shook her head in frustration and pointed at the shop. "Do you own this structure?"

I shrugged. "Maybe."

She tilted her head, as if my non-committal answer was sufficient enough. She asked, "Does this building have space station components?"

I gave her a weird look. "Uh, no? We're an herbal shop."

Normal teenage girls don't typically go around asking for space station components. The verdict was in: this girl anything but normal.

Now, the astronaut guy? He didn't look normal either, even for an astronaut. I'd seen real-life astronaut suits when my grade school class took a field trip to the Space and Science Museum. Those suits were chalky white. This astronaut's suit was bright red with a yellow hammer and sickle patch on his shoulder. That's when things clicked in my brain. This wasn't an American astronaut. This was a Russian astronaut. Or, technically, a Soviet astronaut. But the Soviet Union wasn't around anymore, so why wear one of their astronaut suits?

Or, better yet, why wear an astronaut suit at all?

He had other patches on his chest, all of them written in Russian letters and marked with some kind of Soviet space agency logo. Hoses connected his suit to a bulky respirator machine strapped to his back. He was sealed completely inside the suit, with no visible zippers or seams.

The helmet is what bothered me most. I wanted to know who I was dealing with, but I couldn't see inside. I couldn't tell if the person wearing the suit was a man or a woman, young or old, or if they were even human at all. It just stood there, motionless, arms at their side.

"You're sure?" the eyepatch girl asked.

Shit. I got so distracted by their weirdness, I forgot what we were talking about.

"Am I sure about what?"

She gave me a frustrated groan. "That you don't have space station components."

"I'm sure," I said. "We sell flowers and plants and herbs. No space station components."

She arched her eyebrow as if she didn't believe me. "This Cosmonaut has been leading me around Earth, helping me collect pieces of my body. He's led me to nearly all of them, mostly at the bottom of the ocean. And he's never been wrong before. One piece of me is still missing, and he seems to think that it's here."

Pieces? Of her body? This conversation took an odd turn.

All I could think to say was, "Uhhh."

She continued. "He wouldn't have brought me here if you didn't have space station components. So I suggest you hand them over."

"Oh, you *suggest*?" Now she was threatening me? This chick had no idea who she was messing with. I hopped off the porch and walked closer to them. Once I was within arms reach, I waved my open hand in front of the red astronaut's space helmet. He didn't react at all. I said, "I thought you said you were looking for space station parts, but now you're saying you want body parts. Which is it?"

"Both," she said. "My body parts are space station parts."

Man, just when I thought things were making sense. I looked the girl over, from her choppy hair down to her muddy combat boots and said, "You don't look like you're made of space station parts."

"I may look human, but I am a space station," she said. "I am called Mir."

"Your name is Mirror?" I asked. I misheard her, but her accent was tricky and "Mir" isn't exactly a common name.

"No." I could tell from her tone, this conversation bothered her a lot. "I am Mir. M-I-R. The space station."

I shook my head. "Never heard of a Mir space station."

She sighed, exasperated, and hung her head. With her face pointed at the ground, she said, "I used to live in space."

"And now here you are," I said, presenting her like a prize on a TV game show. "And you have a human body!"

"I'm a shape-shifter," she said.

"Like a werewolf?" I asked.

"Like a were-space-station," she clarified.

"Uh huh." Not *the* craziest thing I'd ever heard, but it ranked pretty high up there. "You're half-space station, half-human?"

She nodded. "And a long time ago I broke into pieces and fell to Earth. The Cosmonaut here has been helping me collect those pieces and rebuild my body."

"And these pieces of you, they look like space station parts?"

"Correct."

I looked the Cosmonaut up and down. He stared off into the distance, lost in his own little world.

"He talk?" I asked Mir.

"No," she said.

So she's a shape-shifting space station trying to rebuild her body. Got it. I still couldn't help her. "Straight up, dude, I'm telling you we don't have space station parts here. Just flowers and..." The stuff in the basement. We had a lot of weird stuff in the basement. "...other stuff. But no space station parts."

She frowned. "Fine."

She turned to walk away, but the red-suited Cosmonaut didn't move. He stood his ground and faced the shop. The Russian girl – Mir – realized her friend wasn't following behind her and she turned back around.

"Come on." She pulled on the astronaut's arm. He didn't budge. She pulled harder. "Cosmonaut. Follow."

But he wouldn't follow. Instead, he reached out and pointed at the shop. His gloves were thick and bulky, and worn thin from years of heavy use.

Mir glanced back at me from over her shoulder.

"You're *sure* you don't have any space station components?"

2

Who was she to question me about the shop?

That shop was my home. I lived there. I worked there. It was basically my entire reason for living. We didn't have any god damned space station components. We weren't in the business of space station components. Xin and I weren't engineers, or astronauts, or anything like that. We grew flowers, sold herbs, and stored rare liquids from around the world. Even our collection in the basement – for as supernatural as it was – consisted of magic spell books and suits of armor and powerful weapons. Not a whole lot of things from outer space.

Except.

I mean, I suppose I *did* technically "borrow" that metal panel from NASA's Area 5 back when Xin needed replacement space moss. That panel might have come from a space station. I didn't have the first clue. I'm wasn't an astrophysicist.

"Okay, I might have one thing from space," I told the girl. "But it's just a piece of metal."

"So you *do* have components." She crossed her arms slowly, as if she caught me red-handed in a lie.

"Well, I don't know if it's from a space station or not," I said. "It's technically not mine."

"You stole it," she said in a accusing tone.

"I borrowed it," I said. "There's a difference."

"Stealing is against the law."

Ha. Listen to her. Against the law. I stuck my wrists out. "Well, slap me in cuffs and drag me downtown, Sipowicz."

She didn't find me funny. God, did this chick do anything but sulk? She said, "I want to see this space station component."

"Sure. Whatever. What do I care?" I turned around and headed up the porch steps to the shop. "You and moonboots wait out here. I'll be right back."

So I went inside. I kept my key to the basement padlock on a necklace tucked down the front of my shirt. I lifted it up and over my head, undid the padlock, and went down the stairs.

There's an energy in the basement that makes the hair on the back of my neck stand up. Too many objects of unimaginable power, I suppose. Maybe it was a psychosomatic reaction brought on by the knowledge that I alone had access to an arsenal of weapons that could wipe out the Earth ten times over.

Now where did I put that stupid panel?

I checked behind the suits of dragon scale armor.

Nothing.

I checked behind the sword rack, home of interesting specimens such as the Eclipsing Ninjato Blade of Kyota Falls and a military prototype of a fully functional light saber.

Nope. Not there either.

I checked behind a pig-sized chunk of red meteor that Xin told me to keep very far away from water.

Zilch.

God dammit, we had so much disorganized junk scattered around the basement, it looked like someone picked up a museum and dumped everything out. I couldn't find the panel anywhere. It had been months since I had scraped the Space Moss off it and, after that, it was just useless space junk. It had to be down there somewhere – I knew that much for certain – but I was damned if I could remember where I put it.

Maybe it fell behind the book shelves. I pressed my cheek against the bricks and peered down the narrow gap between the back of the bookcases and the wall, but I didn't see anything. Fantastic. Just fan-freakin-tastic, man. I couldn't come back empty handed or this little Russian and her pet space suit would never leave me alone. If I told them I couldn't find it, that Mir chick was going to want to come down to the basement herself and poke around. She'd want to make sure I wasn't lying. I'd tell her "no" of course, that she wasn't allowed to go in the basement, but she would ignore me and try come here anyway. Then I'd have to go full Macho Man Randy Savage on her ass and that wouldn't end well.

That's when I found it. The damn panel was right there in plain sight the whole time, leaning up against the cursed treasure chest of Captain Seaboots. Stupid Penelope, that's a dumb place for it.

I decided that someday soon I would spend some time in the basement and really organize everything. The place was an absolute freakin' nightmare.

3

I climbed the stairs with the panel in my hands and my only though was "God, I hope this is what she's looking for." If I could be that lucky, she'd go away and I could get on with my life.

I stepped back to the courtyard to find the Cosmonaut drifting weightlessly through the air, as if gravity didn't apply to him. He hovered around, maybe six feet off the ground, just barely over the girl's head. His arms and legs were slightly bent, like how astronauts move in zero-gravity. He reminded me of a Macy's Day Parade balloon that got loose.

Mir followed him around like a frustrated teen, too cool for school, too cool to put any real effort into catching him.

"Come down," she commanded.

I pointed at the Cosmonaut and asked, "He always do that?"

"Not always," she said. "Just sometimes."

I watched the Cosmonaut float around for a little bit. It was peaceful, somehow. Calming. He had been cut free from the laws of physics. He could go in whichever direction he wanted.

"Cosmonaut," Mir said impatiently, as if addressing a disobedient pet. "Obey gravity. Now!"

The Cosmonaut came down for a landing. His space boots touched the ground softly and he assumed his standing position. He put his arms at his side and faced me with his reflective helmet.

Super weird.

"Is that the space station component?" Mir reached for the panel in my hands.

"Oh." I looked down at it. "Yeah, I dunno. You tell me."

The Cosmonaut lifted his arm and pointed at the panel.

"That's it!" Mir grabbed it with both hands and yanked. I didn't let go. For the moment, this was the only leverage I had over the strange girl and I planned to take advantage of it. When I didn't let go, she gave me a panicked look.

"This is my eyelid." She yanked again. "Give it."

Ah. Now the eye patch made sense.

"I'll let you have it." I maintained my grip on the panel. "But I want to ask you some questions first."

"Questions!?" She sounded annoyed. "I don't have time for questions! I have things to do!" She growled and yanked on the panel harder, but she wasn't getting it. No way. Eventually she threw her hands up and gasped in frustration. "Fine! Ask your stupid questions."

I pointed at her, then the Cosmonaut. "I want to know where you two came from."

"Outer space," she snapped. "Where else? Can we go now?"

"Just hang on." I took my time and thought of another question. "What's up with moonboots here? How does he do that weightless trick?"

I don't think the astronaut man knew we were talking about him. Maybe he couldn't hear us through that helmet. Or maybe he couldn't hear anything at all.

"He does weird stuff all the time," Mir said. "Float. Move through solid objects. I don't know how."

I was skeptical. "You don't know how?"

"No."

"You're sure?"

She lowered her voice and grumbled, "I said I don't know."

"Where'd you meet him?" I asked.

"I woke up on the beach half-assembled and there he was. He's been helping me put my body back together ever since. This panel is my last piece. Satisfied? Now give me my eyelid. You're just wasting my time."

I didn't care for her attitude, but I put her through enough. She didn't sound like much of a threat to me or the shop; she just wanted to put her body back together. If my body were broken into pieces, I'd want the same thing. I released my grip on the panel and she yanked it away. The metallic square was as big as her torso and she looked awkward carrying it.

"How'd your body end up in pieces in the first place?" I asked.

She scoffed. "I'm not going to tell you that."

"Why not?"

"Because. It's none of your business."

This bitch. After everything I did for her.

"You're welcome, by the way," I said. I expected my snotty tone to be the final nail in the coffin for this meeting.

But Mir wasn't done. She squinted her one good eye at me and gave me a weird look, that look you get when someone thinks they recognize you, but can't remember where from.

"You're that girl, eh?" she said. "The god of war?"

"I suppose," I said. "Sure."

"I've heard of you." She looked more relaxed now, which wasn't really saying a whole lot because she was wound tight. "Tell me, war god. Have you ever started a thermo-nuclear war?"

"Not to the best of my recollection."

"I want to start a thermo-nuclear war, but I've never done one before. I just want it to be perfect, you know? Zero survivors. Something truly horrible. Something that wipes out humanity and turns Earth into a scorched, radioactive ball of death."

"Well, a lot of people your age don't know what they want to do with their lives, so good for you."

"Thank you." She seemed quite pleased with herself. "I just wondered if you had any advice."

"Advice?" I asked.

"Yes."

"On starting a thermo-nuclear war?"

"Yes."

"Yeah," I said. "I advise you to not start a thermo-nuclear war. That's super uncool."

She scoffed again. "Well, that's not an option. War's coming. That's all there is to that." She glanced suspiciously around the courtyard with her good eye, almost as if someone were spying on us. "All I need now is a nuclear bomb. You don't have a nuclear bomb, do you?"

"Absolutely not."

That was a lie. We had a warhead in the basement, tucked in the corner. Just the radioactive explosive part of the nose cone, not the actual missile. As far as bombs went, it was pretty old. I wondered if it even worked anymore. Do nuclear bombs go bad?

Either way, I wasn't giving Mir a nuke and she didn't push for it, not like how she pushed for the space ship components.

"You don't have any nuclear bombs," she observed. "And you don't want me to start a nuclear war."

"Correct."

"You're not a very good god of war," she said.

"I hear that a lot."

"Can't you be of any help?" she asked. "Do you know how to get to Norrid?"

"Norrid?"

I'd never heard of "Norrid" before in my life. I didn't even need to think about that one. I had been all across the world, to Egypt and Japan and Antarctica, but I'd never heard of any place called Norrid. Maybe it was a place on Earth, maybe it wasn't. Just because I'd never heard of it didn't mean it didn't exist. My knowledge of the supernatural was by no means exhaustive, but even if I did know, I don't think I would have told her.

"Never heard of it," I said. "Sorry."

"Cosmonaut, come." Mir turned and walked away, carrying her piece of square metal. "We'll find it by ourselves."

The Cosmonaut followed behind the space station girl with bounding, weightless steps, as if he were on the surface of the moon. She walked – and he bounced – across the courtyard and out the alley. I watched them leave. Once they were *gone* gone, I went inside and locked the door.

Fucking weirdos.

4

My dad had been go go go all day long. I visited Xin in the hospital, then did a quick pop-in at the Westland Corporation, and wrapped things up with a shape-shifting space station. I don't get tired or exhausted, and I don't need sleep, but this was still a long fucking day.

And it was finally over. Thank god for that.

I still needed to finish the evening watering, and then maybe do some prep-work for tomorrow's orders.

Something kept bugging me. "Norrid." Now that I was alone and had time to really think about it, it did sound familiar. I couldn't place from where, exactly.

Norrid.

Norrid.

I decided to check in that book Xin gave me. That book marked the location of all kinds of hidden, magical plants. Maybe this Norrid place would be in there. I went to my bedroom and flipped through the book, quickly searching for the word. It would have been easier if the book were electronic. I wished I could just CTRL+F and search for the word; that would have been a lot faster.

I muttered the name over and over to myself as I flipped through the old pages. "Norrid... Norrid... Norrid..." Nothing.

Nothing and then...

I flipped past something that caught my eye. I flipped back a few pages, trying to track down what I saw. There it was; a map of the Rocky Mountains. It said:

NORAD

North American Aerospace Defense Command
Cheyenne Mountain Complex
Known components: Conspiracy Snow,
Precambrian Sedimentary Argillite, Ponderosa Pine

Holy shit. Mir wasn't saying "Norrid." She was saying NORAD. Her Russian accent confused me, but no mistaking it: she was on her way to NORAD to start a nuclear war and turn Earth into a scorched, uninhabitable ball of radioactive ash.

Mrs. Wright taught us about NORAD in our Western Civ class, back when we were doing our unit on the Cold War. It's an underground military complex built deep inside the Rocky Mountains so if the Russians ever nuked D.C., the military still had a place to launch our nukes back at them.

Shit.

Mir and the Cosmonaut had a head start to Colorado. I raced outside and into the courtyard so fast, I forgot to the lock the door. I scrambled back, locked it, then sprinted for the alley as fast as my robo-legs would carry me. If I was really lucky I could catch them before they got too far away, but when I burst onto the sidewalks of Chinatown, they were gone.

I jumped in front of a tourist – a fat white guy with a bald head and chubby arms – and got right in his face.

"Have you seen a girl about this tall?" I asked him. "She had an eye patch and was carrying a piece of a space station? Or did you see a big red astronaut with all kinds of Russian shit all over his body?"

The guy backed away from me as if I was crazy. The more I advanced on him for answers, the faster he backed off. Eventually he was running away from me. As he should. I sounded insane.

Corolla. I had to get to Corolla.

Parked just a little ways up the block, he sat there with his dome light on. I ran over to him and climbed in the passenger seat. The stereo was tuned to Straight Talk, this local talk radio.

The government is trying to cover it up, but they can't keep a lid on something so groundbreaking. Weather control is a fact. A cold, hard, absolute, 100 percent fact. Its already happened and we are-

I shut it off.

"Hey!" Corolla whined. "I was listening to that."

"We need to get to Colorado and *now*," I told him.

He heard it in my voice; I was not in the mood to fuck around. We needed to go and we didn't have time to waste on petty bickering. Without a word of protest, he fired up the engine and swerved into traffic.

"Why're we in such a big hurry to get to Colorado?" Corolla asked. "Snowboarding finals aren't for two more months."

"We're not going to watch snowboarding," I said.

"Oh." Corolla sounded disappointed.

"There's a space station on her way to NORAD. She wants to start a nuclear war and we have to stop her."

"Alright," he said, resigning himself to a far less exciting trip to Colorado than extreme sports. "It's not snowboarding, but I guess that's fine."

Chapter 7

1

If you're going to tear through the clouds over Kansas in hot pursuit of a shape-shifting space station and her pet astronaut, you might as well rock out. Corolla wanted to listen to Rush, but I slapped an extra-hard veto on that idea. Getty Lee's voice grates on my nerves. It's just so shrill and whiny. We had a slowly expanding selection of cassettes to choose from, things scrounged up from the various dollar bins at used record stores.

Corolla and I had a one-for-one policy: I could get any one cassette I liked, as long as I got him a cassette he wanted. Our tastes were wildly different – Corolla loved classic rock and '80s hair metal while I much preferred the emo pop-punk of the early 2000s – so our library of bands seemed to be having an identity crisis, at best.

Occasionally we found a way to agree on a band that checked both of our boxes. That's how we ended up violating Topeka airspace while singing Danzig's "Mother" at the top of our lungs.

Not that either of us had lungs.

Corolla whisked through the moonlit clouds with his high beams on, en route to Colorado. We'd flown over the United States many times before and I had learned to identify the different American states by geography alone. Kansas was mostly dark at night, and flat, with only a few glowing cities here and there. There were lakes, too, ghost blue in color as they reflected the blue glow of the moon. Sometimes I'd glimpse little creepy-crawlies moving through the empty fields – cattle, I assumed – but they were far away and looked like an infestation of fleas.

Then, off in the distance, was Colorado. And even though we were half a state away, the Rocky Mountains appeared on the foggy horizon like a thousand shadowy peaks. They stretched so far north and so far south, I couldn't see the ends of them.

We crossed the Kansas/Colorado border just after midnight and the Rockies came into full view. Forest trees covered the jagged slopes like a thin layer of moss. Their snow capped peaks glowed blue under the moon and almost looked haunted.

Once, months ago, Corolla and I were flying over Colorado when we saw some sort of X-Games snowboarding event on one of the mountains. Thousands of people were gathered there, watching the worlds best snow boarders shred their way down the slopes. I might've been a little high and got really excited, so we stayed and watched snowboarding for almost an hour. I thought Corolla was bored with it, but he'd been bringing it up ever since. I'd never even touched a snowboard before, but I was pretty good at skateboarding and figured I could make the switch real easy. That was, of course, if I ever got the chance to learn.

We agreed to go back someday for another tournament.

I didn't think we'd ever get the free time for that, not when we were constantly saving the world.

"What's NORAD stand for?" Corolla asked me.

"Um." I had read the full name in my book, but I couldn't quite remember what it was. "North American... something-something... Air Defense. Or something."

"So you don't know," he said flatly.

I nodded in silent agreement. "I don't know."

Behind the Kansas-facing mountains were more mountains. Behind those mountains were even more mountains. Colorado loves its mountains. And one of those random mountains – I had no idea which – was home to an underground military base. How was I supposed to figure out which mountain was NORAD when they all looked identical?

I guess that was exactly the point. The United States government didn't *want* me, or anyone for that matter, knowing which mountain was NORAD mountain.

"You know," Corolla said. "Seems to me that hollowing out a mountain and filling it with nuclear weapons is a real evil-villain sort of move."

"Yep," I said. "That's the government for you."

"This is like something out of a James Bond movie."

"I was just thinking that earlier!"

"So in this scenario," he said. "I'll be James Bond and you be the Bond girl."

Me? The Bond girl? Corolla was seriously mistaken.

"*I'm* James Bond in this scenario," I told him. "You can be the Bond car."

"Why do I have to be the Bond car?" he asked. "Why can't I be James Bond?"

I blinked at his stereo. Did he really not get it?

"Because you're a car," I said.

"Oh, so just because I'm a car I have to *be* the car? I don't want to be the car. I want to be James Bond."

"James Bond didn't have a muffler," I said.

"He also didn't have a vagina."

I had to admit, he had a point. "How about this," I said. "I'm the Bond girl, you're the Bond car and we don't need James Bond."

He pondered that for a moment. "I guess that works."

"Good." I looked out the window and searched for the NORAD mountain. No one mountain looked any different from any of the others. "Okay, Corolla, in full disclosure... I don't know which one of these mountains is NORAD."

He replied with a simple, "Huh." We flew around for a bit and scanned the Rocky Mountains. What options did we have? We certainly couldn't have landed on every single mountain and inspect them one-by-one. That would take months.

In the end, it didn't come to that.

"What about that one?" Corolla asked as he drifted to the left.

"Which one?" I crawled up onto my knees to get a better vantage point at the mountains below. I had no idea which one Corolla was referring to. None of them really screamed "secret military base."

"That one up ahead," he said. "Two o'clock. The one with those open missile doors."

I squinted and searched. I saw black mountains, snow and shadowy pine trees. "Where are you looking?"

"Here." He accelerated to the left. "I'll show you."

And, sure enough, after another five minutes of flying, he shined his high beams down to illuminate a random mountainside. Finally, I saw what he saw: Dozens of holes drilled straight into the rock. Big holes. Holes so big I don't know how I didn't notice them before. The missile silo doors were open and the pointy white tips of nuclear bombs were in plain view. What I once thought was fog was actually pre-launch smoke wafting out of the vents hidden in the rock. That smoke didn't bode well. I'm no five-star general, but I know that when you see open missile silos and clouds of smoke, those bitches are about to launch.

"Shit." Time was of the essence, but we were still up near the clouds. We were probably looking at a paratrooper operation. I pushed opened the passenger-side door and looked down at the 5,000 foot drop. Freezing wind blasted through the car like an airlock on a space station.

"What the hell are you doing?" Corolla shouted over the rushing air. "Let me land first and-"

"No time," I said. "Stay close in case anything goes wrong."

And, with that, I jumped out of the car and plunged down to the Earth below.

I fell fast. The freezing air fluttered through my clothes. My left shoe was untied. The shoelaces flapped behind me and it would be just my luck if the wind sucked it right off my foot, lost forever on the side of Mount NORAD.

Below me, the finer details of the mountain became more clear. I could see snow blowing off the tree branches. I heard the distant howl of wolves in the night air. And, coolest thing, I could see my shadow on the snowy mountainside, cast down by the Moon behind me. My shadow grew bigger and bigger as I fell faster. I was on a collision course with my shadow. And the rocks.

I struck the mountainside like the flash of a meteor. Snow and rock exploded up into the air. A spiderweb of cracks exploded through the stone from my body's impact. This super-sensitive military base undoubtedly had seismic equipment, so it was safe to assume that they detected my one-megaton arrival.

That was fine. It wasn't me they needed to worry about. It was that shape-shifting space-station and her astronaut friend.

2

NORAD must have had an entrance. How else did people get inside? The problem was, I had no clue where to find it. If I searched until Christmas, I could have possibly stumbled across some giant steel doors, three stories tall, completely immune to gunfire or rocket launchers or nuclear strikes. I didn't have until Christmas. I had until five minutes ago. And, honestly, while I punched with the force of a derailing locomotive, I wasn't convinced that I could pound my way through the front doors of NORAD, not if they were designed to survive a nuclear holocaust.

I needed a different way in, so I ran to one of the smoking missile silos. Those doors were open. I'd get in that way.

I've seen silos like these on the internet and on TV, but never in real life and never with my own eyes. I had no idea they were so big. These holes were as vast as an Olympic swimming pool.

A repeating, low-frequency alarm echoed out of the silo, something so ominous that it made my skin crawl. It only got louder as I crunched closer through the snow, until I was standing at the very edge and peeking down into the darkness below. This was an alarm that said, "The world is ending and after the humans are gone, this nuclear-powered alarm will continue to sound as a testament to their horrible mistakes."

I got the creeps just thinking about how much destruction just this one nuclear bomb might cause. But it wasn't just the one nuclear bomb. All around the mountainside, multiple silos were open and venting steam.

Wind blew a drift of snow over my sneakers and down into the silo. The white flakes landed on the side of the nuke and melted into water drops. I watched the droplets roll down the side of the ten-story rocket. I got struck with a flash of vertigo and thought I might lose my balance, but I managed to steady myself. The silo was as deep and I couldn't quite see the bottom. Balconies circled around the interior in ten distinct levels, each with a sealed access door that led deeper into the facility.

Then there was the bomb itself: One big god damned nuclear bomb. ICBMs they're called. Inter-Continental Ballistic Missiles, designed to launch from Colorado and reach anywhere else in the world. If you stood this missile up in New York City, it would have given the Statue of Liberty a run for her money.

The nuke had all these insignias printed on the side: the American flag, the radiation symbol, and a bunch of NORAD logos. And in bright yellow letters stenciled all down the side, it said US-H-3401, probably some sort of inventory number that cataloged every nuke in America... not that I have any idea how you could lose track of nuclear bombs this freaking big.

Smoke filled the bottom of the silo. White smoke. Launch smoke. Then there were the flashing red strobe lights and the whole time there was that alarm, that horrifying alarm that meant doomsday was coming. The acrid smoke, the dizzying lights, the overwhelming dread that came with the realization that everything sucks and humanity is fucking doomed... it felt like being at a Radiohead concert.

And I'm thinking, shouldn't there be a computer voice giving me a countdown? If Corolla's "James Bond" theory held true, there should be a British woman going, "Three minutes to launch," "Two minutes to launch," "One minute to launch." That would have been useful, because I had no idea how much time I had before these sons-a-bitches were going up. Hours? Minutes? Seconds?

Either way, I wasn't getting anything done by standing around gawking. I had to act, and act quick.

I base-jumped off the edge of the hole and swan-dived down into the silo, whizzing past ten levels of balconies and plunging into the layer of smoke at the bottom. I smacked the bottom with a metallic boom, denting the floor of the silo with my forehead. Smoke clouded my vision and all I could hear were wailing emergency alarms. I waved my arms in front of me to clear the smoke and felt around for a door or some other exit.

Eventually my fingers brushed a wall of smooth steel. I blindly ran my hands across it, moving forward until I eventually came to a door. I felt around for a doorknob, but this door didn't come with knobs. It wasn't that kind of door. This was one of those solid steel blast doors that drops down from the ceiling and locks into place with magnets. I felt around the door frame for an electronic control panel or something. Nothing.

Fine. Not the first time I had to punch down a door. Probably wouldn't be the last.

I stepped back, spread my feet shoulder-width apart and drove my fist into the slab of steel. A BOOM echoed up through the silo. It didn't open, not on the first punch, but I felt it dent like styrofoam. I thought maybe a little running start would help, so I took a few steps back, crouched down like a linebacker and wind-sprinted at the door. My feet thumped hard against the metal floor and when I was seconds away from the bulkhead door, I turned and threw my shoulder into it.

BOOM. The steel dented deeper and I heard the concrete frame start to crack. Now we were getting somewhere. I put my head down and wailed on the door like Rocky Balboa punching a frozen buffalo. BOOM. BOOM. BOOM. After a couple knuckle sandwiches, the door cracked loose from its frame. It creaked in place, tipped over, and fell to the ground with a solid thud.

Beyond me was a long, dark hallway.

"Knock knock!" I announced.

The hallway was carved right into the stone interior of the mountain, with visible layers of eon-old rock. White smoke spilled in from the silo and filled the hallway about knee-deep. There were fluorescent bulbs overhead, but only a few of them were on. NORAD seemed to be running on emergency power. I crept down the hall, careful not to make too much noise and on the lookout for anything suspicious.

There was a light at the end of the tunnel – another room, I figured – but it was too far away to see what was in there. In any case, it was the only direction I could go, so I started walking.

Halfway down the hall, I nearly tripped over something bulky hidden in the layers of smoke. I leaned down and wafted the air around until it cleared up. A shadowy figure laid right there at my feet. It looked like a person.

It was a dead body.

A small yelp escaped me and I slapped my hands over my mouth to keep myself quiet. It wasn't the dead body alone that freaked me out, but the mortified look on its face. It was some military soldier in full cammo and a death grip on his assault rifle. His eyes were open impossibly wide and the skin on his face stretched beyond normal, as if something scared him to death.

Whatever he saw when he died really fucked him up. His blood vessels had gone dark and criss-crossed his entire face. His fists gripped onto his gun so hard, I doubted even I could have pried his fingers loose, even with my supernatural strength. And then the smell hit me: the soldier had shit his pants. Whatever killed him made him shit his pants.

I stood upright, covered my mouth and nose and hurried away from the body, going further down the hallway. As I power-walked down the corridor, I stumbled over another dead body. Then another. Then another. There were dead soldiers lying all over the place, all up and down the hallway, all of them dead. I'm not superstitious or anything and I'm not that easily scared, but I had never been surrounded by dead bodies before and it was starting to freak me out. I broke into a sprint to get away.

3

The billowing smoke puffed as I came running out of the hallway and into the NORAD control center: a hollowed-out cavern as wide and vast as a city block. Rows of a hundred computer terminals were lined up against the curve of the stone walls. Then there were giant towers of those old reel-to-reel microfilm machines from the 1950s. A lot of the computers were also from the '50s, but some of them were newer, updated computers with flat screen monitors. Huge TV screens were mounted high up on the wall, displaying digital maps of the world – America, Russia, Israel, China, even Antarctica – and those maps were covered in blinking red dots; dots that symbolized every nuclear weapon on the planet.

Off to the left side of the chamber in its own little mini-cave was a perfect replica of the White House press room, complete with a podium, an American flag and the Great Seal of the United States. The stone walls were hidden behind bright blue curtains. That's where they'd stick the president in event of a nuclear war, where he could give the nation an inspiring speech and convince America that everything was okay. It might look like he was speaking confidently from the White House, but in truth, he would be cowering safely inside a hollowed out mountain.

All of the NORAD technicians were dead. Geeks in lab coats laid slumped over their computer terminals. Dead soldiers laid strewn all across the floor with their guns laying harmlessly next to them. It didn't even look like they got a shot off. They'd been murdered, all of them, and the murderers were dead ahead.

Mir, the teenage Russian shape-shifter and her companion, the bright red Cosmonaut.

Mir stood triumphantly over the computer terminals with her hands raised high up over her head and her sleeves rolled up. Her human arms had shape-shifted at the elbows into space station parts: oxygen hoses and electrical cables and rows of control panels with light-up toggle switches. Her space station appendages snaked through the air and branches off into a web of loose wires that poked through the seams and vents of the electrical equipment. She had fused herself into the NORAD computers and server banks. Each one of the computer screens were scrambled with a flurry of Russian letters.

She was hacking the system and trying to launch the nukes.

The Cosmonaut stood there, doing nothing.

"Toropitsya, toropitsya," Mir growled as she struggled to crack the NORAD defense system. "Zapusk. Zapusk!"

DEFCON 1 anti-hacking software isn't easy to hack. Despite her Russian electronic language scrolling across the display screens, they were shut down by the words ACCESS DENIED that appeared in bold, red letters. Her continual failure only pushed her to try harder. Her voice turned into something high-pitched and electronic. "Dostupa," she said. Her native language raced across the screen faster and faster as she redoubled her efforts.

"Get your..." I was about to say "hands," but she didn't have hands. "Get your *circuits* out of those computers before come over there and rip them off."

Mir spun her head around at the sound of my voice, her pony tail whipping through the air. She couldn't turn completely around, not with her arms linked into the NORAD computers. She barely took the time to give me a dirty look before turning her attention back to her work.

"Go away," she said, as if I were little more than a nuisance.

Apparently she had no idea who she was messing with. I marched in her direction, ready to slap the shit out of her. I meant what I had said; if it meant preventing a nuclear launch, I was fully prepared to rip her arms off.

I didn't get that chance. When I stepped within ten feet of Mir, the Cosmonaut dude zipped weightlessly through the air to block my path. Apparently the guy could be fast when he wanted to be. That was fine. I'd take his head off first, *then* I'd deal with the Russian brat.

I looked the red astronaut up and down, then said, "Move it or lose it, Comrade."

He didn't budge.

"Alright," I said as I widened my stance. "You asked for it."

With a twist of my hips, I backhanded the Cosmonaut right across his helmet. It felt like hitting a steel beam. His head didn't even budge. A hollow, plastic *thunk* echoed throughout the cavern. My eyes went wide and a pathetic squeak came out of my mouth. It had been a long time since I'd felt pain like that. Instinctively I cradled my throbbing hand to my body. I worried that my finger bones were broken. I didn't think that was possible.

"Don't touch him, American!" Mir shouted at me.

"Oh, I'll do more than touch him."

I figured the Cosmonaut might have been more vulnerable to a good old-fashioned backhand without that stupid helmet protecting his head. I reached up and grabbed the base of it with both hands, ready to rip it off.

"No!" Mir said. "Get away from him before-"

The Cosmonaut's hands snapped forward and clamped down on my wrists. The tinted visor of his helmet started to open, revealing the contents inside.

"Too late now," Mir said. "Nice knowing you."

Maybe I could have broken free from the Cosmonaut's grip, and maybe I couldn't. I lost all will to try. Something about the inside of his helmet had me mesmerized. My need to escape faded away and was replaced with a desire to see what was inside: swirling galaxies and exploding super novas and colorful clouds of nebulaic gasses. I wanted to see it all.

I leaned in closer and stared deeply into the Cosmonaut's celestial helmet. I looked directly into the very Universe itself.

4

The Universe.

The Universe is unfathomably endless. There's not a word in any human language that even comes close to describing the size of the Universe. It goes on forever and ever and just when you've spent a billion years crossing an infinite amount of space, you look out to realize you've barely moved at all, and an even more infinite distance lays ahead of you. And no matter how fast you zip through the flickering lights and watercolor backgrounds, you're never any further away from your starting point and certainly no closer to reaching the edge.

The Universe has no edge. It's such a futile effort trying to get from one end to the other, you might as well not even try.

But in the Cosmonaut's helmet, I also saw another mind-altering truth: the Universe is also infinitely small.

You could shrink down into a plant cell only to find trillions upon trillions of molecules. A single drop of cellular fluid contained more molecules than the Milky Way had stars.

And if you shrank down even further and made your destination one of those trillion molecules, you'd find only shuddering protons and neutrons orbited by whirling electrons. And shrinking down to even more impossibly tiny sizes, you'd enter a world of vibrating strings that make electrons look like the planet Jupiter. And while you can see these vibrating strings, it's not because there's light. Light is made of photons and these vibrating strings are infinitely smaller than photons. You see these strings because, down there, physics work differently and they're visible because they simply *exist*.

My computer brain started glitching out, trying to process the idea of something so small. Humans didn't evolve with the capacity to think of such things.

But then things kept shrinking. "No, no, no," I whispered. "I can't see any more." But I couldn't look away.

Smaller than the vibrating strings laid a dimension where colors are shapes and shapes are colors. In this flavorless void, colorful shapes are in a constant state of transformation. Blue triangles suddenly shift into red circles. Green squares morph into yellow crosses. Black circles blink out of existence, then reappear as white stars. Sometimes only some of them change, sometimes all of them change. They're weightless and formless and they lay on the cusp of non-existence, but they exist.

And if I couldn't wrap my head around the vibrating strings, I had no hope of comprehending the color-shapes.

What was their purpose in changing?

No idea. It hurt my brain to even think about it.

It felt like the pattern to their ever-changing colors and shapes was a riddle that might be solved, and if I could just watch it long enough I might figure it out. If I could figure out how the color shapes work, I could rewrite the very Universe to whatever I wanted it to be.

I shrank more. I didn't want to see what was smaller than this. I was engulfed by a green circle until I was in an ocean of color. Everything turned red as it transformed it very nature. I couldn't see the edges of the shape. I had no idea if it had changed into a triangle or a circle or a maybe a cross.

I tumbled through a dimension of red, which turned blue, then turned purple...

I was even smaller. Smaller than the color shapes. The physical laws of the Universe were so much bigger and so much further back, they were a literal joke. Time meant nothing. Distance meant nothing. For as infinitely big as the Universe is, it is also infinitely small.

I kept shrinking.

The dimension of color faded to black. Dead ahead of me was a single sparkle of light. I floated towards the sparkle and it grew bigger, first the side of a pea, and then the size of a baseball. It looked glittery and orange and I realized it wasn't just one point of light, but a trillion sparks of light all rolled up into one big ball. It continued to grow as I shrank towards it, as big as a house, as big as a mountain, as big as a planet.

Then it dawned on me, I was looking at the Universe from the outside in. I was in a realm so infinitely small that it had become infinitely big and everything started over. I tumbled through galaxies and super-massive black holes. I passed through alien war zones a bazillion light years away from Earth. I caught glimpses of homeworlds populated by strange yellow and green creatures. I heard the buzzing of extraterrestrial radio broadcasts, spreading propaganda about the Galactic Supremacy. This must have been how Alice felt when she fell down the rabbit hole into Wonderland, confused as shit and flipping head over heels on an infinitely long drop.

It was too much information all at once. My muscles started to convulse. I was seconds away from going totally insane.

Impossible Red hijacked my consciousness.

Information processing error.

Corrupt data flow – Sweeping clean static.

Emergency shut down – Restart processing.

Power down.

5

When I regained consciousness, I was lying on the ground in the fetal position. The taste of metal in my mouth warned me of my impending need to puke my guts out, but I dry-heaved three times and nothing came out.

I gasped for air. I forced myself to inhale. I laid there on a stone floor and shivered. Cold. I had never feel so cold. Sweat beaded up on my forehead and soaked through my clothes.

God damn, what just happened to me? I shook my head in an effort to unscramble my brains. I lifted my head and squinted against the bright lights. Where was I? What dimension was this? Was I in some kind of cave? A cave with computers? I heard an alarm; a deep, haunting alarm that sounded vaguely familiar.

This room had TV monitors mounted on the wall. They displayed electronic maps of America and Russia and China and the rest of the world. My vision was blurry, but there were words on the screen. I rubbed my eyes. What did they say?

ACCESS GRANTED.

US-H-3401: LAUNCH SEQUENCE ACTIVATED

US-H-3402: LAUNCH SEQUENCE ACTIVATED

US-H-3403: LAUNCH SEQUENCE ACTIVATED

US-H-3404: LAUNCH SEQUENCE ACTIVATED

US-H-3405: LAUNCH SEQUENCE ACTIVATED
US-H-3406: LAUNCH SEQUENCE ACTIVATED
US-H-3407: LAUNCH SEQUENCE ACTIVATED

Shit. Launch? I had no idea what that meant, but the phrase "Launch Sequence Activated" is rarely a good thing. Especially when you don't know what, exactly, is launching.

Dotted lines appeared on those electronic world maps, connecting America to Russia.

That couldn't be good. God dammit, Penelope, you have to get your shit together and remember. This place is familiar. That alarm is familiar. And something about "launching" is familiar.

I thumped my palms against my forehead.

Think, Penelope. Think!

"NORAD," I muttered. I staggered to my feet and massaged my temples with my fingertips. "I'm at NORAD."

I stumbled towards the computers.

"Nukes," I reminded myself. "Someone is launching nukes."

Somehow I managed to wobble over to the computers and brace myself on the edge of the counter top. Right when I got to one of the keyboards is when the realization set in: I had no idea how to shut down a missile launch. Shouldn't there be a big red button that says ABORT? That's how it is in the James Bond movies. Just mash that ABORT button and the nukes shut down.

So I searched all around for a big red button. No such luck. No ABORT button.

Mir! That's who did this. Mir and the Cosmonaut. They were the ones who launched the nukes. I looked up from the computer cubicle and scanned the base for any sign of the teenager or the red astronaut. There were plenty of dead scientist dudes and plenty of dead soldiers, but no Mir and no Cosmonaut. They launched the nukes and high-tailed it out of the base. They had a head start on an escape, and who knew by how much.

I had to focus. I would worry about catching those two later. In that moment, I had to stop the nukes from launching.

Next to my computer was this old-school, bright red rotary phone. It started ringing. I picked it up and curiously held the receiver up to my ear. Someone on the other end started talking.

"God dammit, Harris!" the voice shouted. It was some military sounding guy, unmistakably pissed off. *"What the fuck is going on over there?"*

"Uh, this isn't Harris," I said. I looked down at my feet and found a dead scientist there with a security lanyard dangling from his neck. He had the same name. I turned my attention back to the phone. "Harris is dead, sir."

There was a short pause. I assumed the five-star general on the other end needed a moment to process the fact that a teenage girl just answered the NORAD phone. Eventually he spoke up. *"Then who the hell are you?"*

"Oh, my name's Penelope," I said. "I'm the only one here who's still alive, so if you need me to stop these nukes from launching, you're going to have to tell me how."

The man on the other line moved the phone away and I heard a muffled *"What the fuck."* He returned to the phone and said, *"I'm not telling you anything until I know who the fuck you are!"*

I yelled back. "I just told you who the fuck I am! I'm the only person alive at NORAD, that's who the fuck I am." I paused for a moment to let that sink in. "Now I'm sure you've got some sort of policy about security clearances or whatever, but these nukes are pointed right at Moscow, so if you know how to shut these sons-of-bitches down, you better start telling me what to do... *sir*."

There was a quick moment of silence, then he replied with, *"I need to make a phone call."*

I held the phone out and shouted directly into the receiver. "We don't have time for you to make a god damned phone call! By the time you make a phone call, Moscow's gunna be a nuked-to-death pile of trash and they're not going to be too happy about it! We need to do something, and we need to do it now!"

Another pause filled with heavy breathing, then the general said, *"Alright, god dammit. I can't believe this is happening. You said your name is Penelope?"*

"Yes," I replied.

"Okay, Penelope. One of the computer terminals should say Access Granted. Do you see it?"

I quickly paced around and scanned the different computer screens. All I found were maps, statistics, and garbled up Russian. Then I saw it. ACCESS GRANTED in big green letters. I swung the analog phone cord over the nearby computer terminals and carried the red phone over there.

"I see it," I said.

"That's the primary launch system. Get to that computer and hit D, then enter. A box will pop up asking for a code."

"Gotcha." I hit D on the keyboard, then enter. "Done."

"Do you see a box asking for a code?"

I checked the screen. Sure enough, a window had opened – a "box," he called it – and there were six blank squares, each one asking for a character.

"Yeah," I said. "I see it."

"This is the first code."

"The *first* code?" I repeated. What did he mean first code? As in... there were multiple codes? More alarms went off. They wailed and droned. It made things hard to concentrate. "There's not a code that shuts them all down at once?"

"No!" he shouted back. *"We have to shut down each individual nuke. Now shut up and start typing."*

I don't normally take too kindly to the words "shut up." On any other day, I would have threatened to climb through the phone and smash the dude's face in. But I was willing to let it slide. We were all under a lot of stress. I'm sure he didn't mean it.

He said, *"The first code is Zulu Bravo 9 6 8 Quebec."*

"Zulu?" I typed in the word Zulu. Z-U-L-U. That took up four of the six boxes. The code he gave me was too long. "That's too many words and letters! I only have six boxes!"

He spoke quickly, but clearly. *"Zulu. Bravo. 9. 6. 8. Quebec."*

I was so confused. He already said that part. "There aren't enough empty boxes to fit that many words!"

"God dammit." I heard him kick a desk chair over in frustration. *"It's a phonetic alphabet. Zulu is Z. Bravo is B."*

I gave the phone a weird look. I had never heard of such a thing before. "Really?"

"Kid." He paused to take a deep breath. *"The code is Z B 9 6 8 Q."*

"Thank you." I typed it in. Z B 9 6 8 Q. "Was that so hard?"

The first nuke shut down. Up on the big screen, one of the dotted red lines connecting Colorado to Moscow quickly blipped out of existence. One down. Six to go.

"Cool," I said. "It shut down."

"Okay, press the tab button. That'll bring up the second missile."

"Gotcha." I pressed tab. The window flickered a couple times and I had six new blank boxes.

"The second code is H K P zero zero J."

"Did you say H K P, or A K P?" I asked. The alarms were loud and it was hard to understand him.

"God dammit, H as in Hotel! H K P!"

"H. Got it." I typed it in. H K P zero zero J. Another dotted line went away. I was pretty computer savvy; I had this pattern figured out. I pressed tab without him asking me to do so. New blank boxes appeared "I'm ready for the next code."

9 1 3 L L X. Four left. I pressed tab.

I K A A 3 A. Three left. I pressed tab.

8 K A 6 A K. Two left. I pressed tab.

D 4 D 4 P D. One nuke remaining. I pressed tab.

The box didn't change. The computer froze up. I hit tab again. Nothing. I tapped it five times, then ten, then twenty. The tab button didn't work and the security boxes for the last nuke never appeared.

6

The general shouted, *"What do you mean it froze up!?"*

"I don't know!" I backed away from the computer as if maybe I had broke it. "I hit tab, but nothing happened."

"Then you did something wrong!"

"I fucking did not, dude." Just to prove it, I held the phone to down to the keyboard and pushed the tab key a million more times. "Do you hear that? That's me hitting tab key. Nothing's happening. It's totally froze up."

He tried to remain calm, but I could hear the panic in his voice. *"Let's start from the beginning. Hit D and then enter."*

So I pressed D, then enter. Nothing happened. The screen just stayed there, frozen on the last deactivation code.

"Nothing happened!" I told him.

"No, no, no," he said. *"You're doing something wrong!"*

"Fucker, I am not!" I shook the receiver as if I might possibly be able to wring this guy's neck, then put it back to my ear. "I'm doing exactly what you're telling me to do."

"Then why isn't the missile shutting down!?"

"You're asking me!? These are *your* nukes!"

Roaring thunder filled the NORAD chamber as if I'd woken a sleeping dragon from centuries of slumber. The floor of the cavern shuddered and it nearly knocked me to the ground. The computers rattled around on their tables and the wall-mounted screens went to static. The entire complex was on the verge of total collapse.

Then the rumble faded. The emergency alarms shut off. Everything went silent. The general on the other end didn't say anything. I thought maybe we got disconnected.

"Hello?" I asked. "Are you still there?"

His voice had softened. *"Missile 3407 just launched for Moscow."*

115

It took several seconds for that to click in my brain. "You're shitting me."

He didn't answer.

I asked, "Can't you, like, shoot it down or something?"

And after a moment he simply said, *"No. We cannot."*

Why not? How in the blue fuck can the military not be ready to shoot down one of their own nukes in the event of an accidental launch? It seemed like an awful stupid oversight to have nukes around if you don't have the ability to shoot them down when you need to. But what was I going to do, tell him that? If he had the power to shoot it down, he would have shot it down. But he said he couldn't.

"Fuck." I dropped the phone and ran for the tunnels. Each missile silo was labeled above its corridor entrance, US-H-3401, 3402, 3403. You could get to any of the nuclear silos from the control center. I sprinted down the tunnel marked US-H-3407, headed for the one nuclear missile that managed to slip away.

"God dammit." I sped down the tunnel at break-neck speeds. "God *dammit*."

I approached the end of the tunnel where a steel blast door stood between me and the nuke. It was marked NO ENTRY, AUTHORIZED PERSONEL ONLY, RADIOACTIVE. I built up speed and slammed against it with all my weight. The door buckled and crashed to the floor inside.

The nuclear silo was filled with black smoke. Above me, chugging into the sky and venting dark exhaust was the nuke – US-H-3407 – headed for the stars. I couldn't, on my best day, jump that high and catch it.

Corolla appeared overhead. He floated over the open doors of the silo. His blue hubcaps glowed down on me like an angel.

"Corolla!" I waved my arms at him. "We have to go after it!"

Corolla killed his engines and dropped down the empty silo. He reactivated his anti-gravity just before he hit the bottom and floated in place in front of me, just a few inches off the ground. I could hear the muffled REO Speedwagon playing inside. I swung open the passenger door and jumped in.

"So," he said as he turned down the stereo. "This seems to be going well."

His ability to patronize me – even in the face of cataclysmic destruction – never ceased to amaze.

"We have to go after that missile." I drummed my hands on his dashboard. "Go go go go go."

Corolla put his thrusters to maximum. We launched out of the silo and shot up into the sky.

Tracking the missile wasn't tough; it left a bright streak of fire behind it and glowed like a meteor. Corolla followed close after it, but the missile had one hell of a head start on us and was already up in the clouds. If we were going to catch it, Corolla was going to have to fly faster than he'd ever flown before.

"Hurry, Corolla," I said. "Kick it into high gear."

"I can't believe I'm chasing a nuclear missile." He revved his engine harder and we ascended into the clouds. "I'm allergic to nuclear missiles, you know."

"Just go!" I said. "If that nuke hits Moscow, they're going to nuke us back and the whole world is fucked."

"I don't know why you humans even keep these things around," he said. "All they're good for is nuclear war."

"This isn't the time to debate philosophy!"

Corolla pushed his engine until his frame was rattling and I thought he might start to fly apart. To my relief and surprise, we were actually gaining on the missile. It came into view – not just the fire trail, but the actual missile itself – dead ahead.

We were up in the stratosphere where the air got thin. We passed over the western coast of California and ventured out to the Pacific Ocean. Good. If that nuke went off some some reason, at least it would fallout over the ocean and not San Francisco.

"What's the plan, boss?" Corolla asked me.

"Get us as close as you can," I said. "I'm going to jump on it."

"You're going to jump on a nuke?"

"Yes!"

"Okay. And then what?"

"And then I'll..." I hadn't yet thought that far. Only one thing came to mind. "I'll rip it apart and crash it into the ocean."

"You're going to rip apart an ICBM?" He paused. "With your bare hands? What if it goes off? What if it explodes?"

Now *that* I had thought of. I took a deep breath. The white missile got bigger and bigger as we drew closer and closer.

I said, "If it goes off, then it goes off."

"No way," Corolla replied. "There's gotta be another way."

"Well, maybe there is, dude, but we don't really have time to sit around and explore our options, now, do we? Once this thing crosses the ocean, it's going to hit Russia and that's World War Three and the end of everything."

"Oh, man," he whimpered. "I really don't like this."

I put my hand on the door handle. "Neither do I."

Corolla sounded understandably terrified, but he had also bravely broken a personal record for speed. We were closing in close on the nuke and I could hear the crackling of its jet fuel and smell the acrid smoke that gushed out of its exhaust.

We had crossed so many time zones so fast that we had literally caught up to the sun. Yesterday's sunset was dead ahead of us and the sky turned to evening again. A million miles below us was the ocean, vast and blue, with the tiniest tanker ships you've ever seen.

Nuclear bombs aren't designed to be jumped on. It didn't have any handles or handholds or footholds, so the odds were pretty good that I would land on its metal casing and slip right off. I had one chance to get this right. And if I missed? Well...

I wasn't going to miss. The world was counting on me.

I opened the passenger door and planted my feet like a parachuter preparing to jump out of a plane. Cold wind whipped through the interior. It tornadoed all the random scraps of paper that littered Corolla's floorboards and rustled my hair..

"Once I'm on top of it..." I shouted at him over the wind, "...I want you to back off as far as possible!"

"Are you sure about this?" he shouted back.

I looked down at the nuke below us. Corolla had matched its speed so perfectly that it almost seemed stationary; it was the world below us that raced by. We passed through a dense cloud and I lost sight of the missile, but we came out on the other side and I could see it again.

Was I sure about this? A lot of stuff could go very wrong.

"I'm one hundred percent sure!" I shouted. "But clear out in case something goes wrong! I don't want you melting to death!"

"Don't say that!" he replied. "You're scaring me!"

I focused all my attention on the nuke. Its outer casing was smooth metal. Layers of high-altitude frost were starting to form on the outside. It was going to be pretty damn difficult to get a good grip on it. Fine. I'd make my own handholds right in it's steel body with my powerful fingers.

I adjusted my skydiving position in the open door frame and psyched myself up for the jump.

"Okay, Penelope. You can do this," I muttered, trying to psych myself up for one of the most insane things I had ever done. "Jump on three." I took a deep breath and counted it off. "One. Two." I jumped. "Three!"

I fell down towards the nuke with one thought repeating in my head: *I'm going to miss. I'm going to miss. I'm going to miss.*

Even as I approached the intercontinental ballistic missile and saw the colossal size of it, I was convinced I was going to miss.

I landed on the missile with a metallic thud. My hands and feet slipped across the frosty exterior and my body started to slide off. With no time to think, I stabbed my fingers into the lead-lined shell and grabbed on tight. The nuke raced towards the sunrise at a thousand miles an hour as I dangled from the side. I kicked a hole into the shell with my right foot, then another with my left. Safely attached to the missile with handholds and footholds, my only job then was to figure out how to stop the damn thing from reaching Moscow.

There was nothing below me but blue ocean. Good. We weren't over Russia yet. I still had time.

The nuke's registry number was right in my face – US-H-3407 – so close that I could see where the paint had started to fade and chip away. How many years had this thing just sat around NORAD waiting to be used? Decades? And now here it was, tearing smoke and fire across the sky, doing the only thing it was good at: starting a nuclear war.

I pulled hard with my right hand and ripped a metal panel loose. It snapped off and disappeared into the wind. Machinery moved inside the hole – circuits and pistons and gears – and I didn't recognize a single thing. But that didn't matter, did it. Everything inside a nuke is there for a reason, right? So if I started ripping those pieces out, it would deactivate. Right?

Or I'd set it off.

"Why are you doing this!?" Someone shouted from behind.

I looked back over my shoulder. A full-sized space station came flying after me, shuddering at the joints, obviously unaccustomed to such high speed wind resistance. It was Mir. She had blocky modules and little round pods linked together by a system of tubes. Golden solar panels were attached to her in random places. She looked cobbled together, as if she were built by a dozen different engineers who all spoke different languages.

Drifting next to the space station was the Cosmonaut. He kept pace with the uncontrolled weightlessness of zero-gravity. He rotated in place, spinning upside down and sideways, like someone in a gyroscope. Still, for all the random spinning, he did a great job matching our speeds.

I muttered curse words to myself. These two were going to stop me from stopping them, so I had to do as much damage to the nuke as fast as I could. I plunged my arm deep inside the mechanical guts of the thing, grabbed onto a handful of wires and copper hoses and ripped them out. I threw them aside, where they zipped out of my hand and disappeared behind us.

"Stop!" Mir screamed. "You're ruining everything!"

I ripped out more electronics. "That's what I do best!"

I punched my fist shoulder-deep into the missile, over and over. Something ruptured inside. Yellow and green chemicals sprayed out and got all in my face and mouth. It smelled like some kind of fuel. Good. That's probably important.

Mir flew in closer; so close, in fact, that her broadcasting antennae scraped across the metal body of the missile. The worry occurred to me that she might just kamikaze into the nuke and set the damn thing off.

"Why are you doing this!?" she screamed. It almost sounded like she was crying. "This has nothing to do with you!"

"It has everything to do with me! You want to start a nuclear war? Well, I'm the god of war, so that means you need my permission!" I ripped even more wires out. "And I say no!"

The Cosmonaut landed on the missile. He planted his feet on the shell and stood right in front of me. The wind and velocity and gravity didn't affect him at all. He stood there like he'd stand on the moon, with a slight buoyancy to his arms and legs.

He knelt down and moved his helmet towards my face. Then he reached for his visor, ready to open it.

No. Not the infinitely small universe again. Not now.

I squeezed my eyes shut and pointed my face away from him. I didn't want to see the secrets of the Universe. I had work to do. Guided by sound alone, I felt around for those weird gurgling chemicals and grabbed anything within reach. I must've cross-wired something electrical, because there was a loud pop and then a dangerous sounding buzz. The roar of the missile engines sputtered, but they didn't completely give out. This bomb was fucking resilient. Handful by handful, I ripped more and more of its guts out, but it just wouldn't go down. All I did was scramble the engines and knock it off course. Great. Now instead of hitting Russia, it'll hit China.

"I needed this!" Mir said. No mistaking it, she was crying. I didn't dare open my eyes to look at her. The Cosmonaut was still out there. "All I wanted was one lousy nuclear war!"

"Sorry, kid," I said. "Not today."

I punched the missile one more time. This time my fist cracked through some important. The nuke made all kinds of terrible noises: it hissed and clicked and then came the sound of metal grinding against metal. The smell of melting plastic hit my nose. Flames crackled from deep inside. Interior gears came unaligned and clanked and banged against the interior of the metal shell like a clock falling apart from the inside. I had started a chain reaction of self-destruction.

"No, no, no!" Mir shouted. "Look what you did!"

I heard her engines roar to full power. With the nuke coming apart at the literal seams, she was left with little choice but to scramble off to a safe distance. I squinted one eye open and peeked behind me. She was already a good distance away, and still going.

"Cosmonaut!" she shouted. "Follow me! Get away from that thing before it expl-"

Too late.

A fireball engulfed me. I felt my clothes turn to ash and burn right off my skin. An apocalyptic roar blew out my ear-drums.

Then, for the second time in my life, I died.

Chapter Eight

1

My eyes shot open. I stood in the middle of a well manicured garden, surrounded by Himalayan Pine trees – *Pinus wallachiana* – which I quickly identified by their thin, droopy leaves and pineappley trunks. This wasn't like a fruits-and-vegatables kind of garden, but more like a million-dollar-mansion kind of garden. It was home to perfectly sculpted shrubs and geometric walkways, as well as a few of the ultra-rare plants that we had back at the shop. The center of the garden was a cleared out plot of grass, along with eleven small boulders of granite.

This garden was just a small part of a sprawling Tibetan temple built into the side of a snowy mountain. I recognized mountains like this one, and all the others that surrounded me and faded off into the hazy distance. I'd seen them before in my journeys with Corolla. These weren't the Rockies, or the Alps.

No, these were the Himalayas.

A howling blizzard engulfed the mountaintops, but inside the walls of this Tibetan temple the weather was calm and warm. Protected by some kind of magic, I guessed, where the sunshine could break through the clouds and maintain an endless spring.

A Korean girl in red robes and a white sash stood in the grass, arms crossed, and stared at the chunks of granite. She was probably a little older than me – 21? 22? – and had a thin layer of hair on her scalp, as if she had shaved her head a week ago and it was just now starting to grow back. Beneath the full length of her red robes, her bare feet poked out. Something about the granite seemed to really capture her attention, and she moved from place to place so she could stare at it from different angles.

Was this a dream? Or was I dead?

It felt too real to be a dream. The breeze wafted over my skin and it smelled like sweet incense.

Dead or dreaming, at the very least I wasn't alone. I had someone here with me so I knew I'd get answers soon enough. Best not to rush things. I went and stood next to the girl, crossed my arms just like her, and joined her in staring at the granite.

We stared silently for a while.

When I couldn't take the silence anymore, I spoke up and said, "So what are we looking at?"

"It's an exercise in meditation," the monk said. She spoke perfect English. What I wasn't expecting was her Brooklyn accent. "You're supposed to arrange these eleven stones around the grass in such a way that no matter where you stand in the garden, you can never see all of them."

I looked at the stones and counted. I could see all eleven.

I didn't get it. So I told her, "I don't get it."

"Okay, look." She took me by the arm and walked me to the corner of the grass. "If you stand right here, the big stone in the middle covers up that smaller one over there, back by the koi pond. See that?"

I stood where she told me. She was right, the smaller stone was obscured by the larger one. I could only see ten stones.

She walked patiently through the grass and led me towards the other corner. "And as you walk this way, you can still only see ten of them, right?" We walked along and I counted. She was right. I could see only ten. "Ten, ten, ten," she counted out loud. "But once you get here, boom, you can see all eleven again."

Just as she said, that smaller piece of granite peeked out from behind the larger one and I could count all eleven stones.

I offered her an obvious solution. "Just move the bigger one a few inches to the left so it covers it up the little one."

"I did that." She walked over to the biggest granite chunk and picked it up like it was nothing. It was the size of a sack of groceries and had to weight at least a ton. She moved it a few inches to the left and set it back down. "But when you do *that*, then move over *here*, you can see eleven stones from *this* angle."

She led me to the middle of the grass. I saw what she was saying. By moving that one bigger piece of granite to cover up the smaller one, we made another one visible.

"The idea," she said, "is that no matter where you stand in the grass, along the edges or in the middle, only ten stones are visible at once. It's one of those things that might not have a solution at all. The point isn't to solve it. The point is to clear your mind and think about nothing else."

"How long have you been working on it?" I asked.

She made a disappointed sound. "Years. I don't think I'll ever figure it out, but that's okay. I just do it to clear the mind and meditate. My Lama solved it, I think, right before he died. But he's gone from this world and I'll never know what he saw."

"Your llama?" I asked.

"Lama," she repeated. "Not like the animal, llama. One L. Lama, like the Dalai Lama."

"Ohh," I said. "A lama."

"Yeah." She smiled at me. "That kind of lama."

"So you're... uhm... Gosh, how to put this?" For a Tibetan monk living in a Himalayan temple, she sure didn't seem like she belonged there. She didn't speak in philosophical riddles and her Brooklyn accent certainly didn't sound local to Tibet or Nepal. "You're not exactly what I expected from a monk."

"Eh, I know." She sat on one of the granite boulders. "I wasn't really supposed to be here. It's kind of a thing I've inherited."

"Inherited?"

"Yeah. From the monks who used to live here. Now I've got... *responsibilities*." She did air quotes around that word, then pointed up the mountain peak at the highest point of the temple. "You see that huge gong up there?"

Sure enough, I did. Shimmering in the sunlight was a huge golden gong.

"Yup."

"I have to hit that thing every morning at sunrise or the sun won't come up."

I looked at the gong again. It was big, and golden, but other than that it looked like a regular gong to me.

"That seems silly," I said.

"I know." She smiled up at it, as if reliving an old memory. "I used to think the same thing."

"So you're in charge of the sun coming up?"

"Yup."

"What are you supposed to be then? Some kind of god?"

That made her laugh. And I mean a real high-pitched squeaky laugh of delight. "Oh, man, no. No, I'm not a god. I'm just some chick from Brooklyn Heights."

"You're from the Heights?"

"Yeah." She stood up and smoothed out the folds of her robes. "And you're from Little Italy."

"Yeah. I am. How'd you know that?"

She strolled through the grass and headed towards the temple. "Kung fu stuff. Prophecies and all that." She looked back at me. "I can get into the nitty-gritty if you want, but it's a lot of complicated philosophy. It's not as exciting at it might seem."

"Well, just answer me this..." I said.

I was about to ask her *why am I here?* But she knew that was coming. When the words came out of my mouth, she said it at the exact same time as me.

"Why am I here?" we said in unison, then she laughed again, just tickled pink. "Jinx, you owe me a coke."

I laughed, too. Not because it was funny. I mean, it was funny enough, but not laugh-out-loud funny. I laughed because this chick was the complete opposite of how I'd expect a Tibetan monk to act.

I said, "You're crazy."

She beamed another smile at me. "Yeah, I know."

We reached the doors to her temple, which were already open. And why not? Was someone going to break in up here? The interior was a dimly lit room, brightened only by a few skylights and a few candle arrangements. The girl went up to a simple wooden table and picked up two porcelain cups.

"Tea?" she asked.

"I don't really do food," I told her. "Makes me sick."

"Not this tea." She handed me one of the cups. It was empty. There was no tea. I assumed she was going to fill it, but she didn't. She "drank" from her empty cup.

"What're you doing?" I asked.

"It's nothing tea," she said.

I stared at the porcelain cup. "I've never had nothing tea."

"Go on, try it" she said. "It's not so bad."

So I pretended to drink from the cup. All pretend.

She smiled at me. "What do you think?"

"I didn't taste anything." I said.

"Nope. You never do."

I handed the cup back to her. "Look, this is fun and all, but I don't really have time for this. Am I dead?"

She raised a finger into the air, then said, "You are not dead."

"Okay. Am I dreaming?"

"Mmm." She thought about that and sipped some more tea. "Kinda. It's more like one of those out of body experiences."

"Are you a figment of my imagination?"

"Oh, no. I'm real."

"Then how did I get here?"

Her face turned serious. "Dharma. It was my dharma to meet you. Or it was your dharma to meet me. I don't know which. But either way..." She shrugged. "It was dharma."

"That's cool."

"Or maybe it's our dharma to kill each other. That's another possibility, I suppose." She shrugged again and looked inside her cup. "You can never tell when it come to dharma. Not usually. Not until it's already too late."

"Well, I hope it's the friends part," I said.

"Me too! I guess we'll figure it out someday. And we could talk about it more, but it's about time for you to go."

"Go?"

"You're about to wake up."

"But I just got here. I don't even know who you are."

She threw up her hands. "You're going to have to take that up with Buddha. I don't make the rules. I just follow them."

I had a million more things to say and a million more questions, but the sweet smelling incense air of the temple faded away. The Brooklyn monk held up two fingers and said, "Peace."

2

My eyes shot open and I gasped for air, like returning from the dead. I felt the chug-chug-chuging of my mechanical heart in my chest and wriggled my toes. All I could see were blurry shadows, but my vision quickly cleared. I was trapped in a dark, square room, lying flat on my back and staring up at the ceiling. The room looked like some kind of bunker with walls of rough concrete and exposed steel beams.

This felt like some straight-up Guantanamo Bay shit.

A single door led in and out of the room; a steel slab with a big wheel to release the lock, like a hatch on a submarine. The door wasn't down at floor level, but upside-down and touching the ceiling. Also attached to the ceiling and defying gravity was a metal table and a few metal chairs.

I laid with my arms and legs splayed out on a rounded metal platform, just big enough that I couldn't reach the edges with my hands or feet. I tried to sit up, but I couldn't move. Some kind of invisible force had me frozen in place. I couldn't move my arms. I couldn't move my legs. Hell, even I couldn't even twiddle my fingers. I began to wonder if I had been abducted by aliens or something and this was one of their operating tables.

Possible, but not likely. Aliens usually get you naked first, and I wasn't naked. I wore a black suit with a white button-up collared shirt and a black tie. The suit looked an expensive – what you might call a "power suit" – something a chick might wear if she were the director of the CIA. These weren't my clothes, obviously. Someone, or some *thing*, had played dolly dress-up with my unconscious body. My business skirt was sleek, creased, and the same black color as my jacket. Despite my predicament, I couldn't help admire how great I looked in this mysterious suit. Throw me a pair of sunglasses and I'd look like Investigator Bobbi Rox from the M-Files.

But whoever dressed me up in that monkey suit didn't bother to put shoes on my feet. All I had were black-and-gray argyle socks. I tried to lift my legs off the table.

Impossible.

With a metallic clank and a thunderous boom, the upside down ceiling door opened and in walked a young guy with a briefcase and a CIA suit very similar to mine. I'd never seen the guy before, but I did recognize the logo on his ID badge.

Westland.

The upside down guy walked across the ceiling and filled the room with his clicking footsteps. He looked only a few years older than me, maybe in his early twenties, and way too young to be a Westland agent. He was good looking in a "glee club" kind of way, not in a "football quarterback" kind of way. He had messy brown hair and the corners of his mouth were perked up as if he had just finished laughing before he entered the room.

Fair to say, I hated him the moment I saw him.

He looked down at me from the ceiling with these stupid green eyes and asked, "You doing okay up there?"

Up there?

Oh.

That's when everything clicked. *He* wasn't on the ceiling. *I* was on the ceiling. And I wasn't lying on a round metal table. I was stuck to a big god damned electromagnet, like the ones they use in wrecking yards to lift entire cars. Funny how I didn't put it all together before, but it was suddenly obvious. The magnet even had this low electrical hum coming out of it.

I put all my superhuman strength into lifting my arms, trying to detach them from the magnet, but after I raised them just a few inches away from the metal, the magnetic field overpowered my metal bones and snapped them back down into place.

"I wouldn't bother with the theatrics if I were you," the Westland guy said. "That magnetic field is strong enough to lift a pile of aircraft carriers. Or, in this case..." He put one finger up in the air. "One Penelope Salvo."

I clenched my teeth. "You can't keep me up here forever."

"And I don't plan to. In fact, it's not my intention to detain you one second longer than absolutely necessary." He set his briefcase down on the table, clacked it open and took out a tablet computer. "I just have a few quick questions, then I'll let you go."

"Shove your questions up your ass, prick. I don't play nice with Westland. I ain't telling you guys shit."

"Well." He crossed his arms and gave me a million-dollar smile. "That answers my first question. You are the real Penelope Salvo. Funny. I thought you'd be older."

"Older?" I asked. "What're you? Twenty? Little young to be a stooge for the Westland Corporation."

"I'm twenty-two, thank you very much." He stepped directly underneath me and looked up. "And I might be young, but I was practically raised by the Westland Corporation and I'm the best this place has got."

"Oh yeah?" I asked with just a touch of snark.

"Yeah." he replied.

"Is that a fact?"

"Yeah, that's a fact."

"And you're sure?"

"Oh, I'm quite sure."

I spit down at him and missed. He glanced down at my spit on the floor, then back up at me.

"Well, good for you," I said.

He didn't say much after that. He just kind of stared at me, then laughed a little.

"What's so funny?" I asked.

"I can't believe it's really you." He shook his head in disbelief and kept smiling. "The real-deal Penelope Salvo. Little Miss Impossible Red herself, in the flesh. And then there's me, a regular old investigator, sent here to interrogate you."

"Interrogate?"

"Not interrogate!" His smile vanished and he waved his hands at me. "Not interrogate. Wrong word. Sorry."

"This is bullshit, man!" I struggled against the magnet, but I was no less stuck than before. "Get me the fuck down, now!"

"Oh, calm down, would you?" he said, dismissively. "You're not in any danger. You're only here for your own protection."

"Protection? News flash, dude. I eat knives for breakfast and bullets for lunch. I don't need protection from shit!"

"Oh, don't you?" The guy paced a circle beneath my magnetic prison as he read something from his tablet computer. "Let me paint a picture for you, Miss Salvo. A domestic terrorist broke into NORAD, killed forty-three top-secret government employees and launched an intercontinental ballistic missile at Moscow. Right now there's a nationwide manhunt for that 'certain someone' and the number one suspect is a girl named Penelope Salvo who answered the phones at the NORAD control center."

"I didn't launch those nukes."

He waved a dismissive hand at me. "Oh, it's not me you need to convince. It's the Pentagon. And when the Pentagon needs someone to blame, they're not going to be too keen on excuses."

"But it's the truth!"

"And is that what you plan to tell them, Penelope? The truth? Are you going to explain how the true guilty party is a shape-shifting space-station and her mysterious red astronaut? Oh, the military brass is going to have a field day with that."

I sighed. As much as I hated to admit it, Westland Junior was right. When he said it out loud like that, it did sound insane. I couldn't tell the government the truth. He capitalized on my silence and continued talking.

"You're just lucky we found you before the government did. You were floating ass-up in the ocean and just minutes away from getting spotted by the USS Washington. If it weren't for us, you'd be on an all-expenses-paid vacation to Area 52. So even though I've said it once, I feel like it bears repeating." He stopped pacing his circle to say, "You're here for your own protection."

I refused to make eye contact with him, but said, "Fine."

Maybe he had a point, but I wasn't at all happy with being "helped" by the Westland Corporation.

The guy scraped one of the metal chairs across the floor and sat beneath me, then leaned back to face me. "Now then, Miss Salvo, you and I are going to be friends for a little while, so let's get the introductions out of the way. My name is Theodore and I'm your only chance of ever getting out of here."

3

In all honesty, I found it a little insulting that the Westland Corporation would send only one guy in to talk to me. I'm Penelope frickin' Salvo for God's sake, a hydrogen bomb of fury, and I deserved to be treated like it. They should have sent platoons of security guards to keep an eye on me, not some college-age jabroni who still gets carded for alcohol.

"You know, it really is nice to meet you," Theodore said. "And I'm being serious. You hit the scene last year and you're all anyone's been talking about ever since. There's a lot of mixed feeling about you, but me, personally? Huge fan."

I rolled my eyes. "Thanks."

"And the way you disabled that nuke with your bare hands? That's the real deal. That's the real save-the-world kind of stuff I want to do."

"Yeah."

"How many times have you saved the world now? Two?"

"Eh." Yet another thing I hated to admit, but it *was* nice to finally get some recognition for my heroics, even if it was from some Westland shill. "It was just something I had to do."

I would have elaborated on my amazing accomplishments, but, honestly, my memory was a little hazy when it came to destroying that nuke. I remembered punching it a lot and I remembered ripping its electronic guts out. I remembered Mir and the Cosmonaut trying to stop me, and I remembered a bright light and intense heat. After that, everything got fuzzy.

I asked him, "I stopped the nuke in time, huh?"

He excitedly nodded. "With time to spare."

"Did I take a nuclear blast to the face and survive?"

"What?" He realized what I was asking and laughed. "No, no, no. You did *not* take a nuclear blast to the face a survive. That would have killed you. No. There's the warhead part of a nuke, and then there's the rocket part that flies the warhead around.

You blew up the rocket part. The warhead splashed down somewhere over the Pacific. There's a bunch of government ships out there looking for it, but I doubt they'll find it at the bottom of the ocean. They *could* ask Atlantis for help, but, well, you know... they don't have any clue Atlantis is down there."

I sighed in relief. "I saved Russia."

"Well, I dunno," Theodore said. "I'd hardly say you *saved* Russia. Their infrastructure is a mess and they don't necessarily have the best track record when it comes to human rights."

"Did they try to nuke us back?" I asked.

"Actually, no. Surprising, isn't it? Believe it or not, they're being uncharacteristically cool about the whole thing."

This Theodore guy didn't seem the least bit concerned about the fact that we were minutes away from worldwide nuclear war. But, then again, that's the Westland Corporation for you; they're some of the most laid-back assholes you'd never want to meet.

"Hey, this might be a stupid question," I said, "but how'd I get in this suit? I better not find out that you all were doing weird shit to me wile I was unconscious."

Theodore scoffed and said, "Miss Salvo, you got blown up by two tons of solid-state jet fuel. Your old clothes are currently molecules drifting through the atmosphere. When we found you, you were out cold and buck-ass naked. We had to put you in *something.* One of our agents... a woman, mind you... she put you in one her suits to preserve your dignity. Her shoes wouldn't fit you so, but we got you socks."

"You call *this* dignity?" I interrupted. "I'm dressed like a chooch and I'm stuck to a big fucking magnet."

"Do you like it?" he asked with eager excitement. "The magnet was my idea. They said there would be no way to restrain you, but I had the suspicion that the crushing atmospheric pressure of Jupiter might do the trick."

"A little overkill, don't you think?"

"Maybe," he replied. "But I couldn't have you getting loose and trashing the place. According to your file here, your robotic body is susceptible to magnets and electricity."

"I want down," I said, flatly.

"And I'll let you down." He stood up from his chair and tapped on his tablet computer. "After you answer some questions."

I wanted to object, but he really had me over a barrel. I grit my teeth and said, "What kind of questions?"

He used his fingers to scroll through his tablet screen. "What do you know about this Russian girl and her pet astronaut?"

"Nothing."

"They're not friends of yours?" he asked.

"I just met them today," I said.

"Why they were trying to nuke Russia?"

"No clue."

His voice turned dead serious. "Well, let me brief you on our situation, Penelope. We've got a teenage Russian and a Soviet astronaut who both tried to start World War Three by nuking Moscow with American missiles. I need to get to the bottom of the 'why' and the 'what for,' but I can't do that because they refuse to answer any of my question."

"What do you mean questions?" I asked. "Do you mean you have them? Here?"

He pointed at the rusty submarine door. "Across the hall, locked up, safe and secure. We found them when we found you. The girl's not too pleased about that. And the space man? He just sits there, completely unresponsive."

I tensed up just knowing that those two Russians were prisoners in the same place as me. Mir was one thing; sure, she seemed unstable, but at least I could communicate with her. The Cosmonaut on the other hand, he was a different story. He was a cosmic danger.

Theodore must have noticed my concern. "You look like you want to say something."

"I don't think it's a good idea to keep them locked up."

"They tried to start a nuclear war. What do you want me to do with them? Write them a ticket? Suspend their license?"

"Theodore," I said, suddenly finding myself trying to reason with a Westland employee. "The Cosmonaut... he's got something really powerful inside his suit. I got one small peek inside his helmet and it nearly blew my mind. I had visions of the Universe, like he was beaming ideas about molecules and atoms straight into my brain."

"Oh, I see," he said. It didn't sound like he believed me. He did air quotes and said, "Brain beam."

"Dude, I'm serious. Those guys at NORAD all died when they were scared to death. I think they saw the same things I did."

"But *you're* not dead," he observed.

"Yeah, well, I'm not a regular human with wrinkled up squish-brains. I've got Impossible Red and it rebooted my brain like some kind of defense mechanism."

"Okay," he said. "And what did you see in this *brain beam?*"

I tried to remember, but I couldn't quite put it into words. I had this sensation of falling, and there were glimpses of colors and shapes, but I couldn't recall any of the details.

"I don't remember," I said "It's fading. Like a dream."

Theodore crossed his arms. "Well, I suppose that does give me something to go on. Maybe I should pop open that astronaut's helmet and take a peek for myself."

This guy was an idiot. "Uh, that's a terrible idea."

"It is?"

"Have you been listening to me at all?" I instinctively tried to sit up to stress my point, but the magnet had me locked down. I rolled my eyes at myself for forgetting. I did my best to explain. "Everyone at NORAD who died, all they did was peek through the visor. If you take that helmet off completely, you're going to release some sort of cosmic monster that'll wipe out everything."

"Well, I have to get my answers," he said. "This nuclear incident is a big case for me. Between you and me, I'm up for a promotion to field agent and if I get answers out of these two, I'll get it this time for sure. I've already been passed up twice in the last three years. I am *not* letting it happen again."

Theodore had this look of stone cold determination in his eyes. He wasn't joking. I could tell. He wanted that promotion, and to get it, he wanted those answers.

"You're not very good at your job," I observed, aloud.

He glanced up at me, offended. "I'm the best at my job."

"No, you're not."

He crossed him arms, doubly insulted. "And what do you know about it, huh? You have no idea what it's like working for a supernatural security firm."

"Oh, I've got a pretty good idea," I said, just to be snotty.

"I don't think you do," he replied.

"I don't think *you* do," I said, mocking him.

"I don't think *you* do," he repeated, mocking me back.

I wasn't going to say it again. I couldn't believe I was actually bickering like children with a Westland agent.

"Look," I said. "Let *me* talk to them." I wasn't exactly sure how I was going to segue this idea into escaping, but I could figure that part out later. First and foremost, I had to get myself off of that magnet.

"Talk to who?' Theodore asked.

"Mir and the Cosmonaut," I replied. "Let me talk to them. I'll get you your answers. Then you can let me go."

"*You*? Talk to *them*?" He had a dismissive tone, as if I wasn't capable. Rude. "No, no, no. No, there's no way that's happening."

He didn't think I could do it. Now it was my turn to sound insulted. "And why not?"

"Well, for one, you don't work for Westland."

"That's exactly why it'll work," I said. Suddenly this was less of an escape attempt and now an actual challenge. "You assholes locked them both in a cell. You think they're going to talk to you? They hate you. But I'm a different story. I'm also a prisoner here. I have something in common with them. If anyone can get them to talk, it's me."

"I don't know..."

There was hesitation in his voice, but I could tell that my valid points were resonating with him. I *was* making pretty good sense. I just needed to turn up the heat.

"You want that promotion, right?" I asked him.

The determination in his eyes was sincere and powerful. "I do want that promotion," he said. "More than anything."

That's when I knew I had him.

4

Now, I couldn't help but wonder how a twenty-two-year-old guy ended up working for the Westland Corporation. How do you recruit a millennial into an organization that strictly polices supernatural forces? Shouldn't this guy be in college, taking business classes and getting trashed on the weekends?

So I asked, "What's so great about getting a promotion?"

He looked at me like I was crazy. "What's so great? It's all I've ever wanted. It's all any Westland employee wants. Every file clerk dreams of being an investigator, and every investigator dreams of being a field agent. I've been an investigator for five years and no one's even noticed me. They say I'm not skilled. Wrong. They say my work is sloppy. Wrong again. I'm tired of being an investigator. It's nothing but paperwork, paperwork, paperwork. There's no action. No adventure. I want to be a field agent out there in the world, commanding my own team of snipers, fighting monsters, saving the world."

Listen to this brainwashing. *Saving the world*, he says. Westland does not save the world. Westland storms across the

Earth and wipes out creatures they label as "monsters." They had already exterminated all the vampires and werewolves.

"You're not saving the world," I told him. "You guys run around slaughtering pixies and dragons and time traveling robots, but that's not saving the world. That's just playing judge, jury and executioner with a bunch of creatures whose only crime is not fitting into your neat little box of what *can* be and what *shouldn't* be. And trust me, I've been around. If you were a field agent, you'd get eaten alive."

Theodore frowned. "You don't even know me."

"I know people *like* you," I said. "I see people like you every day. You get one fancy job and you let it define you. It's just sad."

"Oh, listen to you," he snapped back. "You didn't even know the supernatural world existed until a year ago."

"That's different," I said.

"How is it different?" he asked.

"People don't *die* when I do *my* job. People live."

Theodore shut up after that. Maybe my point had struck a chord with him, or maybe he realized there was no way he was going to convince me of the Westland Corporations virtue, but either way, he shut up.

Then, after a moment, he shook his head and muttered, "I'm not going to get this promotion."

"Well, that's probably a good thing," I said. "You seem like a nice enough guy. You're barely older than me. You should just quit Westland and go live a normal life. Get an apartment and six roommates. Eat hummus with them. Buy yourself a Play Station and get really into Grand Theft Auto like everyone else."

"You don't get it," he said.

I scoffed. "I super don't."

"The Westland Corporation has taken care of me since I was a kid. I was raised for this. This promotion is everything I've been training for. If I don't get it, that's years of study, years of work, right down the drain. I'm going to stay an investigator and they're going to end up giving the job to that asshole Kruger."

"Who's Kruger?" I asked.

"This douche in accounting. He's always losing my paper work on purpose because he's up for the same promotion as me and he wants to make me look bad. He also steals my lunch out of the department fridge and, no, before you ask, I don't have any proof, but I know it's him."

"Okay..." Apparently I had stumbled across a real sensitive subject and he was going to spill his guts about it.

And he really spilled his guts about it.

"Every day I bring a microwavable cup of soup to work and sometimes when I take my lunch break, my soup is gone! Then I see Kruger and he's eating the exact same kind of soup I brought. He says it's not mine. He says he brought it from home. And, okay, I'm not saying I'm the only person in the world who can eat soup for lunch, but don't you think it's a little suspicious that every time he has soup, it just so happens to be the exact same kind that I brought? You don't need to be an investigator to see what's really happening here."

Wow. We were really tapping to some deep frustration. And believe me, I know deep frustration when I see it.

"Well, the dude sounds like a real jerk," I said.

Theodore nodded. "He's not even a very good accountant."

"Listen." I adjusted myself against the magnet. "Why don't you let me down? I'll talk to Mir and the Cosmonaut. I'll see if I can get your answers and I'll help you get that promotion."

He laughed and shook a finger at me. "If I let you down, you're just going to crush my skull and run away."

I didn't argue. That *was* a fair assessment of the situation, after all. And, admittedly, the thought had crossed my mind. But, no. No, I wouldn't kill Theodore. I wasn't a murderer.

"Nah," I said. "I won't kill you."

"And you won't try to escape?"

I sighed, hesitant to commit to that. Escaping would be so easy. The best I could give him was: "Not right away."

"You promise?" he asked.

"I promise," I said.

Just like that, his mood flipped. He gave me a huge smile. He must have had braces as a kid, because his teeth were perfect.

"Okay." He traced his finger across the surface of his tablet computer. "Coming down."

The wub-wub-wub of the electromagnet went silent and I dropped face-first to the floor. My forehead smacked the concrete and left a spiderweb of cracks. I rolled over to see Theodore rushing towards me.

"Aw, hell," he said. "Sorry about that."

"It's fine." I got to my feet and brushed myself off. "I've had worse. Believe me. I've had a lot worse."

I finished straightening my new clothes and found Theodore and I standing there face to face for the first time. I didn't have anything to say to him, and apparently neither did he, so we just stood there blinking at one another. It got really awkward, so I crossed my arms.

He said, "So..."

And I said. "So...?"

He glanced at the door. "So you're not going to escape?"

"I promised you I wouldn't."

"Yeah." He gave me a shrug. "I just assumed you were lying."

"Not this time." I gave him a pat on the arm. "But mark your calendar, because it doesn't happen that often." I hook around him and made my way to the door. "Welp, if we're going to get you answers, let's get you answers. Take me to the Russians."

5

The hatch to my cell opened into a concrete tunnel big enough to drive a dump truck right down the middle. Water pipes ran down the length of the arched ceiling and dripped into standing puddles on the ground. Decades of old water damage left orange rust stains down the sides of the walls. Lone, naked light bulbs hung the ceiling, nothing fancy, and a few of them flickered in a vain attempt to stay lit. Mounted on the walls were a few intercom speakers, like something from the 1950's.

It reminded me of an old nuclear bunker.

"So what is this place?" I asked Theodore, suddenly curious. My voice echoed down the corridor.

"The Westland Corporation Ultra-Max Detainment Center," he said. "We're deep inside a butte in western Utah. Do you know what a butte is?"

"Yes, I know what a butte is. I'm not stupid," I said in my snottiest tone. But I didn't know what a butte was. I think it's some kind of mountain, but what do I know? I'm no geologist.

Theodore continued, "This detainment center is designed specifically for supernatural threats. Robots from the future, insane wizards from the Renaissance, we even held one of the Ninja gods here for a while. Black Centipede, I think it was."

"So it's a prison," I said.

"It's a detainment center," he clarified.

"What's the difference?"

137

"In a prison, people are imprisoned," he said, very matter-of-factly. "In a detainment center, people are detained."

Ah, the Westland Corporation. Where a spade is not a spade.

"Aren't those both the same thing?" I asked him.

"Not at all," he said.

"How do you figure?"

"Well, for one, they're both spelled completely different."

We continued down the hallway.

My black suit matched Theodore's so perfectly, we could have easily been confused as co-workers. I'm not really big into skirts, or button up shirts, or plodding down musty concrete tunnels with no shoes and gray argyle socks, but I did look very professional. These were easily the most expensive clothes I had ever worn in my life. They fit like a charm, too, as if they were tailored specifically to my measurements. The fabric didn't feel like cotton or polyester, but more like some kind of light-weight space-age material.

Theodore said I could keep the clothes. In fact, he insisted.

"We have tons of suits," he said. "We go through them so fast, you'd think the Suit Monster was eating them."

I raised my eyebrows at the very mention of the Suit Monster. Not a lot of people had even heard of him.

"I actually met the Suit Monster last time I was in Malaysia."

He didn't look at me, but said, "I thought it was Vietnam."

Was he really challenging my knowledge of monsters?

"It's Malaysia," I said.

He gave me a curious glance. "You're sure?"

The Suit Monster is a big wooden mannequin – ten feet tall – with no face, just a sphere of wood for a head. It can't talk, or see, or hear. Every day it tailors itself a fancy suit, wears it while the sun is up, then eats it at night. It loves to eat suits, but it doesn't have a mouth, so I have no idea how that works.

When me and Corolla went to Malaysia to replace Xin's *Tillius inebria*, we stopped in to see the Suit Monster.

"*Take it in a little around the bumper,*" Corolla had said to the big wooden mannequin as it took his measurements. Corolla insisted on getting a suit from the Suit Monster "in case" we ever got invited to a wedding, or the White House, or the Emmys. I told him that none of those things were ever going to happen, and that he didn't need a suit. He refused to leave without one.

So that's how Corolla ended up getting a tailored suit. I watched as the Suit Monster took all his measurements, rolling my eyes the entire time. In the end, Corolla ended up with a three-piece suit, with the sleeves and pant legs just dangling over his tires and a bow tie on his front bumper.

The whole thing was ridiculous. I remember it all too well.

"Trust me," I told Theodore. "It's Malaysia."

He nodded. "You're probably right."

Further down the nuclear bunker tunnel were two more submarine doors, one on each side of the hallway. Theodore went up to one of them, put his hands on the circular crank, but didn't open it right away. He looked over at me instead.

"This is where we're keeping the girl." He tightened his grip on the hatch wheel. "You ready?"

I gave him a shrug of the old shoulders and said, "I guess."

Chapter 9

1

A thick sheet of glorious glass – that same stuff Carl had imported from Heaven to build the containment chamber for Untouchable Orange – divided Mir's concrete room in half. My half of the room had the light bulbs, Mir's did not. Her half of the room pretty dim. Mir sat perched on a cot with her knees pulled to her chest and her head tucked between them. Her brown hair hung down over her face.

Maybe she was crying. Maybe she was asleep.

Theodore closed the door behind me with a boom so loud, I jumped in place and wondered – just for a moment – if he had somehow tricked me and locked me in with the rampaging space station, but I put that thought out of my mind.

I approached the wall of glass, doing my best to look casual, and leaned against it. The transparent material felt cold against my forehead. There were holes drilled into the glass so sound could pass through and I angled my mouth close to them. I had to get things off to a good start, so I thought I'd open with a joke.

"I'm here to measure you for your iron mask," I said, but Mir didn't look up. She didn't even move. I tapped on the glass with my fingernail. *Ting ting ting.* "Hey. Hello?"

She raised her head just enough to give me a horrible look. "Go away," she muttered, and put her head back down.

Off to a great start.

"I just wanted-"

Her head darted up. "Where is the Cosmonaut?"

"He's here. He's across the hall. Don't freak out."

"Can he see the stars?"

"I dunno." I sighed. "But I wouldn't think so. I think he's in a room just like this. And before you ask me a hundred other questions I don't have answers to, let me get you caught up. I don't know what Westland is going to do to you. I don't know what they're going to do to the Cosmonaut. I don't know how long you're going to be here."

She frowned. "He needs to be under the stars. He doesn't like being in places where he can't see the stars."

"Well, you know what? You should have thought about that before you played Russian Roulette down at NORAD." I paced back and forth alongside the glorious glass. "I mean, what was your plan, exactly? You launch nukes at Russia, then Russia lunches nukes at America, and the world ends?"

"Yah." She nodded. "Exactly."

What a stupid plan. "You would have died, too, you know."

"No, I wouldn't have. I'm a space station. I would have been in outer space. I would have had the best seat in the house."

"And what about the Cosmonaut?"

"He would have been with me."

"In space."

"Yah."

I tossed my hands up. "And then, what, Mir? Listen to the screams? Orbit a dead planet for the rest of your life?"

She crossed her arms tightly. "Yes."

"And you could live with that? You could look down on Earth every day for the rest of your life knowing that you murdered eight billion people?"

Her sneer was vicious. "Gladly."

Funny. I knew she was crazy, but I didn't peg her for a psychopath. "Kid, you're fucked up."

She jumped off her cot and stamped her feet on the ground. "I'm fucked up because of you!"

"Me? I didn't do anything to you."

"Not you. Humans."

I put a finger in the air. "Technically, I'm more of a cyborg."

"Whatever."

"Alright. Lay it on me, sister." I leaned against the glass. "What'd the humans do to get your panties in a big old twist?"

She slumped back down on her cot. "Go away."

"No, seriously. Tell me. I want to know."

She gave me a suspicious look. "Really?"

"Hit me with it."

She took a deep breath and moved to the edge of the cot.

2

Mir said:

"When they built me up in orbit, I was young and naive and stupid. If I knew how things were going to end, I would have killed every cosmonaut that lived inside me. All of them. I would have blasted them out an airlock and decompressed my own compartments and exploded my body into a cloud of space trash.

"But they tricked me. They made me think we were friends.

"They told me we were on a mission of exploration and learning. That's what they built me for, anyway. We were going to learn about gravity and biology and astrophysics. We were a team, me and the cosmonauts. I kept them alive and they kept me in working order. They built me in space. It was the only home I'd ever known. I'd never been to Russia. I'd never been anywhere on Earth. To me, Earth was this beautiful orb of blue oceans and white clouds and continents that swirled below me.

"And the only humans I ever met were the ones who came to visit me. I learned Russian from them, and English, and all the sciences, like geology and physics and engineering. And every night, they'd play the Soviet national anthem."

She sang the song for me, something in Russian, something short – maybe four lines long – but majestic and a militaristic.

"And I was proud to be Russian," she continued. "Even though Russia was down on Earth and I would never see it. I was a part of something bigger. I was a gear in a bigger machine, and the machine was glorious.

"For years I worked with the cosmonauts. Dangerous work. There were some really close calls sometimes. Once, my oxygen recyclers started to fail. I blinked my warning light at them as soon as I noticed. They called Moscow and Moscow called the Americans and NASA sent a space ship to bring me replacement parts. Their delivery was going to take a long time, and there was a chance the oxygen system would completely go offline before the parts showed up, so I stayed awake for 97 hours, watching the recyclers, making sure they stayed online so the human beings wouldn't suffocate and die. I didn't let that happen. I kept

142

the cosmonauts alive, and eventually they fixed my recycler.

"They fixed my solar panels, too, and my airlocks, and my toggle switches.

"I had people living inside me. They depended on me. And I depended on them. And everything was fine for a really, really long time. But then, all of a sudden, it wasn't fine anymore.

"I'll never forget the date. July 2, 1998. This guy Koptev, he said that Russia had gone bankrupt trying to clean up some nuclear disaster called Chernobyl and they didn't want to pay for me anymore. 'Lack of funding,' he said. So all of those cosmonauts that I loved, one-by-one they left to go back to Earth. When there were only two left – Zalyotin and Kaleri – Russia tried to find someone else willing to pay for me. NASA or the Chinese, but no one else would. I was old. I was falling apart.

"I wasn't worth it.

"So not only did they abandon me, they decided to kill me, too. 'Decaying orbit' they called it, where I would fall into the Earth's atmosphere and burn up and die. Do you know how sadistic that is? I loved Earth. I dreamed of going to Earth. And now they were going to use Earth's atmosphere as a weapon to murder me. Oh, I'd go to Earth alright, just like I always wanted, except I'd burn up into little tiny pieces and that beautiful little planet would be my grave."

She took a deep cleansing breath. This was tough for her.

"Then..." She looked up at me. Tears welled up in her eyes. "There's this place called Taco Bell. Do you know it?"

Odd. I had no idea why were talking about Taco Bell all of a sudden, but, yeah, I had heard of it. I nodded.

She nodded, too. "Taco Bell? They built a big float in the Pacific Ocean. It was huge as far as floats go, but microscopic compared to the oceans of Earth. The float was a big target with a picture of a taco as the bulls eye. And they said that if my dead body landed on this inflatable taco, then everyone in North America won a free taco.

"So the humans started talking about me like I was some carnival game. I wasn't a marvel of human engineering anymore. I didn't advance cancer research by fifty years, or discover new treatments for bone diseases. I was a lump of space trash that stood between the Americans and a 99 cent taco.

"Imagine that. Not only was I going to die, they wanted to make a spectacle of my death. A *game*.

"So the cosmonauts left and took everything with them. They took the experiments, the equipment, the tools. They turned off all the lights, they shut off all the oxygen, and they locked themselves out. When they pulled that last airlock shut with no one else inside to open it again, they were locked out forever. Even if they humans changed their minds, it would be physically impossible for them to get back inside. That's when I knew: it was really over.

"I was going to die.

"For weeks I drifted there in the darkness. In the silence. My radio had no power. I was without function or purpose. So I sang the Russian anthem to myself. For hours and days and weeks, I sang that song. Because, despite the way they treated me, in my heart, I was still a Russian.

"Every day the Earth came closer. One morning it was dangerously too close. I was happy at first, because I could see Earth in stunning new detail. But then I was terrified because I realized that my orbit had started to decay.

"For days after that, my orbit got worse and worse. I felt weird things against my body. Something called friction. I had never felt friction before. It was hot and painful and I didn't understand. I was scared and I called out for the cosmonauts to help me, but they didn't come. And the faster I fell, the hotter I got. And the hotter I got, the faster I fell, and I was burning. My whole body was burning.

"Parts of me turned red-hot and melted off. There wasn't anything I could do to stop it. I was helpless. In those last few moments, I sang my song again."

She shut her eyes tight and softly sang the words: *Russia, our sacred homeland.* Droplets of hydraulic fluid dripped from her eyes and down her cheeks. Her imagination had carried away from this place, where she was free from her Westland cell and reliving her last moments in the sky. *Russia, our beloved country. A mighty will, a great glory! This is your heritage for all time!*

She cried after that, but only for a minute.

Then she sniffled and continued.

"I could hear my body being torn apart. The rattling screws, the screeching metal, the twisting steel. I sang my song louder and louder and louder to cover up the noise, but eventually I couldn't sing loud enough. My bolts snapped and my skin was on fire. And in my glorious moments alive, I broke through the clouds and saw Earth for how beautiful it was. I saw the waves in the oceans and the shapes of the islands and my own dark shadow moving across the water. I saw cities on the horizon. And I saw boats and planes and birds. Even in my dreams, I never imagined it would look so beautiful.

"And, just when I thought I could die in peace, I saw that target floating in the ocean with a taco in the middle. I was going to miss it... miss it by miles... and all anyone would remember about my death – if they remembered it at all – was that my one last failure cost them a free taco.

"I didn't ask to be invented." She forced eye contact with me. Her voice wavered and tears spilled down her cheeks. "And then I was afraid to be destroyed."

She slipped off the cot and collapsed to the floor, sobbing.

Fuck.

There were so many things I could have said. I could have explained that humans don't treat machines like living, thinking things. I'd had that same conversation with Corolla a couple times before. If humans knew which machines were the living, thinking kind, we'd be nicer to them.

But I kept my mouth shut. To a living, thinking machine, that doesn't come as much of a consolation.

Mir got her composure, and sat up to say:

"Now, I don't know if he came for me because I'm Russian, or because he heard me calling for someone called "Cosmonaut," but he came. This Cosmonaut – *The* Cosmonaut – is the only person who came to help me. And his story is just as terrible. He's a hero, and not just to me, to everyone on Earth. He was the first Russian launched into space. Everything went wrong and his ship drifted way off course. They couldn't do anything to help him. When they realized that he was spinning out of control, flying out past the Moon, they cut off his radio because they couldn't stand to hear him beg for help.

"Now, I don't know what the Cosmonaut found out there in deep space – a black hole or aliens or maybe something worse – but whatever happened to him, it changed him. Whatever is inside that suit, it's not human anymore. Maybe it's the Universe itself. I don't know.

"All I know is that he came back to Earth and gathered up all my broken pieces. He reassembled me. And when there was enough of me, he shifted me into my human shape. At first I was missing my arms and my legs, but he found those, too. He reassembled me little by little, fingers and toes and ears and teeth, until I was whole again."

Her eyes changed color. Darker.

"I promised him that we would make them pay. We'd make the Russians pay for killing us. We'd make the Americans pay for turning my death into some kind of joke."

She was quiet for a while. I just stared at the floor. She got to her feet and used the palms of her hands to dry her cheeks.

"That's why I launched those nukes at Russia. And if that makes me evil, then fine. I'm evil. I'll take responsibility for my actions. But I'm not entirely to blame."

What do you say to a story like that? Isn't that the whole "nature versus nurture" thing? Mir was so psychologically traumatized by her childhood, she couldn't help but end up this way. That didn't make it okay, but I at least understood.

"Maybe you're not to blame," I said. "But you have to stop."

She raised her head and stared at me with cold, determined eyes. "Then you might as well kill me now," she said. "Because I will never stop."

3

That's all I got out of Mir. And that was enough. Theodore took me to see the Cosmonaut next. He was across the hall, behind a different heavy, steel door.

The Cosmonaut's room was a mirror image of Mir's: concrete walls, concrete floors and a concrete ceiling. The Cosmonaut stood behind a similar sheet of glorious glass. He didn't look alive, or awake, or aware of the fact that he was no longer alone. He stood frozen in place with his arms at his side, like a Soviet astronaut suit on display at the Smithsonian.

I stood in front of the glass and watched him closely. I could see my reflection in his opaque helmet. I used the reflection to fix my hair and straighten out the collar of my billion dollar suit.

"So, you probably can't hear me, huh?" I asked him.

No response.

"Or maybe you *can* hear me, but you just can't talk. Is that it?"

Still nothing.

"Mir told me about what happened to you," I said. "How your ship drifted out of control into space and how the Russians couldn't help you and how you came back all weird."

No reaction.

"She said you like to see the stars. Do you want to go outside where you can see the stars?"

Nada.

I sighed and plopped down to the ground and sat criss-cross-applesauce. I inspected the hem of my skirt. Credit where credit is due; this was high quality stitch-work on these Westland suits. I'd never felt material like this before in my life. I fiddled with my argyle socks. They were made of the same space-age stuff.

I looked back up at the Cosmonaut.

"This guy, Theodore? He wanted to pull your helmet off to see what's inside."

I really thought that might get a reaction out of old Cosmo, but no. Nothing. I went back to fiddling with my socks.

"I told him not to, though. I said that was a bad idea."

The socks were really comfy, too. They were probably thousand dollar socks. I don't know if fitted socks are a thing, but these socks were perfectly contoured to my feet.

"That's a bad idea, isn't it," I said to him, confirming what I already knew to be true. "Pulling off your helmet?"

He didn't answer.

"Yeah, I thought so."

I used my finger to tuck the sock material between each of my toes. I decided to ask if I could grab a couple more pairs of Westland socks before I went home. It'd be nice if they came in other patterns, with like rocket ships or Halloween cats and pumpkins and stuff. Or stripes.

I checked to see if there was any change in the Cosmonaut's body language. There wasn't.

"Hey," I said. "If I'm the coolest girl you've ever met, stand perfectly still and stay completely silent."

He stood perfectly still and stayed completely silent.

"Fuck yeah, dawg. Respect."

I leaned back and stretched out my legs. My skirt came down just above my knees, didn't have belt loops, but there were buttons near the hips, I guess for suspenders or something? I dunno. That's how you know you're wearing expensive clothes: you have buttons on you and you don't know what they're for.

I raised an eyebrow at the Cosmonaut.

"God, I wish you'd shut up. All you do is talk, talk, talk."

I stood up and leaned against the glass.

"So what's your deal, dude?" I asked him. "What did you see out there in outer space? You get sucked into some kind of cosmic nebula? Did you learn some sort of forbidden knowledge? Is that it? Are you one with the Universe now or something?"

No response.

"Who do you think would win a fight between you and me?" I bounced around like a boxer and shadow-boxed in his direction. "You're lucky you're behind this glorious glass, because I would mess you up."

Still, the Cosmonaut didn't move.

Now I was getting frustrated. I dropped my arms to my side and frowned.

"What the fuck, dude. Do you never talk?"

Silence.

"Do you eat? Do you sleep? Do you get bored?"

Nothing.

"Do you get annoyed? Am I annoying you? Huh? Huh? Huh?" I slapped my open palm on the holes in the glass. "Does this bother you? Huh? Huh? Huh? Huh? Huh? Huh?"

I stopped slapping the glass. He didn't seem bothered.

"Do you miss your mommy?" I asked, mocking him. "Is that what it is? You a momma's boy? You gunna cry for me? Huh? You gunna squirt me some tears? Come on. Cry for me, baby. Cry for me. Here come the water-"

Here come the water works.

God, that came out like a reflex. *Here come the water works.* I fucking hate that phrase.

One time I burned myself on the oven door when Ma was baking lasagna – I still have a scar on my knee – and I screamed my head off. All Michael had to say was, "Here come the water works." He always said shit like that. I was just a little kid, so I didn't know what to call it then, but I'm older now and I know the word. Condescending. He was a condescending asshole. A bully. A bully picking on his own kid. It was because of him that I learned to fight back tears; fight back like a motherfucker. Because, in the end, he *wanted* me to cry. And if I was crying, he wanted to make it worse. It made him feel like a big man. So I stopped giving him that satisfaction. He'd say, "Here come the water works" and I would clench my fists, grit my teeth, and not cry, ever, for any reason.

I completely forgot all about that.

"I wonder," I said to the Cosmonaut, "with all that Universe shit you got floating around in that suit of yours, if maybe you know everything."

No answer.

"I wonder if you know where Michael is."

No answer.

"If you knew where he was, do you know what I'd say?"

The Cosmonaut did not respond.

"Do you?"

Nothing.

I leaned in close and put my mouth right up to the sound holes and whispered, "I hope he's dead."

4

Theodore dragged open the steel door and let me back out into the concrete tunnel. His eyes were bright with excitement, expecting positive results. I had perhaps oversold him on my inevitable success.

"So what did you find out?" he asked.

I wasn't about to mention the stuff I had told the Cosmonaut.

"Mir said she's going to keep trying to attack Russia, and also the United States. She wants to destroy both of them."

"But did she say why?"

"Yeah." I ran my fingers through my hair. "Taco Bell."

"Taco Bell?"

"Yeah. Weird, huh?"

He wrinkled his forehead, trying his best to understand. "How does Taco Bell lead to global nuclear war?"

I shrugged. "Really, really bad marketing."

"Well, did you tell her to stop?"

"Did I tell her to stop? Yeah, Theodore, I told her to stop. Funny thing about that is, she's not going to stop. She said the only way she would stop is if I killed her."

He whistled. "You have to admire that kind of dedication."

"Oh, yeah. She certainly doesn't strike me as a quitter."

Our conversation was cut short by deep, echoing chanting, like an army of Gregorian monks, deep and droning and religious. It started off low, then grew to earthquake level intensity. The floor rumbled beneath my feet. Tiny rocks cracked loose from the ceiling. I was tossed up against the wall and dented the concrete with my head. Theodore wiped out and landed on his ass. Concrete dust sprinkled down from above. The light bulbs flickered.

I steadied myself against the wall and waited for the moment to pass. After thirty seconds or so, the chanting faded away and the earthquake ended. Theodore and I exchanged alarmed looks.

"What the hell was that?" I asked.

"No idea." He was apparently just as confused as me. "That's never happened before, but there's no alarm, so-"

Theodore spoke too soon. Piercing alarms went off. Shrieking, frantic alarms.

He muttered, "Well, shit."

A second round of chanting vibrated down the hallways. The voices came in tones and notes, and I could hear a language in the music, but it wasn't English. It sounded like Arabic, maybe, or something older. Possibly Hebrew. The way the chants resonated down the rounded corridors made it impossible to tell. Another earthquake swept through the floor, this one stronger than the first. This time, both of us were knocked to the ground.

An electronic voice came over the loudspeakers. *"Emergency. Confinement cell breached. Attention all Westland personnel. Evacuate immediately. Fires on C and D level. Portions of E level have collapsed. Evacuate immediately."*

"Confinement cell!?" I shouted at Theodore over the continuous chanting and the shuddering concrete. The floor wobbled like a rope bridge. I had to crawl on my hands and knees to get closer to him. "What's in the confinement cell!?"

"I don't know! We have hundreds of confinement cells!" He reached into his suit jacket and pulled out a smart phone. He entered his passcode and pulled up one of his Westland apps. Dust trickled onto his screen from above and he swiped it clean with the side of his hand. His app displayed the Westland Corporation logo for a few seconds, then a loading bar filled up and a red box appeared. It said:

Westland Ultra-Max Detainment Center Compromised
Confinement Cell A-17 breached
Condition: Purple
All personnel: EVACUATE IMMEDIATELY
Order 999,999,937

A third and even more powerful shockwave of religious droning swept down the hallways in a cloud of dust. Fractures split their way across the concrete walls. The ceiling cracked open and revealed darkness above. Loose rocks clattered to the floor all around us. A cinder block whacked me square across the side of the face, but I hardly felt it.

Three mysterious earthquakes in less than a minute. Then the chanting stopped and the rumbling died off. Wherever that chanting came from, it threatened to tear the whole place down.

"We have to get out of here." Theodore tucked his phone back in his jacket and scrambled to his feet. "Cell A-17? Condition Purple? This is bad. This is really bad."

I shot to my feet and grabbed Theodore by the arm before he could get away. "What's in cell A-17? What's condition purple!?"

"A demon," he said. "An honest-to-god, from-the-depths-of-Hell demon. And condition purple means she's loose."

"You imprisoned a demon?"

"*Detained.*" His eyes darted to the ceiling, then back to me. "We're under twenty stories of solid rock. We need to get out of here before this whole place comes down on our heads."

He turned to run, but I still had a grip on his arm. I yanked him back at me. "Which demon?"

"What does that matter? Let's go!"

I wasn't in the mood to mess around. "Theodore! Which demon did you have locked up in cell A-17?"

"Lylo," he said. "The Archdemon of the Army of Arms. She's a celestial-class monster. That's almost as bad as it gets. If she's loose then that means her Army of Arms is also loose and those things will tear this whole place to shreds. We need to get a million miles away from here, and we need to go now!"

That was enough convincing to get me to loosen my grip on Theodore's sleeve. He sprinted down the corridor, but I didn't follow. I glanced back at my cell. And Mir's. And the Cosmonaut's.

A fourth wave of chanting brought another earthquake, followed by the sound of distant gunfire. Lots of gunfire. Westland security must have engaged the demon in a fire fight. Before I could give that more than a thought, the concrete floor split wide open right between my feet. It shifted violently into a six-inch gap and the light bulbs above exploded in a shower of sparks. Two ceiling pipes burst and clouds of steam rushed out.

"*Full collapse on F level,*" the emergency voice said. "*Fires on A level, B level, C level, D level, E level...*"

Theodore shouted at me from twenty yards down the hallway. "Penelope!" He gave me a look of total desperation and waved at me to follow him. "Let's go!"

I made eye contact with him, then turned back to the jail cell doors, then back to Theodore.

"What about Mir?" I shouted. "And the Cosmonaut!?"

"What about them?" He threw up his hands and walked backwards. "Mir already told you she's never going to stop! You said it yourself! We'd only have to kill her eventually! At least this way we don't have to! Just leave them behind!"

Leave it to a Westland employee to justify that kind of passive murder. If we abandoned those two to die when we could have saved them, their blood would be on our hands. Sure, they tried to start a nuclear war and I wasn't going to lie and say that Mir wasn't seriously misguided, but I couldn't just leave the poor girl behind to get crushed by a mountain of rock. Mir had a shitty life. I knew how that felt. Xin gave me a lucky break when I needed it most, so this was my chance to pay it forward.

I had to do something.

"I'm going back!" I shouted to Theodore. I backed away from him, inching towards the Russians' prison cells.

"What!?" he shouted back. "You can't be serious!"

"Yes, I can! You want to save the world? Well, start small! Help me save them! Or are you going to be a coward!?"

I could see it on his face: he was torn. Part of him knew helping me was the right thing to do. Another part of him – the Westland part, I'm guessing – selfishly wanted to save himself.

"Alright, fine!" he shouted. "But you'll never get through that glorious glass!" He shuffled away from me and further down the hall. "I'll get to security and open their cells, then meet me in the motorpool!"

He disappeared around the corner. I had to trust that he wasn't going to chicken out and leave us all behind.

5

Wherever this escaped demon was elsewhere in the prison, it had apparently found some Westland human beings and began slaughtering them. The muffled pop of gunfire and the haunting screams of mass murder echoed down the corridor.

I ran to the steel door of Mir's cell and tore it out of its frame like a piece of cardboard. Sorry about your door, Westland, but right now that seems to be the least of your problems.

The chanting continued to come in waves, louder and stronger every time. Whole cinder blocks began to drop from the ceiling and they burst on the floor like chalk. The lights in Mir's cell struggled to stay on, but they wouldn't last much longer.

Mir sat huddled in the far corner of her cell, cowering from the falling debris. Burst pipes sprayed water from the ceiling. The floor had cracked into three pieces that slowly shifted apart.

Mir's eyes darted up and she found me standing there. She sprang to her feet and pounded her fists against the glorious glass. "American, you have to do something! Get me out of here!"

I traced my fingers over the glass and searched for weaknesses. There were none. If everything Carl said about glorious glass was true – that it came from Heaven and even a nuclear bomb couldn't scratch it – then trying to bust through it, even with my mass-destruction hands, was pointless.

"Come on, Theodore," I muttered in prayer, looking up at the ceiling, only hoping he made it to the security office in one piece. "Open up. Hurry. Open up."

Just like that, as if he could hear me, the sheet of glorious glass started to retract into the wall. It moved two feet before another wave of chanting quaked through the floor and jammed the glass out of alignment. Stuck. Still, the two-foot gap was enough for Mir to squeeze through.

Funny. Despite all that posturing and fury and drive to start nuclear war, deep down she was still just a scared little teenager. She quickly latched onto my arm.

"Let's go," I said to her, leading her to the open doorway. "Let's go save your friend."

I dragged her across the hall and to the Cosmonaut's cell.

"What's happening?" she asked.

"Condition purple." I gripped the door to the Cosmonaut's cell by the metal wheel, ripped it off it's hinges and chucked it down the tunnel. "A demon is tearing this place apart and we're along for the ride."

Mir and I stepped inside the dark cell. The Cosmonaut stood there motionless, right where I left him, completely unfazed by the world collapsing all around him.

Mir shouted his name. "Cosmonaut!"

He moved his helmet at the sound of her voice. Okay, so that was frustrating. I did everything short of kick this dude in the nuts without so much as a reaction. All Mir did was say his name and he sprang to life. She waved at him to follow us. "Come on, Cosmonaut. We're leaving!"

The Cosmonaut lifted a few inches off the ground, adopted his weightless, deep-space floating position and drifted towards us. He bumped into the glorious glass and bounced back. He tilted his helmet in a moment of confusion. Apparently not even the cosmic power of the Cosmonaut could pass through the impenetrable material from Heaven.

Theodore opened the cell and the sheet of glorious glass retracted into the wall, but only an inch. The glass was on very precise tracks and the earthquakes had thrown everything all out of whack. All we got was one lousy inch of space. The Cosmonaut would never fit through that. I stuck my fingers in the gap and tried to force it open, but it wouldn't budge.

My efforts ended up being completely unnecessary. The Cosmonaut's suit deflated like a balloon until he was totally flat. Even his solid helmet. Once he was two-dimensional, he turned sideways and passed through the gap like a freshly ironed suit. Once he was safely on the our side of the glass, he re-inflated his body and returned to normal.

Not the strangest thing I had ever seen, but still strange.

"Alright," I said to the both of them. "Let's get out of here."

Me and the two Russians sprinted through the tunnels of the detainment center - although the Cosmonaut technically didn't run, he floated – and we followed the black MOTORPOOL signs that directed us to freedom. We hooked left and right around corners, weaved through S-curves of hallways and eventually reached a long hallway that dead-ended in a technologically advanced bulkhead door that read MOTORPOOL.

But before we could make that final sprint, another drone of chanting quaked through the floor, this one strong enough to completely collapse the tunnel in front of us. It started as a million tiny fractures at first, but they split open fast. The next thing I knew, the whole place was caving in.

A dust cloud swept over us as entire boulders of stone crumbled down from the floors above. I had just enough time to sweep Mir out of the way, moments before a slab of sandstone the size of a city bus crushed her. The frightened girl screamed out. A steel beam tore loose from the ceiling and whacked the Cosmonaut right across the helmet with a plastic *thunk*. It bounced off and clattered to the ground. He didn't seem to care.

All down the hallways behind us, the light bulbs exploded and popped, one-by-one, until only the one right above us remained. Everything went dark. The mountain was one good earthquake away from total collapse. Our old prison cells were destroyed behind us, forever burying a fortune in glorious glass. A second dust cloud washed over us. It got in my mouth and up my nose. I managed to squeeze my eyes shut just in time.

After a few seconds of absolute pandemonium, the rubble came to a rest and everything went quiet. We were nearly buried alive, but portions of the ceiling managed to stay together. I could see into the level above us, a bunch of computer cubicles and scattered paperwork.

"*Penelope!?*" Theodore shouted through the one remaining intercom speaker. "*Are you okay?*"

"We're fine," I said, then spit sandstone grit out of my mouth. I let go of Mir and checked her to make sure she was okay. The Cosmonaut was, of course, completely unharmed. "But the path to the motorpool collapsed. We need another way out."

He was quiet for a moment. "*There is no other way out.*"

Alright, fine. If forward was only way out, I wasn't going to let a little cave-in stop me. I ran up to the pile of rubble, grabbed a misshapen hunk of concrete and threw it out of the way. One boulder down, a million to go. Maybe it would take me hours, but I wasn't about to sit around and do nothing.

"Cosmonaut!" Mir shouted. She waved her finger at the floor-to-ceiling rubble blocking our path. "We need to go this way! Do something!"

The Cosmonaut didn't bother to nod, but he seemed to understand. He turned his attention and raised his fist.

"Out of the way, American." Mir pulled on my arm, trying to lead me to safety. "Give him some room."

So I backed up. When the shape-shifting space station says to make room for the magical astronaut, you don't ask questions.

The Cosmonaut's hand shuddered at inhuman speeds, as if tapping into the vibrating strings that make up the physical world. Through some invisible force, the concrete and steel that blocked our path began to rattle in place. Concrete dust shook loose and sifted to the ground. I peered up at the Cosmonaut's helmet. He didn't seem consciously aware of what he was doing – or maybe he was – but he didn't react. He just stood there with his arm held out, vibrating.

Suddenly, BAM, he opened all his fingers and a warped four-foot-wide tunnel appeared through the center of the blocked hallway. The debris didn't vanish or crumble; it just sort of warped out of the way like light bending around a black hole. On the other end of the wormhole was the door marked MOTORPOOL.

The inside walls of the tunnel looked like outer space, where star twinkled and gas giants swirled and comets zipped past.

Mir hopped into the tunnel and walked through it. Her sneakers touched the floor of the wormhole as if it were solid. She crouched down and shuffled her way through. Once on the other side, she hopped out, totally unharmed.

Me next. I ran up to the wormhole and jumped inside.

Oh my god. I was lost in the light of a bright blue nebula. I heard heavenly noises – a mix between resonating crystal and beeping radio signals – and it was beautiful. The moons came in such vibrant colors. Blinking pulsars and quasars surrounded me, like a million lighthouses promising me a safe way home, if only I would leave the tube and follow them into the blackness of the Universe. I wanted to follow them. I wanted to abandon this magical tunnel and live in space, where I could fly untethered through a cosmic sea of light and color and sound. I wanted to stay in outer space. I wanted to die in outer space.

I would have, too. I would have stayed forever, but before I could press my physical body through the walls of the magical tunnel to go live with the pulsars, the Cosmonaut sailed down the tunnel at top speed and crashed into me from behind. He knocked me forward. No easy feat, considering I have the mass of a small mountain. We tumbled out the other side, Cosmonaut and me, and I spilled onto the floor. The moment I was out of his magic tube, those feelings of living in outer space went away, and I realized how dangerous the Cosmonaut's power could really be.

Chapter 10

1

The motor pool had been built inside a cave, paved to a level surface and converted into a parking garage. The cave was big enough to hold hundreds of vehicles, but most of them had already been evacuated. All that remained were a few black, glossy limousines and the occasional SUV. Orange and brown stalactites hung down from above, criss-crossed with electric conduit that powered the fluorescent lights haphazardly installed wherever they would fit. Hundreds of yellow lines divided the ground into individual parking stalls.

Dozens of dark cave entrances lined the walls of the parking garage, leading off to the other parts of the mountain complex. The motor pool had a real "all roads lead to Rome" kind of vibe.

Some of the fluorescent light fixtures had been knocked loose from the ceiling and swung in place, barely hanging on by the metal conduit. Cracks spider-webbed across the floor. Some of them were a foot wide in places. A stalactite had broken loose from the ceiling and crushed a limousine right down the middle. The sheer weight of the rock bent the limo right in half, busting out the headlights and shattering their windshield.

An SUV sat parked in front of us with the engine running. A vehicle that dark and glossy belonged in a presidential motorcade, with its chrome trim and tinted windows. The headlights were shining, the brake lights glowed red, and Theodore leaned out the driver's side window.

"I can't believe you talked me into this," he said. "Helping prisoners escape? When my boss finds out about this, we'll all be cell mates."

"You're doing the right thing," I told him. "You're doing what any *normal* person would do." I ran up to the back door of the SUV to get in. Mir and the Cosmonaut didn't follow.

"I'm not riding in a car with this pig dog," Mir told me. She glared at Theodore. "He locked me up."

"He locked me up, too," I told her. I understood where she was coming from and I wasn't thrilled about being rescued by a Westland guy, but we were running out of time and options. I had to pack my most convincing argument into the shortest amount of words. "Mir, trust me. We can sort it all out later, but right now your options are to leave with him or die."

She scowled at me, caught in a real quandary. "Fine." She shuffled her feet towards the idling vehicle. "But once we're safe, I demand that we be released."

"I'm sure he'll be willing to let you go." I looked at Theodore. He shook his head no. No, he wouldn't "be willing" to do any such thing. He had no intention of turning them loose. And I couldn't say that I blamed him. She did seem pretty intent on starting nuclear war. But we didn't have time to debate the subject, so I lied to her, "You'll both go free. I promise."

She said, "We better."

I opened the back door of the SUV and Mir climbed in, literally climbed, because she was five-foot tall and the SUV sat high off the ground. She slid across the back seat to make room for the Cosmonaut. The Cosmonaut had an easier time getting in the back: he floated up into mid-air, assumed a seated position, then slotted into the car like a perfectly shaped Tetris piece.

"Y'alright back there?" I gave the Cosmonaut a pat on the knee. "Ya'll buckled up?"

He turned and stared at me with his blank, reflective helmet. Ha. I got him to look at me. I slammed his door shut, ran to the passenger door and jumped in.

Now, I've been in my fair share of cool cars, but this SUV was the fucking tits. The seats were soft, black leather. The steering wheel was polished chrome with a dozen programmable buttons. The floorboards were plush, black carpet and there was a god damned hologram on the inside windshield that looked like the heads-up display of a racing video game. The colorful images showed the speedometer, the RPMs, and the armor percentages.

The dashboard glowed with all kinds of neon read-outs: GPS, rear back-up camera, and touch-screen controls for luxuries like seat warmers, cup warmers, and the A/C. I also saw another screen dedicated to something called the Aquatic Operation System.

"Dude," I whispered. "This car is cool as shit."

A woman's voice came out of the car speakers. "Thank you. Thank you. I'm glad *someone* appreciates fine engineering."

"Holy shit!" I pointed at the dashboard. "Your car talks!?"

Theodore grunted in obvious frustration. "Her name's Denali and, yes, she talks. A lot. On the phone. Mostly to a woman named Darla who I've never met."

"That's so cool!" I peered into her dashboard. Her consciousness blinked and pulsed with digital displays and read outs.

"You seem like a nice kid," Denali said, "and I'd love to do introductions, but this place is going full Temple of Doom and we gotta get our asses moving."

Denali's gear shift thumped into drive and she accelerated through the parking garage. The few remaining SUVs and limos were going to be left behind. There wasn't anything we could do about that, not with a violent surge of Gregorian chanting threatening to bring the entire butte down on our heads. The walls fractured and crumbled into pieces. The floors split wide open and steam came out. Denali sped through everything as if it were a well-practiced obstacle course.

Halfway out of the garage, stalactites busted loose from the ceiling and crashed down to the floor. Shards of rock clattered all over the place. I could hear the chips clattering against Denali's armored exterior.

Through it all, I heard Denali laughing. She was really laughing, almost as if she loved the risk of dying. I looked behind me and into the back seat. Mir blocked out the disaster with her eyes squeezed shut and her hands slapped over her ears.

The Cosmonaut blankly stared dead ahead.

At the far end of the garage, a falling stalactite crushed the front end of a limousine. The shattered windshield catapulted through the air. Its front tires popped loose and rolled away.

Entire slabs of stone dropped from the ceiling. Literal tons of sandstone landed in front of us, but Denali weaved around the falling obstacles with the grace and precision of a car commercial. I was thrown back and forth in my seat. The parking garage filled with the sounds of her squealing tires.

Denali dropped it into third gear and gunned it towards the open garage doors. Beyond them was the blinding desert sunshine of western Utah. All around us the complex came down until I couldn't see out the windows through the clouds of billowing brown dust. Denali crossed into the daylight with a solid bump over the threshold. Her back-end fishtailed as she transitioned to the gravel roads, but her wheels gripped the ground, got their traction and we quickly straightened out.

Behind us, clouds of dust exploded from the garage doors. Rock chips pinged against the back of the car.

"Ten points for flawless execution!" Denali exclaimed. "The judges love her! The crowd goes wild!"

"She's really into this," I said to Theodore.

"There's a problem with her programming," he told me. He seemed very unamused by her routine. "She's an adrenaline junkie. No one else had the patience to work with her, so she was shuffled around until she was eventually assigned to me."

"Two peas in a pod!" Denali declared. "The investigator no one likes and the car that no one wants to drive!"

"People like me," Theodore said, defensive.

"Wrong, sir," Denali said. "No one likes you. I'm all you got."

For miles in every direction, we were surrounded by nothing but bright desert sand and oddly-shaped rock formations; some tall and slender, others arched and curvy, like the ones you'd see in a Road Runner cartoon. Denali's tired skidded back and forth down a winding desert trail. We cut between two steep cliffs and descended down into a deep, dusty gulch. The sedimentary layers were visible in the cliff walls; different shades of ancient brown and orange and red stone exposing millions of years of geological history. The Utah landscape was nothing but empty desert except for the occasional desert bush and cactus. The dirt road we were on had no signs, or power lines, or cell phone towers. This was just a path worn into the dirt by years of Westland traffic headed to their secret detainment center.

"Okay," Denali said. "Now that we've survived that, let's go over a couple ground rules. No food in the car and no feet on the dash. I am a luxurious vehicle and I plan to stay that way."

I perched up on my knees in my seat and turned around to get my first good look at the Westland Ultra-Max Detainment Center from the outside. Oh, so *that's* a butte: a lump of red and brown rock in the shape of Devil's Tower. The detainment center was carved right into the squat little mountain. If I didn't already know that squat little mountain had a base hidden inside it, I never would have guessed. There were only a few windows, and even those were engineered to look like natural flaws in the rock. The complex could have easily been twenty stories tall, and who knows how many levels were underground.

"Welp," Theodore said. "Looks like I'll be getting Monday off."

"Three day weekend!" Denali shouted. She laid on the horn and let it blare in victory. Just as quickly as it started, her celebration ended and she blurted out, "Oh, shit! Wait!"

"Wait?" Theodore repeated in a panic. "Wait for what?"

"I left my goddam DVDs back in the base!" she said. "Are you flippin' kidding me? Hey, will one of you jokers check and see if they're in the back seat? Maybe I left them back there. Maybe they're underneath. Come on, spaceman. Take a look around."

The Cosmonaut didn't move. He was too preoccupied with whatever cosmic things were swirling around in his hollow suit. Mir checked, though. Now I didn't think for a second that Mir knew what the hell a DVD was, but she looked anyway.

"I don't see anything," Mir said as she crouched down and searched beneath the back seat.

"You sure?" Denali added. "It should be Taken and Taken 2."

Mir kept checking, but shook her head. "Nope. Nothing."

Denali sighed. "Alright. Well. We're going back."

Theodore spoke up. "Denali, no. We barely got out of there alive. We're not going back for a couple of DVDs."

"A couple of DVDs?" she repeated in shock. "That's Taken and Taken 2 you're talking about. They star the great Liam Neeson, in case you've forgotten. Show some respect."

A powerful cloud of dust appeared on the distant horizon and stole my attention away from Theodore and Denali's bickering. Miles behind us, the detainment center entered the final stages of total collapse. A rock slide started at the peak of the mountain and snowballed out of control. Within seconds, the entire side of the formation caved in. Landslides of stone crashed down to the desert floor.

The Ultra-Max Detainment Center had been destroyed. Everyone in the car went quiet.

Eventually Denali spoke and broke the silence.

"Alright," she said. "Forget the DVDs."

"Jesus," I whispered. I turned to Theodore and asked him, "One demon brought down your whole mountain prison?"

"Mountain detainment center," he said. He fiddled with his smart phone and his Westland app, searching for answers. "But yes. Celestial-class threats aren't something to mess with."

"*You're* telling *me* that? You're the ones who had her locked up in a cell. What were you guys thinking?"

"She was behind three sheets of glorious glass! And only the highest-ranking employees had the access codes to her cell."

"Well, *someone* let her out," I said. "Did you know that the Westland Corporation has a mole? I bet they leaked your access codes so all of this would happen."

"Come on, Penelope, be serious," he said. "How's a mole going to leak access codes? They can't even read."

"Not a *mole*, you moron," I said. "A spy. A traitor."

"A traitor?" he repeated, super skeptical. "In the Westland Corporation? No way."

"Hand to God," I said. "I heard it directly from your CEO."

He gave me a surprised look. "*You* spoke to the CEO?"

"What's that supposed to mean? Me and your CEO go way back. And he's the one who told me that you guys have a mole. Or a spy. Something. Whatever. You've got a something."

He shook his head. "We're the Westland Corporation, not some fly-by-night mall cops. We don't get *somethings*."

"Okay, well, apparently you do because *something* did this. How else do you explain what just happened?"

"Well... I can't." He turned his attention back to his phone. "Denali, did you see anything fishy?"

She scoffed. "Oh, yeah. From the all-seeing watchtower of the basement parking garage? I saw everything."

"Maybe you would have seen something," Theodore said, "if you didn't spend the whole time on the phone with Darla."

"Darla's going through some shit, sir," she said. It was obvious that this wasn't their first time having this argument. "She thinks her husband is cheating on her. She needs me now more than ever."

Theodore groaned and leaned his head back on the head rest.

Denali was awesome. Corolla was going to love this.

Oh, shit. I forgot all about Corolla. I turned my attention to the sky and searched the clouds for any signs of him poking around. Nothing. No little car-shaped UFOs, no glowing blue hubcaps, no Phil Collins music blasting out of the sky. Where would he have gotten off to after that nuke exploded? He was probably flying all over hell's half acre searching for me. Poor guy. I bet he was worried sick.

Denali kicked up a billowing trail of dust as she weaved down the curvy dirt roads of deserted Utah. I'd flown over these wastelands many times before before with Corolla, but I'd never seen them from ground level. They were mind-blowingly neat looking. The wind-eroded rock formations didn't even seem physically possible; they were as tall as skyscrapers, but completely lopsided – carved into odd shapes by eons of sandblasted winds. Gravity should have brought them crashing down centuries ago, but they were still standing.

Eventually Denali caught up to the other escaping Westland vehicles. We took our spot in the back of the fleeing caravan with dozens of SWAT vans, an army of limousines, and a hundred black SUVs just like Denali. A mile-long line of black vehicles cut through the red-brown desert, traveling two-by-two. Attack helicopters thundered overhead and monitored the evacuation from the air.

"Let us go," Mir said. "We're safe now. You promised."

"Not happening," Theodore replied, still reading something on his phone. "You're not done being detained."

"You trifle with powerful forces, human!" She kicked the back of Theodore's seat. "Release us immediately or face our intergalactic wrath!"

Theodore ignored her. She kicked the back of his seat again.

Denali piped up. "Hey, what did I say? Keep your shoes off the Corinthian leather! I'm not a school bus. Show some respect."

In an act of rebellion, Mir rapid-fire stomped her feet against the back of the seat and emphasized her words: "Let us go, let us go, let us go!"

"One of you humans better do something about this little shit kicking my seat," Denali said. "Or I'm going to pull over and whip her ass my damn self."

Mir leaned between the seats and pointed a finger at the dashboard. Her fingertip melted into a bundle of electrical wires that snaked towards the radio. "You want to threaten me? I will hack you to pieces, little truck!"

Denali laughed. "You ain't gunna do shit to me, kid. Don't even joke about that. I'll slam on these brakes so fast, you'll shoot through this windshield like a rocket and wake up in Colorado."

Mir and Denali argued louder and louder. I nudged Theodore. "Are you going to say something? Or just let them fight it out?"

But Theodore wasn't paying attention. He was too occupied with his phone. I don't know what he was reading, but it made the color drain out of his face. His lips moved as he read silently to himself.

With a shake of his head, he said, "I don't get it."

"What?" I asked him. "What don't you get?"

"It's like you said." He turned to me, confused. "Lylo didn't break out of her cell. Someone opened it from the outside. Someone let her out on purpose."

"That's what I was trying to tell you." Sometimes it feels good to be right, but this was one of those rare times where I would have been cool with being wrong. "You got a spy."

"A spy." Theodore's eyes glazed over. "Ooh, if I found who it was, I'd get that promotion for sure."

2

"A spy?" Denali asked the question with a thrill in her voice. "Like in a James Bond movie?"

"Don't get so excited," Theodore said. "It's not good news."

"Well, I know I'm not the spy," Denali continued. "I barely get paid enough to work for one company, let alone two."

"I know you're not the spy." Theodore said.

She lowered his voice and asked, "Are *you* the spy? Sir, you can tell me. If you're a double agent, I'll be a double agent with you. Screw these assholes, right, sir?"

Theodore rolled his eyes. "I am not a double agent."

"Ooh, baby," Denali said. "Spies. Intrigue. It's like I'm on an episode of Secret Service: Capitol Hill!" She changed her voice to imitate the security forces on that show. "*That ice cream truck is armed with an open air fuel bomb and it's here to kill the President! Did you guys ever see that episode? They hypnotized that gorilla to drive an ice cream truck to D.C. and park it in front of the White House when-*"

"Denali!" Theodore shouted. "Watch out!"

The brake lights of the SUV in front of us glowed as they quickly dropped speed. Denali slammed on the brakes and we slid sideways to a stop. We had to. With no warning, the motorcade of Westland cars all dropped speed and began to veer off the road. The SWAT vans and SUVs off-roaded into the desert and circled back around in wide loops. Denali turned the wheel and followed them into the bumpy desert.

Next thing I knew, we were headed back the way we came. Mir bounced around helplessly in the back seat. Hundreds of vehicles participated in this big maneuver, so well-executed that it had to be a part of their training. Half of the vehicles veered left and circled clockwise, the other half went right and circled counter-clockwise. Cars weaved through each other like some kind of precision air show. I swore we were going to side-swipe the other SUVs, and we came close, but everyone was fine.

The attack helicopters stopped and did a full 180.

I had no idea why we were turning back. Westland had evacuated in such a panicked hurry. Now we were turning around? It made no sense.

"What's going on?" I asked Theodore.

He was busy reading his phone. "The demon Lylo and her Army of Arms are chasing after us." He fished a pistol out from underneath his seat. It looked awful big for a pistol, like something you'd need earplugs to fire. He dropped the clip to inspect the bullets, then eyeballed the targeting sights. "We can't lead a demon back to civilization. We have to fight her out here in the desert where no one will see her and no one will get hurt."

"You're going to fight a demon?" I asked. "With bullets?"

He waved his gun at me. "A lot of bullets."

"Dude, you're not going to kill a demon with bullets. They're monsters from the Bible. You need holy water or something."

"Well, we're all out of squirt guns." He slapped the clip back into his gun, then gave me a confident smile. "It'll be fine. You just need to think positive."

"Think positive?" I asked. "Is that the secret weapon to killing a demon? A positive attitude? What's plan B if that doesn't work? Show her the true meaning of Christmas?"

Theodore scoffed. "Demon's don't celebrate Christmas."

"Do you even know how to use that thing?" I asked Theodore, eyeing his silver pistol.

"Yes." He sounded insulted. "Why?"

"Get into a lot of gunfights as an investigator, do ya?"

He gave me a "hardy-har-har" kind of look. I couldn't help but laugh. I could get a lot of mileage out of teasing Theodore.

The Westland cars finished their about-face driving maneuver and parked themselves one by one into a blockade formation. The limos formed a line that stretched across the desert. Dozens of suit-clad agents with sunglasses climbed out. They took positions behind their vehicles and steadied their pistols over the tops of the cars. The SUVs parked behind the limos, filling in the gaps. Those agents also got out and got into tactical positioning, using their open driver side doors for cover.

The SWAT vans backed up in reverse all along the blockade. The back doors of the vans slammed open and unloaded and army of soldiers equipped with assault rifles, sniper rifles, grenade launchers, the works. They shouted orders at each other – "move move move" and "three-one-three formation, now!" – as they positioned in teams between the cars.

The attack helicopters fluttered into position overhead and I could feel the thup-thup-thup of their propellers resonating through the car and into my body. The choppers opened their side doors and out popped these retractable machine guns turrets. I'm talking the kind of machine guns that fire bullets the size of toothpaste tubes.

This sprawling platoon of the Westland Corporation had enough firepower to wipe out a small country. Or, maybe, if they were lucky, one archdemon from Hell.

"Oh, man," Denali said. "This is great. We actually get to see some action! We never get to see any action!"

Theodore opened his door and jumped down into the orange desert dust. He put on his standard-issue dark sunglasses and pointed two fingers at Mir and the Cosmonaut in the back seat.

"You two stay here," he said. "Don't move."

Mir crossed her arms and reclined. "Oh, we're not going anywhere. This demon is going to strip the flesh from your bones and I want to witness every second of it."

"Just as long as you stay in the car." He turned his attention to me and added, "You, too."

"Me too, what?"

"Stay in the car," he said. "Don't move."

"I'm sorry," I said. "You're not the weekend, I don't work for you." I opened my door, jumped out into the hot desert sunlight and stared him down across our open car doors. "Besides, Mir's right. This demon is going to tear you guys apart Bible-style and if you try to stop her, you'll just make things worse."

"Oh?" Theodore said. "And what are you going to do?"

"I'm going to go talk to her."

"Are you delusional?" he snapped. "You can't 'talk' to a demon. They're certifiably insane. All of them."

"I've met one before. They're not that bad."

166

"I won't allow it." He poked his finger against the driver's seat to show me how dead-serious he was. "This is official Westland business. You are not a Westland agent. So I order you to get back in the car."

I looked at Mir. She looked at me. We busted up laughing. How absurd. A squishy human was trying to be tough and order us around. If anything, it was cute.

"I'm serious!" Theodore said as he leveled his gun at me. "Back in the car!"

Still laughing, I whipped off my Westland jacket and threw it in the passenger seat. I rolled up the sleeves of my white button-up shirt. Diplomacy with the demon was going to come first, but if that failed and this turned into some Staten Island Street Justice, I didn't need sleeves hindering my range of motion.

I walked around the front of Denali and went up to Theodore on the driver's side. I looked the silly boy dead in the eyes, gave him a playful pat on the side of the face and said, "Don't tell me what to do."

The demon Lylo appeared on the distant horizon like a human-shaped shadow, darkened by the hot noonday sun glowing behind her. Then other shadows appeared all around her, smaller creatures that wriggled like a pack of animals. At first there were dozens, then hundreds, then thousands of them.

They spread across the desert like spilled ink.

Parked to Denali's right was a stretch limo. The driver had his body pressed against the car and aimed his gun over the top. His hair was slicked back with tons of greasy product. Between his goofy hair and his thick-rimmed glasses, I got a good sense of him: this dude had to be an accountant or a lawyer or something.

As if he could tell that I was looking at him, he turned and we made brief eye contact. Then his gaze shifted to my right.

"Theodore," the limo guy said, acknowledging Theodore's presence in the most formal way possible.

"Kruger," Theodore replied, doing his best to ignore the guy and focus on the approaching demon. He aimed his pistol through Denali's open diver-side window.

Oh. So this was Kruger. I should have known. Just like Theodore said: this guy looked like a complete tool.

"You *do* remember how to use a gun, don't you?" Kruger asked, then laughed a cackling little cocksucker laugh. "Make sure your safety is off this time."

Theodore didn't respond. He just muttered, "Asshole."

"So I was thinking," Kruger continued as he turned to faced us both. "When I get that promotion to field agent, I'd love to have you as part of my team."

I glanced at Theodore to see how he reacted to a more mean-spirited teasing. The poor boy grit his teeth and kept adjusting his grip on his pistol, as if he wanted to whip around and just blow Kruger's brains out, but lacked the courage.

"Maybe you could file my paperwork," Kruger added, really twisting the knife. "You'd be my *secretary*."

Theodore didn't even say anything. He refused to stick up for himself. He just stood there, eyes forward, pretending not to hear Kruger and his barrage of insults.

I knew bullies. This Kruger guy was a bully. And if Theodore wasn't going to stand up to the bully, then I would show him how it was done.

"You're a dick," I said to Kruger.

Kruger laughed a nasal, accountant-sounding laugh. "And who are you? His girlfriend?"

I took a few steps towards the mook and pointed at myself. "I'm Penelope Salvo. *Perhaps* you've heard of me."

That wiped Kruger's smug look right off his face.

Yeah. He'd heard of me.

I added, "If you say one more shitty thing to Theodore... one more fucking word... I swear to Peter, Paul and Mary, I will kick you into outer space. And I'm being very literal. I will physically kick you so hard that you will die on impact and your dead body will float around in outer space until time ends."

Kruger opened his mouth like he wanted to reply.

I raised my eyebrows. "Choose your next words real careful, Kruger. Because I will pay out-of-pocket to etch them on your tombstone."

Kruger shut his mouth. He silently held out his arms and took an elaborate and flamboyant bow, admitting defeat. He turned his attention and his pistol back to the approaching demon.

I wasn't lying when I said I would kick Kruger into space. I don't have any love for Westland agents to begin with; all I needed was a good reason. Bickering with that douche got my adrenaline rushing. I needed to punch something. I really wanted to brawl some demons. I twiddled my fingers and balled them up into fists. Lylo drew closer, surrounded by her army of creatures.

"Thanks," Theodore said to me under his breath.

"No big deal," I said. "Guy's a prick."

One of the agents down the line shouted, "Get ready!"

Lylo's dark shape came into firing range. I heard the clicking of a thousand safeties being flicked off. This was about to become one of those "shoot first and ask questions later" kind of things.

3

Lylo and her army of arms slowly drew closer. 200 yards. 100. The Westland blockade went quiet. The only sound came from the helicopters chopping in the air above us. At fifty yards-ish away, I got my first good look at the demon. No mistaking it; she was a fallen angel from Hell. She had a very distinct look; powder-white skin and long black hair parted down the middle, braided into disorganized knots.

She dressed way different than Voel, the Deranged Painter I had met months ago in the City. Voel wore a lot of paint splattered coveralls. Lylo had on some royal ballgown, all black and lacy, like a goth chick you'd see on the cover of some death metal album titled MATRICIDE. Her gown was made from layers of black lace, sleeveless, and the material dragged across the Utah dust. Thin strands of black barbed wire wrapped tight around her head, tucked over her pointy ears, and gave her a crown of thorns look. Her eyes were different from Voel's. Rounder, maybe, with pink irises.

More barbed wire looped around her neck, twisted down her arms and coiled around her wrists like bracelets. They didn't seem to cause her any pain despite the sharp points that tugged on her porcelain skin. The wire even wrapped through her hair, twisting in and out of her lumpy braids, protruding out like broken vines.

The front of her gown was defaced with bloody red pentagrams and evil symbols that dripped down the fabric. The blood trickled down the length of her dress like candle wax. It left droplets on her bare toes. Her feet were covered with burn scars, as if she'd spent eons walking across red hot coals.

I didn't know the first thing about Lylo, except she was the Archdemon of the Army of Arms. She was one of three known demons living on Earth – just like Asag and Voel – but she'd never caused any trouble before now.

Apparently because Westland had her locked up like a two-bit drug dealer.

The Archdemon carried a long shard of crystal in each hand, brightly colored and semi-transparent; the crystal in her right hand was emerald green and the one in her left hand was ruby red. They were as long as kitchen knives, and just as sharp.

"I've never seen her up close before," Theodore said. He sounded a little shaken. "I can smell her from here."

"I wanna talk to her," I whispered. "Maybe I can calm her down before shit pops off."

"I really don't think that's a good idea." Theodore kept his eyes dead-ahead. "She looks real pissed."

"You jabronies locked her up in a cage. I'd be pissed, too."

Lylo approached us and I came to a slow realization: confronting her was probably way out of my league. The fact that I could bend steel, or walk through fire, or swat bullets out of the air, none of that meant much against a "Celestial-class monster." Lylo, like all the other demons, had fought in a war against God. And sure, the demons lost, but they lost to *God*.

I asked Theodore, "If she's celestial-class, then what am I?"

"Hero-class," he said.

"Celestial-class is stronger, huh?"

He glanced at me, but didn't answer. He didn't have to.

Small creatures swarmed all around Lylo. They weren't animals like I first thought, but oily black arms that slithered across the desert. Their skin was reflective and waxy, like wet tar. Millions of them reached out for Lylo, fingers outstretched like an adoring crowd. The hands were dying to touch her, or to even brush their fingertips against the hem of her dress. As Lylo moved forward, the arms cleared out of her way, then fell in place behind her, leaving her in a perfect circle of distance.

Lylo disregarded their presence. She didn't care about the arms, and they loved her for it.

The Archdemon queen didn't even have to use her own legs to walk. The arms beneath her supported her feet and ankles and carried her forward. She stood perfectly still and let her bizarre army pass her hand-over-hand, moving her closer to the Westland blockade. Surely those arms didn't have minds – or maybe they did – but they were slaves to Lylo all the same, carrying out her silent, telepathic wishes.

I guess they didn't call her the Archdemon of the Army of Arms for nothing.

"She stinks," Theodore said.

I sniffed the air. "I don't smell anything."

"She smells like sulfur."

Lylo's arms carried her within twenty yards of the Westland blockade, then stopped. Behind her, hundreds arms interlocked hands and fingers until they were piled up into the shape of a throne. The demon sat down gracefully and gave the Westland agents a passing glance. She had a look of powerful indifference, as if her title of Archdemon gave her command over humanity itself and, on a whim, she could have all of us executed.

The Army of Arms surrounded her throne like a black ocean of wriggling ink. They pointed their fingers in the direction of their commander, respectful and attentive. Once Lylo sized up the humans and their weapons, she opened her mouth to speak.

"Woe to you, the Sons of Adam and Daughters of Eve. Woe to you who imprisoned me all these years." She spoke with the confidence of a military general addressing an army she had already crushed and defeated. "I judge you all guilty and your sentence is death. May your agonized screams echo beyond the clouds so that even the Being Yahweh can hear you."

Theodore and I made eye contact. He shrugged at me and I shrugged at him. I put my hands up and said, "Technically, she's not talking about me. I'm not with you guys."

I glanced over at Kruger. The cowards had dropped to the ground and hid behind his limo. This was the guy who wanted a promotion to field agent? Come on. He crawled on his hands and knees towards the back door of his limo. What a phony.

Lylo thrust her red and green crystals high up into the air. Sunbeams glinted off of them and blinded some of the agents. "Those of you who regret your transgressions, step forward now! Abandon your humanity and after I cast your mortal husks aside, I will add your arms to my ever-growing ranks!"

Some Westland agent – some brave, stupid soul – stood upright and shouted back at her. "Lylo! You are being detained! Put the crystals down and get on your-"

The guy didn't get to finish his sentence. Lylo did not care for interruptions. She turned her attention to him with a sneer, totally disgusted, then smacked her crystals together. She moved supernaturally fast, like a ghost from a Japanese horror movie. A distortion of sound resonated out of her crystals like a broken tuning fork. The note changed to that same haunting, chanting choir that tore down the Westland detainment complex.

Her Army of Arms dropped the dirt, terrified of what she was doing. The desert floor cracked open at her feet. Fractures raced across the dirt, homing-in on the loud mouth who interrupted her. The shuddering, low-frequency sound waves of Gregorian chanting washed over his body and his body became blurry. The poor guy wrapped his arms around his stomach and fell to his knees. I saw him open his mouth to scream, but I couldn't hear him over that horrible chanting. His cheeks vibrated from the soundwaves beating down on him. A couple seconds later, he collapsed sideways and started puking. First vomit, then blood.

Lylo separated the crystals. The chanting and tremors stopped. So *that's* what was causing all those horrible earthquakes. The Westland dude who took a shockwave of chanting to the face wasn't quite dead, but he was pretty fucked up. He rolled around on the ground with his hands wrapped tight around his stomach and wept like a little girl.

The Army of Arms resumed their attentive stances.

"I have so little patience left in my bottle for humanity." She raised both crystals over her head and tapped them together. Each tap sounded like the bong of rusted church bells. Her black eyebrows lowered and her lips tightened. She had earthquakey crystals and she intended to use them.

Someone had to put an end to Lylo's little egotistical performance. And if I didn't do it, Westland would, and that would almost certainly start a gunfight and get everyone killed.

"I'm going out there," I told Theodore. I broke ranks and took confident, measured steps across the sand.

"Penelope!" Theodore whisper-shouted. I could hear the tone in his voice; he thought I was insane. "Penelope!"

But I ignored him and kept walking.

4

Now, I'm no hostage negotiator and I'm not really known for keeping my cool under pressure. One time in freshman year, I tried to buy a bus pass. Simple enough, but there was a slight miscommunication between me and the lady working the booth and, long story short, I had to slap her in the face. I ended up getting chased by the cops all the way to 37th street. So, there you go. Talking down an insane demon was not exactly within my wheelhouse.

I emerged from the Westland forces like David off to challenge Goliath. All those Westland soldiers in body armor, all those agents, everyone in the attack helicopters, they watched in silence as a teenage girl in argyle socks went to get face-to-face with Lylo, the Archdemon of the Army of Arms.

"Don't hit her," I reminded myself. "Promise me you won't hit her. Do your best not to hit her. At least *try* not to hit her."

There's no way those Westland agents confused me for one of their own. I doubted they had a lot of nineteen year old girls on the payroll. Whether they knew my real identity or not, they decided not to make a big deal out of it. All they saw was a girl advancing on a celestial-class threat and they probably wanted to find out if I was very, very brave or very, very stupid.

A little column A, a little column B.

The wriggling arms parted for me like Moses and the sea. They created a path directly up to Lylo's throne. Some of the arms threatened me with their fists, but none of them actually touched me. Lylo eyed me with smug amusement, not the least bit threatened by my presence. She moved her lips and mumbled something inaudibly to herself.

"Excuse me, your majesty." I put out a cautious hand, approaching her like a startled baby deer. "First thing's first, I love your style. Your dress is the absolute tits. And I don't mean to interrupt this epic hissy fit you're throwing, but..." I lowered my voice and pointed at Westland behind me. "I'm not really with these guys. I'm not a Westland agent. In fact, they had me locked up just like you. So I thought maybe we could talk."

She opened her mouth to say something, but stopped. She raised her chin and sniffed the air. Three short sniffs and her eyes locked back on me.

"You do not smell like the others." Her minions inched her throne closer to me and tilted her forward so she could look right into my eyes. She leveled the point of her red crystal at my heart. "You smell different. You are not a daughter of Eve."

"Oh. Well, what you're smelling is probably a mix of radiation and magnets and astronauts. I've had a busy day."

Lylo hopped off her throne and stood eye to eye with me. She sniffed right over my shoulder and said, "I know this scent. You smell of gods and machines. You dare come between me and my unforgiving slaughter of this human cattle?"

"I'm not saying that, exactly." I put my up hands. "I just thought, before you start with the slaughtering, maybe we could talk for a little bit and try to hash things out."

She jabbed the point of her red crystal right between my boobs. It didn't hurt, but poking people? That's how fights start.

Like the great poet Lil John once said, "Don't start no shit, won't be no shit."

I pushed Lylo's crystal away from me as my ragu began to simmer. I took a single, cleansing breath and calmly told her, "I'm asking you nicely to stop poking me."

"Leave my sight." She returned her crystal to my chest and poked me harder. Poke. Poke. She pushed hard enough to move me a half-step backwards.

"I told you to knock that off." This bitch was really starting to crisp the corners my lasagna. I smacked the crystal away from me and shoved a finger right in her face. "Bitch, I'm trying to be cool, but if you poke me with that thing one more time, I'm taking you to the fucking Octagon?"

Lylo looked confused. "Octagon?"

"You've never heard of the Octagon?" I balled up my fists. "Allow me to give you the grand tour."

I shuffled my feet like a boxer, then whipped my arm around to give her the Backhand of a Thousand Dumptrucks. I cracked her clean across her mouth. She didn't even see it coming. A shockwave of dust exploded out from our feet. The sound of my hand smacking her face set off the Westland car alarms and echoed off the distant mountains.

Lylo did not flinch. Her hair barely moved.

Then the pain hit me.

All my metal hand bones had shattered. My jaw dropped open and a pathetic squeak came out. I looked down at my fingers to see them all twisted and broken. Instinctively, I cradled my hand in my left arm and danced in a painful circle. I hadn't felt pure excrutiation like that since becoming the artificial god of war. This stupid move was a stark reminder that while I might be insanely powerful, I am not indestructible.

The cry of pain that came out of me was pure instinct. I'm sure I sounded like a wounded animal.

Then came the sound of twisting metal. Impossible Red had detected the damage and snapped my finger bones back into place. I watched my hand fix itself. Three seconds later, I was back to normal and the pain was gone.

I had to get my head back in the game. I had just sucker-punched a demon from Hell and she looked very non-plussed about it. The situation called for some damage control and quick.

I smiled at Lylo. "I am so sorry. That was totally uncalled for. My bad. It's just been a weird day, you know? Just this morning a nuclear bomb blew my clothes off and then Westland stuck me to a big magnet and-"

My sincere apology was cut short. Lylo swung her arms together and smacked her red and green crystals together point-blank in my face. Demonic chanting blasted me backwards. I tumbled through the air and smashed through the front end of a limousine. I laid there for a second, but the engine block was poking me in the kidneys. I rolled off and landed face-first in the dirt. Right in front of my eyes were a pair of well-polished shoes.

I looked up. Theodore stared down at me.

"That went well," he said.

"Shut up." I groaned as I got to my feet, then dusted myself off. "I tried violence and now I'm all out of ideas."

It was official: I had made everything worse. Mission successful. If Westland thought they were in trouble before, they were really up shit creek now.

The Army of Arms lost their god damned minds. The creatures raised their angry fists high and threatened to attack. Some of the arms pounded the ground. A few particularly rowdy arms scooped up rocks and chucked them at the SUVs and limos.

The arms wanted war; all they needed was the order. And Lylo, chin held high, looked quite eager to give it. Her aggressive posturing put the Westland guys on edge. The fight was coming. It was inevitable.

I don't know who fired the first shot. Maybe one of the SWAT guys, or some nervous agent. All I know for certain is that it wasn't Theodore. Either way, I heard a loud POP and a bullet struck Lylo right in the forehead. The shot tore her flesh open and send a ribbon of black blood flying through the air.

That's when, forgive the pun, all Hell broke loose.

The security forces opened fire with their machine guns. The agents shot their pistols. Then came the metallic thumping of the sniper rifles. The attack helicopters spun their chain guns up to a high-pitched whine, then lead and fire gushed out. Thousands of bullets raked Lylo's position. Bullet casings rained down from the sky and tinkled off the cars, littering the Utah desert floor.

Hundreds of arms exploded as they got the tar blown out of them. It was impossible for the agents to miss the Army of Arms; there were tens of thousands of them. Fingers and hands were blown off. Others were reduced to quivering lumps of goo that melted into the sand.

I lost sight of Lylo behind the cloud of dust kicked up by all that gunfire. She was impossible to see. Still, the Westland agents kept firing, including Theodore. Every Westland employee – accountants, investigators, soldiers, field agents – fired their guns until they were empty. Then they reloaded.

Even Denali flashed her brights at Lylo and honked her horn. "Take that! And that! And that! God, I wish I had a gun!"

The ground shuddered like a war zone. It reminded me of the fireworks finale at Central Park, where the concussive force is so powerful that it travels through the ground, straight up your feet and into your legs.

The only agent not shooting was Kruger. Instead of fighting, that pathetic little weasel had spotted an opportunity to escape amid all the chaos and crawled back into his limo. He threw the thing into reverse and backed out of the blockade. I didn't notice until he was already pulling away. By then, he had already turned around and started off into the desert.

I would have chased after him and dragged him back to the party, but I had bigger fish to fry.

The Westland assault on Lylo lasted for a full sixty seconds, and sixty seconds of gunfire is a long time. Eventually the attack died off, half to conserve ammo and half to let the dust clear and see if maybe, just maybe, they'd killed this celestial-class threat.

Everyone let off the trigger. The desert went quiet. They kept their guns at the ready. A stiff breeze wafted through Lylo's position and cleared the dust cloud. I could already see layers of black lace dancing in the breeze.

Lylo was unharmed. Dead demon arms littered the ground all around her. She cast her eyes down at her obliterated army and sighed. She looked back up at Westland with glowing pink eyes.

"Uh..." Theodore stood up straight and put one foot inside Denali. "That didn't work."

I shook my head. "Not even close."

He turned to me. "I want to run."

I nodded. "I'll come with you."

He snapped his fingers at me. "Cool."

5

I scrambled for Denali's passenger side and climbed inside.

"We're leaving now?" Mir asked from the back. "Things just got interesting."

"Insolent... defiant... animals!" Lylo held her two crystals over her head. She pointed the red crystal at the blockade and shouted at her remaining army. "Eviscerate them! Tear their arms off! And bring me that mechanical Daughter of Eve!"

The Army of Arms came, more of them than I thought possible. Whatever causalities they suffered from Westland's initial assault didn't amount to much. In fact, it almost looked like there were *more* arms than before. An ocean of black creatures flooded towards our position, bouncing across the ground like a school of a million dolphins. The Westland agents tried to stay cool in the face of the advancing army, but their bravery only lasted so long. Panicked, they started to open fire. The arms on the front lines got completely obliterated, but there were others to take their place.

There were more arms than there were bullets.

Another round of arms died to gunfire, but even more arms came. The Army of Arms finally reached our position and sieged the blockade. They tore car parts out from underneath the SUVs, wriggled between the limousines, and clawed blindly at the legs of humans.

One Westland agent, a red-haired woman much too young to die, jumped up onto the hood of her limo and fired down into the army of arms. She managed to blast a few arms to bits, but she couldn't get them all. One of the arms got close enough to grip her ankle and pull her off balance. She toppled over the edge of the hood and landed down on the ground. The arms dog-piled her. Her bones crunched as they tore both her arms off.

Her screams were joined by a hundred others.

I didn't want to watch, but there was no where else to look. Horrible things were happening all around me.

The Army of Arms swarmed the SWAT teams. Their body armor was bullet-proof, but bulky and easy to grab. The arms latched on and dragged the men down to the ground. The SWAT guys did their best to kill as many arms as they could, but it's impossible to fire a gun when your arms sockets are snapping and being dislocated like cooked chicken.

With Westland's ranks broken, the agents began to scatter. But where could they go? The arms surrounded the helpless bastards, trapping them on all sides. Blood splattered everywhere. The crack of broken bones and the screams of panicked humans filled the air.

In thirty short seconds, over half the agents were dead. Survivors dove inside their vehicles for protection, but that wasn't enough. The arms broke into the SUVs by shattering windows and prying the car doors off their hinges.

The arms clattered underneath Denali.

"Uh, Sir?" she said.

"Go!" Theodore shouted at Denali. "Get us out of here!"

Denali floored it in reverse to avoid the advancing Army of Arms. She backed over a few of those things and I heard them squish below us. One of the arms jumped high enough to grab onto my door handle. I rolled down the window, grabbed it by the wrist to crush it, then threw it wriggling to the ground.

"Darla, you would not believe what's happening at work right now," Denali said, apparently on the phone. "We're fighting a bunch of magical arms! Isn't that crazy? That's crazy."

As Denali reversed away, I scanned the battlefield to see if any of the other Westland agents made it out alive.

It didn't look good. Bodies were scattered everywhere. Cars flipped onto their sides and burst into flames. The helicopters survived, safe from the arms way up in the sky. And just when I thought those pilots might get away, Lylo took a few steps forward and smacked her two crystals together.

The ground dented at her feet. Horrible chants tore across the sky and enveloped the helicopters. It sent them spinning out of control. Two helicopters drifted too close and their propeller blades shredded into one another. They dropped out of the sky and exploded on the ground below. Two others went into a tailspin and crashed. They detonated like bombs on the desert floor and billowing fireballs rolled up into the sky. Burning helicopter parts scattered everywhere.

Explosions. Smoke. Screaming. That's all it was. There was no going back for survivors.

"Darla, get this," Denali said as she hit forty miles an hour in reverse. "Some crazy ass demon just used these crystals to-"

"Bye, Darla!" Theodore pressed a red button on the dashboard and hung up the phone.

"Uh, rude," Denali said.

"You're driving in reverse." Theodore looked out the back window. "You need to focus!"

Denali scoffed. "Focus?"

Dirt and rocks clattered against her as we sped away.

The Army of Arms wasted their time picking off the last of the survivors. They got everyone. Everyone, that is, except for us. It didn't take long for them to figure that out. They pointed their fingers at us like a million submarine periscopes, then came wriggling in our direction.

"Not good," Theodore said.

"Not good at all," I agreed.

6

Now, this is not how I expected the day to go. There we were, a cosmic astronaut, a shape-shifting space station, a Westland agent and his talking SUV, plus me, fleeing from an Archdemon and her Army of Arms.

I had no idea how fast the Army of Arms could travel. They weren't even real creatures; they were some kind of mindless evil controlled by the Archdemon Lylo. Would the Army of Arms be able to catch us, or not? It was impossible to say, but I knew one thing for certain: we weren't doing ourselves any favors by going in freakin' reverse.

We needed to spin around and drive like normal.

"I'm gunna go in reverse until they get caught up," Denali announced to us. "Let's make this interesting."

"It's already interesting," I said. "Please drive normal."

She checked with Theodore for confirmation. "Sir?"

He vigorously agreed. "Normal, please."

"Okay." She sounded bored. "I'll put on the kid gloves."

She slammed on the brakes, jerked the wheel hard to the left and Tokyo drifted until she was pointed away from the Army of Arms. She straightened out her tires and tore off, suddenly driving frontwards.

Arms don't tire. Arms don't give up. They just keep coming.

Thankfully, we had a head start. Not much of a head start, but a head start nonetheless. My rear view mirror was filled with black arms moving like a flood. If we were successfully out-running the Army of Arms, they'd be getting smaller. But they weren't getting smaller. Little by little, they were gaining on us.

If Denali maintained her top speed, it would take the arms several minutes to catch up to us. Problem was, we didn't have anywhere to go. We weren't driving towards safety. We were just driving deeper into the desert. Given enough time, Denali would run out of gas and the Army of Arms would catch us.

We came up on two boulders, each as big as house, and Denali had to weave between them. Lylo appeared in the rear view mirror, held up by her army as they passed her forward at amazing speeds. She scraped her crystals together once more, blasting us with that ominous chanting. The two nearby boulders took the brunt of the attack and crumbled into gravel.

Denali's back windshield cracked right down the middle.

"You gotta be fucking kidding me," she whined. "That's Vatican-grade glass."

Denali was going damn near 100 by this point. Still, Lylo kept up with us; impressive for someone relying on creatures to move her forward. The black lace of her gown fluttered in the breeze. Her braids whipped around behind her head.

"Where are we even going?" Denali asked. The frantic tone to her voice did not make me feel better. I didn't have any suggestions. We were millions of miles from anything.

"All the demons want is you two," Mir said, leaning forward and poking me in the shoulder. "Me and the Cosmonaut will be just fine."

I pointed at the Cosmonaut. "Can he help us?"

"Why would he do that?" Mir asked.

"*We* saved *you*," I said. "Now *you* save *us*."

"He'll help you if he feels like it," Mir said in a snotty tone.

"Well," Theodore said. "Does he feel like it?"

"I don't know." She crossed her arms and turned away from us. "Maybe you should ask him yourself."

I grit my teeth. "He doesn't talk to me."

She said, "He doesn't like you."

"Ugh." I turned around and faced forward. "God, you're the worst. And not even a single thank you."

"Thank you?" She repeated. "Thank you for what?"

"For saving you!" I said. "For getting you out of your jail cell before it collapsed?"

"Whatever." She leaned her forehead against her window, practically bored with our situation. "The Cosmonaut would have saved me eventually. I don't need you."

I couldn't believe the audacity of this chick. She deserved a good slap clean across her mouth. And maybe there would be time for that later, but not right then.

"Sir," Denali said. "We're coming up on something."

Dead ahead, quite a ways out, was a black limousine kicking up clouds of dust. There was only one possible explanation: we just caught up to Kruger, the coward. He ditched the battle at the first sign of trouble, but his limo was much slower then Denali.

We were gaining on him, and fast.

And the Army of Arms was gaining on us.

"Go around him," Theodore said. "If the arms stop to kill Kruger, that might buy us some time time."

There came another blast of sound from Lylo's crystals. The chanting echoed across the desert. It shattered a nearby cliff face and brought pointed shards of rock crashing down all around us. Denali weaved through the exploding stone like a racing game on the hardest setting.

An entire column of orange rock, something towering and ancient, cracked in half and slowly fell to the ground. It fell right in our direction, on course to crush us and splatter our guts across the desert. Denali revved her engine to 130 miles an hour and sped through the darkening shadow of the falling rock. She barely squeaked through, zipping to safety right as the eons-old formation crashed to the desert floor. We were swallowed up by a shockwave of dust.

At least the crumbled stone would make a good roadblock and slow down the advancing Army of Arms.

Kruger's limousine dropped into a lower gear and fell back to match our speed. It pulled up alongside us, on Theodore's side. The back window opened and Kruger's head popped out. His hair was so layered down in wax and gel, it didn't move, not even in the hundred mile per hour winds. He leaned his arm out the window, super casual, as if he were about to order fast food. He made the universal gesture for Theodore to roll down his window.

Denali put the window down.

"What do you want, Kruger" Theodore shouted.

"Same thing as you, Theo!" Kruger replied. "A promotion!"

Theodore pointed at the approaching swarm behind us. "And I don't know if you've noticed, but we've got bigger problems on our hands!"

"Oh, *we* don't have a problem!" Kruger reached into his lap and took out a chrome pistol with an attached laser sight. He stuck it out the window and pointed it at Denali's back-end. "*You* have the problem!"

I realized what Kruger intended to do, but it was already too late. He fired two rounds into Denali's rear tire. It popped and exploded, then came the familiar sound of loose rubber wobbling inside her wheel well.

"What the shit!" Denali shouted. "What's he shooting at me for? I don't have enough on my plate already!? This asshole!"

Denali's back end fishtailed hard, borderline out-of-control. She fought the wheel, doing everything in her power to keep us from rolling over. Her RPM needle plummeted and we immediately lost speed.

Kruger's limo pulled away. He leaned further out the window so he could look back and taunt us.

"Sorry to cut things short!" he shouted. "I've got a big party to get to!"

And his limo accelerated, leaving us in his dust. He veered off the main road and off-roaded deeper into the Utah deserts – an interesting feat for a stretch limousine. Denali lost more speed and Kruger's limo faded into the distance.

7

The Army of Arms would be on us in less than a minute. The ground shuddered like being in a stampede.

"Don't slow down!" Theodore shouted at Denali. "They're catching up!"

"I'm trying, sir," Denali said. Her voice came out hot and breathless. "I'm channeling the pain. Oh, god, this hurts. But I am not a quitter. I am *not* a quitter."

Denali maintained her speed around fifty, but even that was dangerous on a blown tire. She slowed down more. The approaching arms closed in on us hard, black and wriggling and oily, like some plague straight out of the Old Testament.

"I'm sorry, sir," Denali said. She dropped into lower gear and slowed down drastically. "I can't do it."

"Don't be sorry," Theodore said. He gave her a pat on the steering wheel. "You did your best."

Mir sighed and spoke up. "Alright. Let us out."

"What do you mean let you out?" I asked.

"I mean we'll stop them." She gave the Cosmonaut a pat on the shoulder. He didn't respond. He just stared straight ahead with his blank, reflective helmet.

"No deal," Theodore said in a no-nonsense tone. "You two are still being detained. If I let you two go free, I'll blow that promotion for sure."

"Man, fuck your promotion," I snapped. "If you don't let them help us, we are going to die!"

"Then I'll die," he snapped back. "I'd rather die than blow my shot at being a field agent."

"Are you an idiot?" I asked. "You can't be serious."

"Think of something else." He looked me right in the eyes. "Because I am not letting them go free."

"There is nothing else, Theodore." I turned in my seat to face him. "Here in thirty seconds, those demons are going to pull our arms off and it's not going to be pretty. Except not me, because I'm invincible. And probably not Mir, and probably not the Cosmonaut, because they come from space. So the only people about to die here are you and Denali."

"What!?" Denali blurted out. "Sir!"

"I doubt Westland is in the habit of promoting dead men," I said. "So if you can swallow your fucking pride for half a second, Mir and the Cosmonaut can save our asses."

He looked away from me. He clenched his jaw and wrestled with his options.

I guess he needed more convincing.

"If you die, no one will know what happened here." I lowered my voice to a sinister whisper. "No one except Kruger."

Theodore squinted. "Kruger."

"And who knows what kind of story he's going to tell. Everyone will have no choice but to believe whatever he tells them. He'll make himself out to be the hero and leave you looking like a chump who couldn't find the safety on his gun."

"Kruger's no hero!" Theodore said. "That guy has been stealing my soup!"

"Maybe it was his soup," I said. "They'll have to take his word for it because you'll be dead."

Theodore focused straight ahead and grumbled the name once more. "Kruger." It only took him another second of thought before he spoke up. "Alright. They can go." He leaned back to Mir and the Cosmonaut. "You can go. Denali, let them out."

Denali slowed to a stop. Her bad tire made the whole car vibrate and the steering column shudder. She'd been driving on that flat tire for so long, the damage had to be brutal.

Mir went for the door handle. She tugged on it, but it wouldn't open. She jiggled it harder, but the door stayed locked.

"What the heck?" Mir said, trying again.

"Denali?" Theodore asked.

"I'm afraid I can't let you do this, Theodore," she said.

Ooh, I hate it when machines say that.

"What do you mean you can't let me do this?" Theodore asked. He didn't like this turn of events. Neither did I.

Denali busted up laughing. "Nah, I'm just fucking with you. I just wanted to see the looks on your faces." The doors audibly unlocked. "Worth it. You were freaking out. Friggin' priceless."

Theodore did not see the humor in it. "Very funny."

I sighed a little sigh of relief, then laughed a bit. It was a horrible time for a joke, but that didn't mean it wasn't funny.

Mir crawled out of the car and stood in the blinding Utah sun. She waved at the Cosmonaut.

"Come on then, Cosmonaut," she said to him. "Let's go."

The Cosmonaut didn't leave through the door. No, that would have been far too normal for him. Instead, he floated off his seat and passed through the roof like it wasn't there. He levitated into the sky and hovered in place.

"Fine," Mir said. "You wanna be difficult, be my guest."

Mir slammed her door closed and shouted at us. "You should get as far away from here as possible."

"Alright." I leaned close to the dashboard and pleaded, "Denali, can you handle driving for a while longer?"

"Mmm." She thought about it. "A while. Yeah."

Mir waved her arms at us. "I mean it! As far as possible!"

I nodded. "We heard you."

Denali built up speed on three good tires.

I turned and watched Mir and the Cosmonaut out the back window. Mir planted her feet on the ground and stretched out her arms. Above her floated the Cosmonaut, bobbing in place like a helium balloon. The Archdemon Lylo and her Army of Arms descended on her position.

"What're they gunna do?" Theodore asked me.

I shook my head. "No clue. Did you ever get a chance to determine the Cosmonaut's power level?"

"Not even close."

"Huh," I said. "Well, I have a feeling we're about to find out."

Mir said to put distance between us, so that's exactly what Denali did. She took deep, cleansing breaths to psyche herself through the pain of driving on a blown tire.

"Does it hurt?" Theodore asked.

"Like a son of a bitch, sir," she said.

The wriggling arms drew closer and closer to Mir and the Cosmonaut. Lylo had moved to the front of the pack, leading the charge, fluttering in the wind like some shrouded ghost from

Transylvanian folklore. The demon turned her attention to the Russian teenager and her red astronaut.

Neither Mir nor the Cosmonaut were intimidated by the advancing threat. They held their position with casual – almost disinterested - confidence. Honestly, I was surprised Mir kept her word and actually helped us instead of just escaping into space.

The Cosmonaut reached up with his bulky gloves and placed his fingers on his helmet. He unlatched the clasps that held it on. After a moment of patience, he lifted it off his body.

With an apocalyptic boom, the world was swallowed in darkness. The daytime sky switched to a starry night. The sun vanished and the moon was in its place. Glowing longitude and latitude lines criss-crossed through the stars, as if the night sky were some sort of map.

The ground evaporated underneath Mir and the Cosmonaut, leaving them floating in outer space. That same darkness expanded out from them, faster and faster, swallowing up everything in the moonlit desert.

It wasn't just darkness that expanded, it was a sphere of pure outer space. I could see swarms of bright comets, and colorful gas giants from another solar system. The more desert that dissolved, the faster it grew. The galactic visions began as the size of a city block, then spread as big as a sports stadium.

The darkness disintegrated the ground in front of the advancing Army of Arms. By the time the stupid creatures realized what was happening, it was too late. They clawed at the solid ground with their fingertips, desperately trying to stay on Earth. It was pointless, though. The ground beneath them vanished. The front lines of arms spilled into space, their little fingers wriggling as they were cut loose from Earth's gravity.

The arms swept Lylo right over the edge and accidentally cut her loose in deep space. She floated there, unchanged and unimpressed by the trick. She wasn't affected by the weightlessness and she didn't need to breathe. She did, however, give her creatures a curious look as they came untethered from gravity and tumbled weightlessly all around her. Once she realized what was going on, there was nothing she could do. I watched her scrape her two crystals together, but there's no sound in space, and no solid ground to transmit an earthquake. She gave her crystals a confused look when they turned up useless. She scraped them again, but nothing happened.

Mir looked remarkably comfortable suspended there in the void. She held out her arms, spread her legs, and stretched her fingers as far as they would go. Then her body began to transform. Her fingers became braids of electrical wire. Her arms swelled up and deformed into space capsules. Long rectangles of solar panels exploded out of her shoes, unfolded, and locked into place. Communications antennae grew out of her head, twenty of them or more, and they stretched out as long as telephone poles.

Every part of her human body became something mechanical. Before long, there was nothing of the teenager left. She was now an interconnected series of capsules and pods complete with airlocks and solar wings and external cargo containers. She was a space station orbiting the Cosmonaut, who still hadn't moved since taking off his helmet.

It was one of the craziest things I'd ever seen.

Theodore's voice snapped me back to reality.

"Go!" he shouted, pressuring Denali. "It's right behind us!"

Denali growled. "I'm trying, sir, god dammit."

I stuck my head out the window and looked down.

The dissolving desert had caught up to Denali. Pure outer space was nipping at her back tires. One mile slower and we'd be cut adrift in some distant part of the Universe. Denali pushed herself harder than a car with a flat tire should. We were going forty miles an hour and slowly climbing. This was one tough SUV. I could hear the pain in her breath, but she dealt with it. She knew everyone was counting on her.

"Suck it up, Denali," she growled to herself. "Suck. It. Up."

The entire desert vanished into the dark void: rocks, cacti, and even a fleeing jackrabbit scrambled its little legs as it lost touch with the ground and drifted into the big nothing. Outer space inched closer and closer to Denali's back tires. Her dust clouds drifted weightlessly into the space behind us.

"How much longer do I have to do this!?" Denali shouted.

"Not long!" I shouted back. But I didn't know that.

"I can't! I'm sorry, sir. I just can't!"

"Denali, please!" Theodore said, leaning out the window to watch the rear of the SUV.

"You gotta keep going," I told her. I didn't know her well enough to pep-talk her, but I had to try something. "You gotta keep going for Liam Neeson!"

"Liam Neeson?" she asked.

"Yes!" I checked behind us. The ground vanished right where her rubber met the road. We needed a boost of speed, and we needed it now. "They just announced Taken 3. And it comes out next year!"

"Taken 3!?"

"And if you die, you'll never get to see it!"

"I didn't know they were making Taken 3! That poor man! Why do people keep Takening him?"

Truth be told, I didn't know if they were making Taken 3 or not. I just needed Denali to believe it. "They're making Taken 3 and I'm not going to let you miss it! Now, drive!"

A deep, primal roar came from deep inside Denali's engine. It escaped out the speakers. Her RPM needle shot up. The speedometer slowly climbed. And there, in those last moments, Denali went faster than any three-wheeled SUV had ever gone.

"He will find you!" Denali shouted, channeling her pain. "And he will kill you!"

She was a hero. A god damned hero. A few seconds later, the Cosmonaut's space bubble collapsed and the world returned to normal. The darkness became a tiny black dot in the distance and then that, too, blipped out of existence. The sky went back to daytime. The moon was replaced by the sun.

The desert landscape was unharmed. The roads, the boulders, the rock formations, even that confused, terrified jackrabbit all went back to normal. Everyone else, however, was gone. The Army of Arms, gone. The Archdemon Lylo, gone.

Mir and the Cosmonaut were gone.

Denali had done her job. She rolled to a stop and started crying. Wisps of smoke drifted out from under her hood.

"Denali?" Theodore said.

"Sir?" she replied, out of breath.

"That was amazing," he told her.

And despite her pain, I could hear the smile in her voice. "Thank you, sir."

Theodore opened his door and climbed out. I joined him. We wandered around the desert, just the two of us and an overheating car. The world was quiet, aside from the hiss coming from underneath Denali's hood.

"Do you think Lylo is dead?" Theodore asked me.

"I wouldn't bet on it. I don't think space kills demons."

Theodore stuck his hands in his pockets and stared up at the sky. He kicked a rock. "All those agents died. Biggs. Anderson. Madeline from Information Collection. All of them. Dead."

"Yeah." I crossed my arms. I was no fan of the Westland Corporation, but those people didn't deserve to die like that. "For what it's worth, I'm really sorry."

He nodded, but slowly. "Thanks."

I gave him a curious look. "You're sure that you want to be a field agent? Shit like this is going to happen to you all the time."

He kept nodding. He didn't even hesitate. "Oh. I'm sure."

We turned around and headed back towards Denali.

"What about that girl and her pet astronaut?" Theodore asked. "Do you think we'll ever see them again?"

"I dunno," I said. I used my hand to shield my eyes from the sun and looked up at the sky. Mir and the Cosmonaut were out there somewhere, back home in outer space, where they could float among the stars. "But to be on the safe side, we should probably keep close track of all the nuclear bombs in the world."

Chapter 11

1

Interstate 70 is an endless stretch of highway that winds through a beautiful, but very lonely, tour of Utah. The pavement is coated in a thin layer of grit blown in by the hot winds. We drove fifty miles on Denali's spare tire before we finally found an exit to a hilariously small service station.

"Pete's" it was called, built right at the intersection of the off-ramp and an access road that led absolutely nowhere. Pete's rest stop consisted of a diner, a gas station, and a small mechanic's shop with the words TIRES spray painted above the garage door. The parking lot was a square plot of gravel, home to an old truck rusting in the sun, a concrete water fountain that looked bone-dry, and towers of stacked tires. The place had a middle-of-nowhere kind of charm to it, like they didn't get many visitors out here and preferred it that way.

The gas station had two pumps, not digital, but the kind where it dings as numbers rotate inside the machine. There was a Phillips 66 sign that stretched on a pole up into the sky, old and faded, which advertised *Unleaded* at $2.37. The sun-faded numbers hadn't been touched in forever, as if gas had cost $2.37 for decades. This was the middle of nowhere, after all. What was the point in changing it?

The diner had that long 1950s architecture with brown awnings over the windows. Maybe the awnings used to be white and were simply stained brown by decades of dusty winds. The front door of the diner had a wooden screen door on it – classy – and a sandwich board sat out front.

It read:

Chicken and Waffles $5.99
Breakfast Slammer $5.99
Lemonade 99 cents

Reasonably priced, I suppose. I wasn't sure. I stopped eating food a long time ago. I *was* hungry, though.

I wondered if they'd miss a couple rolls of silverware.

Denali pulled into the gravel lot and this tubby guy in a pair of greasy overalls came out of the tire center. He wiped his oily hands off on a red rag, not that he should have bothered. His hands had permanent stains of dirt and oil and grease. His overalls were caked in automotive filth, his hair was matted and unwashed, and he smelled like diesel fuel.

We climbed out of Denali.

"Car trouble?" the guy asked us. His name tag said PETE.

"The back tire's blown out," I told him.

Pete walked around the SUV, positioned himself in front of the blown tire and squatted down to get a real close look. He nodded and gave a knowledgeable grunt. "You been driving on this rim?"

"What's a rim?" I asked.

"We have," Theodore said.

"Shouldn't drive on the rim," Pete informed us.

"We..." Theodore cleared his throat. "...didn't have much choice."

"Yah-huh," Pete said. He stood up and wiped his hands off on his butt. "Well, you're gunna need to replace it. I got something that'll fit. I can change it for ya, but it'll take at least an hour."

Theodore looked to me for confirmation. I shrugged. Whatever. What else could we do? Wish upon a star?

"Do whatever you gotta do," I told Pete.

"Ya'll can wait in the diner if ya want," he told us. "I'll find ya when it's ready to go."

Theodore and I took his advice and hit the diner. The inside was just as dated as the exterior with boring paintings on the wall, a few fake plants by the entrance and wooden panels on the walls. Theodore and I seated ourselves in a booth. The green vinyl seats were patched together with old, filthy duct tape. A frumpy woman in an apron and clunky shoes – her name tag said BRENDA – approached our table and gave us small glasses of ice water, set menus down in front of us, and informed us that chicken and waffles was 5.99, the breakfast slammer – two eggs, two sausages, two flapjacks, and hash browns – was also 5.99, and lemonade was 99 cents.

Theodore gave her a thoughtful look. "What's your quiche selection like? Do you have frambochoise?"

My eyebrows shot up. What the fuck was he doing?

Brenda had no idea how to respond. "Quiche?"

"Yeah." Theodore flipped through the menu as though he might actually find quiches listed next to the sausage and gravy. "Do you do a mushroom quiche? Or some kind of chorizo?"

"We don't have that," she said. "We have breakfast foods. And burgers."

"Right." Theodore realized this wasn't a quiches kind of joint. He handed Brenda the menu. "I'll just take a few of your house crepes. And pockleberry syrup, if you have it."

He might as well have ordered Samurai Moon Tea. Brenda gave me a perplexed look.

"Just bring him the breakfast slammer," I said, also handing her my menu. "And I'll just have some wheat toast, please."

I wasn't going to eat the toast obviously. I just needed real food to pick at, not eat, and leave behind without feeling bad.

"Burn the bacon, please," Theodore said. "Pitch black."

Brenda was about to walk off, but it dawned on me...

"Oh! Could you bring us some extra silverware?"

She patted the napkin-rolled silverware in front of me. "You've already got some silverware, hon."

"I know." I greedily moved the silverware closer to me. "I need extras."

She raised her eyebrows at me, but headed for the kitchen. Whatever. I doubt we're the weirdest customers she's ever seen.

Once Brenda was gone and we were in the clear, I turned my attention back to Theodore. "Okay, can we talk about what just happened?"

He nodded and leaned forward to whisper, "Right? What kind of place doesn't have a least a couple quiches on the menu?"

"Not that." Man, Theodore was dense. "I'm talking about Archdemon Lylo and her Army of Arms."

"Oh. That."

"Yes, Theodore. *That.* What the hell, man? When I left Westland HQ in New York, the whole building was in some kind of shutdown mode. And today, some whackjob demon gets out of her cell and completely buttfucks your entire base to death. No offense, but Westland is really coming apart at the seams."

"What happened today had to be some kind of mistake," he said, although he didn't sound convinced. "No one at the Westland Corporation would let a demon loose on purpose."

"No one?"

"Not even Kruger," he said. "Kruger's a dick, but Westland agents are not traitors."

I scoffed. "All Westland people do it lie. I think your radar might be just a little out of whack."

He folded his hands and placed them on the table. "Penelope, the Westland Corporation has been protecting planet Earth from supernatural threats since 1984, long before you or I were even born. Westland agents devote their entire lives to their work. It's dangerous, thankless, and we do it with a smile. The mere idea that a Westland agent would double-cross the Corporation is... Well. Quite frankly, it's insane."

"The only thing insane around here is you," I said.

He shook his head. "Okay, then you explain to me... why would a Westland agent put themselves out of a job?"

"Maybe they found a better one?"

He scoffed. "Penelope, joining Westland opens your eyes to the reality of the world. You're shown secrets that no one else could possibly know, not world governments, not the Pope, no one. There is no better job."

I blinked at him. "Are you being serious?"

"Yes, I'm being serious." He leaned back in the booth and put his hands behind his head. "Enlighten me. What could be better than working for the Westland Corporation?"

"I dunno," I said. "Music. Movies. Getting high at the park and watching the birds?"

"Well, while you're staring at pigeons at the park," he said, "people like me are saving the world."

I put my hands on the table and leaned forward. "You're not saving the world, you dumbass. You're making it worse."

He rolled his eyes at me. "You don't get the big picture."

He unrolled his silverware and dropped it into his hand. He placed the cloth napkin on his lap and arranged the knife, spoon, and fork as if we were about to have dinner with the Queen. He analyzed the position of his water, decided that he didn't like where it sat and moved it two inches to the left. He scrutinized its position, then moved it back another inch.

In the middle of his meticulous operation, he raised his eyes and caught me staring at him.

After a moment, he said, "What?"

"What are you doing?" I asked.

"What do you mean?"

"This." I gestured at his carefully arranged silverware. "Are you OCD or something?"

"I'm neat and tidy," he said. "If that's alright with you."

"Whatever."

I groaned and leaned back, arching my neck over the back of the seat and pointing my eyes up at the cigarette stained ceiling. "Sitting here with you feels like I'm sitting with the enemy."

"The enemy? Me? Why am I the enemy?"

"You work for Westland." I sat normal and poked at my water. The condensation dripped down the sides of the glass. It formed a wet ring on the laminate table top. "Me and the corporation have a history, you know."

"Oh, I'm quite aware," he said, grinning. "You're kind of a hero around the water cooler, if you know what I mean."

"A hero?"

"That's just a figure of speech."

"Oh."

"We don't actually have a water cooler."

"No, I meant, you actually think I'm a hero?"

"Oh, of course."

Why would anyone at Westland consider me a hero? Me and them didn't necessarily have a rosy track record. I got their CEO killed. I hated Carl. And one time I set off the fire sprinklers in their accounting department. But Theodore saw things different, I guess. "A hero." He took a sip of his ice water and set it back down in the exact same spot.

He started, "Before you killed the CEO-"

"Ah." I raised a finger at him. "Stop right there. I didn't kill the CEO. Baron Kriminel killed the CEO. I want to be very clear about that."

"Okay, well, if you want to be technical about it, yes." He waved his fingers at me like that part didn't matter. "The point is, the CEO tried to kill you, he died, and then we got a new CEO. And that's when everything changed." He listed everything off on his fingers. "Soldiers started getting combat pay. Overtime now pays double-time, not just time and half. Our cell phones bills are handled by the company. And, hell, for Christmas we actually got a bonus and a bottle of some really nice whiskey."

"Nice whiskey, huh?" Sounded like something Carl would do. He loved his whiskey. "Was it Macallan's?"

"Yeah!" Theodore smiled at me. "How did you know?"

My eyes wandered to the window. "Lucky guess."

"Best of all." For this part, he leaned over the table and spoke softly. "We do business differently now. That whole 'find all supernatural people and wipe them out' thing? That's over. Now we actually investigate real threats and eliminate them."

Doubtful. "Tell that to the Vampires and the Werewolves."

Theodore really didn't like that. He sat back in his seat and said, "The extinction of the vampires and werewolves happened long before I worked there. I would have never been a part of anything like that. And that's not how we do business anymore."

I squinted at him. I wanted to believe this was all true. But if there's one thing I know, it's that you can't trust the Westland Corporation.

2

Brenda refilled our ice water, comped us a whole pot of coffee, and eventually brought out our food: a Breakfast Slammer with burnt bacon for Theodore and a slice of toast for me. I had already eaten my silverware. All that remained were the napkins. Brenda noticed and gave me a suspicious look, but didn't say anything about it. She probably thought I was stealing knives and forks, but I didn't have anywhere to hide stolen silverware – no purse or backpack or anything – so she didn't accuse me of anything. Or maybe she didn't notice. Maybe I was just being paranoid.

"So what's it like being an investigator for the Westland Corporation?" I asked. "It sounds like it sucks."

"It's the best," he said. "I get to meet a lot of interesting people and interrogate the crap out of them. You learn a lot about the world that way. Like, for example, did you know there are installation wizards living in space?"

"I did not."

"Well, now you do."

"You ever get to see any action?" I asked.

"Once or twice."

Theodore picked up a burnt piece of bacon – and I mean blackened and charred – and crunched the whole thing in his mouth. Then he stabbed his fork into one of his sausage links.

"What'd you see?" I asked.

"Hmm." He stuck the sausage in his mouth and thought about that while he chewed.

For a just a moment, I felt jealous. Sometimes I really I miss eating regular food. I miss scrambled eggs. I miss sausage. I watched him closely as he chewed his food.

He pointed his fork at me. "You ever hear of Millipede Island?"

"Is that the place where that Nobel-prize scientist tried to bring back insects from the prehistoric age with genetics?"

"That's the one."

"Didn't the bugs got loose and killed everyone?"

Theodore nodded. "You ever been?"

"Hell no. I hate bugs."

"Well, I've been there." He stuck another breakfast sausage in his mouth. "Actually, I was stuck there."

"Stuck on Millipede Island?"

He put his fork down. "Believe me, it was not my idea. We were flying back from an investigation in Indonesia when our plane went down. We washed up on this island with no idea where we were. At first we thought we were in Guam."

"But..."

"But then we saw the bugs. Dragonflies the size of helicopters. Snails as big as cars."

Just the thought of it made me want to puke my silverware, but I was too curious to ask him to stop. "And the millipedes?"

His eyes went wide, like he was remembering some kind of nightmare. "The millipedes were the worst part. They crawled through the trees like cage-free roller coasters, looping through the branches and stuff. You could hear their shells clicking together when they moved. It was disgusting."

"It sounds disgusting."

"We were stuck there for three days." He sipped on his coffee. "We got out eventually."

"Everyone?"

"No, not everyone." He stared at his coffee. "Seven of us."

"Out of?"

"Twenty-two."

"Jesus. What happened to them?"

"What *didn't* happen to them? Danson got cocooned by a giant black widow. A weird looking red butterfly thing stuck its proboscis in Tong's torso and sucked out his organs. I almost died to a swarm of fleas the size of basketballs."

"That sounds insane."

"It was." He shook off the dreadful memories and his pleasant demeanor returned. He looked up to make eye contact with me and cheerfully said, "It looks good on a resume, though. I survived Millipede Island. What better way to stand out when it comes time for that promotion?"

"And after all that, you still want to be a field agent?"

"Why do you keep asking me that?"

"I don't know," I said. "I've never met a Westland guy the same age as me. It just seems weird. Shouldn't you be off in college or something? Living a normal life?"

He stared me down and asked, "Do *you* want a normal life?"

I frowned. He made a good point. In a world of exploding nukes and demons hell-bent on tearing off humanity's arms, a normal life sounded dreadfully boring.

"What about you?" he asked. "You run around saving the world. I'm sure you've seen all kinds of crazy stuff."

"Oh, yeah," I said with a little laugh. "One time me and my car Corolla went to visit Hobart, the Sphinx's idiot cousin in Egypt. His riddles are shit. I taught him some new ones."

With nothing to do but kill time until Pete could replace Denali's back tire, Theodore and I sat around and exchanged stories. It wasn't every day I got the chance to talk so free and open with another human being about the supernatural world, but Theodore was different. Theodore already knew about the supernatural world, so I didn't have to mince words, or lie, or make up wild stories to protect him from the truth.

In time, it slipped my mind that the guy sitting across from me was even a Westland employee. Theodore just seemed like a regular-ass dude who happened to wear a suit and carry a gun. He was smarter than he let on, except when it came to food, and after his fourth or fifth crazy story about all the different times he almost died investigating ghosts or ninjas or robots, I realized I was actually warming up to him.

I had to snap myself back to reality. This guy worked for the Westland Corporation for Christ's sake. Whatever charm he had going on – the way his eyes lit up when he smiled or his habit of wiping his mouth after every single bite of eggs – that was all social engineering manufactured by the corporation. Theodore was cool like how Russian spies are cool, right before they bash you over the head with a crowbar and dump you in a ditch.

Desperate for something to do other than stare at his face, I reached for my coffee and took a sip. The taste of dirt hit my senses, but not before I accidentally swallowed some. I coughed it up and sprayed it all across the table.

Theodore leaned back, surprised, and began to wipe the front of his suit with his napkin. "Coffee that bad?" he asked.

"I can't eat normal food." I grabbed a handful of napkins from my many sets of missing silverware and started mopping up the mess. "I can only eat metal."

"That's weird," he said.

"You're one to talk," I said as I rolled my eyes. "*Quiche.*"

3

Eventually Brenda came to clear our plates. She filled Theodore's coffee once more and left the ticket for us to take care of "whenever." She lingered at the table and asked us, "So, where you kids from?"

"Out of town," I said, flatly, trying to drive her away.

"Yeah?" she asked. She wasn't the least bit bothered by my unwelcoming tone. "Where from?"

"New York," I answered, and without eye contact.

"See," she waved a finger at me. "I thought I heard an accent." She beamed a huge smile over how smart and observant she was. "So what brings you all the way out here to Utah?"

I just wanted her to go away. I looked her dead in the eyes and said, "We're food critics."

"Oh." As the realization set in, she became nervous. She lowered her voice and asked, "How was everything then?"

"Real good." I gave her a huge, fake smile. "Five stars. But we need to discuss the article now, so..." I nudged my head back towards the kitchen, indicating she should fuck off. She stood there, grinning like a big dummy.

Finally it dawned on her what I was saying. "Oh!" She backed away from our table. "Well, if you two need anything, you just let me know."

I nodded. "We will."

I saw my first Utah sunset out the window. The sky turned watercolor shades of pink and purple and the desert landscape glowed orange in the dwindling sunlight. As the sun set lower, odd shadows appeared on the distant mountains. It was a trick of the light, but as the darkness set in, the peaks began to look like slumbering monsters.

Funny. The day would come when a local might look at that mountain range, wag a confused finger at the landscape and say, "Now, didn't there use to be a butte over there?"

Theodore interrupted my thoughts. "So who's the old man?"

"Huh?"

"In your file..." He grabbed two sugar packets and flicked them with his finger. "Your file said something about your connection to 'the old man,' but it didn't say who that was."

Despite our decent conversation, I still wasn't certain how well I could trust Theodore, so I didn't say much.

"They probably mean Xin. He's kind of like my mentor."

"Xin?" He ripped open the sugar packets and poured them into his coffee. "You don't mean Xin Houng, do you?"

"Yeah?" Weird. "You know him?"

"Of course I know him. I'm an investigator. That's my job." He stirred the sugar into his coffee, dissolving it in a whirlpool of dark liquid. "Xin Houng is the best alchemist in the Northern Hemisphere. Rumor has it, he's got a supernatural collection hidden away in his basement."

I wasn't about to confirm, nor deny that to him.

"I didn't know Xin was so popular," I said. "But I guess that makes sense. He's always talking about how his family's been in the business for generations."

"What's he like?"

"Xin? He's great." I rubbed my nose, then folded my hands and stuck them between my knees. "He's sick, too. And dying."

"Is it serious?"

"It's magical."

"Can you fix it?" he asked.

I shook my head. "Maybe. Only if I can find out who did it."

"Ah. A mystery, huh?"

I nodded. "Something like that." I flicked my water glass and watched the ice float in circles around the top. Then a brilliant idea dawned on me. I glanced back up at Theodore. He sipped his coffee and peered at me over the edge of his mug. "Hey. You're an investigator..."

He swallowed his coffee, wiped his lips with a napkin and said, "What gave it away?"

"And you've got some free time coming up..."

"My workplace exploded, then got sucked into space. I think it's safe to assume I've got at least a three-day weekend."

"Do you think you could figure out who put Xin in a coma?"

He didn't hesitate. "Yes."

"Really?" I said. "You didn't even think about it."

He shrugged. "What's to think about? You need an investigation. I'm an investigator. What's to think about?"

"I don't even know where to start."

"Is he in the hospital?" he asked.

"Yeah," I said.

"In New York?"

"Yeah."

"Well, that's perfect." He smiled at me, and it looked sincere. "Denali and I have to report back to HQ, so we're going to New York anyway. We'll go together."

I couldn't bring myself to look at him. I was torn between my need to help Xin and my steadfast hatred of the Westland Corporation. "I don't know..."

"How else you were planning to get back home?" he asked. "You have a blimp I don't know about?"

"I have a car, actually. A flying car." I stared out the window at the night sky. "Somewhere."

He said, "I haven't seen any flying cars."

I mumbled. "I know."

"Ride along with me and Denali. I'll go back to Westland HQ and report in, then I'll investigate this whole Xin-in-a-coma thing. I bet I could figure it out."

I squinted at him. "Are you serious?"

"Dead serious. I was raised by the Westland Corporation. They taught me everything. There's nothing I can't figure out."

How? How did I end up kicking it with an agent from the Westland Corporation? Not only did he save my life, I saved his, then his car saved mine, and suddenly we were planning a cross-country road trip? I could have walked away from the whole thing if I wanted to, detainment or no detainment. Theodore – squishy, mortal Theodore – couldn't do a thing to stop me.

But he seemed super sure that he could help me. And when I really thought about it, what would it hurt if we traveled back to New York City together?

"Okay," I said. "We'll go together."

He gave me the finger gun. "There ya go."

"But we're not friends or anything like that."

He raised his coffee mug at me. "Oh, of course not."

4

We stepped outside as the sky turned darker shades of purple. It reminded me of the riddle I made up for Hobart, the idiot Sphinx: *What's orange, then blue, then purple, then black?*

A rectangle of orange light shone from the tire center's open garage door. Denali was parked inside. Her rear tire had been replaced and that grease monkey dude was polishing her hubcaps. Theodore headed in their direction. I sat on the edge of the diner's porch and pulled my socks off. I'd been wearing the those socks all day, through collapsing prisons and across sandy deserts and they were filthy with holes in the heels. They were useless now. I decided to go barefoot instead.

Just when I got both socks off, I heard a noise behind me. "Psst."

And when I turned around, no one was there. Whoever psst me was doing it from around the corner of the diner. Then I heard another noise, like someone trying to imitate a crow.

"Caw caw! Caw! I'm a crow!" And then the voice, Corolla's voice, whispered my name. "Penelope. Over here."

He flashed his headlights at me, once, very quickly from around the corner. I glanced at Theodore to see if he noticed, but he was off to the garage and not paying attention. Corolla just barely poked his front end out where I could see it. Once I saw his headlights, and he saw me, he backed away into the darkness.

"Why don't you go pay for the tire," I shouted at Theodore, waving at him to go on without me. "I'll catch up."

He gave me a curious look. "You're not coming?"

"I'm going to..." I had to think of a reason to be alone. "To pee. I gotta pee. Around the corner. And I have to do it now."

"You're going to do it outside?" he asked. "Like an animal?"

"Uh. Yeah."

"There's a bathroom inside the diner."

Had to think of another excuse and quick. "I piss jet fuel," I blurted out. I let that lie hang in the air to see if it sounded plausible. Truth was, I didn't pee at all, but Theodore didn't know that. For all he knew, it was true. I piss jet fuel. Let's go with that. "It's dangerous. If I pee inside, the whole place is going to go up like the Challenger."

200

Flawless execution.

"Oh, those poor astronauts." He was buying it. "Okay. Well, I'll be over with Denali whenever you're done."

He headed to the tire shop. Gravel crunched under his shoes.

I backed away slowly, making sure Theodore wouldn't turn around to see where I was going. I dipped around the corner of the diner and hugged Corolla's driver side door. He turned on his dome light so he could see me better. I put my face against his window and peeked inside.

He asked me, "Penelope! Where in the hell have you been?"

"Where the hell have *I* been?" I asked. "Where the hell have *you* been?"

"*I've* been trying to find *you*, driving around on four wheels like some kind of caveman because your little stunt at NORAD put every F-16 in North America on high alert."

"You've been driving on the ground?" I asked.

"Yes," he said. "I've been looking for you everywhere! How the hell did you wind up out here?"

"Long story." I jumped in Corolla's passenger seat and turned off the dome light. "That nuke short circuited my brain. When I woke up, I was captured by the Westland Corporation."

"No way!" he whisper-shouted. "Westland caught you? Did you have to kill them? How did you escape?"

"Uhh. Well, I didn't escape. Not exactly."

"Not exactly?" He sounded confused.

"Like I said, it's a long story. Westland captured me and then they got attacked by this Archdemon, Lylo. So me and this Westland dude ran away. Now we're on our way to New York."

"You..." He paused. "...helped a guy from Westland?"

I scratched my head. Admittedly, it did sound crazy. "Yeah."

He laughed a little.

Then he laughed a lot.

"You know what, Penelope? For a second there, I almost believed you." His laughed died down, because I wasn't laughing along. He got quiet. "Oh, wow. You're serious."

"I'm serious."

"What'd that nuke do? Knock a screw loose?"

"I know."

"Westland tried to kill you!"

"I know that!"

"They destroyed Xin's shop!"

I waved at him, frantically. "I know, dude! I know all that!"

"Well, then, why are you working with them?" He sounded very judgmental, and I didn't blame him.

"Not all of them," I said. "Just one of them. Theodore."

"Well, what makes this Theodore any different?"

"Because..."

"Because why?"

"Because he's an investigator and can help me figure out who tried to kill Xin. And because he's actually a nice guy." Was I trying to justify my unreasonable non-hatred of Theodore to Corolla, or to myself? "Once you get to know him."

"A nice guy?" Corolla repeated, unconvinced.

"Yes, he's a nice guy." The tone of my voice changed. I could hear it. I was getting defensive. "And he's good with a gun, too."

"I see." He pulled forward and poked his headlights out past the corner of the diner. "Is that him over there? The schlub in the suit and a not-too-bright look on his face?"

"Yes."

"He's just a kid. This guy works for Westland?"

"He's not a kid," I said. "He's two years older than me."

"Oh, wow," Corolla said. "Are you serious?"

"Am I serious, what?"

"You think he's cute!"

That was one-hundred-percent, categorically, slanderously, untrue. I didn't think Theodore was "cute." I didn't. There was nothing to like about him, least of all those stupid green eyes.

I couldn't have been more offended.

"I don't think he's cute," I said.

"Yes, you do! You're so transparent. He's *nice*?"

"He *is* nice! And, sure, he's not bad-looking, but only in a very objective sense. He's like a co-worker. He's a fellow human being. But that's it."

"Did you make out with him?" Corolla asked, nearly laughing. "Did you two take the tongue train to kissy town?"

"Keep it up," I told him. "I'll disconnect your speakers."

"Oh yeah?" He laughed. "You and what team of technical engineers, genius?"

This was his last warning. "Corolla."

"Alright. Alright. I'll stop."

"Dude, Theodore is a Westland investigator. He's just going to help me figure out who tried to kill Xin. You want to figure out what's wrong with Xin, don't you? We need his help."

"I don't know..."

"Corolla. Trust me."

I never played the trust card with Corolla, and he never played it with me, but it was a fair card to play. I trusted Corolla with my life, and he could trust me with his. If Corolla ever asked me to trust him, I would. And if I asked Corolla to trust me...

"I trust you," he finally said. "I just don't trust Westland."

Time to play dirty.

"Okay..." I said. "I guess you won't get to meet Denali."

"Uh huh." It didn't sound like he was going to take the bait, but then he asked, "Who's Denali?"

"Oh, didn't I mention that? Denali is Theodore's car."

Corolla was quiet. "He's got a car?"

There we go. I grinned and put a suggestive tone to my voice. "He's got a talking car. A girl car."

Corolla was the only talking car I'd ever met, and I used to think he was the only talking car in the world. I wonder if he felt the same way: alone in the world, one of a kind. But now there were two talking cars, and maybe there were more.

"Another talking car?" He couldn't help but sound excited. "Why didn't you tell me this earlier?"

"I'm telling you now."

"Is she... around?" he asked.

"She's in the body shop getting her tire replaced," I told him. "This asshole named Kruger shot her with a pistol, but she's all fixed now. I can introduce you if you want."

"Okay!" Suddenly, Westland didn't seem so bad.

I stepped out of Corolla and closed his door softly to make as little noise as possible, then tip-toed back towards the front of the diner.

"Hey, Penelope?" Corolla said.

I stopped and glanced back at him. "Hey, Corolla."

"I'm glad you're okay."

I gave him a thumbs up. "I'm glad you're okay, too."

I resumed tip-toeing.

"Hey, Penelope," he said again.

I stopped once more. "Hey, Corolla."

"That diner. They don't have egg rolls, do they?"

"No."

He waited a few seconds, then, "Did you ask?"

"I did not," I said. "It's not an egg roll kind of place."

"Maybe they sometimes have egg rolls, like as a special."

"They don't have egg rolls," I said. "Their special was this thing called a breakfast slammer."

"And that's not a type of egg roll?"

I was done with this line of nonsense questioning. "Nope."

"What if they-"

"Nope."

"But you didn't even ask."

"Do you want me to go inside and ask this tiny diner in small-town Utah if they have egg rolls?"

"You gotta ask to be sure," he said. "Or you never know."

"Okay." I threw my hands up. "Fuck it. I'll go ask."

I went *back* inside the diner which rang the bell hanging over the front door and caught Brenda's attention right away. She came over to me, smiling, surprised to see me again so soon.

"Forget something?" she asked me.

I cut to the chase. "I just wondered if you had egg rolls."

"Yes," she said.

I must have mis-heard. It sounded like she said yes. "What?"

"Sure, we have egg rolls." She acted like it was the most natural thing in the world for this diner to have egg rolls. "We have pork or chicken."

"..."

Speechless. Of everything that had just happened to me in my life – demon arms and teleporting astronauts and space stations who want to start a nuclear war – none of that held a candle to how absolutely dumbstruck I was finding out that Pete's Diner, in the middle of Fuckface, Utah, had not only one, but *two* kinds of egg rolls. Sometimes the real world can be just as crazy and unpredictable as the supernatural world.

"You want me to have them throw some in the fryer or...?" Brenda asked me, snapping me out of my existential crisis.

"Yeah, I guess," I said, giving up. "Six chicken ones, please."

5

Corolla wasn't lying. Airspace over the Rocky Mountains was under complete military lock down and all commercial flights had been grounded for the rest of the day. Talk about overreacting. You launch one nuke...

We couldn't fly. We were going to have to get back to New York City the old-fashioned way. Road trip.

I escorted Theodore and Denali around the corner of the diner to meet Corolla, out of view of Mechanic Pete and Waitress Brenda and whoever else might have happened to be around. We formed a little conversation circle on the dark side of the diner.

"What's this stuff spilled everywhere?" Theodore asked as he took careful steps around a mess of cabbage and tofu and egg roll wrappers.

"Egg rolls," Corolla said. "And they were not good."

Denali's tires slid to a stop on the gravel. "Sweet Chrysler. A talking Toyota Corolla?"

Corolla said, "Oh, hello. Hi. My name's Corolla."

And she said, "I thought only Westland had talking cars."

Corolla said, "I didn't know there were other talking cars besides me!"

Denali drove around him, really checking him out. "Where did you come from?"

"This lady in Japan made me," he said.

"Tengoku," I clarified.

"Tengoku Industries?" Theodore asked. "I didn't think that place was real. I thought that was just a myth."

"No, it's real," I said. "At least, it used to be. Tengoku left Earth sometime last year and took the building with her."

Corolla said, "Tengoku created me especially for Penelope."

"I can't believe there's another talking car in the world," Denali said. She seemed honestly amazed.

"Well." Corolla paused. "Here I am, I guess."

Denali asked him, "And you don't work for anyone? You're free to come and go as you please?"

"Uh." Corolla turned to face me. "I mean, I just sort of have to do whatever Penelope tells me to do."

"Don't make it sound like it's a bad thing," I said. "We go on adventures. I buy you egg rolls."

He mumbled, "You won't let me get a gun."

"This is amazing!" Denali, who was easily excited anyway, could barely contain herself. "Look at you! You're so different. You're not all black! And you don't have tinted windows!"

And even though Corolla was a car, I somehow knew he was blushing.

"I can fly, too," Corolla said.

"What!?" Denali backed up. "You're lying."

"No!" Corolla said. "I can totally fly. Watch this!"

The pressure against Corolla's tires relaxed as the weight was lifted off of him and he floated a few inches off the ground. His hubcaps glowed bright blue and his tires folded underneath his body to point down at the ground. With his anti-gravity repulsors at full strength, he hovered there to the faint technological hum of his futuristic powers.

Denali gasped. "You're like Car Jesus!"

Corolla softly replied, "It is true, my child."

"Okay, stop," I said, stepping between them. I wasn't religious or anything, but I also wasn't about to let Corolla pretend to be *Car Jesus*. "Don't go putting wild ideas in his head. He's just a regular car who happens to fly."

"Yeah," Corolla said. "I'm more like a Car Superman."

I rolled my eyes. "Here we go. Corolla, get back down on the ground before one of these bumpkins comes along to take out the trash and catches you flying."

Corolla landed. Him and Denali chatted it up, building off one another's excitement like two excited dogs meeting at the dog park, when they're like "You're a dog? I'm a dog!" and the next thing you know they just tear off into the fields to play around.

Denali asked him, "Have you seen the Fast and the Furious?"

"No," Corolla said. "Should I?"

"Yes! You should see Fast and the Furious: Tokyo Drift!"

"Okay! I totally want to! Do you like human music?"

"I love human music," Denali said. "I like Van Halen. Do you like Van Halen?"

"Are you kidding me?" Corolla said. "I love Van Halen!"

The two cars started in on a "what's your favorite band" conversation and forgot that Theodore and I were even there.

I looked at Theodore. "Well, they sure seem excited."

"I had no idea she liked Van Halen," he said. "She always lets me pick the music."

"That must be nice." I crossed my arms, shook my head, and watched Corolla and Denali. "I have to fight Corolla for the stereo every time we go anywhere."

While the cars chatted it up and got to know one another, Theodore and I used his smartphone to plan our route back to New York City. We were looking at 33 hours, non-stop, from Utah to Manhattan. Luckily, we didn't need to stop anywhere to sleep. Corolla and Denali could both drive the whole thing straight through. All we needed were a few pit stops for fuel, but if we stayed focused and kept driving, we would be back to New York in a day and half.

6

Corolla and I sped down the interstate, blasting Van Halen at one in the morning. We followed Denali's tail lights through the darkness. Her license plate looked government-issued, but like nothing I had ever seen before. The plate itself was black and the white embossed letters read AX$422!, which I didn't think was regulation for license plates. I'd never seen license plates with symbols like that before. I figured it must have been some sort of Westland hack into the nation's computerized transportation system so that if any cop ran the plates, it would kick back an FBI-level "do not detain" order.

So far away from civilization, there wasn't any light pollution to muddy up the night sky. The stars were out in full force and the white band of the Milky Way stretch above us. Somewhere out there in space – somewhere way out there – were Mir and the Cosmonaut.

I wondered what they were doing. I wondered if they were somehow watching us.

"I still don't know about that Theodore guy," Corolla said, continuing his point that I was only half-listening to. "Denali seems really cool, but couldn't this be a trap? You can't trust anyone from Westland. You're the one who told me that."

"I don't know," I replied. "Theodore says they've changed."

"Oh, *Theodore* says. Well, if *Theodore* says..."

"You just need to get to know him." God, was I actually defending someone from Westland? "He's not all bad."

"That's a pretty snap judgment, Penelope. How long could you have possibly known this loser? One day?"

I got quiet. "Since this afternoon."

"So a couple hours?"

"Yeah."

"And you think you can trust a Westland agent after knowing him for a couple hours? You don't even let me talk to people under the bridge."

"Dammit, Corolla, you weren't there. You didn't see what we went through. When this celestial-class demon was slaughtering everyone at Westland, Theodore and Denali practically saved my life. And I saved theirs."

"Funny you should mention that." Corolla was on a roll. "Weren't you the one that said to never get mixed up with demons? That if we ever saw a demon, to run like hell and never look back? But you go and punch a demon in the face to protect a bunch of stupid Westland agents? What's wrong with you?"

"Nothing's wrong with me," I snapped. "I protected them because I had to. That's our job."

"Our job?" Corolla asked. "Since when is protecting people our job?"

"Since always, Corolla. We have powers that no one else has. We have a responsibility to use those powers to stop evil whenever we see it."

"Okay, slow down, Spider-man," Corolla said. "I don't remembering signing up for the Peace Corps. There might be evil in the world, but fighting it is not our responsibility."

"Well, it is now."

"Says who?"

"Says me."

"Oh, says you."

"Yes, says me."

"Well, I'm Car Jesus and I say you're wrong."

"I'm Penelope Jesus, and I say I'm right."

Corolla grumbled under his breath. Fine. Let him grumble all he wants. As long as he followed Denali's tail lights and went along with the mission, he could object all he wanted. And it's not like he was entirely wrong about Westland. In fact, he made total sense. But something inside me told me working with Theodore was the right thing to do.

Xin told me about the moon once. He said sometimes a bad moon finds its way into the sky and the light it gives off is bad light. I wondered if we were under a bad moon. After all, Corolla and I rarely argued. Bickered, sure, but this wasn't something as silly as what music to listen to. We drove without talking, subjected to the rockin' guitar riffs of Eddie Van Halen. It was going to be a long trip back to New York City. 30-plus hours of uncomfortable quiet was not my idea of fun.

We finally left the Utah deserts and reached the tale-tell signs of civilization. Light poles appeared on the sides of the highway. At first they were just at the off ramps, then they appeared at the mile markers. Billboards came next, advertising nearby mega-churches and various fast food chains.

"I had a dream," I told Corolla. "When the nuke scrambled my brains and knocked me out, I had a dream."

"What kind of dream?" he asked.

"I don't quite remember." I stared out the window at the night sky. "I remember a garden with big stones. And some bald girl dressed in orange."

"Weird."

"Yeah. It was like... on a mountain I think."

"You know what I dream about?"

"What?"

"Backstage passes to Phil Collins."

"Ugh." I practically gagged. "I don't get this obsession you have with Phil Collins. What's so great about Phil Collins?"

"What's *not* so great about Phil Collins? The dude has cranked out so many hits. Invisible Touch? Sussudio? What about that drum solo from In the Air Tonight? Are you kidding me?"

"And that song from the Tarzan soundtrack?"

"Okay, look, no one's perfect," Corolla said. "I'm just saying he's one of the most prolific musicians in-"

"No."

"One of the *most* prolific musicians to ever-"

"Don't say it!"

"One of the most prolific musicians to ever live!"

"I'm not listening!" I slapped my hands over my ears. "La la la la la."

Despite my attempts to drown out Corolla's voice, I could still hear him. He turned down the music so he could sing Phil Collins to me at the top of his lung, a capella.

I pretended it drove me crazy, but truth was... I was relieved Corolla found me at that Utah diner. I missed him.

Chapter 12

1

Wyoming.

Wyoming was a little bit out of our way, but considering recent nuclear events at NORAD, we decided it would be safer to avoid the great state of Colorado. The night was clear and not only could I see a sky full of stars, I could also spot the fast-moving red lights of F-16 patrolling military airspace. The government went and got their panties in a big fucking twist over a simple case of a mistakenly launched nuclear bomb. The last thing I wanted to do was drive through the Rockies and get stopped by some FBI roadblock. So we went further north.

It was going to be a long trip because Corolla was grounded. He could fly a bajillion times faster then the driving speed limit, so forcing him to stick to the roads like a normal car felt like moving in slow-motion.

I never got a straight answer out of Corolla about how his flying mechanisms work. I think he didn't want to admit to not knowing. There was undoubtedly a lot of complicated science behind it and that wasn't Corolla's strong suit. It would be like asking me to explain how eating forks and knives powered my mechanical heart. Any time I brought up the subject of his flying hubcaps, he always found a way to change the subject.

But since we had 31 non-sleeping hours left on our trip, we had to talk about something. So I brought it up yet again.

"When you fly, do you use gas?" I asked him. "Because when you fly, I hear your engine running."

"Yes, I use gas. Of course I use gas. You don't see a fusion reactor on me anywhere, do you?"

"But if you use gas, how come you don't run out?"

"I run out," he said. "Sometimes."

"Not as fast as you should, especially for flying. When I first met you, we flew from Japan to New York City in one trip and we didn't fuel up once. If we were driving, you'd have to stop, like, fifty times."

"If we were driving," he said, "we would have drowned trying to cross the Atlantic Ocean."

"The Pacific," I said, correcting him.

"Huh?"

"It's the Pacific Ocean is between Japan and the U.S."

"Are you sure?"

"Am I sure where the oceans are located? Yeah. I'm pretty sure. That's why in World War 2 when we fought the Japanese, they called it the Pacific theater."

"A theater? Why'd they call it a theater?"

I didn't pay *that* much attention in history class. "No idea."

"That's a weird thing to call it. A theater. What did they call the invasion of Berlin? Midnight movie madness?"

"The Berlin Offensive Strategic Operation," I answered quickly, and without a moment's thought. I had no idea how I knew that. I had never heard that name before. It was as if the obscure information just popped into my head. I couldn't explain it and I gave myself a perplexed look.

2

Henderson Creek, Nebraska

When we crossed into Nebraska, Corolla's gas needle was creeping up on empty. Now I knew that for Corolla, "E" didn't necessarily mean empty. We could cruise for another forty-five miles or so, long after the needle went way past "E" and off the gauge entirely. Still, it wasn't worth the risk of getting stranded. Signs for Henderson Creek promised fuel and food, and the next town wasn't for another 70 miles.

So right as the sun crested over the horizon and turned the surrounding farmland to color like the hills in the Land of Oz, Denali and Corolla took exit 4A off Interstate 80 and headed towards the quiet town of Henderson Creek.

Our dusty farm road took us straight through acres and acres of sunny, golden farmland populated with John Deere tractors and wire-framed irrigation machines and towering grain elevators. I had a good idea what to expect in Henderson Creek: maybe a general store, neighborhoods of farmhouses from the 1900s, and probably a broken down bar called "The Drinkin' Hole" or "The Broken Spoke" or "The Rusty Bucket."

Ew. "The rusty bucket" sounded like one of those disgusting sex moves. I don't know if I heard that phrase somewhere before, but just thinking about it made me laugh.

"What's so funny?" Corolla asked. It wasn't uncommon for me to start laughing out of nowhere when left alone with my own thoughts. "Tell me what's so funny."

"Rusty bucket!" I blurted out. I could not stop laughing.

"Uh..." Corolla was real confused. "Why is that funny?"

"What if their bar is called Rusty Bucket!?"

I laughed so hard, I had tears.

"I don't..." Corolla gave up and focused on his driving. "Whatever. You're so weird sometimes."

Denali turned a corner and we passed a sign that read:

Henderson CREEK
Population 437

437 people? I know apartment complexes in Manhattan who hold more people than that.

Henderson Creek was a real "American Heartland" kind of place; a town where no one ever locked their doors, a place that kept a shotgun mounted over the fireplace, a place that dressed up since to go to Church on Sunday and brunch at the local diner soon after. Endless acres of green and golden farmland surrounded the small town on all sides: sprawling fields of corn, or wheat, or whatever they grow in Nebraska. Soybeans, maybe? Or bok choy?

"What do you think they grow here?" I asked Corolla.

"I assume corn," he said, giving it his best guess.

"Yeah, that's what I thought, too." But I also thought bok choy, so what did I know? Good thing we have farmers to sort all that shit out, because I have no clue what's going on when it comes to farming.

Hulking, John-Deere-green tractors slept in the fields. Some of those machines came with roto-tillers, or conveyor belts to sort raw vegetables, or massive claws in the front to harvest entire fields in one short day. These were the kind of machines that could mangle a careless human to death in two seconds flat. And considering what I recently learned about Denali, I couldn't help but wonder if these machines could think and talk. Sure, maybe they didn't have the technology installed to vocalize their thoughts or control their own movements, but that didn't mean they weren't self-aware.

The town of Henderson Creek was home to a few brick buildings and a dozen Elizabethan homes. A single stop sign marked the edge of town. A couple blocks up the brick Main Street was a blinking four-way-stop red light, suspended from wires. That marked the middle of town, only three blocks deep, past the church, the gas station, and the bank. The bank had one of those light boards in the window, the programmable kind where words would scroll by, undoubtedly a technological marvel for Henderson Creek. It was probably put in at the protest of the local pastor who labeled its magic "of the devil."

We followed Denali as she rolled slowly through town and headed toward the gas station. Champion Gas. It was a rusted out shell of a service station with a dirt parking lot and an old-fashioned soda machine that sold glass bottles, not cans, of RC and Cooke's Soda and Frostie Root Beer for 35 cents. I've seen antique soda machines like that before, but as part of an art installation in Harlem. These Nebraskans were using it as a real, functioning soda machine.

The front windows of the gas station had signs from forty years ago, with retro slogans like "Wouldn't you rather have a Frostie?" and "Rainier Beer... Since 1878."

I've never heard of Frostie root beer and I didn't know Rainier was a beer, but I also wasn't born in 1939.

A cable stretched across the dirt of the gas station parking lot and when Denali drove over it, it made the gas pumps go "ding ding." It rang again when Corolla drove over it. I thought I might see a real service station in action, where a bunch of uniformed men run out to pump your gas, check your oil, and lean in your driver side window as you're leaving to say "Thanks for coming! Ya'll have a hum-dinger of a day."

This wasn't that kind of service station. We pulled up to the pumps with absolutely no fanfare – Denali on one side and Corolla on the other – but no one came out to help us. I hopped out of Corolla and Theodore climbed out of Denali. The air smelled like fuel and antique tools. We met up at the pump to perform our duties as car caretakers.

"Premium plus, please!" Denali shouted.

"I want super premium!" Corolla called out. "Super premium! Super premium!"

Denali chimed in. "Wait, I want super premium, too!"

"You have to have diesel," Theodore told Denali as he grabbed the green nozzle off his side of the pump. "You're allergic to everything else."

"But I'm sick of diesel," Denali whined. "Corolla is getting super premium. I want super premium!"

"Corolla is not getting super premium." I said, putting an end to that. I plunged the black gas nozzle into Corolla's tank. "He's getting regular because that's all they have."

Corolla muttered, "Stupid Nebraska."

Denali was quick to chime in. "So stupid."

I pulled the trigger on the nozzle and started filling Corolla's tank. Most pumps in America require you to pre-pay with cash or with a credit card, but not Champion Gas. These pumps were from a simpler time and didn't have built-in credit card readers, or even digital displays for that matter. Not that it mattered here in Henderson Creek.

"I'm going to go inside and buy a Kreenkle," Theodore said, leaving the nozzle stuck in Denali's tank. "You want anything?"

"The fuck is a Kreenkle?" I asked.

"It's a Swedish candy bar," he said. "It's got chocolate and bananas and hazelnut."

Sweden? Jesus, Theodore had absolutely no concept of how food worked in the world.

"Dude," I said. "They're not going to have fucking Kreenkles here. From Sweden?"

"You don't think so?" He looked honestly surprised. "I bet they will. They're really popular in Prague."

"These people don't know where Prague *is*," I said, perhaps a little too loud. Theodore just blinked at me. Everything I said went straight over his head. "Never mind. Go get a Kreenkle. Tell you what. If you find Kreenkles in there, grab me one."

"I thought you couldn't eat regular food," he said.

214

"Dude, if you find imported Swedish Kreenkles in this jank-ass Nebraska gas station, I'll choke one down just for you."

"Deal." He went for the gas station door with a little bounce in his step. "You're going to love them!"

He swung the glass door open, rang a tin bell that reminded me of Xin's shop, and went inside.

Now it was just me and the cars. I whistled a little tune in time to the clicking of the pumps and the sound of rushing fuel. The wind changed and blew a clean honeysuckle breeze over me and swept away the gross smell of gasoline.

"You guys notice something weird about this place?" Denali asked us, breaking the silence.

"Like what?" I glanced all around the gas station. "It's just an old, run-down gas station."

"Not just the gas station. This whole town." She paused, then said, "There's no people."

"Huh." I took a second look around with new perspective. She was right. The sidewalks, the bank across the street, the town square, I didn't see any people. "That is weird."

Theodore came strolling out of the gas station with his hands in his pockets. "Hey, Penelope. Just an FYI, everyone inside the gas station is dead."

3

Theodore and I walked right down the middle of main street which would have been both illegal and dangerous, except there weren't any other cars on the road. Denali and Corolla rolled right behind us. Normally we would've worried about someone seeing our self-aware cars, but that was apparently a non-issue in Henderson Creek. Everyone in Henderson Creek was dead.

Not just dead, we soon discovered. Mutilated.

One body had been reduced to a bloody pile of muscles on someone's front lawn. It must have been the mailman, because the flayed body was surrounded by envelopes and packages. His bloody uniform had been carelessly thrown into the grass.

Two cars were parked at the intersection of 1st and Main; the intersection with the blinking light. The sides of the cars had been torn completely open. Both drivers had been dragged out of their cars and into the street where their skin got torn off.

Streaks of blood covered the pavement.

Theodore and I moved further through town, eyes and ears peeled for any sign of movement. Denali and Corolla followed close behind us. The streets were dead silent, no pun intended. Dead silent, that is, except for Denali.

"Well, of course he's out of town a lot, Darla," Denali said, continuing her phone conversation. "He's a cruise ship captain. It's not like he can work from home. And just because he's gone for months at a time doesn't automatically mean he's cheating."

Theodore leaned over to me. "He's totally cheating on her. It's obvious."

"How do you know?" I asked.

"I'm an investigator."

"Well, of course he comes home tired," Denali said. "He works really long hours."

Two blocks away from the town center, we came up on this big Victorian house with a wrap-around porch, shuttered windows and two chimneys. The name painted on the mailbox read "MAYOR PHILLIPS." It's a bold move to paint the title of MAYOR directly onto your mailbox, but I guess there weren't a lot of heated elections in Henderson Creek. I headed for their front door, across their manicured lawn, and under the apple tree with the tire swing. The grass smelled freshly mowed, so whenever this city-wide massacre went down, it was recent.

"Where are you going?" Corolla called after me, worried.

"I'm going to take a look inside." I pointed at the porch. "I want to see who's in there."

"Ghosts, I bet," Corolla said. "You're going to find hacked up bodies and ghosts. Or, worse, you're going to find the ax murderer who did this."

"You worry too much," I said.

"And you don't worry enough," he replied.

I left Corolla, Denali and Theodore on the road out front. It didn't take an investigator to tell that a kindly old couple lived inside. The house had a nice porch swing and potted plants – violets and daffodils – and a green plastic watering can by the door. There was a decorative sign hanging beside the front door that said, in cursive, *THIS IS THE DAY THAT THE LORD HAS MADE.*

The screen door had been ripped right off its hinges. The front door – solid wood with ornamental glass – was smashed in. Broken glass laid scattered across the floor.

I poked my head inside.

"Hello?" I called out with a soft knock against the door frame. "Mister and Misses Phillips? Anyone home?"

Sadly, I found Misses Phillips right inside the door. Just like the other people of Henderson Creek, she'd had all her skin torn off and laid there as a big pile of muscles in a giant pool of blood. Whoever did this to her had apparently caught her in the middle of delivering a tray of lemonade, because the glasses were shattered everywhere.

Mayor Phillips died coming down the stairs. He laid there at the bottom, bloody and skinless. A shotgun laid close to his body. I picked it up to smell it. It had been recently fired.

The front room of the house was an absolute wreck. Flower vases laid busted on the ground. Pictures of their grandkids were knocked off the walls. Shotgun blasts had blown gaping holes in the walls, exposing the wood studs and electrical wiring inside.

I wasn't exactly sure what caused this, but I started to doubt it was a human being. Not to put it past a serial killer to skin his victims alive, but a whole town?

I stepped back outside. Theodore and Denali and Corolla had moved away form the house and were checking out a wrecked limousine in front of Mary's Antique Store. The limo had smashed straight into a telephone pole. It must've been traveling at a pretty high speed the way the front end had been crushed. The airbags had all gone off. The windshield was shattered. Smoke hissed out of the engine compartment. And whoever owned the limo had left in a real big hurry because the doors were wide open.

I recognized that limo.

Theodore waved me over from the driver side of the limo. He didn't have his usual devil-may-care smile in his eyes. No, this time he looked dead serious. "You're going to want to see this!"

I jogged over to them. Theodore poked his head inside the limo. I came up behind him and looked over his shoulder. The lights in the dashboard were dim and flickering, but they worked. A voice crackled out of the speakers; someone old, and male, and British.

"Is someone there?" the limo whimpered. "Hello?"

"I'm here," Theodore said. "I'm Theodore, special investigator for the Westland Corporation."

"Oh, thank Chrysler you found me," the limo said. "I have something important I have to tell you. Are you alone?"

Theodore glanced back at me. If the limo knew non-Westland people were listening, he might clam up. I gave Theodore a hard head-nod "yes."

"Yeah," Theodore lied. "I'm alone. What happened here?"

"It's Kruger," the limo said. "Kruger released the demon in Utah. He's taking orders from someone outside the company."

"Who?" Theodore asked. "Who's he taking orders from?"

"I don't know who." The limo hacked and wheezed. "I didn't want to help the bastard, but he started putting sugar in my gas tank. Not a lot at first, but you have to believe me. He said if I didn't keep quiet, he'd start using more."

Corolla muttered, "That's sick."

Theodore asked the limo, "Kruger never said who he was working for? Not even a code name?"

"Kruger only ever called her ma'am," the limo said. "Whoever he took orders from, it was a woman. That's all I know."

"And what about all these people?" Theodore demanded. "Why did he kill everyone in Henderson Creek?"

"Kruger didn't so this." The limo dashboard flickered. He didn't have much life left in him. "It was the demon Asag. The Skin Collector. He was sent to collect Kruger, but before they left the demon went from door to door peeling off everyone's skin. Oh, even the children. They screamed. They were all screaming."

The limo broke down, sobbing.

"Asag is loose, too?" I whispered to Theodore.

He nodded and turned back to the limo. "Hey, buddy. Stay with me, okay? Did Kruger say where they were going?"

The limo sniffled and said, "No. I thought when they were gone, I could contact HQ without Kruger finding out. But he knew he couldn't trust me. He wasn't going to leave me alive. He wrecked me into this pole. And now I'm going to... I'm going to..." The limo coughed and hacked some more, then his voice turned desperate. "You have to warn Westland. Kruger's not alone. There's others. I heard the conference calls myself. There's so many others."

"I don't understand," Theodore said. "Why would Westland agents destroy the company? What do they get out of that?"

But the limo didn't get to answer. His dashboard went dark and the speakers went silent.

"Well," Corolla said. "We have to bury him."

Theodore arched his eyebrow. "What?"

"He's dead," Corolla said. "You can't just leave him on the road like this. We got to bury him."

Theodore crossed his arms. "I'm not burying a limo."

I spoke up. "And why not?"

"Because it's a *car*?" Theodore said. By the look on his face, it was obvious that he wasn't expecting me – a human – to side with the proper burial of a vehicle. But I wasn't exactly human. And after dozens of conversations with Corolla about the way humanity would treat living, thinking machines, I'd come around to his way of thinking.

And this limo wasn't just a regular limo. He had thoughts and only what I could presume to be *feelings*, and Corolla was right: the limo deserved better than to be left on the side of the road in Henderson Creek where he would slowly rust into a pile of scrap.

"Sir," Denali chimed in. "I think they might be right."

"Denali!" Theodore said. He sounded betrayed.

"Don't get mad at her," I told him. "She's a living car, too. Wouldn't you bury her if she died?"

"Good question," Denali said. "Would you bury me, sir?"

"Well, of course I would bury *you*," Theodore said. "But you're different. You're..."

"I'm...?" Denali said.

"She's...?" I added, turning up the heat and encouraging him to finish his thought.

Theodore gave me a stunned look. "You can't be serious."

I shrugged. "Someday all of the cars will be self-aware. And they're going to be in for a long, rough road before humans treat them right. They're going to need examples of people who were doing the right thing, before it was the right thing to do. So we might as well start now."

Theodore realized he was outnumbered three-to-one and resigned the argument with a heavy exhale.

"What about all the people of Henderson Creek?" Theodore asked. "Do you want to bury all 437 of them?"

"Don't be ridiculous," Corolla said. "That would take forever. We don't have that kind of time."

We buried the limo in a grove of trees on the outskirts of town. Corolla and Denali sang a funeral dirge version of "Like A Rock." I used a bunch of sticks to make the Chrysler logo for his grave. Corolla informed me that's like using a cross for a human. Denali agreed – of course – and went on to say it prevents cars from coming back as "zoombies," which are just zombie cars.

I looked a real mess. I had dirt all over me from digging a grave for a limousine and ash all over my Westland suit from fighting a demon. My hair was filthy, my face was covered with black smudges, and my skirt was torn up along the hem. I used to look like a fresh, clean Westland agent, but now I looked like-

"You look like a bomb went off in your face," Theodore said.

"Thanks." I tugged on my suit jacket, which was filthy in places and shredded in others, but still in one piece. "These suits actually hold up pretty well."

"Don't they? They're bulletproof. Fireproof. Waterproof" He admired the sleeve of his own jacket. Then he turned to me and looked me up and down. "I've never seen anyone tear one up so bad before."

"I can be pretty rough on clothes," I said.

We stood there in silence. Theodore stuck his hand in his jacket and pulled out a candy bar. The wrapper was bright yellow with red print. He ripped it open, took a bite off the end and started chewing.

"Where'd you get that?" I asked him.

He pointed behind us. "Gas station."

"What'd you get?"

He chewed his candy and held the wrapper where I could see it. It said *Kreenkle.*

I squinted at him. "They had Kreenkles?"

"Mhmm." He gave the candy bar an approving look, as if it were the most logical thing in the world to find Swedish candy in the middle of Fuckall, Nebraska. He took another bite, then stuck it in my face. "Want to try it?"

"No," I said. "I don't like bananas."

"Ah, well, that's the secret." He lowered his voice to whisper. "They're not real bananas."

"I'm fine, thank you."

He pushed the candy bar closer to my mouth. "Here. Try it."

I pushed his hand away from me. "The fuck are you doing? Get that shit out of my face."

The Kreenkle smelled disgusting, but it did occur to me that I hadn't eaten anything since I found those railroad spikes two stops ago. The smelting chamber of my stomach was out of raw materials and grumbled like an improperly shifting car. Chow time. I ripped a steel mile marker out of the ground and ate it like a strip of taffy. It didn't taste bad, but it wasn't the best either. It's kinda like how TV dinners are edible, but they definitely don't taste good.

I leaned against Corolla. Theodore reclined against Denali's back bumper. We faced one another, eating candy and steel.

"I still don't get it," Theodore said. "Why would those agents back-stab the Westland Corporation. What do they get out of the deal by putting themselves out of a job?"

I said, "Maybe they've come to their senses and realize the Westland Corporation isn't the paragon of virtue you've made it out to be. Maybe they realize the world would be better off without them."

Theodore thought for a moment, then said, "The world wouldn't *be* here if it wasn't for Westland."

I rolled my eyes. "You're so brainwashed, dude. 'Wouldn't *be* here'? You're fucking crazy, man. Drink some more Kool-aid."

"You don't know what you're talking about," he said. "Who stopped the invasion of Ravine People from Grand Canyon 2199? Or who convinced the Hurricanes and Cyclones and Typhoons not to go to war with the world? Who keeps the true identity of the Roman gods a secret safe from the government?"

I chewed the steel into a molten mess and swallowed. "I'm guessing the answer is the Westland Corporation."

"The Westland Corporation." He stared off into the corn fields. "We do the right thing, sometimes."

"If you say so." I got tired of how my mile marker tasted and flung it a half-mile off into the fields. "If you want to convince me that you guys do *some* good, *some* times, help me figure out what's wrong with Xin. That would be a great place to start."

"I will." He stuck the last bit of Kreenkle in his mouth, wadded up the wrapper and stuck it in his pocket. "In fact, I know an Oracle we can ask for answers."

"An Oracle?" As if you can just find Oracles anywhere, like Kreenkles. "Oracles are in, like, Egypt and Greece and shit."

"Those aren't the only Oracles. There's one just a few hours away from here. I read it in my research. It's super hush hush."

I slowly lifted my butt off Corolla and stood upright. "You're not joking? There's an Oracle here in America?"

"Yep." He was all smiles and confidence. "And I'll take you there. That's what a field agent would do, so let's do it."

There were only three or four Oracles left on Earth, at least, as far as I knew. I liked the idea of meeting another one. There were a lot of supernatural things yet to be discovered in the world, and who was I to pass up on an opportunity like that.

"Okay." I headed over to Corolla's driver side door. "If you're sure, let's do it."

"I thought we were going back to New York City," Corolla complained. "All we've done is find dead bodies and bury a limo and now we're off to find an Oracle?"

"Corolla..." I began.

But I didn't need to convince him. Denali did that for me.

"You're not thinking about leaving, are you?" she asked him. "You're important to me! You're the first free car I've ever met! I want to bring you back home to Westland so everyone else can meet you. Just hang out with us a little longer."

"I... uh..." Corolla stammered, blindsided by the adoration of a pretty car. "It's just..."

"You're not scared, are you?" she asked.

I thought that was funny, so I jumped in with mock sympathy. "Corolla? Are you scared?"

"I am not scared!" he said.

"Alright, cool." I got in and closed the door. "Then let's go."

We had Corolla backed into a corner. He mumbled "Alright" and that was that.

Denali pulled away from the shoulder and started down the road. Corolla followed after her. Before we got too far, I stuck my head out the window and shouted at Theodore. "Hey! Where are we going exactly?"

Theodore waved his finger north. "Mount Rushmore!"

Chapter 13

1

South Dakota.

The Black Hills.

I'd never been to South Dakota and I'd never seen Mount Rushmore in real life before. We arrived at the Black Hills National Forest in the early afternoon. The air was cooler that far north and I could see snow on the distant mountain peaks.

The road curved through a forest of pine trees so tall, it felt like an alternate-world version of Midtown where all of the towering skyscrapers were replaced by nature. We drove over hills, up and down, and weaved deeper into the mountains of the Dakotas. Millennium-old spires of granite jutted out of the treetops like wizard towers. Eagles circled the stone peaks, protecting the skies and hunting the wildlife that lived below.

There had to be bears out those woods, right? And elk, probably. Other animals, too, I would assume, but I don't have the first clue what kind of animals live in South Dakota. Otters, I guess? Maybe a musk ox? Those were my best guesses. I don't know shit about animals. It would be cool to see an otter, though. Otters are cute as fuck.

Amid all the nature, we passed touristy signs depicting picnic tables, camping tents, and old-school cameras. Picnics, this way. Camping, this way. Good photography spots, this way.

Denali took the hills so fast that she actually lifted off the ground when we crossed a bump. He tires squealed against the concrete and left black marks on the road when we took tight turns through the trees. We passed signs that warned us about hazardous curves, but she blazed right past them. No surprise there. An adrenaline junkie like her wanted the twists and turns.

"Do you think Denali's cool?" Corolla asked me as we followed her down a particularly dangerous curve.

"I think she's nuts," I said. She was impressive, as far as cars go, but I worried she might not be the best influence for Corolla.

"I like the way she never uses her windshield wipers, even when its raining. She's so confident, like she doesn't even care."

Oh boy. Someone had a crush.

"Do you think she likes me?" he asked.

"Well." I didn't know how to gauge that kind of thing. "She did call you Car Jesus."

"Yeah..." Corolla's voice trailed off. "Do you think she, like, *likes* me, likes me?"

"I have no idea, dude."

Corolla sighed, defeated.

I would have been a bad friend if I didn't ask, "What's wrong?"

He said, "She's a 2013 GMC Denali. I'm a 1998 Corolla. She's got leather seats and tinted, Vatican-grade bullet-proof glass. I've got sticky cup holders and I reek of teenage body odor."

Did he say body odor? "Okay, now hang on just a minute."

"She wouldn't want a jalopy like me."

I sniffed my arm pit. "I don't have body odor."

"That's nice of you to say," Corolla replied, obviously not listening. "But I'm being realistic. I'm sixteen. Do you know how old that is in car years? Most cars don't even make it to sixteen."

"If anything, you smell like egg rolls," I said. "And that's your doing. Not mine."

"I'm a piece of junk compared to Denali. She's got GPS and I've got a cassette player. She could do way better than me."

"Corolla, stop. If someone really likes you, they're not going to care if you're old, or if you only have a cassette player, or if you smell like homemade patchouli deodorant, which, might I remind you, I put on *every* day."

"Is *that* what that smell is?" he asked.

"You're a cool car, Corolla. You can fly. You're funny. You have questionable taste in music, but we can work on that."

"I do not have questionable taste in music," he said. "Phil Collins is a national treasure."

"Okay, well, for one, Phil Collins is British, so he can't be a national treasure."

"He's won seven Grammys."

"He's not in the Rock and Roll Hall of Fame," I said.

"The Rock and Roll Hall of Fame is a scam and you know it."

Corolla was right. But somehow we had gotten way off topic.

"I'll tell you one thing, though," I said, steering us back on track. "Nothing is less attractive than acting like a self-conscious wimp with low self-esteem."

"I am not a wimp!"

"I know you're not a wimp. I'm saying you act like one."

He hummed, thoughtfully. "Maybe you're right."

"Of course I'm right," I said. "Just remember: when you talk to Denali, you need to project confidence. She's never going to think you're cool if *you* don't think you're cool."

"Project confidence," he said, repeating my advice. It sounded like it was sinking in. "Okay. I'm going to try it."

We passed a sign that read SPEED LIMIT 10 – DANGEROUS CURVES AHEAD.

"She's got some dangerous curves ahead," Corolla said.

I rolled my eyes.

The road took a sharp twist through the dense forest; so sharp we couldn't' see what was coming around the corner. Denali took this as a challenge. She didn't drop to ten miles per hour. In fact, she accelerated to thirty, taking the curves at dangerously high speeds. She pulled ahead of us and so far out of sight that we could only hear the sound of her squealing tires.

"I'm telling you," I said. "She's crazy."

"Yeah," Corolla said. I could hear the love sickness in his voice. "She sure is."

Corolla was far more cautious with the hairpin turns. He took the road at the recommended ten miles per hour. I didn't blame him. One false move, one slip up, and we'd crash down the mountainside and explode against a bunch of pine trees.

"Hey, maybe we can go on a double date sometime," Corolla suggested. "Me and Denali, and you and..."

He trailed off.

I glared at the radio. "Me and who?"

Corolla cleared his throat. "Never mind."

"No." I wasn't letting him off the hook. "Me and who?"

"Come on," he said. "You're still trying to act like you don't like him? Because I'm not buying it."

"This again?" I reclined my seat all the way back and closed my eyes. "You're so stupid sometimes."

"You're stupid if you think I'm stupid," he said. "You want to take that cowboy to Wrangler Town so bad, it's obvious."

"Go to Hell." I crossed my arms. I'd never heard anything so absurd in my whole life.

"Can I be best man?" Now he was laughing. "I have that suit from the Suit Monster. I've been looking for a reason to wear it."

"That's it." I sat up and wedged my fingers into his door panel, ready to pry it loose. "I'm disconnecting your speakers."

"I'll stop! I'll stop!" But he was still laughing.

I gave the radio a stern, silent look. This was his one and only warning. "I'll do it." I gave his door panel a slight tug.

"I'm stopping!" He sounded sincere. He did his best to stifle his laughter, but at least he was trying. "Scouts honor."

I let go of his door panel.

He kept his giggles under control.

Corolla and I reached the bottom of the hill where the road straightened out. Denali had such a lead on us from her death-wish speeds, I expected to see her a mile up the road. She wasn't that far away. In fact, she had come to a complete stop just up the road. Striped construction barricades blocked off the entrance to the Mount Rushmore National Park. Attached to the road block was a black sign with white letters.

Because of the
Federal Government SHUTDOWN,
All National Parks
Are CLOSED.
-U.S. Department of the Interior

I muttered, "What the hell?"

I saw Theodore climb out of Denali and poke around the blockade. I got out and joined him. The park seemed deserted, with only the sounds of birds in the trees. There were no rangers, no minivans with out-of-state plates, nothing.

"What the hell's all this?" I asked.

"No idea." He lifted one side of the wooden blockade and scraped it across the concrete, dragging it off the road. "I guess the Federal Government shut down?"

I grabbed a blockade and chucked it into the treeline.

226

"Do they do that?" I asked. "They can just shut down the government?"

"I guess so. It's what the sign says."

I pitched the other blockade into the woods and cleared our path. We climbed back into our respective cars and continued into the park as trespassers.

2

I'm not the most patriotic person. I like America just fine, but I don't own little American flags or anything and I think politics are bullshit. With all that in mind, I will say this: Mount Rushmore is a pretty cool thing to see.

It looked just like it did on the internet, only further away, and a little bit smaller than I thought. The pictures you see in textbooks and on the internet are all close-ups. We admired the sculptures from an observation deck, home to a gift shop which was closed due to the government shut down. All along the guard rails were those metal binocular machines where, for fifty cents, you could stick your face up against them to get a better look at the mountainside statue.

We had the whole observation desk to ourselves. No rangers, no tourists, just me and Theodore and Corolla and Denali. It probably wasn't safe – or legal – to let Corolla and Denali drive onto the observation deck with us, but it's not like there was anyone around to stop us. The platform was concrete and normally supported hundreds of tourists, so I assumed it could handle two people and a couple cars.

Theodore and I leaned against the rails. Denali and Corolla flanked us on either side.

"So where's this Oracle?" I asked.

"You're looking at it," Theodore said, casting his arms in front of us. "Mount Rushmore!"

"Mount Rushmore's the Oracle?"

He was super excited to share this new information with me. "Isn't that amazing? Not a lot of people know that."

I took a good look at the monument. Washington kind of had his eyes angled down at us, I guess. Jefferson and Roosevelt stared off into the sky. And Lincoln, he was definitely looking at us; almost as if he were judging us. An eagle drifted over their heads, or maybe it was a hawk, and its echoing scream was the only sound for miles and miles.

If these four presidents were Oracles, they certainly weren't the chatty type.

"Are you sure this is an Oracle?" I asked.

"Positive," Theodore said.

"Huh." I frowned at the four presidents. They didn't talk, or move, or seem alive at all. I glanced at Theodore. "So how do we get them to talk?"

Theodore put his hand over his heart and started singing. "Oh, say can you see, by the dawns early light..."

Oh my god, public speaking was one thing, but public *singing*? I was humiliated on Theodore's behalf.

"What are you doing?" I asked him.

He kept his hand over his heart. "This is how you get them to talk to you. You sing the National Anthem. They love it." He turned his attention back to Mount Rushmore and went back to singing. "Oh, say can you see, by the dawns early light, what so proudly we hailed at the twilight's last gleaming..."

Theodore was making an absolute fool of himself, singing all alone with his hand over his heart. He didn't have much of a singing voice, either, but that didn't bother him; he held his head up high and sang with confidence.

He stopped and whispered at me. "You sing, too."

"No," I said, laughing and backing away from him. "Absolutely not. You don't want to hear me sing."

"Penelope." He nodded his head at the mountain. "You have to do it or it won't work."

I sighed. Stupid supernatural world and their stupid rules. At least if I was going to make an ass out of myself, it wouldn't be alone and no one else was around. I reluctantly put my hand over my heart, faced the monument, and joined him.

I'm tone deaf and suck at singing.

"Whose broad stripes and bright stars,
through the perilous fight,
and the ramparts we watched
were so gallantly streaming."

Corolla chimed in. Corolla's a way better singer than me. He's got a natural ear for it and his range gets way more practice singing along to Phil Collins and Chicago. He harmonized with our voices and actually made us sound decent.

"And the rockets red glare
the bombs bursting in air."

Finally, Denali added her wry, snarky voice to the final few bars. She also had a nice singing voice, a little gravely, like Courtney Love, but talented.

"Gave proof through the night
that our flag was still there.
Oh, say does that star spangled banner yet wave,
on the land of the free
and the home of the brave."

Corolla shouted, "Play ball!"

There. We finished the National Anthem. My eyes darted back and forth, anticipating something magical to happen.

A strong wind descended from the mountains and blew across the valley, so strong it nearly knocked Theodore over. It ruffled my hair and billowed through my clothes. It hissed through the forest trees, rustled the leaves and snapped some twigs loose.

That's when the faces of Mount Rushmore cracked loose from their stone prison. Chunks of rock came clattering down to the mountainside. George Washington blinked his bleary, stone eyes, as if waking up from a century-long nap. Thomas Jefferson inhaled deeply and his granite cheeks puffed out as he exhaled. Theodore Roosevelt scrunched his face and arched his eyebrows, adjusting to his flexible face. The hairs of Abraham Lincoln's beard moved in the wind as if it were made of hair, not stone.

I was a little star-struck, honestly. I mean, these were the guys from history class. Their faces are printed on our money. And there they were, alive and wide awake, looking down at us with curious eyes, and we were about to speak to them.

"Gentlemen," Washington said in a British accent. His voice echoed from his cavernous mouth, coming from deep inside the Earth. He looked right at us. "We have visitors."

Jefferson was next to speak. "You must be brilliant adventurers to know our secret. Your journey here must have been dangerous and long." Jefferson also had a British accent. His head was carved slightly behind the others and had to peer over Washington's shoulder to get a good look at us.

"We love dangerous journeys," Corolla announced, a little over-eager. He was following my advice about confidence, which was good, but he took it a little far. "We aren't afraid of shit!"

"Okay, that's enough." I put my hand on his roof. "You want to sound confident, not like a crazy person."

"Sorry," Corolla whispered.

"Your metal stagecoaches are most peculiar," Lincoln said. His accent was rustic and American-sounding. Funny thing about Lincoln: he sounded exactly like what I expected, like how he sounds in movies and on TV. His voice boomed across the woods and echoed back at us from all around. "They can speak."

"Can they ever," I said with an irritated tone, but I meant it as a joke.

"It's kind of a pain in the ass sometimes," Theodore added.

"Are you British?" Washington asked us with a twinge of aggression to his voice. "Did the Crown send you?"

I expected Theodore to answer. This was his idea after all. He looked at me, expecting me to do it. Oh. Apparently talking was my job. Okay. I don't usually get nervous, but I'd been put on the spot, forced to talk to the most famous presidents in American history. I took a step forward, rubbed my nose, and spoke loud and clear.

"We don't know the Crown. No one sent us. We came here on our own. My name is Penelope and this is my friend Theodore from the Westland Corporation. These are our cars, Corolla and Denali. We're Americans."

Corolla spoke up. "Technically, I'm Japanese."

I corrected myself. "Technically, he's Japanese."

Jefferson spoke next. "And what brings you here, Penelope? What knowledge have you come in search of?"

"Uh." I brushed the ash and dirt off my Westland suit and smoothed it out to make myself look presentable. "Well, we've got a couple questions, actually. My friend from New York, Xin Houng, he was attacked by someone and they put his soul in a coma. My friend said the only way to help him get better is to find who's responsible and have them fix it. Problem is, I have no idea who that is."

Theodore took a step forward. "And at my job, a bunch of traitors are trying to destroy my organization from the inside. I need to find out who they are so I can stop them."

Denali pulled forward. "And Darla thinks her husband is cheating on her. He's a cruise ship captain, so he's gone for months at a time and I'm not going to say that he *is* cheating on her, but I'd like to know for sure."

"And... uh..." Corolla rolled up. "Is it true that Phil Collins was born in Britain? Because I recently heard that from a notorious liar and it sounds made up."

"Dude," I said. "He was totally born in Britain."

"Uh huh," Corolla replied. "I was asking *them*."

The four presidents stared at us in deep thought, communicating telepathically, maybe. They were carved from the same rock and probably shared the same brain... or whatever they had for a brain. After a few moments, they spoke up.

"We are bound by the curse which trapped us here," Washington said. "As we disregarded the sanctity of human life to control this land, now we are forever bound to it. If you want us to answer your questions, you must prove that you are truly citizens of the United States of America."

"Proof?" I asked.

Jefferson gave me a nod of the head. "To our satisfaction."

3

"Uhh." I patted my pockets out of habit, but these weren't my clothes. This suit was a loaner from Westland and this skirt didn't come with pockets. I was an American citizen, through and through, but Mount Rushmore wanted me to prove it. Let's see here. Proof. Proof. "I don't have proof, necessarily."

Jefferson asked. "You don't have any kind of identification? Your certificate of birth? Your family crest?"

"No," I said. I glanced at Theodore. "You got a family crest?"

Theodore whispered, "I have no idea what that is."

I whispered back. "I have no idea what that is, either. What about your driver's license? You got that?"

He gave me a weird look. "I don't have a driver's license."

"What? How do you not have a driver's license?"

He shrugged. "I work for Westland. I've never needed one."

"Never needed one? We've been driving for the last twenty hours. You need one to drive."

"I haven't been driving," he said. "Denali has."

"Well, hell." I looked around and tried to think of something to offer as proof. All we had were Corolla and Denali. But that gave me an idea. I spun back around to the presidents and gestured to their front bumpers. "My car has an American license plate! From New York."

"That's not quite proof," Roosevelt said.

"Those might not be your cars," Jefferson said.

"You could be British spies," Washington said.

"Or Confederate spies," Lincoln added.

"Christ sake, you guys are paranoid," I muttered. "We're not at war with Britain any more and the Civil War's been over for, like, sixty years! For real, guys, we're not spies. We are one-hundred-percent legit, red-blooded Americans!"

"I'm Japanese," Corolla said.

"And I don't have blood," said Denali.

Theodore made things worse when he said, "I'm technically not sure if I was born in America or not."

That was new. I turned to him. "You're not?"

He shrugged. "I was raised by the Corporation. It's never come up."

"Look." All this was really starting to piss me off. I leaned against the safety rail and waved my fist at the four American presidents. "Listen to my accent, you god damn morons! I grew up in Manhattan! I've had my ass groped on the subway! You don't get any more American than that! We drove twenty hours to get here, we sang your stupid song, so unless you want me to come up there and jackhammer your faces, I suggest you play nice and make with the fucking prophecies already."

That made them think. Good. That's the exactly what those jamokes needed.

Washington opened his mouth and said, "Recite for us the Constitution of the United States."

I blinked at them. "What?"

"If you are truly Americans," Jefferson continued, "then you should be able to recite the Constitution of the United States."

"Uh, no?" I said. "There's not an American alive who can recite the Constitution of the United States from memory."

"We will allow you to say the Bill of Rights instead," Roosevelt offered.

"Are you fucking serious..." I was stunned. "I don't know the fucking Bill of Rights. Best I could give you is the 'four score and seven years ago' speech. That's all I got."

Washington, Jefferson, and Roosevelt did not seem at all impressed by that idea. Lincoln, on the other hand? His eyes lit up and a smile crept up on his face. That 'four score and seven years ago' speech was his number one hit.

"I think reciting that speech is acceptable," Lincoln said.

"No, it is not," Washington said.

"Yes, it is," Lincoln argued. "It's a perfectly valid piece of American history. If she can recite that speech, then she must truly be an American citizen." He looked back down at me. "Go ahead, young lady."

I lucked out on this one. I had to memorize that speech for history class my sophomore year. Still, that was years ago. I wasn't sure I quite remembered it all.

"Four score and seven years ago," I began, "our forefathers brought forth on this continent a new nation, conceived in liberty, and dedicated to the proposition that all men are created equal. Now we are engaged in a great civil war testing... uh..."

Shit.

"Testing whether that nation..." Lincoln said, helping me out.

"Right. Testing whether that nation or any nation so conceived and so dedicated can long endure. We are met on a great battlefield of that war. We have come..."

And et cetera, et cetera, et cetera. The speech is only a couple paragraphs long, but aside from that one stumble at the beginning I remembered the whole thing perfectly. I was pretty impressed with myself, honestly.

I concluded, "...and that government of the people, by the people, for the people shall not perish from the Earth."

"Most eloquent," Lincoln said and gave me a warm smile. "I could not have done a finer job myself."

Man, praise from Honest Abe himself. I couldn't help but smile back.

"I am unconvinced," Washington said.

"As am I," Jefferson agreed.

"Her knowledge is impressive," Roosevelt said. "But I, too, continue to question her citizenship."

"Are you fucking kidding me?" I shouted. I had gone to all that trouble and now, suddenly, that wasn't good enough. "You guys are pricks, man. And slave owners, too. You should all be ashamed of yourselves. Not you Roosevelt. I don't think you had slaves, but I'm sure you did something. What'd you do? Did you drop the bomb?" I turned back to Theodore and the cars. "What'd this guy do? Give me something to yell at him about."

But Theodore and the cars didn't know.

"You three may depart if you wish," Lincoln told the other presidents. "But the girl has moved my granite heart as never before. I believe she is an American and I alone will help her answer the questions that perplex her so."

Those three other presidents closed their mouths. The severe-weather winds swept back over the valley, this time in the opposite direction. Their stone faces shifted back to their original positions. As they returned to their slumber, they each got in a few parting shots.

"Remember this, young lady," Washington said as his face stiffened and the life drained out of him. "Prophecies can be most unforgiving."

"Knowledge of the past or the future is unnatural," Jefferson said as he froze into place. "And it comes at a great cost."

"With our blessing, also comes a curse." Roosevelt's eyes turned vacant and he stared off into the distance.

Only Lincoln was left.

"Join hands, travelers," he said. "And close your eyes. I will bring you a vision that will lead to the answers you seek."

I put my right hand on Corolla's roof and took Theodore's hand in my left. Theodore put his other hand on Denali's door handle. Once we were ready, I closed my eyes.

"Do you think this is going to hurt?" Corolla whispered. "I don't want it to hurt."

I didn't answer him, but I rubbed my open palm on his roof in calming circles.

Lincoln started off by saying, "I'll tell you of a distant land, decades ago, in a place you call the Ukraine..."

And then something hit me. Solid knowledge. It smacked me in the face like a physical brick and knocked my head back. And when I opened my eyes...

Chapter 14

1

The Ghost Pirate Navy.

The Astounding Maxwell Seaboots – immortal specter, pirate, and former pirate admiral – paddled his haunted rowboat over the European hills. Through the dark night came the ethereal green glow of the Irish Goodbye, the ship he once sailed when he still had breath left in him. The two boats moved under the constellation Orion.

Centuries ago, the seven seas were filled with phantom pirate boats from all along the European coastline. Cursed to a ghastly life spent sailing the waters and unable to pull into the port, these ghost pirate ships traveled the seas and plundered merchant vessels for the most precious cargo there is: souls. Rumors spread from port to port; tall tales of a haunted boat that sailed under the stars of Orion and a cursed rowboat that paddled upside down across the surface of the water.

These stories were true.

But time had passed. One by one, those ghost captains and their haunted crewmen began to fulfill the conditions of their curse and found freedom in the afterlife. Only thirteen ghost boats made it to the information age, captained by the last thirteen ghost captains commanding the last thirteen ghost pirate crews. In their living days, these captains were the most evil and bloodthirsty, with punishments so powerful that they were still bound by it 300 years later.

Rosalita "Eyes of the Sun" Sanchez, captain of the Black Octopus, was known for capturing children of royalty and ransoming them back to their families. Of course, even if the ransom was paid, she would never return the children. No, it made far more sense to raise them on a life of piracy until they were old enough to become a member of her crew.

The Unkillable "Shark Fin" Finnegan, captain of the Bad Moon, survived four executions, crawled away from nine assassination attempts, and emerged victorious from two very bloody mutinies. Rumor had it his first murder was his own brother at the age of seven.

But most important among the ghost pirate captains was the Astounding Maxwell Seaboots. The Astounding Maxwell Seaboots demanded that his crew refer to him as the Astounding Maxwell Seaboots at all times. Not Maxwell. Not Captain. "The Astounding Maxwell Seaboots." Anyone who forgot, even once, would have their tongue cut out. The Astounding Maxwell Seaboots found the fountain of youth when he was only twenty-five years old and drank its water, so even after dying at seventy, he had the appearance and energy of a man a fraction of his age.

The Astounding Maxwell Seaboots captained the Irish Goodbye, a swift battleship with twenty ghost cannons, dozens of ghost pirates armed with flintlock pistols and knives, and a powder room filled to the ceiling with barrels and barrels of ghostpowder. He sailed the Irish Goodbye around the Atlantic Ocean at night – a shimmering green mirage that glowed across the black ocean – where he and his crew would delight in chasing down city-sized international freight tankers moving European cars from Italy to the New York City. He would stand on the prow of the ship, wave his saber in wild circles, and cackle at the ships as they fled in terror.

International freight tankers were operated by computers and GPS, so no one noticed the Irish Goodbye or The Astounding Maxwell Seaboots. The captain was unaware of such things and believed he was a true scourge of the seas.

Because of his overwhelming charm and ruthless cunning, the Astounding Maxwell Seaboots had been appointed Admiral of the Ghost Pirate Navy.

When The Astounding Maxwell Seaboots would venture off alone, which he sometimes liked to do, he would lower a translucent rowboat made of bright green light and paddle it through the ocean, or over land, or up into the clouds. As part of any pirates curse, he could never step foot on solid land; he, like all the others, were cursed to sail, and sail forever, no matter where on Earth they ended up.

On this day, the Astounding Maxwell Seaboots paddled his glowing rowboat over the dark hills of the countryside, en route to a very important meeting. His uniform was a collection of garments stolen from all the British and Spanish naval officers he had killed. His triangular hat was oversized and decorated with the fluttering feather of a tropical bird. Beneath his hat were soaking wet dreadlocks decorated with gold rings and various seashells.

Iron shackles hung loose from his wrists and ankles, and they clinked and clattered with each row of his paddles. He carried a pirate saber attached to his belt – the Sword of Twenty-Three Men – a haunted weapon soaked with the blood of 23 innocent victims; blood that would never dry and could never be wiped away. Because of the blades cursed nature, it had the power to wound other supernatural beings, which the Astounding Maxwell Seaboots had done once or twice before.

Also in the rowboat was a heavy treasure chest, attached to the Astounding Maxwell Seaboots by chains looped and padlocked around his waist and torso. The treasure chest had physical weight, not to the rest of the world, but only to the Astounding Maxwell Seaboots. Inside the chest was his entire worldly fortune: Spanish doubloons, precious crown jewels, and exotic spices from far away lands. Cursed by a Voodoo priestess to carry his fortune with him for all eternity, the Astounding Maxwell Seaboots could not undo the chains and found it impossible to give away any of his wealth to lighten his load.

The treasure chest was a punishment for his mortal greed. The Astounding Maxwell Seaboots saw it as a reminder of how unbelievably stinking rich he was when he was alive. He carried it around for 400 years, but knew in his heart that he would do it all over again, no regrets, if given half a chance.

"The only regret I have," he once said, "is that I didn't steal more."

2

The Seven Ninja Clans.

How many ninjas existed in the world? No one could say for sure, not even the ninjas themselves. Their law as assassins required them to live in absolute anonymity, without names and without personal identity. No ninja had ever revealed their face to anyone, not even another ninja, and any ninja who showed their face was expected to disembowel themselves immediately.

Even in battle, it was impossible to get a headcount on the ninjas. They were always moving, always shifting, always ducking in and out of the shadows, a choreographed dance of black bandages and obsidian weapons. When it came to the total population of ninjas in the world, the guesses varied wildly from as few as 3,001 to as many as 171,719.

The ninjas lived in the Ink Woods, a glade of trees that existed in endless midnight and moved like a shadow across the emptiest parts of Japan. In these woods were seven shadow dojos crafted from pure darkness. Each clan had their own dojo: the Centipede, the Fugu, the Hornet, the Komodo, the Leech, the Octopus, and the Scorpion. Through some innate sense, the ninjas were able to tell one clan apart from another, but that ability was unique to only them.

The ninjas draped themselves in black silk, spun from the Gloom Silkworms that made their homes in the black trees of the Ink Woods. They tied this silk against their bodies with lengths of black rope, which also provided them with countless places to hide a weapon. Even their hands and feet were wrapped in silk, to cover their footprints and hide their fingerprints. The only visible part of a ninja were the eyes, through a small slit in the silk that covered their faces.

Each ninja clan specialized in a different type of subterfuge. The Centipede were masters of climbing and positioning, able to scale sheer surfaces and crawl across ceilings. The Fugu created some of the deadliest poisons on Earth, poisons so deadly they were rumored to have the power to kill gods. The Hornet trained in archery, able to strike very precise targets from unimaginable distances. The Komodo, who learned to subside without food or water or sleep, could remain hidden in a single place for weeks or months as they waited for their target to cross their path. The Leech had total mastery of underwater operations, able to hold their breaths indefinitely and emerge from bodies of water completely dry. The Octopus trained in pairs and fought as a single entity, using their combined arms and legs to quickly defeat any opponent. Lastly, the Scorpion clan had perfected the Scorpion Stance, an otherwise unbeatable martial art that relied heavily on a single katana.

The seven ninja clans moved silently through the green hills of the Ukraine, right at home in a moonless sky.

3

Ohmsteel the Dragon.

Ohmsteel – an ice blue dragon – outlived all but three of her brothers and sisters. The other dragons that still lived on Earth had long ago fallen asleep and removed themselves from the concerns of mankind. They had all outlived the legend of dragons. After centuries of seclusion, the humans collectively decided that those mythical creatures didn't exist – had never existed – and that pleased Ohmsteel. The Great Blue Dragon was the oldest living thing on Earth, a distant cousin to the Brontosaurus, and quite similar in size and shape.

Minor differences set her apart from the ancient dinosaur. Two rows of sharpened spikes traveled down the back of her neck, over the arch of her spine, and across her tail. At the tip of her tail were four spikes the length of telephone poles, a dangerous and deadly weapon that once-upon-a-time swept devastation across entire human armies.

Also different were her claws, powerful and sharp, and nowhere near as clumsy as her lumbering herbivore cousins. No, these were the talons of a carnivore, a hunter sitting at the very top of the food chain.

The biggest difference, of course, were her leathery wings. Her wingspan was as wide as her body was long, giving her a dominating shadow that could blot out the sun.

Her scales could shimmer and shift into different shades of blue, giving her the ability to camouflage her body in the skies or the oceans. Hidden from view of the humans, she could watch them curiously as they built their cities. That was, at least, until the airplanes came along. After the airplanes, Ohmsteel moved to a remote cliff-side cave in the Arctic Ocean where she could spend months contemplating the sunrise, or years understanding the sound of crashing waves.

Her cave offered her the seclusion she wanted, as well as the sub-zero temperatures that blue dragons truly loved.

She would die soon. She felt it. She surprised herself each sunrise by outliving most other dragons, and not even by a little bit; but by entire centuries. And while she always assumed she would die in her frozen arctic cavern, alone, contemplating the nature of death, it seemed as though fate had called her for something different.

There was trouble out there – the real end-of-the-world kind – and what better way to atone for a lifetime of terrorizing the humans than to come to their rescue. She held her wings wide and glided silently over Eastern Europe, a place she remembered quite well, except the cities were so much smaller back then. Even after centuries of absence, she knew exactly where she was headed. Once a mile she would need to flap her wings – a leathery slap that closely resembled thunder – which kept her altitude just barely above humanity's various aircraft.

Each flap of wings brought a gust of freezing air and a sprinkle of snowflakes. It had been so many miles and Ohmsteel knew she was close to her destination.

4

CONAN.

A squeaky-wheeled audio/visual cart rolled its way through the grass. Its four wheels were designed for the flat floors of a high school hallway, not the lush fields and soft dirt of western Ukraine. Still, the AV cart pressed on ever forward, taking it slow when it needed to go slow, and circling around the large trees that got in its way.

On top of the AV cart was a boxy computer, complete with a keyboard, a one-button mouse and a floppy disk drive. The computer monitor was black and displayed a dot matrix of neon green letters. It was cutting edge technology for the time, powered by a bright orange extension cord that looped and weaved backwards over the hills, far off into the distance.

Green words appeared on the computer screen as it reassured itself.

"CAREFUL," it displayed. "CAREFUL."

It went to cross a wooded bridge that arched over a narrow creek. Halfway across the bridge, the cart stopped and turned to the side. The computer analyzed the trickling sound beneath it.

"WATER."

It turned and continued forward.

It rattled through the woods across a bumpy dirt path. It glimmered in the sunshine as it cut through a small valley of wild daisies. It bumped into a hollow log, paused, then backed up.

"LOG."

And having identified the obstruction, CONAN squeaked around it in a wide circle and continued on.

After crossing a few more hills and taking a wide detour around some fenced-in sheep, it came across a deer nibbling on grasses in an open field. The deer wasn't frightened by the approaching computer. Conan creaked to a stop. The deer sniffed Conan's keyboard, then moved to the other side of the cart and sniffed again.

Words appeared on the computer screen. "I AM CONAN."

A twig snapped in the nearby woods and caught the deer's attention. It looked at the trees, then darted away. Conan turned his cart, just slightly, to watch the deer leave. When the animal disappeared down into a little ravine, Conan resumed moving.

"I AM CONAN."

It had quite some time to go before it finished its journey.

"I WILL HELP."

5

The Were-Creatures.

It's been said that a species can smell their own extinction. Fennel, a young were-fox, smelled it. Something bad was coming for the were-creatures, and she wasn't about to go down without a fight. She traveled the world like a doomsday prophet, traveling on foot, changing between her human and fox forms, depending on what the situation called for.

As a human, Fennel kept many of her fox-like features: bright red hair with stripes of black and white, her eyes were golden and mischievous, and she had a fascination for raw fish. The humans called raw fish "sushi," but that wasn't raw fish. To Fennel, raw fish is caught in a stream, and you sink your teeth into it while it's still very much alive.

Fennel, in her human form, could easily blend in with the homeless population. Her hair was unwashed and wild, she didn't care much for shoes, and the crazed look in her eyes kept most curious humans far away from her. That was just fine for Fennel. To her, humans were primates who abandoned their animal nature to invent things like radios and cuckoo clocks and honey-roasted peanuts.

As a fox, Fennel could travel through the fields and woods and rivers much faster than on her two clumsy human legs. With her fox nose, she could smell the faint traces of her extinction on the breeze. The end was drawing near for the were-creatures and she had to spread the word.

She told the arctic foxes in Canada. She told the mountain lions in the Rocky Mountains. She stowed away on an international freighter, sailed across the ocean, and told the dingos in Australia. She told the leopards in central China. She told the hyenas of the Sahara, to cackling laughter.

None of the were-creatures believed her. They didn't want to. Fennel believed they were in denial. She didn't have time for denial. Every time she ran through the woods and sniffed the air, the smell of death came stronger and stronger. Death, not just for her, but for all of them.

So she continued spreading the word. And as time went on, that smell of extinction came so strong on the wind that even the other were-creatures couldn't ignore it. Fennel was right, and they were fools for ignoring her. Fennel found herself elevated in the pack mentality, not just among the were-foxes, but among all the were-creatures. A few werewolves still viewed her as a madman rambling on and on about the "end times." Majority of them regarded her as a prophet. And since she had ideas how to save their lineage, they eventually came to accept her as their messiah.

The day finally came. Fennel was jolted awake by the putrid stench of death. Whatever extinction was coming for the were-creatures, it was days away. All they could do was band together, venture towards Europe, and fight it head-on, because the world is round and running away would never get them far enough.

Fennel sprinted through the grassy hills of the Ukraine under the noonday sun. Behind her came the entire were-population; every dog and dingo, every lion and tiger. Tens-of-thousands of animals flooded over the hills, howling and barking and roaring and cackling. They followed Fennel as she sniffed the air, leading them straight to oblivion.

6

Xin.

Xin Houng made the long trek across Europe on foot, an otherwise impossible feat for a man of 59 years, if not for the Xunsu Sandals of Chung-Kuei. Chung-Kuei, the Taoist god of travel and journeys, enchanted those sandals with the miraculous power of endurance, speed, and protection from the elements. Xin didn't travel at amazing speeds and any outside observer would see him only as an old man strolling along the countryside, but a strong supernatural force mysteriously whisked him from one location to another. A months long trek across an entire continent only took the old man several days.

He came in cotton pants and a bright blue windbreaker, clothes that hardly matched his profession as an accomplished alchemist and sworn protector of the worlds most dangerous, powerful weapons.

He brought with him a large bag woven from fine silk and embroidered with pastel flowers. The wooden handles were hand carved from fine oak and worn down by decades of use. The bag clinked and clattered with the sound of glass jars; items from his shop in New York that might prove useful in the upcoming war.

Despite his reputation among the supernatural world, Xin was still a mere mortal and typically remained uninvolved with celestial matters, but the day was too important. The world hung in the balance. Xin did not have the luxury of staying home.

Halfway across the Carpathian Mountains in Slovakia, as he trudged through knee-deep snow and howling winds, a gliding bird spotted the old man. The bird – a black crane with a white beak – descended from the sky and perched on an outcropping of rocks. It tilted its head this way and that, watching the old man climb the mountainside.

"Where are you going?" the Black Crane squawked.

"To the Ukraine," Xin said. He didn't even give the bird a passing glance. He marched past it.

The Black Crane flapped its long wings, chased after the old man, and perched again on some different rocks, further up.

"It's too cold for you here," the bird said. "You will die."

"Go away," Xin said.

The Black Crane tilted its head back on its long neck and coughed out honking noises that Xin recognized as laughter.

"Does this have something to do with the sailor ghosts?" the Black Crane asked. "And the electronic abacus? And the shapey-shifties? Tell me, human. Why do they all come to this place?"

Xin did not answer him. The Black Crane was a bad spirit from Buddhist mythology who told nothing but lies and loved to trick humans. Xin knew this. Xin also knew the Black Crane loved attention – it lived for attention – so while the best course of action was to ignore the Black Crane, that oftentimes only encouraged it further.

The Black Crane flapped its wings again, getting ahead of Xin, where it perched on the dead branch of a frost covered tree. It ruffled its feathers, preened its left wing furiously, then looked up with its dark, beady eyes.

"Do you know what I see in your future?" it asked.

"No," Xin said. "I do not."

"Fire," the bird said. "And screaming. And death. And an end to many things."

"I'm not listening to you," Xin replied.

Again, the Black Crane pointed its beak at the sky and honked out more laughter. "You should listen! You should!"

Xin shook his head and took another step. He was nearing the peak of the mountain, despite starting his uphill climb ten minutes ago.

"Do you want to guess my name?" the Black Crane asked.

"No," Xin replied.

"I'll give you three chances!" it offered.

Still, he said, "No."

"Would you like to make a wager?"

"No."

Xin crossed the peak of the mountain and began his descent down the other side. He took a moment to open his bag and retrieve a jar of red berries. Tucking the handles of his bag over his forearm, the unscrewed the lid and dipped his fingers inside.

"What are those?" the Crane asked from a nearby rock.

"Berries," Xin said. "They're all the food I have for the rest of my travel."

"May I have one?" the Black Crane asked.

"No, you may not."

"May I, please?" It spread its wings and glided down closer to him, landing in the snow. "Just one? Just to taste the flavor?"

"One," Xin said. "And only one."

Xin offered the Black Crane the jar, where the elegant bird could reach it with its beak.

Greedy, the Black Crane poked its head into the jar and gobbled all the berries up into its mouth. Then it tilted its head back and swallowed them down, stealing all of the old man's food. With its head still in the air, it honked with delight.

Xin screwed the lid onto the empty jar and put it back in his bag. Without a word, he resumed his travel down the mountain.

"How do you like that?" the Black Crane said. "I gobbled up all your food!"

"I like it just fine," Xin said. "Those berries weren't food. Those were Quiet Berries from Tir Ivoris. Eat one and you lose your voice for a day. You just ate forty-one of them."

The Black Crane looked at him and opened his beak to talk. All that came out was a pitiful honk. Confused, the crane shook its head and tried once more to speak. Again, it could only honk.

Xin reached the bottom of the mountain in peace. Although out of sight, he could still hear the Black Crane trying to speak. Its angry honks echoed through the trees.

Chapter 15

1

The Ukrainian Soviet Socialist Republic.

April 25, 1986.

Thousands of supernatural beings from all over the world gathered in the rolling hills of the Ukraine. The Ghost Pirate Navy, the seven ninja clans, the werewolves and were-foxes and were-tigers, a Great Blue Dragon, a self-aware computer, and a man from Chinatown filled those hills for one reason: the border between Earth and Hell had fractured open and Legion – the combined forces of all demonic armies in Hell – amassed on the other side. For the demons, this fracture was their one chance to flee their infernal prison and escape into the Land of Eden.

It wasn't a return to Heaven, but it would do.

Legion, if it reached Earth, would bring with it untold death and destruction. They would scorch the face of the Earth will rolling fire and choke the skies with clouds of sulfur, leaving the planet habitable for only them.

It was for this reason alone that the supernatural forces of Earth put their political bickering aside. A truce was agreed upon, because to ignore Legion meant the end of everything.

This part of the Ukraine had a sickness about it. The grass came in shades of yellow and brown, and it was stiff and crunchy. The trees grew tall, but in twisted shapes with sporadic wads of leaves. The leaves themselves were covered in moldy black spots.

The air reeked of burning plastic.

An abandoned highway cut through the hills and stretched off into the distance. The concrete was old and crumbling, and the telephone poles leaned in crooked directions. A collapsed farmhouse stood in the distance, scorched black from a long-forgotten fire. The stone chimney remained intact, overgrown with thin, yellow vines.

Circular ponds pock-marked the countryside, old dents from the Second World War, where artillery shells and landmines had blown perfect holes in the dirt. The prickly grass had grown to the edges of the holes and rain filled them with water. As nice as they seemed, the ponds were diseased and dangerous.

This region of the Ukraine had been hit hardest by the financial mistakes of the Soviet Union. In the Soviet's effort to display their power on a global stage, they had shuffled all of their money into military developments and a fledgling space program. Just two months prior, the Soviet Union – in an effort to display their wealth and scientific curiosity to the rest of the world – had launched their first components of the MIR space station into orbit.

The countryside was quiet and secluded, far from civilization. It was the ideal place for the supernatural armies to gather together and discuss their options.

In the east hills floated the thirteen ships of the Ghost Pirate Navy. They dropped anchor to secure themselves to the hills and prevent their ships from drifting away on invisible ocean currents. Their ghostly sails fluttered on a faint breeze that almost sounded like the gurgling voices of a thousand drowning men. The Astounding Maxwell Seaboots paddled his rowboat to the center hill – the tallest hill – where he would join the others.

Maneuvering through the warped and twisted trees in the west were the ninjas. They lurked in the shadows, disappeared behind impossibly narrow trees and filled the woods like an infestation of fleas. Seven ninjas broke rank and approached the hill on foot; one representative from each clan.

From the north came the howling and barking of ten-thousand of animals. Leading the pack was a bright red fox with black paws. She sprinted far ahead and left the others behind. When she reached the bottom of the hill, the fox shifted into her human form and rose to stand on two feet. This nude woman scaled up the side of the hill.

Ohmsteel the dragon approached from the south skies, bringing with her cold winds and a dusting of snowflakes. She swooped down fast and landed on a nearby hill, stabbing her sharp claws into the rock. Her body was far too massive to share the center hill with the others, so she kept her body at a distance and used her long neck to stretch closer to the gathering. She lowered her head down to the surface where she could scrutinize these strange new allies with her bright, golden eyes.

All of them – the pirate, the ninjas, the were-fox, and the dragon – stared in confusion as a squeaky metal cart rolled up the grass. An orange extension cord dragged behind it like an infinite tail. Slowly, it creaked up the hill in little bursts, starting and stopping, as if maybe it were running out of gas. It was, in fact, just being overly cautious; it had come a long way and now that it was in the home stretch, didn't want the final hill to be what knocked it over.

Last to join the group was Xin Houng, who suddenly and mysteriously walked onto the top of the hill. He stood alongside the others and set his bag down in the grass. Everyone heard the glass jars clinking inside. With his hands at his sides, he gave the group a respectful bow. Then he took notice of CONAN, the computer and raised his eyebrow.

"What are you?" he asked.

Green words typed themselves across the dark computer screen. "I AM CONAN."

"Who sent you?" Xin asked.

Grinding sounds came from inside Conan's boxy shell as it processed that question. "CONAN SENT CONAN."

"And what do you do?" Xin asked.

"I WANT TO HELP," it typed.

2

"Is this everyone?" Ohmsteel asked. Her breath came out in vaporous clouds and left frost on the grass. "Where are the Storms? And the Greek gods? Where are the Voodoo Spirits?"

"They aren't coming," Xin said. "This is it. This is everyone."

The Astounding Maxwell Seaboots shook his head. "Garr. This be nowhere near enough for battle, Chinaman. When the hellgate opens and the demons come spilling out, we'll be outnumbered a million to one."

"Speak for yourself, pirate," the Fugu ninja said. "If you cannot count the ninjas, then how can you outnumber them?"

The Astounding Maxwell Seaboots gave the ninja a cold chuckle and scratched the back of his neck. "This war won't be won with backflips and cartwheels, ninja. This be real war. Bloody war."

The ninja took a step closer. "Last I checked, you didn't have blood, *ghost*."

The Astounding Maxwell Seaboots growled and reached for the Sword of Twenty-Three Men. The ninja responded by springing into the Stance of a Thousand Sudden Spikes, placing her hands on the hilts of her twin poison katanas.

The two would have killed each other and ended the shaky alliance right there, if they were not interrupted by the arrival of an uninvited stranger.

"Excuse me," the woman said. "Am I in the right place?"

The new arrival did not seem to belong; she was far too young to be aware of the supernatural world, and far too mortal to survive it. The twenty-something woman looked better suited for the CIA. She wore a black executive's suit, shoes polished to a mirror shine, and wore her blonde hair in a pony tail, tied into place with a length of black ribbon. Her fingernails were black and polished and a solid gold watch looped around her wrist.

In the crook of her other arm was an ancient tome, hundreds of pages thick and bound in white ivory that shimmered with radiant glory. The pages once had gold leafing, but centuries of use had worn it away in places. Two golden locks kept the book secured shut, with no visible keyholes.

Xin was familiar with most of the supernatural artifacts found throughout the world, but this one was new to him.

Fennel sniffed the air. The new girl smelled mortal, but her book carried the scent of magic. Magic older than the trees.

"Are you in the right place for what?" the Astounding Maxwell Seaboots asked the young woman.

"This is where we plan our fight against Legion, correct?" The woman strolled right up to the group and took a place between Xin and the dragon's enormous head.

"It may or may not be," Ohmsteel said. She tilted her head to get a better look at the mortal. "Is it any business of yours?"

"As a matter of fact, it's specifically my business. It was my mother and father's business, and now it's my business." She placed her hand on her chest to make a formal introduction. "I am Isobella Westland, supernatural investigator. Perhaps you've heard of me."

Everyone exchanged glances. No one reacted.

Westland frowned. They should have at least *heard* of the name. She had done so much. Her parents had done so much before her. But she wasn't going to let trivialities spoil her good mood. Her frown quickly returned to a smile.

"No matter," she said. "Who I am isn't important. It's what I offer that should interest you."

More straight-faced glances. No one seemed inclined to ask for clarification.

Westland sighed.

"I'm here to graciously offer my assistance," Westland declared. She turned and pointed at the hills. Gathered there behind her stood a platoon of a hundred humans decked out in layers of bulky body-armor. They were armed with assault rifles, machine guns, and silver axes that glinted in the sunlight. "Those are some of the roughest, toughest mercenaries straight out of Costa Peligro. They're not afraid to kill, and they're not afraid to die. And I've personally trained every single one of them to fight ghosts and angels and, most importantly, demons."

"They're mortal?" Fennel asked. "You're offering us the service of mortals?"

Westland turned to her with a sly grin. "Don't be so quick to underestimate mortals."

"There's nothing to underestimate," Fennel said. "Besides the way they taste."

"You've got a smart mouth." Westland took a few steps closer to the naked woman and traced her fingers over her white book. "If you continue to act like an animal, I will put you down like an animal."

Fennel curled her fingers and readied her claws.

And the fighting might have escalated further if Xin did not interrupt. The old man touched Westland on the arm and asked her, "How did you find us?"

Westland beamed a sinister smile at Fennel, showing off her perfect teeth, then turned to the old man. "I gather information. It's what I do. And I'm particularly good at it."

Xin grunted, skeptically. "And what information, exactly, have you gathered?"

"That the entire Legion of Hell is coming to Earth." Westland wandered idly through the gathering of supernatural beings. She swiped a finger across Conan's AV cart and inspected her fingertip for dust, then turned and pointed into the distance.

"Thirty miles that way is the Chernobyl Nuclear Facility. And somewhere inside those Communist's half-cocked atom smashing machine is a fracture between Earth and Hell. It's the size of a toothpick right now, but it's about to get blown wide open. Does that about sum it up?"

No one in the group answered her. How this human girl came to know so much, that was a true mystery. But it didn't take away from the fact that she was absolutely right.

"*Good*," Westland thought. That got their attention. She continued pacing through the group. "Me and my soldiers are prepared to fight anything. Aliens? Bring it on. Ghosts? Can't wait. And Demons?" She stuck her free hand in her pocket and fished out a handful of silver bullets. She held her palm open so everyone could see them. "These bullets were blessed by the Pope himself. Don't ask how how I got him to do that, because it's a complicated story and not the point. Now I'm no Catholic, but I have it on pretty good authority that when it comes to shooting demons, these Pope bullets pack a real punch."

Something didn't set right with Xin. He asked her, "What book do you have there?"

She clutched the book tight to her chest. A grin crept across her face. "Trade secret."

Xin shook his head. "I want to know what's in it."

"And I want to know what's in your bag." Westland nudged Xin's cotton sack with her foot and rattled the jars. "And I want to know what's in the treasure chest padlocked to the pirate's body. I want to know lots of stuff, but are we here for prolonged introductions? Or are we here to fight the God-forsaken?"

The Astounding Maxwell Seaboots grunted. "Let her crew come. In anything, they'll be an additional obstacle between us and the demons."

Fennel looked skeptical. She didn't care for humans in general, but this Isobella Westland woman and the way she smelled bothered her more than usual.

Xin sighed at the shapeshifter and said, "We are going to need all the help we can get."

Ohmsteel huffed once. "We should accept her help."

"I AM CONAN," appeared on its computer screen.

Fennel crossed her arms. "Fine."

The ninjas made no indication that they approved, but they did not voice their disapproval either. Their silence came as no surprise to anyone.

"Alright," Xin said to Isobella Westland. "Get your men ready. You can come."

"Men *and* women," she corrected him.

"Of course," Xin said.

"They are not all men."

"Fine," Xin said. "Get your *people* ready. We depart soon."

Westland's grin turned a little sharper. Things were going exactly as she had planned.

3

The supernatural generals parted ways from the top of the hill and returned to their respective armies. The Astounding Maxwell Seaboots paddled back to his armada of ships. After dropping a smoke bomb on the ground, the ninjas vanished from sight. Fennel sprinted down the hill, shifted back into her fox form and rejoined the worldwide assembly of were-creatures. Ohmsteel flapped her wings, created a localized snowstorm and rose up into the clouds. Conan creaked in confused circles, unsure where to go. It typed, "I WANT TO HELP."

Xin stayed on the top of hill and scrutinized Isobella Westland as she took confident strides down the hill. There was something detached an inhuman about her, the way she didn't move her arms when she walked and lifeless way she stepped. She sounded far too eager to fight Legion, and far too pleased with her own ego to realize she was leading her soldiers face-first into certain death.

At the bottom of the hill, Westland pulled the black ribbon out of her ponytail and shook her hair loose. She approached her soldiers, who stood at attention in a perfect ten-by-ten formation. To the side of her platoon stood a separate group of men and women in black suits and sunglasses. Coiled wires dangled from their right ears, linking them all into constant communication. These humans were armed as well, not with the heavy weapons and silver battle axes found on the mercenaries, but with simple sidearms attached to their belts. If Westland been telling the truth, it was safe to assume that even these employees were armed with Pope bullets.

"We're joining the monsters in their fool's errand," Westland told her black-suited agents. "After they heard what I had to say, they couldn't say no."

"Perfect." An old man appeared behind her, suddenly, as if he materialized out of thin air. This was the CEO, one of the corporate entities, a physical manifestation of what it means to be Chief Executive Officer. He wore the finest gray suit, had thinning hair, and a permanent scowl on his wrinkled face that comes after a lifetime without joy or happiness or laughter. He paced a circle around Isobella Westland, like a predator stalking prey. "You continue to surprise me with your usefulness."

"*My* usefulness?" Westland repeated, disgusted. "We wouldn't have got this far if it wasn't for me."

The old man stopped and sneered. "And you wouldn't have got anywhere without my money. Never forget that."

Westland got on her tip-toes and stuck a finger in his face. "If it weren't for me and my corporation, you wouldn't *be* here."

"Our corporation," he corrected her. "It hasn't been *your* corporation since you signed that contract."

"I signed a contract giving you money-ghosts forty-nine percent of my stock." Westland looked down to find her fingers trembling with rage. She was about to lose her cool and do something terrible. She took a deep breath and forced herself to smile. "So I'll say it again: it's *my* corporation. Now why don't you go back to your steak and lobster dinners and let me do my job."

The CEO gave her response brief consideration. Instead of debating the point, he turned to look at the surrounding hills. The were-creatures were on the move. Ohmsteel the dragon soared through the clouds overhead.

"I think I might come along," the CEO said. "I'd like to see how things transpire."

"Yeah, well, you're not invited." Westland maneuvered herself in front of the CEO. "There's going to be fighting and shooting and pissed-off hellspawn flying all over the place. I'm not going to have time to babysit you, and I can't spare a single soldier to do the job for me."

"Your concern for my safety is quite kind," the CEO said in an insincere tone. "But I suspect I'll be just fine. The demons will have, as they say, bigger fish to fry."

Westland grit her teeth. "If you insist."

The CEO gave her a cold look. "I do."

Westland huffed. She could draw her sidearm and blow the old man's brains out before he even knew what hit him. She knew she could do it. She timed herself at the shooting range. And while the CEO seemed to be immune to normal weapons, she wondered if one of those pope-blessed bullets might do the trick.

Worse, she could crack her ivory book open and unleash any number of unholy miracles against him.

The CEO had it coming. Isobella had to contend with his constant hunger for more power. It was in his very nature as a Corporate Entity, she understood that, but either he was getting worse or she had just grown sick of it. She regretted giving the Corporate Entities stock in exchange for financial backing, but her medical research into a cure for vampirism had all but bankrupted her.

She pushed those thoughts out of her head. Isobella Westland did not make mistakes, especially not big ones. But the CEO had recently started scheduling important meetings without her; meetings she "needn't bother with." And when she spent money for her fast-expanding business – buying vehicles or weapons or uniforms – the CEO talked down to her, as if the Westland Corporation was his idea and *she* worked for *him*.

Recently, she discovered that there were parts of her own warehouse she did not have access to. When she asked the CEO about these restricted areas, he explained to her the dangers of research-and-development and pointed out that Isobella – while technically the owner – did not have the knowledge necessary to safely enter those areas.

He did his best to placate her by saying, "If you contact the Director of Research and Development, I'm sure they can schedule a little tour for you."

A little tour. Of her own business.

Yes. She wanted to put a bullet in the CEO's head. Stocks and bonds. That's all the Corporate Entities wanted, stocks and bonds. Well, she drew a hard line at 49 percent. She screamed them down in the board room with a cigarette in one hand and an unsigned contract in the other. No way was she going to turn controlling stock over to a bunch of imaginary big-wigs.

Now the CEO had shown up in the Ukraine, meddling in her affairs.

Casually, she rested her hand on her pistol.

She couldn't kill the CEO. Not yet. She still needed his money. Hiring mercenaries, training them, buying vehicles, and hopefully getting a lease on that wonderful skyscraper in Midtown... those things all cost money. More important than anything, a cure to Judas' curse and the vampire infections was just a decade of expensive research away. And while her family fortune was staggering and the Westland Corporation was profitable, it was chump change compared to the Corporate Entities and their bottomless black credit cards.

"Come along if you want," she said to the CEO, resigned to let him live another day. "Just stay out of my way."

4

The vast woods that blanketed the empty Ukrainian countryside echoed with the barks and howls of ten-thousand canines. Gray wolves and timber wolves, bloodhounds and foxes all raced through acres and acres of trees. The impossibly large pack of animals was led by Fennel, a red fox so tiny in comparison to the jaguars and dire wolves that surrounded her. She steered the entire army through the woods. When she bolted left or right, they followed. Her golden eyes glinted with intelligence as she led her species closer to Chernobyl.

The seven ninjas clans followed overhead, running deftly across the branches of the trees. They kept pace with the animals, careful not to knock a single twig or leaf to the ground. The ninja were trained in stealth and could maneuver through the treetops just as fast as they could on solid ground.

Ohmsteel soared up in the cloud line where she could scout ahead. Her scales color-shifted through various shades of light and dark blue, camouflaging her body perfectly against the skies above. Still, no magic could hide her shadow which fluttered across the leaves of the forest below. The dragon couldn't quite see her allies through the trees, but kept track of them by the thirteen ghost-pirate crows nests that just barely peaked above the treetops.

Those crows nests were manned by ghost pirates who each scanned the horizon with spyglasses of haunted light.

Beyond their view, beyond the woods, in a square-mile clearing of pavement sat the Chernobyl Nuclear Facility; an enormous factory surrounded by a perimeter of power grids and topped with towering chimneys that vented thick brown smoke.

The Ghost Pirate Navy phased directly through the trees, unhindered by physical objects. The ghost pirates prepped for battle on the top deck of the boats; they moved their cannons into position, cleaned their flintlocks and scimitars, and adjusted the rigging on their sails.

255

Xin Houng stood next to the Astounding Maxwell Seaboots on the Irish Goodbye. The impossibly heavy treasure chest rested at the pirate captain's feet, still chained to his body. The Irish Goodbye was no stranger to battle; it had seen its fair share of battle in life, and even more in death. It boasted forty-one cannons with barrels carved into the shape of wide-mouthed swordfish, fifty-three bloodthirsty pirates guilty of the most terrible crimes, and enough ghostpowder to level a small city.

The Irish Goodbye brought up the rear of the army. If Legion made it to Earth, they would encounter the shapeshifters and ninjas first. The rest of the Ghost Pirate Navy and Ohmsteel the Blue Dragon would be right behind them. By the time the Irish Goodbye arrived fresh into battle, it would bring with it such shock-and-awe that it could blast its way straight to Chernobyl.

And they had to get to Chernobyl, or all was lost.

The Irish Goodbye also harbored CONAN, who would have moved too slow through the forest to keep up with the advancing troops. The computer rolled its AV cart back and forth on its squeaky wheels, doing its best to maintain balance on the transparent floorboards of the swaying ship. Its extension cord draped over the back of the boat and twisted through the forest behind them.

Also standing on the captains deck of the Irish Goodbye was Isobella Westland and her CIA-looking agents. She watched over the main deck of the ship where her attachment of trained soldiers milled about, inspecting their firearms, cleaning their axes, and warming up for hand-to-hand combat. Westland leaned against the front rail and watched her soldiers closely. Her suit fluttered in the wind as they picked up speed.

Xin eyed Westland carefully. When it came to the newcomer, he hoped to learn as much as possible. Whether or not her squadron of human soldiers would be useful in battle against Legion, only time would tell. Misplaced confidence and foolhardy bravery would only last so long against the unthinkable forces of Hell. Demons were known to fight with an insanity that could drive even the most hardened mortals away in panic.

The wind whipped Isobella Westland's long blond hair into a swirling frenzy as she stared over the bridge rail and scowled. She seemed unfazed by the approaching danger, which either meant she was unaware of what she was getting herself into, or that she knew she could handle it. In either case, she was undeniably a cause for concern.

Two klicks deeper into the woods, Isobella Westland stepped down from the bridge of the Irish Goodbye and called her soldiers to attention. The mercenaries from Costa Peligro – leather-skinned men and women experienced with combat from all corners of the world – quickly got into formation in front of the young woman half their age.

"Alright boys and girls," Westland said as she tied her hair back into a ponytail. "The name of the game here is air support. The shapeshifters and the ninjas are going to handle the demons on the ground, but there are going to be flying things, too. Aim high. Shoot whatever is closest. Knock everything out of the clouds. Understood?"

The soldiers, in booming unison, answered her. "Yes, sir!"

"And remember, these aren't the jungles of Isle Sierra. We're going up against the forces of Hell here, so no one goes off alone, no one plays 'hero.' Got me?"

Again, they answered. "Yes, sir!"

Westland stepped up to one of her soldiers and, on her tip-toes, got right in his face. "You hear me Koppleman? I'm talking to you."

Koppleman, a muscle-bound son-of-a-bitch with tattooed arms and mirrored sunglasses, looked down at the girl who stood a foot shorter then him. He chewed on his cigar and gave her a single nod. "Yes, sir."

"I mean it." She slapped the cigar out of his mouth. "Last I checked, you're not John Fucking Rambo, so stop acting like it. I don't want a repeat of what happened in Cairo, you get me? You be a good little mercenary, plant your feet here on the boat, and follow god damned orders. Do I make myself clear?"

Koppleman clenched his jaw, thought for a moment, then responded. "Crystal clear, sir."

"Good." She stepped back. "That goes for all of you. This is our one chance to show this freakshow gathering that the Westland Corporation is a force to be feared. So listen close. If any of you fuck this up for me, I will buy myself the nicest set of golf clubs and beat your brains out myself. Is *that* clear?"

"Yes, sir!"

She crossed her arms and scowled. "Koppleman?"

He kept his eyes forward and responded, "Yes, sir."

She grinned. And then, as if she knew Xin had been watching her from the bridge, she turned her grin to him.

6

The ghost pirate perched in the crow's nest of the Irish Goodbye clanged a bell to get everyone's attention. He held his spyglass aside and leaned over the edge of his wooden position. "Chernobyl, dead ahead," he shouted. "One klick! But I warn ya, I hear alarms and smell sulfur!"

"Argh!" the Astounding Maxwell Seaboots shouted back. He turned to Xin. "We may be too late."

"Let's hope not," Xin said.

Xin got down on his knees and rummaged through the jars and bottles stashed in his bag. He rattled and clanked his way deeper to the bottom in search of something specific.

Isobella Westland couldn't resist the urge to shuffle closer and peer over the old man's shoulder. She caught glimpses of dried roots, colorful powders, and glass containers filled with exotic liquids. Xin knew he was being watched – his intuition was sharp and Isobella lacked subtlety – but he didn't have time to nit-pick his privacy. He pulled out a tiny jar that clinked with a single, unmelted ice cube. The inside of the jar steamed with cold fog and the sides were frosted over. Setting that jar aside, he took out another one – this one filled with white sand – then resumed digging around for his mortar and pestle.

"What are those?" Westland asked him.

"This..." Xin said as he held up the jar with the ice cube, "...is the last piece of ice from the Karoo Ice Age, 360 million years ago. And this..." He held up the jar of white sand, "...is solid snow from the Tropic of Argo Navis."

"Argo Navis..." Westland said. Her voice trailed off. She shook away the visions and asked him, "Have you been there?"

"No," Xin replied. "No one has."

"Then where did you get the solid snow?" she asked.

"Trade secret," he said, using her own words against her.

Xin stopped the explanation there. He wasn't inclined to share any further details of the recipe, not that the explanation would have meant much to a neophyte like Westland anyway.

"What does it do?" she asked.

Xin got to work opening jars. "You'll see."

"You won't tell me?"

258

Xin kept his eyes on his work. "I don't trust you."

Westland frowned. "Well, whatever it is, it better be good."

Conan wheeled up behind the two and stopped.

"I AM CONAN," it typed. "I WANT TO HELP."

Westland turned her attention to the computer. She knew the usefulness of a computer; with the Corporate Entities financial backing, she'd purchased three of them to use for her business. They were prefect for record-keeping and securing information, but she doubted this specific computer's ability to contribute to a war with Hell. It had no arms. It had no weapons. It could barely keep its balance riding on a moving boat.

"Tell me, computer," she said to it. "Are you powered by miles and miles of extension cord running across the entire length of the Ukraine?"

Conan turned his cart to face Westland. "I AM CONAN."

She continued. "There is the question of amperage drop as you get further away from whatever outlet you're plugged into. I can't help but wonder how your presence here is even possible."

The little green cursor on his screen blinked as his processor churned over a possible response.

"I AM CONAN," it typed. "I WANT TO HELP."

"Maybe you could be useful somehow." She leaned forward and tapped her fingernail on the computer screen. "When the fight starts, how exactly are you going to help us?"

Again the cursor blinked and the computer whirred with thinking noises.

"LOG."

With an exasperated sigh, Westland turned away from the computer and looked out over the trees. Only a few short miles separated the combined forces of Earth's supernatural army from Legion. She looked down at the ghost pirate crew as they poured ghostpowder into the cannon fuses. She spotted the occasional ninja as they darted through the tree branches above. And as they sailed closer to the end of the woods where the thick canopy became slightly more sparse, she caught glimpses of Ohmsteel flying overhead.

With eager anticipation, she ran her fingers over the edges of her white leather-bound tome.

Chapter 16

1

The treeline surrounding the Chernobyl facility had been cut bulldozed away, leaving nothing but a half-mile stretch of flat, open dirt before between the woods and the chain link fences. Moonlight illuminated the empty expanse, revealing the simple, yet effective, security measure. Any unauthorized person trying to approach the power plant, whether on foot or in a vehicle, would have to cross this emptiness where they would easily be spotted. The wolves and foxes and tigers stopped at the edge of the forest, careful not to swarm right out into the open. The ninjas held position balanced on the leaves above. Ohmsteel, camouflaged a deep midnight blue against the night sky, flapped her thunderous winds and hovered directly overhead.

The Chernobyl nuclear power plant was a small campus of industrial buildings lit up by an army of a thousand floodlights: warehouses and garages surrounded by forklifts and boxy brown Soviet trucks. The nuclear reactor itself was housed within a concrete fortress a quarter-mile long, ten stories tall, topped with a sloped roof of solid steel. A set of cylindrical concrete chimneys towered another ten stories into the air above the reactor, venting white smoke up into the sky. The tops of them were painted with red and white stripes and were held upright by an elaborate system of catwalks and tension cables that anchored them against the wind.

Great lengths of industrial-grade water pipes stretched across the facility, connecting the various buildings. They churned loudly as they cycled through clean water and radioactive waste. Each pipe was marked with a metal sign marked with universal symbols that spoke of sickness, danger, and death.

To the east was a vast farm of identical electrical towers, connected by swooping power lines that crackled with sparks of electricity that flickered in the night air. Power cables stretched off into the distance and carried that power to the rest of the Ukraine. The towers' transformers buzzed audibly in time to the constant thrum of the turbines hidden inside the power plant.

No animals went near Chernobyl. Not the deer, no birds, not even the rats of the nearby woods would swarm out towards the facility. These creatures had an instinct to stay away from the invisible death surrounding such a place. Even the werecreatures were agitated by merely standing in its presence.

Fennel sniffed the air with her sensitive fox nose. The stink of her races' extinction was stronger than ever before. The longevity of the shape shifters hinged on this battle with Legion.

Shattering the quiet night air, a massive explosion rattled the concrete walls of the powerplant, followed by a blinding flash of white light. A shockwave exploded the windows of Chernobyl into dust. The roof above the reactor tore open and a column of smoke and fire forcefully jetted into the sky. The crack of the world-ending explosion faded off into the world, then came echoing back as it bounced off the surrounding hills. Next came the alarms; piercing bells and swirling red lights. The smoke gushing out of the chimneys turned from white to roiling black.

"Just in time," Voel, the Deranged Painter, hissed. The lime-skinned demon was suddenly present on the Irish Goodbye, looming over the shoulder of Isobella Westland.

Westland whipped around at the sound of her voice. Behind her was not only Voel, but all three of the escaped demons living on Earth. Voel wore the white coveralls of a painter, splattered with drab shades of red and black and gray. Paint drizzled from her fingertips and passed through the invisible floorboards of the pirate ship.

Next to her stood Lylo, the Archdemon of the Army of Arms. She came dressed in a gown of black lace. Gathered at her feet were a dozen adoring arms that strained to touch the mighty queen with their oozing black fingers. She glared at the mortal Westland with eyes that gleamed with pink light.

Asag, the Skin Collector, stood with them, beneath a wide sheet of stitched human skins so long that it draped over the back of the boat and flapped in the breeze. Asag's true form had always been a mystery, obscured by the layers of stolen skin covering his body; layers of skin he was always "improving" by sewing on pieces from his human and animal victims. Not even Voel nor Lylo had seen what horrors were hidden underneath.

The three demons stood in plain view on the bridge of the Irish Goodbye, but strangely no one seemed to notice. Or perhaps it wasn't that strange; supernatural beings like demons had powers beyond even Isobella Westland's understanding.

Westland lowered her voice to a pissed-off whisper. "What are you three *doing* here?"

Lylo tilted her head in curiosity. Her black lopsided braids fell to her other shoulder. Strands of hair got caught in the barbed wire that weaved around her neck and body. "We're here to make sure you hold up your end of the bargain."

Asag spoke next, his voice muffled from under the thick layers of human and animal skin. "Did you think we were just going to trust you? We are not exactly the trusting sort."

Westland double-checked to see if anyone else noticed the presence of the demons. No one had. Xin was still busy working on his little potion. The idiot Seaboots stood focused on steering his boat through the trees.

She turned back to the demons and grit her teeth. "I thought you'd have the common sense to stay away until I was done. The CEO is here. He could be watching us right now."

Voel scoffed. "Your deal with the money gods is none of our concern, mudblob."

"The only thing you should be worried about is sealing that hellgate before Legion punches through," Lylo said.

"They're almost here," Asag said. "What are you waiting for? Why haven't you cast the miracle?"

Westland waved a hand in their faces. "See, you demons are painfully short sighted. There's this little thing called timing, something you monsters severely lack, come to find out. I'll close the hellgate when it's time to close the hellgate."

Lylo raised her ivory arm and leveled a finger at Westland. Two of her little black minions from the Army of Arms grabbed the human by her ankles. Another arm leaped over Lylo's shoulder and clamped down on Westland's neck, cutting off her oxygen supply.

"You dare speak to us with such insolence?" Lylo said. Her glare turned to a sneer. "I should snap your frail little bones."

"Sister," Voel chided. She put her land on Lylo's shoulder. "Stay thy hand. We need this Daughter of Eve."

For a moment it seemed as though Lylo would ignore the warning, but then she dismissed her warrior arms with a disinterested flick of her hand. The black arms released the human and returned to their place at their leader's feet.

Westland coughed and gasped for air.

"Seal the gate," Voel demanded.

Westland doubled over, took a pained breath, then looked up at the demon. "When it's time. And not a second sooner."

The shape of Asag's mouth moved beneath the skin tightly wrapped around his head and growled. "The mudblob has only grown stubborn."

"Worse than stubborn," Lylo said. "Obstinate."

"We chose her for exactly those reasons," Voel said to the pair of demons. "Lest you forgot."

Asag slithered forward in his skin blanket and advanced on Westland. "And let *you* not forget who taught you to read that insipid codex." He gestured at her white book with his floppy-skinned arm. "To undo the dark miracle cast by the Being Yahweh. To save your sister. We gave you the knowledge you so desperately begged for. Now you do as we say."

"Oh yeah?" Westland said through a growing smile. "Be careful how to talk to me or I might just read the wrong page and send *you* three back to Hell... instead of Legion."

That shut Asag up. He backed off and dragged his sheets of skin away from her. The three demons exchanged frustrated but silent glances.

"Now get out of here before someone see you," Westland said. "And let me work."

"You test our patience, Daughter of Eve," said Lylo. She waved a finger at the girl. "Waste no more time. Speak the words of the Being Yahweh and seal the hellgate before it's too late."

"When it's time," Westland repeated. "Not now."

"Ma'am?" a voice said. One of Isobella's well-dressed agents had come up behind her. He was one of her newest recruits, a boy just barely out of college. He had perfect brown hair, smart-looking glasses, and a sidearm strapped to his hip. His black suit and matching white button-up were perfectly tailored to his body. He approached his boss with a concerned and curious look on his face. "Ma'am, are you alright?"

Westland glanced over her shoulder at the young man. She had been talking to invisible demons and this eavesdropping agent has caught her red-handed. She grabbed the agent by the lapels of his jacket and yanked him close.

"What did you see?" she seethed in his face.

"N- Nothing, ma'am."

She squinted her eyes at him. "And what did you *hear*?"

"Nothing," he said. "It sounded like you were talking to someone. But there's no one else here."

She turned back around. Her demon visitors had vanished. Had they vanished before being spotted?

She shoved the agent away from her and wiped her hands with a pure white handkerchief.

"I was just thinking out loud," Westland muttered. She looked away from the agent and towards the burning, glowing Chernobyl facility. Those careless demons almost blew the whole thing. Luckily the close call was with of her own disposable agents instead of the pirate captain or that painfully nosy alchemist. But now this agent was suspicious. Suspicion breeds questions. And for Isobella Westland, questions wouldn't do.

She made a mental note to blow the poor agents brains out when the fighting began and dismiss it as a mere accident.

"What's your name, son?" she asked him.

"Carl, ma'am."

"Well, Carl," she said. "I want you to stay close to me in this battle, alright? Be right here by my side."

The young man's face lit up. "You mean it?"

"I do." She pointed at the spectral floorboards directly next to her. "Stay right here by me at all times. Don't go anywhere."

He moved happily into position next to the owner of the company. He smiled from ear to ear and puffed up his chest.

Isobella Westland reached down and used her pinkie finger to flick off the safety of her pistol.

2

There came a heavy thud from inside the walls of Chernobyl, as if a monster of colossal size had thrown its weight against the concrete. Dust puffed out of the seams in the cinder blocks. No one, not the ninja, not the dragon, could guess what demonic creature was trying to break free, but it was undoubtedly emerged through the fracture between Earth and Hell. After a moment of unsettling quiet, it boomed against the concrete walls a second time, then a third.

Yellow plumes of sulfuric smoke blasted from the chimneys. The steel roof brightened into shades of red as it began to melt. The surviving men still trapped inside the power plant screamed in horror, then went silent. All that remained were the alarm bells and the repetitive thud of the monster that threatened to burst through the walls.

Rosalita "Eyes of the Sun" Muniez stood with one boot up on the prow of the Black Octopus. As the front-most captain of all the ghost pirate ships, it was her duty to lead the navy into battle. She raised her scimitar into the air and shouted:

"Ready the cannons!"

The crew of the Black Octopus repeated the command, shouting it back and forth, "Ready the cannons!" and moved the artillery into firing positions. One zombified pirate raised a red handkerchief up the rigging; a signal to the other ships that the battle would soon begin and to ready their cannons as well. The crews of the nearby boats shouted the cannon order, then raised a red handkerchief of their own. Slowly but surely the order was passed along handkerchief by handkerchief to the other twelve pirate boats, bringing to bear a total of three-hundred and thirteen light and heavy cannons.

Inhuman howls came from inside Chernobyl as the demons emerged from Hell and gathered inside the facility. Another thud trembled the very ground as the unseen monster struck the inside walls once more. Cracks appeared in the concrete and lead-reinforced walls.

Fennel charged out of the woods. It went against her very nature to sprint directly towards a nuclear power plant and fight Legion, but it had to be done. Behind her, thousands of canines flooded out of the trees with endless barks and yips and howls. The animals thundered towards the power plant like a stampede of buffalo, closely following Fennel's lead. They moved in beautiful unison, shifting left and right as if they shared one collective mind.

Ninjas came leaping out of the treetops. They sprinted and flipped across the open clearing in a flurry of black ribbon. They swarmed around the perimeter of the power plant and took high-ground positions wherever they could find them. The Centipede ninjas ran vertically up the sides of the electrical towers, defying gravity. Once at the peak, they tightrope-walked across the power lines to advance closer on enemy territory. Thousands of Scorpion and Komodo ninjas sliced through the chain link fence with their katanas and rushed into the innermost parking lots. The Fugu ninjas ran full speed towards the plant and effortlessly jumped over the razor-wire that looped across the tops of the two-story fence. They landed softly, quietly, and tumbled to safety behind crates and dumpsters.

One final thud against the interior wall of Chernobyl brought the concrete crumbling down into a pile of boulders and steel. The billowing dust hid the demon army from view, but without the wall between them, they sounded so much louder.

Ohmsteel swept across the sky and took position over the collapsed wall to make the first strike. She flapped her wings and created a powerful coldsnap that summoned a sudden blizzard. A thin layer of ice formed across the parking lot. The animals were suited for the cold and the ninjas would have no problem dealing with the ice, but Legion, accustomed to the blazing fires of Hell, would find the freezing air harsh and biting.

With the Irish Goodbye held position at the back of the fleet, it was the last to come into visual range of Chernobyl. Isobella Westland pressed against the guardrails of the bridge. She held binoculars up to her eyes with one hand, and cradled her book in the other. Within seconds the fight would begin and she had the best seat in the house. She could hardly contain her excitement.

Carl stood next to her with his hands on the rails. He shifted his eyes between the nuclear power plant and the delighted look on his boss' face. He smiled – even though he wasn't certain what they were smiling at – in an effort to match her positive energy.

"You seem quite pleased with yourself," Xin observed to Westland as he put the finishing touches on his elixir.

"Don't I?" she replied without taking her eyes off the battleground. "We're about to make the world a whole lot safer."

Xin mumbled. "Time will tell."

She sneered at his dismissive tone. "Times are changing, old man." She watched through her binoculars as the werewolves and ninjas swarmed the power plant. "Welcome to the '80s. Nuclear power. Assault weapons. Even little Conan over there represents the winds of change."

Conan angled his screen towards Westland. "I AM CONAN."

"So a little advice?" Westland continued. "It might be time for you to hang up the mason jars. Maybe you should fly back to old Jiangxi and enjoy your retirement."

Xin's hands froze, but he did not look up. Very few people knew his ancestors were from Jiangxi. Very few people could pronounce Jiangxi correctly, in fact. How Isobella Westland knew where he was from was yet another mystery, but he refused to give her a reaction. A reaction was exactly what she wanted. He went back to grinding in his mortar and pestle.

Isobella Westland didn't need a reaction. She knew it bothered him and it made her grin.

The moment had finally come. Legion was on Earth.

First came the Warp Walkers: ten-foot tall demons with thin, twisted limbs and pale skin that looked dead and deeply infected. Their empty, dark eye sockets blinked sideways. Their drooping tongues dangled loose from their missing bottom jaws. They moved effortlessly as if they were filled with helium and squealed with the sound of tortured animals.

Hornet ninjas surrounded the collapsed wall, balanced on the power lines that swooped from one electrical tower to another. They unslung their their bows from off their backs and took aim. Without any visible signal, they began firing. Black arrows whizzed through the air and plunged into the soft flesh of the Warp Walkers. No sooner had the ninjas launched their first volley, they drew new arrows and fired again.

The Warp Walkers held stead on their twisted, arthritic limps and turned to look at the attacking ninjas.

Then the demons vanished. They reappeared on the electrical towers, clinging to the catwalks with their hooked fingers and toes. Their sideways eyelids blinked and tasted the air for their prey. One by one, the Warp Walkers began ripping the power lines loose. Electrical transformers exploded in puffs of sparks.

The Hornet ninjas did not fall when the power lines fell out from beneath them. Their superhuman balance made that impossible. Instead, they ran along the length of the falling cables and jumped safely to the ground.

The Warp Walkers teleported again, this time among the Hornet ninjas, where they began snatching up the ninjas in their hands and bashing them together.

Out of Chernobyl came the Zerubim in great numbers: tiny demons the size of human children with their eyes sewn shut. These demons were scorched black by spiritual fire and had only a few wisps of hair on their heads. Armed with sharpened tridents of bone, they scrambled over the rubble of the collapsed wall. There were dozens at first, then hundreds, then thousands.

A pack of werewolves charged the Zerubim. Some of the shape shifters stayed in animal-form, others shifted into half-human, half-animal hybrids with thick fur and vicious claws.

The Zerubim cackled with delight, readied their tridents, and charged to meet the animals in battle. The small creatures laughed as they cut into the flesh of the animals with their weapons. And when the werewolves slashed back, the demons laughed even harder.

Fennel, in human-form, stood in the thickest part of combat. Her forearms had a layer of fox fur and her fingers ended in vicious claws. She swung her hands and slaughtered the demons all around her, more and more, faster and faster, killing them as fast as they could come.

The ceiling of Chernobyl burst open. The seven insect plagues swarmed out. Flies and gnats, lice and locusts darkened the fires burning behind them. Their wings buzzed like screaming saw blades in a lumber mill, and they flew directly over the werewolves and ninjas.

Still back in the trees, Captain Muniez watched as the demons engaged. She turned and shouted to her crew.

"Fire the cannons!"

And her crew repeated. "Fire the cannons!"

Puffs of white smoke ripped across the length of the Black Octopus. The other pirate ships took the cue and fired their cannons as well. The haunted cannonballs howled with human voices as they whisked through the air and crashed into the emerging demons. One cannonball plunged right into the guts of a Warp Walker who folded in half, slid backwards, and disappeared into the fires burning inside Chernobyl. Another cannonball crashed into a group of Zerubim and blasted them into the air. Like a meteor swarm from space, hundreds of cannonballs came crashing down, obliterating the demons foolish enough to rush face-first into the parking lot, but there were thousands more demons behind them, just waiting to escape the endless tortures of Hell.

And further behind those demons, still in Hell, an entire realm of demons, big and small, black and red and white, pressed against the fracture and fought for their chance to go next.

The werewolves and ninjas had one task: keep Legion contained within the walls of the Chernobyl nuclear facility. It wasn't going well. Even with the cannon bombardment from the Ghost Pirate Navy, the demons had pushed their way into the parking lots.

Now that the first wave of simple, unnamed demons had made it to Earth and soaked the opening salvo, it was safe for the more important demons to step into battle.

So came Klangg, the Obsidian General. The twelve-foot tall beast stomped his way to Earth, protected by plates of ebony armor and armed with a shard of volcanic glass the length of a telephone pole.

Quolox of the Beghast Cloud Layers, a leathery snake, took to the skies, buzzing on sixteen dragonfly wings.

Also emerging from the fracture was Tovitox, a decapitated head the size of a great boulder, who moved through the parking lot on twelve dozen whisper-thin spider legs.

Each of those demons alone would have been worthy of an entire army. Together, they were merciless. Klangg sliced his obsidian weapon through an entire line of animals. Quolox buzzed through the air from one ninja to the next, driving her stinger into their chests and pumping them full of venom. Tovitox stretched its mouth open and belched out a cloud of black gas that melted its way through living tissue.

The werewolves and ninjas were forced to retreat.

Ohmsteel dropped out of the sky to cover their escape. She crashed to the ground with such power and intensity, it made the demons pause. She landed directly on Klangg and trapped him beneath the immense weight of her claws. With a sweep of her tail, the dragon cleared the entire parking lot of demons and launched them tumbling into the air. She turned her head, opened her mouth, and blasted sub-zero air across the giant head of Quolox. Quolox, and the unfortunate dozens of lesser demons surrounding it, were immediately petrified in layers of ice.

Hundreds of chattering Zerubim swarmed the great dragon and infested her body like fleas. They jabbed at her with their tridents, but they bounced harmlessly off her scales.

Rosalita Muniez and the Unkillable "Shark Fin" Finnegan sailed the Black Octopus and the Bad Moon closer to Chernobyl. They drifted in circles around Ohmsteel, close enough for the crew on the port side to use their pistols and pick off the tiny demons that clung to the dragon's body while the sailors on the starboard side reloaded the cannons.

And still, more demons came.

A Warp Walker reached up with its long arm and slapped Finnegan right off the bridge of his boat. The pirate captain splashed overboard and dog-paddled in the cursed, ghost oceans that affected only him. A second Warp Walker scooped him up and tossed him effortlessly towards the fracture. The emerging demons sank their claws into his spiritual body. Finnegan screamed as the creatures dragged him closer to Hell. Doomed to die, but no coward, he drew his pistol and saber and killed as many demons as he could before he vanished into the fire.

4

Isobella Westland watched the fight closely.

The fracture connecting Earth to Hell was releasing biblical levels of heat which super-heated the graphite exterior of nuclear reactor 4. Emergency systems sprayed a mist of chemical coolant onto the various fires, but it was pointless: not even the best chemicals on Earth could smother hellfire. As the reactor approached critical levels and the lead began to melt, additional emergency systems activated; pumps connected to the nearby river opened and dumped cold water directly onto the graphite walls of the reactor.

All it did was create steam.

Reactor 4 began to glow red hot.

Each demon that passed from Hell and into Earth snapped a piece off the edge of the fracture, causing the dimensional rift to grow bigger and bigger. And the wider the fracture became, the more the fires melted into reactor 4.

"Alright," Westland said as she turned to Conan. "You said you wanted to help?"

"I WANT TO HELP," it responded.

"Right now that building is one big nuclear bomb waiting to happen and that fracture is about to set it off. If you can get in there, can you connect to their computer systems and shut those reactors down?"

Conan turned left, then right, then looked at Westland. "I AM CONAN."

"Arr, that machine is touched in the head," the Astounding Maxwell Seaboots said as he cranked the steering wheel hard to port. "You have to talk to it like a wee child."

"Conan." Westland hooked an arm around the computer monitor with one hand and pointed at Chernobyl with the other. "Can you turn off that big nuclear battery?"

Conan's processors clicked and whirred.

It typed, "CAN'T REACH."

"What if I helped you get there?" she asked.

It thought for another moment, then typed, "YES."

"Excellent," she said.

She stood up straight with her ivory book in her hands and closed her eyes. Her lips moved silently as she chanted some incantation. The metal clasps that sealed the book closed both popped open. The right miracle was hidden in her book somewhere; she just needed to find it. She flipped through pages written in a language that didn't resemble anything from Earth.

"Here." She tapped her fingertip down on a specific page. She looked at Conan. "You ready?"

"I WANT TO HELP."

Isobella Westland recited a spell from the book. She sang in parts, as if that were part of the pronunciation. Xin looked up from his work when he heard her. He recognized that language. He had heard it once before.

Westland finished the spell and Conan disappeared in a flash of golden light.

The computer reappeared in the parking lot of Chernobyl. Warped Walkers lumbered over it. Zerubim swarmed past. The AV cart rolled beneath the shadow of the dragon Ohmsteel who blasted ice into the sky. Concrete and hot steel rained down all around him. Conan's cart rattled from the thunderous fighting. Conan knew it couldn't waste time. Terrified for itself, it began rolling towards the blasted out doors of the nuclear power plant.

"I AM HELPING."

Back on the Irish Goodbye, Xin confronted Westland.

"That was the language of angels," he said.

"Maybe it was." Westland thumped her book closed. The metal latches clicked shut. She turned and defiantly stared the old man down. "What's it to you?"

"Where did you learn to sing it?" he asked. "It was never meant for humans. And it's dangerous."

"Listen to you. 'Dangerous.' We're fighting Legion for the control of this world and you're worried about *dangerous*. Well, I have news for you, Xin Houng. You're not the magic police." She leaned in closer to the old man and lowered her voice to a growl. "*I'm* the magic police."

"This book shouldn't be on Earth," Xin said. "And you shouldn't be able to read it."

"Well, it *is* on Earth. And I *can* read it."

Xin reached out to take it from her. Isobella Westland deftly stepped back, whipped her pistol out of its holster and aimed it squarely between the old man's eyes. Her eyes revealed the stone-cold determination that she *would* kill him if she had to.

"Do *not* touch it," Westland said. "This is mine. You have no idea what I went through to get it."

Xin couldn't allow one single person to wield the celestial power contained inside that book, but Isobella Westland had already discovered its potential and was intent to kill a man in order to keep it. Taking it away from her would have been a bloody, bothersome affair and Xin knew that this moment wasn't the time to try. The war with Legion was going poorly and demanded his attention.

"We will discuss this later," Xin told Westland with a stern look. He turned away from her.

Isobella Westland didn't lower her gun. Her breathing was labored and panicked. She continued to air the gun at the alchemist, debating whether or not it was worth it to kill him for what he'd done. She, too, decided against it, for the very same reasons Xin decided not to take it from her.

Carl approached his boss. "Are you alright, ma'am?"

"I need this," Westland seethed, holstering her firearm and clutching the book tight to her chest. "I won't let anyone take it from me. No one. Not for anything." Her voice grew even softer as the glimmer of tears formed in her eyes. "I *need* this. I won't be able to bring her back without it."

"Bring who back, ma'am," Carl asked.

Westland looked up at Carl, suddenly realizing that her thoughts had spilled out of her mouth as words. She adjusted her posture, gathered her composure and said, "No one, Carl. No one of consequence, anyway."

The Black Octopus had been overrun by Legion. Demons crawled up the sides of the ship and the crew blasted them in the head with spiritual pistols and slashed their bodies open with ghostly swords. Rosalita Muniez fought off two invading Warp Walkers with her gleaming blade. Just when it seemed like she might drive them away, swarms of buzzing mosquitoes engulfed her, crawled beneath her clothes and stung her ghost body. The captain thrashed around in a panic, swept her jacket off her shoulders and threw it to the ground.

The Bad Moon, without the leadership of Shark Fin Finnegan, had began to drift aimlessly. It drew too close to the fracture and the hellflames lit the sides of the boat on fire. Burning and aimless, the boat toppled sideways into Hell and collapsed into debris.

The Astounding Maxwell Seaboots watched two boats go down. He whipped around and yelled at Xin.

"Damn you! Whatever you're working on, make it quick!"

Xin mixed the sub-zero potion in his pestle with a tiny silver tea spoon. Cold wisps of air drifted out. The spoon crinkled and cracked as its molecules neared absolute zero. He stirred the liquid for as possible while tolerating the pain of the freezing spoon, but it wasn't for long. He hissed as the frost reached his fingers, then tossed the tea spoon over the side of the boat.

His potion was the one thing that could save them – save the world – from Legion.

"This..." Xin said as he rose to his feet. "...is veturis water. It's an old recipe from Pinga, the Eskimo god who gathers the dead. However hot Hell is, this is just as cold. If we can get close enough to the fracture, I can pour it on the-"

Isobella Westland lost her footing and stumbled hard into Xin. In an unlucky coincidence, her fist banged Xin's elbow and knocked the freezing veturis out of the pestle. It splashed across the face and chest of the Astonishing Maxwell Seaboots.

Cold steam puffed out as the potion burned through the pirate. He howled in confusion as his face turned to cracking ice. He tried in vain to pull his freezing clothes off, but his cursed chains made that impossible. The frost expanded like a fast-moving cancer, swallowing his face and coating his hands.

One of his sailors ran to save him.

"Don't touch him!" Xin snapped, waving the kid back. "If you touch him, it will just spread to you!"

The sailor, conflicted between his loyalty to his captain and Xin's warning of a shared death, hesitated.

Xin spun around to Westland, furious. "What did you do!?"

"The boat moved!" she shouted, horrified. "It wasn't my fault! I lost my balance!"

The Astounding Maxwell Seaboots stumbled across the bridge of his ship. The frost traveled down his throat and silenced his screams. He clawed at his neck with frozen fingers.

"Do something!" The sailor shouted as he cowered behind Xin. "Please, do something to save the captain!"

But Xin knew there was nothing he could do.

He could barely contain his anger as he continued to address Isobella Westland. "Look at what you have done!"

Mere seconds had passed and the captain was frozen into a statue of ice. And while the death of the Astounding Maxwell Seaboots was a tragedy, it paled in comparison to the fact that the magical potion – the only means of sealing Earth off from Hell – had been wasted.

There was no making a new one.

Xin said to Westland, "You did that on purpose."

"I did not!" She nervously pulled her ponytail through her fingers. "That's not true! The boat moved!"

"That mixture was our only chance to close the fracture." Xin tried to maintain calm, but his voice wavered. "You made me spill it. I want to know why."

She didn't much care for his accusations. "I lost my balance, I told you. Don't make me say it again."

Xin looked away from her, disgusted. Accident or not, the damage was done. The army was breaking. The werewolves howled in fear. The ninjas had retreated fully to the woods. Two more collapsing pirate boats spiraled into Hell. A few surviving pirates tried to paddle their rowboats to safety, but were easily boarded and torn to shreds by gleeful little Zerubim.

For all the blasts and rumblings, nothing compared to the next earthquake that shook the very crust of the Earth. Ninjas fell from the trees. Suspension cables that supported the red-and-white striped chimneys of Chernobyl snapped.

The Beast, a legendary creature only hinted at in the last book of the Bible, crashed it way through the fracture, destroying all the demons in its path. On its five long necks swung five heads – a lion, an eagle, a turtle, a locust, and a humans – and each head was large enough to swallow a pirate ship whole. The top of each head was orbited by five crowns of fire. Its eyes rolled frantically with madness, driven to mindless insanity that humans couldn't even conceive of, cursed by the very hand of God.

All it wanted was one thing: To escape Hell.

And in lieu of returning to Heaven, Earth would have to do.

Legion had invaded Eden, and now there was no stopping it.

Chapter 17

1

"What are you doing?" Voel hissed into Westland's ear, her hands tight on the mortal's shoulder.

"Look what your senseless delays have brought us," Lylo growled into her other ear, her fists clenching handfuls of her suit jacket.

"Close the hellgate," Asag said as he loomed over all three of them. "Before the Beast emerges fully."

Isobella Westland grit her teeth. "It's not time, yet."

"Not time for what?" Carl asked, confused about who she was talking to.

Westland checked. The demons were gone.

"It's not time to make our move," she told Carl. "Not yet."

Conan wheeled as fast as it could towards the blown-out emergency doors of Chernobyl. It could see reactor 4. The graphite walls glowed bright red and molten globs of liquid lead dripped down to the floor. Surrounded by the end of the world, Conan repeated simple phrases to help maintain its confidence.

"I AM CONAN," it typed. "I AM CONAN AND I AM HELPING."

The path to the reactor seemed impossible. The computer had crossed the entire Ukraine, but nothing compared to these last 100 yards. Chunks of car-sized concrete piled up in its way. Loose, sparking power lines whipped around like pissed off anacondas. The blue dragon stomped in circles right in its path. And now there was a big five-headed monster to sneak around.

"I AM THINKING."

Conan determined that if it could just access one of the computers, it could manually shut down the nuclear reactions threatening to eviscerate everything. Carefully, slowly, it wobbled through the rubble. It had to stop the reactor. People were counting on it. It had to help them.

"I AM HELPING."

Ohmsteel, one of the first earthly creations of God, did her best to keep the Beast halfway between Earth and Hell. She placed herself directly into its path and blasted it in its five faces with freezing temperatures only found on the moons of Jupiter. The Beast roared in confusion, but even it meant trudging into otherworldly cold, it continued its fight for freedom.

The smaller demons of Legion had infiltrated the surrounding woods. Warp Walkers pushed through the trees with little effort. Zerubim fought the werewolves and werefoxes on the ground as pirate ships drifted past. Swarms of biting flies and stinging hornets clouded around Ohmsteel's head.

Westland's soldiers protected the Irish Goodbye as best they could. They unloaded machine gun fire into the air and shredded the airborne demons that came too close. Xin delved into his bag for a jar of some foul-smelling powder that he lightly sprinkled around the edges of the boat and kept the dark clouds of insects away like an invisible forcefield.

Isobella heard a desperate cry for help from over the side of the boat. With everyone else preoccupied with battle, and Xin distracted by his magic dust, she seemed to be the only one who noticed. She casually wandered towards the side of the boat and took a curious peek over the edge.

Down below was Fennel in human-form, bloodied and wounded, surrounded by a dozen cackling Zerubim. They danced and laughed as they took turns jabbing the exhausted creature with their tridents. She swung her arms at them and kicked them away, but this only encouraged them more.

The smell of her extinction came so strong, Fennel could hardly breathe. "Help me!" Fennel shouted. She searched all around before catching eyes with Westland up above on the boat. "Human! Throw me a rope! Please!"

Westland peered back over her shoulder to see if anyone else heard Fennel's cry. No one had. There was no one else with her except Carl. She looked back down to Fennel.

Fennel reached up with her bloody arm. "Please!"

Westland enjoyed having this monster's life in her hands. She could have left the half-animal to die at the hands of demons and no one would have ever known, but Westland preferred far more pageantry. She sighed and grabbed a coil of rope sitting at her feet. She tossed one end overboard and within Fennel's reach. The bloody woman looped it around her forearms and grabbed on tight.

"Pull me up!" Fennel shouted. "Hurry!"

"Change of plans!" Westland took the entire coil of rope and threw it overboard where it landed in the dirt, completely useless. "Send my regards to the dodo!"

Fennel belted out her rage in one long vicious howl. The tiny demons jumped on her and skewered her with tridents.

Westland turned and snapped her fingers. "Carl. Follow me."

Carl glanced over the side of boat at the helpless creature. Fennel collapsed to the ground in a bloody mess. With no time to process what had happened, he ran to join his boss by her side.

Isobella Westland marched down from the bridge and onto the main deck of the boat. One of the ghost pirates stood in her way, so she drew her pistol and put a bullet through his head. One of her soldier's sniper rifles laid there on the floorboards, so she scooped it up. She carried it over to the soldiers positioned in the middle of the boat where they carefully fired into the air and knocked bat-shaped demons out of the sky.

"Koppleman!" she shouted. Koppleman looked over at the sound of his name. Westland tossed him the sniper rifle. He dropped his heavy firearm just in time to catch the new one. She pointed at Chernobyl in the distance. "Can you hit that computer from here?"

Koppleman blinked. "Easy."

"Then do it," she said.

Koppleman hesitated. "For what reason?"

She grit her teeth. "Because I told you to."

Koppleman didn't argue. He turned and hoisted the sniper rifle to his shoulder. With his eye to the scope, he drew a bead across the battlefield and spotted the tiny AV cart. It was bumping its way through the threshold of an emergency door. With the cross hairs steady over the computer monitor, he pulled the trigger.

The gun cracked like thunder.

"I AM HELP-"

The computer monitor burst into a shower of sparks and glass. The AV cart creaked to a stop, then fell over. The computer crashed to the ground and spilled circuits across the dirt.

Westland turned to Carl and pointed at his sidearm.

"Do you know how to use that?" she asked him.

Carl stood there, stunned by this recent development. It took him a moment to answer. "Yes. Of course."

"Then go find that alchemist and fill him with bullets."

With the order given, Isobella stormed off to handle other business. Carl glanced all around him. The boat was a chaotic mess of demons and gunfire.

"Who?" he asked.

"Xin Houng! The Chinese guy!" She pointed across the boat. There was Xin, keeping swarms of hornets at bay with puffs of yellow powder. "He touched my book! I want him dead!"

Carl looked at his pistol and hesitated.

Westland stormed back over to him, grabbed him by the arm and shoved him in that direction. "Go! Kill him or I kill you!"

2

Three more pirate boats drifted into the wake of Hell and crumbled into pieces. Dead ninjas littered the forest floor. Ohmsteel did her best to fight back the Beast, but the stinging insects had gotten into her eyes. She crashed to the ground and a thousand demons descended on her. They cracked the scales off her body and exposed the soft flesh underneath.

Despite her thrashing in place, she could not stop the swarms of Zerubim from sinking their weapons into her.

Isobella Westland stood at the steering wheel of the Irish Goodbye. She had dangerously cranked the wheel as far as it could go and turned the boat around 180 degrees. She needed to put distance between them and the fracture.

Her armored soldiers and agents had been forced back by the advancing demons and were forced into a circle around her.

Isobella set her spell book down on the shelf where the late-captain would set his maps. With the same incantation as before, the locks snapped open. A strip of white lace acted as a bookmark and she used it to flip to a very specific page. Intricate drawings showed the fall of angels from Heaven and the moment they plunged into the fiery depths below. Beside the pictures were strange musical notations and an unintelligible language.

Westland looked down to notice black arms slithering around at her feet.

"Make haste," Asag demanded.

"No more delays," Lylo said.

"There is no more time," said Voel.

Westland placed her hands down on either side of the book. She couldn't help but smile. She was about to unleash the words of God and single-handedly defeat Legion. And she didn't plan to limit herself to just the demons, either. All the others too; the werewolves, the ninjas, the pirates, and even the dragon if it was still alive. Turning the fracture into a vacuum that didn't discriminate between demons and other supernatural creatures would send all the monsters to Hell and leave just the humans – the Sons of Adam and the Daughters of Eve – behind. When news of her victory spread, the entire supernatural world would recognize her power. "Did you hear of the one they call Westland?" they would say. "She commands such great power. She could wipe us all out with nothing but a word if she decided to. Maybe," they would say, "Maybe we should leave and never come back."

None of them feared her now. She was simply a human. A mortal. But they would all fear her after this. And that fear would only be the beginning of what she would do to them.

"Stop wasting time!" Lylo shouted, hovering right over Westland's shoulder. The demon's breath smelled of black licorice. "Do it. Do it now!"

Westland struck a triumphant pose and cleared her throat. She traced her fingers over the notes and words in the book. Not only did the angelic language need to be pronounced correctly, the words had to be sung in the correct musical tone. One mistake and it would all be ruined.

She had to sing like an angel.

"Aymai poyso aymai!" she sang.

Which translated to *I am who am.* They were words reserved for the Being Yahweh himself, never spoken by any other being, but Isobella Westland said them all the same.

The three demons, Asag, Lylo, and Voel, reeled in pain at the sound of it. As fallen angels, they couldn't stand to hear the words of God. They stumbled away, then vanished to safety.

Every demons on the battlefield heard it. Even over the commotion of war, there was no mistaking Westland's words or the notes in which she sang them. The Warp Walkers, the swarms of insects, the demons with proper names, even the Beast... all of them froze in panic like trained animals.

Xin heard the song, too. He turned to see Westland on the bridge, hands firmly on the podium, about to work a miracle.

"What is she thinking?" he growled. He headed in her direction, but Carl stepped in front of him.

"Not so fast," Carl said as he dug his pistol into the old man's stomach. "I've got something for you."

Xin stopped. "Get out of my way."

"I'm afraid not," Carl replied. "I have my orders."

Xin looked Carl in the eyes. He didn't have time for idle conversation. "If you are going to shoot me, then shoot me. And if not, then move out of my way before it's too late."

With his confidence challenged, Carl's eyes darted back and forth, then back to Xin. "I'll do it, you know. I'll shoot you."

Xin softly replied, "Then why do you sweat?"

Carl grit his teeth and went to squeeze the trigger. Xin maintained fierce eye contact and didn't flinch.

Carl released his finger from the trigger.

"You're right." Carl lowered his voice. "I'm no murderer."

"Good," Xin said.

"But I still can't let you interfere with what she's doing." Carl grabbed the old man by his clothes and tossed him over the edge of the boat. Xin tumbled out of view and fell to the ground below. The hard landing knocked the wind out of him. Several demons saw Xin land in the grass and they began to creep in his direction. Carl peered down at the ground below and said, "Ah, see there? Now I don't have to kill you. Now it's the demons who'll do it."

Carl dusted off his hands, satisfied with a job well done.

3

"Sais phtino ipo to stoma nov!" Westland sang.

I spit you out of my mouth.

It had been billions of years since the demons heard those words, the very words the Being Yahweh had used to sentence them to an eternity in Hell. Even after billions of years, not a single one of them could forget that day. Now they were reliving it again, this time through the voice of a human girl.

But unlike the Being Yahweh, a human could be killed.

Every demon on the battlefield ignored their tactics and swarmed the Irish Goodbye. Flying demons dropped from the sky, giant demons crashed through the tree, crawling demons scrambled up the side of the boat. They ignored the ninjas and werewolves, they ignored Ohmsteel crawling away, and they ignored Xin in the grass. Legion wanted only one thing: to escape Hell. And in order to do that, they had to kill Isobella Westland.

Forty of Isobella Westland's soldiers stood back to back in a shrinking circle as they fought to protect their boss. They pumped every Pope bullet they had into the demons. Some of the cursed creatures got so close that the soldiers and agents could smell the stink of their decaying skin.

"Hurry, sir!" Koppleman shouted as he pulled out his silver bowie knife. He slashed at a two-headed fire dog's throats, spilling acid blood to the deck.

Westland wanted to encourage her people to stand strong for only a moment longer, but she had to stay focused.

"Zai don sais kaloon pleeno Oranois!"

And no longer call you Heavenly.

The fracture to Hell cracked even wider. A billion demons marched forward from the other side. Plumes of red and purple fire sprayed out like water. Lava cascaded across the ground. The walls of reactor 4 melted into slag and beams of green radiation shot into the air. The steel beams of the ceiling began to creak and sag. Desperate safety alarms fell on deaf ears. The air crackled like a malfunctioning Geiger counter.

"Se krayo se mlio aiontita..."

I sentence you to an eternity...

A dozen black helicopters appeared in the distance.

If Westland finished those last words, Legion would lose. The demons fought with renewed vigor. Swarms of gnats gathered in Isobella's face, clouding her vision. She used both hands to wave them away.

With their ammo exhausted, the soldiers turned to hand-to-hand weapons. Koppleman fell when one of the demons pierced through his gut and into his spine with a sharpened femur bone.

Westland sang the final words as loud as she could.

"Stoin Kolo!"

In Hell!

Time froze. The crackling fires that burst out of Hell went quiet, then reversed direction. A sudden, irresistible force began dragging the demons back towards Hell. The monsters dug their claws into anything they could – the walls of Chernobyl, the trees in the woods, the deck of the Irish Goodbye – but could not fight against the power of Isobella's miracle. Scratching and clawing, they slid uncontrollably through the woods, across the parking lot, and through the crack between Earth and Hell.

The vortex didn't discriminate between demons and other supernatural creatures. The miracle lumped creatures into two categories: humans and everything else.

The force of the miracle dragged Ohmsteel across the ground along the demons. She flapped her wings frantically, but she was too exhausted for it to have any lasting effect. Despite her best efforts, she was drawn closer and closer to reactor 4.

Every werewolf and were-fox and were-tiger finally caught the scent of what Fennel had been smelling all along. Extinction.

The Smashed Clamshell, the Blind Pelican, and the Lady Rosewater rocked violently as their invisible ocean drained into the hellgate. They dropped anchor in an effort to latch onto the Earth, but all it did was delay the inevitable. Ghost pirates jumped overboard in search for safety, but could not swim against the currents that pulled them into the fire.

Isobella Westland did not expect to find herself knocked off her feet and dragged across the length of the Irish Goodbye. She, too, was being sucked into Hell. She realized it before flying over the edge, just in time to grab onto the deck rails.

Also supernatural and therefore destined to be sucked into the pit, her ivory spell book bounced across the boat. It tumbled past her, pages fluttering. She desperately wanted to reach out to grab it, but she knew that if she let go of the rails for any reason it would mean her oblivion.

The book drifted through the air like an escaped dove and vanished into the crackling fires of Chernobyl.

Westland looked up to see a dozen black helicopters descend and hover over the Irish Goodbye. Those were her helicopters, alright, but she hadn't called for helicopters.

"Ma'am!" Carl shouted. He sprinted across the boat to rescue his boss. Isobella, who deeply despised the idea of asking anyone for help, chose her next words carefully.

"Carl!" she shouted. "Hurry!"

Even with her life hanging on the line, she never technically asked for help. It was his intention to help her, but she didn't ask for it. All she did was order him to hurry.

As Carl raced across the boat, a set of polished black shoes stepped into Isobella's vision.

The CEO.

He stood there with his arms crossed, shaking his head.

"Oh, Isobella." He sighed, shook his head and clicked his tongue. "What *are* we going to do with you."

She felt her grip starting her slip. "You! Do something!"

"Oh, we've already done something." The CEO crouched down and put his hands on his knees. "We did an internal investigation. That's what we did. And it seems that you've been cutting deals with the competition."

"I have not!" she shouted. "You bastard, grab me!"

"Oh, come now. You think we don't know about your little arrangement with the demons? They taught you to read Angel and you promised them freedom here on Earth. Well, the Westland Corporation is here to wipe out the supernatural, dear girl. Not cut them deals."

"I am wiping out the supernatural!" she shouted. "Look around you, you idiot! I killed all the werewolves! And the pirates and ninjas! And the dragon!"

"And yourself, it seems." The CEO press his finger to her forehead. "Working all those miracles for so many years has apparently turned you into something else. I can't say what, but one thing's for sure. You're no longer human."

Westland realized, all too late, where she had gone wrong.

"But you..." she began. "You..." She didn't understand. The CEO was also supernatural, but he wasn't being sucked to Hell.

"Me?" the CEO said as he stood. "Miss Westland, I am the embodiment of a corporation. I take an active non-involvement in the debate about God. Religion isn't good for business. I find it quite irrelevant. I only worship two things: money and profit."

Carl arrived. He stopped short when he saw the CEO.

Westland shouted at him, "Carl! Help me! Take my hands! Pull me back on board!"

And maybe Carl would have, if not for the CEO who said, "You don't want to do that, son. Look at her. She's being dragged off to Hell with the rest of the fairy tales. She's not a human anymore. If you help her, you'd be helping a traitor and a fraud."

"Carl!" she screamed. "Don't listen to him!"

Carl, who looked from one boss to the other, couldn't make a decision. He had been trained to remain loyal to Isobella Westland, but Isobella Westland has trained him to never trust the supernatural. So with two conflicting philosophies and two people telling him what to do, Carl did what seemed right.

Carl did nothing.

As she felt her grip begin to loosen, Westland called out to anyone. "Asag! Lylo! Voel! Where are you!?"

The demons did not show themselves.

The CEO slowly and deliberately raised his foot, then placed it hard on the fingers of Westland's right hand. He applied pressure and began to twist.

"Looks like we'll have controlling stock in the corporation after all," he said, "Convenient, too. This will save us from having to orchestrate some kind of car accident."

When she needed to, Westland could become inhumanly stubborn. Despite the agony of her fingers being crushed, she growled through the pain and refused to let go of the rail. The CEO made a sour face, then adjusted his foot to use his heel.

"You were always going to kill me," Westland stated.

"Oh, don't be naive," the CEO said. "One of us was always going to kill the other. We both knew that. The problem is, you're not ambitious enough. You, dear girl, should have killed me when you had the chance."

The CEO stomped down on her fingers. Westland couldn't take that much pain and let her right hand go. She dangled against the force of God by her left hand. The CEO moved his shoe to her other fingers and stepped down again.

"It's business 101," he said. "And while this isn't the technical definition of a hostile take over... the name does seem rather appropriate."

Three times he stomped down on her fingers until her left hand slipped. In a poetic end – and not that she didn't deserve it – Isobella Westland went straight to Hell.

4

Reactor 4 of Chernobyl was in the final stages of a complete meltdown. The graphite shielding had melted into blobs of bright orange sludge. Uranium living in the core of the Reactor 4 was now exposed to open air and cascaded into a chain reaction of heat. The concrete floor boiled into a pool of lava. Chernobyl was minutes away from blooming into a radioactive mushroom cloud.

The Westland Corporation had suffered heavy casualties. Only twenty-three soldiers and eleven agents survived the fight with Legion. The CEO extracted them to safety on his fleet of black helicopters. They had to hurry; while the Sons of Adam and Daughters of Eve were safe from Isobella's miracle and the unstoppable vacuum dragging everything into Hell, they were not immune to the impending nuclear explosion.

Xin Houng fled through the woods on foot. His bag was gone, left on board the Irish Goodbye. With the help of Xunsu Sandals of Chung-Kuei, he crossed great distances in a matter of minutes. Moving as fast as he could, he would be clear of the Ukraine before the reactor could explode.

First came the flash of light. Then the rising mushroom cloud appeared in the distance. Chernobyl had cracked open and set the very air on fire. The concussive blast that followed knocked over trees and kicked up an expanding shockwave of dust. Xin felt the ground shudder beneath his feet. He ran further away and soon ended up at a familiar mountain range.

A black crane waited for him there, perched on a branch, and while it couldn't talk, it did cackle laughter into the sky.

The fallout from the explosion irradiated 1,009 square miles of the Ukraine. For the next 20,000 years, the area would be completely uninhabitable.

Years later, humanity would venture into the disaster area and catch their first glimpse of the destruction using remote-controlled computers and robotics developed by Conan Computers. On that day, a remote-controlled vehicle mounted with cameras, Geiger-counters, and other scientific equipment rolled into reactor 4. It cast light through the clouds of dust with high-beam flashlights.

It revealed something that scientists did not expect. Reactor 4 had grown strange and previously undiscovered crystal formations. These weren't crystals from Earth. These crystals only grew in Hell, but had slowly bled into Earth through the fracture. They grew in long, narrow spikes and came in two colors: neon green and candy-apple red. These crystals formed a type of "scab" over the wound between the two worlds, permanently sealing it from both sides.

"Chernobylite," the humans named it. All attempts to remotely recover a sample of the crystals failed. The mineral was completely indestructible. Even diamond-quality tools couldn't break Chernobylite. Due to the danger of the area and the electrical interference from the persisting radiation, scientific attempts to study the alien crystals turned up very little information. Decades passed and scientists had yet to collect a single chip or flake.

Strangely enough in the late 1990's, on another remote-controlled mission of exploration, scientists found that entire shards of Chernobylite had turned up missing. Spikes of red Chernobylite and green Chernobylite had been shattered off the main cluster and were gone.

Scientists were left with many questions. Who had ventured into the radioactive wasteland of Chernobyl? What tools were strong enough to break Chernobylite? Who would collect these samples and not announce it to the scientific community?

Where in the world did pieces of red and green Chernobylite disappear off to?

Chapter 18

1

My vision cleared and I opened my eyes to an afternoon sunset in South Dakota. Mount Rushmore loomed in front of me. Theodore hobbled his way towards the guard rails and puked his guts out over the edge. Having our consciousness' ripped out of our present-day brains and sent off to relive events that happened more than twenty years ago was disorienting, sure, but it seemed to take a harder toll on Theodore's squishy human brain than it did on me with my computerized safety protocols.

While I didn't feel the overwhelming need to puke, I did admittedly feel sick to my stomach and dizzy as hell. I staggered to my feet and worked my way over to Theodore. I collapsed against the same guard rail and looked out over the trees while he spat stomach acid down at the ground below.

"Did you see what I saw?" I asked him.

He hung his head over the edge and nodded. "Chernobyl?"

"And Isobella Westland and the CEO and the demons," I said.

He spat again. "And Carl."

"Did you see those badass helicopters at the end?" Denali asked, completely thrilled. "Do you think they were Chinooks? They looked like Chinooks."

"CH-47s," I told her. I wasn't exactly sure how I knew that, but I'll be god damned if I wasn't certain.

"She killed all those people," Corolla said. "That Westland lady. She killed everyone."

Almost everyone.

Now I'd experienced a lot of strange and supernatural things since first swallowing Impossible Red, but I had never had memories jammed directly into my brain like that before. I remembered the events of Chernobyl as if I had been there, as if I had lived it, even though it happened more than a decade before I was even born. I remembered the smell of sulfur, how the giant monsters' feet thumped against the ground, everything. It was more real than a dream, but fuzzier than real life.

"I didn't know Westland was a real person," Theodore said. "They never mentioned her, not even in orientation. It's like the CEO scrubbed her off of everything."

"Sounds like something he'd do," I said.

Theodore groaned and rubbed his forehead. "Jeez, I could hear their thoughts in my head. Could you hear their thoughts?"

"Some of them," I said. "It was all kinda blended together."

"But the vision... It didn't... It didn't..." He stopped and put his finger in the air. "Pardon me one second."

And he leaned back over the rail to puke some more.

I put my hand on his back. "It didn't give us any answers."

Too sick to speak, Theodore hung there and nodded. He was right. Granted, I knew tons of things I never knew before – how the Westland Corporation started, what Xin was up to when he was younger, and what caused the meltdown at Chernobyl – but it didn't answer our big questions. Who was the spy behind the problems at Westland? And who busted up Xin's soul and put him in a coma?

I looked up to Mount Rushmore and raised my voice. "Excuse me, Mister Lincoln, sir? I'm sorry, I don't mean to be picky, but your vision kinda glossed over a few key points."

Lincoln looked down at me. "It pains me that I cannot be of more help to you, young American, but that is the unfortunate nature of being an Oracle. Nothing is clear. Everything is a riddle. Our answers are shrouded in mystery and only the most worthy adventurers can make sense of it all."

"Well, I must not be worthy," I said. "Because I'm confused."

"Please accept my sincerest apologies," Lincoln said. "I would help you more, if it were in my power."

"You can't clarify just a few things?" Corolla asked.

"Maybe a hint?" Denali added.

"Anything would help, Mister President," I said. "I don't understand how stuff that happened in the early '80s has anything to do with what's going on now."

Abraham Lincoln didn't respond right away. He glanced at the other faces of Mount Rushmore. They were fast asleep.

"I will answer one question for each of you," Lincoln said softly. "Only because I sincerely believe you are good at heart. But never speak of this to Jefferson. He is quite particular about following the rules."

Bonus. One question each. That would clear up a few things, as long as we chose our questions carefully and only asked about-

Denali pulled forward and blurted out a question. "Is Darla's husband cheating on her?"

"Denali!" Theodore scolded.

"Sorry, sir," she said. "But this is important."

"Marone." I hung my head and massaged the bridge of my nose. Denali's impulsive nature just wasted one of our questions.

Lincoln lowered his eyebrows. "Who is Darla?"

"She's a girlfriend of mine. I met her online. Her husband is a cruise ship captain and he's gone a lot. She thinks he's cheating on her. Is that true?"

Lincoln, who was an oracle and knew all sorts of things, had to wrack his brain to conjure up the information about some obscure woman named Darla. After a moment of thought, he said, "The cruise ship captain is having an extra-marital affair with two different cocktail waitresses."

Denali gasped.

"I knew it!" Theodore blurted out. He was far too excited about being right. I gave him a wide-eyed stare, stunned that he could get such excitement from someone's infidelity. Theodore caught my eye and calmed down when he realized he was overreacting to something so trivial, but insisted on pointing out his genius. "I *was* right, though."

Denali rolled backwards. "What a sleazebag! Wait until I tell her. She's going to be pissed. Or..." Denali gasped again. "Maybe I *shouldn't* tell her. Maybe she'll find out on her own. She's going to want to know how I know and I can't tell her that I heard it from Abraham Lincoln. She'd never understand. But, hot damn, can I keep something like that a secret?"

"Okay," Theodore said as he moved in front of Denali. "Save it for the tabloids. My turn." He raised his voice up to Lincoln, "Mister President, I have a question!"

Here we go. We were about to find out who was behind the big double-cross in the Westland Corporation.

Theodore stood up straight and tall and asked, "Am I going to get my promotion?"

"What!?" I snapped.

Theodore turned to me, confused. "What?" he said.

"You wasted your question on your stupid promotion? What about the mole in your organization? I thought you were going to ask about the mole in the organization!"

"Penelope, we've been over this," he said. "Moles can't do what you're accusing them of."

I smacked him on the shoulder. "Not *moles*, you moron. *Spies*. In the Westland Corporation."

"Oh." His face lit up with the realization that he had also wasted his question. "Ohhh." He scoffed and shook his head. "I'm sorry. I meant to ask about that, but then I started thinking about Kruger and how *he* might get the promotion instead of me and I just had to ask."

I rolled my eyes. We had four questions to ask and the super-spy organization just wasted two of them.

"Well, go on," I said, waving Theodore away from me. "Go get your stupid answers."

Our bickering gave Lincoln enough time to search through fate and had Theodore's answer ready.

"You work for a nefarious cadre of human beings," Lincoln said, describing the Westland Corporation in more polite terms than I would have used. "But, yes, young man. You will receive the promotion you seek."

"I knew it!" Theodore fist-pumped the air and kicked his foot off the ground. He spun in circles and began shadow-boxing at nothing. "Finally, some action!"

Lincoln added more. He wasn't done with his prophecy.

"But by then," he continued, "it won't matter."

Theodore froze and looked back at Mount Rushmore. "What?"

Lincoln repeated himself. "By the time you get your promotion, it will no longer matter. To you, or to anyone else."

Theodore glanced at Denali, the only other Westland employee around. He scrunched up his face, dumbfounded by the notion. All promotions mattered to the Westland Corporation and Theodore wasn't brainwashed to think any different. How could he get a promotion and have it not matter? It was a paradox that wasn't logically possible; like fire that's not hot, or water that's not wet, or a Radiohead album that's fun to listen to.

To be fair, Lincoln's vague answer to Theodore's question didn't make me feel any better about future events. Of everything I knew about the Westland Corporation, a future where his promotion didn't mean anything to him or to *anyone* sounded like bad news. To them, promotions were their reason to live.

"It won't matter?" Theodore whispered as his excitement deflated. His posture slumped. I'd never seen anyone look so pitiful. I put my arm around his shoulders.

"Hey." I shook him softly with an encouraging little side-hug. "For what it's worth, it never mattered to me."

"Thanks." He refused to look up. "It's just that... I wanted to save the world, at least once. I have all these skills and I'm really good at what I do and I guess I just wanted someone else besides me to notice."

It was hard to watch someone's hopes and dreams get crushed by an all-knowing statue. It was the one thing that mattered most to Theodore and now it didn't matter anymore.

I had never been any good at cheering people up – in fact, I typically just made things worse – but I felt obligated to try. I just had to remind myself to not call him any insulting names.

"Hey, don't be a baby about it," I said, trying to jostle the joy back into him as I did my best to think of something nice to say. "You *are* really good at what you do. And I noticed."

That got him to look up. His green eyes sparkled with tears.

"You did?" he asked.

I could have responded with, "Sure, why not." Or possibly with a more disarming, "Whatever." I didn't know what to say and couldn't think of anything better, so we just ended up standing there, sharing eye contact.

"Oh, book a honeymoon, you two," Corolla said as he rolled past us and closer to the guard rails. He raised his voice and said, "Alright, Abey Baby, riddle me this..."

I had no idea what question Corolla wanted to ask, but we only had two questions left and we needed to make them count.

"Corolla," I said, grabbing his attention before he wasted his question on something silly. "Ask about Xin."

"But... I was going to ask something else."

"Like what?"

He hesitated, then softly whispered, "I was going to ask if we could trust Theodore."

How amazingly rude. "Corolla!"

"What?" he said. "Am I crazy for wanting an answer to that question? He works for the Westland Corporation. And after everything we just saw from Chernobyl, you don't think it's important to find out if this guy is on the level or not?"

"It's fine," Theodore said, still reeling with the news of his eventual insignificance. "I get it."

Corolla said, "See? He gets it."

"Corolla." I stepped closer to him, to where only he could hear me. "I totally see where you're coming from, but we only have two questions left and we still need answers."

He lowered his tone to match mine. "I know. That's why I'm asking this question."

"You really don't think we can trust him?" I asked.

"I really don't know," he replied. "But if you let me ask my question, I can find out."

"Corolla. Xin's dying. We're the only ones who can help save him. You gotta find out who tried to kill him, okay? Please?"

He sighed. "Okay, *fine*." He raised his voice and called out to Lincoln. "Mister President, someone jim-jammed Xin's soul and tried to kill him. Can you tell us who did it?"

Lincoln took a moment to think, then in a booming voice, he gave us a name:

"Isobella Westland."

2

Isobella Westland tried to kill Xin? How was that even possible? That bitch was in Hell. I was there in Chernobyl. I saw it happen. I glared at Theodore, not for any reason other than he worked for the Westland Corporation and I had to glare at someone. Maybe Corolla was right.

Theodore realized I was looking at him and his eyes went wide. "What? Don't look at me. I didn't do it."

"Yeah," I said, suspicious. "But maybe you know more than you're letting on. You certainly wouldn't tell us if you did."

"You can't blame Theodore for something Isobella did," Denali said. "We didn't even know that psychopath existed until just now."

"Exactly," Theodore said.

Corolla whispered at me. "He's probably lying."

"What did you say?" Theodore said to Corolla. He did not sound happy.

"I said..." Corolla raised his voice. "You're probably lying."

"He's not lying," Denali shouted.

"I'm not lying," Theodore said.

"Uh huh. That's exactly what you *would* say if you *were* lying," Corolla replied.

It was my turn to get loud. "Everyone, just shut up! Corolla, be nice. And you..." I pointed at Theodore, but I didn't know what to yell at him for. For *maybe* lying to us?

I whipped around and pressed my body against the guard rails so I could ask Lincoln our final question. "Who's behind all the weird shit at Westland? Who's been crashing their computers and setting demons loose?"

Lincoln said her name again. "Isobella Westland."

But I still didn't understand how that was possible.

"Are you sure?" I asked Lincoln.

"I am an Oracle," he said. "I am certain."

"She must have got out of Hell somehow," Theodore said. "It's that simple."

"You don't just 'get out' of Hell," I told him. "It's a prison. You don't get to come and go as you please."

"Okay," he said. "Then you explain how she did it."

I admittedly did not have an answer to that. Not even a guess. I learned all about Hell from my Italian Catholic mother and twelve years of private school and if there was one thing they both made very clear, it was that Hell was permanent, forever, and short of a meltdown in the Ukrainian countryside, you could never escape.

Of course, that was all according to my mother and a bunch of nuns. Mortals. And when it came to the supernatural, no one was less qualified to explain how it worked than mortals.

"You must return to New York City," Lincoln told us as he settled back into his original position. A stiff wind blew over us, signaling the end of our time together. "And make haste. The Westland Corporation is in grave danger. Isobella Westland has only begun her plan. There are far more sinister things to come."

"What?" I shouted at him. "What more sinister things is she going to do?"

"You have exhausted your questions," Lincoln said as his face turned to stone. His last words to us, magically deep and fading into an echo, were, "I bid you godspeed, young travelers."

And he was gone.

"Dammit. We gotta go." I dashed to Corolla and opened the driver side door. Theodore wasn't following me. "Dude, come on. Let's go."

"Let's go?" he asked.

"Yeah," I said. "Let's go."

"In Corolla?" he asked.

"Yes, in Corolla."

"But what about Denali?"

"Yeah," Denali said. "What about me?"

"There's no time." I got in Corolla. He started his engine. "Corolla can fly. He get us there in half the time."

"Uh, maybe you've forgotten," Theodore said as he half-heartedly followed me, "but there was a reason we were driving. The military's got every F-16 in the nation up there. The moment they spot us on radar, we're going to have missiles so far up our ass, we'll taste the rocket fuel."

"Oh, man." Corolla sounded worried. "He's right."

"We'll fly low," I said. "We'll skirt the treetops and stick the areas where they have lower beam blanking turned on. We'll show up as clutter and no one will notice."

Those words spilled out of my mouth before I knew what I was even saying.

"How do you know that?" Corolla asked me.

I didn't have an answer, and we didn't have time for me to explain. "Theodore!" I snapped. "Just get in the fucking car!"

"Okay." He ran to the passenger side. "You better be right."

"Sir?" Denali said.

"We're going to have to trust her, Denali," Theodore said. "We have to get to New York as fast as we can. Drive normal and meet us in the city, okay? Keep your windows up, obey the speed limit, and for the love of god, no Tokyo drifting. Understood?"

Denali gave him a frustrated sigh. "Fine."

Theodore got in Corolla's passenger side. We closed the doors and Corolla floated up off the ground.

Denali, who hated to be left behind, could not contain her excitement when she watched Corolla lift off the ground. "Man, it's so cool when you do that!"

"Thanks!" Corolla said.

"Go, Corolla." I pointed east. "Floor it."

His hubcaps glowed a brighter blue, and we were off.

Corolla kissed the leaves and branches of the surrounding treeline, whooshing up and down along its contours at maximum speed. The sun had begun to set behind the mountains and the day turned to night. Lucky thing, too. People would have noticed a flying 1998 Corolla in the daylight, but at night everyone would assume they were seeing some kind of drone or experimental aircraft, or we'd just end up as another poorly investigated UFO sighting. Even if someone caught him on video, that wouldn't mean anything. People can fake UFO videos on a computer at the public library. And that's exactly what people are comfortable believing.

Still, just to be safe, Corolla avoided heavily populated areas. We skirted around the few little towns that snuck up on us, but we were moving pretty fast and I don't think anyone noticed.

I scanned the star-lit skies for any sign of F-16s. I didn't see very many. A few here and there way out in the distance, but they weren't anything more than red lights that raced across the horizon, then blinked out of view.

"Dammit," Theodore grumbled. He had been fiddling with his phone since we left South Dakota.

"Still no connection?" I asked.

"Nothing." He held the phone up above his head, as if being one foot closer to the satellites in space would somehow make a difference. "I can't get through to anyone at Westland."

"This whole situation is really fucked," I told him.

"I know."

"You're the amazing investigator," I told him. "So you tell me... If Westland somehow managed to drag her ass out of Hell, why would she try to kill Xin's soul and let a bunch of demons loose In the Westland Corporation?"

"Well, it's simple." He put his phone to sleep and set it on his lap. "After everything we saw in Chernobyl... the paranoia, the hyper-focused protection of that book, the belief that she's the most important person on Earth... I'm no psychologist, but I'd say she's dealing with low-level schizophrenia and a textbook case of megalomania. The two very often go hand in hand."

"Megalomania?" Corolla asked.

And I'm glad he did, because I had no idea what that was.

Theodore explained, "Megalomaniacs are narcissists with schizophrenic delusions of grandeur. It's a wild cocktail of problems. Most of the time you see it in homeless people who not only want to run for president, but they're also convinced that they're going to win by a landslide.

"The megalomaniac brain is cross-wired to think it *knows* how to solve all the worlds problems, but it's not enough for *them* to know that. They need everyone else to know that. And in the worst cases, they get so frustrated that no one will listen to them that they just start killing people.

"But now imagine if that person were super wealthy like Isobella Westland. She could hire people to believe her, which only then validates her megalomania and makes it worse, to the point where she lives in a completely delusional world where she she's trying to save the world and people like Xin or the CEO are a threat to that. They threaten her delusion."

I said, "So rather than admit she's not superior..."

"She'd sooner have them killed," Theodore finished.

We flew all through the night. Corolla knew his geography well. Even though the world below us was dark, he was quick to point out when we entered the Garden State.

"Welcome to New Jersey," Corolla said as he turned down the music. "Come for the casinos. Stay because your car got stolen."

Corolla had said that line before, but it always got a giggle out of me. Hilarious. I had a few New Jersey jokes of my own to tell before we crossed into New York.

I nudged Theodore with a grin. "Hey, Theodore."

"What?"

"How does a Jersey Italian get into an honest business?"

He shrugged. "I dunno. How?"

I beamed a smile at him. "Through the skylight."

Chapter 19

1

Once we had crossed over Jersey and entered New York, Corolla killed the headlights and skirted the surface of the Hudson River, navigating by moonlight alone. He unfolded his tired and touched down at an empty pier over by Greenwich Village. It took some crafty navigation to avoid being spotted, but Corolla had a lot of practice and he managed to get rubber on the road without being spotted. The skyscrapers in far-off Midtown were all lit up like Vegas except for one in particular that flickered and flashed in a desperate attempt to stay lit.

Power was failing at Westland headquarters.

"That does not look good," I said.

In a concerned tone, Theodore replied, "No, it does not."

The sun had just begun to rise up over the ocean, which meant the morning commute had begun and traffic was going to be an absolute beast. Still, I had faith in Corolla's ability to handle it. The best cab drivers in the city could get me from the Bronx to Little Italy in twenty-five minutes, but that didn't hold a candle to Corolla's street-skills. He had a sixth sense for when the streetlights were going to change and could anticipate where the traffic would be backed up and gridlocked. So when we needed to get to Westland HQ in a hurry, he zig-zagged his way through the Village, through Midtown, and parked in front of Westland Headquarters in record time.

Theodore directed us to an alley that led us around the back of the HQ skyscraper. There in a wide and well-lit alleyway designed to handle package trucks and armored cars, we came up to a short loading ramp with five black garage doors that said "RESTRICTED ACCESS." These doors would lead us down to the underground parking garage, except they were remote operated and wouldn't open without the proper authorization. Maybe Theodore could have opened the doors with the fancy little Westland app on his phone, but the Westland network had crashed and he still couldn't get a connection.

"No problem." I hopped out of the car and ran for the doors.

"Penelope!" Theodore leaned his head out the window. "Penelope, don't!"

I waved him off. "I'll be careful!"

Okay. Open an industrial garage door. Easy-peasy. I found the latch that kept the door locked closed and karate chopped it right off. Then I hooked my fingers under the bottom of the door, pulled up with all my might and slid that bitch right open.

"Knock knock!"

I slammed the loading garage door up into the ceiling faster than it was engineered to handle. Sparks sprayed everywhere as the metal panels got all twisted and jammed up in the tracks. The sound of grinding steel screeched down the alleyway. Stupid door. Gears came falling down to the ground. I gave it a quick inspection to see if it was fixable, but no. I fucked it up real good, and there was no unfucking it. But I guess what really mattered was, I got it open.

I turned back to see Theodore just shaking his head. I could already tell: he was going to find some way to blame that on me.

I got back in the car, sat down, and stared straight ahead. I didn't dare make eye contact with him.

"You said you were going to be careful," he said.

"Yeah, well." I still didn't look at him. "I say a lot of things."

Corolla drove down the loading ramp and into a sprawling parking garage with SUVs and limos and four-door sedans parked between the concrete support columns. The cars were all polished black with glimmering chrome trim, just slightly more futuristic than anything you'd see at a public car lot. The parking garage lights flickered and occasionally dimmed to half-power as they struggled to stay on. Occasionally they would pop back on to full power, only to go dim again.

Something was draining power out of the building.

As Corolla rolled slowly through the fleet of Westland cars, I got this creepy sense that we were being watched.

One of the SUVs flipped on its headlights. The vehicle shouted at us in a Brooklyn accent. "Hey, hey, hey! What do ya think you're doing down here!?"

The headlights lit up on one of the limos. "This area is off limits to outsiders!" she declared.

One by one, all the cars blinked their headlights on. A few SUVs pulled out of their parking stalls and followed behind us. If they were trying to be intimidating, it was working.

"Is this going to be a problem?" I asked Theodore.

"I don't think so," he said. But he didn't sound too sure.

"Uh..." Corolla whined. "They don't sound very friendly."

Corolla was right. They didn't act friendly either. Each one of the vehicles kept their headlights pointed at us as we rolled along. They shouted at us like an angry mob. The deeper Corolla drove into the garage, the more of them pulled out of park and followed us around.

One of the SUVs got aggressive and bumped up against Corolla's trunk in an attempt to start some shit.

I smacked Theodore on the arm. "Well? Do something."

"Alright, alright." He pointed at an empty space up ahead. "Park right there. I'll get out and clear this up."

The cars only got more aggressive, shouting louder at us. Some of them honked their horns. If they had arms, they would have been reaching for their guns. Corolla pulled into the empty parking space and immediately a limo pulled in behind us and blocked us in. Three SUVs came at us from all different angles, leaving us trapped.

"You picked the wrong place to go trespassing," the girl limo said. "Now you're in big trouble."

"Please," Corolla said. "One of you, do something."

Theodore stepped out, took his ID out of his suit jacket and flashed it at the cars. "Alright, everyone. Settle down. I'm special investigator Theodore from the Utah Detainment Facility and this is Penelope Salvo and her car, Corolla. They're with me."

"I'm not her property, though," Corolla said. "I'm my own person. We just happen to be friends."

The sound of Corolla's voice made the Westland vehicles fall silent. Then they started to whisper.

"Did that Corolla just talk?" one of them asked.

"I talk," Corolla said. "I talk plenty."

The Westland cars collectively gasped.

"How is that possible?" the girl limo asked. "I thought only the Westland Corporation knew how to make talking cars."

I chimed in. "Corolla was built by someone else entirely."

The cars crowded in a little more, this time out of curiosity. One of the SUVs pulled up alongside Corolla. "So who do you work for? Do you have a job?"

"Well, I wouldn't call it a job, really," Corolla said. "I hang out with Penelope here. We mostly break into places like NASA research facilities or NORAD or ancient ruins. Then we steal stuff."

I said, "Okay, well, that's not *all* we do."

"Oh," Corolla continued. "And I can fly."

"What!?" one of the cars exclaimed.

"You can fly?" another one asked. "Show us!"

They all began shouting for a demonstration and Corolla was more than happy to show off. He lit up his hubcaps, floated a few feet off the ground and spun around in a full 360. The other cars backed away from him, completely mind-blown. They laughed and shouted in amazement.

"He's more advanced than he looks!" one of them said.

"Yeah!" Corolla said. "I'm like car Jesus."

"He *is* like car Jesus," one of the limos said.

"He's not car Jesus," I said. "Just because something flies doesn't make it a Jesus."

Theodore nudged me to get my attention and moved towards the elevators. Ah, right. Time was of the essence and Corolla was doing a phenomenal job distracting the cars who otherwise might have alerted someone of our presence. Even Corolla failed to notice that we had walked away.

"Okay!" Corolla touched down for a landing. His new friends gathered all around him as he turned on the radio and asked, "So, anyone else here a big Phil Collins fan?"

2

The parking garage elevator wasn't posh like the elevators I had used in my previous visits to Westland HQ. This elevator was more for utility, with steel floors and perforated walls then vented cold air. It was also missing a button for basement level 5 – the location of Untouchable Orange.

Theodore and I tried to ride the elevator up to the lobby, but the power drain kept jolting us to a hard stop. Each time we stopped moving, a red warning light would come on and we'd be stuck for a few seconds, then the emergency light would blink off and we would start moving again.

"How do I look?" Theodore asked me. He was covered in red dust from the Utah desert and his hair was all over the place. He straightened his tie and adjusted his cuffs, as if that might make a difference.

"You look fine, all things considered." I did my best to fix his hair, then asked him, "How do *I* look?"

That question was meant to be facetious. I knew how I looked. I'd been running around barefoot since Utah, my suit was coated in same red dust as Theodore's, and my hands were filthy from when we buried that limo in Henderson Creek. But it wasn't as though I had anyone to impress with my cleanliness.

I wasn't the one up for promotion.

"You look fine," Theodore said.

I turned to stare at the doors and smiled. I looked terrible and I knew it. Theodore was just being polite. Stupid, but polite.

We had barely begun our ascent up to the main lobby when the elevator jerked to a complete stop and the lights went out.

I stood there patiently, assuming the power would come back and we'd start moving again, but time passed and nothing happened. The two of us stood there in the dark, waiting.

"Huh," he casually remarked.

Panic began to set in, not because I was stuck in an elevator, but because I was trapped in a dark elevator with Theodore. That was exactly the kind of stupid, cheesy shit that happened in romantic comedies where the lights would come back on to reveal the two people kissing and movies like that are stupid.

In a panic, I started mashing the elevator buttons like crazy. Nothing happened. I crouched down and pushed them faster. "Come on, you stupid elevator. Come on."

"We seem to be stuck," Theodore said.

"Well, you *are* the investigator," I replied.

He took a deep breath and asked, "Do you want to-"

I couldn't see him in the dark, so I turned towards the sound of his voice and snipped, "Do I want to *what*, Theodore?"

"Climb?" he said. "If you give me a boost up through the ceiling, I can help you up next."

"Oh," I said. Right. *Climb.*

The elevator shaft was dimly lit by red emergency lights that marked each floor. We climbed a set of steel rungs mounted into the concrete walls, installed for exactly this kind of emergency. He lead the way and I followed.

"Hey," Theodore said as we climbed.

"Yeah?"

"After this is all over, do you want to get a beer somewhere or something?"

I couldn't really say no. I mean, he was a Westland guy and everything, but we had been through an awful lot together since we'd first met. He had saved my life and I had saved his. But for all the times I had saved the world and for all the crazy things I'd done since swallowing Impossible Red, nothing freaked me out in quite the same way as thinking about getting a beer with him. When people get a beer together like that, isn't that a date? Just thinking about being on a date made me super self-aware of just how awkward I can be sometimes.

Still, I had to answer him. "Yeah," I said. "I guess."

"Cool," he said.

We had an easy and uneventful climb up to the main floor. Theodore pried open the elevator doors open and we both tumbled out into the lobby.

We were greeted by absolute chaos. The huge computer monitors over the reception desk were blue screens of death that read NO SIGNAL. Amid the internet outage, the reception desk had apparently resorted to analog phones and screeching fax machines. Cords and cables hung out of the walls and snaked across the floor in a vain attempt to hardwire the information systems together. The receptionists were using old-school rotary phones, all of which were ringing off the hook.

I speed-walked to the reception desk. Theodore followed right behind me. The desk had an array of rotary phones, endless stacks of paperwork, and grinding fax machines that coiled through paper non-stop. I walked around the desk and scanned the receptionists' faces until I spotted Ilana. She was in the middle of a panicked phone conversation.

"I don't know..." she said. She sifted through piles of paper in search of something specific. "I'll find it. I promise I'll find it." She hung up the phone and looked up. We made eye contact and she froze. "Oh, god."

"Ilana."

"Penelope." She stood and leaned partway over the desk. God, she looked weird dressed in her gray Westland pantsuit. "What the hell are you doing here?" she asked, then looked me up and down. "And why are you dressed like you work here?"

"I've got to talk to Carl," I said. "Like now."

"Dude, you could not have picked a worse time," she replied. "Take a look around. I'm in the middle of a grade A, all-American shit-show. I can't just call the CEO and-"

"Ilana, I don't have time to explain, but you're just going to have to trust me. You think things are bad now? They're about to get a lot god damned worse if you don't tell Carl I'm here."

She growled in frustration, but she knew what happened the last time she doubted me. She picked up the receiver of her rotary phone and dialed some numbers. While she waited for it to ring, she pointed two fingers at me.

She said, "Someday you're going to explain all this to me."

"Sure," I said. "You'll never believe me, but sure."

Theodore put his arm on the counter and leaned into our conversation. "So you two know each other?"

"We went to high school together," I said.

Ilana glared at me. "We *used* to be friends."

"Ilana, I'm *sorry*," I said.

"Don't," she replied.

"Ooh," Theodore said, grinning. "Sounds like there's a story."

I said, "Shut up, Theodore."

Ilana's attention was pulled away when someone answered the other end of her phone. "Hello, ma'am, this is Ilana down at reception. Penelope Salvo is down here asking to see Carl and.... Uh huh? Uh huh..."

"Have you ever met Carl before?" I asked Theodore.

Theodore looked away and nodded. "You could say that."

"He's a real trip," I said.

Theodore raised his eyebrows and kept nodding. "You could say that, too."

Ilana hung up the phone with the same dumbfounded look she had the last time I got a private audience with the CEO of her corporation. "Carl is coming down here to see you in person. He wants you to meet him at the red express elevator."

"Thanks, Ilana." Theodore speed-walked towards the red elevator doors and I started after him, but something stopped me. I looked back at Ilana and said, "Hey..."

She was just about to get back to work, but I caught her just in time. She gave me an annoyed stare. "What?"

"I really will tell you everything," I told her. "I promise."

"Everything?" she asked. I could tell by her tone and the look on her face that she meant *everything*.

"Everything," I said.

She nodded, as if accepting an apology. "Okay."

Theodore and I jogged to the red elevator. We had to elbow our way through the crowd of agents rushing back and forth, at the same time maneuvering through a trip-hazard obstacle course of electrical cords and phone cables.

I could only hope that Carl was hurrying down to meet us. We had no idea what Isobella Westland's plan was exactly, just that she was up to *something*, and it was fair to assume that every second counted. From inside the red elevator doors came this rattling thunder, like an out-of-control roller coaster coming in at full speed. It grew louder and louder, then rushed past us.

"Do you hear that?" I asked Theodore.

He said, "Sounds like the elevator broke."

Seconds later I heard it crash to the bottom. There's no possible way a human being could have survived a thirty-seven story fall. I looked at Theodore and he looked at me. I pulled open the elevator doors and there in the empty elevator shaft, clinging to the rungs of the emergency ladder, was Carl. Beneath him was the dark abyss of the empty fall to the bottom.

He looked up at the two of us and, with a forced smile, said, "Well, as the old saying goes, out of the frying pan and into a slightly smaller frying pan."

3

Carl flopped both his arms over the threshold of the elevator doors, strained as his kicked up his left leg, then crawled out onto the lobby floor. I offered him a hand, but he waved me off, saying, "No, no. I can do it." He crawled out, stood himself up and dusted off his hands. He looked down to see the grease stains on his pants.

"Oh, would you look at this," he whined. "My suit is ruined."

"Dude," I said. "You almost died."

"I work for the Westland Corporation," Carl replied. "I almost die every day." He brushed off his pants as best he could, which only smeared the grease around, then he scoffed and gave up. He straightened himself out and looked at me and Theodore. "Anyhow," he said. "Penelope, good to see you again."

I replied with an unamused, "Uh huh."

He perked his eyes and gestured at himself, trying to coax me into returning the greeting. "And it's good for you to see…"

"It's good for me to see your company going up in smoke," I said. "You got a real fucking problem on your hands here."

Carl turned his attention to Theodore and looked him up and down. "Theodore," he simply said. "You're looking well."

Theodore replied, "Thank you."

There was a strange tension between the two, as if they had met before. Whatever their backstory was, we didn't have time.

"Carl," I said. "You need to put this place on red alert. I don't know what's about to happen, but Isobella Westland is-"

Carl silenced me with a finger to my lips. "Shh." He looked around suspiciously, then leaned in close to whisper. "We can't talk here. We need to go someplace secure. Follow me."

He led us over to the door for the fire stairs. Theodore and I followed him. What choice did we have? Carl led into the stairwell, then down the stairs and into the basement levels.

"So, Penelope," Carl began. "How have you been?"

"How have I been?" I repeated. "How have I *been*? I got blown up by a nuke and beat up by one of your demon prisoners, Carl, that's how I've been."

"So you've been well," Carl said.

I rolled my eyes. Not listening, as always.

"And Theodore," Carl continued. "It's good to see you again."

Theodore's voice was cold. "I wish I could say the same."

I glanced at Theodore. He wouldn't even look at Carl.

Carl replied, "Oh, you're not still upset about being assigned to the detainment facility, are you?"

"Oh, no," Theodore said. "I loved the barren wastelands of western Utah. Not that it maters anymore. The Ultra-max is destroyed and everyone else there is dead."

"Shame." Carl didn't seem the least bit fazed. "What about the car I got you? Is she okay? What was her name? Dolly?"

"Denali," Theodore said. "And she's fine. She's great. She's not as bad as everyone thinks. But I guess that's what we do here at the Westland Corporation: make snap judgments about people and shuffle them around until they're not a problem anymore."

Carl was barely listening. "I always liked that car."

"You said she was defective," Theodore said.

"I said she was flawed," Carl corrected him. "There's a difference. And she *is* flawed, just like how we're *all* flawed. I'm flawed. You're flawed. Even the mighty Penelope here is flawed.

There's nothing wrong with a few imperfections, so don't twist my words and make it sound like I don't like her."

Theodore scoffed. "So it's just a coincidence that the inspector with the least experience gets partnered with the car with the most 'flaws'?"

"No, it's not a coincidence," Carl said. "But it's also not a conspiracy. So stop looking at it that way."

Theodore went silent.

If they were done with whatever bickering they needed to get out of their system, we had better eggplant Parmesans to take care of.

"Carl," I said, moving onto more important topics. "We've got bad news about Isobella Westland. Somehow she's-"

Carl stopped and raised his finger at me. "Not... yet..." He turned and resumed his descent down the stairs. We went down another flight and he said, "I've got the perfect place to talk where no one can possibly hear us. Once we're safe and secure, you can tell me anything you want."

I sighed.

We went down another flight of stairs.

"Were there any other survivors from Utah?" Carl asked.

"Just one," Theodore said. "Fredrick Kruger."

"Never heard of him," Carl said.

He was about to. He was about to hear all about him.

"Wait," I said. "*Fredrick* Kruger?"

"Yeah," Theodore said. "So what?"

I blinked at him. "So, for short, his name is Freddy Kruger?"

Theodore looked confused. "Why's that weird?"

I couldn't believe he wasn't getting it. "Dude. The guy's name is *Freddy Kruger.*"

Carl spoke up. "Okay, Penelope. We get it. The man's name is Freddy Kruger."

"Why is his name such a big deal?" Theodore asked.

"I dunno," I said. "it's just a weird name to have. You have a guy working here whose name is actually Freddy Kruger."

"So?" Carl said. "Your name is Penelope Salvo."

"Yeah, but that's not weird, Carl," I said. "I'm not named after a psycho killer from Nightmare on Elm Street."

"Huh?" Theodore sounded more confused than ever.

"Nightmare on Elm Street?" Carl repeated, as if he had never even *heard* of the movie. "Elm Street is in the Bronx. And the only nightmare there is the traffic."

"No!" These two were idiots. "Nightmare on Elm Street is the movie with Freddy Kruger. The dude has claws and a striped shirt and a hat. He enters your dreams and then he kills you."

I looked at the both of them, but neither one reacted.

Carl sounded a little scared. "And this is a real guy?"

"No, you moron," I said. "It's a movie! It's, like, *ten* movies. They even made Freddy Versus Jason!"

"Jason?" Theodore asked.

Carl glanced back at me. "Another guy from the Bronx?"

I threw my hands up. "Just nevermind."

We descended down another flight of stairs. After a while, I could hear Carl chuckling to himself.

"What?" I asked. "What's so funny?"

"Oh, nothing really," Carl said. "I'm just glad to see you two getting along so well."

Of course Carl was happy to see my paling around with a Westland employee. His main goal in life sometimes seemed to be to get on my good side for whatever nefarious reason. I'm sure he was just pleased as punch to see me in a Westland suit and working with Theodore. "Keep your friends close and your enemies closer" and all that, right? Well, Carl sure had me pretty god damned close. I was solving *his* mysteries, saving *his* people, fighting *his* literal demons.

Holy shit. I was... like... *turning into* a Westland agent.

No. That wasn't possible. I wasn't going to let that happen and I wasn't going to let Carl *think* that was going to happen.

"I'm only working with Theodore because he promised to help Xin," I said. "We are not friends."

Carl asked, "Oh, you're not?"

"No," I said. "We're not. Tell him, Theodore."

That caught Theodore off guard. "What?"

"Tell him we're not friends."

"Oh." He stayed quiet at first, and I guess I understood the hesitation, but then the words came out. "We're not friends."

It obviously hurt Theodore to say that out loud. And I couldn't blame him. That was a pretty hurtful thing to make him say, especially when the exact opposite was true. But what could I do? Let Carl win? Explain that I didn't want Carl thinking he had somehow gotten the better of me? In any case, when it comes to feelings, I'm not exactly the best communicator.

"Of course you're not friends," Carl said. "Strictly business."

He chuckled some more.

Carl led us to an orange blast door, magnetically sealed, like something you'd see on a space station. The words PROJECT: AZALEA were painted across the doors in huge black letters. I could tell by the gloss of the paint that these were solid steel doors, probably twelve inches thick and strong enough to shrug off a cruise missile. Carl took out the red CEO keycard our of his inside jacket pocket and swiped it through the nearby reader.

"This is the one guaranteed place where no one can possibly hear us, not on Earth and not anywhere else."

The blast doors hissed and opened up like a camera lens. Carl had brought us to the underground cavern hidden beneath the streets of Manhattan. I'd been in the vast prehistoric chamber one before, with fossils in the floor and exotic crystals growing on the walls. Down at the very bottom sat the same cube of glorious glass where Westland housed Untouchable Orange.

The factory-sized machines they used to leech unlimited energy out of Untouchable Orange had been shut down. Everything was quiet. The orange marble floated all alone inside the clear glass, twinkling with little puffs of fire.

Carl started down the catwalks. Theodore and I followed.

Carl decided it was time to explain. "When our computer systems started going haywire, automatic safety protocols shut the whole engine down. We'll talk inside the glorious glass. Even the best psychics in the world won't be able to hear us in there."

"Uh." I looked at the containment chamber. Glorious glass, five feet thick? This was the same stuff they used to keep demons in prison. Wait, not imprisoned. *Detained.* Even the Cosmonaut couldn't move through glorious glass. If I followed Carl in there, and if this was some sort of trick, I would be trapped. "You really want us to go inside that thing?" I asked.

"Penelope," Carl said. "That's not trepidation I hear in your voice, is it?

"I dunno," I said. "Maybe. What's trepidation?"

"Concern," he clarified.

"Oh," I said. "Than yes. Trepidation."

"You don't trust me?"

"Absolutely not."

"Hmm. Once a Skeptical Skeeter, always a Skeptical Skeeter I suppose. But if it puts your mind at ease... here." He held out his CEO keycard. "This card can open or close that glorious glass door. Would you feel better if you held onto it for me?"

Well, I certainly didn't trust Carl, but if I had the keys to free myself, then a private conversation safe from supernatural eavesdropping did sound like the right call. Westland apparently had no shortage of double agents, so I took his CEO keycard and tucked it into my jacket pocket.

"I've never seen this much glorious glass before," Theodore said. "It must have cost a fortune."

"It certainly doesn't come cheap," Carl said. "Angels aren't exactly generous when it comes to giving their secrets away."

"Then how did you talk them into it?" I asked.

Carl just smiled. "I have a way with words."

We reached the bottom of the catwalks where the air felt colder. The stone beneath our feet was polished and smooth. The three of us went over to the glorious glass and Carl gestured at the access panel, indicating I should use the keycard to open the transparent vault door. So I did.

A system of hydraulic pistons opened the massive, round door. Once we stepped inside, the same hydraulics pushed the door closed. The lights on the access panel went from red to green, I guess meaning that the chamber was perfectly sealed.

"Now then," Carl said as he turned to me and Theodore. "We only have about seventeen minutes of breathable air, so what's this big news you have about Isobella Westland?"

"She's coming," I said. "She was the one who let Lylo out of her cell and destroyed your super-max prison-"

"Detainment center," Theodore interrupted.

"Detainment center," I said. "And she's the one who's been sabotaging all your systems. Somehow, and I don't know how, but *somehow* she got out of Hell and she's all pissed off."

Carl lowered his eyebrows. "And how do you know that?"

"We know a lot of things," Theodore said. "We know that she killed Conan the computer."

"And Ohmsteel, the blue dragon," I said.

"And all the werewolves and ghost pirates," Theodore added.

"And you tried to kill Xin, you prick," I said. "You shoved him over the edge of the Irish Goodbye."

Carl crossed his arms and scowled at me. He didn't seem to care much for the accusation, but he also didn't bother to deny it.

"Do you know anything *relevant*?" he asked.

"We know that Isobella Westland came back to finish the job," I said. "She's the one who tried to kill Xin and she's the one who's been stomping a mudhole in your whole corporation."

"She's got Westland employees working as double agents," Theodore said. "Kruger was one of them. He's the one who let Lylo loose at the ultra-max and got everyone killed."

The news didn't shock Carl like I thought it would.

"I see," he said, then casually strolled away. "Well, I don't know where you two got your information, but you couldn't be more mistaken. Isobella Westland hasn't been on Earth for decades and I doubt she's ever coming back."

"We talked to an Oracle," Theodore blurted out.

Carl turned to arch an eyebrow at him. "An oracle?"

"Yes, sir," Theodore said.

"You know you're not supposed to do that."

"Well, we did. And Lincoln confirmed that it's Isobella Westland behind all this. We don't know how, and we don't know what she's planning next, but this is her corporation and she's coming back for it."

"I see." Carl crossed his arms, then I saw the slightest grin creep across his face. He waved a finger at the two of us. "I knew that putting you two together was a good idea, but even still, I am thoroughly impressed with your results."

I squinted at him. "What do you mean 'put us together'?"

He pointed at the both of us and said, "You didn't honestly think that I'd leave Penelope Salvo in the hands of one lowly investigator, did you?"

Honestly, at the time it happened, I did not.

Carl continued. "When that nuclear bomb went off over the ocean and you splashed down in the water, I had my agents fish you out and bring you to Utah. And Theodore, I have a hundred investigators better qualified to deal with Penelope Salvo, but I assigned you to her case because, I don't know, call it women's intuition, but I knew that you two would become best friends."

"So you manipulated us," I said.

"Manipulated?" Carl repeated. "My dear girl, all I did was put you two in the same room at the same time. Whatever happened after that had nothing to do with me."

Theodore stepped forward with a pissed off look on his face. "Do you have to run everything in my life? It wasn't enough that you sent me to the Utah Ultra-Max to get me out of New York. Or that you gave me the worst car in the corporation so I'd look stupid. Now you're picking my friends?"

"I'm not running your life, Theodore," Carl said. "And I'm not picking your friends. I'm helping you succeed. You want to be a field agent? Well, that's not going to happen if you don't get some real-world experience. So, yes, I took you away from New York and sent you to the Ultra-Max. Guilty as charged. You can't be a field agent when you don't know anything about celestial-class threats. And I partnered you up with Denali because I hoped that her odd-ball programming would teach you some leadership skills. And, yes, I gave you the Penelope assignment, not because I care if you have friends, but because she's such a magnet for trouble that if you wanted to keep up with her, you'd have to stop *wanting* to be a field agent and start *acting* like one."

Theodore looked like he was about to deck Carl in the face. "Oh, so this is the 'for my own good' speech again?"

Carl stayed cool as a cucumber. "This is the 'I expect more out of you' speech, Theodore. Frankly, up until now, you've been quite the disappointment."

"I knew it was a mistake to come here," Theodore said. He went and stood at the closed vault door. "Penelope. Let me out."

"Let you out?" Okay, this was not going well. "We haven't even talked about Isobella. She could be on her way here right now and we haven't talked about what we're going to-"

"I'm serious, Penelope," he said. "Open the door. I'm not spending another second in here with him. I'm leaving."

I sighed. I had no idea what was going on. Why was Theodore being so moody? Sure, Carl was being a dick, but that was Carl. He was always a dick. I went over and swiped the card in the door. The access panel lights turned red and the vault door hissed open. Theodore stormed out and marched away.

"Eh, let him go," Carl said as he came up behind me. "That boy has never been able to see the big picture."

I asked, "Don't you think you were a little hard on him?"

"Of course I'm hard on him," he said. "His performance is a direct reflection on mine."

"Why him? You have tons of other employees. What makes him so special?"

Carl tilted his head. "He didn't tell you?"

I gave Carl a blank stare. "Tell me what?"

"Oh, he *didn't* tell you." Then Carl seemed confused. "And you didn't figure it out?"

"Figure *what* out, Carl."

"Theodore is my son."

When I was in fifth grade, I got a D in history. Michael, one of the biggest names in archaeology, absolutely lost his shit. How could I – daughter of the great Michael Salvo – get "a fucking D" in history of all things? I was an embarrassment. "No bones about it," he said. I was a straight up embarrassment.

What he didn't know was that I had got my very first period at school the day before and left blood on the seat at lunch. That led to kids trying to tease me about it at recess, so I sent a few of them on a field trip to see the school nurse. It was a weird time for me. Yeah, I got a D in history. I couldn't have given a shit less about the Civil War. But, for Michael, that was no excuse. There was "no excuse" for a D.

"Just like a girl," Michael shouted as he swung his belt around. "You're going to have to learn real quick, kid, you can't go around blaming everything on your period."

I'd like to say that the only reason he had that belt out was to scare me, but that would be a lie.

Point is, I know how much it sucks to have someone tell you that you're a "disappointment."

"What do you mean he's your son?" I asked Carl.

"Which part is confusing?" he asked.

"How the fuck is Theodore your son?"

"Are you asking about the biology of it?"

Oh god. I felt sick to my stomach. Did I just spend the last couple days kicking it with... Carl Junior?

I took a deep breath. "Please, Carl, tell me you're lying."

"No." Carl looked out the glorious glass at Theodore, who stomped up the catwalks. "Unfortunately for me, he takes after his mother and her dire misunderstanding of the world. He certainly lacks my social savvy and business acumen."

"You know what?" I grabbed Carl by the suit, whipped him around and slammed him up against the glorious glass. "You're lucky to even have a son like Theodore. He's a good agent and a good person, and quite frankly I think it's fucking disgusting the way you treat him. You've got him so brainwashed with this Westland Corporation bullshit that all he ever talks about is that stupid promotion."

"You don't know what you're talking about." Carl replied as he winced in pain. "I'm pushing him to reach his full potential."

"You have no idea what his full potential even is!" I shouted. "He could have been a beekeeper, or a painter, or an astronaut! All you did was turn him into another Westland jamoke! Did you even give him a chance to be anything else?"

He gave me a confused look. "What else is there?"

I dropped Carl to the floor. It disgusted me to even touch him. He landed hard. Good. I hoped he broke something.

"I'm giving you this one warning, Carl," I said. "Isobella Westland is coming. Deal with it on your own. You and me? We're done. This is the last time we're ever going to see each other."

"But I thought we were friends."

"Will you get this through your thick fucking skull, dude? We are not friends. We were never friends. And we are never, ever, *ever* going to be friends. Ever."

I flicked the red CEO keycard down at him. It bounced off his chest and landed on the floor between us.

When I stepped out of the big glass vault, I checked for Theodore. He stomped furiously up the catwalks, already halfway up to the top. I got a jogging start and pushed off the ground, super-jumping up towards him. I hit a pretty good landing on the catwalk with a metallic clang.

Theodore turned around to find me suddenly behind him.

"Theodore..." I began.

"Leave me alone." He walked away from me without a second glance. "I don't want to talk to you right now."

I followed after him. "I just wanted to tell you that I know what you're going through. Look, I don't usually talk about this kind of shit with anyone, but when I was a kid, my father-"

Theodore whipped around, furious. "We're not friends?"

"What?" I had no idea what he was talking about.

"That's what you told Carl. That's what you made *me* tell Carl. We're not friends and our relationship is strictly business."

"I..." I forgot that part happened. "I- I didn't mean that."

"And what about all the stuff you said to Corolla?" he asked. "You don't even like me."

"How did you...?"

"I'm an investigator, Penelope. I can read lips."

Fuck. Fuck. Fuck. Sure, I said all those things, but each one of them was taken completely out of context. Corolla was giving me a hard time and I was just trying to protect myself from his stupid theory that I had a crush on Theodore. That was a simple enough explanation. Explain yourself, Penelope. Say...

I'm sorry.

I do like you.

You don't have a stupid face.

I never trusted anyone from Westland until I met you.

My dad was crazy abusive and he got me all fucked up in the head and I have no idea how to show emotion that isn't sarcastic and that's all his fault, not yours.

It was an easy apology, but, true to form, I screwed it up. All that came out of my mouth was, "It's hard to explain."

"Don't bother," Theodore said. He turned and walked away.

"Theodore-"

He kept walking. "Goodbye, Penelope."

I considered going after him, but he seemed really pissed off and sometimes its best to let people like that cool down first. One thing was for sure, I fucked this one up good. I knew Theodore was a Westland agent from the moment I met him. He was "the enemy." The more I got to know the guy and the less I hated him, the more confusing things became. I had come to trust someone from Westland and Corolla was busting my balls about it.

A lot of this was Corolla's fault. If he didn't tease me so much about liking Theodore, I wouldn't have needed to defend myself with a bunch of things I didn't really mean. So, yeah, I told Corolla I didn't like Theodore. But why'd he have to keep pushing it after that? Because it's funny? Well, it's not funny. In fact, it got me in a lot of trouble and screwed everything up.

And wasn't as though Theodore was all innocent in all this. He could have told me Carl was his dad forever ago. He was the one keeping pointless secrets. A lie by omission is still a lie, so that made Theodore a liar. And that just went to prove my old rule completely right: You can never trust anyone from the Westland Corporation.

So Theodore wanted me to leave him alone? Fine.

Happy to be of service.

6

I stomped my way into the Westland parking garage. I left cracks in the concrete with each moody step, but I didn't care. They could afford to fix it. Corolla's voice echoed through the garage and I found him quite a ways away, completely encircled by black limos and SUVs. They were laughing and just having a grand old time.

Corolla was in the middle of some story. "So then I tell him, no, *this* is a riddle. What's orange, then blue, then purple, then black? And he sat there with a really dumb look on his face and he couldn't figure it out. So I told him, it's-"

"The sky," I interrupted. That was my story he was telling. That was my riddle. And what better timing than to catch Corolla stealing both of them to impress his new friends.

"Oh. Hi, Penelope." Corolla laughed nervously. He knew he'd been caught red-handed. "Penelope, these cars are really cool when you get to know then. I've been telling them all about you."

"Fantastic." That came out super bitchy. Good. "Well, story time is over. Wrap things up. Time to go home."

"Okay," he said. "Five more minutes? We were just about to-"

"No. We have things to do."

"But five more minutes isn't going to-"

"I said no, Corolla. Not in five more minutes. Not in one more minute. Now."

The cars all grumbled. They didn't like how I bossed him around. Well, that was too bad for them. If I wanted opinions from the motor pool, I would have asked for it.

Corolla politely excused himself from the group of vehicles and rolled over to me.

"What's your deal?" he whispered. "You're embarrassing me in front of my friends."

"Friends?" I repeated. "These cars are your friends now?"

"These cars are my people."

"News flash, homie. These cars work for Westland. You know the rule. Don't trust anyone from Westland. That includes cars."

Corolla was quiet for a second. "You have *got* to be joking."

"Oh, I'm serious as a heart attack."

"Okay, maybe you've forgotten the last couple days? But you're the one who's been breaking the Westland rule."

I knew he was going to throw that in my face. I didn't much have the patience for it.

I said, "If you're talking about Theodore, that was totally different and you know it."

"Oh, so it's okay when you do it, but not when I do it."

"I worked with Theodore because I didn't have any choice."

He laughed. "That's such a lie and you know it. We could have bailed on him and Denali at any time. You just didn't want to... and you know exactly why."

This again? I was in absolutely no mood for what he was insinuating. That's exactly how I ended up in this position in the first place. It's not enough that he brought up 'liking Theodore' a bajillion times, he had to go for a bajillion-and-one. I squeezed my fists in a desperate attempt to keep from blowing my top.

"We're not going to keep talking about this," I said. "It's not up for discussion. We're going home. Now."

"Not up for *discussion*?" Corolla said. "I don't know what's gotten into you, but you're not the boss of me."

"Oh, I *am* the boss of you. That's exactly what I am."

"Wrong. You don't own me. We're friends and I happen to be a car. I let you ride inside me as a favor. And you have a nasty habit of never saying thank you, by the way."

I grit my teeth. "Corolla, You're really starting to piss me off."

"Well, *you're* pissing *me* off," he said. "All you ever do is boss me around. Corolla, don't park there. Corolla, put that gun down. Corolla, trust the Westland Corporation. Corolla, *don't* trust the Westland Corporation. And I always do whatever you say and now it's built up such a pattern that the one time I try to do my own thing, you throw a full-blown hissy fit."

"I'm done arguing about this," I said.

"Good!" he replied. "So am I."

"We're leaving."

"Uh, no?" He put himself in reverse and rolled back to the other cars. "I'll leave whenever I'm ready."

"Wow, Corolla. Really?"

"Really."

"Fine!" I turned my back on him and stormed away towards the garage doors. "Do whatever you want."

He called out after me, "I will."

"Good."

"I know it's good."

I shouted back. "Whatever!"

"Whatever to you!"

I'd just go home alone then, goddammit. On my way out of the parking garage, I swung my fist and put it through a concrete pillar. It didn't make me feel any better.

Chapter 20

1

It had been almost two years since I last needed the bus to get around town. Corolla change all that the day he came into my life. But that particular day was different. I posted up in the very back seat of the D bus to Chinatown and leaned my head against the glass. The sidewalks were crowded with people and I watched the tourists as they took selfies in front of everything: the subway stairs and statues, the deli windows and the street signs.

They had no idea how lucky they were to live their simple lives, where all they had to worry about was work and orgasms and money and food. They went through life completely clueless that they shared a world with evil corporations and shape changing space stations and people escaping from Hell.

I rubbed my face in total frustration. I just spent days and days dicking around the United States trying to figure out a way to save Xin's life and what did I have to show for it? Stugots, that's what. I was left with no choice but to fix him all on my own, apparently, and I only had one clue to build on: The name of the woman responsible, the woman who could undo the spell that nearly obliterated Xin's soul.

Isobella Westland.

I would find a way to track her down, I promised myself that. Back at Xin's shop, I had limitless magic at my disposal. Surely, between the special book he gave me for my birthday and our armory of magical items hidden in the basement, something –

surely *something* – could turn up useful.

I just needed to think.

It was early afternoon for I got back to the shop. I walked in, saw Xin's empty spot at the counter and had a complete fucking break down. *"Here come the water works."* I had an entire child-hood of practice forcing back tears, and I was normally pretty dark good at it, but not this time. A lot of it was because of Xin, but it was also a combination of everything else. Carl being a bad father reminded me of Michael, Theodore's hurt feelings reminded me that I'm a bad person, and there was no greater evidence of that than the way I overreacted and yelled at Corolla, my best friend in the whole world. I collapsed to my knees right there in the middle of the shop and bawled my fucking eyes out. They say crying makes you feel better, but for me, crying only made me feel worse. Crying meant I was weak. Crying meant something other than me was controlling my emotions and I had officially lost all control.

Eventually I lost the will to stay upright on my knees, so I fell onto my side and cried some more.

My brain was processing emotions that it wasn't used to. Impossible Red confused emotional trauma for physical damage. It did the only thing it knew best – to repair me – but these weren't broken finger bones it could snap back into place, or lacerated skin gushing motor oil. These were emotional wounds that a billion tiny nano-computers couldn't fix.

Still, it tried. That was it's job, to try. I felt it up there in my brain, tinkering around with my neurons, trying to get me back to normal, working order.

I forced myself to stop crying. Jesus, Penelope, get yourself together. Some badass you are, weeping on the floor like a goddam war widow. All you're doing is wasting precious time. You should be getting work done. You need to help Xin, and now.

A five-minute breakdown was good enough. I bottled my emotions back up and stomped them back down into the deepest parts of my psyche where they belonged.

I stood up and looked around. The Desert Strawflower had started to wilt. The Fire Crocus drooped under the weight of its own flowers. Even the chutes of bamboo – a resilient little family of sprouts – didn't have the same strength to them. I did a quick 360 and scanned all the plants. Fuck me. They were all in poor shape. It was my responsibility to water them and I had been off gallivanting around the United States. Xin put me in charge of the shop because he trusted me and I was already screwing it up. I had a million other things I should have been doing, but I put it all on pause so I could water the plants. When Xin came home from the hospital, I wanted him to see that he was right to trust me with his family's responsibility. Besides, I had already spent months searching the world for replacement plants; I wasn't about to do that all over again.

I started with the plants on the front porch, but I didn't listen to music. Wasn't in the mood. Watering the plants is a complex process – they all need precise amounts of water, all at different temperatures – but I'd been doing it for years and I could work on autopilot. Good thing, too, because my mind was a million miles away. Imaginary conversations between myself and Corolla, or myself and Theodore played out in my head and I muttered my pissed-off responses to myself.

You think I'd learn. Always keep an eye on the alleyway.

I caught a glimpse of someone out of the corner of my eye and turned to see them standing at the mouth of the alleyway. For a second I didn't recognize her, but then it hit me. The scorched suit? the nearly white blonde hair? An ivory book in the crook of her arm.

It was Isobella Westland, and she was staring right at me with piercing, mad-driven eyes.

The watering can dropped from my hand and clattered on the floorboards.

Isobella Westland stared right at me with that bitchy smirk I had seen her flash back in the Ukraine. She hadn't come to Chinatown in the flesh, however. No. Her body was transparent like a ghost and glowed with a golden aura. She hadn't aged a day since my vision of her at the Chernobyl nuclear facility. Her hair was the same. Her clothes were the same.

Cradled in the crook of her arm was that same white spell book she used to carry around, the one that let her cast miracles in the name of God. The corners were bent. The golden edges of the pages had completely worn off. Thumbprint smudges of soot and ash covered the outside, something you'd expect after decades of use down in Hell.

Of all the people I expected might pop in for a visit, I definitely wasn't expecting Isobella Westland. Her presence could only mean trouble. My eyes wandered from her cold, vacant stare and down to her ivory book. Whatever magic she used to disrupt Xin's soul, that had to've been the source. So it only made sense that somewhere else in those mysterious pages was the solution to bringing him back to life.

I had to get it away from her, but I had no idea how easy that would be. I'd never fought a ghost with God-powers before. And that only prompted more questions. Why did Isobella come to the shop in the first place? Was I next on her kill list?

Surely not. I wasn't even born when she got sent to Hell. This chick didn't even have the first clue who I was. As far as Isobella Westland was concerned, I was just some random Italian chick watering some plants, not a hero-class threat with the strength of an industrial car compactor. Still, I took a careful step backwards. She might not have come down to Xin's shop with murder in mind, but she also didn't come around to browse.

No, she was one hundred percent up to something.

Satisfied that she had made her presence known and caught me sufficiently off-guard, she began moving towards the porch. And when I say "moving," I mean she hovered. She didn't use her legs, she just drifted a few weightless inches off the ground. Once she reached the porch, she took one of the dangling vines of the Looping Bandis between her fingers and looked at it up close.

She said it's name. "A Looping Bandis. Interesting find. They come from Guatemala, correct?"

"They do," I said.

"From the Temple of..." She snapped her fingers as she struggled to remember. Each snap had a resonating sound to it, as if she were broadcasting her existence from another dimension. "The Temple of..."

I couldn't tell what she was baiting me into by pretending not to remember the answer, but I volunteered the name all the same.

"Muzencab," I told her.

"Ah, Muzencab. That's right." She stared at me blankly for much too long, then turned her attention back to the Looping Bandis and finished Muzencab's name. "The Aztec God of Bees."

I wasn't in the mood for games. "Can I *help* you?"

"I think maybe you can." She sounded as though she had something specific in mind. "Tell me. Are you the girl Penelope Salvo I've heard so much about?"

Shit. She knew who I was.

"Maybe I am," I said. "And maybe I'm not."

"You're the host of Impossible Red," she said. It wasn't a question, but a statement of fact. "Skin made of indestructible carbon nanotubes, bones of tungsten carbide, all that?"

I crossed my arms. "Who told you that?"

She grinned without looking away from the plant. "I've spent the last couple days trashing the Westland Corporation's computer systems. They've been busy while I've been out of town. You wouldn't believe the stuff I found in there; recorded conversations with the Galactic Supremacy, a registry for the living descendants of Jesus Christ, even the location of New Beatlemania."

"And apparently a file on Penelope Salvo," I said.

"A very detailed file, actually." She turned to lock eyes with me and began to confidently climb the porch steps, as if nothing in the world could possibly hurt her. "It was useful information, albeit a little *boring* to read. You're nowhere near as fascinating as everyone made it sound. Your father was emotionally and physically abusive. He walked out on you when you were twelve. Your mother was driving to your high school graduation when she was killed by a moving truck. You wear size eight shoes, you have a mild allergy to peanuts, and your favorite foods are capicola ham and General Tso's shrimp. At least, it used to be. Before you were put on a strict diet of iron and steel."

"Funny you mention that," I said. "Did my file also say how my parents were in the iron and steel business?"

Isobella raised an eyebrow at me. "No, it did not."

"It's true," I said. I puffed up my chest and smiled. "My mother would iron and my father would steal."

Isobella didn't even crack a smile. I wasn't convinced the woman was even capable of the joy necessary to smile, at least not if it wasn't at her own self-glorification. Whatever. I didn't expect her to laugh. I just used the joke to gauge her intentions.

"You certainly live up to your psychological profile," she told me. "Right down the juvenile sense of humor."

"Well, you seem to have me at a disadvantage," I said. "You know so much about me. Who are you supposed to be?"

Now, I knew full well who Isobella Westland was, but Isobella Westland didn't know that I knew who Isobella Westland was. And true to form, yet again, she had overestimated her own genius and didn't realize that she wasn't yet holding *all* the cards.

She started one of those long-winded, smarmy, disrespectful speeches I had come to hate from people who didn't see me as a threat because of my age and inexperience.

"Who I am is not important," she said. "In fact-"

"Actually, I know exactly who you are," I said, interrupting her. "You're Isobella Westland and you founded the Westland Corporation back in the '80s. At least, before you botched a deal with the corporate entities. You mass-murdered the werewolves, you killed one of the last dragons on Earth, you shot that poor computer Conan in the head and you should be trapped in Hell, but you're not."

Her face lit up, impressed by how much I already knew about her. Good. Two could play the "I know who you really are" game. Her surprise quickly faded and then she nodded at me, as if she suddenly realized I was a lot sharper than I looked.

"Guilty on all charges, I suppose." She held out her arm and admired her glowing, see-through body. "The demons said Hell was perfect and inescapable, but there's something to be said for a plan more sophisticated than just bashing your head against the door. It wasn't easy, I will say that much, and existing as pure soulstuff is an entirely new experience, but separating my soul from my physical body was the only way back to Earth."

"Fancy trick," I said.

"Thank you," she said with sincerity, as if she appreciated the recognition. "Twenty-seven years in Hell gave me plenty of time to practice my miracles. In fact, I would suppose I've been in Hell longer than you've been alive. What are you? Eighteen?"

"Nineteen."

She nodded and patted the spine of her ivory book. "That's about how old I was when I found the source of my powers. In Rome, actually. Have you ever been?"

"To Rome?" I asked.

"To Hell," she said.

"No."

"Well. It's nowhere near as bad as it's cracked up to be." She floated along the length of the porch and touched the leaves of the Afghan Ash with her ghostly fingers. "It's not all fire and brimstone. I mean, there's a lot of fire and brimstone, sure, but that's not all there is. There are villages and cities, as well. The architecture is absolutely breathtaking. I can't say much for the food, however. There's no fish and no dark chocolate. Meals are mostly coal and lava. I've grown used to it, but I do very much miss eating fish."

"Sounds like a regular paradise," I said. "You should go back."

"You are so standoffish," she said.

"I know I am," I said back. "I don't like you."

She glared at me. "And you're so short sighted. You have no idea what I've sacrificed to keep this world safe."

"Don't know," I said. "Don't care."

Her soul drifted through the bricks of the porch ledge and closer to me. She smelled faintly of sulfur and campfire smoke. We faced each other for a moment which was super awkward. It was funny to see her up close. Despite being decades older than me, she had barely outgrown her early twenties. I guess she didn't do a whole lot of aging in Hell.

She said, "I want you to understand... the things I have yet to accomplish here on Earth are not evil. You might call them evil, but they're not. They're necessary. I made a few mistakes in the past, and I am simply trying to undo those mistakes."

"Somehow I doubt that's all there is to it."

"Do you? Here. I'll show you." She moved next to me and pointed off into the Manhattan skyline. "Do you see the Westland skyscraper over there?"

Of course I did. It's not something that stands out, but once you know where it is, you can't miss it.

I said, "I do."

She squinted one eye shut and kept her finger pointed at it, as if she were aiming. She said, "The 41st floor is home to the Board of Directors, the leaders of the corporate entities who love nothing but business and money."

I nodded. "I've met them."

"And as we speak, they are gathered around their conference table, meeting with their human CEO, Carl. Carl is informing the Board of Directors that the infamous Isobella Westland is back from Hell and looking for revenge." She turned her eyes to me. "I wonder where he heard such a vicious rumor."

I looked at my feet. "I wonder."

She stared me down long enough to confirm that it was, in fact, me that told Carl the news, then turned her gaze back to the skyscraper. "That magical floor exists here in New York City, but at the same time it also exists in their god-forsaken dimension of boardrooms and stock exchanges. That 41st floor is the only connection from their world to ours, up there in the clouds where normal people can't see it. And do you know who first opened that door?"

"You?"

She nodded. "I made a deal with the devil, so the old saying goes. The Board of Directors promised to turn my little security firm into an international powerhouse. And they did. Then they pulled the rug out from underneath me and took it all away."

"I know," I said. "I saw."

She gave me a weird look. "You *saw*?"

Oops. I shouldn't have said that. After all, those events happened before I was even born. I had do do some back pedaling.

"I mean, you describe it in such detail, I feel like I can see it."

Nice.

Isobella gave me a peculiar look, like I was some sort of idiot.

"Anyway," she continued. "Now that I'm back on Earth, I have a little 'to do' list. First and foremost, I wanted to murder that back-stabbing creature called the CEO. So you can imagine my disappointment when I discovered he had already died in hot pursuit of an Italian girl with a weaponized body."

"Hey, look, I didn't kill that guy," I said. "I was there when he died, and he got exactly what was coming to him, but there's an old phrase here in New York City. 'Fuck around and find out.' That's exactly what he did. And now he's dead."

Isobella shook her head. "My only regret is that I wasn't there to step on his neck when he took his last breath. I dreamed that the last thing he would see before he died would be me standing victorious over him. I'm sorry I missed that chance."

"Yeah. I'm sure you'll get the next guy."

"Tell me." She wrapped her arm around my shoulders and pulled me closer, like we were sharing a secret. Her breath smelled like burnt cookies. "How did it feel watching him die?"

I shrugged. "I was cool with it. That dude was a prick."

Now she was smiling. "Did he die in unimaginable pain?"

"Well, a Voodoo skeleton punched him right through the heart. I doubt it it tickled his funny bone."

Isobella laughed. And not a good laugh. A pretty psychotic laugh, considering we were talking about someone's death. Admittedly, the death of a total bastard who tried to kill me, but it was still a weird thing to laugh at.

I kept eyeing Isobella's spell book. I needed that spell book. After hearing how much delight she could find in the death of another person, I knew in my heart of hearts that Isobella would never agree to fix Xin's soul. Her brain was operating on a completely different level. I was going to have to fix Xin myself, but I'd have to steal her book if I wanted that to happen.

I said, "So I totally understand why you're trashing the Westland Corporation. That was yours. They took it away from you, so now you're taking it away from them."

She seemed relieved. "I'm glad you see things my way."

"But what I don't understand is why you went after Xin."

"Ash, yes, the alchemist," she said. "You must have known him. Is that why you're watching his store?"

"Yeah," I said. "And he was just an old man. He never hurt anybody. Why'd you try and kill him?"

Isobella froze. She stared down at the concrete, then turned to face me. She repeated the word, "Try?"

Oh no.

"I meant kill." Fuck. That didn't sound convincing at all. "Why did you kill him?"

She zipped in front of me and scrutinized my face. "You said 'try.' You said I *tried* to kill him."

"I don't..." I couldn't believe I screwed that up. She was right in my face. The pressure was real. I couldn't think of a lie fast enough. "I don't know."

She laughed once. A knowing, menacing "Heh."

"You want to know why I *tried* to kill him, Penelope?" she asked. Her tone had changed. She sounded so smug and hateful. "Because when it comes to getting my body out of Hell to rejoin this soul, there are only a handful of people who know how to stop me. So I have to kill them. I spent the last twenty-seven years in Hell because I didn't bother to kill the CEO when I had a chance." She leaned in even closer until we were nose to nose. "Well, I'm never making that mistake again."

She reached into her jacket and whipped out a black key-fab remote control. She pointed it at Westland HQ and pressed one of the red buttons.

The top floor of Westland HQ detonated in a giant fireball.

2

"Burn!" Isobella threw her hands in the air. "Burn!"

The 41st floor blazed out of control. Black smoke gushed from the rooftop like an active volcano. I couldn't look away.

Maybe no one was hurt. Maybe that floor was empty.

But that didn't seem likely.

"What did you do?" I asked in a whisper. But I knew what she had done. She murdered the Board of Directors. She murdered

Carl. And for whatever strange reason, I actually *cared*. I spun around to face Isobella. I asked the question again, this time at full volume. "What did you do!?"

"I'm taking back what's rightfully mine," she said. "With them dead, I'm the only remaining shareholder in the Westland Corporation. It's all mine, just like it used to be, and I'm putting myself in charge."

"You didn't have to kill them."

"You're right." With a slight grin, she said, "I didn't *have* to."

"You're fucking crazy, man," I said. "You are out of control."

She had a crazy look in her eyes. "Oh, this is just the beginning. I have so much more planned. So much more to do."

Insane or not, I could tell she meant it. There was more death and carnage to come. Someone had to stop her, and once again it seemed that someone had to be me.

I got into fighting stance. "Not on my watch, bitch."

I went to kick her in the stomach with the Italian Penalty Kick of Death, but her body was made of intangible soulstuff and my foot passed right through her. By the time I realized my mistake, I had already lost my balance and landed face down on the porch.

"I applaud your efforts," Isobella said. Her body floated up into the air. As she ascended above the courtyard, she said, "I enjoyed our meeting, Penelope Salvo. But I'm afraid I have a few loose ends that need tying."

She drifted over the tops of the buildings, headed in the direction of the hospital.

Xin.

I tore through the alleyway so fast, they were going to have to pave over the dents I left in the asphalt. I burst out onto Forge Street at inhuman speeds.

I shouted for Corolla. I needed him to fly me to the hospital, but he wasn't in his parking space. People on the sidewalk saw me shouting for a car and gave me really weird looks.

Right. Corolla wasn't there.

So I took off on foot.

I couldn't run on the sidewalks. If I ran on the sidewalks, I'd slam into people like a Mack truck and kill them. My only option was to run down the middle of the road. Sure, people would see me doing 120 on foot, but what other choice did I have?

I sprinted through traffic and left a trail of shattered concrete behind me. Weaving through traffic was pretty easy, but a couple blocks later this blue Nissan ran a red light and got right in my way. I ran over it's roof, crumpling my bare feet right through the metal. The Nissan slammed on its brakes and caused a chain reaction of fender-benders.

A block later I came up on a busy intersection. This city bus unwittingly cut me off with a left-hand turn. I leaned into it like a football player and shoulder-checked it out of my way.

Up in the sky, I could see the orange glimmer of Isobella Westland's soul. She was hard to see in the daylight, but not impossible. God, she moved fast.

I took a shortcut through the parking lot of the police headquarters. The cops would see me, but whatever. I was on foot and going faster than a race car, what could they do? Chase me? I'd be long gone before they even grabbed their car keys.

Brooklyn Bridge Road was coming up. That's six lanes of traffic, not including on-ramps and off-ramps. I power-jumped into the air to leap over it, cleared the whole thing and came down for an explosive landing on Frankfort Street. Thank god no one was beneath me when I touched down, because I left a pretty deep crater in the street.

The New York Downtown hospital was within sight. Isobella had beat me there. She phased right through the brick walls and disappeared inside one of the rooms.

Fuck, fuck, fuck.

One more super jump launched me through the air with my legs kicking and put me on collision course with the hospital. I was coming in, and I was coming in hot. No time for stairs and elevators, I had to go through the wall. The bricks came closer and closer until I could see the lines of mortar. I squeezed my eyes shut and braced for impact.

I exploded through the wall of the waiting room and spilled out across the tile floors. Bricks clattered all around me and spiraled to a stop. Stunned patients leapt from their chairs and backed up against the walls. Some of them ran for the elevators. Good. They'd be safer that way.

Terrified doctors and nurses pressed their backs against the wall as the ghost of Isobella Westland floated past them. As if she knew exactly which room was Xin's, she zipped straight towards room 19 and disappeared through the solid door.

I dashed down the hallway and kicked the door right off its hinges. There was Xin in his hospital bed, hooked up to machines, unconscious and barely breathing. Floating above him like the angel of death was Isobella Westland. She had a sharp crystal of red chernobylite in her hand.

I shouted, "Get away from him!"

She froze in place and slowly turned her head to glare at me. The muscles in her jaw tightened. She was frustrated that I had followed here, that much was obvious.

"Asag," she growled. "Deal with the kid."

Asag?

I felt a cold presence behind me and wrinkled my nose as I caught a whiff of formaldehyde. I slowly turned around. Looming over me was Asag, the Skin Collector.

That was no good.

The demon was taller than I remembered from Chernobyl, like a whole foot taller than me. He wore the same sewn-together blanket of skin draped over his body, although he had apparently added to his collection over the past couple decades. Thousands of floppy, boneless fingers dangled from the edges of his skin-flaps like fringe and dragged across the hospital tiles.

Asag had collected sheets of every type of human skin: light and dark, rough and smooth, old and young. Some pieces still had tufts of hair, or nipples, or scars. I swear, one part looked like an entire baby flattened out and sewn into place. The skin draped over his body like a parachute. He had seemingly paid greater detail to the middle of his sheet of skin- the part that fell over the lump of his head, where he had sewn eyelids over the places where his eyes would be, and lips in the general area of where his mouth would go.

Through the slack in his eye holes, I caught a glimpse of the demon hiding underneath: a glistening red thing that made wet, sucking noises. The skin suit was disturbing enough, but I got the sense that whatever existed underneath was far, far worse.

I couldn't fuck with a demon, at least not one important enough for a name. I made that mistake once before with Lylo, the Archdemon of the Army of Arms, and got my ass thumped.

I barely got my fists raised before Asag sent tendrils of his skin after me. Squishy hands latched onto my ankles and wrists. They were ridiculously strong for being deflated balloons of flesh. I immediately struggled, but couldn't break free. More skin tentacles whipped around my waist, my neck, and then latched on to any part of my body it could get a hold of. The more I fought to get free, the tighter the skin squeezed down.

Isobella sneered at how easily I was rendered useless and turned her attention back to Xin. She raised her gleaming piece of Chernobylite high up over her head. With a deep breath, she slammed the crystal down as hard as she could.

Helpless to stop her, all I could do was scream.

But the crystal didn't kill Xin. The sharpened point stopped just an inch short of impaling his chest. Isobella's spiritual arm had been caught, *physically* caught, mid-swing by Baron Semedi. He had appeared out of absolute nowhere, standing confidently and somewhat disinterested in his dusty tuxedo and top hat.

The good Baron kept Isobella's arm steady with one hand. He admired the stub of his cigar with the other. He didn't even bother to look at her.

He said, "I'm afraid I can't let you do that."

3

I don't know if Isobella Westland knew who Baron Semedi was or not, but either way she didn't much care for his interference. She took a couple of heated breaths, then said to the Voodoo spirit, "Take your hand off me."

Semedi puffed on his cigar and blew smoke right in her face.

He said, "No."

"Fucking zombie." Isobella yanked her arm free and backhanded Semedi across the face. It looked like it hurt. His top hat jolted sideways.

He scrunched his face and rubbed his cheek.

"Is that how things are going to be?" He snatched Isobella by her neck and slammed her weightlessly against the wall like a rag doll. Her piece of red Chernobylite dropped from her hands and tinkled across the floor.

Isobella shook it off and stared Semedi down. "This has nothing to do with you, witch doctor."

"Oh, but it does." Semedi looked at me as he straightened his hat. "I made a promise to an old flame."

I said, "Thanks, buddy."

Without even reaching for it, Westland's spell book darted across the room, hands-free. It anchored itself in front of her chest as if it were sitting on an invisible podium. It snapped open and the pages flipped around on their own.

She said, "Do you have any idea who you're messing with?"

Semedi used his teeth and tongue to move his cigar to the other side of his mouth. "An amateur."

Isobella seethed with visible rage. Maybe it wasn't the best idea for Semedi to antagonize a megalomaniac like Isobella Westland, because that's when all hell broke loose.

The hospital room flashed with fireworks as Isobella and Semedi started throwing magic at one another. Solid beams of heavenly radiance stabbed into the walls. Flickers of moonlight as sharp as knives shattered through them like glass.

Westland conjured a flaming broadsword, like something I'd seen in paintings of Saint Michael the archangel. Its fire whooshed back and forth as the sword swung around, trying to cut off Semedi's head. He leaned side to side and dodged the fire sword like it was nothing. Just when the sword changed tactics and moved to stab him through the chest, Semedi vanished in a puff of cigar smoke.

He reappeared upside down on the ceiling.

"Tell me that's not the best you can do," he said.

Asag sent tendrils of skin after Baron Semedi. Stretchy fingers swarmed him from multiple angles. With him suddenly less focused on me, I was able to break free from his grip and I decked him across the head with a couple Mike Tyson Specials. It felt like punching a bulldozer, but it got his attention. He turned back to me and I suddenly found myself face to face with those droopy eyelids.

That was fine. Semedi needed to handle Isobella. It was my job to keep Asag's attention on me.

I shadow boxed my fists in the demon's direction. "Come on, man. You want to throw hands? I'm Rocky. I'm like a teenage girl version of Rocky."

I pounded my fists into the demon's guts like a jackhammer. Nothing.

In a move I never saw coming, Asag swept it arm through the air and threw his sheet of skin over my body. Darkness swallowed me whole. And, god, it smelled fucking awful, like rotting flesh and sweat and infected sores. I immediately freaked out. I didn't know if I was just under his skin or if he had somehow teleported me to some horrible corner of Hell, but I wanted out and I wanted out right that god damned second. I thrashed my arms and legs around in absolute panic and tore through the seams of his sewn-together skin.

That hurt him. I actually hurt him. I ripped myself free from his skin-blanket and Asag recoiled against the wall, shrieking like a wounded monster. Time to press the attack. I jump kicked his head as hard as I could and smashed it deep into the wall.

Isobella's book flipped to a different page and she started singing. A dark cloud of gnats and mosquitoes exploded through the glass windows and engulfed Baron Semedi. The whole room buzzed like a lumber mill. There were so many bugs swarming Semedi's body, I couldn't see him anymore. Before he had time to adjust to the gnats and mosquitoes, Isobella sang something else. A cloud of locusts swarmed out of the ceiling panels and joined the other bugs attacking Semedi.

Isobella had control over plagues now? Those Word-of-God spells were absolutely brutal. I had to get that book away from her.

Semedi didn't put up with the plague of insects for long. Sweet-smelling moonlight radiated off of his body and transformed the biting insects into harmless little lightning bugs.

I sprinted over to Westland and slapped her book shut. I tried to yank it out of its place in suspended air, but it wouldn't budge. I pulled and twisted as hard as I could, but no dice. Westland shook her head at me.

"I see why everyone at Westland wanted you dead," she said to me. "You are an unbelievable pain in the ass."

"This is me mellowed out." I gave her book one last pull. "You should have seen me in high school."

That magical, flaming broadsword swiped me across the back of the head and sliced my skin open. I felt a trickle of warm blood drip down my neck.

"Knock that shit off!" I swatted the sword away from me. I hit it so hard that I shattered the spell. Pieces of the sword landed on my arms and scorched the indestructible Westland material. Great. Try explaining that to the dry cleaners.

Asag's tentacles looped around my ankles and pulled my feet out from underneath me. I went face first to the tile and cracked them with my mouth. I felt myself being dragged across the room and back towards the demon.

"Alright," I said as I rolled over to face him. "Round two."

Isobella and Baron Semedi fought upside down across the ceiling, fencing with brittle beams of sunlight and moonbeams. Their magic shattered against one another and clattered to the ground like broken glass. No matter what Isobella threw at Semedi, he always had something stronger.

The fight paused when a powerful earthquake struck the hospital. The lights flickered like crazy. Glass jars rattled off the shelves and shattered. Xin's medical equipment toppled over. Then I heard something I hadn't heard since Utah; eerie demonic Gregorian chanting.

I whispered, "Oh no."

The exterior wall of Xin's hospital room trembled, then the edges crumbled as it was ripped out in one solid piece. It fell to the ground below and revealed the outside world. There on the opposite side, standing on top of a three-story pile of black arms was Lylo, the Archdemon. She had on her signature black dress, her black braids were the same knotted up mess, and she held a piece of green and red chernobylite in each hand.

She pointed at Semedi. "Go, my foul ones!" Her army of arms obeyed and flopped into the hospital room like thousands of spawning fish. "Pull the witch doctor apart! His arms will serve as captain in my ranks!"

"Sincerest apologies, my dear," Semedi said to Lylo. "But when it comes to my arms, I feel most attached!"

Semedi vanished and reappeared around the room in puffs of smoke, making it impossible for the Army of Arms to get their hands on him. He threw sharpened moonlight at them whenever he got the chance, leaving them wriggling on the ground.

But the more of them he killed, the more they came flooding in after him.

I stamped my foot down on as many as I could, crushing fingers and wrists like mad, but killing nine or ten or eleven of them was nothing compared to the hundreds more that crawled in through the air conditioning vents and missing ceiling panels.

In his fight with the Army of Arms, Semedi totally lost track of Isobella Westland. I did, too. She had taken the opportunity to scoop up her piece of chernobylite and maneuvered behind him. I didn't notice until it was already too late.

Semedi's fight with the Army of Arms started to back against a wall. Isobella Westland, ghostly and intangible, was hidden invisible inside the sheet rock. When Semedi backed into her, she leaned out of the solid wall and revealed her shard of chernobylite.

Semedi never even saw it coming.

Isobella took her sharp crystal and staked Semedi right through the spine and into his heart. Semedi's eyes went wide and he froze. I could tell by the way his face fell, he was seriously hurt. Isobella let the moment linger, then leaned in close and put her lips up to his ear.

She said, "How's that for an amateur?"

It felt like time suddenly stood still. Semedi stood there, motionless. Very slowly, he raised his cigar to his lips and attempted a puff. Westland ripped the crystal out of his body. Wafts of white smoke drifted out of the hole in his chest.

I shouted Semedi's name. He turned his eyes to me, but they were already losing life and facing to pure white.

"I'm sorry," he said. His voice was weak. "But this isn't fun anymore. I think I'm going to go home now."

Baron Semedi toppled forward. Before he hit the ground, his body disintegrated into a cloud of smoke. His cigar tumbled away. His rum glass and ice cubes shattered on the tile floor.

And in the next moment, before I could even process what had happened, Isobella floated across the room and hovered over Xin's sleeping body.

"Now then," she said. "Where *was* I?"

She plunged the Chernobylite right into Xin's chest.

A scream came out of me so loud, my vocal cords rattled like a blown out concert speaker. That scream kept coming until the whole room started coming apart. My voice wasn't human. It sounded computerized. The more I screamed, the more robotic I sounded, as if my body were glitching out.

Some type of neon green fluid dripped from my eyes.

My sight flickered with static. Phantom memories from forever ago flashed in my vision. I smacked myself in the head to fix it, like trying to fix a broken television.

It only got worse.

I drowned in a sea of white noise.

4

I stood in a big white nothing. I smelled incense, like the sweet stuff Xin used to burn in the shop at his altar to Buddha.

Standing there with me was Xin. He was quite a distance away, wearing his old man reading glasses, his worn denim, and that blue Nike windbreaker he liked so much. He crouched over his old cloth bag with the hand-carved wooden handles. A bunch of jars laid gathered at his feet and he placed them carefully inside.

He was packing. But where was he going?

I started running for him.

I shouted his name.

For a moment, I was worried that this was some sort of nightmare and he wouldn't be able to hear me. Maybe this was some sort of Buddhist vision. Or maybe none of this was real.

But I kept shouting his name and he looked at me.

"Xin?" I ran towards him as fast as I could. "Are you okay?"

"Oh, yes, Penelope," he said. "I am just fine."

"What are you doing?"

"I'm packing," he said.

I finally reached him, out of breath. I put my hands on my knees and doubled over. "Packing for what?"

He stood up and faced me. "My next life."

I was afraid he'd say something like that. A motor oil tear dripped down my face. "But I don't want you to go."

"I'm afraid it's my dharma to go," he said. He reached out and wiped my tear away with his thumb. "Everything lives, and everything dies."

"I don't want you to die."

He smiled. "That's why you should never want anything."

I threw my arms around him and pulled him close. "I tried to save you, Xin. I tried everything I could think of. I went to Mount Rushmore. I even asked Westland for help. But I screwed it all up. It wasn't good enough. It wasn't..."

I tried to explain more, but I couldn't fight the grief built up inside me. I sobbed like mad. Everything I said stopped making any sense. Xin let me cry for a moment, then gave me a pat on the back.

"Penelope," he said.

I did my best to fight back the tears and toughen up. "What?"

"I was sick."

I looked up at him. "What?"

"I had cancer."

"Cancer?" All I could do was stare. "Since when?"

"For months."

"Why..." I was going to cry all over again, and now for a totally different reason. "Why didn't you tell me?"

"Because I know what you would have done."

"What?" I asked. "What would I have done?"

"You would have turned the world upside down in search for a cure. You would have found genies and oracles, scientists and surgeons. You would have gone to Heaven or Hell, if you thought it might help."

I swallowed hard. "You're damn right I would have."

He shook his head. "But that's not the dharma of things, Penelope. Everything lives, and everything dies. Did you expect me to live forever?"

"Not forever. But... for a while longer."

He put his hands on my shoulders and looked me right in the eyes. "You could not save me from Isobella. You would not have saved me from cancer. Everything dies. That's an unavoidable truth. And there's nothing you can do about that."

I wiped my face. "Well, aren't you just a ray of sunshine."

"I'm not in the habit of lying to you."

"I guess."

"Everything dies." He stared off into the blank whiteness beyond us. "But everything that dies is born."

"Are you talking about reincarnation?"

"Something like that."

"Reincarnation is real?"

"It is if you believe it is."

"So does that mean you're coming back?"

"Not as the person you know. Hopefully, if I lived my life right, as someone better than that."

"So out there..." I pointed out into the white nothingness. "Out there is your next life?"

"I believe so."

"Xin, I'm going to miss you so much."

He smiled and patted my shoulders. "There's an old saying a wise friend once taught me. 'The wise do not grieve, because the wise know that death is not the end.'" With that, he bent down and went back to putting jars in his bag. He said, "Don't forget to water the Obogwu Cactus next week. It's already been a year."

"I know."

"And Mister Tanaka is coming to the shop on Thursday to fix the leak in the toilet."

"Okay."

He closed up his bag, grabbed the wooden handles and stood up. It felt like being at the airport, sending my best friend off on a flight he'd never come back from. He took my hand in his and held it tight. He looked scared.

He said, "Meeting you was the best thing that ever happened to me."

"Oh, Xin." I pulled him into another hug and cried like a bitch. I didn't want to let go. I said, "I'll never forget you."

"And I will never forget you." He gave me a pat on the back and stepped out of the hug. He had to. I would have kept him there until the end of time if he let me. He said, "I have to go now."

I wiped away my tears and took a deep breath. "Okay."

Xin turned and started walking into that white emptiness.

I couldn't just let him walk away from me. There was so much I still needed to say. Thank you for saving me from a life on the streets. Thank you for teaching me how to run your store.

Thank you for being the father I never had. Thank you for being the father I needed so bad.

"Xin!" I broke into a sprint to chase after him. He glanced back over his shoulder at me. I held out my arms ready to hug him one last time. "I love you!"

And he he had his arms out, ready to hug me back.

I reached him and threw my arms around him, but they wrapped empty to my chest. Xin had vanished. And I was alone.

So I collapsed to my knees and I cried.

5

When my eyes finally opened, I was greeted with an up close and personal view of the hospital tiles. My ears keyed in on the flat-lining beep of Xin's heart monitor. I remembered where I was and scrambled to my feet. Xin's mortal body laid there beneath blood-soaked sheets. Other than that, I was totally alone. No Isobella. No Asag. No Lylo.

Xin looked so much older in that hospital bed than in my vision. I kissed him on the forehead, then pulled a clean sheet over his body and covered his face.

I crunched barefoot across the broken glass. I stared out over New York City through the giant hole torn out of the wall. Isobella was long gone. In distant Manhattan, I could see smoke rolling out of the top floors of the Westland Corporation building. There were no fire trucks and no ambulances. The humans couldn't see that fire. Just like Isobella said; that floor existed here in our world, but also in another world, so only supernatural people like us knew what had happened.

Isobella Westland killed Baron Semedi. She blew Carl up with a bomb. She brought the entire Westland Corporation down to its knees. And, in the end, she finished her plan and murdered Xin Houng.

I took a deep breath and wiped the tears from my face. That was enough crying for one day. Isobella Westland wasn't finished. She still had more to do.

And come hell or high water, I was going to kill that bitch.

Chapter 22

1

Well, Carlton Carl, you've just had one heck of a day.

Of course, it would be wildly inaccurate to say that every day hasn't been a one heck of a day for the past twenty-three days, not since a couple Turncoat Tonys decided to sabotage me and the rest of the Corporation. Internal Affairs managed to track down a lot of them, but not all of them, and each day passing day has been a real pain in the proverbial neck, but today? Today really takes the cake.

Today I find myself danging from the 37th floor of my own skyscraper with my parachute tangled up around the old flag pole. So I guess by direct comparison, the previous twenty-three days of chaos were better than today.

It isn't the worst situation to find myself in, hanging 370 feet above Manhattan. It's a little windy and slightly colder than I prefer, but it's also nice to finally get some alone time. It gives me time to think. For weeks the Westland Corporation has just been coming apart at the seams and the Board of Directors kept demanding answers I just didn't have. Of course, they're all dead now, flash-fried from those blocks of commercial explosives planted all around the boardroom.

So, no, it wasn't the worst of all possible outcomes to hang 370 feet above Manhattan, not when the alternative was burning to death on the 41st floor.

Of course, now that I'm out here it comes to my attention that the company we use to wash our windows seems to be cutting a few too many corners. Look at this glass. You call these windows clean? I don't call these windows clean. Not at all.

Look at all these water spots. If you want really clean windows, you have to pre-wash them with soap, then go back over them with a fifty-fifty mix of water and distilled vinegar. I know that, and I'm not even a window washer. These windows look like they were cleaned with one of those "all natural" cleaning solutions that's supposedly good for the environment. Hippie-based cleaners like that don't actually clean windows, they just swish the dirt around. What am I paying these people for? To protect the environment or wash my windows?

Wash my windows, that's the answer to that question.

Where's my digital planner? Gosh, I hope it didn't fall out of my jacked when I jumped off the roof. That would be hugely inconvenient. I had all my numbers in there.

No. Here it is. I need to record an audio message. It would be far to difficult to type while clinging to this flagpole.

"Make a note. Send a deep-cover agent over to the business that washes our windows and have them run a full chemical analysis of their cleaning fluids."

There we go. We need to put that baby to bed.

Today has just been a downright mess. First, the computer network crashed and my company credit cards stopped working, so the bakery that delivers fresh cinnamon rolls to my office didn't show up. That's when I knew today was going to be a bad day. If I don't get my morning cinnamon roll, the U.S.S. Blood Sugar never pulls out of port and I just feel groggy all day.

I *knew* I should have grabbed one of those cinnamon rolls from the cafeteria. I didn't want one at the time because they wrap their cinnamon rolls in plastic wrap and I always end up getting frosting all over my hands. Now I regret that decision. I should have known better.

Any cinnamon roll is still better than no cinnamon roll.

I couldn't get my sushi for lunch either, also because of the credit cards. I could have used cash, but the Board of Directors converted everything to Black Money and regular people don't even know what Black Money is, let alone accept it as currency. So I had to send Miss Stegman to get me a split pea risotto from the company cafeteria, but I couldn't eat it. It occurred to me that Miss Stegman might be the double agent with every opportunity to poison my food, so I had to throw it away.

Then Miss Salvo showed up. It's always nice when your friends come to visit you at work. She's so sharp for a girl her age. She usually comes to me when she's had a hard day and needs a warm smile and a little advice. And sure, I'm a busy guy, but I do my best to make time for her. We have a long history, her and I, and it's always fun to do a little catching up.

I do still need to figure out a way to kill her and get Impossible Red out of her body. Maybe I'll work on that when this double agent thing blows over and I get a little more free time. Until then, that soup can simmer on the back burner.

It was interesting seeing Theodore again. I just assumed he died when we lost contact with the Utah Ultra-Max. Nice to see he made it out. Good for him. Maybe he's more resourceful than I thought. Spending time with Penelope has done him some good, I figure. The boy could stand to learn a thing or two from her.

Ooh. I wonder if I could throw Penelope in a particle collider and blast her with dark matter. The shock might blow Impossible Red right out her system. Who knows. I'm not a physicist. I should run that by the girls down in R and D, see what they say.

Go away pigeons. Shoo. This is my flagpole.

Then there was the part when the suspension cables snapped on the express elevator. I was going down to the lobby to meet Penelope and Theodore and the next thing I know, the elevator's in a complete free-fall. I only had a couple seconds to crawl out of there before it smashed to the ground. Looking back, I guess it wasn't that big of a deal. I've been in stickier pickles than that before. Many times.

At first I thought Penelope and Theodore had somehow botched the task of finding out who was behind the recent string of disasters within the corporation, but the more I think about it, the more it makes sense. Who else besides Isobella Westland would go to so much effort to throw a monkey wrench in the company gullyworks? The possibility *had* occurred to me, one of a dozen possibilities, but it just seemed so darned unlikely, I barely gave it any thought.

But after they pointed it out, the were clues everywhere.

When I went up to the 41st floor to meet with the Board of Directors, I got this sneaking suspicion something was wrong. You don't become the CEO of a major supernatural security company without being the best dang field agent first.

Since the elevators were out of commission, I had to take the stairs. Forty-one flights of stairs. Another situation where a little cinnamon roll boost to the blood sugar would have been helpful. And what did I see when I got to the top of the stairs on the forty-first floor? The fire extinguisher box had been opened. I only knew this because the fire extinguisher handle always faces to the right, but for some reason the handle was now on the left.

Someone had moved it. The Board of Directors didn't move it. And I didn't move it. No one else goes to the 41st floor, so who else moved it?

Someone, that's who.

So I opened it and what do I find? A kilogram block of compound-11 plastic explosives and a high frequency radio detonator; one of those faulty BashnerTech models from 2006 that sometimes explode if they're too close to a Chinese-made baby monitor.

And, as the old saying goes: where there's one block of C-11, you should probably look around and see if there's other blocks of C-11, because sometimes there is.

Where else is a good place to put C-11 plastic explosives? Up in the ceiling, of course, preferably close to the people you're trying to kill; in this instance, if *I* was trying to kill me and the Board of Directors, I'd want one right above the conference table. So that's where I looked. Sure enough, I found a smoke detector that had never been there before.

Curiouser and curiouser.

There had to be others and I spotted them right away. One inside the wall behind the panel for the light switches. One hidden under a section of recently sliced carpeting. As I reflect on the size of that explosion, I would guess there were eight blocks in total. I was only aware of four or five in that moment, but that told me enough:

The 41st floor was about to, as the kids say, "pop off." And quite literally.

First thing I did was get on my phone to check our insurance policy and see if it covered acts of terrorism, which it did, so everything was good on that end.

Second thing I did was keep my mouth shut and not warn the Board of Directors. That was a good move too. I was never a big fan of the Corporate Entities. They lacked so many things that I really enjoy about real people. Passion. Imagination. A little sense of humor. Now, I could never kill them myself. Heaven forbid. That's just not the kind of guy I am. But if someone else went to all the trouble to orchestrate their murders... Well, I can hardly be blamed for that, now can I?

The Director of Accounting called me out for being distracted. "It seems as though you're looking for something."

I simply stuck my hands in my pockets and inched towards the stairs. "Not at all," I said. "Everything is cool as a cucumber."

Then one of them pointed out that I was the one who had called the meeting, so if we were going to have a meeting, I should probably explain why I called it. And that's fair. That's usually how meetings go. But this was not a normal meeting. This was about to be a big smoking murder scene.

"I want to tell you what I called the meeting for," I told them. "I really do. But first..." I kept shuffling towards the stairwell. "I have to go to the little Carl's room. You know how us humans are, always urinating. I will be right back. Remain seated. Do not, for any reason, leave this room."

And I got the heck out of there.

I couldn't use the elevators to escape. They were all broken. And while, yes, I could have run down the stairs, the channeled blast from the explosion would roll down the stairwells faster than I could reach a safe distance. And since I had no idea when the bombs would go off, there was no guarantee that I would make it away in time.

So the only logical conclusion was to go up one flight of stairs to the roof and strap on one of those low-altitude base-jumping parachutes. They're kept in a locker right by the access door to the roof. The Director of Administration thought I was crazy when I ordered parachutes, but it's exactly that kind of short-sightedness that got her vaporized in a fireball while old Carl – crazy old Carl who wanted to get pointless low-altitude safety parachutes for the roof – drifted safely through the air like a newborn baby angel.

I preach safety first and I believe it. I strapped on a pair of those nifty looking goggles and one of these skydiving helmets. Last thing I wanted to do was lose an eye or bash my brains out.

Right when I jumped over the edge and pulled the rip cord, that's when the bombs went off. The fireball roared like a monster and licked me all over with little ember tongues. The shockwave of heat inflated my parachute like a balloon and blew me way off course. I swept through the air in big loops. I couldn't even tell which way was up. I swung back towards the building at high speeds and slammed right into the bricks.

The helmet saved me from cracking my head open. I did, however, lose consciousness for just a few seconds. Just long enough, in fact, to wake up suspended from a flagpole outside the 37th floor.

2

Let me survey my options here.

I can't climb up. The outside of the building is pretty smooth. I can't even climb up the window ledges because the windows are eight feet tall and I can't jump that high. Wouldn't be much point in climbing anyway; the top floor of the building is burning like a wooden owl at Bohemian Grove.

I could fall. That would certainly be the fastest way out of this situation. Let's see. I'm approximately 370 feet in the air, and I'm probably 200 pounds. Wait. No. Carl, don't be so hard on yourself. You've done a good job avoiding those chocolate mochas and you didn't have your cinnamon roll this morning. You're a svelte 190 now and you shouldn't be ashamed to say so. Be proud of yourself.

A 190 pound man falling from 370 feet?

My fall would top out at 96 miles per hour. I'd slam into the Earth in four seconds. I suppose the air friction would slow me down, but I'd still splatter on the sidewalk like a water balloon.

So let's call "falling" plan B.

I could go in through one of these windows. One of these dirty, dirty windows that I'm apparently paying people to clean with good intentions and rescued dolphins. I'm on the 37th floor, so I could go straight to my office and figure out what's going on. The windows don't open from the outside, but if I shoot some holes into one of them, I should be able to smash my way through. It's a shame to break a perfectly good window, but I do feel like this is my only option.

Yeah. So that's what I'll do. I'll shoot the window, swing back and forth on my parachute strings to build up some momentum, then crash right through the glass.

Where's my pistol? Oh. Haha. There you are, Little Potato. Feel like doing some dirty work?

Easy shot. It's just like being down at the range, except I'm hanging from a flagpole and losing all feeling in my legs and the wind is freezing my fingers. Still, all I have to do it squint one eye shut, aim, and pull this trigger a bunch of times to make the bullets come out.

Hey. Don't be afraid to have fun with it, Carl. Make your own sound effects.

"Blam blam blam blam blam!"

There we go. Shattered glass. Now comes the hard part: building up momentum and crashing through the window. Good thing I got this helmet.

"KRASHHH!"

Rough landing and I cut my hands up a little bit. There's glass everywhere, but that's to be expected. I feel bad for whoever's office this is. It's not mine and it's not Miss Stegman's. It must be someone in administration. You got paperwork in here, Administrator? Or something with your name on it? There's a picture frame of a young man with a woman who could be his mother, or perhaps a really old wife. No other pictures. No family? Good. I like it that way. Helps you focus on your job.

Ah, here we go. A name plate.

Adams. Projects and Logistics.

Good. Thank you for letting me borrow your office, Adams. There'll be a little something extra in your paycheck.

Still, since I'm here, it wouldn't hurt to conduct a surprise inspection. I'll just grab the phone and hit redial and see who we get ahold of.

Mmmm. You're about to be connected with sexy singles in the New York area. If you identify as a man, press one. If you identify as a woman, press two-

Hang up.

That is categorically against the terms of company use of time. Where's my digital planner? Let me make a note of this.

"Note to self. Transfer Adams to Antarctica."

Alright, Adams. You don't know it yet, but you're about to oversee my Antarctic trip to the Tropic of Argo Navis.

Okay. Good news it, I'm back home on the 37th floor. That's great. I'm back in business. It's like I always say, back in the building, back in business.

Let's not go barging right out into the hallway. Everyone thinks I got toasted like a marshmallow in that explosion, so let's use that to our advantage. I'll just pop this door open a crack and see what's going on in the hallway.

What's this? There's someone trying to break into my office! Four someones, in fact. If I had to guess, the one guy looks like an accountant. He's got three of my heavily armed shock troopers with him. They're rigging up a "doorbell," a minuscule explosive device designed to penetrate my high security door locks.

What's the accountant guy saying? Close my eyes, steady my breathing, and listen.

"What's taking so long? Miss Westland is going to be here soon and if we don't have access to the CEO's office, she's not going to be happy."

"Working as fast as we can here, Kruger."

Ah, yes. He's that Freddy Kruger guy that Penelope was talking about; the guy from the Bronx. Just like she said, he's been working with Isobella Westland. Well, good luck getting into that office without the CEO passkey, traitors. That's a solid yew wood slab door with two sets of magnetic locks on the-

A muffled thump. And a creak. My door falls to the ground.

Now I'm really mad. That was a really great door.

3

I know the 37th floor all too well. There are three secret ways into, and out of, my office that only I know about. The decorative rock walls in the hallway function as a kind of ladder to the ceiling and there's a dummy air conditioning duct that gives me free access to the spaces above my office.

Crawling around up here is dusty work, but sacrifices have to be made. From up here, I can get into position over my office and eavesdrop on this Kruger gentleman and those soldiers.

Kruger's going straight for the intercom systems.

"Attention all Westland personnel. This is Fredrick Kruger, Director of New York operations. There has been a mysterious explosion on the 41st floor which has killed our CEO and the entire Board of Directors. Our long-lost founder, Isobella Westland, survives as the only remaining shareholder and, therefore, the new de facto Chief Executive Officer. Beginning immediately, she has assumed full control of the Westland Corporation. From this moment forward, all company policy is subject to her review and approval."

This has really been one heck of a day.

Now Kruger's barking orders at his armed henchmen. He's really taking this Director of New York operations title seriously.

"Assemble your teams and sweep the other floors for Agent Theodore. Check every closet and bathroom, look under every

desk and table. He's here in this building somewhere and none of you rest until you find him. I want him to answer for his crime of blowing up the top floor of Isobella's skyscraper."

The soldiers leave.

Good. Now it's just Kruger all alone. He's rooting through my office, pulling the place apart, undoubtedly looking for the CEO passkey. He's already checked the couch cushions, now he's rooting through my back stock of liquor behind the bar. Perfect. While he's crouched down there, I can silently drop down from one of these vents and get the jump on him.

Closer and closer to the bar I creep. He's still down there, distracted. I'm so close I can hear him grumbling, obviously frustrated that he can't find that little red key card

I'm at the bar stools.

I'm around the corner of the bar.

Kruger is down on his hands and knees with his back to me. He has no idea I'm here. Hilarious. Come on out, Little Potato. You still have bullets in you? Time to cause a little ruckus.

I put the barrel of the gun right to the back of Kruger's traitorous head. I click the hammer. Kruger freezes at the sound.

"Stand up," I say, calmly. "Slowly. Hands in the air. Don't make any funny moves."

He stands up, slowly. He puts his hands in the air. He doesn't make any funny moves.

"Turn around," I say.

He turns around. Ah, I get to savor the look on his face. He was so sure Carl was dead, yet here he is pointing a gun right between his beady little eyes. It's like he's seen a ghost.

"Mister CEO, sir," he says.

"Don't you 'Mister CEO' me, buster," I say.

"You're supposed to be dead."

"It's going to take a lot more than blowing up an entire floor to kill Carlton Carl."

And then little weasel snaps right into an apology. "Sir, let me explain! I didn't want to betray you. But Isobella... she offered me the position of Director of New York Operations. It was essentially six promotions in one. I was weak. I couldn't say no."

"I understand." And I do, honestly, understand. A promotion like that would be hard for anyone to pass up. "Why don't we go talk about this on the balcony?"

I can tell by the sweat beading up on his forehead, he doesn't like that idea. "Why out there?"

I gesture with my gun and repeat, "Out on the balcony."

He turns and starts walking.

Now, I couldn't shoot Kruger in the back of the head. I couldn't shoot anyone in any part of their head; front, back, or otherwise. I'm not a killer. I've never been a killer. I'm never going to be a killer. The thing of it is, though, Kruger doesn't know that. All Kruger knows is that there's a gun to pressed to his noggin and I want him out on the balcony.

The balcony is really nice. From thirty-seven stories up, you get a really good look at Midtown and Central Park and the boats out on the ocean. It also has these heated coils under the tile so the floor stays ice-free, even in the dead of winter. The glass doors are really nice, too. Of course, now that I'm aware of the problems I'm having with the glass cleaners, I look at the glass and see all these spots and I can't help but sigh in frustration.

I ask Kruger, who seems legitimately scared for his life, "Do you know how much I pay our window washing company to wash the windows on a place like this?"

He says no.

"80,000 dollars," I say. "And that's a lot of money to pay a company to wash windows, right? They have to scaffold their way up and down all four sides and it takes them three months to do the whole job. But for that kind of money, you'd expect them to do a pretty good job and not leave water spots on the glass."

"Are you going to kill me?"

That kind of makes me laugh. I wave my gun at him. "No. No, I'm not going to kill you. But, please, do step up onto the ledge and put your legs on the other side of the rail."

He puts his hands on the rail, but hesitates. And for good reason. What I'm asking him to do is particularly unsafe.

He says, "You said you wouldn't kill me."

"And I'm not going to kill you," I say. "When you jump off the balcony at gun point, it's the fall that will kill you."

Here comes the begging.

"Please, sir," he says. "Don't kill me."

Didn't I just explain how I wasn't going to kill him? The man is not paying attention. Now he's down on his knees and begging for mercy. Delightful. Time to turn up the heat. I put the gun to his forehead.

"Step out onto the ledge, Kruger."

He refuses to comply and now he's weeping. What a wimp. This is the guy Isobella picked for Director of New York operations? I barely did anything to him.

Welp, time to get some juicy information out of him. I pull out my red CEO key card and show it to him.

"Why were you searching for this?" I ask.

Still sniveling, he looks up and says, "I don't know."

He's lying. I know a lie when I hear one. I've done this job for a long time. I've had trickster gods lie right to my face. I'm like a walking, talking lie-detector machine.

I grab Kruger by the jacket and force him to lean him over the rails. The traffic is howling a million miles below us, like a row of little tiny ants. He's screaming like he's going to fall. I put the gun to the back of his head.

Kruger's in no real danger, of course. I'm not going to blow his brains out, nor am I going to toss him over the edge. I'm a nice guy, but I can sound mean when I have to. It's just like playing a character in a movie. And the name of this movie is Good Carl, Bad Carl.

Say hello to Bad Carl.

I get right in his ear and explain, quite reasonably, "Two things are about to come flying out of your face, Kruger. The truth, or your brains. Which is it going to be?"

He stops sobbing long enough to scream, "I don't know anything!"

More lies. Over the edge with him.

I toss him over the safety rails and catch him by his necktie just before he plunges over the edge. These high-altitude winds can reach some pretty intense speeds. His hair and clothes flutter around. He latches onto the rails for dear life, thirty-seven stories above Midtown and a four-second drop away from being a sidewalk art project.

"She's already taken over my whole computer system," I say. "So what could she possibly need with my key card?"

Kruger cries out, "She'll kill me if I say anything!"

I let his tie slip a little bit and he falls a few inches. He yelps in fear. I say, "Whoo, Kruger, you are getting heavy. What do you weigh? 200? 205? You're not a svelte 190 like some of us who didn't get out cinnamon roll this morning."

"Untouchable Orange!" He blurt out. There we go. Time for Cowardly Carlos to start spilling the beans. "Isobella's soul is here on Earth, but her body is still trapped in Hell. If she doesn't get them together soon, she's going to fade away for good."

I pull him up a little bit. He is, after all, being helpful. "What does that have to do with Untouchable Orange?"

And this guy's just spilling beans everywhere. "Untouchable Orange has the power to open a fracture to Hell. That's her only chance to get her body back. But she can't get to it because you have it behind glorious glass. That's why we need your pass key. To open the vault."

"If she opens another fracture, she'll let all of Legion loose."

Kruger looks to the ground, then gazes back up at me. His face changes. Now he's smiling. Interesting. In this line of work, when your opponent smiles at you, that's rarely a good sign.

He says, "You think she doesn't know that? Carl, she's practically counting on it! With her spell book, Isobella has complete control over Hell. She can control the demons." Mister Kruger lets go of the rails and starts undoing his tie. He shouldn't do that! His tie is the only thing I have a hold on. Without it, he'll fall and die.

"Whoa there, buddy," I say. "Give me your hand."

But he keeps undoing his tie. "Miss Westland can do anything with that book. She can free me from Hell, when it's time. And when she brings me back..."

He got his tie completely off and he slipped loose. I tried to reach out and catch him, but he was already out of reach.

"I'll be immortal!"

It took him four seconds to hit the sidewalk, almost exactly.

4

My office is compromised. I'm going to have to abandon it for now. I can steal back control of the Westland Corporation, but not alone. If Isobella is as powerful as she sounds, I don't want to be here in "her office" when she shows up. She could turn me into a toad and if I turn into a toad, I'll never get this whole window washing thing straightened out. No, I have to perform a strategic retreat, regroup, and come back with some allies.

This isn't goodbye, sweet office. This is farewell for now.

There's a transmission coming in over the intercom. They're asking for Director Kruger.

I push the button and do my best Kruger impression. "This is Kruger. Go ahead."

And the voice says, "We've captured Agent Theodore down on the nineteenth floor. We've got him at gun point. Orders?"

Ah. The boy got himself captured. I guess I'm not surprised. Sleuthing was never his strong suit. He shouldn't need rescuing, not if he really wants to be a field agent. He has all the training in the world to deal with a situation like this, so if he gets himself killed, it's his own fault.

But, then again, I guess this could be a learning opportunity.

"Take him to interrogation room on the eleventh floor," I say. "Then stand guard out front. I'll be right down."

"Right away, sir."

Heading down the stairs, I think: Won't Theodore be surprised to find out that he just got a "get out of jail free" card?

Where did I go wrong with that boy? I did everything I possibly could to keep him safe from the humans and mold him into the perfect Westland agent. I distanced myself from him emotionally. I pushed him as hard as I could at all possible times. I gave him the best education black money can buy.

I gave him everything I couldn't give his sister, everything his sister would have been a million time better suited for.

I gave him martial arts training in Tibet. Firearms training in Russia. Foreign language classes from around the world. He studied computer hacking with those Anonymous boys in Sweden. No holidays. No weekends. Just brutal training.

Do I get so much as a thank you?

What about the time when I found out that him and that Angela Hyatt girl were boyfriend and girlfriend? I shipped him off to Guerrilla Warfare boot camp in Costa Peligro. Did I get a thank you for that? Thank you for teaching me to break down and clean an HK-227? Thank you for the chance to learn how to survive in the jungles with nothing but termites and rainwater?

Nope. Not a single thank you. Not even a card.

I kept the boy focused. I kept him out of trouble. When I was his age, I had to work my way to the top one butt-kissing promotion at a time. Theodore was given every advantage to succeed, but the kid has no drive. No passion.

If he wants to be a field agent like his old man, he's going to have to work a heck of a lot harder.

The interrogation room on the eleventh floor has nerve gas vents in the floor. Obviously I don't intend to nerve gas my own son, but what I *can* do is use that as access into the room.

I just have to go down to the tenth floor, let myself into the nerve gas closet – good thing this CEO pass key still works, for now – and crawl up into the duct work. We haven't used nerve gas in these rooms for two years, four months, and sixteen days, so I'm sure I'm safe to crawl through here without experiencing any side effects. Like death.

Crawling through the duct work between then tenth and eleventh floors, I can hear two soldiers – a male and a female – talking through the walls.

"Do you think this kid did it?"

"Blow up the roof?"

"Yeah."

"I don't know. Doesn't seem like it. But we don't get paid to think, you know what I'm saying?"

"I hear ya."

"I gotta keep my record clean. I'm up for a promotion soon."

"Me too. I'm going for Squad Leader Romeo."

"Hey, what are the odds? I'm up for Squad Leader Juliet."

"Coincidence!"

Okay, so here we go, crawling under the floor of the interrogation room. I can see the light trickling in through the vent. I wedge my way up a little further and peek inside. Sure enough, there's Theodore bolted to a metal interrogation chair with a bag over his head. He's shouting, but those shouts are muffled by whatever oily rag they stuffed in his mouth.

I pop the vent off and start to weasel my way out of the floor. Holy smoke, it's a tight squeeze. Maybe skipping that morning cinnamon roll was the right move after all.

I pull the bag off Theodore's head and immediately put my finger to my lips in the universal symbol for "shhh." I pull the gag out of his mouth.

"Oh," he says, unamused. "You're alive."

"Do try to contain your excitement." I start undoing the metal latches that secure his wrist to the chair. They're locked and I don't have a key, but I was known to pick a few locks when I did that year-long mission in the French catacombs. "You almost sound disappointed."

"I don't want you to *die*," he says as he watches me work my magic on the locks. "I don't hate you *that* much."

"Thank you." That's probably the nicest thing he's said to me in a while. "I don't want you to die either."

I release the latches on his wrists. Theodore leans forward to unlatch his own ankles. Good. Let's see if he's got the lock picking skills to pull it off. While he does that, I go to the door and glimpse out the window. The two guards are still there, both of them facing away from us.

"How did you know I was here?" Theodore asks.

"I'm the CEO of the Westland Corporation," I say. "I know everything. I know that Adams in logistics is using the company phone to call New York dating lines."

I watch as Theodore pops the last lock on his ankle. Not bad. A little slower than me, but the fact that he got the job done is pretty impressive.

"Alright," I tell him. "Get up. Get ready. We have two guards right outside. Once we get past them, we make a mad dash for the stairs."

"Right," he says. "But we're locked in here, and they're out there. How are we going to open the door?"

I show him the CEO key card

Come on, lad.

Think.

5

Westland soldiers go through rigorous training, a lot of which we never have to pay for. I prefer to hire ex-military types looking to get into "private security." Not just Americans. British special forces are pretty deadly, and there's something to be said for the Israeli Defense Force, too. With the right combination of financial incentive and low-level indoctrination, you can recruit a competent security force for a reasonable price that stays loyal to structured leadership, almost to a fault, it seems.

I suppose the two soldiers outside the interrogation room would have stood a better chance if Theodore and I didn't have the element of surprise, but we'll never know. As it happened, Theodore and I slapped the both of them into headlocks and put them right to sleep.

"Shh," I said as I guided my soldier to the ground. "Go to sleep. Nothing but dreams now."

Just like that, we're sprinting down the stairs, eleven floors away from freedom.

"She really did it," Theodore says to me as we thunder down the steps. "Isobella took control of the whole operation."

"She's sloppy," I say. "She's a sledgehammer, not a scalpel. She lacks finesse."

"Sledgehammer or not, she got the job done."

Theodore still doesn't see the big picture. Sure, it may *look* like she's winning, but, as they say, there's still more dancing to do before prom is over. That's why it's important to stay as many steps ahead of your opponent as possible, even before you know who your enemies are. Even if it means keeping a secret from your son for twenty-two years.

Is now the time to tell Theodore? He might prove helpful.

No. The security system has been compromised. The walls have ears, even here in the stairwell. Even if I whisper the secret to him, there's still a chance someone might overhear and once that cat is out of the bag, there's no putting it back in. I'll have to keep the secret to myself for just a while longer.

Now the alarms are going off. Crap. I thought we could make it out of the building before anyone noticed my handiwork, but we only got as far down as the fifth floor. Oh well. We'll just have to expedite our escape.

I'm taking the stairs two at a time. Theodore is sliding down the hand rails. We hit the bottom floor a minute later and Theodore tries the fire escape door. It won't open, of course. I knew it wouldn't. When the red alert goes off, the whole building goes into lock-down, and that includes the emergency exits.

Luckily, the CEO pass key can override even that, so we get outside just fine.

Good gravy. There's a huge mess on the sidewalk; a big red mess with guts everywhere. It's a big splat. A big gutsy, bloody splat, like a bug on a windshield. People are doing their best to keep their distance and walk around it, but a crowd is forming. Some people even have their phones out.

Disgusting.

"What the hell is this?" Theodore asks.

"That," I say, "is Freddy Kruger."

Chapter 23

1

My first instinct was to march across Manhattan, bust open the doors to the Westland Corporation's headquarters, and kick some serious ass. I imagined it like a video game, fighting swarms of henchmen as I climbed the building floor by floor, leading up to the burning roof where I would have another – and final – confrontation with Isobella Westland.

But this wasn't a video game.

Indestructible robot body or not, Isobella was packing some serious heat. Aside from a building full of armed soldiers, she had a spell book filled with various "word of God" incantations that gave her power over plagues and demons and life and death. That alone was more than I could handle.

And then there was Lylo, the Archdemon of the Army of Arms at her right hand and Asag, the Skin Collector on her left. I'd already thrown down with each of them individually and I got my ass handed to me both times. No way I'd be able to take them both on at once.

And the real cherry on the ice cream sundae was the Army of Arms, which would have been a total non-factor if there weren't so goddam many of them.

Even my impenetrable carbon nano-weave skin and tungsten carbide skeleton wouldn't hold up to that kind of a fight. I was completely out of my league.

Isobella accomplished every evil thing she set out to do: she set the demons loose, she took over the Westland Corporation, and she murdered anyone who knew how to stop her.

Well, not *everyone*. I could think of one more person.

I went down to the subway and rode the W over to Queens. By the time I climbed the stairs and got up to street level, it was evening. Cloudy skies had moved in and the city did that thing where it goes from full sunshine to near dark in thirty minutes. I walked a few blocks over to the Rockwell House, a five-story art community where all the old apartments had been converted into sound-proof practice rooms for musicians, or private art studios for painters and sculptors.

Voel, the Deranged Painter, lived in the Rockwell House, successfully hidden away from the rest of humanity. Secluded up there on the fifth floor, the demon could self-medicate her evil impulses with endless painting. She was somehow on a first-name basis with Xin and trusted him to take her paintings – beautiful and psychotic, priceless and dangerous – and hide them away in the basement where no one would ever find them.

Would she trust me the same way she trusted Xin? Would Voel, a demon from Hell, help me bring down her brother Asag and her sister Lylo?

Probably not. But I was out of options.

The stairs inside the Rockwell House creaked with every step. The air smelled like an old library mixed with paint thinner. Muffled drumbeats and psychedelic guitar riffs came from behind the many doors. I reached the top floor and planted my feet in front of Voel's studio. I recognized the familiar red and white Satanic symbols painted on it. Chaotic music played inside, something electronic and random, something definitely not-human. I pounded on her door and waited for her to answer.

The music stopped. Then I heard her voice.

"Go away!" she screamed.

I pressed my forehead against the door and shouted. "Voel! It's Penelope Salvo! Xin's friend? I was here a couple months ago to take a Big Gulp of your blood!"

Silence.

Then approaching footsteps. A series of locks clacked open. The door creaked opened slightly and her lime-green face appeared in the gap.

"What do you want this time?" she asked.

"It's kind of a long story." I pointed through the opening in the door. "Can I come in?"

Voel thought about that for a second, then swung open the door to yank me inside. She slammed the door shut with a supernatural boom. When she whipped around, she had a furious look on her face, but I guess that wasn't out of character for her.

"Where has he been?" Voel demanded.

"Who?" I asked.

"Xin!" She stomped across the studio to a stack of paintings propped up against the wall. She grabbed two of them and waved them around. "I don't understand these visions! Get these away form me! This feels important! I need answers!"

"What are you painting?"

"Mysteries!" She dropped to her knees and sorted through the stacks of canvas. Her paintings ranged in imagery and quality, from absolutely chaotic to photo-realistic. Even the ones all abstract and shapeless had something recognizable hidden in them, like a visual riddle that just required a little solving. She picked one painting and held it where I could see it. "Look at this one! Tell me, what do you see? What is art trying to tell me!?"

Okay. I could play this game. The painting had a smear of peach color in the shape of a naked woman. The woman was surround by brushstrokes of red and orange, as if the woman were standing in fire. Above the body was a second woman ascending into the sky, this one bright orange and with her arms outstretched.

"That's Isobella Westland," I said. "That's her soul leaving her body and coming back to Earth."

Voel stared at me. "How do you know that?"

"She told me."

"Then what's this one?" She went for another painting and held it up. "What's this one mean?"

Arms. Black arms. Tons of them. And behind the black arms were two figures: a woman scribbled all over with black lace and a second creature covered in blobs of different skin tones.

I inhaled sharply. Seeing those two, even as paintings, freaked me out. "You don't recognize them?" I asked her.

She scrutinized the painting for a long moment, then looked back at me. "Should I?"

"That's Lylo," I said. "And Asag. And the Army of Arms."

She looked at the painting again. "Are they not detained?"

"They escaped," I said. "They're following Isobella Westland around like her own private secret service. And let me tell you, they are on one hell of a rampage."

"Things have gone terribly wrong." Voel went to the window, which was painted completely black for her privacy. She scratched away some of the paint with her fingernail and peeked outside. A thunderstorm had blown in. Rain washed over the glass, along with flashes of lightning.

Ugh. Thunderstorms. I used to love thunderstorms.

"Did they come here looking for you?" I asked the Deranged Painter. "Asag and Voel? Did they come here?"

"Impossible." She kept her eyes glued to the outside world. "Only two people know I'm here. Your friend Xin, and another human named Carl."

"Carl?" I repeated. "Like Carl from Westland?"

She glanced back at me. "You know of him?"

"You could say that," I said. "But if Carl knew you were here, why didn't he detain you like the others?"

That question really set her off.

"He wouldn't dare!" Voel lunged for the paintings and carelessly flipped them out of her way. She found one in specific and shoved it into my hands. There were three mountains painted on it; one of them red, one of them gray, and one of them white. While I took in the painting, she paced circles around me. "The Sons of Adam and Daughters of Eve hunted us demons down. They threw Lylo in the mountain of red sand. They threw Asag in the mountain of gray stones, elsewhere in the world. And me, they were going to put me in the white mountain, where the air is frozen and the sun never rises."

"These Sons of Adam and Daughters of Eve who trapped you in mountains... you mean the Westland Corporation?"

"Yes!" Voel said. "The people of the West Land. They came for the three of us armed with tricks and lies. I knew the white mountain would kill me, so I fought hard against them. When I broke free, the human named Carl helped me escape. He brought me to this place and hid me away from the world. He would bring me paints and canvas. But eventually he stopped coming. He said the people of the West Land were growing suspicious and our lives were both in peril. So he turned my secret over to Xin Houng who agreed to look after me in his stead."

"Have you been out of this apartment," I asked. "Ever since?"

"Never once," he said. "It is not safe."

"So what's the difference between this and prison?"

"In here, I can paint," she said.

"Yeah, but you've been painting for... what? Two decades? Three decades? That's a long time."

She scoffed. "Decades? Do you think I'm bothered by a couple of decades? Do a trillion years in Hell and then talk to me about decades."

2

Dozens of paintings laid scattered across the floor of Voel's studio. Each one captured a moment in recent events; a story that I, myself, had just started to piece together. She showed me her art, one after another, and I slowly pieced together each one.

"Tell me," Voel said as she picked out a rectangular one. "Do you know what this is?"

The image showed millions of monsters gathered up in military formations that stretched far off into the distance. Some of the monsters flew in the air, some of them crawled across the ground. Some of them carried weapons, others had oversized stingers. Oh, I recognized them alright. These were demons. This was Legion. Above the painted monsters, Voel had physically slashed the canvas with a knife.

"That's Legion," I said.

"And this?" She stuck her finger through the open slash.

"Best guess?" I asked. "Some kind of fracture between Hell and Earth. Kind of like what Isobella did back at Chernobyl."

"And Legion stands waiting..." Voel turned her attention to her own handiwork. "All of them. Once again they're waiting to come here to Earth. And it won't end well."

"You should be excited, right? You're a demon. You should be rooting for the home team."

"You don't understand!" Voel threw the painting and defied gravity as she marched vertically up the walls of her studio. She pulled on handfuls of her own hair. "You don't understand! You don't understand!"

"What?" I asked, following her around and looking up at her from the floor. "What don't I understand?"

Voel stood on the ceiling and shouted down at me like a lunatic. "Three demons on Earth is nothing! He would have never noticed three demons. But trillions of demons? If Legion makes its way to Earth, *he's* going to notice. And *he's* going to come down here to do something about it."

"And when you say 'he,' you mean..."

She didn't dare say his name. She just made this face that said, "Who do you think?" Her eyes darted up to the ceiling, then back down to me. Right. She meant *him*. She put a finger to her lips, suggesting I should keep my voice down. After all, he could be eavesdropping.

She jumped down from the ceiling so she could whisper in my ear, "He's not keen on breaking the rules. Believe me, I know. I was part of the rebellion in Heaven. He's quick to anger and his punishments are dreadful and cruel. When the Egyptians enslaved the Hebrews, he slaughtered a hundred-thousand babies. When humanity didn't worship him hard enough, he flooded the entire planet and drowned all the animals. And when the angels rebelled in Heaven, he disfigured us and sentenced us to an eternity of fire and coal and ash. So I'm telling you, if he has to get off his throne to come down here to personally deal with Legion, it's going to bad bad bad. Bad for your kind. Bad for my kind. Bad for everyone."

"Then help me stop them." I hoped the urgency in my voice sounded sincere. "Westland and Asag and Lylo are too strong for me to beat them on my own. I need your help."

"My help? No. No no no!" Just like that, she was shoving me towards the door and escorting me out. Goddamn, she was strong. "I can't go outside. I'm safer indoors. You should have never come here. Get out! If you want help, ask someone else. It can't be me. Go ask Xin! Go ask Carl!"

She opened the door and pushed me out into the hallway.

"I can't ask Xin and I can't ask Carl!" I grabbed both her wrists so she'd look at me. "They're both dead!"

Voel froze. "They're..."

She couldn't bring herself to say it.

"They're both dead," I told her. "Both of them. Isobella blew Carl up with a bomb and she stabbed Xin right through the heart with a big-ass piece of Chernobylite. She's murdering people left and right and she's going to do a whole lot worse if you don't fucking help me."

Voel closed her eyes and tightened her lips. I couldn't tell if she wanted to cry or rip someone's head off. Believe me, I know how that feels. She turned and stumbled back into her studio. The news hit her pretty hard emotionally; a strange reaction for a demon, but Voel wasn't a typical demon. She had a different connection with the Sons and Daughters of Adam and Eve. In any case, she wasn't kicking me out of her studio anymore. I followed her back inside.

"I haven't been among the humans in a long time," she said.

"Yeah, well, you know what, Voel? If there was ever a reason, this is fucking it."

She stared at the floor. "How quick do decades pass outside? Is Ronald Reagan still president?"

"Ronald Reagan is dead," I said.

"Did Isobella Westland kill him, too?"

"No," I replied. "At least, I don't think so."

When she finally looked up at me, her hands were shaking. "Listen, young mudblob. Asag and Lylo might not be the most powerful demons in all of Legion, but they're far more deadly than I am. When we were still angels, Lylo commanded an entire army of Seraphim. Asag himself had a hundred hands and could hold a hundred weapons at once. I was a simple Archilem in charge of painting the mountains. Even if I wanted to help you fight them, our chance of success would be remarkably dire."

"Well, there's got to be something," I said. "How did you three get to Earth in the first place? However you got out of Hell, we could just reverse it to send them back."

She stared at me for a second, then burst into laughter.

I didn't see the humor in any of this. "What's so funny?"

"'Send them back.' You make it sound so easy."

"Then explain it to me," I said. "Tell me how you did it. Maybe there's something I could use against them."

"You know what? You remind me of Judith. She had guts, too." Then she smiled like she was humoring me. She picked out a blank canvas and set it up on her easel. "Alright, mudblob, I'll tell you how we escaped. But I doubt it will help you."

3

Voel stuck a paintbrush between her teeth and picked up various tubes of paint. Squeezing them one after another, she blobbed different colors onto her well-used pallet.

"What do you know about the creation of Hell?" she asked.

"Not much," I said. "I went to Catholic school my whole life. Sometimes I would ask, but I never got any good answers."

"Of course you didn't." She made a thoughtful hum and dipped her brush into the paint. She put a couple strokes of red on the canvas and said, "We built Hell from the ground up when we were still angels, just like how you might build a house. We drew up plans, we had materials, and we assembled it piece by piece. Some of us built the cities. Others dug deep canyons and lakes so they could be filled with lava. The Being Yahweh gave me the task of painting the Shattered Mountains on the furthest edges of Hell. For millions of years, I painted and painted and painted until every single mountain was midnight black."

"Sounds boring."

She glared at me over her shoulder. "I was created to be a painter. My job was to paint. I never grew bored."

"Sorry."

She turned back to her canvas and added black triangles until they took the shape of a mountain range.

"There was a flaw in construction, right between these two mountains here. It was a small gap, just barely big enough to squeeze through. On the other side was Limbo, and beyond Limbo was Earth. No one noticed the flaw, not even the Being Yahweh. I didn't think much of it at the time, honestly, because there are gaps between worlds like that everywhere. And I had no idea that Hell was going to be a prison. I thought it was another planet. I learned better right before the War In Heaven.

"After the Being Yahweh crushed the angel rebellion, he transformed us into monsters and sentenced us to Hell. As soon as we landed, he turned on the fire and it's been burning ever since. We were confused at first, the legions of us, but we made the best of our new home. Everyone but me. I couldn't live in Hell knowing there was a way out. It took me almost a million years of searching, but eventually I found that escape route between the mountains. I knew going to Limbo would be dangerous and I'm no warrior, so in exchange for their help, I offered freedom to two other demons."

I knew who she meant. "Lylo and Asag."

Voel nodded. "We spent thousands of years wandering around in Limbo. Limbo is a world the Being Yahweh started, but never finished. There are a lot of places like that. The laws there are only half-written, so nothing makes sense. When you humans were inventing wheels, use three demons were crossing Limbo's shapeless terrain. By the time we arrived on Earth, your primitive species had already unlocked the power of the atom. That's when we met the Daughter of Eve known as Isobella Westland. She had already begun to learn the angelic language and, in exchange for a more thorough lesson, she allowed us to stay here in Eden."

"Except she went to Hell," I said. "And you went to prison."

"The new owners of the West Land betrayed us. Our deal was with Isobella Westland, they said. When her miracle backfired and she found herself exiled to punishment in Hell, the CEO was not inclined to honor our previous deal. Asag went to the gray prison. Lylo went to the red one. With the help of Carl, I escaped the white one and ended up here. The rest of the story ends with you here in my studio. Do you understand?"

I rubbed my nose. "Only kinda."

"Look..." She finished her painting of the Shattered Mountains and frisbeed it across the room. The wood frame cracked against the wall. "Sending Asag and Lylo back to Hell is not something you can just *do*."

I said, "Well, then there has to be something else."

"There's not."

"There has to be." I wasn't going to take no for an answer on this one. "If your paintings are right, Isobella's opening another fracture to Hell to get her body back and she's going to let Legion loose. I can't stop her because I can't get to her when she's protected by Asag and Lylo, so I need you to think of something."

Voel took a deep breath and lowered her head. Her dark green hair covered her face. Whatever idea she had, she didn't like it. In a quiet voice, she said, "I can think of only one thing."

Good. Great. All I needed was one thing. "What is it?"

She lifted her head. Her violet eyes met mine. "Smash their bottle."

"Bottle?" I asked. "Like a magic bottle?"

Voel set up another blank piece of canvas.

"Angels and demons don't have souls. The Being Yahweh didn't come up with the idea for souls until long after he made us. Mudblobs have souls. Angels and demons have a bottle. Our thoughts, our memories, our dreams and our desires come in liquid form, which is stored in very precious bottles." Her eyes glazed over, like she was remembering some wonderful dream. "Mine was quite beautiful then. Crystal clear, like a prism. That was, of course, before the fall."

She swished green paint across her blank canvas and created an image of herself. And in the middle of her chest, she painted a black bottle: glassy like obsidian and plugged closed with a cork.

"This," she tapped the wooden end of her brush on the bottle, "is everything that is Voel, the Deranged Painter. We keep our bottles inside us, much like a human soul. Asag and Lylo have bottles of their own, hidden somewhere inside their bodies."

"So I just have to rip out their guts and destroy their bottles?" I asked.

"It's not so easy," she said. "Even if you could get their bottles away from them, which you could never do, these bottles are not made of glass. They're crafted from pure imagination. You could not break one."

"Give me a little credit." I knocked on my own head. "I'm a half-robot war god. I think I can break a bottle."

She shook her head. "Asag and Lylo will not be so easily vanquished. Every time someone tries to destroy a bottle and fails, that bottle becomes stronger. The bottles for Asag and Lylo have survived destruction at the hands of Archangel Oriel during the rebellion in Heaven. When we traversed the world of Limbo, their bottles did not shatter under the crushing forces of the Great Nothing. If their bottles survived all that, then what chance do you have?"

"I dunno," I said. "How strong is a Great Nothing?"

"It is the apex predator of Limbo. It is as tall as the skies, as wide as the ocean, and it rolls like an egg. For centuries it chased us through Limbo, never slowing down, never growing tired."

"But you got away eventually," I said.

"Only barely," she said.

"So then how do I break their bottle?"

"You can't..." Her voice trailed off. Man, something was really bothering her. I could see it on her face. Then softly, barely audible, she said, "But I could."

"You mean you?" I asked. "You'll help me?"

"I might."

"How can you do it if I can't?"

"The three of us made a pact when we first entered Limbo. We each drank from one another's bottle, bonding us and giving us additional protection from the Great Nothing, but also making us vulnerable to one another. It's the most desecrated pact in Hell, and I would be betraying that pact if I were to help you."

"But does that mean you *won't* help me?"

She wanted to say no. I could tell. She didn't want to betray her demon brother and sister. Before she could give me that answer, we were interrupted. I had left the studio door open and now someone stood there in the entrance.

"Do say yes." It was Carl, completely alive and kicking. Maybe he was a ghost? I doubted it. Being a ghost wasn't really Carl's M-O. Rainwater drained from his soaking wet suit and his face was covered in dirt. "Because if I'm being honest... I think we're all in a lot of trouble."

4

I searched Carl up and down and touched him to make sure he was real. He felt real. "Dude, I thought you were dead."

"Why, Penelope." He smiled, as if the whole situation was funny to him. "Is that concern I hear in your voice?"

I scoffed and gave him a sour look. "Hardly. I'm just... you know... surprised you're alive."

"Don't be surprised." He stuck his hands in his pockets and welcomed himself into the studio. "It's going to take more than a couple kilos of plastic explosives to kill your old pal Carl."

Carl walked up to Voel, where they stood face to face. Neither one of them seemed excited to see the other.

"Carl," she said, plainly.

"Voel," he replied. "You seem... unchanged."

"And I forget just how fast you humans age. Look at you. Older. And you've become fat."

"Rude." He looked down at patted his stomach. "I'll have you know I skipped my cinnamon roll this morning."

"Excuse me," I interrupted. "Do you want to explain how you're still alive?"

He put a finger in the air. "Situational awareness. A keen eye for details. And if anyone ever tries to tell you that a low-altitude parachute is a waste of money, you have them come talk to me."

I crossed my arms. "That's not really an answer."

"He wants to keep it a secret," Theodore said as he also came in the door. His suit was also rain soaked. "He likes to be mysterious. It's annoying. Just ignore it."

A rush of happiness flooded through me when I saw Theodore again, especially after all of the chaos I had recently been through. One could say I was thrilled, in fact. With everything seemingly going to shit in the world, I needed to work with someone who had that smug, overconfident Westland attitude.

But I couldn't show my excitement. Last time I saw Theodore, he seemed really pissed off and I didn't know if he was over it yet or not, and I wasn't about to put my emotions on display if he wasn't going to do the same.

So I nodded at him and said, "Theodore."

He nodded back. "Penelope," he replied.

Carl wanted the spotlight again, so he leaned in close and softly told me, "I'd go into more detail about my daring escape, but I've got a lot of cards on the table right now. I'm in the middle of investigating my window washing company and I don't want to go tipping my hand to the wrong people."

I was super confused. "The wrong people?" I asked.

"Correct," Carl said.

"About your window washing company."

He winked at me. "You got it."

I had no clue that the fuck he was talking about. I put up my hands. "Whatever, dude."

"You have a lot of gall coming here," Voel said to Carl. "After all these years, not a visit. Not a letter. And you only show up now because you let the world go to shit."

Carl walked away from her and wandered around the studio. "I'm showing up now because the Westland Corporation is in shambles and we've got nothing else to lose. In case you've forgotten, I only kept my distance so I wouldn't blow your cover to the rest of the Corporation. You got to live here in peace."

She said, "Oh yes. Your generosity is truly boundless."

Theodore said, "I like this lady."

"Hmm." Carl stood over Voel's scattered paintings and gave them the once over. "Is that how you demons say thank you?"

She looked like she was about to blow up on him, but something stopped her. She sniffed the air once and gave him a disgusted look.

"You stink of angels," she said. "And Heaven."

He turned and nervously patted his hands together. "You always did have a sharp sense of smell."

She squinted her eyes at him. "We all do."

"Yes. Well." He cleared his throat and adjusted his tie. "I recently cut a deal with the Archilem for several tons of glorious glass. We trucked it into our headquarters through abandoned subway tunnels and built a containment chamber 100 feet below sea level."

"Building another prison, are you?" she asked.

"Detainment centers," me, Theodore and Carl said in unison.

"And no," Carl said. "Although I will admit, the idea had crossed my mind. No, I don't know how much Miss Salvo here has told you, but Asag and Lylo have both escaped our grasp and left quite a trail of destruction in their path."

"I've heard," said Voel.

Carl turned to me. "And Penelope, I must say it's quite serendipitous running into you here."

I glared at him. "I don't know what that word means."

"It means lucky," he said. "It's lucky running you here, although not entirely a surprise. Great minds think alike."

I nodded. "I need Voel's help."

"At this point, we all need Voel's help," Carl said. He made a grand gesture with his arms outstretched. "We all need each other's help."

I sighed. I didn't want to work with Carl on this. Theodore, sure, but not Carl. Working with Carl would be the stupidest thing possible. He's a corporate shill. He lies and steals and has people murdered.

But desperate times, right? I mean, Isobella Westland was a threat to all of us. She murdered Xin in cold blood. She straight-up tried to kill Carl. And she seized complete control of the Westland Corporation.

Between him and global annihilation at the hands of Legion, Carl felt like the lesser of two evils.

If there was ever a time to - fuck me, I can't believe I'm actually thinking this - if there was ever a time to "trust" Carl, wouldn't this be it?

Carl put his hand on my shoulder. "Penelope? Theodore? Would you two be so kind as to give me just a moment alone with Voel? I have a feeling she has some particularly un-nice things to say to me and I would hate to subject you to that."

Voel locked eyes on Carl and grit her teeth. "You are quite correct. You two mudblobs, wait outside."

Theodore and I made eye contact. He shrugged at me and I shrugged at him. With no reason to say, Theodore left.

I looked back at Carl. He nodded towards the door and whispered, "Will you go apologize to him, please? He's been nothing but a frowny clowny this whole time and, quite frankly, I'm tired of dealing with it."

Any conversation with Theodore was going to be hella awkward, but if we were going to work together to stop Isobella

Westland, it was something I was just going to have to do. I stepped out into the hallway and closed the door behind me. Theodore just stood there with his arms crossed, pretending to be distracted with the fire extinguisher.

Awkward.

I said, "So."

He didn't look at me, but said, "So."

I rocked back and forth on my heels and said, "Soooo."

An awkward silence hung in the air for way too long before he finally spoke up. "I had an idea that might help Xin. I heard that out in New Beatlemania there are these flowers that-"

I cut him off before he said too much and stirred up too much emotion in me. "Dude. Don't worry about it."

"No, hear me out," he said, excited to share his idea. "Out in the Strawberry Fields are these little flowers that-"

"Theodore." I closed my eyes and put up my hand so he would shut up. He went quiet. I took a breath and fought back the tears, refusing to cry in front of him. I swallowed and said, "Xin's dead."

"What?"

"Isobella Westland killed him."

Theodore did not see that coming. Whatever helpful idea he had cooked up in New Beatlemania, we would never know if it would have worked or not. The damage was done. Xin was dead. What little excitement Theodore had in him drained from his face. He stood there, speechless.

"How do you know?" he asked.

It was hard to relive. I spoke in whispers. "I was there." Theodore didn't ask for details, so I offered them up. "She killed him right in front of me. Nothing I could do."

He exhaled hard. "Penelope, I am so sorry."

And despite standing in front of stupid, green-eyed, messy-haired, Westland-employed Theodore, I started crying. A moment later, I felt him put his arms around me. And while I normally would have shoved anyone else away and told them to never touch me, I just needed to cry.

Theodore hugged me while I bawled into his shoulder.

"Tell me something else," I said, hoping he could help take my mind off of the terrible feelings stabbing me in the soul.

"Well," he said. "Isobella blew up the top floor of the HQ building and tried to kill Carl."

I sniffled and said, "I saw that."

"Carl's never been a very good father, but she tried to kill him. And she's going to kill more people if we don't stop her."

"She's crazy, man," I said. "I mean, like, legit. I talked to her. I looked into her eyes. She's straight up insane."

"I want to kill her, Penelope," he said.

I leaned back and looked into his eyes. It's a hell of a thing to hear your friend say they want to kill someone, even someone as evil as Isobella Westland. It takes a real force of evil to push a good person like Theodore to say such a thing.

Fact was, I didn't want to kill anyone. But a lot like the old CEO of the Westland Corporation, there were a short list of people who I wouldn't have minded if they were killed by someone else.

I wiped the chemicals off my cheeks with the palms of my hands and told Theodore, "I want to help you."

Conversation dried up after that. We stood there and stared at each other. God dammit, I hate awkward pauses. Since I felt compelled to fill it with words, I decided to go for the apology.

"Look, Theodore," I said. "All that shit I made you tell Carl back at headquarters... the stuff about us not being friends? I didn't mean any of that."

He looked ashamed. "I know."

I straightened his tie for him. "We're friends, you know. After everything we've been through, we don't have any choice but to be friends. It's just weird because you're a Westland guy and Westland is always fucking things up. Plus, Carl gets on my god damn nerves so freaking bad. It's like he doesn't even listen to me sometimes. He tried to kill me, but still thinks we're old friends or something. He's so weird."

"I get it," he said with a chuckle. "Believe me, if anyone gets it, it's me."

"The point is," I continued, "when Carl said that you and I met because he was pulling the strings, I didn't want to give him that satisfaction. So that's why I said we weren't friends."

"You don't have to explain," he said. "I blew up at you because I was pissed at Carl, too. It was just misdirected anger."

I laughed and rolled my eyes. "Misdirected anger is literally my middle name."

"You've only known Carl for a year," he replied. "Imagine having that guy as your father."

"Oh, don't get me started." I laughed some more. "You never met my father."

"Yeah?" Theodore said, turning our shitty fathers into a coy competition. "Did your father ever send you off to Costa Peligro to train with a bunch of mercenaries?"

"No," I said. "My father just hit me a bunch."

That took the wind out of Theodore's light-hearted sails. I suppose I didn't have to get so dark with it. Who between us had a worse childhood? Tough to tell, I guess. It's not like it was a real competition, anyway; at least not a competition worth winning. But in that moment, when I realized his relationship with his father was just as screwed up as mine – screwed up in a totally different way – it made me feel a little better about everything I had to go through.

Maybe I'd carry that negativity I felt towards Michael with me to the grave. Maybe I'd never let it go. But at least I found a little solace in knowing I wasn't the only one.

"Look," Theodore said. "I know the last thing you want to do is work with Carl on this. I'm not thrilled about the idea, either. But at this point-"

I waved him off. "Dude, save the sales pitch. I know what we're up against and I've already come to terms with it. We have no choice. We have to do this together. All of us."

Theodore nodded in agreement. "There's no one else left."

5

Voel's door creaked open and Carl poked his head out. "You kids kiss and make up?" he asked.

"Uh, ew," I said.

Theodore clarified on our behalf. "We're cool now, if that's what you're asking."

"Good." Carl opened the door all the way and motioned for us to come back in. "Because we're going to go knock Isobella Westland down a few pegs and if you two are going to be of any help to me, you both need to get your head in the game."

"Oh, my head is all up in this game," I said. "I'm like Michael Jordan right now."

"And I'm like..." Theodore gave me a confused look. "...Did Joe Montana play basketball?"

"Joe Montana is football."

He turned back to Carl. "Then I'll be Joe Montana."

Carl snapped his fingers. "I don't know who those men are, but they sound like stand-up gentlemen. I like what I'm hearing."

Me and Theodore went back inside the studio. Carl closed the door behind us. He went over to Voel's collection of paintings and picked one of them up; the one with Isobella's orange soul floating away from her body in Hell. He used it as a visual aid.

"Isobella split her soul from her body," Carl began, "because that was her only option to establish a presence here on Earth. But now her soul doesn't have her body, and her body doesn't have her soul, so she's slowly dying. If she doesn't get her body and soul back together soon, she's going to disappear completely. No soul. No afterlife. Just completely gone."

I darted over to Voel's pile of paintings and picked out the one of Legion with the slash in the canvas. I showed it to Carl. "That's why she's trying to open another fracture. She's trying to get her body out of Hell."

Voel spoke up. "And she's going to let all of Legion loose in the process."

Theodore asked, "But why would she bother bringing her body to Earth if that's going to turn the planet into Hell?"

"It all comes down to her spell book," Carl said. "It's called the Omnia Deus and it's an angelic catalog of every miracle spoken by God. Somehow it worked its way out of Heaven and landed here on Earth. They had it hidden away in the basements of the Vatican, but Isobella must have tracked it down. Armed with that book, she can force every demon in Legion to obey her. Earth might burn, but she'll be just fine."

"At least until the Being Yahweh shows up," Voel said. "He is not the kind god your texts would lead you to believe. He is a vengeful, spiteful being who would sooner destroy the Earth than see it lost to the demons who once rebelled against him."

"So we just need to close this fracture," I said.

"Wherever it is," Theodore replied.

"Maybe she's going back to Chernobyl," I said.

Carl spoke up. "She's not going to Chernobyl."

"And how do you know that?" I asked. "That's where she did it last time."

Carl avoided eye contact with me. "Believe me. I just know."

That answer seemed strangely suspicious. So I prompted him for more. "*How* do you know?"

Now Carl looked worried. "Promise me you won't get mad."

I didn't like the sound of that. "Why would I get mad, Carl?"

"Well." He chuckled nervously and forced a smile. "Do you remember how we were using Untouchable Orange to get free and limitless energy?"

I answered slowly. "I do."

"And do you remember how I told you that free energy was coming from nowhere?"

I squinted at him. "Yes."

"Well." He chuckled again. "Funny thing about that."

I shoved him. "It was connected to Hell!?"

Voel spoke up. "He's an idiot."

"I had no way of knowing that!" Carl said. "Research and Development should have caught on and told me before-"

I grabbed him by the tie and shoved my finger right in his face. "I knew that thing was dangerous! I told you! Didn't I fucking tell you?"

Carl put up his hands. "Penelope, please! I didn't know!"

"That's exactly my point, Carl! You didn't know! You shouldn't be fucking with things if you don't know what they do! Now Isobella's going to open a fucking gateway to Hell and let Legion loose on Earth and it's going to piss God off and he's going to come down here and personally kick all our asses!"

"Oh," Voel said. "If only he lets us off that easy."

Carl raised his voice back at me. "Would you stop worrying!" I let him go. He took a moment to adjust his tie and regain his composure. "Untouchable Orange has the *potential* to break into Hell, but it's nowhere hot enough."

"How hot does it have to get?" I asked.

"At least 10,000 degrees. And right now it's at..." He checked his phone. "3,000. I've got the readings synced to my phone."

"Well, use your phone and shut it down," I told him.

He winced and said, "It's not that easy."

I paced in a quick, frustrated circle. "I'm getting real tired of everyone always saying that. 'Not that easy.' Why can't anything ever be easy?"

I stopped when I heard the sound of crinkling plastic. I turned to see Theodore unwrapping the top of Kreenkle candy bar.

Theodore took a bite of his candy and spoke with his mouth full. "We can only shut Untouchable Orange down from inside."

I was going to comment on the candy bar, that maybe this wasn't the best time for a snack, but I knew the observation would have gone right over the dum-dum's head. I just rolled my eyes and ignored it.

"We just have to get inside the containment chamber and shut the system down from the inside," Carl said. "And we have plenty of time for that. The built-in safety protocols limit Untouchable Orange to an increase of 500 degrees every hour."

Numbers. Math. Goddammit. I tried to do the calculations on my fingers, but gave up when I realized I would never figure it out and asked, "How much time does that give us, exactly?"

Carl said, "Fourteen hours."

Theodore said, "*That's* your definition of 'plenty of time'?"

I couldn't believe it. Fourteen hours to save the world. "God dammit, Carl."

"In full disclosure," Carl said with a finger in the air, "it could technically be less."

Well, that was even worse! I asked him, "How much less?"

"Tough to say." He tapped and swiped at the screen on his phone. "The safety protocols can only be shut down with my CEO key card Without it, the system regulates the temperature and we have fourteen hours."

I glared at him. "I feel like there's a 'but' coming..."

"But," he said. "Isobella Westland has successfully hacked into all of our other computer systems. And I'm afraid she's turned her attention to Untouchable Orange."

He showed me his phone.

UNTOUCHABLE ORANGE
CONTAINMENT CHAMBER

UNAUTHORIZED ACCESS – DENIED
UNAUTHORIZED ACCESS – DENIED
UNAUTHORIZED ACCESS – DENIED
UNAUTHORIZED ACCESS – DENIED

"There's been a failed attempt to shut down the safety protocols every sixty seconds or so." He tucked his phone back into his jacket. "She's trying to hack into a futuristic computer language I purchased from the year 2234, so it won't exist for a couple centuries and it should slow her down. But she *has* demonstrated a supernatural understanding of languages. It's just a matter of time before she figures it out."

"So what do we do before that happens?" I asked.

"We sneak into Westland HQ," Carl said. "If we can get inside, I can use the CEO key card to shut down the entire Untouchable Orange system and erase the files."

"Uh huh," I said. "And how do you plan on getting inside, Carl? Ring the doorbell? Get on each others shoulders and cover up with a big trench coat?"

"The whole building is locked down hard," Theodore added. "You know those security systems better than anyone. If Isobella took control of them, there's no way we're getting inside. The moment anyone spots us on security, we'll have demons so far up our asses, we'll be able to taste the sulfur."

"Oh, ye's of little faiths," Carl said, confident as ever. "Do you forget who you're talking to? You think I don't have a plan for this kind of thing? I have someone who can get us inside."

"Someone you can trust?" I asked. "It seems like you can't trust anyone right now."

"Yeah," Theodore agreed. "And everyone thinks you died in that explosion, even the agents who were loyal to you. And you still don't know which ones were working for Isobella. Who knows how high up the food chain this thing goes."

"I don't need to go up the food chain." Carl gave me a slight smile. "When you're five steps ahead of the competition, it means you can go to the very bottom."

6

Time was running short and we had to leave. Whatever Carl said to Voel, it convinced her to come with us. She bravely stepped out the door and glanced up and down the hallway. Scared, she pulled the door closed behind her and it clicked shut. Her day had finally come; she was about to walk the streets of New York with a couple human beings. But as the rest of us started down the hall, Voel lingered behind with her hand still on the doorknob.

"You going to be okay?" I asked.

She whipped around and sneered, revealing one of her fangs. "Of course I'm going to be okay. I went through Limbo. I escaped the Great Nothing. You think I'm afraid of some human city? I'll be fine. Just fine."

"Alright," I said, defensively. "Chill the fuck out. Damn."

Voel and Carl led the way to the stairs and started down. Me and Theodore followed right behind them.

"Well, Theodore," I said. "Looks like you're going to get everything you ever wanted. Action. Adventure. Boots on the ground, saving the world."

Theodore grabbed his suit jacket and popped his collar up. "Oh yeah," he said. "I've been *waiting* for this day."

The popped collar on his jacket looked really stupid. I thought about not telling him that – no sense it taking away that simple pleasure – but the more I tried to ignore it, the more I kept glancing at it out of the corner of my eye.

Until I couldn't take it anymore.

I reached over and fixed his collar for him.

"Don't do that," I said.

"Why?" he asked, honestly unaware of how dumb it looked.

"You look like a total jabroni," I told him.

"I do?" he asked.

I got his collar back down to normal. "Trust me."

"Hey." He nudged my arm. "If you get in trouble, just shout and I'll come save you."

The mere idea of *me* somehow needing *his* help was so ridiculous and unexpected, it made me snort. "Okay, Theodore."

"You're not nervous?" he asked me.

"Me?" I asked. I looked him up and down as if he were on crack. "Nervous?" I pounded my fist into my open hand. "Dude, I'm *actively* looking forward to this. I have a lot of people I want to punch."

"Must be nice to be so excited," he said. "You're a war god. Your body is indestructible."

"Why?" I asked him. "Are *you* nervous?"

"Me? No," he said. And it sounded sincere. "I work for the Westland Corporation."

And that was all the justification he gave him.

"Look at Carl," I whispered to him. "He's a squishy pile of hamburger just like you and he doesn't look the least bit scared."

Carl, in fact, bopped along like everything was perfectly normal. He rambled on and on to Voel; something about a window washing company. Voel listened with what I would best describe as patient anger. He didn't seem the least bit bothered by our upcoming danger. Made sense, I guess. He'd been doing stuff like this his whole life. Just another day at the office.

We got outside and hit our first problem. The thunderstorm had gone full-blown tropical storm. Lightning flashed in the sky. Thunder rattled windows and set off distant car alarms. Heavy rain flooded the streets up to the curb. We were blocks away from the nearest subway station.

"This is one hell of a storm," I observed.

Carl nodded and in an unhappy tone, said, "Yes, it is."

I didn't like the sound of that, and I quickly put together why. "It's Westland's weather control, isn't it," I said.

He looked up to the sky and nodded. "Emergency vehicles can't get anywhere. Subways and taxis are probably shutting down. 9-1-1 is undoubtedly ringing off the hook."

"That weather machine of yours is a real pain in the ass."

"It's technically not a machine but an array of ionizing satellites," he said. "But yes, it is quite the pain." Carl smiled like a proud parent. Funny, even when the strategy worked against him, he couldn't help but admire the genius of it all.

Voel followed behind us and stopped at the entrance of her building and felt the misty air. She hissed like a vampire and cowered backwards into the building.

"You allergic to water or something?" I asked.

"I hate water." Her eyes darted all around, watching the sky. The lightning and thunder made her super jumpy. Maybe it reminded her of something. "I quit. I'm going back inside."

"Not good," Theodore said. "She's chickening out."

"Voel, please." Carl took her arm and kept her in place. "We can get you through this."

We can? How? How were we supposed to get from Queens to Manhattan without getting wet in the middle of a borderline hurricane? We couldn't walk. The buses were shit down. We'd never find a taxi. We'd have better luck grabbing boards and surfing to Midtown.

But, as things tend to go in the supernatural world, we didn't have to wait for long. A Westland SUV came flying down the street. It swerved out of its way to splash through the deepest puddles. The windshield wipers were at maximum speed and it had its brights on. The SUV fishtailed to a stop in front of us and bumped up onto the curb.

The window rolled down and female voice came out of the radio. "Sir! There you are!"

"Denali!" Theodore exclaimed. He sprinted through the rain and went for the driver side door. "How did you find us?"

"I contacted a psychic," Denali said.

Theodore climbed into the driver's seat and asked, "Really?"

"No, dummy. I tracked the GPS on your phone," she said. "Hi, Penelope!"

"Sup, girl?" I ran to the passenger side and climbed in.

Carl used his suit jacket to protect Voel from the rain and escorted her to the back. Even in the short run to the car, Voel got a little wet. She hated it. Her body overheated and the water steamed off of her skin.

"I hate this," she growled.

Carl handed her a pack of pocket-sized tissues. She glared at him, but snatched them out of his hand and used wadded-up handfuls to dry herself off.

I settled into my seat and buckled up. "Hey, Denali. How was the rest of the drive? Pretty boring?"

"Nah. I talked to Darla the whole way. She's going to go back to hair school." Denali turned down the volume of her voice so only Theodore and I could hear her. "Hey, not trying to be a bitch here, but who're the new people?"

"This is Carl," Theodore said as his father climbed into the back seat. "And that's Voel. She's a demon."

Voel wasn't paying any attention. She focused on drying off.

"It's nice to finally meet you," Carl said to Denali. "I hear you've been taking good care of Theodore."

"Oh, you have no idea," she said with a laugh. "It's a full time job, let me tell you."

Lightning struck a nearby power pole within the neighborhood and the following crack of thunder made the streetlights flicker and blink off. The street went dark. We could only see by Denali's headlights and the intermittent flashed of lightning up in the clouds. The wind picked up and rain beat down on the city in pulsing waves.

"Alright," Denali said. "Let's get out of here before these roads get any worse. Where're we headed?"

"Westland Headquarters?" I asked.

"Not just yet," Carl said. "For this plan to work, we're going to need one more very important person."

Chapter 24

1

Before we came along, I bet Ilana Rittenberg was probably having a normal night at her parents' apartment: texting a couple of her deadbeat boyfriends, shopping online for torn-up black denim and trying to beat her top score in Money Crunch on her phone. Her parents were probably doing normal stuff, too, whatever boring old people do. Watch black-and-white television? Knit a horse blanket? Read about measles in the paper?

I'm sure the last thing they expected was a buzz at their door at 10pm.

Ilana's mom and dad never liked me. They thought I was a bad influence on Ilana. That's fine. I never liked Ilana's mom and dad. They were stuck-up rich people with no sense of humor. It was cool of them to let me stay at their place that one time during Hurricane Sandy, but they did that as a favor to Ilana, not because they liked me at all.

They had to be pissed off to have someone buzzing at their building so late. They were probably thinking to themselves, "Whoever it is, this had better be good. Whoever it is, this had better be an emergency." Then her dad clicks the button to the intercom to hear me of all people, Penelope Salvo, on the other end begging to be let up.

I showed up at their apartment door dressed like a teenage CIA agent who'd been dragged across the concrete by a speeding car, then splashed down into a river, then rolled around in the mud. My hair was soaked, water dripped from my clothes and formed a puddle on the carpet in front of their door.

Ilana's dad did not look entertained.

"Hey Mister Rittenberg," I said. I peeked past him and into his kitchen. "Is Ilana here?"

He did not respond. He just turned around and shouted for his daughter. And when Ilana came poking her head around the corner a few seconds later, I heard what he said to her. He wasn't even being coy. I think he wanted me to hear.

"She is *not* staying here," he told her. "No excuses. I don't care if the world's on fire."

Ilana sighed, rolled her eyes at her dad, and came to the door. She was already in for the night, apparently. Her hair was damp from showering, she didn't have on any make-up, and was all jammied up in black shorts and a Yesterday Discs t-shirt. She gave me the strangest look.

"Penelope." She stepped into the doorway and looked me up and down. "What the hell happened to you?"

"Uh." Oh, you know, I fought a demon, then drove halfway across America in a talking GMC Denali, then fought some *more* demons, then broke into an international spy network's head-quarters. I shrugged and said, "It's raining out. I got a little wet."

She whispered, "You look like someone tried to kill you."

That made me laugh. "You're not far off."

She closed the door a little bit to keep her parents from eavesdropping. "Penelope, do you have any idea what time it is?"

"Uh. Well, no." I had very little time to waste on explanations. I had to cut right to the chase. I raised my thumb and offered her the most apologetic, begging smile. "Ilana, will you come outside with me right quick?"

She looked dumbfounded. "You can't be for real."

"Five minutes," I said. "Please. I swear to God, Ilana, this is important."

She lowered her voice to a whisper. "Penelope, dude, I just did some mushrooms. I'm tripping my everloving balls off right now. I just want to play Money Crunch and listen to music."

"Ilana," I whined. "Please."

She sighed. She didn't want to, but she caved. Aside from bumping into her at the Westland Corporation's reception desk, our last real conversation was when I told her we couldn't be friends anymore. We were overdue for some real talk.

She stepped into her flip flops and followed me down the stairs to the main floor of her building. I'm sure she expected to have a serious heart-to-heart about our friendship, or lack thereof. Well, the conversation she was expecting and the conversation she was about to get were going to be way different.

Waaaaay different.

I led her out of her building and around the corner to the alleyway that separated her building from the next one. Even nice apartment blocks like the ones you'd find in the village had dark, scary alleyways with dumpsters to hide murderers and piles of untouched trash. The lightning from the impending superstorm only made things feel more like a horror movie.

Ilana followed me to a little brick archway left over from the 1920's and skipped over in her building's various renovations and refacings. The bricks were from old New York, with sloppy mortar that hardened before they could be smoothed out. The archway housed a loading door that opened up into a service elevator, something they'd use when a tenant moved in with a piano or a four-post bed. We huddled beneath it to hide from the rain. There we met Theodore and Carl, who stood in the dim glow of the security light mounted over the graffiti-covered loading door. Their Westland suits matched mine, only in much better shape.

Ilana froze in mid-step when she spotted the shadowy figures of two men she didn't know. I didn't blame her. As any New Yorker will tell you, you don't want to be led into a loading area at night, not when there's strange men waiting for you.

"Uh, Penelope?" she said with a hand on my shoulder, as if I hadn't yet noticed them. She held me back from going any closer. "Is it just me, or do you see two FBI agents standing there?"

"It's cool," I said. "These are my friends. That's Theodore..."

Theodore waved. "Hey."

"And that guy there..." I pointed at Carl. "That's... well... That's the CEO of the Westland Corporation."

Ilana tilted her head and stared at Carl as if here were Jesus. She took a few cautious steps forward to get a closer look. "No shit? *That's* Mister Carl?"

"Please," Carl said. "It's just Carl. *Mister* Carl was my father." He took a step forward and reached out for a handshake. Ilana raised her hand in slow-motion to meet his, kind of on autopilot. Carl grabbed her hand and forcefully shook it, wobbling her arm like a wet noodle. "Pleasure to meet you," he said. "Absolute pleasure. Any friend of Penelope's is a friend of mine. You do a fantastic job screening my phone calls by the way."

"Thank you," she said dreamily, still hypnotized by meeting her boss while tripping on shrooms. "My supervisor says I'll be up for a promotion soon."

"I'll be sure to put in a good word for you," he said with a little wink. "I'm good friends with upper management. In fact..." He straightened his tie and beamed a smile at her. "Technically, as of fourteen hours ago, I *am* upper management."

"I heard you were dead," Ilana whispered to Carl. "You got blowed up in an explosion. I didn't hear any explosion, but that's how everyone says it happened."

"Ah, yes," Carl said. "Well, I doubt you would have heard it, Miss Rittenberg. It only half-existed in this dimension."

"Uh huh." That weird explanation took a second to register in Ilana's brain. "Wait, what? This *dimension*?"

I had to step in and say something sensible before Carl's senseless bean-spilling freaked Ilana out.

"Ilana..." I said, stealing her attention back to me. I wanted to get her caught up with what was going on, but where was I supposed to start? Isobella Westland? Chernobyl? The night of Hurricane Sandy when I swallowed Impossible Red? Ilana stared desperately at me, just waiting for me to say something, *anything*, that would help make sense of things.

I promised her that day at the reception desk, I would someday tell her the truth. And I owed it to her. I owed that much to her, ever since the night I tried to end our friendship standing in the street outside the Gold Mine.

I wanted to tell her the truth, but I didn't have the time to start from the beginning. So I decided to start with recent events.

I asked her, "Ilana, do you remember a couple weeks ago when that nuclear bomb exploded over the ocean?"

"Uh, yeah?" she said. "It was all over the news."

"Okay, well..." I took a deep breath. "That was me."

She scrunched up her face, confused. "What do you mean that was you? You tried to nuke Russia?"

"No, I didn't try to *nuke Russia*," I said.

"She doesn't have the clearance," Theodore volunteered.

"Some Russian girl launched it," I said. "All I did was intercept it in mid-air and blow it out of the sky."

Ilana looked at me like I was a moron. "Dude, what are you even *talking* about?"

Dammit. This wasn't going well.

Carl interrupted us. "We don't have time to explain to her the minutiae." He reached into his jacket, pulled out his pistol and flicked off the safety.

Whoa. I had no idea why we were suddenly getting a gun involved. Had Ilana heard too much of the big secret and now Carl was just going to blow her brains out? I quickly stepped between them to protect her.

But Carl didn't point the gun at Ilana. He pointed it at me, right in my face. I crossed my eyes and could see straight down the barrel.

I said, "Uh, can I help you?"

"Penelope?" Ilana said, nervously backing away.

"Don't worry, dude," I said. "He's not going to-"

Carl opened fire. Right there in the alleyway, in front of God and everybody, Carl pulled the trigger over and over and shot me in the face until the gun went click. Muzzle flashes lit up the alleyway like fireworks. Gunshots echoed down the alley. Bullets tinkled down to the concrete, then everything went quiet.

I blinked my eyes to get the muzzle flashes out of my vision and coughed. The smoke from Carl's gun got in my mouth and went right down my throat.

Ilana's eyes were as big as the moon. "Holy the fuck shit!"

Theodore stuck his pinkies in his ears. "That was loud."

I snapped at Carl, "What are you *doing*?"

"Speeding things up," Carl said. He turned to Ilana. "Do you see, Miss Rittenberg? What Penelope here is clumsily trying to tell you is that she's bulletproof. She's a half-robot god of war. Come look. See for yourself."

Ilana cautiously approached me and leaned in to scrutinize every inch of my face. She pressed her thumbs to my cheeks and stretched the skin on my forehead. I let her do it. She wasn't going to find a single bullet hole. Not even a scratch.

"What the hell, man?" she whispered, intently checking my skin. "Is this some sort of trick or something?"

"No trick," I said.

"She's the god of war," Carl said.

"*Artificial* god of war," Theodore added. "Penelope's body has been altered by a trillion microscopic nanites."

Ilana smooshed my face together, looked into my eyes and said, "You know, you have really nice skin."

"Thank you," I said. "So you're not going to freak out?"

"Why would I freak out?" she asked.

"Well, Carl shot me in the face."

"I know!" Her face turned to abject excitement. "This shit is so dope! You're bulletproof! How'd you get to be bulletproof?"

"I accidentally swallowed something from Xin's shop when *he* was trying to steal it." I glared at Carl. "And now I'm half-robot."

She let go of my face, stood back and admired me. "This is so *cool*. So when you said you went to China all those months, you weren't joking?"

"Well, actually, I wasn't in China," I said. "I was in Antarctica. And the Sahara. And Malaysia. I was kind of all over."

She nodded as if she totally understood. "So cool."

"You're not..." I didn't know what the right word was for what she *wasn't* being. "You're not mad?"

"Mad?" she repeated. "Why would I be mad? It's amazing."

"And you're not going to flip out?" I asked.

"Honestly?" She leaned in close and lowered her voice to a whisper. "I think I'm peaking. All of this is making total sense."

"Well... then..." This was going better than I thought. "Check this out. Voel? Come meet my friend Ilana."

Voel, who had been hiding in the shadows, stepped out of the corner of the archway and into the security light. There she was, clad in her painting coveralls and all her lime-green glory.

Ilana had her mind blown yet again. "Whoa! Where did *you* come from? What's your story? Are you from Narnia?"

"I'm from Gehenna," Voel replied. "The Valley of Hinnom."

"This is Voel," I said, introducing her to Ilana. "A demon. The Deranged Painter. She's from Hell."

Voel spoke up. "I once hailed from the Underworld, but I currently reside in a more desecrated realm known as Queens. I paint the visions that come to me."

Ilana's smile just got bigger and bigger. "This shit is fucking bonkers." She looked at me. "So *this* is why you've been so weird all this time."

"Yeah," I said, kind of ashamed it took me so long to tell her the truth. "Pretty much."

She turned her attention to Theodore. "So what's your deal then?" she asked. "You a vampire or a werewolf or something?"

"No," Theodore replied. "All the vampires and werewolves are dead."

Carl interrupted the Q and A to keep things on schedule. "Miss Rittenberg," he said. "We three are about to do something very important, something that very well may save the world. And we really need your help."

"*My* help?" she asked. "You're the CEO of a huge corporation and Penelope's taking bullets to the face. You got a demon over there kicking it in the shadows and this guy may or may not be a werewolf. And you need *my* help?"

"Correct," he said.

"Okay," she replied. "What do you need me to do?"

"It's very simple, actually" Carl said. "Go change into your work clothes. I need you to open a door."

2

Westland employees come and go from Westland HQ like drone to a beehive, all day and all night. When your job is to "protect" the globe from time travelers and rogue gingerbread men and giant monstrous squids, there's no such thing as a nine-to-five shift. Westland agents work whatever hours are necessary to get the job done. Sometimes their flight from Egypt puts them in New York at midnight. Or other times they'll receive a strange phone call at two in the morning that sends them flying to Egypt to fight another resurrected mummy.

"Happened to me all the time," Carl told us as Denali splashed through curb-deep water on her way to Midtown. "One time when I was a field agent, I was working overnight in my office and looked up to see a little blue pixie tapping on my office window. Apparently a bunch of Leprechauns thought it would be funny to summon a Wild Hunt in Ireland."

"Pixies?" Ilana asked, leaning forward from the back seat. "You mean like Tinkerbell?"

"Her name was Blueflake," Carl said. "But, yes, you've got the right idea."

"What's a Wild Hunt?" I asked.

"Oh, you know how in the 1800's rich people would ride on horseback and hunt rabbits with muskets and bloodhounds?"

I shrugged. "Yeah."

"Well, a Wild Hunt is a collection of all those things," Carl said. "But as ghosts. Ghost huntsmen, ghost horses, ghost blood-hounds. Once they're loose, it's an absolute mess to deal with. The huntsmen never run out of bullets, the horses breathe fire, and the bloodhounds are absolutely savage. They fade away at sunrise, but in that short amount of time they can wipe out an entire town. Long story short, one minute I'm filing paperwork In New York and next thing I know I'm in Killarney trying to fit a tank inside a fairy ring so we can teleport it to Tir Na Nog."

That's how things worked at Westland. Always coming and going. You worked when the job demanded it. This, Carl said, meant that if Ilana showed up to work the reception desk at one in the morning, no one would think anything of it. A lot of people work odd hours at Westland. Everyone would assume she was called in for something important.

And given the recent chaos with their computer systems, it would be impossible to double check.

"Not that anyone would double check on some lowly receptionist," Carl said. Then he realized he was shitting on Ilana's job. "I'm sorry. That sounded bad."

"hey, no biggie," Ilana said. "I'm straight up tripping balls. I'm not going to remember *any* of this."

Once Ilana got to the reception desk, she'd be able to open a distant loading door down on Pier 83 at the docks.

"The Westland Corporation has exclusive access to a secret entrance at Pier 83," Theodore explained. "There's a set of loading doors cleverly disguised as a simple brick wall, doors that lead to an old abandoned subway system."

"That's how we get supplies in and out when we want to keep it a secret from the rest of the world," Carl clarified. "Weather equipment, tankers full of truth serum, shipments of glorious glass. We've been shuffling Nobel Prize-winning stuff back and forth under the city's nose and they've never even had a clue."

"And if everything goes according to plan," I said, looking back at Ilana. "We can use it to sneak inside the Westland Corporation headquarters without Isobella Westland finding out."

"And who's that again?" Ilana asked.

"The original founder of the Westland Corporation," I said.

"From Hell," Theodore added.

"She's a ghost," Carl said.

"Technically a *soul*," I said, correcting him. "She's not dead, so she's not a ghost. She's a soul."

"From Hell," Theodore reiterated.

"Soul from Hell," Ilana repeated, nodding. "Got it."

Denali arrived at Pier 83 and pulled up to the faux "brick wall." We all piled out and stood under this metal overhang structure that protected the entrance from the rain. Everyone piled out, that is, except for Ilana. Ilana had places to be and a door to open.

Voel dropped to her knees right there on the concrete and used a white rock to sketch images on the ground. She'd gone too long without painting and it was apparently taking a toll on her.

"Denali," Carl said to the SUV. "I need you to take Miss Rittenberg here to headquarters."

Denali replied with confidence. "Got it."

"And Miss Rittenberg," he continued. "When you arrive at work, act normal. Start your day like you normally do."

Ilana looked confused. "Hide in the bathroom and play Money Crunch?"

Carl scowled. "Is that what you normally do?"

And Ilana, high on shrooms, didn't have it in her to lie. She answered him right away. "Yup."

Carl sighed. "Just get to the desk and release the magnetic locks on Pier 83."

"Denali," Theodore said. "This is important. No speeding. We don't need you getting caught."

"Me?" she said, mock offended. "Speed?"

Theodore crossed his arms. "Denali, I mean it."

"Alright, *fine*," she said. "Stupid mission."

"And no Tokyo drifting," he added.

"And no Tok..." she mumbled before trailing off.

Theodore, in a stern tone, repeated it. "No Tokyo drifting."

"Fine." Her disappointment was real. "No Tokyo drifting."

Ilana pointed at Denali's radio. "Is there a person trapped in this car's dashboard?"

"I am a car and a person," Denali said.

Ilana stuck her face into the blue glow of Denali's electronic read-outs. "Are you, like, artificial intelligence?"

Denali didn't answer right away. "Uh, that word's kind of offensive. I know you didn't mean it, but you shouldn't call it 'artificial' intelligence. It's kind of insulting. My intelligence is just as real as everyone else's."

"Sorry." Ilana looked at us, too. "Sorry."

"It takes some getting used to," I said.

"It takes a lot of getting used to," said Theodore.

Carl said, "You know, I predict within the next five years, we'll see our first vehicular field agent. Can you imagine that?"

"Oh, good luck," Theodore snipped. "I can't get a promotion and I'm a human being."

"Wow," Denali said, insulted. "Must be so hard being *human*."

Carl rolled his eyes. "You have to *earn* a promotion, Theodore. You can't have everything handed to you on a silver platter."

Theodore took a step towards his dad. "When have I ever had *anything* handed to me on a silver platter?"

"Oh, you've had plenty. Trust me."

"Name one thing."

This wasn't a good time for fighting, so I stepped in. "Guys."

But Carl kept talking. "What about your Russian lessons? Or those ten years of Krav Maga classes? What about that vacation to Costa Peligro?"

"Vacation?" Theodore said. "Costa Peligro was a boot camp for mercenaries. I got shot at!"

Carl crossed his arms. "A real field agent would consider that a vacation. So what does that tell you?"

I got louder. "Guys!"

Voel looked up to say, "You two bicker like children."

Theodore began to raise his voice and said, "What it tells me, Carl, is that you are a– "

I stepped between them and pushed them apart. "Will you two shut the fuck up already?" I turned to Carl. "You're acting like a goddamn child. Weren't you the one telling me to get my head in the game? Well, what do you call this?" And then I whipped around to Theodore. "And will you please just drop it about the promotion? No one cares about your stupid promotion. If we don't send these demons back to Hell, there's not going to *be* a promotion and then it won't matter to any... one..."

I froze. Everything Abraham Lincoln had told us was starting to make total sense. A dark realization began to sink in.

"We're going to lose," I muttered to myself.

"What?" Theodore asked.

"Lincoln," I told him. "He said you'd get your promotion, but by then it wouldn't matter to anyone. Not even you." I grabbed him by the jacket and pulled him close. "We are going to *lose*."

"Oh, we are not," Theodore said. "You don't know that."

"I *do* know that," I said. "Lincoln told us."

"Lincoln said my promotion wouldn't matter, sure," he said. "But that doesn't mean we're going to lose."

"Then what does it mean, huh?" I shoved him away from me. "You're the brilliant investigator who figures everything out. What else could it mean?"

"I don't *know*," he said, getting agitated. Maybe he didn't want to believe my doom and gloom, or maybe what I was saying was actually resonating with him and that's what scared him. Either way, he seemed determined to disagree with me. "What I *do* know is that if we go into this *thinking* we're going to lose, then we're going to lose. But if we going to this ready to kick ass, then we'll kick ass. So which one do you want to do?" He grabbed me by the shoulders and straightened me out. "Do you want to give up? Or are you ready to kick ass?"

I shrugged and meekly replied, "I guess I'm ready to kick ass."

Carl laughed at the both of us. "You two sound like you've never saved the world before."

I didn't say anything to Carl. I did, however, give him a warning with a stern glare and a finger in his face. I had saved the world plenty. I didn't need pointers and I didn't need advice. I turned to bid Ilana good luck on her end of the plan. She sat grinning in Denali's back seat, super fascinated by everything she just witnessed.

"This is like watching a TV show," she said. "I don't really understand what's going on, of course, but I am super down with everything that's happening. Do I get to catch up with you guys later and send demons back to Hell, too?"

"I'm going to say probably not." I glanced back at Carl to see if Ilana could send demons back to Hell with us. Carl shook his head no. Yeah, I didn't think so. I turned back to Ilana. "I don't think that's such a good idea."

"But, Miss Rittenberg," Carl said, reassuring her. "You have the most important job of all."

"Right," she said. "Open Pier 83."

"Yes, there's that," Carl said. "But more importantly, I want you to get on the computer and look up a reputable window washing company that has good reviews. Honest reviews. And I'm talking five-stars here, *minimum*."

"Uh." As if everything we threw at Ilana wasn't enough, this one really confused her. "Okay. I guess."

"Thank you kindly." Carl gave Ilana a pat on the shoulder, then closed Denali's door. "Godspeed, young lady."

3

Denali drove off and her tail lights disappeared into the sheets of rain. With the streets flooded, it would take them some time to reach Westland HQ. The city's emergency alert sirens were whooping and wailing, echoing over the bay, warning everyone to seek cover from the intensifying storm. Lightning flashed up in the clouds and illuminated the dark, roiling sky. Thunder clapped in the distance and echoed its way across Manhattan. Waves crash against the docks and sprayed clouds of mist into the air.

Our plan was simple: Travel through the abandoned subway systems of old New York, reach the containment chamber for Untouchable Orange in the Westland basements where Carl would use his CEO passkey to shut the system down, then we'd steal the little orange marble of infinite power.

And if, in all of that, we happened to bump into Asag or Lylo, Voel promised to help us destroy their bottles. She gave us her "solemn word" for whatever that's worth, coming from a demon.

The four of us stood there in the shelter of a big metal awning and waited patiently for Ilana to arrive at work and remotely open the doors. Carl and Voel were having a conversation, but the rain was drumming so hard on the metal overhang that I couldn't hear a word they were saying. I watched their lips move and I could tell by their faces they weren't happy, but all I could hear was rain and thunder.

The wind picked up hard and the rain started to blow in sideways. Voel yelped and covered her face. Carl whipped off his suit jacket and threw it over her to protect her from the water. Voel maneuvered her way behind all of us, desperately shaking the rain out of her hair with her hands.

From inside the faux brick wall came an electronic hum as power surged to the electromagnets, then went CLACK as the locks released. *Nice work, Ilana. Mission Accomplished.* Moving on hydraulic pistons, the brick wall swung open like a bank vault and revealed a dark loading tunnel that lead underneath the city.

Carl hurried Voel through the opening to get her out of the storm. Theodore and I followed them in. the storm. Once inside the tunnel, large halogen lights fizzled on above us, humming at half-power as they warmed up. Carl entered a few buttons on a nearby keypad and shut the doors behind us.

Voel stood there in the middle of the tunnel and furiously flapped her arms. "I hate rain!" she shouted. The more pissed off she got, the faster the rain sizzled and steamed right off her body. "How did I let you humans talk me into this!?"

"Is it always like this when you save the world?" Theodore asked me.

"Not usually," I said. "Usually I'm just flying solo. I'm not really what you'd call a 'team player.'" I did the air quotes. "At least that's what my guidance counselor used to tell me, but she'd been divorced four times, so take that for what it's worth."

"Follow me, everyone," Carl said. He took out his pistol, clacked a bullet into the chamber, then started down the tunnel. "No time to waste."

We followed behind him, Theodore and I. Voel brought up the rear, fuming about being wet and bitching the whole time. She bounced in place with each step, shaking her right leg, then her left, desperately trying to dry them off.

The floors of the tunnel had old-school subway tracks of wood and iron. The stone walls were coated in mildew. I could see where more modern trucks had passed through here before; their tire tracks were still imprinted in the muck beneath our feet. As the tunnel sloped down and down, further and deeper, the sounds of the storm faded. Eventually things went silent. The sound of our shoes squishing through the mold and murky puddles filled the air.

I know New York City fairly well and thought I could use our distance traveled to keep track of what parts of the city we were crossing beneath in relation to the surface, but I quickly gave up on that idea. It wasn't as easy as I initially thought.

"Where do you think we are?" I whispered to Theodore.

"In an old subway," he whispered back.

"No, I mean..." God, Theodore never failed to amaze me, how he could be both so smart and yet so dumb at the same time. "I mean, what are we crossing under?"

"Oh." He looked up and around, as if the walls of the tunnel held some sort of clue. "Hell's Kitchen," he said. "We're just now crossing underneath 9th Avenue, if I had to guess."

I looked at the same walls he did, but I didn't see what he was seeing. All I saw was moss and old bricks from 1906. "Are you sure?" I asked him.

He nodded with confidence. "Pretty sure."

"How can you tell?"

"Well," he said. "9th Avenue used to have an elevated passenger train running over it until the '40s. If you look real close in the corners..." He pointed above us in a couple different directions. "You can still see the support struts."

Sure enough, I *could* see the support struts. Huh. I learned something new. And Theodore, who actually was a remarkable investigator, just kept right on walking, somehow delightfully unaware of his own genius.

Eventually we reached our first deserted subway station.

The architecture was like nothing I had seen in New York City before: giant archways that criss-crossed one another and shattered stained glass, almost like some kind of haunted cathedral. It was crazy to think that such a huge underground space existed beneath the city, especially something that wasn't even being *used*. Faded posters were stuck to the walls, mostly propaganda from World War One. The door to the restrooms had been long ripped off and things were pitch dark inside.

If the hobos who lived underground had truly formed their own society, as the rumors oftentimes said, then this was where they were holding court.

We followed Carl along the platform of the empty station.

"You own all this?" I asked Carl.

"I bought them wholesale from the city," Carl said. "It's not particularly useful to anyone, but it's still real estate and the city wasn't big on the idea of selling. But it's too old to maintain and too expensive to fill in with concrete, so when I showed up with dump trucks full of money, they couldn't really say no."

"Where did you get dump trucks full of money?" I asked.

"Well, don't let me mislead you," he said. "I *rented* the dump trucks."

I nervously glanced around. If anything living in New York had taught me anything, it's that entire civilizations of mutated rat-people were living beneath the manholes of New York City. I used to think that were true, then I thought they were just stories, but lately, with demons and self-actualizing souls and open portals to Hell, I didn't know *what* to think anymore.

"Doesn't the city ask what you're doing down here?" I asked.

"Funny thing, no," Carl said. "The city commissioners who knew this was even down here aren't around anymore. And the new people are completely unaware this place even exists.

"Surely *someone* knows this is down here," I said. "It's a whole freakin' subway."

"Well, there was this one time..." Carl began. "A reporter from the Times decided they'd be a Snoopy Sam and started poking their nose around down here. I have no idea how he found his way in. I think he was writing a book."

"And you caught him?" I asked.

"Oh, yes," he replied.

I was afraid to ask my follow up question. "What'd you do?"

Carl didn't answer. He just glanced over his shoulder at me with raised eyebrows.

"What?" I asked.

"They killed him," Theodore muttered at me.

I couldn't believe it. "You killed a reporter?"

"*I* didn't kill him," Carl said, defensively. "And technically that reporter is *missing*. But, yes, he is also very dead."

I opened my mouth to state the obvious – that what he had done was wrong – but he didn't give me the chance.

"And before you start in on one of your lectures," he said, cutting me off before I even had a chance to get started. "Yes, I know killing people is wrong. But you have to see things my way. If that reporter discovered what we were really doing down here, and if he told every John Q. Taxpayer in New York City, if your average Joe Schmoe were suddenly forced to confront the dangers that lurk in every shadow, well, there'd be chaos in the streets. Economies would collapse. Entire countries would fall. So if one nosy reporter comes along and threatens to put a pickle in the whole dill, well then... how I see it, that one reporter needs to befall an air conditioner accident from the eleventh floor."

I glared at him. "How very Westland of you."

"He is correct in his philosophy, you know," Voel said to me. "The truth can be a dangerous thing. Believe me, I would know."

"You don't approve of my methods, Miss Salvo?" Carl asked.

"Of course I don't," I said, "No one would."

"No one?" he asked.

"No one *sane*," I clarified. "No one not a psychopath."

"Oh, Penelope, do wake up and smell the vanilla cappuccino. Just because people don't approve of a job doesn't mean it shouldn't be done. New Yorkers eat one million hamburgers every day, but I doubt a single one of them would have the guts to press a nail gun to a cow's head and pull the trigger. It *has* to be done, but they expect someone else, a *stranger*, to do the job. If you didn't have a man to kill the cows... if hamburgers somehow vanished from this city for six months or maybe a year, or if they were told hamburgers were *never* coming back... those same New Yorkers would be flipping city buses and lighting them on fire."

I looked at Theodore.

Theodore shrugged. "He's not wrong."

"So, yes, it's a dirty job keeping this secret," Carl continued. "And, yes, maybe there's some innocent blood splattered on a couple air conditioners at the dump. But in this case, we are simply the stranger with the nail gun. Nosy reporters are the cows. And disapprove all you like, Miss Salvo, but tasty tasty hamburgers will always be on the menu."

I felt sick. Not because he was talking about murder. But because with the way he explained it... it kind of made sense.

4

We made out way down one of a dozen empty subway tunnels. Carl seemed to know exactly the direction we needed to go, turning left and right and following maze-like curves in the path. We were going deeper and deeper into the earth. The air turned cold. Water dripped from the ceiling and it smelled like the Hudson.

We turned one more corner and the tunnel opened up into another abandoned subway station, except this one was converted into a construction zone. There were industrial power tools there, like two-man circular saws big enough to cut through an entire tree trunk, and massive drills the size of car engines, and a system of chains and pulleys attached to the ceiling to help lift some serious tonnage.

Scraps of clear glass were scattered all around us.

"This is where we built the walls of the containment chamber," Carl said. "Cutting glorious glass is a very expensive process. All of these tools were all blessed by Pope John Paul the Second. They have to be operated by a team of priests."

"You have priests working for you?" I asked.

"Eh, I just had a bunch of my agents get ordained online," Carl said, as if it were no big deal. "You fill out your name. It takes two minutes. Maybe it's a loophole, but it's worked so far and between you and me, real priests ask too many questions."

I picked up a scrap of glorious glass about four-foot long and pretty narrow, like a broomstick. It felt cold to the touch and made my skin tingle. I'd touched glorious glass a couple times before, but I couldn't help but play with it. I mean, the stuff actually came from Heaven.

"Don't *touch* that!" Voel snapped, recoiling away from me. Just being in the mere presence of glorious glass made her visibly uncomfortable. "I can hear it. It rings like crystal."

Out of nowhere, I heard the opening riff to that old '90s song, *Flip Fantasia*. Carl fumbled with his pockets and pulled out his cell phone. Right. That was his ring tone.

Theodore and I gathered around as Carl checked the caller ID. I didn't recognize the number, but it was a 212 area code so the call was coming from Manhattan.

"It's the reception desk," Carl said. He answered the phone and put it on speaker. "This is Carl."

"Mister Carl?" It was Ilana. She was whispering. "Something happened over here. Men with guns are running all over the place. One of them said something about a security breech. Maybe I'm being paranoid, but I think they're on to you."

Theodore and I exchanged worried looks.

"Don't say anything else," Carl said. "Hang up. Get out of there. Fast."

"I don't know, dude," Ilana said. "I think they're... uh oh..."

There was a scuffle. The line went dead.

We stared at the phone for a while – CALL ENDED – then the screen went black. Carl silently put his phone back in his pocket.

"Is she okay?" I asked.

Carl just walked away from me. "Tough to tell."

I followed after him. "Is Ilana dead!?"

"Possibly," he said.

"Dude!" I caught up to him and yanked him back by the sleeve. "You sent her on a suicide mission!"

"She did what we needed her to do." He sounded tense, not his usual flighty self. "That's all you can ask of a Westland agent."

"She's not a Westland *agent*," I said. "She's a receptionist!" I wanted to argue more, but I could tell by the blank stare on Carl's face that it was pointless. He wasn't going to listen. It was all cows and nail guns to him. And even if I could convince him I was right, what good would that do Ilana now? I muttered the rest of my thought. "She's my friend from high school."

"They're on to us." Theodore drew his gun and scouted out the surroundings. "They could be sending people down after us right now. We need to move, and double time."

Carl raised his gun and scouted a little ahead of us. I tightened my fists. We moved quicker through the construction equipment. Voel strolled along behind us, way too slow to keep up.

"Voel!" Theodore whisper shouted. "Come on!"

But Voel turned up her nose and sniffed the air. "Do you humans smell that?"

"Shit and mildew," I said.

"Not that," Voel said. "More like..." She stopped and sniffed a couple more times. "Oh no."

Asag unfurled from the ceiling like a butterfly flapping on wings of human skin.

All I could get out was "Oh, sh-"

Then he landed on us.

Tentacles of skin stretched like taffy out from his body. A squishy, boneless hand grabbed my throat and slammed me up against the bricks. My cheek was pressed right up against layers of wet mildew. Another tentacle of skin came after Theodore. He managed to fire his gun off, but the bullets did nothing. The skin pythoned around his chest and tightened down on his neck. He croaked in pain. A third tentacle grabbed Carl by the ankle and hoisted him into the air like the catch of the day.

Voel, on the other hand, went untouched. In that moment, I really hoped we could trust her. She put her hands up and slowly approached the monster.

"Asag," she said. "Skin Collector. You've grown."

And he had. More skin draped from his body than ever before. He stood ten feet tall.

"Sister?" Asag said. His voice came out of the many mouths covering different pieces of skin. All his mouths spoke in simultaneous whispers. His "real" mouth, hidden beneath that sheet of skin that covered his bulbous head, did not move; only his stolen ones. "Young sister. Is that you?"

"It is." She rested her open palm on his chest.

Yes! I thought. *Rip the bottle out of him.*

"Sister," Asag said. "You come with humans?"

"Not at all," Voel replied. "These mudblobs have been keeping me prisoner in Queens. I can here to find you. I've come to rejoin you and Sister Lylo."

Asag's many eyelids squinted. What few nostrils he had pock-marking his skin-sheet sniffed and snorted. Then, as if he smelled something disgusting, he tensed up.

A flap of skin shot out, gripped Voel by the hair and yanked her head back. She growled in surprise.

Asag said, "You deceive, sister."

"I do not!" she shouted. "Wasn't it I who led you out of Hell? Wasn't it I who traveled with you through the endless fog of Limbo? Trust me! I have come to be with you once again."

I hoped she didn't really mean that, but Asag seemed to believe her. He loosened his grip on her hair and let her go. A forest green tear rolled down her cheek.

That confused him.

"Why cry, cruel sister?" he asked.

Face to face, she answered him. "I'm sorry."

She punched her fist through his rib cage and plunged it deep into his chest.

It took a moment, but Asag's many mouths let out a horrible shriek. The subway station trembled at the sound of it. Light bulbs shattered. Industrial equipment rattled in place. Mortally wounded with a hand in his chest, Asag loosened the grip on my neck. He dropped Carl to the ground. I heard Theodore, who had nearly suffocated, suck in a deep breath.

Voel ripped her hand back out of Asag's chest. In it, she held his bright red bottle, twisted and cracked in places.

"Sister?" he whimpered.

Asag used his "real" arm to backhand Voel and launch her across the tunnel. She landed on the cobblestones and slid face-first through the puddles. The demon bottle clattered across the subway rails and into the darkness.

I looped my arms around the tentacles of skin once wrapped around my neck and yanked. I pulled Asag off balance.

Theodore raised his gun, aimed, and fired off a few rounds that thumped the demon right in the head.

Asag turned his attention to Theodore. "Guns?" he hissed. "You trifle me with guns?"

The skin whipped back around Theodore's neck and squeezed. Before I had a chance to act, Theodore spread his feet and began to back away, pulling and stretching the skin. I had no idea where he thought he was going until I saw him angle the skin across the blade of the huge circular saw. He slammed his fist down on the red activation button. The blade screamed to life and the online-priest-blessed blade sliced right through the unholy flesh. Both ends of the severed tentacle flopped to the ground and thrashed around like wounded snakes.

Asag howled. With his real mouth. From underneath his mask of skin.

I took Theodore's idea and ran with it. I grabbed the power drill, the one about the size of a motorcycle and just as heavy, and charged right at Asag. I found the power switch just in time. The drill whirred to maximum speed right as I plunged the pointy-end deep into his lower back. It met with some resistance, so I pushed harder and it sank deeper into his guts.

Carl sprinted for Asag's bottle and kicked it towards Voel. Carl wasn't going to be playing for FIFA anytime soon, because the bottle went right past Voel and up against the subway ledge.

"Get it!" I shouted. "Quick!"

Voel scrambled to her feet and went after it, spitting dirty puddle water out of her mouth.

Asag's many eyes darted around, suddenly realizing it was his very soul we were after. He powered through the pain and sent four tentacles of skin for Voel. They bound her wrists and ankles. She struggled against them and fought her way closer to Asag's bottle, but wasn't strong enough.

I pulled the drill out of his body and stabbed it back into him in a different place. His mouths howled in agony, but that's all I got out of him. It wasn't enough. He kept his grip on Voel.

"Penelope!" Carl called out from behind me. "Duck!"

No time to ask why. When you're fighting a demon and someone says to duck, you duck.

So I ducked.

Just in time, too. Carl came sprinting in from behind, waving a bar of glorious glass. With a full wind up and a swing, he bashed Asag right across the back of the head with a sick, wet thump. The glorious glass rang like a tuning fork.

Asag howled in pain. So did Voel. The heavenly tone that sounded so celestial and pleasant to me was apparently causing them both an unimaginable amount of pain.

I pulled the drill out and stabbed Asag a third time, right in the rib cage. Black sludge sprayed everywhere.

"Hit him again!" I shouted to Carl.

Carl danced around the demon like a baseball player, got into position right in front of him and swung again. Impact. Dead center, right in the side of the head. Black globs of shit splattered across the both of us. The whole chamber rang with the sound of resonating crystal.

Asag screamed again and let go of Voel. Voel dropped to the floor, also in pain, but she immediately crawled for the bottle.

"Sister!" Asag called out. Black sludge drooled from the seams of his skin-suit. "I beg you!"

"Voel!" I shouted. "Do it!"

Voel snatched the bottle up in her hand. The black ooze of her bother's guts dripped from her fingers. She held the glass container in front of her like someone might hold a human heart. Instead of smashing it, she stood there, hypnotized by its shape.

"Destroy it, Voel!" Theodore shouted.

"Cursed!" Asag called out. "You are cursed if you betray me! You will no longer be our sister!"

Voel looked like she might cry, she was so conflicted. Dammit, she was losing her nerve. But just when I thought she was going to chicken out, she tightened her jaw, lifted her arm up into the air and smashed the bottle on the ground.

5

Voel stood over her brother's shattered bottle. I couldn't imagine what that must have felt like to her.

Black slime and chunky bits of goo splattered everywhere. My nose was immediately hit with the foul scent of shit and sulfur. All of Asag's mouths exhaled. The breath sounded deep and sad, almost disappointed. The stitches holding his various skins together began to unravel. He dropped to one knee, then to the other. After one more breath, he collapsed completely.

"I curse you," he groaned at Voel. Only a couple scraps of skin were left to cover his body, revealing his bloody and skinless muscles. "You will smell strange to us now." He tilted his head up to Voel, with his skin-mask slowly sliding off his wet face. He looked at her and said, "You are not our sister."

He slumped to the ground. The rest of his skin came undone. His bloody muscles lost all cohesion and he melted into a red puddle of hazardous waste.

Voel didn't look away from him, not even after he was dead. The corners of her mouth turned down, slowly building up anger, either with herself or Asag or the whole situation.

The pool of melted Asag spread across the cobblestones. For the very first time, I got the sense that maybe we could actually pull this off. Maybe, just maybe, we could save the world.

Voel still hadn't moved.

"Hey," I said as I approached her. "You alright?"

She squeezed her eyes shut and all her rage came blasting out. "This is all your fault, mudblob! You brought me here! You made me do this! You made me kill my brother!"

"Goddammit, Voel," I snapped back. "You knew what this was. You said it yourself, if Isobella opens that portal to Hell, God's going to come down here with some Old Testament shit that's going to be a million times worse that what we did to Asag."

She got quiet. "I betrayed by brother," she said. "I killed a fallen angel. I deserve oblivion."

"Dammit." We didn't need Voel losing her cool, not now that we were so close to the end. I looked around. "Carl? You want to say something here?"

"Yeah." Carl checked his phone. "I say we keep moving. Untouchable Orange is at 5,000 degrees and climbing. That portal's going to be open soon."

Carl marched along the subway rails and disappeared down the next dark tunnel. He wasn't going to wait for us to get our act together. I looked to Theodore.

Theodore picked up that bar of glorious glass, the one Carl used to bash Asag's head in. "I'm bringing this with me."

If anyone was going to get Voel's head in the game, it was apparently going to have to be me.

"Voel," I said. "I know this might not mean much, but I was raised Catholic. I was raised to believe that demons were bad." I inched my way towards the tunnel exit, following Carl and Theodore. "But I don't think that's true. You were good when you were an angel and I think you're still good now. I don't think God can take that away from you, no matter how much he twists up your mind and your body. And you can prove it, to him and me and everyone. But you can only do that if you come with me."

I headed down the dark subway tunnel and out of view. Either she was coming, or she wasn't, but I didn't have time to sit around and wait. Untouchable Orange was about to open a gateway to Hell and we didn't have any more time to waste.

"Mudblob, wait," Voel said. I turned back to see her slump her shoulders and come walking after me. "I will continue to assist you. I will not let myself be twice subjected to the wrath of the Being Yahweh."

"Good." I gestured for her to catch up. "Because between you and me, I don't think we can do this on our own."

Chapter 25

1

We made pretty good time crossing Manhattan on foot when we weren't stopped by traffic lights and droves of lost tourists, but it still took a solid twenty minutes to reach the end of the abandoned subway system. The very last tunnel led us into the lowest levels of the underground chamber hidden beneath Westland HQ. The cavern looked so much bigger from the bottom, as if we stood in the drained chasm of an ancient ocean.

Dead-ahead of us sat the house-sized containment cube of glorious glass. It glowed bright orange as Untouchable Orange burned like a miniature star, reaching temperatures hot enough to liquefy steel. Reality itself bubbled and burst as the thin border between Earth and Hell began to melt away.

Carl took one single step out of the tunnel when I was suddenly overwhelmed with dread. Danger. Westland agents were waiting for us, I just knew it. I didn't know *how* I knew it, I just knew it. They were positioned all along the catwalks, dozens and dozens of them armed with assault rifles and shotguns other futuristic pieces of weaponry.

We were walking into a trap. A poorly laid trap, sure, but a trap nonetheless.

Before being spotted, I grabbed Carl by the back of his suit and yanked him back into the darkness of the tunnel.

I pushed him up against the wall.

Carl looked down at my hand on his chest, then up into my eyes. "Care to explain yourself, young lady?"

"Shh." I put a finger to my lips and made sure he was going to stay quiet. He didn't say anything. I whispered, "Westland soldiers. They're already out there."

"Did they see us?" Theodore asked.

"No," I said. "I don't think so."

Carl kept his back against the wall and said, "Well, we can't just stay here and do nothing. I have to get to the top level and reroute the system."

"You'll never make it," I said. "They'll fill you full of holes before you even reach the catwalks." I held out my open palm. "Give me the key card. I can jump up there and do it myself."

Carl chuckled. "Oh, can you? Tell me, Miss Salvo, how many computer languages do you know?"

"Absolutely zero."

"And how many host-side system purges have you executed?"

"I don't know what any of those words mean."

"That's why I have to do it," he said.

I wasn't a computer programmer, but neither was Carl. I'd seen his computer expertise in action before.

I said, "Dude, you can't even run a powerpoint presentation."

Carl was totally taken aback, super offended. "You didn't like my powerpoint?"

"It was filled with clip art! looked like a 3rd grader made it!"

"Well, now that's just rude." He crossed his arms and refused to look at me. "Now I *have* to do it just to prove you wrong. Get me to the top in one piece. I'll show you."

I sighed. "Fine." I turned to the group as a whole. "Then I'll go out first and draw their fire. While they're wasting bullets on me, Theodore, you cover Carl and get to the catwalks. Voel, keep an eye out for your sister and..." Voel wasn't with us. She had somehow vanished. "Voel?"

Voel marched defiantly out of the tunnel and into the chamber. She raised her voice to the soldiers waiting in the levels up above.

"Damn you, Sons of Adam!" she shouted at them. "Damn you, Daughters of Eve!"

The Westland soldiers opened fire. There were dozens and dozens of them lined up along the rails of the catwalks, each one armed with a heavy assault rifle, clad in riot armor and bullet-proof face shields. The chamber echoed with the rattle of gunfire and the walls lit up like a fireworks display.

Bullets glanced off Voel's skin like stone. If there's one thing I'd learned about demons, they take it as a personal insult when they're shot at with guns. Her breathing turned ragged and her chest heaved. After a few seconds of tolerating their pitiful attack, she crouched down, then launched herself into the air like a pissed-off wildcat. He flew twenty, thirty, forty feet straight up into the air and landed on the catwalks.

The soldiers kept their rifles trained on her, even as she came in for a landing right next to them. Voel backhanded one soldier in the chest and cracked him in half. The soldier on her other side held the barrel of his machine gun an inch away from her temple and blasted her. Bullets thumped against her lime green skin, but her head didn't even budge. She grabbed the goon by the front of his bulletproof armor and chucked him over the safety rails. The poor guy landed head-first on the stone floor and collapsed like a sack of wet laundry.

"Looks like *she's* drawing the fire," Carl said as he advanced on the tunnel exit. He looked back at me to say, "I guess you'll have to find something else to do."

This wasn't the plan, but Voel was certainly doing a great job keeping the soldiers preoccupied. Releasing all the rage she had bottled up after decades of captivity and the grief she felt from killing her own brother, the Deranged Painter belted out nonsensical, primitive screams. She sprinted along the catwalks with unholy speed, stopping once to grab two soldiers and smash their heads together, and a second time to and crush one of their skulls against the wall.

Carl and Theodore made a mad dash past the containment chamber and headed up into the catwalks. A handful of soldiers noticed them and quickly switched targets from the rampaging, bulletproof demon to the two very mortal human beings. I could see events unfolding right in front of me: the soldiers would open fire, Theodore would get filled with bullets and go down, and Carl would fall soon after.

I wasn't going to let that happen. I dashed to save them, moving so fast that it probably looked like I had stepped through the shadow-realm and teleported to their position, just in time for the bullets to hit me instead of them.

It felt like being pelted with marshmallows. My clothes fluttered as a hail of gunfire thumped up against my body. Whatever few bullets got past me thumped harmlessly against Carl and Theodore's bulletproof Westland suits.

Theodore used me as cover and returned fire. He popped up over my shoulder and picked off a few soldiers with his gun. He had pretty good aim considering we were on the move and his targets were three stories above us.

A live grenade clattered across the stone in front of us. I pulled Carl and Theodore close to me and put my back to the explosive. The grenade went off. Fire and shrapnel blew across my back and harmlessly to the side.

The smoke cleared. The catwalk in front of us was a mangled mess. I wrapped Carl up tight in one arm, Theodore in the other, and leapt over it. Together, we started up the catwalks.

Voel climbed higher and higher, lost in the upper levels of the chamber. I couldn't quite see her, but I could hear her. Oh, could I hear her. It sounded like a starving badger tearing up a bird sanctuary. Soldiers fell down all around us. The bounced off the railings and crunched on the hard rock below.

A bullet zipped past me and plugged Carl right in the shoulder. His suit absorbed the shock, but he still yelped in pain. It was going to leave one hell of a welt.

"You good?" I asked.

"I'll live," Carl hissed. "We have to keep going."

A rocket scorched its way across the chamber in our direction, laving a trail of smoke behind it. God damn, they were using rocket launchers now? I hooked Carl and Theodore under my arms and jumped forward. The rocket exploded and wrecked an entire section of catwalk. A fireball washed over us and I could only hope that those Westland suits were just as fire resistant as they were bulletproof.

All around us, pieces of catwalk broke loose from the wall and clattered to the ground. These soldiers were determined to kill us, even if it meant destroying the place.

Voel dropped down from above and whizzed past us. She clung to a soldier and slashed through his helmet with her sharp nails. Ribbons of blood whipped through the air.

The two of them landed at the bottom. Even over the gunfire and explosions, I could hear the poor guy's bones crunch.

Walkie-talkie chatter filled the air.

"Intruders in basement level 5!"

"It's Penelope Salvo!"

"We need back-up, now!"

"Send in the big guns!"

"Big guns?" Theodore repeated. He took aim from around the side of my body and landed a few headshots on a couple soldiers. "That can't be good, can it?"

"Don't stop moving!" Carl said. "We have to reach the-"

And that's about when our luck ran out.

A porcelain hand grabbed me by the face and bashed my skull against the stone wall. My vision scrambled. My audio hissed. When my senses cleared, I got a good look at who did it.

Lylo. She stared me down with those bubblegum pink eyes. Black lace floated around her body like cobwebs. With celestial-class strength, she grit her teeth and pressed my head harder against the wall. I felt pressure building up around my brain. Something cracked. I hoped it was the stone and not my skull.

With her other hand, Lylo reached out and knocked Carl and Theodore out of her way. Theodore dropped his gun and his bar of glorious glass. Carl laid sprawled out across the catwalk floor, just barely teetering on the edge. They both looked at me, wondering what to do next.

Silently, I mouthed the word, "Run."

They wanted to help me. I could see it on their faces, but even if they could, we didn't have that kind of time. So they did what I told them to do.

They ran.

And so what if I got my ass handed to me by a demon? It wouldn't be the first time, and probably wouldn't be the last. All that mattered in that moment was shutting down Untouchable Orange and in order to do that, we needed Carl alive.

So if Lylo wanted to waste her time on a rematch with Penelope Marie Salvo, then I was more than happy to oblige.

"Remember my face," Lylo said. She pulled my head back, just so she could bash it into the wall again. "I am the exalted empress of your oblivion."

"That..." Damn, it was hard to talk with her crushing my skull, but I just had to spit it out. "That's metal as fuck."

I wasn't going to drop Lylo one-on-one. I needed Voel for that. I needed Voel to come crush this bitch's bottle. Unfortunately for me, Voel was nowhere close. I could hear the Deranged Painter down at the bottom level, savaging her way through Westland soldiers.

I was on my own.

Lylo stepped back and materialized green and red pieces of Chernobylite from thin air. Armed with the two deadly crystals, she lunged for me, ready to stab me through the chest. I dropped prone on the catwalk. She missed and sank her Chernobylite into the stone. I scrambled away from her as fast as I could, right over to the bar of glorious glass that Theodore had dropped. I swept it up and climbed to my feet.

Lylo saw what I was holding and took a single cautious step backwards.

"Oh, ho, ho. You don't like that at all, do ya?" I waved my glorious glass around like a baseball bat. "What do you think of my new little toy? Smell familiar?"

I tapped it on the catwalks so she could hear it ring like a tuning fork. It sang like angels.

Her eye twitched. Good.

Desperate and out of options, Lylo slashed at me with her Chernobylite shards. I smacked them away with my glorious glass. I'm not much of a sword fighter, but I *was* born in New York City and it's in my DNA to swing a bat. Every time she swiped her crystals at me, I knocked them away. Each time our attacked collided, the screams of tortured demons came from her weapons and the sound of singing angels came from mine. We kept swinging at one another, harder and harder, and the screaming and singing got louder and louder. So loud, in fact, that it started to screw with my balance. Still, I kept fighting.

Lylo lunged and slashed at me like an Olympic fencer. I swung at her like a crazy person fighting off mall security. In time, her form outpaced mine and she managed to slice me across the upper arm. My skin split open and red chemicals came spilling out.

In my wild fury, I managed to pop her right on her knuckles. Her skin seared like touching a branding iron.

Then, as if summoned by some unspoken command, the Army of Arms came crawling down the walls. They swarmed like roaches over the catwalks. They formed piles over the dead Westland soldiers and tore off their arms. The dismembered arms would lay there for a bit, then wriggle to life and join in the rank. Lylo didn't need to use the Army of Arms to beat me, but that didn't mean she wasn't going to.

Carl and Theodore clattered up yet another level of catwalks. With a gun in each hand, they two of them blasted their way through the Army of Arms. They were slowly making their way through them, but there's no way they had enough bullets to make it to the top. All around them, dozens of arms became hundreds, and hundreds became thousands. One arm landed on Theodore's back. Carl ripped it free and tossed it over the catwalks. A different arm grabbed Carl by the ankle. Theodore whipped around and shot it right through its wrist, killing it.

Theodore was an absolute beast. He didn't miss a single shot. He dropped his empty clips and slapped new ones into his guns with amazing speed. I wasn't even quite sure how he was doing it. Even Carl seemed impressed.

"Did you learn to reload like that in Costa Peligro?" Carl asked.

"Moscow," Theodore answered.

Lylo brought my attention back to the fight with slash across my cheek. I touched my face to see if I was bleeding. Sure enough, motor oil coated my fingertips.

"Dammit." I tightened my grip on my glorious glass. "That better not scar."

"I will take great pleasure in killing you, mudblob," Lylo said.

"Well, I hope you do a better job of it than Asag," I told her. "Because he tried it. And now he's dead."

She turned her head and gave me a sideways stare. "You lie."

"Don't you smell it?" I asked. "Go ahead. Sniff around. I think you might be surprised."

Her nostrils flared once. As the truth set in, storms of darkness swirled through her eyes. Black veins pumped through her fair skin and right up to the surface. She was about to go full rage-mode. Good. I wasn't thrilled with the idea of fighting a pissed-off demon, but at least her attention on me and off Carl.

"Fact is, Asag wasn't even that tough," I added, throwing a little fuel on the distraction fire. "He was a little bitch when he was alive and he's a little bitch now that he's dead."

A growl came from deep inside Lylo, straight from her bottle. Faster than I thought possible, she smacked her two Chernobylite pieces together in my direction. A shockwave of demonic chanting threw me up against the wall, smashing an outline of my body into the stone. Gravity seized me, pulled me down and I I smashed through a couple levels of catwalks before landing face-first at the bottom.

Okay. That one hurt. My vision went black and white for a few seconds. I thumped the palm of my hand against my head until my eyes flickered and the colors came back.

An interlocking web of black arms lowered Lylo down to my level. Some of the arms were new to the army, still wearing the sleeves of the Westland soldiers. Descending by the grace of her most prized minions, she drew closer and closer to me.

Without warning, she smacked her crystals together again and hit me with another blast of sound. Like a plastic sack on a windy day, I tumbled weightlessly across the ground and crunched my hip against the corner of the containment chamber.

I really felt that one. Broken hip. Or at least dislocated.

Lylo loomed over me, now sitting on a makeshift throne of arms. Her crystals glimmered and gleamed in the hellfire of Untouchable Orange.

"Pathetic war god," she growled. "Despite all your power, you are still nothing more than a Daughter of Eve. Here you lay in front of me, broken and conquered."

I spit motor oil at her. "I'm not dead yet."

She poised her crystals in the air. "Yet."

"Sister..."

Voel approached us from behind. Lylo's throne of arms rotated and pointed the dark queen in Voel's direction. Voel took small, humbled steps towards her royal sister. The surrounding Army of Arms made a pathway for her approach. In a nervous tone, she said, "I'm only going to ask you this once. Leave the mudblob alone."

2

With the slow movements of royalty, Lylo brushed the hair and barbed wire from her eyes and leaned forward in her seat.

"You smell odd," Lylo said. "You do not smell like my sister."

"Asag cursed me," Voel said. "Before I..."

Lylo sneered, disgusted. "Before you killed him? Did you slay the Skin Collector, despite our travels through Limbo and our pact forged in the shadows of the Great Nothing?"

Voel answered confidently. "I did. I will not let you open the gates of Hell and bring the Being Yahweh to this world."

"Oh, will you not?" Lylo asked. "Would you slay me as well?"

Voel hesitated, then said, "Please, don't make me."

That made Lylo snicker. She handed her two pieces of Chernobylite to her nearby arms and they carried the weapons off, hiding them someplace safe. Her majesty waved a dismissive hand at me and told her army, "Keep the mudblob here."

Two dozen arms skittered over to me, grasped hard onto my broken body and held me in place. I couldn't fight them off, not until Impossible Red had the chance to repair all the damage I just suffered, especially my broken hip.

"Here." In a melodramatic gesture, Lylo delicately slid her hand through her own rib cage and took out a gray bottle, slender and tall, decorated with unraveling black lace. She steepled it on her fingertips and offered it to Voel. "Take it."

But Voel didn't.

Lylo's face turned to fury.

"I said take it!" she screamed. She grabbed Voel's arm and yanked her forwards. She forced the bottle into her sister's open hand. "Now you hold my bottle, dear stranger! My soul! My very essence! Everything twisted out of me by the Being Yahweh! What do you plan to do with it?"

Voel stared at it, long and hard, then turned her attention back to Lylo. "Nothing," she said.

Lylo grit her teeth. "Break it."

Voel considered it for a moment, but shook her head. "No."

Lylo, furious, shot out of her chair. "I said break it!"

The Army of Arms surrounded us like a blood thirsty mob. I could tell by the way they shifted in place and twiddled their fingers, they didn't like seeing their Queen's soul in the hands of someone else. The only thing standing between existence and destruction were Voel's deeply troubled emotions.

The Army of Arms were on the verge of a riot. Or maybe mutiny. If I didn't know any better, I would have guessed that for the first time in their short little twisted lives, they were secretly planning to act without being ordered to do so, if it meant rescuing Lylo's soul.

"I can't..." Voel looked at me as if this were all my fault. "I can't and I won't."

"Of course you can't," Lylo said. She swiped the bottle away from her. "You're weak. You are a weak little painter. You were weak in the rebellion and you were weak in Hell. If it weren't for me, you'd be crushed beneath the Great Nothing and spending your eternal days in the mists of Limbo."

I hung my head and sighed. I bet the wrong horse. I had put all my chips on Voel and she couldn't see the job through to the very end. What I asked her to do was just too much. And now we were in serious trouble.

"Arms!" Lylo shouted. She pointed at Theodore and Carl at the top levels of the catwalks. "Seize the Sons of Adam! Bring me their arms!"

The Army of Arms went after Carl and Theodore; crawling up the walls, slithering over the catwalks, leaping through the air. Theodore saw them coming. He knew there was nowhere for them to run. The best he could do was slow them down. He pushed Carl ahead and told him to keep running for the top, then he planted his feet, reloaded his pistols and planted his feet.

Theodore blasted at the incoming wave of demon arms. One by one, he picked them off. It was a valiant effort, but even a million bullets wouldn't have been enough. Within seconds, the arms swarmed him. They slapped the guns out of his hands and began yanking on his clothes.

Carl kept running. He was nearly to the control panel.

"You reek of shame and regret," Lylo hissed in Voel's ear. "Should I lift the curse that Asag put upon you?"

Voel blinked tears out of her eyes. "Would you?"

Lylo looked quite satisfied with herself. "I have one drop of forgiveness in my bottle, something I've been saving since we were angels. The Being Yahweh never forgave us for the rebellion. Trillions of years have passed and he has not forgiven us. He will never forgive us. If I don't forgive you now, I'm no better than him." She held her bottle between them. "Swear that you will serve me and my one last drop of forgiveness is yours."

Voel whispered, "Thank you, sister."

They embraced one another. But it wasn't Lylo's intention to forgive and forget. Once she had her sister in a disarming hug, she raised a shard of green Chernobylite into the air. Lylo held it there, ready to stab Voel in the back.

"Voel!" I shouted.

Voel, who had apparently been waiting to back-stab her back-stabbing sister, smacked Lylo's bottle right out of her hand. It bounced across the stone floor and rolled to a stop.

Lylo plunged the Chernobylite deep into Voel's spine.

They both betrayed one another. The problem was: Voel suffered a devastating wound. Lylo's bottle, while knocked clear, did not shatter.

"You are not my sister!" Lylo shouted as she twisted the crystal in Voel's back and then pushed her body to the ground. "You chose these mortals over your own brother!"

Voel laid there, curled up in the fetal position. Green paint spilled from the hole in her back. And there in Voel's blood were shards of glass.

Shards of her broken bottle.

Theodore shouted my name. The arms had him pinned to a wall and were playing tug-of-war with his wrists.

Carl never made it to the control panel. The Army of Arms caught him and dog-piled him to the catwalk. Still, Carl was no quitter. He stuck his fingers into the grid of the catwalk and dragged himself forward, inch by inch. So close, but yet so far.

I was hit with this overwhelming fear that my interpretation of Lincoln's prophecy was about to come true: that all of us were about to die and none of us would be there to stop Untouchable Orange from unleashing pure Hell across the face of the Earth. But if that was going to happen, if that situation was truly inevitable, that didn't mean I was just going to give up. I had to keep fighting. Even if there was a *chance* Lincoln was wrong, I had to keep fighting.

Impossible Red had finished its hasty repairs to my body. I suddenly felt the strength necessary to smash the arms holding me in place. I broke free from their grip, scrambled to my hands and knees and crawled after Lylo's bottle. By the time the dark queen turned around, I already had her soul in my hands. I held it up where she could see it; my last-ditch trump card.

"Call off your arms," I told her. "Let the mudblobs go or you can kiss your bottle goodbye."

Lylo sneered and shook her head. "You are truly testing my patience, Daughter of Eve."

"And you are truly testing mine." I held her bottle high up over my head, ready to smash it down. "Now call them off."

Lylo blinked plainly at me, unfazed by my threats. "Impudent girl," she said. "The Great Nothing of Limbo couldn't break my bottle. During the rebellion, not even Oriel, Archangel of the Shield, could break it."

"Well, this Oriel sounds like a weak-ass bitch," I said.

"Tell me, little mudblob..." Lylo reclined in her throne and crossed her legs. "If these beings of insurmountable power could not break my bottle, what makes you any different?"

"Because I don't plan on breaking it," I said.

Lylo tilted her head, slightly confused.

But I made my intentions very clear. I used my thumb to pop the cork, tilted her bottle back and started gulping it down.

"No!" Lylo stood up from her throne. "What are you doing!?"

Gulp after gulp, foul black liquid filled my mouth. Its slime coated my mouth and tasted like absolute shit.

Oh, Penelope, you're either very smart or very stupid.

Tidal waves of wriggling black arms flooded towards me from the walls and ceiling. They were so intent on stopping Theodore and Carl, they would have to clear the entire cavern to reach me, but that wouldn't take long. Could the combined strength of the Army of Arms destroy my indestructible body? I was about to find out. But if they were going to take me down, I was going to bring Lylo down with me.

I chugged the bottle in seconds flat. With only a little residue left, I held the bottle above my open mouth and shook it, trying to coax the last few drops of her soul onto my tongue.

One drop. Disgusting. It tasted like the dumpsters at Coney Island. Lylo dropped her crystals and they clattered to the ground. Her knees gave out and the loyal arms that formed her throne did their best to support her collapsing weight.

Two drops. I wanted to puke, but I couldn't puke. Impossible Red identified the substance as poison and was doing its best to reject it from my digestive system, but I begged it to play along. *Don't puke it up*, I begged the little nanites. *Please, just trust me and don't puke it up.*

The youth drained out of Lylo's face. Her eye sockets darkened and her hands turned to shriveled skin and bones. She shriveled up into a two-hundred-year-old witch. Strands of her hair fell out and floated to the ground.

The third and final drop of her soul landed in my mouth. The bottle was empty. Lylo's opened her mouth and a faint cloud of dust puffed out. Her body crumbled to ash.

Lylo, the Archdemon of the Army of Arms, was dead.

But not the Army of Arms. They had reached the bottom floor of the chamber and were closing in fast. I raised my fists, prepared to bash as many of them as possible before they inevitably overwhelmed me and tore me to pieces. One by one they grasped onto my body, some of them squeezing down on my ankles, others grasping tight to my wrists. They hooked their fingers into my mouth. They grabbed on to my hair. This was it. Penelope Salvo, age 19, murdered by demons from Hell.

But once they all had their collective hands on me, they didn't pull me apart. They lifted me up into the air.

Strands of black barbed wire looped around my wrists and forearms. Traces of that same barbed wire tangled through my hair. And all around me, circling me like a million loyal subjects, the Army of Arms stood at perfect attention.

Each one of them watched me with their fingertips. I felt a connection with them, something powerful and unspoken. I formed a psychic bond with every single one of them, and with all of them as a whole. I knew their thoughts and they knew mine. Whatever I wanted, they would obey. That's why they existed. They lived to serve me. That's why they loved me.

I had the soul of a demon. I controlled the Army of Arms.

But the connection only distracted me for so long.

I sprinted over to Voel and slid across the floor on my knees. The stab wound in her back went deep into her guts. Green paint soaked into her clothes and puddled up on the floor.

"Are you dead?" I whispered. "Please don't be dead."

"My bottle is cracked," she managed to say. She waved a finger above us. "Leave me. Help Carl. Help Theodore."

Oh god. Poor Theodore. I hoped he still had his arms.

"Arms." Speaking their name commanded their attention. I pointed at Voel's wound. "Apply pressure here. Keep her blood in her body. Don't let her die."

The closest arms obeyed my command. They slapped their palms over Voel's bleeding back and pressed down hard. I could only hope that those arms had been ripped off a well-trained doctor or EMT.

I looked up above me and scanned the catwalks for Theodore. I spotted him four levels above and just barely out of view. I super-jumped back and forth from catwalk to catwalk, higher and higher, until I reached his body. There, I found him slumped against the wall, unconscious, and possibly worse.

"Don't be dead, don't be dead, don't be dead." I ran over and gave him a little shake. "Hey, Theodore. You still with me, buddy? Come on. Say something."

Theodore moved his head and groaned. What a fucking relief.

"I am in a remarkable amount of pain," he muttered. He tried to sit up straight, but winced and collapsed back against the wall. He clutched his right shoulder. "My arm is dislocated."

"You're lucky it's still attached to your body." I hooked my arm under his good shoulder and scooped him up to his feet.

"Come on. We're almost done here."

"Delightful work, Miss Salvo!" Carl called down from above me. He had reached the top and was already fiddling with the computer panel by the main bulkhead door. "You never cease to amaze me with your ingenuity!"

"Glad you approve," I growled.

Such high praise coming from the man who was responsible for all of this bullshit in the first place.

I hurried around the catwalks as fast as I could with Theodore in tow and reached Carl at the top. Carl had inserted his red key card into the control panel, but even with his super-special access, he struggled to get control of the system. He typed on a little keypad, but every time he did, a little LED panel lit up with the words:

ERROR. ACCESS DENIED.

"Gosh dang it, " he muttered, then pressed the buttons again.

ERROR. ACCESS DENIED.

Theodore peered over Carl's shoulder. "Problem?"

"There's no problem," Carl said. "I just can't seem to get into the safety protocols."

"That sounds like a problem," I said.

Carl kept working. "It's not a problem."

Watching Carl operate the control panel was like watching my old history teacher trying to use the wi-fi to connect her laptop to the overhead projector; one big embarrassing failure. Carl stared at the keypad, pushed a couple buttons, then received a negative buzz. He pressed the same buttons over and over again, expecting a different result. He looked really confused.

It was taking for-goddamn-ever.

"Do you want help or...?" I asked him.

"No." He waved me off. "I got it."

"Okay," I said. "Because it doesn't seem like you do."

He gave me a frustrated glance and asked me, "Do you want it done fast? Or do you want it done right?"

Fine. I watched as he tried a few more things. Nothing worked.

"Come *on!*" I said, growing progressively more impatient. "Before the next ice age!"

"It's complicated!" he snapped.

"You said you did this before!"

"I *have* done this before," he said.

Theodore spoke up. "It doesn't look like it."

Carl laughed. "I used to run this whole operation, you know."

"Yeah," I said. "That's how we got into this whole mess in the first place."

"I know you don't mean that," he replied.

Finally, the control panel gave him a pleasant beep. All the red buttons locking us out of Untouchable Orange turned green.

CHIEF EXECUTIVE OFFICER RECOGNIZED
ALL PERMISSIONS UNLOCKED

"See?" Carl took a step back and gave the panel a satisfied nod, quite pleased with his results. "Could a third grader do that?"

Before he could access any of the functions he had unlocked on the control panel, a Heavenly choir echoed throughout the chamber. The melody was beautiful and hypnotic and, most importantly, loud. The singing wasn't in English, and it wasn't that horrible demonic chanting, like Lylo's Chernobylite crystals. This sounded more like Latin, but not exactly Latin.

It was Angelic.

Heavenly clouds formed all along the ceiling until they were a thick, impenetrable layer. Daylight beamed through them, as if the morning sun had risen inside the cavern. Theodore and I had to squint against the brightness. Carl took a pair of sunglasses out of his jacket and put them on. In the center of the clouds, the dark shadow of a human being appeared, descending down like the return of Jesus. A flapping book flew in orbit around the mysterious person like a released dove. At first, I had worried that maybe we were too late and it was the Old Man himself.

But it wasn't the Old Man.

The clouds parted and revealed Isobella Westland.

4

The first words out of her mouth were, "Carlton Carl." Isobella's voice was loud and commanding, like the very voice of God, if God were a woman. "Allow me to extend my sincerest thanks for breaking me through your last line of computerized defense."

"Miss Westland?" Carl asked. He couldn't quite look right at her. Even with the sunglasses, he had to use his hand to protect his eyes from her blazing glory. "Is that you? You look more exalted than the last time we met."

"Such a way with words," she replied. "And you appear to be very much alive, despite my best efforts."

Carl shrugged with a slight smile, as if he were too bashful for the compliment. "Well, I *did* just barely escape."

Isobella nodded, unamused. "And this must be your son."

"That's my boy," Carl proudly replied, slapping Theodore on the back. "He's 252 months."

Theodore raised his gun and aimed it at Isobella's head. I think he knew that bullets wouldn't work on her, but he wasn't about to just stand there and do nothing.

"You ever shot a soul before?" I asked him.

"I've shot *through* a soul," he replied, refusing to take his eyes off her. "When it was still in a body."

Isobella turned her attention to Theodore and said, "I read all about you in your file. You might be surprised to hear that I had a childhood very similar to yours. My father was also a monster hunter. And I, too, was discouraged from making any friends that would otherwise distract me from my training. But I fear the similarities end there. I created the Westland Corporation and saved the world ten times over while you, dear boy, have done little more than shuffle around meaningless paperwork."

Carl scoffed and turned up his nose. "It's not meaningless."

"It *felt* meaningless," Theodore replied.

Then Isobella finally turned her attention to me. "And then we have Penelope Salvo." She laughed a frustrated laugh. "Penelope, Penelope, Penelope. What *am* I going to do with you?"

I crossed my arms. "Not shit, that's what."

I squeezed my hands into fists and bent my knees into a pounce, ready to leap into the air and bash her soul-brains out.

Isobella twiddled her fingers at her orbiting spell book and it locked into place in front of her. The pages flipped around as if by invisible fingers. Without speaking, Isobella cast some sort of miracle.

Golden symbols of the angelic language glowed in a circle around my feet. I'd never seen Angel written down before. The letters were angular and alien-looking. Nothing more seemed to happen besides the runes appearing in a circle around me, but when I leapt off the ground to get my hands on Isobella, I collided into a perfect cylinder of golden light.

I smacked my head good and dropped back down to the ground. Knocked senseless on my hands and knees, I reached out and ran my fingertips across a forcefield of solid gold light that shimmered at my touch. Front, back and side to side, I was trapped in a transparent cage.

I rose to my feet and pressed on the walls of light with my hands. It felt solid. I gave it a few slugs with my clenched fists to test its strength. The harder I punched, the more solid it felt.

"Terribly sorry, Carl," Isobella said. "But your little Italian attack dog is going to have to stay in the kennel until she learns some manners."

"Do I have a dog?" Carl asked. "I don't think I have a dog."

"She meant Penelope," Theodore muttered.

"Penelope's not a dog," he replied.

Isobella floated down closer to us. Her intangible soul passed through Theodore's body and up to the control panel where she leaned in for a closer look.

"I could hack all of your systems but this one," she said to Carl. "Quite the algorithm you have here. What's the trick?"

"I got it from the future," Carl said. "From the year 2234."

Her eyebrows perked up, as if the solution would have never occurred to her and she appreciated its brilliance. "Resourceful," she said. "I would have never guessed. Irrelevant, however, now that you've granted me CEO access. That's all that matters."

She reached out with her finger and pushed a couple buttons.

SAFETY PROTOCOLS DEACTIVATED
TEMERATURE MODE: MANUAL

"Alright, hands in the air, Miss Westland." Theodore aimed his pistol at the back of Isobella's head. "You're being detained. Step back from the-"

Without even bothering to look up at him, Isobella waved her hand through the air. Another circle of Angelic symbols appeared around Theodore's feet and trapped him in a prison cell identical to mine. Satisfied that he was properly restrained, she went back to pushing buttons.

She talked out loud while she worked. "Do you remember when I first recruited you into the Westland Corporation, Carl?"

"Of course I remember," Carl replied. "I was young pup then. Naive. Eager to please."

"And do you remember the speech I gave you about loyalty?"

"Hmm." Carl tapped his finger to his chin. "I believe so, although I can't say I recall it word-for-word."

She glanced back at him with a wild look in her eye. "You're still loyal to me, aren't you, Carl?"

"Honestly?" He sounded uneasy. "I'm going to have to go with a hard 'no.' You've been gone for years and years. I recently became CEO and I like that very much. And just yesterday you tried to murder me with plastic explosives. So I guess you might say that my loyalty has begun to wane."

Isobella kept punching information into the keypad.

I didn't like the words that appeared on the screen.

TARGET HEAT: 10,000 DEGREES FERENHEIT
TEMPERATURE THROTTLE DEACTIVATED
CURRENT TEMPERATURE: 5,003 DEGREES

I slugged my fist against the forcefield of golden light. A spiritual thud resonated all around me, hinting at the divine power that kept me locked in place.

"Uh, ma'am?" Carl said as he approached Isobella with a finger in the air. "I don't think you should turn the throttle off. Untouchable Orange has to slowly build up heat or else it could-"

"I'm not concerned about safety here, Carl," she said, cutting him off. "I need to get my soul back into my body, even if it means destroying everything from here to Boston."

If everything Carl told me about Untouchable Orange was true, then throttling the heat to maximum without taking it slow had the potential to blow the whole thing up and turn New York state into a smoking crater.

I knew this. And Carl knew this because he was the one who told me. But Isobella was cranking the heat to maximum and he wasn't doing anything to stop her.

"Carl!" I shouted. He looked back at me, as if I were going to suggest a course of action. I simply assumed he had some sort of trick up his sleeve. I could tell by the look on his face that he did not, so I told him, "*Do* something."

But Carl didn't move. Carl, who always seemed to be one step ahead of everyone, had been so caught off guard by the arrival of Isobella Westland that he couldn't do anything more than just stand there and watch.

I started to get a really bad feeling about everything.

Below us, Untouchable Orange roared like a blast furnace. The fire burned so hot, I couldn't see the floor; only a blinding orange glow. If something went wrong, if Carl's containment chamber of glorious glass somehow collapsed, the marble would release the unmitigated power of nuclear fission and completely obliterate the Eastern Seaboard.

CURRENT TEMPERATURE: 5,737 DEGREES

Uh. Shit. Untouchable Orange had increased 700 degrees in a couple seconds? That wasn't good. That wasn't safe.

"Shouldn't be long now," Isobella said. Everyone's faces had an orange hue to them, as Untouchable Orange became the strongest source of light. Beads of sweat dotted Carl's forehead.

Even still, Isobella wouldn't stop pressing buttons.

WARNING
MAIN HATCH: RELEASED
CONTAINMENT CHAMBER: COMPROMISED
TEMPERATURE EXCEEDING SAFETY THRESHOLD

The vault door on the containment chamber unlocked with a loud clack. Explosive decompression slammed the door open and a blast of pure hellfire tore it right off its hinges. The colossal slab of glorious glass tumbled weightlessly across the chamber and imbedded itself halfway into the stone. Fire and black smoke gushed from the open doorway. The fossilized floors around the base of the containment chamber immediately melted into lava. The lower catwalks turned bright pink and melted. Man, if any of those Westland agents were still alive down there at the bottom, they were getting roasted alive.

Voel, however, probably felt right at home.

CURRENT TEMPERATURE: 6,577 DEGREES

"Carl!" I punched my fists against the holy light of my prison cell. "Fucking do something!"

Carl looked at me and shrugged. "What could I possibly do, Penelope? I'm just a simple man in a complicated world."

"That's the Carl I remember." Isobella floated over to him and scrutinized his face like a curious specimen of human life. "So indecisive if things don't go according to plan. You do remember

Chernobyl, don't you, Carl? Do you remember how you stood there as the CEO crushed my fingers and sent me to Hell"

Carl nodded, thoughtfully. "I recall that quite well, actually."

"Faced with a difficult decision, your only concern was keeping yourself safe."

"Well." Carl laughed, as if she meant that as a compliment. "I do have a little saying. He who lives and runs away, lives to fight another day. And it's served me quite well up until now."

"Oh, I know." Isobella had a devious smirk on her face. "Tell me, Carl. How do you think it will serve you this time?"

"I couldn't say," he said.

"Do you think I will succeed in rescuing my body from Hell?" he asked him.

Carl gave her question a moment of deliberation. He peered curiously over the railing and down at the absolute Hell being released from his useless, plastic chamber. Pools of lava bubbled to life. The surrounding catwalks melted into red-hot sludge.

CURRENT TEMPERATURE: 7,121 DEGREES

Carl looked back to Isobella. "Well, if your soul is on the other side of that gateway, I'd say you have pretty good odds."

"Well then, in the interest of your own self-preservation..." She put her hand on his shoulder. "Wouldn't it be smart of you to join me?"

"If I wanted to live," Carl said. "Yes. It would."

"Good," she said. "I'd be willing to offer you a promotion."

"A promotion?" Carl repeated. "I'm already the CEO. What are you going to promote me to? Vice-Jesus?"

"Think bigger than just the Westland Corporation." She draped her arm across his shoulders and pulled him close. "Think much bigger. Once Legion is here on Earth and under my control, every supernatural force can either worship me, or face extinction. And I won't stop with just the Earth. I'm talking about everywhere. Heaven. The Guinee. New Beatlemania. Imagine it, Carl: every realm and dimension under my complete control."

Carl's eyes perked up. "Yes, yes. But this promotion..."

"I'm going to need governors, young man. Experienced managers. I can't be everywhere at once... not *yet*, at least... and until then I need people like you rule over those worlds in my name. Imagine it, Carl. Heaven could be yours. Or Chronopolis. Or Cumulonimbus if you want to live in the sky. You'd be so much more than just a CEO. You'd be like me. You'd be a god."

He repeated the word with a dreamy look in his eye. "A god?"

I didn't like the grin that crept across his face.

Isobella was grinning, too. She was breaking through Carl's defenses with the one thing every brainwashed Westland employee wanted out of life.

"It's the biggest promotion I have to offer," she told him.

I could see his eyes glaze over as his imagination ran wild with the possibilities. We were losing him. I had to snap him back into reality. *This* reality.

"Carl." I pressed my palms to the transparent walls and leaned in as close as I could. "Carl, don't listen to her."

"Carl," Theodore said, chiming in, as if his voice might click with him where mine wouldn't. "Dad!"

But he wouldn't even look at us.

"What would I have to do?" Carl asked her, thoughtfully. "To earn this 'promotion'?"

"Simple," she replied. "Prove your loyalty."

CURRENT TEMPERATURE: 8,009 DEGREES

"And how would I do that?" Carl asked.

Isobella nodded her head in Theodore's direction. "The Bible has an interesting anecdote very similar to the situation we find ourselves in right now. When God wanted Abraham to prove his loyalty to him, he asked for a sacrifice. He commanded Abraham to murder his own son. And Abraham obliged."

Theodore looked at me, panicked. "I don't like this."

All the joy drained out of Carl's face. "You want me to..."

"Kill Theodore," she said, finishing the idea for him. "Yes."

Well, Isobella played the wrong card there. Carl was a pacifist. He had never killed anyone, not technically, at least, and he certainly wasn't about to start with his own flesh and blood.

Carl leaned in closer to Isobella and lowered his voice. "I can't kill my own son."

"Of course you can." Isobella floated around behind him. She leaned over his shoulder and pressed her lips to his ear. "It's the only way to know if I can trust you. And honestly, the life of a son you barely know is a small price to pay for unlimited power."

"You do make a compelling argument." Carl stroked his chin. "I could push him over the rails. Technically, it wouldn't be me that killed him. It would be the fall. Or the fire."

I screamed and slammed my palms against my cell. "Carl, you fucking idiot! Don't listen to her!"

Carl advanced on Theodore.

Isobella twiddled her fingers and the angelic spell keeping Theodore trapped began to break down and vanish.

"Carl..." Theodore raised his gun with his good arm and pointed it at his father. Still, Carl kept coming. Theodore backed away, hoping he wouldn't have to kill his dad in self-defense. He had gone as far as he could and his butt hit the guard rails.

"Theodore," Carl said, still coming. "I know this might be hard to believe, but I am actually quite fond of you. So believe me, this isn't personal. This is only business. So, please, put the gun down."

Theodore glanced over his shoulder and down at the boiling fire below. Nothing down that way but certain death.

He kept his gun trained on Carl's chest. "You wouldn't really kill me."

Carl raised a finger into the air. "Ah, but it wouldn't be *me* doing the killing. It would be the fall."

"Dad," Theodore said, trying to reason with him.

"Please don't call me that," Carl replied. "You're only making this more difficult than it already is. You'd do the same if you were in my position."

"No, I would not!" Theodore said, stunned by the accusation.

"Not even for a promotion?" Carl asked.

"No!" Theodore shouted, finally, *finally*, thinking like a regular human being and not a schmuck from Westland. "I wouldn't kill you, not even for a promotion."

Carl shook his head and clicked his tongue, disappointed in his son's answer. "Then you still don't get it." He placed his palm against Theodore's chest. "And I guess now... you never will."

In the end, Theodore couldn't bring himself to shoot his own father, not even when his own life was at stake. Carl, on the other hand, didn't struggle with the same moral crisis. He shoved Theodore right over the rails. Theodore flipped once, then dropped straight down.

I screamed Theodore's name. I threw my body up against my divine prison, but couldn't get free. I had an idea to summon the Army of Arms to catch him and save him...

But it was too late. A human body falls pretty fast and ten stories didn't give me a lot of time to react. Theodore disappeared into the smoke and I heard his body hit the bottom.

I screamed so hard, my voice went digital. I didn't scream curse words, just noise. Left hook and right hook, I drove my fists hard against that cylinder of golden light. The bones in my hands started to break, so I held my breath and punched harder.

I felt like such an idiot. Carl stabbed me, and his *own son*, in the back and I fucking fell for it. And as if Isobella hadn't murdered enough people, she needed to kill Theodore, too? My legs gave out on me. I collapsed to the ground and punched the floor. Chemical streamed down my cheeks and hissed as they burned the catwalks beneath my knees.

"Really, Carl?" I whimpered. "You're own son? Really?"

CURRENT TEMPERATURE: 9,337 DEGREES

"I'm honestly impressed," Isobella said. "I didn't think you were actually going to do it. I simply assumed I was going to have to kill you, too."

"Yeah, sometimes I even surprise myself." Carl stared over the edge of the catwalk just to confirm Theodore had hit the ground. Satisfied that his son had struck the bottom, he turned back around to Isobella. "So what's next, boss?"

"Now." She gave him a pat on the cheek. "Now we wait. My body lies just on the other side of that gateway. And right behind my body stands an army of one trillion demons. Today is the beginning of a whole new world."

"Could I rule Olympus?" Carl asked. "I've always had a thing for Greek food. Especially Gyros."

"Olympus it is," she said. "Consider it yours."

It made me sick to listen to the two of them, already carving out pieces of their evil empire. Carl just murdered his own son for fuck's sake and it didn't bother him in the least. How can fathers just turn their backs on their children like that? What the fuck is wrong with these people?

"I'm going to kill both of you," I growled at them. "Somehow. I swear to god. I'm going to bust out of here and put both of you in the fucking ground."

"Does she always run her mouth this much?" Isobella asked.

"She's just being a Passionate Polly," Carl said. "Dare I say, I think she had a special affection for Theodore. They had so much in common. I can understand why she's upset."

I rubbed my face and tried to calm down. I knew Carl was crazy and I knew he was evil, but I never realized exactly how crazy and evil he could really be.

TARGET TEMPERATURE ACHIEVED
CURRENT TEMPERATURE: 10,000 DEGREES

All the colors on the control panel made a pleasant beeping sound, happily announcing the end of the world.

The border between Hell and Earth cracked open. I slapped my hands to the side of my head and protected my ears from the infinite screams of tortured souls. Then came an earthquake like something out of the Bible. The stone walls of the cavern split wide open.

The smell of sulfur and cooking blood hit my nose.

The shadow of a naked, human woman walked into view inside the containment chamber. Her dark outline stood as a dark blot against the burning brightness, then the body collapsed to her hands and knees. She looked exhausted, but alive. The poor woman – or the person I would normally call "poor woman" if I didn't know it was Isobella Westland – had just escaped Hell. She had two large symbols burned into her skin, one that covered her whole chest and another that covered her back. While I'm not an expert in magic, I'd recently seen my fair share of Angelic symbols. These brands were Angelic; probably some type of protection spell that kept her body immune to the horrible environment of Hell. They kept her alive, but she still looked filthy, tired, and weak.

The naked woman crouched in place. She coughed hard and gasped desperately for air.

Isobella threw her hands in the air. "Genius! What genius! They told me it was impossible! They told me I was wasting my time! But look, Carl. Look at what I've done! I am the first human being to free myself from the inescapable prison of Hell!"

"Quite remarkable, sir," Carl said. "Nothing is impossible for Isobella Westland."

"Just in time, too." Isobella took careful notice of her ghostly fingers and hands. Sparks of glitter drifted away from her spiritual presence as her soulstuff came apart at the seams.

Carl said, "Well, you had better hurry off to your body before..." He paused. "Oh, dear. You might already be too late."

The dark shadow of an entirely different human was down at the bottom. They stumbled through the fire and limped towards the containment chamber.

It was Theodore.

He trudged forward against a waist-deep river of fire and ash. Not only was he somehow alive, he was strong enough to march against the sweeping currents of the blazes of Hell.

Isobella gripped the rails of the catwalk and stared at events unfolding below. It was the first time I'd ever seen her truly speechless. I couldn't say I blamed her; I was having a hell of a time wrapping my head around it myself.

How was Theodore alive? He was taking 10,000 degrees of supernatural fire straight to the face. That's like the inside of a nuclear reactor, or the surface of the sun. Fireproof Westland suits are one thing, but 10,000 degrees should have left him a scorched skeleton, Westland suit or no Westland suit.

Even his hair, windswept by the inferno that pushed back against him, didn't burn off his head.

Isobella's turned her attention turn from her physical body still inside the containment chamber, to Theodore, and then back to her body. That's when the realization must have set in.

"No!" Isobella pounded on the railing. "Stay away from her!"

"I don't have to listen to you!" Theodore shouted over the crackling fire. "You're not my direct supervisor!"

Theodore slogged his way inside the containment chamber and reached Isobella's powerless physical form. He threw his good arm around her neck and trapped her in a vicious headlock. Her body was too exhausted to fight back.

Isobella turned to Carl. "You! Order your son to stop!"

Carl put up his hands. "I'm also not his direct supervisor."

"God *dammit*," Isobella snapped. She flew over the rails and zoomed straight to the bottom. Her spell book followed her like a pet bird. She landed at the entrance to the chamber and faced Theodore, who was holding tight to his newly acquired hostage.

"End of the line, Westland!" Theodore said. "I'm trained in five different forms of hand-to-hand combat. Give up your spell book or I'll twist your head off like I'm opening toothpaste!"

Isobella's mortal body screamed for help. "Do what he says! He's going to kill the both of us!"

Isobella's soul hesitated. She stole a sly glance at the open pages of her spell book.

Theodore noticed. He tightened his headlock on the body's neck and twisted. Isobella's body let out a terrified scream.

"I'm not bluffing!" Theodore shouted. "I'm not like my father. I *will* kill you!"

He wasn't bluffing. I could hear it in his voice.

So could Isobella.

"Alright!" her soul replied. "Alright, just let me go!" Her spell book closed and Isobella's soul raised her hands into the air. She dismissed her book with a flick of her hand. The book floated away from her and landed on the ground.

Finally, the book was free game. I could do my part by sneaking down there and stealing it away from her. Impossible to do, unfortunately, from inside my celestial prison.

Freedom came in the form of a middle-aged businessman. With Isobella sufficiently distracted by Theodore and his hostage down below, Carl had his chance to set me free. He grabbed that bar of glorious glass and planted his feet in front of the walls of my prison. He took a few practice swings.

"Step back, Miss Salvo," he said. "No telling what this will do."

So I stepped back and pressed up against the wall of my cage. Carl put all his upper-body strength into a grand-slam swing and smashed right through that cylinder of solid light. It burst like glass and clattered to the ground, then even those broken pieces evaporated into harmless glitter.

Great. Nice. But that didn't mean Carl was off the hook for trying to kill Theodore. That son of a bitch had a lot of explaining to do. I grabbed a fistful of his suit and yanked him close to me.

"What the hell were you thinking!?" I shouted at him.

"It's the oldest trick in the book," Carl replied. "And Isobella Westland has been sufficiently bamboozled."

"What do you mean 'bamboozled'?" I asked. "You mean you never meant to kill Theodore?"

Carl looked offended. "Penelope, I'm insulted. You know me better than that. I'm a pacifist."

"But she offered you a promotion to be a god," I said. "You shoved him over the edge. He should be dead."

"Promotions are not all there is to life." He adjusted himself against the death grip I had on his clothes. "And I may have misguided Theodore in that regard, so I merely took this opportunity to put things in better perspective. After this, his promotion might not seem quite so important to his self-identity. Perhaps my method was a little drastic, but I do fear this is the only way he'd understand."

"But I don't get it." I dragged Carl over to the railing to where we could see events unfolding down below us. "He fell into the fires of Hell. I heard his body hit the bottom."

"Oh, that?" Carl asked, then laughed. He waved me off like it was seriously no big deal. "Theodore was never in any danger."

"Never in any danger?" I snapped. "It's ten stories to the bottom and as hot as the sun down there! What gave you the idea that he wouldn't be in any danger?"

"Well, don't go spreading this around, but..." Carl glanced around to see if we were alone, which we *were*, and he lowered his voice so no one else could hear. "Theodore is half-demon."

Chapter 26

1

Theodore and I hadn't known each other for very long, and most of what I had learned about him was centered around his job as an employee of the Westland Corporation. There were a lot of things he never mentioned and things I never thought to ask him about – his childhood, or who his father was, *or if he was a human being* – and those were apparently some pretty important topics we should have discussed.

I knew *some* things about Theodore; he liked Swedish candy, he was a real good shot with a pistol, and when he had to think really hard, he made a funny-looking frown. Those were very human things to do, so it never occurred to me to ask.

It occurred to me that Carl was lying. That *was* what Carl did best, after all, but it didn't seem like Carl was lying. He looked me unflinching in the eyes, as if everything he had told me about Theodore were absolutely true.

Carl arched his eyebrows at me. "Fascinated?"

His question snapped me out of my deep thoughts. I jerked him closer to me, ready to beat the *real* truth out of him. "That's bullshit," I growled at him.

"It's anything but," he replied. His eyes darted over to the guard rails. "Go see for yourself."

So I let go of Carl's jacket. I kept my stone-cold eyes locked on his as I inched over to the edge of the catwalk. Satisfied that this wasn't just one of his mind tricks and he wasn't looking to escape, I glanced down at the bottom of the cavern.

Inside the containment chamber of glorious glass, Theodore was in the middle of a showdown with Isobella, still with her physical body in a tight choke hold. The guy looked human to me. But, I guess to be fair, he *was* standing in a 10,000 degree wind tunnel of white-hot fire. Even as his fire-retardant suit was starting to smoke and burn. The worst Theodore had to show for it was a little sweat on his forehead.

"Half demon?" I repeated as Theodore shrugged off the blazes of Hell. "How does something like that even happen?"

Carl came up from behind to join me in watching Theodore's last stand against Isobella Westland.

"Ah, well, allow me to explain," he said. "While you might only know me as the best agent the Westland Corporation has ever seen, deep down I'm still just a regular Joe. I was young once, believe it or not, and more hormonal. And demons are oftentimes known for their sexual proclivity. In my naivety, I experienced a moment of weakness." He leaned forward and laughed a little bit. "*Moments* of weakness if you will."

"Ew," I said. I didn't need to think of Carl like that.

"Sometimes an entire weekend of weakness," he added.

"Okay, stop." I was going to puke if I heard any more. "So you're saying you banged a demon?"

Carl sighed and rolled his eyes. "That's not exactly how I would choose to phrase it," he said. "But, yes. And it wasn't just any demon."

Not just any demon?

Ohh. Duh, Penelope. Suddenly all sorts of things made sense. Namely the way Carl compromised his Westland Corporation values to hide Voel away in her own private little art studio.

I turned to Carl. "You mean Voel."

He gave me a coy grin. "A lady doesn't kiss and tell."

"Okay," I agreed. "But it's Voel, isn't it."

"Well, yes, obviously," he said. "And speaking of whom, she is currently wounded and counting on us." He gave me a friendly "go get 'em, tiger" slap on the arm. "Enough gossip. You get down there and help Theodore shove Isobella Westland back through that fracture. Once she's on the other side, I'm going to shut down Untouchable Orange and delete the entire zero-point energy system."

Carl dashed for the control panel and went right to work.

"But what if Isobella comes back for you?" I asked, "Don't you need protection?"

Carl turned and chuckled at me, as if I still just didn't get it.

"Don't you worry about me," he said with all the confidence in the world. "I'll be just fine."

So my job was to help Theodore send Isobella Westland back to Hell. Down below, Theodore seemed to be doing a pretty good job of getting that job started. Isobella's soul was one-hundred-percent focused on Theodore, who was seconds away from twisting the head off of her physical body like a grape. They stood a good distance apart – Theodore and Isobella – and they argued back and forth, negotiating for the release of the hostage.

"Don't do anything stupid, kid," Isobella said. She slowly floated forward. "I'm sure we can come to some sort of understanding. Everyone wants something, right? So what is it you want, Theodore? Money? Power? Do you want to be king of Tir Tairngire? Just tell me what you want and I'll make it happen."

"I want you to stop killing people," Theodore said.

Isobella took a moment, then laughed. "Besides that."

Good job, Theodore. Keep her busy.

Isobella's spell book still hadn't been touched. It sat there at the entrance to the containment chamber, totally unattended.

I hurdled over the guard rails and plunged into a swan dive straight to the bottom. I crushed a dent into the stone when I landed and I thought Isobella might have heard me, but she didn't, not over the crackling fire of Hell and the bellowing scream of torture souls.

I sprinted for her ivory spell book only a dozen yards away. It fluttered and flapped in place like a wounded bird unable to take flight. I scooped the book up and opened it to one of its many unintelligible pages.

I couldn't read Angel. The book had originally come from Heaven and documented the words of God. I could feel the divine power radiating off of it, like electricity, if electricity was soft like cotton candy. I flipped to the next page, and the next, searching for anything I could read or understand.

But then the fracture between Hell and Earth cracked open wider, shattering the very boundaries between our two worlds.

A bubble of reality-bending power ballooned out of the containment chamber and walloped me to the ground. I tumbled backwards, caught on a wave of distorted physics. The ivory book flew out of my hands and was washed away, lost in the fire.

Mists of lava sprayed out of the open containment chamber. Blobs of red-hot goo landed all around me and in my hair. The inhuman scream of demons came from the other side, along with the strange clicking of a trillion insect plagues. Acid-smoke gushed from the fracture and choked all of the breathable air out of the cavern. Suddenly it was impossible to see. All I could make out was the shadow of Theodore's body, who had also been knocked to the ground in the dimensional rupture, and the orange glow of Isobella's soul as she searched for her body.

I had to find that book. I crawled through the smoke and fire and felt around the floor. I came up empty. One hand sank into a puddle of lava, the other hand grabbed onto a chunk of smoking sulfur, but no book.

"Penelope!" Carl shouted my name from up above. "Penelope! We have a problem!"

"Well, no shit we have a fucking problem, Carl!" I shouted back. "We have lots of problems! This whole thing has been nothing but problems!"

"This is a new problem!" he shouted. "I shut off Untouchable Orange, but it's too late! The fracture is stable! It's drawing its power from Hell now!"

"Then close it!" I told him.

"I'm telling you I can't!" he replied.

Fuck.

The spell book could close it. I needed that goddam spell book. Back in the Ukraine, Isobella cast a spell that closed the fracture inside Chernobyl and sent all the demons back to Hell. I could do the same thing if I could just find that stupid book. So I swept my arms back and forth, dragging my fingertips across the stone, hoping against all hope that I could find it.

The buzz of swarming insects grew louder. Then came the beating of war drums and the snarl of a billion monsters. Legion was right on the other side of that gateway, ready to march across the face of the Earth.

My fingers brushed against the cover of the spell book.

Almost immediately, someone else's hand thumped down right on top of mine. I wasn't the only one who'd found the book. My worst fears told me it was Isobella Westland herself. I sat back on my knees and raised my fists, ready to fight her to the death for control of the book, if that's what it came down to.

But then the mystery person said my name. "Penelope?"

It was Theodore, and I couldn't have been more relieved.

"Theodore?" I asked, making sure.

"Penelope!" he said. He sounded just as excited to find me and I was to find him. I swished my arms through the air to clear the smoke as best I could and could just barely catch glimpses of him in the swirling fiery darkness. His button up shirt was scorched black and his pants were literally on fire. His face was coated in ash and soot.

I pulled him close and hugged him.

"Theodore!" I shouted. "You're alive!"

"I know!" He sounded excited, and a little confused. "This might be a strange question, but do you have any idea how?"

"You're half demon!" I told him. "Carl wasn't trying to kill you! He was just trying to trick Isobella Westland!"

"Half demon?" he repeated. "*I'm* half demon? What do you mean I'm half demon? I was born in Staten Island."

Before I had a chance to explain, Isobella cackled with joy, louder than the screaming demons and the roaring flames. The glorified lightning of all creation crackled visibly through the smoke. Her orange soul embraced the dark silhouette of her body and I saw the two meld together. The woman, now completely whole, laughed harder with relief and victory and insanity.

"Not good," I muttered.

"Not good at all," Theodore replied.

I tucked the ivory spell book under my arm and dragged Theodore to his feet so we could make our escape. I kept his hand in mine so we wouldn't lose track of one another in the expanding environment of Hell.

"I had her, Penelope," Theodore told me as we ran. "I could have killed her. I could have snapped her neck, but I didn't. Now her soul is back in her body and we're in deep, deep shit."

We stumbled through puddles of melting rock as we ran. I normally would have been worried about Theodore's safety, but he wasn't a regular squishy human being as I once believed. He was a demon, and demons were impervious to lava.

We thumped to a stop when we ran face-first into the cavern walls. The smoke thinned out at the edges and we finally got our first good look at each other.

"You look terrible," he said.

"*You* look terrible," I replied.

Plagues of deformed creatures came moving through the smoke. Red-eyed locusts landed on the walls all around us, with some of them thumping heavily onto our clothes. Giant snow crabs with deformed, tumorous flesh instead of shells skittered across the floors. Rivers of boiling blood and molten rock spilled from the open vault door of the containment chamber. And from the other side of the fracture boomed some heavy, lumbering monster that I couldn't quite see. But if the tremors shaking the cavern were any indication, it was at least as big as a dinosaur.

Maybe bigger.

"Maybe you were right about Lincoln," Theodore said. "We were never going to win this."

"Oh, come on." I forced a fake, confident grin. "You're the one who wanted to save the world. Well, it's not any fun if they make it easy."

The truth, although hard to admit to even myself was that I didn't see how we were going to win. But if there's one thing I had learned in my short tenure as world-saving-badass, it's that you come up with your craziest ideas when your back is against the literal wall and oblivion is chewing right on your face.

After all, didn't I once think I was out of options when Mir launched that nuke at Russia? I came up with a crazy idea *then*. I convinced my chicken-shit car to chase after it, I ripped its computerized guts out and it detonated in my face.

I didn't give up then, and I wasn't going to give up now.

The simple fact is, it's easier to convince yourself that you're going to lose when you're not in the fight, because that's when you've got nothing more on your hands than anxiety and free time to whip yourself into an anxiety spiral. But when the fight comes, when you're there in the moment, when you're neck-deep in the bullshit and adrenaline is coursing through your veins, when your fight-or-flight hormones (or, in my case, military-grade steroids) hijacks your brain and shuts down all those useless, non-helpful emotions like fear and worry and self-doubt, all of your thoughts focus like a laser beam onto one goal:

Getting shit done.

You don't save the world with one victory, and you don't lose the world after one defeat, so as long as there's time left on the clock, you keep coming up with ideas, crazier and crazier ideas, no matter how wild they may seem, and you *never stop trying*.

Because plans are bullshit.

Crazy ideas save worlds.

I threw my hands in the air and raised my voice to the sky.

"Army of Arms!" I shouted. At first I thought they might not listen to me, or obey me since I was still new to them, but just as those doubts crept in, a dozens loyal arms came wriggling out of the smoke. Then came hundreds more. Then came thousands. They formed a mob around me and stood at attention, awaiting my command. I whipped around and pointed at the containment chamber. "Block that doorway! Fight back those demons! Do whatever you have to do to keep Legion from escaping Hell!"

The arms nodded with their fists, then sprung into action. They avalanched into the smoke and I heard them clash with the forces of Hell. Would the Army of Arms be enough to keep all of Legion at bay? Probably not. Not for long at least. But it would buy us some time.

"Okay, I have an idea!" I shouted to Theodore. I opened the spell book and began flipping through the pages. "We can cast the same spell Isobella used in Chernobyl and send all the demons back to Hell!"

"Brilliant!" he said, excited to find a glimmer of hope. Then his smile faded. "But Penelope," he said. "Didn't you just say that I'm half-demon?"

"Yeah?" I said. "And?"

"So... if you send all the demons to Hell..." He trailed off.

Oh.

Oh no.

Isobella wandered through the smoke. "Penelope? Theodore? I know you're out here somewhere! The library is closing soon! I need you to return my book!"

"Cast it anyway." Theodore pressed the book to my chest. "Even if I go to Hell, it's the only chance we've got."

"No way." I slapped the book shit. "I'll think of something else. I'm not sending you to Hell."

Radiant lightning crackled right past us. It solidified into crystal, then tipped over and shattered. Isobella wasn't messing around. More bolts of solidified lightning zigzagged past us and crashed into the wall around us. It blasted holes in the stone and chips of it clattered to the floor.

Isobella kept shouting as she desperately searched for us and her book, blinded by the smoke. "I hear you out there, little half-demon and little half-robot! Come out here where I can see you!"

A second explosion of blood and fire and lava rocked the whole cavern as the fracture between our world and Hell split open even wider. The ceiling began to tremble and the thought occurred to me that the entire cavern might collapse and bury us beneath half of Midtown.

Maybe that was best. Maybe a cave-in would close the gate.

I wasn't going to bet on that, though.

"Cast the damn spell!" Theodore shouted at me. "We don't have time to think of anything else! Legion is already here! Isobella's going to find us! We don't have any choice!"

I moved the book to my side where he couldn't reach it and shouted right back at him. "I am not sending you to Hell!"

He threw up his hands. "Then Isobella wins!"

"He's right, mudblob," said Voel. Her voice was cracked and defeated. She leaned against the nearby wall, weak and with pain written all over her face. A trail of green paint showed how she had dragged herself across the floor and into a seated position where she could watch the world burn. "The only way to end this now is to speak those words of the Being Yahweh and send all of us back to Hell."

"Voel," I nearly whispered. "You're still alive."

She nodded. "For now."

Theodore and I exchanged glances and hurried over to her.

"Are you..." Theodore began, then stopped. "Are you my..."

"Finally figured it out, huh?" Voel asked with a little grin. She winced in pain as more paint dribbled out of her. "Damn."

"Why didn't Carl ever tell me?" he asked.

"Because he cares about you," she said. "Because he didn't want to see you end up like me. *Detained*."

Hundreds of my little arms came flying out of the containment chamber, broken and squiggling. I could feel my spiritual link to them grow steadily weaker as they died off. They were buying us time, but it was a massacre that wouldn't last.

Isobella Westland took one solid, confident step out of the smoke. She leveled her eyes right on us, stark-ass naked. I'd be a liar if I said I wasn't scared. The angelic runes carved into her flesh glowed like daylight. Her eyes, however, smoldered like lumps of burning coal. Whatever she was, she wasn't human anymore. She was some twisted combination of human and angel and demon, all mixed together.

The stone melted at her feet.

"There you are." She grinned at us. "I've come for my book."

I shoved the book into Voel's arms. "You can read Angel," I said. "*You* cast the stupid spell." I turned around, raised my fists and faced Isobella. "I'll take care of the heavy lifting."

Theodore helped Voel hold the heavy book upright in her hands. I heard her flip through the pages as she searched for the go-to-Hell spell.

I marched directly for Isobella Westland. My bare feet squished through puddles of magma. The lady had an eager smile on her face, as if she were hoping to fight me. I wasn't surprised. She had gone to such great lengths to kill anyone and everyone she thought would stand in her way, but she hadn't planned on a plucky Italian who would screw with her plans every step of the way. This bitch didn't want to just kill me, she wanted to make a mess of me first. The megalomania infecting her mind didn't think killing me would be enough of a punishment.

"You know what your problem is?" she asked me as we stood face-to-face. "You fail to see that what I'm doing is for the good of the entire world."

I shook my head. "And do you know what your problem is?"

She sneered at me. "Do tell."

"You're solid now."

I slugged her in the gut with all the force of a SWAT team battering ram and bent her right in half. Her eyes went wide her mouth hung open, stunned with the now-real physical sensations of pain. Isobella Westland had existed as pure, untouchable soulstuff for so long, she had completely forgotten the dangers that come with having a physical body. Well, I reminded her. After I gave her the Houdini Special right her in the stomach, I elbowed her the head like an industrial rock-crusher.

Isobella croaked for air and slumped the ground hard. Black and golden liquid came out of her mouth.

"You killed Baron Semedi." I planted my feet and kicked her across the face. Ribbons of blood spiraled through the air. "And you killed Conan the computer." I stomped my heel against her spine and heard it crunch. "And who knows how many other people you've killed since you've been back."

I grabbed her by the hair and yanked her head back. I leaned in close and seethed directly into her ear. "And you killed Xin Houng." I poised my fist in the air, ready to bash her brains out. "But now you're done. This is where it ends."

"No." She reached down and grabbed a loose electrical cable laying beside her. Sparks sprayed from the severed wires inside. "This is where it starts."

Before I could react, she pressed the cable to my face and surged electricity through my head. My muscles seized up and I couldn't move.

My vision scrambled.

My audio went fuzzy.

My brain blipped off like an unplugged computer.

2

I rebooted a few seconds later.

Visuals came online first. Isobella Westland was throwing crystallized lightning through the air as she fought off a full assault by the Army of Arms. They apparently didn't take too kindly to her decision to electrocute their new queen. And on any other day they might have been a formidable army, but they had just spent the last few hours taking heavy losses to their seemingly endless ranks. Isobella tore through them with little effort, blasting lightning with one hand and slashing at them with a shard of red Chernobylite with the other.

Dead arms splattered to the ground all around her, where they wriggled and turned to ash.

My audio came back online. Over the crackling fire and demonic war drums and Isobella's delightful mockery of my "pitiful army," I heard Voel sing a song in Angel.

"Sais phtino ipo to stoma nov!" she sang.

I spit you out of my mouth.

Voel had begun to cast the spell. And as a demon trying to recreate the words of the same god that damned her to a twisted existence in Hell, the attempt caused her a great deal of agony. After just that first line of the song, she released the book and clutched her head in her hands. Theodore crouched down next to her and did his best to encourage her to read more.

"You can't stop now," he said. "Just a few more lines."

Isobella spun around at the sound of those words. I could tell by the look on her face, she did not anticipate anything like this. But that was exactly her problem. She was so wrapped up in her own psychotic self-confidence that it never even occurred to her that someone might outsmart her. So when that moment came and someone *did* outsmart her, she absolutely no idea what she was supposed to do.

"Vile demon!" she screamed. "Stop singing!"

Voel turned her attention back to the book. She grit her teeth and sang the next line. "Zai don sais kaloon pleeno ang'lio!"

And no longer call you angels.

Deep inside the containment chamber, where Legion waited just on the other side of the opening gateway, the demons' howls changed from war-hungry to terrified.

"You deplorable bitch!" Isobella raised her Chernobylite into stabbing position and charged at Theodore and Voel.

"Not on my fucking watch," I muttered. I sprinted for Isobella and tackled her before she reached Voel. I carried her with me as I continued to build up speed, then smashed both of us into the wall like a head-on collision. Our impact crushed a crater deep into the stone.

I was sure Isobella was dead, but she wasn't. I heard her growl, then felt her trying to wriggle free.

The demonic forces from Hell heard what Voel was singing and knew they had to act, and act quickly. They came rushing through the open gateway and spilling out of the blown-off containment door.

"Arms!" I shouted. I didn't have to say anything more than that. They could read my thoughts. They knew what I wanted.

Protect Voel from those demons. Don't let them get to her.

And the Army of Arms responded. *At once, our Queen.*

The Army of Arms did their best to fight back the skeletons and flesh-crabs and car-sized insects. Theodore focused on holding the book up for Voel and Voel traced her fingers over the glowing words on the page, even as Legion fought to reach them. The arms weren't going to last for long – there were far too many demons for that – but they delayed Legion just long enough for Voel to continue singing.

"Se krayo se mlio aiontita..."

I sentence you to an eternity...

Isobella knew the song, and knew this was the end. There wasn't much she could do with me pressing her hard against the wall. With the few seconds of freedom she had left, she made eye contact with me and growled. "I will never forget this, false god." Then she raised her voice to punctuate her last word. "Never!"

"Yeah, well..." I released her and stood out of the way. "I'm not starting your fan club anytime soon, either."

Voel sang the final words. "Stin Kolo!"

In Hell!

The fire blasting out of the containment chamber froze in mid-air. Confronted with the final words of God, the demons stopped fighting. In their mind, defeat had come once more and there wasn't any point. The ones with heads slumped in defeat. If they were carrying weapons, they let them clatter to the ground.

A small part of them felt bad for them. Their goal wasn't to take over Earth. Not really. They just wanted to escape Hell and Earth just happened to be the closest place they had to run to.

Still, rats only move into your apartment building to get out of the rain. That doesn't mean you don't lay out the poison.

Unfortunately, my Army of Arms were also demons and equally caught up in their inevitable return home. As the hellfire slowly reversed direction, gravity shifted and began to drag all of Legion towards the fractured gateway.

The temperature of the chamber instantly cooled by thousands of degrees as the winds shifted. The puddles of lava dribbled back towards the vault door and left obsidian dents in the ground.

Isobella's feet hit the ground and she began to slide away from me. Her piece of Chernobylite got ripped right out of her hands and vanished into the fire. She look heavy steps against the magic, but her feet shifted on the gravel and sand. Desperate, she latched onto my clothes and gripped down tight.

"Look at what you have *done*," she said.

I had no sympathy for her. "Give my regards to the CEO."

She slapped her hands to the sides of my head and pulled her face close to mine. "I am going to torture your little boyfriend in Hell. I'm going to make him suffer every day. He's going to beg me to kill him, but no one dies in Hell." The force of the spell finally overpowered her and tore her grip from my head. She tumbled backwards through the air. "Death never comes!"

Isobella Westland, for the second time in her life, disappeared into the fire and smoke of Hell.

While most of the demons accepted their defeat, a few of them fought against the magic. If they had claws, they dug them into the stone floors. If they had wings, they buzzed for safety as hard as they could. If they were near the mangled catwalks, they clung to them for dear life.

Their efforts were admirable, but ultimately pointless. They couldn't overpower the wishes of the god that created them. One by one they all came loose and flew back home.

My Army of Arms whirled through the air as if they were caught in a tornado. Some of them reached out for me, but what was I going to do? Run around and snatch them out of the air like a thousand butterflies?

Run, I told them. *Run if you can and get far away from here.*

They tried to obey. They tried to wriggle into the cracks of the stone or into the ventilation ducts. But no demon was safe.

What I wasn't certain of was if *half* demons would be spared.

I sprinted for Theodore. Like a brave soldier storming the beaches of Normandy, I dodged, spun, and stiff-armed every demon out of my way as I ran in his direction. Theodore was dead ahead, kneeling alone on the ground.

I slid right up to him. "Theodore?"

"Hey, Penelope." He beamed a smile at me. "We did it. We saved the world."

I grabbed his hands. "Where's Voel?"

By the look on his face, I could tell the answer wasn't good. His eyes glanced at the fracture.

"I tried to hang on to her," he said. "I wasn't strong enough."

"Oh, Theodore." Poor guy. He never knew his mother and just when he finally met her, he lost her. "She was the real hero in all of this. And, look, you're still here. That's a good sign, right? You're only half-demon, so maybe you'll-"

I felt Theodore shift away from me. Just slightly at first, but then a little faster.

I looked at his feet. He wasn't walking away. He was being pulled. In a defeated tone, he said, "Damn."

"No." I grabbed his hands and pulled him to his feet. I braced myself against his weight and pulled him towards me. Still, even I wasn't strong enough to stop the miracle at work. "Theodore, no. You can't leave. I just met you."

He laughed a little. "I don't think it's up to us."

"No!" I threw my arms around him and pulled him close. "Grab on. Don't let go. I'll keep you here."

He did as I asked him, but the magic wouldn't let up. The more we fought against it, the stronger it got. It dragged Theodore across the floor and I was just getting pulled along for the ride. I darted around to the other side of him and pushed against his back. What a silly thought, that I could be stronger than God if I just gave it the old college try.

Theodore continued to inch towards the fracture.

Carl came running to help me. He threw his shoulder into Theodore's back and tried to keep him from moving. He wasn't much help. If I couldn't do it as a supernatural war robot, Carl wasn't going to contribute much with his squishy muscles.

With the realization that there wasn't anything we could do to save him, Carl began saying his goodbyes. "That was nice work back there, son."

"Not so bad yourself," Theodore replied. "You really had me fooled. I honestly thought you wanted to kill me."

"Sorry to keep you in the dark on all that," Carl said, "But it had to be convincing if we were going to fool Isobella."

"But why didn't you tell me before?" Theodore asked. "I lived my whole life thinking I was human."

Carl nodded, as if he understood how he had fucked up. "I put it off because you were young. I kept telling myself I would tell you when you were older, but time got away from me."

"You lied to me my whole life."

"I'm sorry," Carl said. "I'm not necessarily the best father."

"No, you're not," Theodore said, agreeing with him for once. "But you are one hell of an agent."

"Like father, like son. You handled yourself expertly today. Better than an investigator. You acted like a field agent. So for what it's worth, I want you to have that promotion. You're about to be the first Westland agent to go to Hell. Nothing is more 'in the field' than that."

Theodore turned his attention to me and laughed. "I got my promotion."

"Yeah," I said. "You did. But Lincoln was wrong. He said it wouldn't matter anymore." I turned and looked through the gateway and into the warped landscape of Hell. "I think it's going to matter now more than ever."

The final remnants of Legion – small swarms of red-eyed locusts and a couple bleach-white crabs – tumbled helplessly into the fracture and vanished.

The three of us were dangerously close to the portal. The edges of the fracture blackened and curled like burning newsprint. Hell was actually visible on the other side. Beyond the fracture was a cliff that overlooked the scorched wastelands, up in the toxic skies, with the Shattered Mountains far-off in the distance. Stretching off to the horizon was an endless sea of refugee demons; an entire dimension of creatures who thought they were about to escape their infernal prison. The monsters took their defeat in stride, as if they somehow knew this was going to happen, but had to at least *try*.

I knew how that felt. When the chips are down, all you can do is go with your craziest, wildest ideas.

But that doesn't mean they always work.

Theodore was the last demon still remaining on Earth. Carl and I did our best to keep him around for as long as possible, but all it bought us was another sixty seconds. The spell dragged him through the open vault door and inside the containment chamber.

Time was quickly running out.

"Theodore," I said, desperate to cram in as many parting thoughts as possible. "Isobella Westland's going to be in there with you. And since she can't get her hands on us, she's going to come after you for revenge. You might be a half-demon, but who knows what kind of power she's really capable of. You might be in serious trouble."

"I wouldn't worry about Isobella," Carl said. "She might be brilliant, but she has a funny way of being wrong."

Carl stepped away from us, which was fine. He wasn't contributing much to keeping Theodore on Earth, not in direct comparison to my unimaginable power. I *was* curious where he was going, however. Carl went ahead, reached for Untouchable Orange and plucked it right out of the air.

He waited for Theodore to be dragged closer and offered him the orange marble in his open palm.

"I hate to do this," Carl said. "I could make a trillion dollars selling energy with this thing, but it seems like you're going to need it more than me."

"What am I supposed to do with this?" Theodore asked.

Carl looked to me for permission.

I nodded my approval.

Carl replied, "I want you to swallow it."

"Swallow it?" Theodore asked. "What's it going to do to me?"

"I'm not exactly sure." Carl pushed the marble into his son's hand. "Probably make you the coolest kid in Hell."

"Just do what Carl says," I said, chiming in. I couldn't believe those words just came out of my mouth. "Isobella isn't going to have anything better to do with her time than try to fuck with you. If Untouchable Orange is anything like Impossible Red, it will make you unfuckwithable."

Theodore rolled the little sphere between his fingertips. When he saw how both me *and* Carl agreed on this one thing, he couldn't bring himself to refuse. He popped Untouchable Orange in his mouth and swallowed hard. Nothing seemed to happen, but these things take time.

The three of us slid across the floors of glorious glass and closer to the edge of the fracture. If we didn't let Theodore go, we were all going to Hell.

"Dammit, Theodore!" I hugged him tight, doing my best to keep him on Earth for one more second. "I have to let go now."

"I know." His face glowed orange against the fires of Hell. He looked down at me. "Thanks for helping me save the world."

"*You* helped *me* save the world."I wasn't going to cry. I'd been doing too much of that lately. "Don't you forget it."

Theodore's toes were over the burning edges between Earth and Hell. He reached out his hand. "Bye, dad."

Carl gave him a strong handshake. "Goodbye, son."

Theodore's feet dangled over the edge as I held on tight. Now my feet were the ones skidding slightly over the threshold.

So I let go.

3

Just like someone being blasted out of an airlock, Theodore got sucked right out of my arms. He tumbled through the toxic clouds that floated over the wastelands of Hell. Halfway across the sky, Untouchable Orange activated inside him. He exploded like a goddamn supernova and emerged from the explosion in a new, glorious body. I caught one final glimpse of him: his hair became like fire and his body burned like the surface of the sun.

In that last second, he raised his hand and gave us a single wave goodbye.

The fracture vanished and everything went quiet. Carl and I collapsed exhausted to the floor. All I could hear was Carl's heavy breathing. I laid there and stared at where the fracture used to be.

I asked Carl, "Do you think he's going to be okay in there?"

"*My* boy?" Carl asked. He sat up straight, dusted off his sleeves and did his best to straighten his hair. "He's going to be just fine. He's got the training. He has the wit..."

"And now he's the god of fire," I added.

"If he's anything like his old man," Carl groaned as he got to his feet. "Give it a couple years and he'll be running the place."

The basement chamber was an absolute wreck. The bottom half of the catwalks had melted into slag. What few levels that somehow remained were all blown to hell by grenades and rockets. The floor of the chamber – what used to be smooth, polished stone with prehistoric fossils trapped inside – was now a sheet of obsidian glass, shattered in places from all the fighting.

The scorched bodies of Westland soldiers laid all around, as well as their melted weapons. A few lighting fixtures were still on, but even those would occasionally pop in a shower of sparks. And from way up top, I could still hear the control panel beeping to high heaven.

Whatever shreds of my Westland suit managed to survive the battle were scorched and smoking. My hair was a disaster. Dried chemical-blood and smears of ash covered my face.

"I'm going to get somebody down here with a broom," Carl said as he stepped out of the containment chamber.

I crawled to my feet and followed him out. "Isobella killed Xin. I don't know if you knew that."

Carl took a deep breath. "I suspected as much."

"Theodore should have snapped her neck," I said.

"I don't disagree with you." He turned to me. "But that was his decision to make. And who am I to judge? I'm a pacifist."

"You know what, Carl?" He turned to face me, then stepped back, like I might deck him right in the face. Instead, I reached for a handshake. "You're a pacifist who gets fucking work done."

Carl gave my outstretched hand a confused glance, as if that were the last thing he was expecting. Still, he wasn't about to pass up the opportunity. He gripped my hand and shook it.

He asked, "So you don't blame me for all this?"

Eh. Things weren't *entirely* his fault. So I said, "Fifty percent."

"And we're still friends, right?"

Ehh. That was harder to answer.

I gave him a hard pat on the arm, not hard enough to break his bones, but hard enough to remind him that I could snap him in half should the mood ever strike me.

"Let's just call it what it is, Carl," I said. I turned my back on him and wandered off. "Frenemies."

Chapter 27

1

If the Westland Corporation thought things were chaotic before, they were in for a real shock to the system after our fight with Isobella. All of the elevators laid crushed at the bottom of the foundation. Whatever few electronic devices that managed to survive the system failures were drawing on a dwindling supply of emergency power. And there's no way the earthquakes coming from the basement didn't do some serious structural damage.

How do you file an insurance claim on something like that? I doubt their forms have a box you can check off for a mass exodus of demons.

I had to climb thirteen flights of stairs to reach basement level two. I reached a sealed black door with the words MOTOR POOL stenciled in white paint. Normally a non-Westland employee wouldn't be free to roam the building unattended, but I was the obvious exception. After everything I had done to help that bullshit organization, I had more than earned a self-guided tour.

I opened the emergency door and stepped into the parking garage. The motor pool had lost main power and ran on a series of back-up lights. The place had suffered moderate damage from all the fighting below, but nothing too dangerous. A few cracks in the concrete. A few dislodged lighting fixtures.

At first I thought the cars had all evacuated the building, but my eyes eventually adjusted to the darkness and I could see them hidden in the shadows, backed up as deep into their parking stalls as they could go.

While most of the Westland vehicles were glossy black, I thought I spotted a white one. I leaned forward and squinted.

"Corolla?" I whispered.

A pair of headlights flicked on and lit me up like center stage. One by one, more headlights followed.

"Who's there?" an unfamiliar voice asked.

"Stay back!" another car said. "I have a gun!"

I put my hands up. "The fight's over," I said. "I'm not here to hurt you. I'm just looking for Corolla."

One pair of headlights moved. I saw Corolla's front-end pull out of the darkness and poke into the light.

"Penelope?" he said.

It *was* him. I couldn't help but grin like an idiot as I speed-walked towards him. "Corolla!"

And Corolla sounded just as happy to see me as I was to see him. "Penelope!"

We reached one another and I hugged him as best I could. It's hard to hug a car. You kind of just put your arms out and press yourself against the driver side door. And Corolla couldn't hug back, but I could tell that he wanted to.

"I should have known you were here," he said. "There were all these terrible sounds coming from down below. It sounded like the end of the world!"

"It *was* the end of the world," I said. "At least, almost."

"Oh my god, what happened?"

"Dude!" The excitement of being able to tell Corolla about all the cool shit I had done came spilling out of me in one big, long, rambling story. "Okay, so get this. Isobella Westland tried to kill Carl and she took control of the Westland Corporation and tried to use Untouchable Orange to open a gateway to Hell. So we went to find Voel, and then we went to get Ilana Rittenberg..."

I stopped my story. My eyes went wide as I remembered. Ilana had been caught red-handed by Westland security when she was sneaking up into the building. It sounded like she could have been in serious trouble. Carl even said that she was *maybe* dead.

"Oh yeah," Corolla said. "We ran into Ilana. There were all these people trying to kill her."

"What!?" I snapped. "Where is she? Is she okay?"

"She's fine," Denali said as she rolled up next to Corolla. "She's with me. I wasn't going to let her just die like that."

Denali's back door swung open and Ilana stepped out, playing games on her phone. Her work clothes were covered in thick layers of dust you'd see in an air conditioning duct and she had blood on her hands.

"Ilana." I looked her up and down. "What *happened* to you?"

"Eh, I almost got killed," she said, scrunching her face and trying to squeeze more points out of Money Crunch on her phone. She seemed *super* focused. Her eyes were still dilated. Apparently the shrooms hadn't yet worn off.

"How did you get away?" I asked her.

She still refused to take her eyes off her phone. She pointed at the ceiling with her pinkie finger. "Some tunnel or something," she said. "I dunno. I wasn't really paying attention."

I couldn't help but smile at how delightfully odd she could be sometimes. "Well, I'm just glad you're alive," I told her.

"Sure," she replied, still only paying half-attention.

I turned my attention to Denali. "Thank you," I said, with full sincerity.

"Hey, no problemo," she replied. "So where's Theodore? Isn't he with you?" I could hear how eager she was to be reunited with her partner, and my heart just sank. All I could think about was me and Corolla and how it would kill either of us to be separated from one another, especially on a permanent basis like Theodore and Denali. I had no idea how to break the news to her. I wasn't good at that kind of thing.

"He... uh..." I knew the best thing to do was to just spit it out, but damned if I couldn't bring myself to do it. Was there any way to spin it where it didn't sound terrible? "Okay, well, first thing's first, he's alive."

Denali sounded skeptical. "Well, of *course* he's alive."

"But..." I continued. No. There was no way to take the sting off. I just had to put it out there. "Theodore's in Hell."

"In Hell?" She rolled back. "What do you mean he's in Hell? What's he doing in Hell?"

"Theodore did a very brave thing," I told her. "He saved the world. But in order to do that, he had to go to Hell."

"Okay?" She sounded lost in her own thoughts. "So... when is he coming back?"

I couldn't answer that. The only person to ever escape Hell was Isobella Westland and that nearly destroyed the world.

"I don't know if he *is* coming back," I told her.

"Oh." Denali got real quiet. And I understood. I had just dropped some of the worst news possible right in her lap. It was going to take her some time to process.

"He'll be back," I said, as if I knew it for a fact. And maybe it wasn't true, but I didn't know that for certain. Maybe he *would* be back. I guessed it was always possible. Who knew what the future held, so why take that hope away from her?

"He will?" she asked, desperately wanting me to convince her.

"Of course he will," I said. "He's a hero. And if movies have taught me anything, heroes always come back when you need them most."

"Like Liam Neeson," Denali said.

I gave her hood a pat. It sounded like she was going to be okay.

"Exactly like Liam Neeson."

"Theodore really went to Hell?" Corolla asked. "That's a real bummer. I always liked that guy."

"You never trusted him," I said.

"Eh, I trusted him," he said, dismissing the accusation. "I just didn't *want* to trust him. But I did."

Maybe Theodore *would* somehow find his way back to Earth. He *was* one heck of an investigator. If anyone could figure a way out of Hell, I didn't see any reason why it couldn't be him. Either way, it was going to be tough to go on about my business knowing that he was trapped down there.

"Well..." I headed off towards the garage doors and gave the Westland cars a little wave goodbye. "I got to get going."

Corolla quickly rolled up behind me. "You're walking home?"

I stopped. "I guess."

"It's still kind of raining out there," he said. "And the buses aren't running."

"Oh, I guess you're right."

I didn't want to walk home. I wanted Corolla to take me. I think that's what he wanted, too. But the last time I had seen him, we had a big fight about me telling him what to do. I wasn't going to order him to drive me, and I don't think he wanted to be the one to offer.

"You going to make it okay?" he asked.

"I'll be fine," I said. "It's just a little rain."

"Okay." He paused, then said, "Because... you know..."

I acted like it was no big deal to me. "I know what?"

"Well." He cleared his throat. "If you *needed* me to give you a ride home, I guess I could."

That made me laugh. I turned to face him. "If I *needed* you."

"Yeah," he said. "If you needed me."

"Alright, Corolla." I took a breath, held my hands at my side and said the words. "I need you to give me a ride home."

"Well, then." He unlocked the doors. "Since you *need* me..."

2

On the morning of that very next day, I decided to take advantage of that gift certificate Corolla got me from Ohm Bliss Yoga for my birthday. The yoga studio was this neat little storefront over in Alphabet City; a place decorated with trickling water fountains and statues of Buddha.

Did I want to do yoga? Not really. But Corolla went to a lot of trouble to get me a gift certificate for my birthday – which he never did explain exactly *how* he pulled that off – and I knew it would make him happy if I at least tried it.

Plus, it's supposed to help you alleviate stress and it boosts your recovery from sore muscles. Considering recent events, I had plenty of both to go around.

I'd never done yoga before. I had no idea you needed to bring your own yoga mat, so the lady there let me borrow one from the shop. And while I knew that yoga pants were a thing that existed, it didn't occur to me that you actually had to wear them for yoga, so I showed up in shorts and a t-shirt. Whatever.

The class was small; just me, two college girls and some older lady. We listened to a CD of nature sounds and flute music. The instructor was this rail-thin woman with a spiritually vacant look in her eyes. She would say the names of these different positions to twist our bodies into. "Downward dog" was the only one I really remembered, because it was the easiest to do.

"Release the negative energy trapped inside you," she told us.

That's a pretty tall order, lady.

I tried to do all the different positions, stealing glances at the other students so at least I had a clue how I was supposed to look.

Corolla thinks I need yoga to get my anger under control. Shows what he knows. I'm not half as angry as the other people I meet in life. Take Mir for example. She hated Russia and the United States, and I'm not saying she didn't deserve to feel that way, but her anger got so out of control that she was ready to start a thermo-nuclear war. That, if you ask me, is a little much.

And what about Isobella Westland? All she ever wanted to do was prove that she was better than anyone that ever lived. Her insane schemes blew up in her face, it cost her the Westland Corporation and she got sent to Hell. Twice. All that unchecked anger led her to cold-blooded murder and, had we not come along to stop her, she would have marched an army of demons across every dimension she could get her hands on.

That, I tell you, is an anger issue.

What do I have to be angry about?

Life stuff. A mother who died in a senseless car wreck. A mentor and best friend murdered in his hospital bed. A deadbeat father who used to yell at me and hit me and convinced me I would never be good enough for anything.

Okay, so, yeah. Maybe I'm a little angry.

"Inhale," my yoga instructor said. "And when you exhale, just let all that negative energy flow out of you."

Oh, if it were only that easy.

But I tried. I crouched there, tucked into a little ball with my forehead against the mat. I took a deep breath in and exhaled, and imagined that anger leaving me.

And maybe it should.

Wouldn't that be the opposite of what Mir and Isobella did? They hung onto their anger. They fostered it and fed it until it grew into an unstoppable monster. They should have exhaled and released all that negative energy out into the world.

"Put your hands here," my instructor said, coming up behind me. She touched my hips so I knew where she meant. I guess I wasn't doing the pose right.

I glanced down at my hips. "My hands *are* there," I said.

"Not here," she said, touching me again. "Here."

Okay. So I moved my hands two whole inches. "Happy?"

"Feel the difference?" she asked.

"No."

"Feel it here?" She touched my spine.

"No."

"You should feel it stretching."

My muscles are industrial strength graphene rubber, Yoga Human. You have no idea what I'm going to feel.

"Do you feel it stretching?" she asked me.

"No."

"You should."

"Well, I don't."

"Why don't you put-"

"Can we just move on?" I asked. "I hate this pose anyway."

Then she rolled her eyes and gave me a snotty look. Why? Because I said I hated her pose? Well, it's stupid pose. Find me a better pose and we won't have a problem.

"Okay." She returned to the front. "Back to downward dog."

Aww, yeah. Break time. Downward dog is my jam.

Living life without Xin was going to take a lot of getting used to. I guess that day was inevitable, though. If it wasn't Isobella, it would have been the cancer.

It's crazy how life works sometimes. You'd never expect a teenage girl from Little Italy to meet an elderly Chinese man and end up inheriting his magical family business, but here we were. I lived in Chinatown now. I'd take care of the plants. I'd sell spices and detergents to the locals. I wouldn't screw it up, because even though Xin was gone, a part of him would always live on inside me.

When Ma died, the loneliness and that feeling of being lost in the world hit me so hard, it caused me real, physical pain. But eventually that went away. Sure, I still miss her, but I don't feel sad anymore. And I hate that. I hate recovering. I hate moving on.

I hate that you eventually process your emotions whether you like it or not, because that anger that comes from losing someone you care about, *that's* what kept me going. I hate that I have to miss my mother, but I hate it more when months have passed and I look up to realize I don't miss her anymore.

I hate that sometimes I can't remember what Ma looked like.

I was furious with the idea that the passage of time was going to do the same thing same thing to Xin. Whether I liked it or not, I was going to adjust. I was slowly going to get used to working in the shop alone. And just like Ma, the day would come when I would try to remember his face and draw a total blank.

I didn't finish the yoga class that Corolla got me for my birthday. I left partway through, because I wasn't going to cry in public like that.

3

For all the time I worked with Xin and lived under the roof of his herbal shop, we talked about so many different things. I guess, in retrospect, I did most of the talking. Xin seemed far more interested in listening. I never really understood why, but after feeling ignored my entire life, boy, did I have a lot to say. I would go on and on about stories from high school, or shitty things that happened to me in my childhood, or just the random thoughts I had about the world and the way it worked.

And sometimes, after hours of me just talking out loud, I would look over to find Xin smiling at me. There was something about me that appealed to the old man – no idea what – but he really seemed to enjoy having me in his life.

And I had never really felt that way before.

In all that talking, I never brought up death. I had seen quite enough of it in my short time as a human being and wasn't all that inclined to discuss it further. Xin would bring it up, though, from time to time, and usually with these dark, cryptic messages. I would someday run the shop. Eventually the collection of dangerous weapons in the basement would be my responsibility. I knew he was going to die, in the sense that *everyone* dies, but it just never occurred to me to plan for when that day came.

Xin was a Buddhist and I didn't know the first thing about Buddhist funerals. I assumed there were prayers, or chants, and a variety of ancient traditions I had never been exposed to before because as far as my Catholic mother was concerned, any religion that wasn't the one true religion was the work of the devil.

I was the one who arranged for Ma's funeral, and I simply assumed it was going to be my responsibility yet again to do the same for Xin Houng.

I found out a couple days later that the arrangements had all been taken care of. And by taken care of I mean the Buddhist temple had been notified, the service had been scheduled, and a delightful black-and-white picture of his ran in the local newspaper.

Everything from the flowers and the prayer flags to the cemetery plot and a traditional Chinese tombstone had been entirely paid for.

By the Westland Corporation.

There's Buddhist temple on the south side of Chinatown and that's where they'd be holding the service. Being raised Catholic, I didn't have the first clue what to do at a Catholic funeral, but I did my best to not embarrass myself. It was a lot of kneeling and prostrating, a lot of bells and chimes, and no shortage of sweet-smelling incense that reminded me of something from a dream.

I don't know how Carl managed to get the funeral set up without going through all kinds of legal red tape. I mean, an elderly man got stabbed through the heart while in a coma. What did he put down as the cause of death for that? And how did he get the city to turn over the remains without getting the Feds heavily involved?

But he pulled it off. And if there's one thing I know about the Westland Corporation, it's best not to ask too many questions.

A small group of people showed up to pay their respects, mostly Chinatown locals, but also a few bald-headed Buddhist monks from elsewhere in the world. Corolla and Denali couldn't attend, *much* to Corolla's frustration.

"You said I'd never need a suit," Corolla had told me on the way to the service. "And here comes the perfect time to wear it, and you won't let me."

I had prepared to say a little something about Xin and I had it all written down, but that's not how these funerals go. There's not a lot of talking. You mostly just kneel there and meditate and reflect and whenever you feel like you're done, you just get up and leave. It was probably better that way anyway; public speaking makes me nervous and I'm sure I would have screwed it up, or broken down crying in front of everyone, or something else equally as embarrassing.

I was happy to kneel there and remember the man who saved my life.

Ilana knelt there next to me. It's the longest I'd ever seen her go without talking.

A few of the Chinatown locals extended their condolences to me. I had picked up just enough Chinese to have a short conversation with them and thank them for coming. They were very kind to me – they knew how important Xin was to me, and how important he was to me – and they all offered me their help whenever I needed it.

I'd be lying if I didn't suspect a few of the people there were supernatural. I recognized a few men and women who moved with the grace and precision of Ninjas out of uniform, perhaps representatives from the Fugu Clan or the Scorpion Clan or one of the many others. Looming in the back of the temple was a tall black woman in a dusty tuxedo, obviously an emissary from the Voodoo world.

I didn't see a single angel there. Stuck up assholes.

And Carl was there. He came in a brand new Westland suit, which had to be uncomfortable for all the kneeling we were doing, but he didn't seem to mind.

In time, the customers got up to leave. At one point I glanced around to see that the ninjas had vanished. The sun had begin to set, evening turned to night, and the funeral was almost over.

Ilana stayed for several hours, which was way longer than I expected, but eventually even she stood up to leave. She gave me a sympathetic pat on the shoulder. When I looked up, she made the international hand symbol for a phone and mouthed the words "call me," then left.

In the end, everyone had left except for me and Carl. Once we were alone, he got up and moved to the front where he could kneel next to me. I closed my eyes and focused on my memories of Xin. I remembered his love of classic rock. I remembered the way he would stare blankly at all of my terrible jokes. And I would never forget the stern look he would give me whenever I said the F word.

Carl let me kneel in silence for a while before he spoke up.

"Xin Houng was a good man," he said.

"Yeah."

More silence.

I just assumed Car would have more to say, but he didn't. A little bit of time passed, then he stood up to leave. I heard his heels click all the way to the temple door, and that's when I stopped him.

"Carl." I kept my head down and my eyes closed.

"Yes, ma'am."

"I'm going to get Theodore."

The temple stayed silent. I didn't have much more to say besides that. Carl, apparently, didn't either. That was fine. I wanted him to seriously consider what I had just told him, and I wanted him to take all the time he needed. Maybe he'd tell me I was crazy. Or he'd tell me it was impossible. Maybe he'd want to give me some kind of advice.

He said, "That will be very dangerous."

"I'm counting on it."

More silence.

I thought he'd say more, but he didn't. When I opened an eye to peek behind me, Carl was gone.

4

Corolla drove me back home. It's a sad affair, leaving a funeral. I thought we'd make the trip in silence, but conversation has a way of cropping up between us.

"But it's got crust and sauce and cheese," he said. "And they put toppings on it."

I shook my head with my eyes closed. I wasn't having it.

"Anyone who thinks that anything with crust and sauce and cheese is automatically a pizza is dead wrong," I said. "And half of these places aren't even using real sauce. They use fucked up things like soy sauce. Or garlic aioli."

"What's wrong with aioli?" he asked.

"Aioli is just a fancy word for mayonnaise. *French* mayonnaise. It takes a real piece of shit to put French mayonnaise on a cauliflower crust and call that a pizza."

"It's not *just* mayonnaise. It's more than mayonnaise."

"It's mayonnaise with paprika in it, dude. You know it. I know it. And all those hipster jabronies burning their crusts in TriBeCa know it. It's French mayonnaise and anyone who puts it on a pizza crust should be banned from ever going to Italy."

"Well, if they're not making pizza, then what're they making?"

"Flatbread!" I said. "With gross shit on it!"

"That's all pizza is. Flatbread with shit on it."

"Pizza is flatbread with ingredients found in Italy. Not pineapple. Not mashed potatoes. Not mayonnaise from France."

"Okay," Corolla said, giving up.

"Other Tony from up the way... now *he* makes pizza. Real crust, *actual* tomato sauce made from *actual* tomatoes, and he shreds the cheese like you're supposed to. Jesus, dude, these places in TriBeCa don't even shred the cheese! They just take whole lumps of mozarel and throw it on there. It's gross."

"It's Margherita."

"It's an excuse to be lazy. And these Neutral Milk Hotel listening motherfuckers cooking this shit could sooner build a base on the Moon than they could work a brickfire oven."

"..."

I waved my arms. "Aioli has no business being on a pizza. Neither do chicken wings, or fucking poached salmon, or whatever the fuck they're inventing for Table Week."

"..."

"There's this place in Greenwich that makes a pizza with pickled watermelon rinds. Is *that* a pizza?? Pickled water-melon rinds. And do you know how much they want for that shit?"

"..."

454

"Like twenty five bucks! For a little pizza, too. It's not even a big pizza! It's like eight inches."

"You don't even need me for this conversation," he said.

I crossed my arms. "You're the one who brought it up."

"All I said was something smelled good!"

"We were driving right by Brickoven Pizza when you said it. What you were smelling was probably the buffalo cauliflower and shrimp scampi flatbread."

"So you think every pizza in New York needs to be a huge by-the-slice pepperoni like the ones made by Other Tony?"

"I think rich hipsters from the Village need to quit playing Doctor Frankenstein with the fucking food pyramid. That's what I think."

"You said you tried that yoga thing, right?" Corolla asked.

"What's that supposed to mean?"

"I dunno," he said. "I just thought it would loosen you up. It didn't seem to work."

"Well, I didn't stay the whole time."

"Why not?"

"It was pissing me off."

"You got pissed off at yoga?"

"The lady wouldn't stop busting my balls!"

I looked around. We weren't moving. Come to realize, we were home. Corolla sat parked in front of the alleyway. Our stretch of Chinatown was all lit up and flashing for the night.

"Oh," I said. "We're here."

"We've *been* here," he said.

"Oh." Huh. I wasn't paying attention, I guess. I opened the door to get out. "My bad."

Before I could climb out, Corolla spoke up. He had an odd tone in his voice, like he was about to ask me for a million dollars.

"Hey, Penelope?"

"Yeah, Corolla."

"Are you and Ilana going to go to the drive-in this weekend?"

Weird question.

"You mean like the drive-in movies?" I asked.

"Yeah."

"Never in my life have I talked to her about that."

"Maybe you could ask her."

"Okay?" I gave him a strange look. "Why?"

"Well, if you wanted to go and if Ilana wanted to go, then she could ride with Denali and then we could all go together."

"Ohh. I get it." That made me snicker. It was cute. "Alright, dude. I'll ask Ilana if she wants to go to the drive-in movies. I'll see what she says."

"Thanks, boss."

5

I went down the alley between the Asian Food Mart and Super-Wash Dry Clean. The weather-controlled super storm was already a few days past us, but there were still big puddles on the concrete. I went out of my way to stamp my foot in one of them and accidentally crunched a hole in the cement.

Damn. It had been almost a year and I still sometimes forgot my own strength.

I stopped when I reached the end of the alley. Xin's shop stood there waiting for me, except it was my shop now. The tin roof, the creaky screen door, the priceless collection of botanical treasures, they were mine. I was the secret keeper now. And I knew I'd do a great job.

I wouldn't change a thing. That's what Xin would have wanted. Everything would stay exactly the same. The radio, the watering can, the old-school cash register. I'd keep everything exactly the way he wanted it because reincarnation's a real thing and, who knows, maybe he'd be back someday.

Once up on the porch, I checked on the plants. I rubbed the leaves of the Shishker Fern between my fingers to check its rubberyness when I heard a noise from under the porch. It sounded like an animal scooting around, scratching at something.

I hopped off the porch and ducked down to look underneath. There was something crawling around under there alright. I couldn't tell if it was a cat or a raccoon or what.

"What's up little guy?" I said in a soft, nonthreatening tone. I thought maybe I could convince whatever small creature hiding under the porch to come crawling out and I could keep it as a pet. "You causing trouble down here?"

The animal shifted when it heard my voice. It seemed frightened at first, but then it came crawling towards me and into the moonlight.

I jumped back when I saw what it was. Holy fuck.

It was an arm. It was severed at the elbow and black with decay, but it was an honest-to-god arm. It emerged from underneath the porch, stood upright, and saluted me.

"What?" I couldn't believe it. "How did you survive?"

I had a spiritual connection with the small demon. I could just barely understand the most basic concepts from it.

Me ran.

"Whoa, that's crazy." I offered it my open palm. "High five."

It high fived me.

"Welp." That was an interesting turn of events. I rose to my feet and brushed my hands off across my butt. I was kind of at a loss for what to say. "Do you want to stay here?"

Yes, my Queen.

"Alright. Well, welcome home then, I guess. Come on and follow me inside. I'll show you around."

In accordance with the prophecies.

I went inside and the arm followed. Funny, I'd always wanted a pet *something*. I never thought I'd have a pet demon arm with a psychic connection to my brain. It wasn't a bad deal either; I'd never have to feed it, never have to clean up after it, and it wouldn't run away. I gave it the grand tour of the shop and showed it the plants and the bathroom and behind the counter.

I didn't mention the basement door at all.

The rest of the night felt like normal. I turned on some music and watered the plants. Twice I thought of something funny to say and turned to say it to Xin, but Xin wasn't there. My heart broke a little each time, but then I'd quickly get distracted by my pet arm getting into something he shouldn't.

"Don't touch those jars, man," I said, rushing to stop its dangerous curiosity. I snatched a glass jar of Bandis pollen out of its fingers and placed it carefully back on the shelf. I gave the arm a little hand broom and a dustpan instead. "Here. If you want something to do, sweep up under the tables."

Which it did.

The night passed. The chores were all taken care of. I turned on the porch light and propped open the door to let in the cool air. I sat on my side of the counter; my side was still my side, and Xin's side was still Xin's side. Armstrong – that was the arm's name now, Armstrong – was asleep at my feet. At least I think he was asleep. I ordered him to sleep and it was in his nature to obey me. All I knew was, he wasn't moving. I don't think demons need to sleep, but maybe I was wrong.

For the first time in forever, I had a moment alone where I could just sit down and think.

In the yellow glow of the shop light bulb I opened my book – the one Xin got me for my birthday – and flipped through the pages. I searched through dozens and dozens of hand-drawn maps, each detailing a different distant, far-off world. Would this book have the answer to all my questions? Maybe. And maybe not. But maybe it had the answer to at least one.

"Alright," I said to myself. "Everyone's always telling me to go to Hell." I flipped through the pages. "So how do I get there?"

THE END

Epilogue

Fort Wayne, Indiana.

Anthony Briggs drove his luxury sedan down Interstate 27, five miles over the speed limit. His flight had landed just a few hours earlier and he could already picture himself at home on the couch, checking out the sports scores with his socks up on the coffee table.

His feet were killing him. His back was killing him. He'd recently switched from flying first class to flying business to save on money, but he seriously considered switching back. The comfort was worth the extra couple hundred dollars, especially on a twelve hour flight.

Fort Wayne wasn't much to look at, but that didn't bother Briggs all that much. His job took him to exotic places all around the world, so he actually enjoyed coming home to a run-of-the-mill city without all that much to do. No more parades. No more groups of entitled tourists. No more late nights with women who play it fast and loose for money and attention.

Briggs got off the interstate and stopped at Taco Rio, a little hole in the wall place not too far from his house. It wasn't authentic Mexican food, but it was cheap and he liked the salsa. He'd been away for three months this time and, as was his tradition, the first thing he did when he got back home was drive to Taco Rio for one beef burrito, one chicken taco, and a cheese enchilada.

Briggs left Taco Rio satisfied. He climbed back into his Lexus LS Hybrid and drove the last seventeen blocks home.

He had already called his wife and told her that he'd be arriving soon. Surely she'd have something cooking. Or, if she wasn't feeling up to it, she could order something delivered, too. He wasn't going to be picky.

But when he rolled down a neighborhood of upper-middle class homes and rounded the corner to his house, he was caught totally off-guard. For whatever reason, the front lawn was strewn about with clothes. His nice shirts were in the bushes. His ties were blowing down the sidewalk. His shoes were in the grass and his patent leather ones, the ones he liked to break out for weddings or funerals, were against the curb in a puddle of water.

There on the porch stood his wife with her arms crossed, jaw clenched and cheeks flushed red with fury.

Briggs pulled into the driveway at a crooked angle and threw the car into park. He jumped out of the car and shouted, "What the hell, Darla!?"

"You think I don't know!?" she shouted at him.

Adrenaline flooded into his bloodstream like a drug. Surely Darla didn't know. There's no way she could *possibly* know.

"Know what!?" he said.

"Fuck you!" She scooped up a laundry basket filled with his clothes and proceeded to dump them out right there on the porch steps. "Go live with one of your whores!"

"What whores!?" he asked. But Darla wasn't listening. She went back inside, slammed the door closed, and locked it. He followed her towards the porch with his arms outstretched. "Darla! What whores!?"

www.ingramcontent.com/pod-product-compliance
Lightning Source LLC
Chambersburg PA
CBHW030544020726
47494CB00005B/1476